E V E R Y M A N ' S   L I B R A R Y

EVERYMAN,
I WILL GO WITH THEE,
AND BE THY GUIDE,
IN THY MOST NEED
TO GO BY THY SIDE

EMILE ZOLA

Germinal

Translated from the French by Leonard Tancock

EVERYMAN'S LIBRARY

24

First included in Everyman's Library, 1991
Translation © Leonard Tancock, 1954
Published by arrangement with Penguin Books Ltd.
Introduction, Bibliography and Chronology © David Campbell
Publishers Ltd., 1991

ISBN 1-85715-024-4

Distributed by the Random Century Group Ltd.,
20 Vauxhall Bridge Road, London SW1V 2SA

Printed and bound in Germany

INTRODUCTION

Why *Germinal*? Only after various alternatives had been considered by Zola ('Fire Below Ground', 'The Fourth Estate', etc.) did he finally decide on this title which as he later said occurred to him 'by chance', and which he at first rejected, thinking it 'too symbolic, too mystical'. Today we should judge it ambiguous, or at least polyvalent, since it can be interpreted in at least three ways. Germinal was the name given in 1793 to the seventh month of the new calendar, intended by the revolutionaries to replace the Gregorian calendar introduced by Pope Gregory XIII in 1582; used as the title of Zola's novel, it has therefore revolutionary connotations and may suggest a new revolution destined to be marked by the same bloodshed and devastation as had stained the first one. In the second place, Germinal refers to the season of the year in which both the opening and closing of the novel take place. The revolutionary months had no exact correspondence to those of the old calendar, since it had been decreed that the new year should start on 22 September, the anniversary of the declaration of the Republic. The month of Germinal ran from 21 March to 19 April and was associated with the variable weather experienced at that time of the year in the northern hemisphere, as the last frosts of winter give place to the first flowers of early spring. In the first paragraph of the book there is reference to 'the March wind blowing in great gusts like a storm at sea, icy cold from sweeping over miles of marshes and bare earth'; while the last chapter, in which Etienne is shown walking away on his journey back to Paris, is clearly set at the other end of the month: 'the April sun was now well up in the sky, shedding its glorious warming rays on the teeming earth'. The entire action of the novel thus takes place between the first and last days of the month Germinal, in different years of course. And thirdly, most importantly from Zola's point of view, Germinal suggests germination, the germination of the seeds of life underground and the germination of the underground workers, better educated, growing

v

more aware of their condition and destined to emerge shortly from obscurity into the light of day when, as he writes in the last line of the novel, 'their germination would crack the earth asunder'. Thus to the cycle of the seasons revolving from year to year corresponds the revolution in human affairs which he foresaw.

Germinal was the thirteenth of the twenty-volume cycle which was Zola's principal contribution to literature, a saga tracing the fortunes of a fictional family, *les Rougon-Macquart*, living in the middle of the nineteenth century. The double-barrelled name points to the family's division into a legitimate and an illegitimate branch, the former, the Rougons, adopting various middle-class professions, medicine, the law, high finance, while the Macquarts, descended from a drunkard, ill-educated and suffering from a vitiated heredity, have to struggle for their living as ill-paid manual workers, shop-keepers, and assorted social outcasts, a failed artist, a prosti-tute; they include Etienne Lantier, the central character of *Germinal*, whose mother was born a Macquart. Each novel was written with one particular member of the family as protago-nist; but it is significant that the novels concerned with the Macquart branch have, from a literary point of view, weath-ered better than the others and in fact Zola's first major success, *L'Assommoir*, relating the pitiful life of Gervaise Mac-quart, was also the first novel in French literature to deal exclusively with the poorer classes of Paris. It may have been the sensation it caused, both as a work of fiction and when dramatized for the stage, that encouraged Zola to return some eight years later to the oppressed underclass in *Germinal*.

But the two novels were very dissimilar. The question of class conflict, barely raised in *L'Assommoir*, is basic to *Germinal*. The miners in *Germinal* are all working in the same industry and constitute a recognizable proletariat; whereas in *L'Assom-moir*, although the numerous characters live hugger-mugger in the same working-class district of Paris, they all follow differ-ent trades, as laundress, roofer, blacksmith and so forth; thus their interests are divergent and they have no shared social grievances or political aims, as have the miners in *Germinal*, to encourage them to make common cause against the class enemy. Another important difference was that Zola was already well acquainted with working-class districts in Paris, having lived in them when he was struggling at or below subsistence level in his early twenties, whereas the Anzin coalfield in north-east France was an environment he had never set eyes on until his first trip there in February 1884. He might as easily have chosen a large factory or a steel-works as the setting for the new novel; he fixed on this region near the Belgian border because the colliers there had just come out on strike and he needed a strike to provide the violent clash between capital and labour on which the whole drama of *Germinal* was to turn.

Having taken a room in the principal town, Valenciennes, he made contact with local guides who agreed to take him down the coal mines and explain to him the various tasks the workers had to perform; he also visited the company cottages where they lived and looked in at a few of the beer parlours where they took their recreation. After no more than ten days of this fact-finding tour he returned with full notebooks to start work on the novel, well armed with technical details but with a large margin left for the play of the imagination. The experiences of this visit must have been overwhelming: the swift descent down the mine shaft, the labyrinth of ill-lit underground galleries, the scattered villages above ground in this vast treeless plain crossed by roads stretching in straight lines to the horizon, the sense finally of an almost military discipline in the gangs of workers, of commands handed down from above that must be obeyed unquestioningly. It was a world apart, of which he would need to convey the eeriness, the brutality and the underlying horror, since his readers, for the most part, knew nothing more of the conditions under which these men and women laboured than he had himself before he arrived to investigate. He achieved the effect he wanted by a very simple device, one which he had used before in several novels and was to use again in later ones: he chose a newcomer to the environment, showing the whole scene through his eyes so as to convey the full impact of surprise and shock. Etienne Lantier, the unemployed railwayman wandering into this strange land looking for work, would experience the same kind of aghast astonishment that Zola himself must have felt on his first arrival. Later, of course, after Etienne has been engaged in monotonous physical work for weeks and months, he forgets his earlier sense of bewilderment, he becomes as accustomed to this world as his mates and hardly notices his surroundings; the novelty, as we say, has worn off and so at this point he loses the privileged position in the novel of the 'seeing eye' and Zola, after this first part, takes over from him as narrator.

But, throughout, the organizing mind remains Zola's. He has not merely to describe the vicissitudes of the strike but to show what lies behind it, the sense of bitter injustice in the workers, the conflicting ideologies of those who try to inspire and organize them, the indifference, merging into indignation and finally panic, of the representatives of the middle class. Possibly because he had not at this stage fully made up his mind as to the rights and wrongs of the case, more probably because he was still guided by the aesthetics of the realist doctrine which aimed at objectivity or a 'scientific' approach, he strove from the beginning to adopt as far as possible a neutral stance. Zola's own class loyalties were mixed. His father had been a self-made man, a builder of railways and canals, but his premature death had left his son finally penniless with a widowed mother to support. After a period of dire poverty in his early twenties, he fought his way up again, as a freelance journalist and writer of hack fiction, until finally by dint of perseverance and natural genius he succeeded in rejoining the professional middle classes. It was a period when a best-seller could earn its author thousands, and thanks to the royalties accruing from *L'Assommoir* in 1877 he was able to acquire a small country estate near Paris with a house which he was continually building on to. Thus the author of *Germinal* was not a man with a chip on his shoulder; money troubles were a thing of the past, but he was aware, as most of the bourgeoisie were not, of the flimsiness of the social fabric and felt that if his new novel was to have a specific message for the middle-class reading public, this would be to warn them against disregarding the grievances of the underprivileged and allowing their misery to swell until the resultant explosion could plunge the country into a new and even bloodier revolution than that which had started a century before.

But how to ensure that *Germinal* should not be dismissed as a piece of blood-curdling left-wing propaganda? Zola thought he could achieve this end by giving as much attention to members of the middle class as to his working-class characters and by apportioning sympathy and blame even-handedly. Whether or not he succeeded in so doing is open to dispute. In the second part of the work we are shown, very simply and without comment, the enormous gap between a famished working-class family and a comfortably circumstanced middle-class one. On the one hand there are the Maheus, husband and wife, with seven children and Maheu's ageing father Bonnemort crammed into one small cottage, everyone working in the mines who was of age to do so; on the other hand the two middle-aged Grégoires, with their single daughter Cécile, with cook and maidservants to relieve them of domestic work, living not far away in a pretty country house, with nothing to do but to lead a tranquil existence on their large unearned income. The two are brought face to face in the most natural way possible: Maheude, the mother of this large brood, desperate for a few francs to buy provisions at the grocer's, has made up her mind to walk over with her two youngest to beg for charity. She remains throughout the interview as conciliatory as she can, knowing that to act differently would only set the Grégoires against her. Having exposed their pitiful circumstances she concludes: 'Oh, I don't mean to complain. That's how things are and we have to accept them, especially as however much we struggled we probably shouldn't be able to alter anything.' In the end she is disappointed. The Grégoires are not uncharitable, but they make it a rule never to give money, only warm clothing for the winter, for money given to the poor will only go straight on drink, it's a well-known fact.

Maheude's passive hopelessness, her conviction that they are beaten in advance and that nothing can be done about it, is what Etienne in particular will have to overcome if he is to arouse the miners to revolt. He had not arrived in the area with any idea of acting as an agitator, but the revelation of the

wretched conditions to which the miners' families are condemned serves as the catalyst to his conversion to militant
socialism. His ideas are initially confused, a hotchpotch of
theories derived from his reading of various left-wing publica-
tions and from his correspondence with one of the leaders of
the socialist movement in Paris; but as he talks to the Maheus
in whose house he is lodging, he discovers in himself a talent
for drawing seductive imaginary pictures of the future utopia
that might be established once the 'social problem' had been
solved. Even Maheude begins to lose her former mute resignation; 'there are times,' she says, 'when the injustice of it makes
me mad'.

Etienne is not the only 'advanced thinker' in the neighbourhood: there are two others whom he sees regularly at the
village pub, and each represents a different aspect of the
general movement. Etienne's ideas, as they eventually crystal-
lize, centre on organizing a general strike which he optimisti-
cally thinks will lead to the downfall of capitalism, since the
system depends in the last resort on labour and would soon
crumble if labour were withdrawn. The publican Rasseneur
who until Etienne's arrival enjoyed the reputation of being the
miners' friend and had achieved over the years some better-
ment in their conditions, is a believer in putting forward
'reasonable claims'; a strike would achieve nothing and would
probably leave the workers worse off than before; much better
to negotiate than to raise inflated expectations. Finally there is
Souvarine, who says little, smoking one cigarette after
another, stroking his pet rabbit, lost in a mystic dream. A
political refugee from Russia, he has no faith in socialism, nor
has he any sympathy for Rasseneur's belief in step-by-
step improvement. He stands for something new, something
that did not begin to manifest itself in France, thanks to
various well-publicized outrages, until some time after
Germinal appeared: anarchism. Intelligent and well educated,
Souvarine realizes that in the current depression, with factories closing down everywhere, the market for coal has shrunk,
the company is obliged to stockpile it and would probably
prefer a strike which would relieve them of the necessity to

continue paying wages out of their shrunken profits. Souvarine is in favour of making a clean sweep: blowing up the mine, killing off the idle profiteers, destroying everything and starting afresh from the 'primitive commune'; he represents the ultimate nightmare of the bourgeoisie, the wrecker, the bomb-toting terrorist.

These three men, representing however vaguely three possible directions the labour movement might take in Zola's view, are neatly offset by three representatives of the capitalist system, equally divergent though more because of their conflicting interests than their underlying ideologies. Grégoire, rubicund, self-satisfied, totally unaware that there is any problem, stands for the average shareholder, quite content to live his comfortable life at the expense of the 'toiling masses' and seeing nothing amiss in the arrangement. After all, if it had not been for the investment originally made by his forefathers, there would be no mine and no employment for the miners; so it is only right and proper that he, as their heir, should continue to reap the rewards of their foresight. When Négrel, the mining engineer, warns him teasingly at a dinner party that he risks having his house looted by the strikers since he is the 'accursed capitalist' and has no right to his wealth, he practically has an apoplectic fit. The looting of the Grégoires' house never takes place, but Zola visits a far more terrible punishment on them at the end when Cécile, carrying out one of her usual charity visits, calls at the Maheus' cottage and finds no one in but the old grandfather Bonnemort, now paralysed and in his dotage but who nevertheless summons up the strength to strangle her, thus obscurely avenging the generations of colliers who have slaved to keep her and her parents in comfort. Then there is Deneulin, the old-fashioned, paternalistic pit-owner; he has modernized his mine, is respected and even liked by his workers, but the big Company is secretly manoeuvring to buy him out. In the end the plan succeeds when the strikers, determined to close all the mines in the area, attack his, smash the machinery, forbid further work at the pit and so effectively ruin him beyond all possible recovery. And finally there is Hennebeau, no capitalist, simply as he insists a salaried employee of the Company, the local administrator who has to deal with trouble at the source. In a key scene (Part 4, Chapter 2), where he faces a deputation of aggrieved miners, he puts it to them finally that the Company has no control over wage levels. If it raised wages it would have to cut the shareholders' dividends; they would then withdraw their investment and bring about the financial collapse of the Company. To remain competitive it must retrench, and in a labour-intensive industry like coalmining there is no other way of retrenching except by cutting wages. 'Why don't you face the facts,' he asks them, 'instead of blaming the Company? But you won't listen, you refuse to understand'; to which Etienne replies in a low voice but in accents trembling with conviction: 'On the contrary, we understand perfectly well that there is no chance of improvement for us as long as things go on as they are now. Indeed, it is for that very reason that sooner or later the workers will see to it that things are managed differently.' The implied threat in the remark is that a new revolution cannot long be deferred.

In fact, after the strike ends the miners are shown to be no better off than they were and the Company to have been damaged but not destroyed. The revolution seems as far off as ever. But Zola never pretended to be a social economist, with a programme ready to hand and just waiting to be applied. As he wrote even before he began on the novel proper, all he wanted to do in *Germinal* was to deal with 'the struggle between capital and labour. That will constitute the importance of the book, presaging the future, posing the question which will be the most important question of the twentieth century.' The most important question? Certainly *an* important question, though from the vantage point of the last decade of the twentieth century most readers will be able to think of certain others just as important which await solution if they are not to destroy us.

As the problem of the struggle between capital and labour has lost its priority over the years, to be replaced by others more urgent, so *Germinal* itself seems a little old-fashioned if one restricts one's view of the novel to the aspect we have been considering hitherto, the aspect, that is, of a dramatization of warring ideologies. Nowadays the tendency would be to dismiss such matters as being chiefly of historical importance but hardly of enduring human interest, and *Germinal*'s continuing hold on its readership must be accounted for in other ways. The principal drama derives no doubt from the strike itself and its vicissitudes, from the suffering it causes and from its final failure; but there are other more private dramas quite unconnected with the major one, in particular that involving the trio Etienne–Catherine–Chaval which is constantly in the background and occasionally occupies the foreground. The theme of the woman placed between two lovers – a predicament explored more from her point of view than from theirs – is one of the constants in Zola's fiction, beginning with his two early novels, *Madeleine Férat* and *Thérèse Raquin* and recurring in several of the later ones, including *L'Assommoir*; it was a sort of obsessive triangle that haunted him in much the same way as the pattern of the girl sought simultaneously by three suitors in Hardy's fiction, in *Far from the Madding Crowd*, in *The Trumpet-Major* and in *The Hand of Ethelberta*. Etienne is normally a pacific man, but when roused he 'sees red', literally, and can with difficulty control himself sufficiently not to kill his antagonist. New to the pit, he is befriended by Catherine, the elder daughter of the Maheus who, although only fifteen, is considered old enough to work underground as a haulage girl in her father's gang of which Chaval is also a member. He and Etienne take an instant dislike to each other; correspondingly, Catherine and Etienne are drawn to one another, he out of pity for this overworked adolescent, she out of a sense of his innate refinement and gentleness; but Chaval considers he has a prior claim on the girl. Etienne, too shy or too honourable to declare his feelings, has two fights with the other man, both in Catherine's presence. In the first of them she comes to Chaval's assistance, striking Etienne over the face and shaming him into letting her lover go; on the second occasion, in Rasseneur's inn, the quarrel begins with mutual insults and degenerates into a fist fight until Chaval, knocked down, draws a knife; this time Catherine cries out a warning to

Etienne. In the ensuing struggle Etienne gets hold of the knife and is seized by a 'sudden, insane desire to murder a man, a lust for blood. He had never felt it so badly before' but fought it 'with the frantic paroxysms of a man mad with lust struggling on the verge of rape. He managed to get himself under control, threw the knife behind him, and muttered hoarsely: "Get up and get out!"'

The third and finally fatal encounter takes place underground, after the strike has collapsed and the miners have agreed to resume work. A desperate act of sabotage carried out in secret by Souvarine has weakened the lining of the main shaft that insulates it from the underground water level; the passage of the cages widens the leak and in an hour or so the whole mine is flooded and part of the labour force is trapped below, among them Etienne, Catherine and Chaval, all three caught in an air-pocket, safe from drowning but with the prospect of dying from hunger and in darkness when their lamps run out of oil. The old sexual rivalry flares up for the last time; to a taunt from Chaval, Etienne responds by jerking a lump of schist from the rock face and dashing out his opponent's brains with a single blow. It is a prehistoric act of murder, one man killed by another for a woman in a cave, but a cave from which they cannot escape unless the rescuers reach them in time. Catherine dies finally in a delirium brought on by starvation and exhaustion, but not before she and Etienne make love for the first and last time. Etienne survives, but it is as 'a skeleton with hair as white as snow' that he is carried out by the rescue team.

Zola's imagination appears to have been haunted by scenes of this type, where death and sexual passion, Eros and Thanatos as a Freudian critic has called them, are conjoined: beginning with the linked suicide of the guilty lovers at the end of *Thérèse Raquin*. In *The Beast in Man* (1890) the central character, Jacques Lantier, is an engine-driver, a brother of Etienne, secretly responsible for a series of murders for which he is never brought to book. Originally Zola had intended to give this part to Etienne who, we should remember, is said in *Germinal* to have worked on the railways before joining the mining community in Montsou; he changed his mind when he decided – possibly influenced by the widespread morbid interest in the contemporaneous exploits of Jack the Ripper in Whitechapel, gloatingly reported in the French press – to turn his protagonist into a sort of sexual maniac, a man who cannot conceive of desire for a woman except in terms of knifing her. This kinkiness was not easily reconcilable with the Etienne he had imagined for *Germinal*, though it is noteworthy that he attributes Jacques' deviancy to the same cause – an alcohol-sodden heredity – as he had Etienne's less pathological fits of rage.

Since the social problem to which Zola wished to draw his readers' attention – the dangerous gulf yawning between haves and have-nots – no longer preoccupies people to the same extent as it did in the 1880s, and since the brutal melodrama of his triangle of doomed lovers appears less shocking to us after decades of fictional violence have blunted our sensibilities, it might be thought that *Germinal* would have lost much of its power to fascinate the modern reader. That this is far from being the case is due to other aspects of the work, on which criticism has increasingly concentrated in recent years. To start with, there is the special eeriness associated in many people's minds with what lies below the surface of the planet. It is a region that can be explored by speleologists and has from time immemorial been burrowed into by men searching for veins of metallic ore or fossilized fuel; but it remains mysterious, more uncharted than the deeps of the ocean; it is the source of occasional volcanic eruptions when the fiery plasma always churning beneath the crust is forced up to the surface, but that is all we know about it for certain. The ancients made it the seat of Hades and of Tartarus, while medieval Christians located there the infernal regions to which the damned were consigned. Being so myster-ious, it can serve as a metaphor for the locus of all instinctual processes. The subconscious and the subterranean are in this sense transposable, the subconscious being the source of dreams and nightmares but also of all creative drive, so that the artist must, as we say, tap the subconscious to bring to the light of day whatever lies buried below, exactly as the miner with his pickaxe taps the subterranean vein to extract the coal that fuels all the engines of the industrial world.

In this sense *Germinal* is, apart from all else, a dramatization of the act of creation, and a much more effective one, it must be admitted, than the novel Zola wrote immediately afterwards about the artistic life, entitled *The Masterpiece*. It is this metaphor, actualized, that is responsible for such nightmarish scenes as the one just discussed, coming at the end of the novel, but horror, terror and the monstrous are meant to grip the reader from the very start. If we return to the opening chapter, where Etienne is first introduced, chilled to the bone, starving, plodding through the gloom in a state of exhaustion where things appear not as they are but as they might appear in a bad dream, we saw him enter into conversation with the old haulier, Bonnemort, who explains to him, as the newcomer stands warming his frozen hands at the fire, that what he can see, looming through the darkness, is in fact a pit; in time Etienne can indeed make out the various details. But it still seems to him something uncanny and threatening. 'With its squat brick buildings huddled in a valley, the chimney sticking up like a menacing horn, the pit was evil-looking, a voracious beast crouching ready to devour the world'; and the exhaust pipe working away, 'the long, heavy monotonous panting' he could hear, had seemed in his stupefied state of mind 'the snoring breath of a monster'. And so, having learned what he could from Bonnemort, Etienne struggles on towards the pit buildings while, 'huddled in its lair like some evil beast, Le Voreux crouched ever lower and its breath came in longer and deeper gasps, as though it were struggling to digest its meal of human flesh'. He arrives at the works, and having explained he is seeking employment, is advised to wait for the arrival of the supervisor; to pass the time, he watches at the pit head the cages as they zoom up bearing the newly cut coal and a moment later descend with a cargo of colliers, a load of human flesh. His earlier impression of a carnivorous monster is reinforced by this spectacle at close quarters. 'The shaft went on with its meal for half an hour, gulping men down more or less greedily according to the depth of the level they were bound for; but it never stopped, for the hunger of this gigantic maw could swallow up a whole people.'

Once Etienne is accepted as a coal-face worker and himself becomes habituated to the daily round, these nightmare visions fade; and when they recur, at the end of the book, it is not through his thoughts that they are presented but through those of the narrator, describing the final effects of Souvarine's act of sabotage. As the underground galleries fill with water, the soil beneath the pit-works subsides, dragging the buildings and machinery down, the thirty-metre chimney last of all, 'swallowed whole by the earth, like a giant candle that had melted away. Nothing was left showing, not even the point of the lightning conductor. This was the end. The evil beast, crouching in its hollow, sated with human flesh, had drawn its last long heavy breath.' Etienne's initial imaginings have been absorbed here into the descriptive vocabulary of the narrator, Etienne himself being absent from the scene, scurrying in desperation along the underground passages rapidly filling up with water. But it was artistically necessary that the mine, presented earlier as the gullet of a monstrous carnivore to which generations of workers had yielded up their lives, should meet its own death in this ultimate apocalyptic catastrophe.

There are other embodiments of evil in *Germinal*, betraying the author's constant concern to break free of the trammels of realism and create his own world of symbolic entities, monsters and dark gods controlling the fate of hapless humans, much as they are seen to do in primitive Celtic or Scandinavian mythology. One of the most striking of such cases is Zola's presentation of free-enterprise capitalism – not a thing of bricks and mortar like Le Voreux, but a complex enmeshing of economic forces, supply and demand, an abstraction in other words but none the less potent – as a remote idol exacting pitilessly its tribute from its hapless devotees. This image makes it first appearance in answer to the simple question Etienne puts to Bonnemort in the opening chapter, staring at the dimly perceived coalfields dotted with extraction plants: 'who does all this belong to?' Bonnemort's answer lacks precision. 'Who does this belong to? God knows... People...' he says, indicating some vague spot in the darkness. 'His voice had taken on a kind of religious awe, as though he were speaking of some inaccessible tabernacle, where dwelt unseen the gorged and crouching deity whom they had all appeased with their flesh but whom nobody had ever seen.' The same image reappears at the end of Hennebeau's interview with the strike committee. After much argument he tells the delegates he will transmit their demands to the board of directors and let them know the response. Etienne asks innocently why they cannot present their demands in person instead of through him. Hennebeau smiles, telling them unhelpfully that if they don't trust him they'll have to go down yonder, pointing vaguely through one of the windows. They suppose he means Paris, 'but they could not say for sure; the whole question was receding into some distant and terrifying place, some far-off, metaphysical region where the unknown god was crouching on his throne in the depths of the tabernacle. They would never see this god, but they felt him as a power, weighing down from afar on the ten thousand miners of Montsou. And when the manager spoke, he had this hidden power behind him and pronounced its oracles.'

The final impression left by *Germinal* on a reader of today, less likely than Zola's contemporaries to see it as a tract for the times and be troubled by his vatic warnings of disastrous class conflict, may well be of an immense and sombre fresco dominated by a limited chromatic system, mostly black, white and red. Each of these colours serves not merely to paint the scene but possesses in addition a nexus of symbolic values. The entire novel is set in what was known as the 'black country' (*le pays noir*), and blackness refers firstly to the coal hewn from the seam, piled up on the surface awaiting transportation, and floating in the form of fine dust in the atmosphere, dirtying the miners' skins and entering their lungs (Bonnemort's spittle is not blood, as Etienne supposed, but coal dust mixed with phlegm). Blackness is also the colour of darkness and of night. It has been calculated that only ten of the forty chapters in *Germinal* take place in broad daylight; six are sited in the mine underground, where the only light comes from the colliers' Davy lamps; the remainder take place in twilight or at the dead of night. The association here is with dark deeds plotted or accomplished. The secret meeting of some three thousand miners at which the decision is taken to halt work, by force if necessary, in the mines that are still open, takes place at night in a dark forest clearing lit only by the rising moon. The castration of the grocer Maigrat by the village hags is effected similarly at nightfall; and Jeanlin's senseless murder of the Breton sentry is also committed at night, at a moment when the clouds are obscuring the full moon. Lawlessness and violence are the daughters of night, and it is almost inevitable that Etienne's braining of Chaval should take place in the bowels of the earth, in the blackness of the flooded mine, with only a single lamp glimmering in the darkness.

White comes in more than one form. The silvery hair of the elderly Grégoires, the milky white of Cécile's neck that tempts Bonnemort, suggest good health, well-being and wealth: the French word for money is in fact the same as that used for the metal, silver. But there is also an unhealthy, chlorotic white, bluish or yellowish, the colour of poor Catherine's skin discoloured by coal dust and by an inadequate diet. And thirdly there is the dead white of winter snow under the clouds, covering the countryside at the height of the strike, when the miners sit crouched round empty hearths with empty bellies and when Alzire, the Maheus' angelic hunchbacked child, fades away and dies for lack of food. 'No shadow darkened the bare whiteness of the snow. The village had relapsed into the deathly silence of starvation in the intense cold.' Whiteness stands for final annihilation, and it is perhaps significant that with every appearance of Souvarine in the novel there is some reference to his pallor: his white hands and teeth, his very fair hair, his light blue eyes. He is, of course, a man of the north, an alien, taciturn and with a hint of the otherwordly about him; one might almost imagine him to incarnate the angel of death.

As for red, it has been the colour of revolution since long before the red flag and the red star were adopted by the communist régimes of the east; in the earliest days of the French Revolution, the National Assembly was said to be divided into the reds, urging extremist policies, and the blacks, favouring more conservative ones. More literally, red is the colour of fire and of blood: the fires dotted over the plain that

Etienne sees in the opening chapter as so many red points in the darkness, the blood that flows when the soldiers posted to guard the pit entrance, exasperated first by the insults and then by the half bricks thrown by the miners, let loose a volley which kills fourteen of them, including two children and three women. But the colour is also used metaphorically, as when Etienne, in a fit of homicidal fury, 'sees red'; or else shades and variants combine at certain moments to give a general impression of scarlet, orange and purple pigments running together, as in the description Zola gives of the enraged strikers stampeding across country towards Montsou: 'the last rays of the setting sun bathed the plain in blood, and the road seemed like a river of blood as men and women, bespattered like butchers in a slaughterhouse, galloped on and on'. Those who witness this frenzied march are Hennebeau's wife, Deneulin's two daughters, and one man, Négrel, who was driving them to dinner at Montsou: four members of the bourgeoisie, cowering in a wayside barn, watching the dramatic scene. It is clear that Zola was thinking here of the historical precedents, in particular of certain well-documented scenes of the French Revolution, the march of the famished women of Paris to bring the royal family back from Versailles in 1789, the invasion of the Tuileries in 1792 and the ensuing bloody massacre of the Swiss guards. The constant cry, the slogan of this uncontrollable mob: 'Bread! We want bread!'; the singing of the Marseillaise, first composed under the French Revolution and banned under the Second Empire which is the supposed historical setting of *Germinal*; the single axe, held aloft above their heads 'like the blade of the guillotine' – these are so many direct evocations of the events of 1789–94. But it was not just a re-enactment of the past: 'what they saw,' continues Zola, 'was a red vision of the coming revolution that would inevitably carry them all off one bloody night at the end of this epoch'.

The whole of this paragraph reads almost like a prediction of what is shortly to come to pass: the phrase 'at the end of this epoch' for once fails to translate exactly what Zola wrote, 'de cette fin de siècle', i.e. at the end of this (the nineteenth) century. Just as in the 1990s some find it fascinating to speculate what the coming century holds in store, so it was in the 1880s and 1890s. H. G. Wells' *Time Machine*, published ten years after *Germinal*, similarly deals with the problem of class conflict, but in Wells' fantasy what lies ahead is not chaos and anarchy, but a total separation of the two classes: the Eloi, ultimate descendants of the bourgeoisie, an effeminate, decadent but beautiful race, have inherited the daytime, while the dreaded Morlocks, who live underground and provide the technological support for the Eloi's life-style, emerge at night to raid them and drag them down to the caves where they devour them. Mankind has split into two species, one vegetarian, the other carnivorous if not cannibalistic. Both novels offer terrifying visions of the future, but their starting-point is the same: the division of mankind between parasites and workers, between the idle dwellers on the surface of the earth and those who toil underground.

However, it is important to note that this 'red vision of the coming revolution' is presented not as Zola's own, but as the embodiment of the fears of his middle-class characters – and no doubt of Négrel in particular, an educated man if not an intellectual. At the end of the book there is another, far more optimistic vision, that of Etienne as he leaves the mining area, with all his experiences behind him, and the bright spring sunshine to lift his spirits, 'going forth fully armed as a fighting missionary for the revolution', welcoming this revolution as 'the real one, whose fires would cast their red glare over the end of this epoch even as the rising sun was now drenching the sky in blood'. Which vision is the true one, that steeped in Négrel's pessimism or that infused with Etienne's optimism? Zola leaves the question open. *Germinal* is not after all a prophetic book like *The Time Machine* or like the utopian novels Zola wrote towards the end of his life under the heading *The Four Gospels*, one of which, entitled *Work*, suggests a final solution which is neither the collectivist one that Etienne appears to favour, nor the status quo gradually humanized which seems to be Rasseneur's preference, but the fusion of the two classes assisted by a technological revolution in which the 'toiling masses' are relieved of their hardships by the intelligent application of the new source of power, electricity. In *Germinal* he was wiser, accepting the uncertainty of the future, concentrating instead on the present which includes, of course, people's hopes and fears for the future, which the future, when it arrives, usually shows to have been misconceived, because they failed to take into account other developments still latent which no one could have foreseen at the time. Extrapolation of one strand, when so many are tangled together, is almost certain to confound the prophet.

F. W. J. Hemmings

SELECT BIBLIOGRAPHY

GRANT, ELLIOTT M., *Emile Zola*, Twayne, Boston, 1966. A critical appraisal, in which *Germinal* has a chapter to itself entitled 'The Top of the Ladder'.

— *Zola's 'Germinal', a critical and historical study*, Leicester University Press, 1962. Concerned in part with Zola's source material and the planning of the novel, in part with an analysis of the characters.

HEMMINGS, F. W. J., *Emile Zola*, 2nd edn, The Clarendon Press, 1966. Includes a chapter ('Cry from the Pit') on *Germinal*.

— *The Life and Times of Emile Zola*, Paul Elek, 1977. A biography with numerous illustrations.

KING, GRAHAM, *Garden of Zola*, Barrie and Jenkins, 1978. Sprawling but readable. Includes a chapter on *Germinal*, 'The Pitiless Pit', and another of some interest on the initial reception of Zola's novels in Victorian England.

KNAPP, BETTINA L., *Emile Zola*, Frederick Ungar Publishing Co., New York, 1980. A brief account in the 'Modern Literature Monographs' series. Contains a useful list of recent translations of the novels into English.

PETREY, SANDY, *Realism and Revolution*, Cornell University Press, Ithaca & London, 1988. A suggestive final chapter, 'Performance and Class in the month of Germinal'.

WALKER, PHILIP, *'Germinal' and Zola's Philosophical and Religious Thought*, John Benjamins Publishing Co., Amsterdam & Philadelphia, 1984. An unusual and valuable contribution.

— *Zola*, Routledge and Kegan Paul, 1985. Biographical.

WILSON, ANGUS, *Emile Zola: an introductory study of his novels*, Secker and Warburg, 1952. Still the best presentation of one novelist by another.

CHRONOLOGY

DATE	AUTHOR'S LIFE	LITERARY CONTEXT
1840	Birth of Emile Zola in Paris.	Sainte-Beuve: *Port-Royal* (to 1859). Births of Daudet and Thomas Hardy.
1843	The Zola family move to Aix-en-Provence.	
1844		Births of Nietzsche and Verlaine.
1845		Publication of Edgar Allan Poe's *The Raven and other stories* and *Tales*.
1846		Balzac: *La Cousine Bette*.
1847	Death of Zola's father.	Publication of Thackeray's *Vanity Fair*.
1848		Death of Chateaubriand.
1849		Death of Poe.
1850		Turgenev: *A Month in The Country*. Death of Balzac. Birth of Maupassant.
1851		Goncourt brothers: *Journal* (to 1896).
1852		
1854		Gerard de Nerval: *Les Chimères*.
1856		Publication of Hugo's *Les Contemplations*.
1857		Publication of Flaubert's *Madame Bovary*. Birth of Gissing. Death of Alfred de Musset. Baudelaire's *Les Fleurs du mal* put on sale.
1858	The Zolas move back to Paris.	
1859	Zola fails twice at his baccalauréat. Gives up the idea of law studies.	Darwin: *The Origin of Species by Means of Natural Selection*.
1860		
1861	Period of unemployment and severe poverty (until 1862).	Dickens: *Great Expectations*.

HISTORICAL EVENTS

Birth of Monet.

Expedition against Madagascar. Potato famine in Ireland. Wagner's *Tannhäuser*.

Verdi's *Macbeth*.

Outbreak of February Revolution. Louis Napoleon President of France.
Marx–Engels *Communist Manifesto* first published in England.
Rome proclaimed republic and then taken by French.

Louis Napoleon proclaimed Emperor Napoleon III.
Crimean War.

Crimean War ends. Birth of Freud.

Franco-Austrian War.

First Italian Parliament. Lincoln becomes President of USA.
Victor-Emmanuel becomes King of Italy. American Civil War starts.

DATE	AUTHOR'S LIFE	LITERARY CONTEXT
1862	Zola enters Hachette's publishing firm.	Turgenev: *Fathers and Sons*. Hugo: *Les Misérables*.
1863		Death of Alfred de Vigny. Tolstoy: *War and Peace* (to 1869). Taine: *Histoire de la Littérature anglaise*.
1864	Working intermittently as a newspaper columnist (to 1881).	Death of Thackeray. Goncourt: *Germinie Lacerteux*.
1865	Zola leaves Hachette and decides to support himself by literature alone. Publishes first novel: *La Confession de Claude*.	
1866-8	Defends Manet and the pre-Impressionists in the press.	
1867	Publication of *Thérèse Raquin*.	Marx: *Das Kapital* I. Death of Baudelaire.
1868	Zola makes his plan for the Rougon-Macquart cycle thanks to his studies on heredity and experimental science.	Flaubert: *L'Education sentimentale*.
1869		Death of Lamartine. Daudet: *Lettres de mon moulin*.
1870	Marriage to Alexandrine Meley. Leaves for Marseille and Bordeaux.	Death of Jules de Concourt. Death of Dickens.
1871	Back to Paris. Appearance of the first volume in the Rougon-Macquart cycle: *La Fortune des Rougon*.	Birth of Proust. Hardy's first published novel: *Desperate Remedies*.
1872	Publication of *La Curée*.	George Eliot: *Middlemarch*.
1873	Publication of *Le Ventre de Paris*.	Rimbaud: *Une Saison en enfer*. Tolstoy: *Anna Karenina* (to 1877).
1874		
1875		Taine: *Les Origines de la France contemporaine* (to 1894).
1877	Publication of *L'Assommoir* which gives rise to a tough polemic and birth of Naturalism campaign. Zola is supported by Flaubert, Turgenev, Daudet...	
1878	Zola purchases a country house (Médan).	

CHRONOLOGY

HISTORICAL EVENTS

Bismarck becomes Prussian Premier.

Death of Delacroix. Metropolitan Line opened.

Lincoln assassinated. End of Civil War. Slavery abolished in USA.

Suez Canal opened.

Franco-Prussian War and downfall of Second Empire. Siege of Paris.

Fall of Paris ends war. Paris Commune set up and suppressed. Bismarck *Kulturkampf* against Catholics.

Death of Napoleon III.

Impressionists' first exhibition in Paris.
France becomes Third Republic.

Pasteur starts to work on cause of infectious diseases. Edison invents phonograph.

Afghan War.

DATE	AUTHOR'S LIFE	LITERARY CONTEXT
1880	Publication of *Nana*, sequel to *L'Assommoir*. Death of Zola's mother. Publication of essay 'Le Roman Expérimental'.	Dostoyevsky: *The Brothers Karamazov*. Death of Flaubert.
1882		
1883	Publication of *Au Bonheur des dames*.	Death of Turgenev. Nietzsche: *Also sprach Zarathustra*. Trollope: *Autobiography*. Maupassant: *Une Vie*.
1884		First translation in French of Dostoyevsky's *Crime and Punishment*.
1885	Publication of *Germinal*.	Publication of Marx's *Kapital* II. Death of Victor Hugo. Maupassant: *Bel-Ami*.
1886		Tolstoy: *Death of Ivan Illich*.
1888	Publication of *L'Œuvre*. First performance of dramatized version of *Germinal*. Zola's works are the cause of his English publisher's imprisonment.	Strindberg: *Miss Julie*.
1889	Beginning of Zola's lifelong liaison with Jeanne Rozerot. Birth of daughter, Denise.	
1890	Publication of *La Bête humaine* (*The Beast in Man*).	Gissing: *The Emancipated*.
1891	Publication of *L'Argent*. Birth of Zola's second child with Jeanne Rozerot: Jacques.	Hardy: *Tess of the D'Urbervilles*. Gissing: *New Grub Street*. Deaths of Melville and Rimbaud.
1893	Completion of the Rougon–Macquart cycle with *Le Docteur Pascal*.	Death of Taine. Death of Maupassant.
1894	First volume of Zola's trilogy *Les Trois Villes: Lourdes*.	Death of R. L. Stevenson. Kipling: *The Jungle Book*.
1895		Hardy: *Jude the Obscure*.
1896	Publication of *Rome*.	Death of Edmond de Goncourt.
1897	Conducts a press campaign for the rehabilitation of Dreyfus.	Conrad: *The Nigger of the 'Narcissus'*. Death of Daudet. Rostand: *Cyrano de Bergerac*.

CHRONOLOGY

HISTORICAL EVENTS

Europeans massacred in Egypt. Navy bombards Alexandria. Cairo occupied.

Decazeville's coal-mine strikes. Miners arrested.
Wilhelm II becomes Kaiser.

Bismarck resigns. International anti-slavery conference in Brussels.

Nicholas II becomes Tsar.

DATE	AUTHOR'S LIFE	LITERARY CONTEXT
1898	Loses libel case over publication of 'J'Accuse'. Condemned to a year of imprisonment, Zola spends eleven months in exile in England. Publication of *Paris*.	
1900		Conrad: *Lord Jim*. Deaths of Nietzsche and Oscar Wilde.
1901	Publication of *Travail* (*Work*).	
1902	Death of Zola.	
1905		
1908	Ashes in Pantheon.	

CHRONOLOGY

HISTORICAL EVENTS

Curies discover radium. Death of Bismarck. War between Spain and the USA.

Russia occupies Manchuria.

Death of Queen Victoria.

First Russian Revolution.

Introduction

On 10 August 1932 André Gide wrote in his *Journal*: '*Germinal*, which I am reading for the third (or fourth) time, seems more admirable than ever.' He chose it as one of the ten best novels in the French language.

On the other hand it has frequently been pointed out that this novel (and indeed many others of Zola) is unsubtle and crude, oversimplified and melodramatic, psychologically rudimentary and improbable ... and many other equally unpleasant-sounding things. The picture it draws, we are told, is bestial and insulting to our dignity as human beings, its language coarse and obscene, its style repetitive and emphatic. Nor have the psycho-analysts failed to find in the violent sexual matter clues to Zola's own spiritual and bodily condition.

It is a pity that so many professional critics devote their ingenuity to explaining how an artist could have done something quite different much better, how he could have improved his work out of all recognition by doing what he never intended to do. Such critics tend to forget that the critic's job is not to indulge in irrelevant smartness at the artist's expense, but to try by patience and insight to find out what the artist meant to do, and then to estimate how well he has succeeded in doing it. To accuse *Germinal* of indelicacy of matter and coarseness of form is as irrelevant as to blame *Alice in Wonderland* for avoiding the harsh facts of life in nineteenth-century industrial England.

Fortunately Zola's own notes and preliminary sketches set out his intentions unmistakably:

To get a broad effect I must have my two sides as clearly contrasted as possible and carried to the very extreme of intensity. So that I must start with all the woes and fatalities which weigh down on the miners.

5

Facts, not emotional pleas. The miner must be shown crushed, starving, a victim of ignorance, suffering with his children in a hell on earth – but not persecuted, for the bosses are not deliberately vindictive – he is simply overwhelmed by the social situation as it exists. On the contrary, I must make the bosses humane so long as their direct interests are not threatened; no point in foolish tub-thumping. The worker is the victim of the facts of existence – capital, competition, industrial crises . . .

Nothing could be clearer than that: broad effects, the social problem set out in its crudest form, yet an attempt at impartiality based on the view that neither side is really to blame for the hopeless situation which springs from human nature itself and the inevitable tragedy of life. For *Germinal* is an episode in the tragic struggle between capital and labour, indeed it is a tragedy in the narrow sense of the term, for the drama plays itself out in a closed environment from which there is no escape and which progressively brutalizes all the actors. Nobody is really responsible, the employers being caught up in the system as much as the employees. But if *Germinal* be placed in its context we can understand its author's intentions still better.

*

Published in 1885, *Germinal* was the thirteenth to appear in the great series of twenty novels to which Zola devoted nearly twenty-five years of his life, for he began working on *La Fortune des Rougon* well before the outbreak of the Franco-Prussian war of 1870 and completed *Le Docteur Pascal* in 1893. The full title of the series: *Les Rougon-Macquart. Histoire naturelle et sociale d'une famille sous le Second Empire*, indicates Zola's twofold purpose: to study the effects of heredity and of environment upon the members of a family. With characteristic enthusiasm for the fashionable scientific doctrines of his day, Zola unquestioningly ascribed to physiological determinism the role played in earlier literatures by fatality, human or divine. Henceforth, thanks to science, it was to be recognized that a man's heredity, blood and nervous system are his doom. This physiological doom may be modified by the man's environment – his social position and his daily work – but it cannot be escaped. Zola proclaimed that in the modern world the novelist, like everybody else, must be a scientist in the sense that like the experimental scientist he simply 'observes' phenomena. The scientist in his laboratory puts his substances into contact in a suitable container (environment) and then plays no further personal part, but steps back and merely notes down the inevitable reactions. In exactly the same way the modern scientific novelist should bring together certain human types, whose hereditary composition is known, put them together in a suitable environment and then report impersonally what must happen because scientific laws dictate each reaction. It follows from this theory of the 'experimental novel', as Zola called it, that the novelist, being a scientific observer of contemporary society (for the historical novel, being a work of imagination, is ruled out as unscientific), cannot be held morally responsible for what happens in his novel any more than a chemist for what happens in his test-tube. Moreover, if he has to 'observe' diseased or depraved beings in a corrupt society, not only must he put down faithfully what he sees, but he can no more be accused of bad taste, obscenity, or nastiness than the doctor who uncovers a man's nakedness and examines his sores in order to diagnose his disease.

With these aims and methods in view Zola set out in 1868 to document himself by reading all the available medical and scientific books and taking copious notes about conditions in this and that walk of life, for by making members of a large and complicated family seek their living in various ways and rise or fall in society, it would be possible to examine the principal professions, trades, classes, political, religious, or artistic groups, and so on. The grandiose scheme was thus not only to follow out the workings of heredity, but at the same time to give a complete and scientific documented picture of every level of society in France during the Second Empire. Let us make the acquaintance of those members of the family who explain the heredity and background of the hero of *Germinal*, Étienne Lantier.

*

The common ancestress of all the family was Adelaïde Fouque, known as Tante Dide, born in the eighteenth century and great-grandmother of Étienne. She was a passionate, hysterical creature whose weak and uncontrolled nature ultimately brought her to the madhouse, where she was to live on and die as a centenarian, having been a silent and uncomprehending witness of the passions and follies of her numerous descendants. She lived at Plassans, in Provence, which is of course Aix-en-Provence, where Zola spent his childhood and youth. Adelaïde married Rougon, a stolid and hard-working peasant, but soon lost him, after the birth of their son Pierre Rougon. Soon she gave herself to a violent, drunken smuggler named Macquart, and from this irregular union came two children, Antoine and Ursule Macquart. Hence the two branches of the family: the legitimate line, the Rougons, and the illegitimate, the Macquarts. All the members of the family have one trait in common: violent appetites and a desire to have, hold, and enjoy to the full the things of this world. But whereas the Rougons, in whom Adelaïde's volatile, passionate blood is thickened by the heavier stuff of the peasant Rougon, are intelligent, energetic, and generally successful in life (often unscrupulously), the Macquarts, being cross-breeds from two equally unstable and neurotic ancestors, whose instability is aggravated by alcohol, are violent, exaggerated in their reactions, criminals, lunatics, or (since these things are closely allied) artists and geniuses. The family story is complicated still further at one point when the two branches fuse by a marriage between Rougon and Macquart cousins and three 'mixed' children result.

Antoine Macquart, born of Adelaïde and the smuggler in 1789, was a soldier, then a wastrel and blackmailer, who lived to a great age in the neighbourhood of Plassans without doing a stroke of work because he knew all the details of his successful half-brother Rougon's rise to a position of wealth and civic power. He and his wife were chronic alcoholics. Their second daughter, Gervaise, born in 1828, the most pathetic figure in the whole saga of novels, inherited her parents' fecklessness and their alcoholism. At fourteen she had a son, Claude, by a smart and handsome ne'er-do-well named Lantier. Two more boys followed in rapid succession,

Jacques and Étienne (born in 1846). When Lantier's mother died, in 1851, he took Gervaise and two of the boys, Claude and Étienne, to Paris. But as soon as they had spent his inheritance, he abandoned her and the children in their lodgings and went off to sponge on another woman. Gervaise might have made good in her job as a laundress, but she married a labourer named Coupeau who took to drink while recovering from an accident. This example was too much for her weak nature and inherited tendencies, and she sank into drunken squalor and died in misery (*L'Assommoir*). Étienne's brother Claude became an artist of genius destined to kill himself in an insane fit of artistic frustration. It is probable that into his portrait of Claude Zola put some traits of his childhood friend Cézanne (*L'Œuvre*). The other brother, Jacques, who had been left behind at Plassans, became a railway engine-driver and homicidal maniac (*La Bête humaine*), whilst the half-sister of these three, Anna Coupeau, called Nana, brought up in a Paris slum in an atmosphere of drink and sexual promiscuity, seized the earliest opportunity to leave home and embark on a career of prostitution (*Nana*). Our hero Étienne, conscious of his terrible hereditary taint, manages as a rule by self-discipline to master his own murderous tendencies and is the least abnormal of his family.

*

So much for the 'natural' history of Étienne Lantier. It is not very important, and *Germinal* would not lose its value or interest if the reader had never heard of Rougons or Macquarts, for Étienne is merely a literary device, a point of view. Zola's object being to study the whole question, not only of coal-mining in northern France, but of working-class conditions, the clash between capital and labour and the value of the various remedies and solutions put forward by labour organizations and political parties, he must have an eye-witness who is himself a worker and knows the miner's life from the inside. But in order that this observer may see with fresh eyes and be able to appreciate suffering and injustice with some detachment and sense of comparison, he must come to this life from the outside and have just enough advantage in education and intelligence over his work-mates to enable him to pity them, judge, and ultimately lead. Hence the remarkable construction of the book. Étienne arrives at Montsou a penniless down-and-out with no mining experience. He obtains an unskilled job and has to learn his trade from the beginning. For eleven chapters, or nearly one-third of the book, Zola is concerned with the first day of Étienne's sojourn in this mining community, and he succeeds in telling the reader a great deal about pits, conditions of work, living conditions of the miners and their families, the social hierarchy of a mining area, while keeping the action constantly on the move and introducing a wide circle of people representing every aspect of the miner's life and every influence brought to bear upon him.

It is not a pleasant picture. Not only are the workers exploited and so underpaid that the ordinary occupational diseases of their life are aggravated by malnutrition, and the daily life of wives and mothers is haunted by debt, but bad housing conditions, over-crowding, and lack of any sort of amenities leave drink and sex as the only possible diversions. The Church is either frankly on the side where good food and company are to be found, and lazily indifferent to the people's sufferings, like abbé Joire, or else, like his successor abbé Ranvier, utilizes those sufferings in its own blackmailing interests. Charity invariably goes to the wrong address, for kindly folk like the Grégoires, with their food parcels and woollies for the children, are always taken in by the clever or artful Pierronnes of this world, who look 'respectable' and 'deserving'.

*

Can this terrible indictment be accepted as it stands? Was Zola playing quite fair? Was he not taking advantage of the fictional Rougon-Macquart framework in order so to confuse the issue with overlapping anachronisms that his readers in 1885 might take *Germinal* for an exact picture of the mining industry at that time? Was he not playing the age-old trick of the political and social agitator which consists of painting a horrifying picture of the scandals of long ago and omitting

10

to say that many of them have long since been put right? Of course up to a point he was prisoner of his own self-imposed limits, and events in the real world had been unkind. Before 1870 he had committed himself to a long series of studies of French society in the Second Empire, that is to say of contemporary society, and like many of his literary colleagues he was opposed to the reactionary selfishness of the régime. But before he had published the first of the series, *La Fortune des Rougon*, the Franco-Prussian war had sent Napoleon III into exile and the Second Empire had passed into history. So that almost from the outset Zola was no longer writing novels of contemporary life, but historical novels, no longer describing a living organism, but dissecting a corpse. And for the next twenty-three years he was to be dealing, at least theoretically, with a society that had come to an end in 1870. This circumstance was to have several very interesting results. It is true that the collapse of France in 1870 gave Zola the magnificent closing scene which art and his social ideas required, and he seized the opportunity and wrote one of the world's great war stories, *La Débâcle* (1892). But in real life this necessary closing scene had come inconveniently early, and in the short space of eighteen years (1852–70) from the beginning to the end of the Second Empire, Zola had to account for all the generations of his vast family. As a result some of the chronology of the Rougon-Macquart novels is specious in the extreme, and the lives of some of his characters are full ones, to put it mildly. Nana, for example, conquers the music-hall stage, becomes the most sought-after of Parisian *cocottes*, corrupts and ruins half the nobility of France, compromises at least one European royalty, travels widely, becomes a race-horse owner on the grand scale, and finally dies worn out and diseased in a hotel bedroom on the Boulevards just as the 1870 war is breaking out. Her age, according to the genealogical tree, is eighteen.

But nobody objects overmuch to a little foreshortening of chronology – indeed, nobody would object at all were not Zola so self-consciously scientific. Other results are more serious. With the passing of the Second Empire passed the

11

danger of political censorship and legal proceedings against hostile writers (Victor Hugo spent the whole of the Second Empire in exile). Now it was safe for left-wing writers to express themselves freely. Who could resist the temptation to get a little of his own back? Not Zola, whose picture of the Second Empire now became frankly socialist in its bias, and in fact a retrospective indictment of a hated society rather than a judiciously realistic portrait. Furthermore, since nothing is more boring than yesterday's newspaper, unless it be last month's, Zola found that his social problems were becoming less topical as the Second Empire was receding, and it was vital to inject some new interest. This he did partly by adding more and more matter of a brutal or erotic nature, so that his novels became world-famous for being 'strong' and 'daring', and partly by dealing more and more frankly with *contemporary* conditions and problems, at the risk of being anachronistic. For instance, in *Au Bonheur des Dames* (1883), on the development of the modern department store, he described methods of publicity and display of goods far in advance of anything known in the sixties, when the action was supposed to take place. The mischief begins, from the point of view of social and political truth, when the unwary reader is presented with a mixture of past and present, of conditions which applied twenty years previously but are no longer true and other conditions and doctrines which had scarcely been heard of twenty years before and are the latest thing today.

This is what happens in *Germinal*. Étienne's age and his family tree date the action at about 1867. Zola accordingly darkens his picture of life in the mines by harrowing descriptions of the agonies of women and children used as beasts of burden, but at the same time, omitting to state that most of this has since been put right, he makes the general industrial slump governing the actions of the Directors of the Montsou Company depend upon all sorts of international factors, such as a radical change in the American market, which did not yet apply in 1867. The Russian anarchist visionary Souvarine, with his doctrine of total destruction as a necessary preliminary to the establishment of a new society, with his scorn for the International, his bombs and his dynamite, is a character compounded of Bakunin and Kropotkin, and the various anarchist outrages of the late seventies and early eighties which culminated in the assassination of Alexander II in 1881. The resulting composite picture of events at Montsou contains old abuses long since modified or put right and modern developments of socialism unknown in 1867. It is a grandiose epic poem of human misery and the revolt of the oppressed, but in no sense a true account of affairs as they could ever have existed at a given time.

*

If this were all, *Germinal* would be a mere political pamphlet containing all the half-truths, exaggerations, and over-simplifications familiar in any work of propaganda. It would not be a work of art. A work of art must have some fundamental human truth; it must not merely make a number of puppets dance to a political tune. Or, to put it another way, *Germinal* is a tragedy, and in tragedy both sides of the struggle have a certain amount of justification and believe themselves to be right. Zola is not merely concerned with demonstrating some theory of his about trades unions or socialism, but with universal human nature, the conflicts of self-interest, the instinctive motives of gain and self-preservation which underlie all men's actions, and which so many political theorists ignore. *Toute politique*, as Valéry has said, *tend à traiter les hommes comme des choses.* Zola does not fall into the trap, and he does not allow his political enthusiasms to blind him to psychological realities and a sense of fairness. The struggle at Montsou is not simply a revolt of oppressed and innocent workers against wicked and tyrannous employers, for life is never as simple as that except in Hyde Park oratory. All these people are caught in the web of a system that is beyond their control, and nobody's motives are disinterested. There are two sides to the question which is at the bottom of the strike of the Montsou workers – the method of payment for timbering. For obvious reasons the miners insist on a piece-work system of payment. That means that time spent on timbering as they cut into new

13

seams is money lost, and therefore they regularly neglect or scamp the timbering. Hence terrible accidents and loss of life. Hence the firm tries to devise a system of payment which will force the men to timber better *for their own safety*. But the men will not sacrifice their more lucrative piece-work, and so· it goes on. Unlike some emotional champions of the underdog, Zola sees that laziness, bad faith and vice are not to be found only in the rich bourgeois and capitalist employers, and that the workers are not always above criticism. Whatever the conditions or the political régime, any community of workers will have its wasters who live in vice and squalor like the Levaques, and its sneaks who feather their own nests and always get the best of everything, like the Pierrons. The tribunes who lead their mates in the struggle are not free from such motives as trying to impress a girl and rise above their station (Étienne), jealousy of younger and more successful tribunes, coupled with the need to attract customers to their pub (Rasseneur) or the downright careerism of Pluchart, with his gay, well-dressed life as a delegate, his congresses, dinners, lunches, and speech-making tours with all expenses paid and never an hour of honest work. And as the little anecdote of the Marseilles hat-makers reminds us, there is not one of these men who, if he won the lottery, would not instantly invest his winnings and become an entrenched capitalist. If the employees are not angels neither are the employers devils. Hennebeau has his terrible personal worries, and his livelihood depends upon his carrying out the policy of the Board of Directors. Deneulin faces ruin and humiliation; he has sunk his all in modern improvements to his pit, his workpeople respect him, but these things avail him nothing. All are the victims of the distant, anonymous power crouching, as Zola says, like some malignant god in his impenetrable shrine. A great sadness, the tragedy and pain of life itself, overwhelms all these poor mortals who suffer as though playthings of the gods. It is significant that the bravest, and in the end most unselfish person in the book is the devil-may-care, philandering engineer Négrel who in the sufferings of others discovers his own humanity. Here is the simple

14

moral of the book: Négrel toils night and day to save the life of his arch-enemy Étienne, and when he has succeeded these two men fall into each other's arms and weep together.

Humanity, then, is the real hero of *Germinal*, and the most successful pages those in which Zola handles crowds of poor people, whether enjoying themselves at the Bank Holiday fair, wandering about the countryside in the search for bread, wreaking terrible vengeance upon machines or men (the vengeance of the women upon Maigrat is one of the most horrible pages in literature), or scattering in panic before the soldiers' guns. As Mr Angus Wilson has said: 'Nowhere, perhaps, have scenes of mass action been more deftly managed, nowhere the confused emotions and thoughts of simple people, treated like beasts and driven into self-defence that is often bestial, more directly made lucid without losing reality.'

Note on this Translation

I HAVE followed the text and chapter arrangement of the standard Bibliothèque Charpentier edition (Paris, Fasquelle) which has appeared in successive reprints ever since Zola's time.

In translating the novel I have tried to keep before me the principle of fidelity to the *tone* of the original, or what Dr E. V. Rieu has called the 'law of equivalent effect', that is to say the duty of a translator to try to reproduce upon English readers the effect which the original had upon its readers when it was published. Now *Germinal* is a brutal and angry book about brutal and angry folk whose language is coarse, direct, and often obscene. Any attempt to make it refined and 'literary' would have betrayed the author's intentions.

But translation of coarse dialogue full of oaths is a delicate matter. The crude words for certain parts of the body and their functions present no difficulty, although such words may pain the high-minded reader, but often swear-words lose their point if transposed directly, simply because the scale of values and the social standing of these words are quite different in one language from another. For instance, some of the strongest French oaths used in this novel are more or less blasphemous variations and elaborations on the *Nom de Dieu!* theme. I have frequently substituted for this sort of thing language more likely to be used by Englishmen of a similar type in similar circumstances.

Zola's style in this novel, as indeed in his other novels of working-class life, such as *L'Assommoir*, has certain peculiarities. In order to maintain uniformity of tone and to suggest that things are seen through the eyes of his characters, he frequently uses the slangy, ungrammatical language of these people even in descriptive or explanatory passages where it is the author who is speaking. But he is not consistent in this, any more than he is always logical in the dialogue of his illiterate characters who, like Maheude, sometimes deliver themselves of passages of a highly poetic and 'literary' nature quite out of keeping with their station, unless it be assumed that in their apocalyptic moments they are vouchsafed a gift of tongues far transcending their normal parlance. I have not considered it my business to try to improve upon Zola in this respect. But there are one or two flagrant discrepancies in the ages of characters, notably old Bonnemort (58 at the beginning of the book but later 50 – since his son Maheu is 42 he must have been precocious indeed!), and on these occasions I have corrected the error in the text and indicated the point in a footnote.

A translator has to adopt an arbitrary policy about proper names. In order to avoid obvious absurdities I have left all personal and place names in French and followed Zola's practice of using the style Monsieur and Madame only for the socially superior characters. But there remained the problem of the miners' womenfolk. Zola prefaces their names by the article *la* and uses wherever possible a feminine form of their surnames (Maheu's wife is la Maheude, Mouque's daughter la Mouquette, etc.). Here I have used the simple feminine form with no prefix, though Ma Brûlé seemed more suitable for that termagant. There is no feminine form of Levaque, and Havelock Ellis's device in his translation of referring to

16

that slatternly creature as 'the Levaque woman' is clumsy and monotonous. I have left her as la Levaque.

Once or twice Zola mentions the temperatures which human beings had to endure in this underground hell. In order to convey the right impression to English readers I have used Fahrenheit equivalents and indicated the original centigrade figures in a footnote.

A work on a subject as technical as coal-mining is bound to have a somewhat specialized vocabulary, and a translator without first-hand knowledge of life in the pits must constantly choose between words for the same thing which are quite different in different British coalfields. How is he to decide between a *collier*, *hewer*, *getter*, *breaker*, let alone a *pickman* and *pikeman*, bearing in mind that in the pre-mechanized mines of Northern France seventy or eighty years ago the very methods of extraction and the jobs of the various workers were totally different from what they are in this country today? In the above case *collier* is clearly the most general term, but in some more debatable cases I have kept to the word most likely to be understood by the general reader, at the risk of incurring the derision of, say, a Black Country miner when he sees a term smacking of South Yorkshire. In this matter, as in many others, I am most grateful to two friends and colleagues, Dr Gordon Hall and Dr R. E. Asher, who have put their long experience of life in mining areas at my disposal. Married men will understand my desire to mention at this point the debt I owe my wife, Kathleen Tancock, for ungrudging help and patience without end. Such flaws as remain are due to my ignorance or obstinacy, or both.

March 1954   L. W. T.

Part One

░░

[1]

On a pitch-black, starless night, a solitary man was trudging along the main road from Marchiennes to Montsou, ten kilometres of cobblestones running straight as a die across the bare plain between fields of beet. He could not even make out the black ground in front of him, and it was only the feel of the March wind blowing in great gusts like a storm at sea, but icy cold from sweeping over miles of marshes and bare earth, that gave him a sensation of limitless, flat horizons. There was not a single tree to darken the sky, and the cobbled highroad ran on with the straightness of a jetty through the swirling sea of black shadows.

The man had set out from Marchiennes at about two. He strode on, shivering in his threadbare cotton coat and corduroy trousers. He was having trouble with a little bundle done up in a check handkerchief, which he held against his ribs first with one elbow and then with the other, so as to keep both his hands deep in his pockets, for they were numb and raw from the lashing winds. Being out of work and homeless, he had only one thought in his mind, and that was the hope that the cold would get less intense when daylight came. He had been tramping like this for an hour and was within two kilometres of Montsou, when to his left he saw some red flares – three braziers apparently burning in mid-air. At first fear held him back, but the urge to warm his hands for a minute was too painful to resist.

The road ran into a cutting and the fires disappeared. To his right there was a fence, a sort of wall of heavy baulks of timber shutting off a railway track, while to his left there rose a grass bank with some sort of roofs on top, like a village with low gables all the same size. He walked on about two hundred paces and suddenly, as he rounded a bend, the lights re-appeared quite close, yet still he could not make out why they were burning high up in the dark sky, like smoky moons. But his eye was caught by something else at ground level; it was the solid mass of a block of low buildings, surmounted by the silhouette of a factory chimney. Here and there a light showed through a grimy window, while outside five or six dismal lanterns were hanging on blackened timber-work which stood like a row of gigantic trestles. Out of this weird, smoke-black vision there came a single sound: the heavy, laboured panting of an unseen exhaust-pipe.

Then he realized that it was a pit. His nervousness re-turned: what was the good? there was sure not to be any work. Instead of making for the buildings, he decided to venture up the slag-heap where the three coal fires were burning in buckets to give light and warmth to the workers. The rippers must have worked late, for the waste was still being brought up. He could now hear the labourers pushing their trains along the trestles and pick out moving shadows emptying the tubs near each of the fires.

'Morning,' he said, going up to one of the fire-buckets.

The haulier, an old man in a mauve jersey and felt cap, was standing with his back to the fire, while his big, cream-coloured horse stood like a statue, waiting for the six tubs he had pulled up to be emptied. The man at the tip, a lanky, red-haired fellow, was in no hurry and looked half asleep as his hand worked the lever. Up above, the icy wind redoubled its fury with great regular gusts like the strokes of a scythe.

'Morning,' the old man answered.

Silence. Feeling himself looked at with a resentful eye, the man said at once who he was.

'My name is Étienne Lantier and I am a mechanic. Any work going here?'

The firelight showed him up: he looked about twenty-one, was very dark, handsome and strong-looking in spite of his slight build.

The haulier, reassured, shook his head.

20

'Work for a mechanic? No. Two of them tried yesterday. No, nothing doing.'

A gust of wind interrupted them. Then, pointing at the dark mass of buildings at the bottom of the slag-tip, Étienne asked:

'This is a pit, isn't it?'

But the old man could not answer at once for he was choked by a violent fit of coughing. In the end he spat, and his spittle showed up as a black patch on the ground reddened by the glow.

'Yes, it's a pit all right. Le Voreux. Look, the village is just over there.'

Pointing in his turn into the darkness, he indicated the village, the roofs of which the young man had guessed at. But by now the six tubs were empty, and he walked off after them on his stiff, rheumaticky legs; as for the big horse, he started off on his own, without needing any crack of the whip, plodding heavily between the rails, with the hair of his coat blown up on end by a fresh gust of wind.

While Étienne lingered by the fire warming his poor raw hands, Le Voreux began to emerge as from a dream. He could now pick out each part of the works: the tarpaulin-covered screening shed, the headgear, the huge winding-house, the square tower of the drainage pump. With its squat brick buildings huddled in a valley, and the chimney sticking up like a menacing horn, the pit was evil-looking, a voracious beast crouching ready to devour the world. As he stood looking at it, he thought of himself and the wandering existence of the past week while he had been job-hunting. He saw himself hitting the foreman in the railway shop and being kicked out of Lille, kicked out of everywhere. On Saturday he had reached Marchiennes, where they said there was work at the Forges; but there was nothing, either at the Forges or at the Sonneville works. Sunday he had had to spend hiding under the timber in a wheelwright's yard, and now the watchman had chucked him out, and at two in the morning. Nothing left, not a penny, not even a crust; what was he to do now, on the road with nowhere to go and no idea even where to find shelter from the wind? Yes, he could see it was a mine now, for the scattered lanterns showed up the yards, and a door which suddenly opened gave him a glimpse of the furnaces in a blaze of light. He could understand it all now, even the exhaust of the pump, the long, heavy, monotonous panting, like the snoring breath of a monster.

The tipper, bending over his work, had not even looked up at Étienne, who was just going to pick up the little bundle which he had dropped, when a fit of coughing heralded the return of the haulier. He was slowly emerging out of the shadows, followed by the cream horse with six more loaded trucks.

'Are there any factories at Montsou?' asked the young man.

The old chap spat black and then shouted into the wind:

'Oh, plenty of factories, and no mistake! Should have seen them three or four years ago. Everything humming, couldn't find enough men, never were such profits. And now we're all tightening our belts again. The whole place is a misery: factories closing down and people being sacked right and left. . . . I suppose it isn't the Emperor's fault, but what does he want to go off fighting in America for? To say nothing of the animals dying of cholera, same as the men.'

And then they both went on grousing, in short sentences as the wind caught their breath. Étienne told him about his week's useless tramping round. Had he just got to peg out with hunger, then? Soon there would be nothing but beggars on the roads. Yes, the old man agreed, it was bound to end up in a row, for, by God, you couldn't throw all these decent people out on the streets.

'It isn't every day you see any meat.'

'If you even got bread. . . .'

'Yes, that's a fact; if you even got bread.'

Their voices died away as the squalls bore off the words in a dismal howling.

'Look,' shouted the haulier at the top of his voice as he turned southwards, 'that's Montsou over there.'

Holding out his hand again, he pointed to some invisible places in the darkness and named them one by one. Over on that side, at Montsou, the Fauvelle sugar refinery was still working, but the Hoton sugar people had cut down staff, and there was hardly anything else working except the Dutilleul flourmill and the Bleuze cable works. Then with a sweeping gesture he indicated half the northern horizon: the Sonneville building firm had not had two-thirds of their usual orders, only two of the three blast-furnaces of the Marchiennes Forges were burning and there was a strike threatened at the Gage-bois glassworks because there was talk of a wage-cut.

'Yes, I know, I know,' said the young man at each bit of information; 'that's where I've just come from.'

'It's all right for us so far,' went on the haulier, 'but still, the mines have reduced output. Only two batteries of coke-ovens working at La Victoire, which you can see over there.'

He spat again, and went off after his sleepy horse which he had harnessed to the empty tubs.

Étienne now commanded a view of the whole district. It was still very dark, but the old man had peopled the darkness with untold sufferings, which the young one could sense all round him in the limitless space. Could he not hear a cry of famine borne over this bleak country by the March wind? The gale had lashed itself into a fury and seemed to be blowing death to all labour and a great hunger that would finish off men by the hundred. And with his roving eye he tried to peer through the gloom, with a tormenting desire to see and yet a fear of seeing. Everything slid away into the dark unknown, and all he could see was distant furnaces and coke-ovens which, set in batteries of a hundred chimneys arranged obliquely, made sloping lines of crimson flames; whilst further to the left the two blast-furnaces were burning blue in the sky like monstrous torches. It was as depressing to watch as a building on fire: as far as the threatening horizon the only stars which rose were the nocturnal fires of the land of coal and iron.

'You come from Belgium, don't you?' It was the haulier's voice behind him. He had come back again.

This time he had only brought three tubs. There had been an accident to the cage, a broken nut, which would hold up work for a good quarter of an hour, but at any rate these three could be emptied. At the bottom of the tip there was not a sound to be heard, and the continuous rumbling of the labourers on the trestles had stopped. All you could hear was a hammer banging on sheet metal somewhere down the shaft.

'No, I'm from the south,' answered the young man.

The tipper had emptied the tubs and sat down, glad about the accident. Still surly and taciturn, he looked up at the driver with his big dull eyes as though he was put out by all this talk. And certainly the old man was not usually so chatty. He must have taken to this stranger's face, and had one of those urges to talk about themselves which sometimes make old folk ramble on out loud even when they are alone.

'I belong to Montsou,' he said; 'name of Bonnemort.'

'Is that a real name?' asked Étienne with surprise.

The old chap grinned with satisfaction, and pointing to Le Voreux:

'Yes, yes . . . three times I've been brought up out of there in pieces. Once with all my skin roasted, once stuffed with earth right down to my gizzard, and the third time with my belly blown out with water like a frog. So when they saw that I didn't mean to kick the bucket, they called me Bonnemort, just for a joke.'

His mirth redoubled, like the screech of pulley that wants oiling, and it ended up in a terrible fit of coughing. By the light of the fire-bucket you could now see his big head, with its sparse white hair, and his flat features, livid, with bluish blotches. He was short, with a powerful neck, his legs turning outwards and his toes turning in, and his square hands hung at the end of long arms right down to his knees. Like his horse, who stood motionless without appearing to mind the wind, he seemed to be made of stone, unconscious of the cold and the hurricane whistling about his ears. He coughed, a mighty, scraping hawk which seemed to tear out his inside, and then spat by the side of the fire. It turned the ground black.

Étienne looked at him and looked at the blackened earth.

'Have you been working in the pit for long?'

Bonnemort threw out both arms.

'For long? I should say so. I wasn't eight when I first went down – it was in Le Voreux, as a matter of fact – and now I am fifty-eight. Work it out for yourself. . . . I've done everything in my time: began as a pit-boy, then haulage man when I was strong enough to push, then eighteen years as a collier. Then because of my perishing legs, they put me on ripping, then packing, then repairs, until in the end they had to bring me up above ground because the doctor said that if they didn't I should stay down for good. Well, that was five years ago, and they made me a haulier. Fifty years as miner and forty-five of them underground. Not so bad, is it?'

Every now and again while he was talking, a live coal would fall out of the bucket and light up his pale face blood red.

'They say I've got to rest,' he went on, 'but I'm not having any. What do they take me for? No, I shall stick it out another two years till I'm sixty and get the hundred and eighty pension. If I walked out today they would at once grant me the hundred and fifty, the artful buggers! And anyway I'm pretty tough, apart from my legs. You see, I've been so soaked with water down in the workings that it has got under my skin. Some days I can't move my foot without shouting out.'

He was cut short by another fit of coughing.

'And that's what makes you cough as well?' said Étienne.

But he shook his head vigorously, and when he could speak again went on:

'No, no. I caught cold last month. I never used to cough, and now I can't shake it off. And the funny thing is that I spit and I spit. . . .' He hawked again and spat black.

'Blood?' by now Étienne felt he could make bold to ask.

Bonnemort slowly wiped his mouth with the back of his hand.

'No, coal. I've got enough in my carcase to keep me warm for the rest of my days. And I haven't set foot down there for five years! It seems I had it in store without knowing it. Oh, well, it keeps you fit.'

There was a pause. The distant hammer went on banging regularly down in the pit, and the wind went on wailing like a cry of weariness and hunger rising from the depths of the night. By the light of the leaping flames the old man went quietly on chewing over his memories. Oh yes, it wasn't yesterday that he and his had begun picking at the seams! His family had worked for the Montsou mine ever since the beginning, and that went back a long way, a hundred and six years. His grandfather Guillaume Maheu, then a lad of fifteen, had found soft coal at Réquillart, the Company's first pit, now disused, over there by the Fauvelle sugar refinery. It was common knowledge in the district, and the proof was that it was called the Guillaume seam – after his grandfather. He hadn't known him himself, but they said he was a big, strong fellow who died of old age at sixty. Then his father Nicholas Maheu, nicknamed Red, had stayed at the bottom of Le Voreux when he was barely forty; they were excavating it then. Roof fell in, flattened him right out; the rocks had drunk his blood and swallowed his bones. Later on, two of his uncles and his three brothers had ended down there too, and he, Vincent Maheu, was considered a wily old bird because he had got out of it with a whole skin, except for his gammy legs. What could you do about it, anyway? You had to work. You did this job from father to son, just like anything else. His son Toussaint Maheu was killing himself at it now, and his grandchildren and all his lot; they all lived in the village, up there. A hundred and six years of cutting, the kids after the old ones, and all for the same firm. Plenty of posh people couldn't have said as much, eh?

'All right so long as you can find something to eat,' murmured Étienne again.

'That's what I say. So long as there is something to eat you can keep going.'

Bonnemort fell silent as his eyes turned towards the village, where windows were lighting up one by one. Montsou church tower chimed four and it felt colder than ever.

'Is your Company rich?' asked Étienne.

The old chap raised his shoulders and lowered them again, as though he were weighed down by an avalanche of coins.

'Oh yes, oh yes! . . . Perhaps not quite so rich as the Anzin Company – that's our neighbour – but even so, millions and millions. You lose count. Nineteen pits and thirteen of them in production – Le Voreux, La Victoire, Crèvecœur, Mirou, Saint-Thomas, Madeleine, Feutry-Cantel and others besides;

and six for drainage and ventilation, such as Réquillart. . . .
Ten thousand employees, concessions stretching over sixty-
seven parishes, five thousand tons lifted every day, all the pits
linked by rail, and workshops, and factories. . . . Oh yes,
there's plenty of money!'

The big cream horse pricked up his ears at the sound of tubs
running along trestles. The cage must have been repaired
down below, for the labourers had started on the job again.
As he harnessed his horse for the downward journey, the
driver affectionately said to him:

'Mustn't get into the habit of gossiping, you lazy devil!
Suppose Monsieur Hennebeau knew how you are wasting
time!'

Étienne looked thoughtfully at the blackness around him
and asked:

'So all this belongs to Monsieur Hennebeau?'

'Oh no!' the old man explained. 'Monsieur Hennebeau is
only the manager. He is paid, same as we are.'

The young man waved an arm at the unfathomable darkness.

'Who does all this belong to, then?'

But just at that moment Bonnemort was choked by such a
violent fit of coughing that he could not get his breath. At
length, after spitting and wiping the black foam off his lips, he
said into the howling wind:

'What? Who does this belong to? God knows. . . . People.
. . .'

And he pointed to some vague unknown distant spot in the
night, where these people lived for whom the Maheus had
been hacking at the seam for a hundred and six years. His
voice had taken on a kind of religious awe, as though he were
speaking of some inaccessible tabernacle, where dwelt unseen
the gorged and crouching deity whom they all appeased with
their flesh but whom nobody had ever seen.

'If only you could eat your fill,' said Étienne for the third
time, without any obvious transition.

'Lord, yes! If you could always eat you would have nothing
to grumble about.'

The horse set off, and its driver disappeared too, with the

27

dragging gait of a sick man. The man by the tip had not moved, but was still curled up in a ball, with his chin between his knees and his big dull eyes staring into space.

Étienne picked up his bundle, but still did not go away. The wind felt icy on his back, but his chest was being roasted by the big fire. All the same, it might be as well to apply at the pit, for the old man might not know anything about it; and besides, he was not particular, he would take on any sort of job. Where was there to go and what was to become of him in a land ravaged by unemployment? Was he to leave his corpse behind some wall, like a stray dog? And yet here on this naked plain, in this thick darkness, he had a feeling of hesitation; Le Voreux struck fear into him. Each squall seemed fiercer than the last, as though each time it blew from an even more distant horizon. No sign of dawn; the sky was dead: only the furnaces and coke ovens glared and reddened the shadows, but did not penetrate their mystery. And, huddled in its lair like some evil beast, Le Voreux crouched ever lower and its breath came in longer and deeper gasps, as though it were struggling to digest its meal of human flesh.

[2]

VILLAGE Two Hundred and Forty, surrounded by its fields of corn and beet, was slumbering in blackest night. Its four great blocks of little back-to-back houses could just be made out: they were like hospital or barrack blocks, geometrical, parallel, separated by three wide strips of land divided into regular garden plots. The only sound in this desolate plain was the moaning of the wind through gaps in the fences.

At the Maheus', number sixteen of the second block, there was no sign of life. The one proper first-floor room was wrapped in thick darkness, which seemed to weigh down on the sleeping beings, their presence felt rather than seen, who lay there all of a heap, open-mouthed, knocked out with fatigue. Although it was so cold outside, the air was heavy with the warmth of living things, the stuffy heat of even the best-kept bedrooms when full of human flesh.

The cuckoo clock downstairs struck four and still nothing could be heard but the gentle sound of light breathing, accompanied by two deeper snores. And then, suddenly, Catherine got up. In her sleep, she had instinctively counted the four strokes, through the floor, but had not found the strength to wake up properly. She dragged her legs out of bed, felt for a match, struck it and lit the candle. But there she sat, and her head felt so heavy that it toppled from shoulder to shoulder, yielding to an invincible urge to fall back on to the pillow.

The candle lit up the square room with its two windows. It was almost filled by three beds, but there was a cupboard, a table and two old walnut chairs, which stood out dark against the cream-painted wall. That was all; clothes hanging on pegs, a jug on the floor beside a red earthenware basin to wash in. In the bed to the left the eldest son Zacharie, a fellow of twenty-one, was sleeping with his brother Jeanlin, who was nearly eleven; in the right-hand one two children, Lénore and Henri, the one six, the other four, were asleep in each other's arms; whilst Catherine shared the third bed with her sister Alzire, who was so puny for her nine years that she would not even have noticed her by her side, had not the poor deformed creature's humpback stuck in her ribs. Through the open glass door could be seen the landing passage, a sort of cubby-hole where the parents slept in a fourth bed, against which they had had to put the cradle for their last-born, Estelle, scarcely three months old.

Catherine made a desperate effort, stretched, and ran her hands through her red hair, which was tousled on her neck and forehead. She was slight for her fifteen years, though as she was entirely covered by her tight-fitting nightgown, the only parts of her that could be seen were her feet, tattooed in blue by coal, and her delicate arms, the milk-white colour of which contrasted with her muddy complexion, already ruined by constant washings with soft soap. She opened her mouth wide in a final yawn, and showed her fine teeth set in pale, chlorotic gums. Her grey eyes were weeping as though they had soap in them, and they had the tired, careworn expression that

29

comes from fighting back sleep. This seemed to give her whole body a puffy look.

At that moment there came from the landing a sort of growl. It was Maheu's voice, thick with sleep:

'God! it's time. . . . You lighting up, Catherine?'

'Yes, Dad; it's just struck four downstairs.'

'Look sharp, then, you lazy faggot! If you hadn't danced quite so much yesterday, being Sunday, you would have woken us up a bit earlier. There's a lazy life for you!'

He grumbled on, but sleep got the better of him too, and his remarks got mixed up and then tailed off into renewed snoring.

The girl moved about the room barefoot, in her shift. When she came to the bed of Henri and Lénore, she pulled up their coverlet which had slipped down, but they did not wake out of the deep sleep of childhood. Alzire, with her eyes wide open, had turned over without a word into the warm place left by her big sister.

'Come on, Zacharie! And you too, Jeanlin, come on!' said Catherine several times, as she stood over her two brothers sprawling there with their heads buried in the pillow.

She had to get hold of her elder brother by the shoulders and shake him; and then, while he was cursing and swearing, she decided to pull the bedclothes off them. It amused her to see the two boys' bare legs kicking about, and she laughed.

'Leave me alone, you fool,' growled Zacharie in a surly voice when he sat up; 'don't you try to be funny, I don't like it. O Christ! to think it's time to get up!'

He was thin and lanky, with the fair hair and anaemic pallor of the family, and a suggestion of beard made his long face look dirty. His shirt was up to his middle, and he pulled it down, not out of modesty but because he was cold.

'The clock's struck downstairs,' she repeated; 'come on, up you get. Dad's getting angry.'

Jeanlin, who had curled up again, shut his eyes and said: 'Go to hell! I'm asleep.'

She went off into another healthy peal of laughter. He was so tiny, with his thin limbs and huge joints swollen with the scrofula, that she picked him up bodily. He kicked out; his face, like a small, frizzy-haired monkey's, with its green eyes and big ears, was white with humiliation at being so weak. He said nothing, but bit her right breast.

'You beastly tike!' she muttered, stifling a scream, and dropped him on the floor.

Alzire, holding the sheet up to her chin, had not gone off to sleep again but, with the intelligent eyes of an invalid, silently watched her sister and two brothers dressing. A fresh quarrel broke out over the basin: the two boys, complaining that their sister was dawdling over her washing, began shoving her out of the way. Shirts flew through the air, and they shamelessly relieved the night's distension with the calm familiarity of a litter of puppies brought up together. Catherine was ready first. She stepped into her miner's trousers, put on her coarse linen jacket and fastened her blue cap over her knot of hair. In these clean, Monday-morning clothes she looked like a little man, and the only trace left of her sex was a slight swing of the hips.

'The old chap will be pleased to find the bed all mucked up when he comes in,' said Zacharie spitefully. 'I'll tell him it was you.'

The old chap was their grandfather Bonnemort who, as he worked on nights, went to bed in the morning. In this way the bed never got cold; there was always somebody to snore in it.

Without answering, Catherine set about pulling over the coverlet and tucking it in. But meanwhile noises had begun next door, through the wall. These brick walls, built as cheaply as possible by the Company, were so flimsy that the slightest breath could be heard through, and no detail of private life was hidden, even from the children. A heavy foot had stumped on the stairs, and then there was a sort of soft thud followed by a sigh of contentment.

'Here we go!' said Catherine; 'Levaque goes down, so up comes Bouteloup to join la Levaque.'

Jeanlin sniggered, and even Alzire's eyes sparkled. Every morning the threesome next door tickled them like this. A collier taking in a ripper as a lodger; that gave his wife two men, one for nights and one for days.

'Philomène is coughing,' went on Catherine, after another listen.

31

She was referring to the Levaques' eldest daughter, a gangling girl of nineteen and Zacharie's mistress, by whom he had had two children already. With it all she was so weak in the chest that she worked as a screener, never having been fit to work underground.

'Don't you believe it!' said Zacharie. 'She's asleep. She doesn't care a damn. Fancy sleeping on until six o'clock, the lazy pig!'

He was pulling on his trousers when, on a sudden impulse, he opened one of the windows. It was pitch black outside, but the village was waking up, and lights were peeping one by one between the slats of the shutters. And that started off another argument: he was craning his neck to try to see whether the overman of Le Voreux would come out of the Pierrons' opposite, for he was said to sleep with Pierronne. But his sister kept on shouting that since yesterday Pierron had been on the day shift at pit-bottom, so that Dansaert could not have slept there that night. All this time, as they got more and more vehement about the truth of their information, the wind was coming in in icy gusts; and then a burst of crying came from Estelle. The cold was upsetting her.

That woke Maheu. What was the matter with his old bones? He dropped off to sleep again like a good-for-nothing. And he swore so loud that the children in the next room hardly breathed. Zacharie and Jeanlin finished washing with weary slowness, while Alzire still looked on wide-eyed. The two babies Lénore and Henri, locked in each other's arms, had not stirred, but went on breathing softly all through the hubbub.

'Catherine, give me the candle!' roared Maheu.

Buttoning up her jacket, she took the candle into the little room, leaving her brothers to find their things by the glimmer coming through the door. Her father was getting out of bed. She did not stop, but felt her way downstairs in her stockinged feet, lit another candle in the living-room and began to make the coffee. The clogs of the whole family were under the dresser.

'Will you shut up, you little varmint!' shouted Maheu, exasperated by the continual yelling of Estelle.

He was a sturdier edition of old Bonnemort, short, with a

big head, flat pale face, and close-cropped fair hair. The baby bawled louder than ever, frightened by his big sinewy arms waving about above her head.

'Leave her alone, you know she'll never stop,' said her mother, stretching herself out in the middle of the bed.

She too had just awakened and felt peevish; it was so silly never to get a night's sleep. Couldn't they get themselves off quietly? Snuggling down under the clothes, she showed only her long face with its strong features, handsome in a heavy way but already worn out at thirty-nine, owing to her life of poverty and the seven children she had had. While he was dressing she kept her eyes on the ceiling and went on talking slowly, for now neither of them so much as heard the baby who was crying fit to choke.

'You know, there isn't a penny left, and it's only Monday: six more days to go till pay-day. . . . It can't go on like this. You bring in nine francs between the lot of you. How do you expect me to make do with ten in the family?'

'Nine francs, I like that!' Maheu countered. 'Me and Zacharie, three each: that makes six. . . . Catherine and the old man, two: that makes four; six and four, ten. . . . And Jeanlin one, that's eleven.'

'Yes, but there are Sundays and days lost. It's never more than nine, I tell you!'

He didn't answer, but busily groped about on the floor for his leather belt. Then, as he straightened up:

'Mustn't grumble, I'm still pretty tough. Quite a few of them are drafted to repairs by the time they are forty-two.'

'That's as may be, my dear, but it doesn't get us any bread. What am I going to do, eh? I suppose you've got nothing?'

'A couple of coppers.'

'Keep them for a drink. . . . Oh Lord! what *am* I going to do? Six more days! They'll never end. We owe Maigrat sixty, and the day before yesterday he turned me away. Of course I shall go back and try him again all the same. But if he keeps on refusing . . .'

And she went on in a doleful voice. Her head never moved, but now and then she blinked her eyes in the dismal candle-light. She told the tale of the empty cupboard, the kids asking

33

for bread and butter, even the coffee running short (and the water gave you the colic!), and all the day long you pretended to satisfy hunger with boiled cabbage leaves. She gradually had to raise her voice so as not to have her words drowned by Estelle. The noise was getting unbearable and Maheu suddenly seemed to become aware of it, for he picked the child out of her cradle and flung her on to her mother's bed, shouting in a frenzy of rage:

'Here, you take her; I could bash her head in. . . . The brat has got every bloody thing she wants, she has a suck of milk whenever she likes, and yet she grouses louder than anybody else!'

True enough, Estelle had begun to suck. She was now snugly hidden under the warm bed-clothes, and all that was left of her was a greedy smacking of lips.

'Didn't the gentry up at La Piolaine say you could go and see them?' said Maheu after a pause.

His wife pursed her lips with a look of dreary scepticism:

'Yes, they met me . . . they take round clothes for poor children. . . . Oh, well, I'll take Lénore and Henri up there this morning. If only they would give me a hundred sous!'

Silence fell again. He was ready now, and he stood still for a moment and then wound up with his expressionless voice:

'Well, what do you expect? That's how things are. Try and fix up something for the soup. . . . We shall never get any forrarder talking about it; much better be getting on with the job down there.'

'Yes, of course,' answered his wife. 'Blow the candle out. I don't need to see what colour my thoughts are.'

He blew out the candle. Zacharie and Jeanlin were already going downstairs and he followed them, the wooden treads creaking under their heavy, stockinged feet. Behind them darkness had fallen again in the landing-room and the main bedroom. The children were asleep and even Alzire's eyes had closed. But the mother stayed there with her eyes staring into the darkness while Estelle, pulling at her worn-out, pendulous breast, was purring like a kitten.

Catherine's first job downstairs had been to see to the fire. A coal fire burned night and day in the cast-iron kitchen range

34

with its grate in the middle and ovens on each side. Eight hectolitres of *escaillage* – hard coal picked up off the roads – were issued to each family per month. The stuff was hard to light, and Catherine, whose job it was to cover the fire at night, had only to poke it up in the morning and add a few bits of specially selected soft coal. Then she put a kettle on the grate and stooped down to look in the cupboard.

The room was fairly big, occupying the whole of the ground floor. It was painted apple green and kept with Flemish cleanliness, with its flagstones washed down and sprinkled with white sand. Apart from the varnished deal cupboard, the furniture consisted of a table and chairs of the same wood. Stuck on the walls were some highly-coloured prints – the standard portraits of the Emperor and Empress presented by the Company, soldiers and saints with plenty of gilt on – which contrasted violently with the bare lightness of the room. The only other ornaments were a pink cardboard box on the cupboard and the cuckoo clock with its gaily painted dial. Its heavy tick seemed to fill the empty spaces near the ceiling. Beside the staircase door was another leading to the cellar. Although the place was so clean, a smell of onions, shut in since the day before, pervaded the hot heavy air, already acrid with coal fumes.

Catherine was pondering in front of the open cupboard. All there was left was a bit of bread, plenty of cream cheese but only the merest shave of butter; and sandwiches had to be made for the four of them. At length she made up her mind, cut slices of bread, spread one with cheese, scraped a little butter on the other and clapped them together. This was the *briquet*, the sandwich taken every morning down the mine. The four *briquets* were soon set out on the table in a row graded with strict justice, from the biggest one, which was father's, to the smallest for Jeanlin.

Although she seemed wholly taken up with her housework, Catherine must have been turning over in her mind Zacharie's tales about the overman and Pierronne, for she opened the front door and peeped out. It was still windy. More and more lights were appearing in the squat houses, for the village was all agog with an indefinable atmosphere of getting-up. Doors

35

were already banging and shadowy lines of workmen disappearing into the night. But how silly she was to be standing there getting cold, when for certain the onsetter was still asleep as he did not go on at pit-bottom until six! But there she stood, contemplating the house across the gardens, and when the door opened her curiosity was aroused. But of course it could only be Lydie, the Pierron child, setting off for the pit.

A hissing of steam made her turn round. She shut the door and ran, for the water was boiling over and putting out the fire. As there was no fresh coffee left, she had to pour the water on to yesterday's grounds. She then put some brown sugar straight into the coffee-pot, and by that time her father and two brothers were coming down.

'Lumme!' declared Zacharie, sniffing at his bowl, 'this lot won't give us a headache!'

Maheu shrugged with a resigned air.

'Never mind, it's warm; it'll do you good.'

Jeanlin had collected the crumbs from the sandwiches and was making a sop. When she had finished her coffee, Catherine emptied the rest of the pot into their tin flasks. All four were standing up in the light of the guttering candle, swallowing at full speed.

'Aren't we nearly ready?' said father. 'Anybody would think we were gentlemen of leisure.'

From upstairs a voice came down through the open door. It was Maheude calling:

'You can take all the bread. I've got a little vermicelli for the children.'

'Right-oh!' shouted Catherine.

She covered over the fire and stood some left-over soup on the corner of the hob to be hot for grandfather when he came in at six. They took their clogs from under the dresser, slipped the strings of their flasks over their shoulders and each one put his sandwich down his back, between his shirt and his jacket. And off they went, the men going first and the girl last, when she had blown out the candle and locked up. Darkness reigned again.

'Hallo! We can all go along together,' said a man who was shutting the next front door.

It was Levaque with his son Bébert, a lad of twelve and a particular crony of Jeanlin's. Catherine was a little taken aback and stifled a giggle as she whispered to Zacharie: 'What? doesn't Bouteloup even wait for the husband to be out of the house nowadays?'

Lights were going out now. A last door banged and everything relapsed into slumber; women and children were settling down to have their sleep out in roomier beds. And all along the road from the silent village to the panting Le Voreux a line of shadows tramped slowly through the blast. The colliers were off to work with shambling gait and folded arms, for they did not know what else to do with them. Each one had his *briquet* on his back. Though they were shivering in their thin clothes, they did not quicken step, but plodded on, strung out along the road like a trampling herd.

[3]

HAVING at last come down from the slag-heap, Étienne had gone into the works, but the men he asked about a job shook their heads and told him to wait for the overman. He was left free to wander round the ill-lit buildings, with their gaping black holes and eerie maze of rooms on different floors. He had climbed a dark and rickety staircase and found himself on a shaky gangway, then crossed the screening-shed, where it was so pitch dark that he held his hands out in front of him for fear of banging into something. Suddenly two huge yellow eyes stared at him out of the shadows. He was under the headgear, at the pithead, the shaft yawning in front of him.

One of the deputies, old Richomme, a big man with a grey moustache who looked like a kindly policeman, happened to be making for the checkweighman's office.

'I suppose you don't want a man for any sort of job?' Étienne asked again.

Richomme was going to say no, but he hesitated, and as he was moving away said what the others had said:

'Wait for Monsieur Dansaert, the overman.'

There were four lanterns standing there, and the reflectors, which threw all the light towards the shaft, lit up the iron railings, signal levers and bolts and the timber guides between which the two cages slid up and down. The rest of the great building faded off into darkness, like the nave of a church haunted by monstrous flitting shadows. But at one end the lamp-room was a blaze of light, while a guttering lamp in the checkweighman's office looked like a waning star. The winding had started up again and so had the incessant rumbling of the tubs of coal over the sheet-iron flooring. You could just make out the long bent backs of the labourers in all this confused movement of black and noisy things.

For a moment Étienne stood still, deafened and blinded. There were draughts blowing in from all sides and he was frozen. Then his attention was caught by the shining steel and copper of the engine, and he went across to have a look at it. It was set back some twenty-five metres from the shaft and on a higher level, and so securely built into its brick cradle that, even when going at full speed and exerting all its four hundred horse-power, the huge, perfectly oiled crank rose and fell without a sound and not the slightest tremor could be felt. The engineman stood at his regulator, listening to the signal bells and keeping his eyes on the indicator; on it the pit, with its different levels, was represented by a vertical slot in which lead weights, for the cages, went up and down on strings. And each time the engine started, the drums – two immense wheels of five metres radius, by means of which the two steel cables were wound and unwound in opposite directions – turned so fast that they looked like clouds of grey dust.

'Look out!' shouted three labourers who were dragging an enormous ladder.

Étienne had nearly been flattened out. As his eyes got used to the gloom, he looked at the cables flying through the air, more than thirty metres of steel ribbon, leaping up into the headgear to pass over the pulleys and drop sheer down the shaft to the cages. The pulleys were supported by an iron framework like the skeleton of some lofty church tower. This prodigiously heavy wire, capable of lifting up to twelve hundred kilogrammes at ten metres per second, was ceaselessly moving to and fro with the swift, smooth, silent flight of a bird.

'Look out, for God's sake!' the labourers shouted again as they moved the ladder over to one side to inspect the left-hand pulley.

Étienne went slowly back to the pithead, feeling giddy with all this mighty flying about over his head. Shivering in the draughty shed and deafened by the rumbling tubs, he watched the loading and unloading of the cages. Next to the shaft was the signal, a heavy hammer on a hinged lever, which fell on a block when pulled by a rope from pit-bottom, once for stop, twice for down, three times for up. The tumult was dominated by these unending hammer-blows, together with the high-pitched ringing of a bell, whilst the man in charge added to the din by bellowing orders to the engineman through a megaphone. In the midst of the hurly-burly cages came up and dived down, emptied and filled, and Étienne had no idea what all these complicated movements were about.

There was only one thing he did see clearly: the pit gulped down men in mouthfuls of twenty or thirty and so easily that it did not seem to notice them going down. The descent to work began at four; the men came from the locker-room barefoot and lamp in hand, and stood about in little groups until there were enough of them. Like some nocturnal beast the cage, with its four decks each containing two tubs, leaped noiselessly up out of the darkness and settled itself on its keeps. Banksmen on different landings brought out the tubs and re-placed them with empties or tubs already loaded with timber, and the miners piled into the empties, five at a time, making up to forty in one journey when all the space was free. A muffled and unintelligible order was bellowed into the mega-phone and the rope was pulled four times – the 'meat-call' as it was termed – to warn them at the bottom that a load of human flesh was coming down. Without a sound the cage would first make a little jump and then drop like a stone, leaving nothing behind but the vibrating cable.

'Is it deep?' Étienne asked a miner who was standing by, looking half-asleep.

'Five hundred and fifty-four metres,' he answered. 'But

39

there are four levels before the bottom, and the first one is three hundred and twenty.'

They silently watched the cable which was now coming up again. Étienne spoke first.

'Supposing it breaks?'

'Oh well! – it just breaks. . . .'

The miner finished the story with a gesture. His turn came; the cage had come up again with its easy, tireless movement. He crouched inside with his mates and down it went again, to reappear less than four minutes later and swallow another lot of men. And so the shaft went on with its meal for half an hour, gulping men down more or less greedily according to the depth of the level they were bound for; but it never stopped, for the hunger of this gigantic maw could swallow up a whole people. More and more loads went down into the pitch blackness, and up came the cage out of the void, always silently asking for more.

In the end Étienne felt the same uneasiness coming on as he had felt up on the slag-tip. Why keep on trying? This over-man would send him packing, the same as the others. Sud-denly a fit of panic seized him, and he made off and did not stop until he was outside, by the boiler-house. Through the open door he could see seven boilers with double furnaces. In the midst of white clouds of steam from hissing safety-valves a stoker was feeding one of the furnaces, and the white-hot fire could be felt right out beyond the door. The young man, glad to feel the warmth, was moving up when he ran into a fresh group of miners just arriving. It was the Maheus and Levaques. Catherine was in front, and the sight of this gentle-looking boy gave him the superstitious idea of making one last attempt.

'I say, mate, I suppose they don't want anybody here for any sort of job?'

She looked round, a little startled by the sudden voice out of the darkness. But Maheu was just behind, and he answered and stopped and talked for a minute. No, there weren't any jobs. He felt sorry for this poor devil on the tramp, looking for work. As they moved on he said to the others:

'You know, we could easily be in his shoes. We ought

40

to be thankful. It isn't everybody that's worn out with work!'

They went on and made for the locker-room. The walls of this huge shed were roughly plastered, and padlocked cupboards stood all round. In the middle was an iron stove, a sort of oven without doors, which was red-hot and so tightly packed with incandescent coal that the pieces spluttered and fell out on to the earthen floor. This was the only light in the room, and the blood-red reflections danced along the greasy woodwork and up to the black, grimy ceiling.

As the Maheus came in the overheated room was ringing with laughter. Some thirty men were standing with their backs to the stove, having a luxurious warm. Everybody came like this and made sure of a good skinful of warmth to take down and face the damp of the pit. But on that particular morning the mirth was more noisy than usual, for they were chaffing Mouquette, an eighteen-year-old haulage girl. She was a strapping wench, with a bosom and buttocks that almost split her vest and breeches. She lived at Réquillart with old Mouque, her father, who was a ponyman, and her brother Mouquet, a banksman; but as their hours of work were not the same she came to the pit on her own, and took her fun with the young man of the week, in summer in the cornfields and in winter against a wall. Everybody in the pit had had a go: a real free-for-all among pals and nobody minded. But one day, when somebody had accused her of going with a nailmaker from Marchiennes, she had nearly exploded with indignation, declaring that she had more self-respect, that she would cut off one of her arms if anyone could claim to have seen her with anybody else but a miner.

'So you've given up that lanky Chaval?' sneered one of the miners; 'and you've taken on that little tich instead. But he'd have to have a ladder! I saw you behind Réquillart. I know, because he got up on a milestone.'

'Well, what about it?' grinned Mouquette. 'What's it got to do with you? Nobody asked you to give him a push!'

This good-natured obscenity made the men laugh louder than ever, as they stood there stretching their shoulders half roasted by the fire; whilst she, shaking with giggles, strutted

41

about among them in her indecent attire. The bulges of flesh, exaggerated to the point of deformity, were both comical and exciting.

But the laughter stopped. Mouquette was explaining to them that Fleurance would not be coming any more: she had been found the day before laid out stiff on her bed – some said a heart-attack, others a litre of gin swallowed too fast. Maheu was furious; more bad luck – now he had gone and lost one of his haulage girls with no hope of replacing her yet awhile! He worked on a contract system – four colliers together on the face, himself, Zacharie, Levaque, and Chaval. With only Catherine left to move the stuff, the job would be slowed down. Suddenly he cried:

'Half a minute! What about that chap who was looking for a job?'

Dansaert happened to be passing the locker-room. Maheu told him what had happened and asked permission to take the man on, using as an argument the Company's policy to replace haulage girls by men, as at Anzin. The overman's first reaction was a smile, for as a rule the miners objected to the plan to exclude women from underground work, being much more concerned about jobs for their daughters than about hygiene and morality. But after a moment's hesitation he gave his permission, subject to ratification by Monsieur Négrel, the engineer.

'Anyhow, if he's still running he will be miles away by now,' said Zacharie.

'No,' said Catherine, 'I saw him stop by the boilers.'

'Go along, look sharp!' said Maheu.

She rushed off, while a wave of miners moved on up to the cages, leaving their places by the fire to others. Without waiting for his father, Jeanlin went and got his lamp, with Bébert, a great ninny of a boy, and Lydie, a puny girl of ten. Mouquette had set off in front, and she was screaming in the dark stairway, calling them dirty little brats and threatening to clout them if they pinched her.

In the boiler-house Étienne was talking to the stoker shovelling coal into the furnace, for the thought of having to go back into the night chilled him to the bone. He was making up his mind to move on when he felt a hand on his shoulder.

'Come this way,' said Catherine; 'there's something for you.'

At first he did not understand. Then he seized her hand and shook it violently in an outburst of joy.

'Thanks, chum! You're a good sort, and no mistake!'

As she looked at him in the red glare of the furnaces she began to laugh, for it seemed so funny that he should take her for a boy, though certainly she was still slight and her hair was hidden under her cap. He on his part was laughing with relief, and there they stood for a moment, cheeks aglow, laughing at each other.

In the locker-room, Maheu was crouching in front of his locker, taking off his clogs and thick woollen stockings. When Étienne arrived everything was fixed up in a few words: thirty sous a day, hard work but easy to pick up. The collier advised him to keep his boots on and lent him an old round leather cap to protect the head – a precaution he and his children scorned. Tools were taken out, including Fleurance's spade, and when he had locked up his clogs and stockings, together with Étienne's bundle, Maheu suddenly burst out in a rage:

'What's up with that bloody Chaval? One more girl up-ended on a heap of stones, I suppose! We're half an hour late today.'

Zacharie and Levaque calmly went on toasting their shoulders, but in the end Zacharie said:

'You waiting for Chaval? He got here before us and went straight down.'

'What! You knew that and didn't tell me? Come on! Come on! Get a move on!'

Catherine was warming her hands, but had to fall in behind the rest. Étienne let her go in front and followed after. Once again he found himself in a maze of stairs and dark passages, in which the miners' bare feet made a flopping sound like old slippers. They came to the lamp-room, a glasshouse full of racks, with hundreds of Davy lamps in rows one above the other. They had all been cleaned and inspected the day before, and the whole place was ablaze like a *chapelle ardente*. Each man, as he passed the window, took his own lamp, stamped with his number, examined it and closed it himself, and the timekeeper at his table entered the time in his book. Maheu had to apply for a lamp for his new man. As a final precaution everybody had to pass a checker who saw that lamps were properly closed.

'Lumme! it's none too hot,' said Catherine, shivering.

Étienne only nodded back. Once again he was by the shaft, in the middle of the huge draughty shed. He thought he was brave enough, but what with the rumbling trucks, bumping signals, megaphones bellowing indistinctly and cables ceaselessly flying past as the drums wound and unwound at full speed, a nasty feeling seemed to grip him by the throat. The cages slid up and down stealthily like beasts of the night, and went on swallowing men as though the pit were a mouth gulping them down. As his turn came he felt very cold, and his silent tension called forth a sneer from Zacharie and Levaque, for neither of them approved of taking this stranger on – particularly Levaque, who was offended at not having been consulted. So Catherine was glad to hear her father explaining things to the young man.

'You see, up above the cages there is a safety catch; iron hooks catch the guides if the cable breaks. It works . . . well, sometimes. . . . Yes, the shaft is divided vertically by planking into three compartments: the middle one has the cages, on the left is the well for ladders. . . .' But he broke off to grumble, though not too loud:

'What the hell are we doing here, anyway? Keeping us standing about freezing like this!'

Richomme, the deputy, was on his way down too, his open lamp fixed by a nail to his leather cap, and heard him complaining; being an ex-collier himself whose sympathies were still with his old friends, he muttered paternally: 'Careful! You never know who's listening. Besides, the unloading has got to be done. . . . Well, here we are! Get your lot in.'

The cage was waiting for them, resting on its keeps. It was fitted with fine wire netting, reinforced with strips of sheet-iron. Maheu, Zacharie, Levaque, and Catherine slipped into a

44

tub on the further side, and as there was supposed to be room for five Étienne went in too. But the best places had gone and he had to squeeze in beside Catherine, one of whose elbows stuck into his stomach. His lamp got in his way and he was advised to hook it into a buttonhole in his coat, but he did not hear and went on holding it in his hand, clumsily. The loading went on above and below; it was like shovelling in a lot of livestock pell-mell. Still no move! What was the matter? He seemed to have been fuming there for minutes on end. At length he felt a jerk, everything turned over, the things round him flew away and a sickening sensation of falling tugged at his bowels. This lasted as long as there was any light, while they were passing the two pithead landings and their flying beams. Then, in the darkness of the pit, he was stunned and lost any clear idea of his sensations.

'Here we go!' casually remarked Maheu.

They were all quite calm. He wondered at times whether he was going down or up. There were moments when there was a sort of stillness – that was when the cage dropped sheer, without touching the guides. Then there would be sudden tremors as it bobbed about between the beams, and he was terrified of a disaster. In any case, he could not see the walls of the shaft although his face was glued to the netting. At his feet the huddled bodies were hardly visible, so dim were the lamps, but the open lamp of the deputy in the next tub shone out like a solitary beacon.

But Maheu was going on with his instructions: 'This one is four metres in diameter. It's high time it was re-lined – the water is coming in everywhere. We are getting down to that level now; can't you hear it?'

Étienne was already wondering what the noise was. It was like pouring rain. First a few heavy drops had pattered on the cage roof, like the beginning of a shower, but now the rain was streaming down faster and faster, turning into a real deluge. The roofing must have been faulty, for a trickle of water on his shoulder went through to the skin. It was intensely cold; they were sinking into wet blackness. Suddenly they went through a blaze of light: in a flash there was a vision of a cave with men moving about. And then the void again.

45

'That was the first level,' Maheu was saying. 'We are three hundred and twenty metres down. Look at the speed.'

He held up his lamp and shone it on to one of the guide-beams which was flying past like a rail under an express train, but apart from that nothing could be seen. Three other levels went by in glimpses of light, and the deafening rain lashed in the blackness.

'What a depth!' murmured Étienne.

The plunge must have been going on for hours. He had taken up an awkward position and did not dare to move, and this was particularly painful because Catherine's elbow was sticking into him. She said nothing, but he could feel her warm against him. When at last the cage stopped at the bottom, five hundred and fifty-four metres below ground, he was amazed to learn that the descent had taken exactly one minute. But the clang of the bolts and the feel of solid ground beneath him suddenly cheered him up, and he light-heartedly chipped Catherine:

'What have you got under your skin to make you so warm? I've got your elbow in my stomach. . . .'

What a donkey he was to go on taking her for a boy! Had he got his eyes bunged up, or what? She burst out:

'I'll tell you where you've got my elbow – in your eye.'

At this there was a general storm of laughter which quite mystified the young man.

The cage was emptying and the men crossed the bottom landing, a hall hewn out of the rock, with the roof reinforced with masonry, and lit by three large open-flame lamps. On-setters were hurrying loaded tubs along the iron floor. The walls exuded a smell of cellars: a cold saltpetre smell mingled with the warmer breath of the stables nearby. Four galleries yawned in front of them.

'This way!' said Maheu. 'You're not there yet; we've got two good kilometres to do.'

The miners separated into groups and disappeared into the black holes. Some fifteen of them had made their way into the one to the left, and Étienne brought up the rear, behind Maheu, who was behind Catherine, Zacharie, and Levaque. It was a good haulage-road, running through such firm rock that it had needed timbering only here and there. They went on and on in single file by the light of their little lamps, and uttering never a word. At every step the young man stumbled and tripped over the rails. He had been puzzled for some little time by a dull roar like the rumbling of a storm, distant at first but, he thought, growing in violence, and coming from the bowels of the earth. Was it the thunder of a fall, which would bring crashing down on their heads the enormous mass between them and the light of day? The blackness was suddenly broken by a light, the rock trembled; he flattened himself against the wall like his mates. A big white horse went by, close to his face, pulling a train of tubs. Bébert was sitting on the first, holding the reins, whilst Jeanlin was running along barefoot, holding on to the last one.

They resumed their tramp. Further on they came to a junction where two new galleries opened out. The party divided up again as the miners gradually spread themselves out over all the workings of the pit. The road was now timbered, the roof supported by oak stays and the loose rocks lined with planking, between which could be seen strata of shale, sparkling with mica, and the duller masses of rugged sandstone. Trains of full or empty tubs were continually passing him and passing each other, and their thunderous rumbling was borne away into the darkness by phantom animals, trotting along unseen. On a siding a stationary train was slumbering like a long black serpent. The horse snorted; it was wrapped in such deep shadow that you would have taken its vague outline for a block of stone fallen from the roof. Ventilation traps slowly opened and closed. As they went on, the gallery became narrower and lower and the roof more and more irregular, so that they had to keep their backs bent.

Étienne gave his head a nasty bang. But for the leather helmet his skull would have been split open. And yet he was imitating even the slightest movement of Maheu in front of him, whose dark shape stood out in the glimmer of the lamps. None of the others ever hit anything; doubtless they knew every bump, every knot in the timbers, every bulging rock by heart. To add to his troubles, the slippery floor was getting wetter and wetter: sometimes he walked through real pools, which could only be descried by the churned-up mud all round. The most surprising thing of all was the sudden changes of temperature. At pit-bottom it was very cold, and along the main tram-road, which ventilated the whole mine, the confined space between the walls had turned the icy wind into a hurricane. But further on, now that they were penetrating into other roads which had only a small share of the ventilation, the wind had dropped and the heat was increasing, a suffocating heat, as heavy as lead.

Maheu had not said another word. He now turned to the right along a new gallery, simply calling back, without turning his head:

'The Guillaume seam.'

The face they were working on was in this seam. After the very first steps Étienne bruised his head and elbows. The sloping roof came so low that he had to walk bent double for twenty or thirty metres at a time, and always ankle-deep in water. They did two hundred metres in this way, when suddenly Levaque, Zacharie, and Catherine vanished. They seemed to have melted away into a narrow crack in front of him.

'We have to climb,' said Maheu. 'Hang your lamp to a button-hole and grab the beams.' And then he disappeared too.

Étienne had to follow. The chimney was a private way left through the seam, by which miners could reach all the secondary roads. It was the same width as the coal seam, scarcely sixty centimetres, and it was as well that he was thin, for in his inexperience he hoisted himself up with needless waste of energy, pulling in his shoulders and haunches and moving up by sheer strength of arm as he clung to the timbers. The first gallery was fifteen metres up, but they had to go on further, as the face on which Maheu and his gang were working was the sixth – up in hell, they called it. The galleries, spaced one above the other at fifteen-metre intervals, seemed to go on for ever, and the climb up this narrow fissure was scraping the skin off his back and chest. He was gasping for breath as though the rocks were crushing his limbs beneath their weight, he felt as though his hands were being torn off and his legs were black and blue, while the lack of air made his

48

blood seem ready to burst through his skin. In one of the galleries he dimly made out two creatures, one small and the other big, crouching as they pushed tubs along: it was Lydie and Mouquette, already at work. And two more faces to climb! Blinded with sweat, he despaired of keeping up with the others, whose agile limbs he could hear brushing along the rock.

'Cheer up, here we are!' said Catherine's voice.

And there he really was, when another voice called from further along the coal face:

'Well, what the hell? You don't seem to care a damn! I've got two kilometres to walk from Montsou and I'm here first!'

It was Chaval, angry at having been kept waiting. He was a man of twenty-five, tall, thin, bony, with strong features. When he saw Étienne, he asked with pained surprise:

'What's that supposed to be?' And when Maheu had explained the story he muttered:

'So the men pinch the girls' jobs now!'

In the glance that the two men exchanged there flared up one of those sudden instinctive hatreds. Although he had not quite understood, Étienne felt that an insult was intended. There was a silence and they all set to work. Gradually all the seams had filled with workers, and there was activity at every face on all levels, and right to the end of every road. The greedy pit had swallowed its daily ration of men; nearly seven hundred of them were now toiling in this immense ant-hill, burrowing in the earth, riddling it with holes like old, worm-eaten wood. In the heavy silence down in the deep seams, you could put have your ear to the rock and heard these human insects busily at work, from the flying cable raising and lowering the cage to the click of tools picking away at the workings.

As he turned round, Étienne once more found himself pressing against Catherine. But this time he became aware of the curve of her young breast, and suddenly understood.

'So you are a girl?' he murmured in amazement.

She replied in her gay, straightforward way:

'Yes, of course! What a time it has taken you to find out!'

[4]

THE four colliers had spread themselves out, one above the other, to cover the whole coal-face. Each one occupied about four metres of the seam, and there were hooked planks between them to catch the coal as it fell. The seam was so thin, hardly more than fifty centimetres through at this point, that they were flattened between roof and wall, dragging themselves along by their knees and elbows, unable to turn without grazing their shoulders. In order to get at the coal, they had to lie on one side with twisted neck, arms above their heads, and wield their short-handled picks slantways.

Zacharie was at the bottom, with Levaque and Chaval above him and Maheu at the top. Each cut into the bed of shale with his pick, then made two vertical slots in the coal and finally drove an iron wedge in at the top, thus loosening a block. The coal was soft, and in its fall the block broke up and rolled in pieces all over the men's stomachs and thighs. When these pieces, stopped by the planks, had collected beneath them, the men disappeared, immured in the narrow cleft.

Maheu had the worst of it. At the top, the temperature went up to ninety-five degrees,* air could not circulate, and he was stifled to death. In order to see, he had to hang his lamp on a nail so near the top of his head that its heat set his blood on fire. But it was the wet that really tortured him, for the rock, only a few centimetres above his face, incessantly dripped fast and heavy drops with maddening regularity always on the same spot. Try as he might to twist his neck and bend his head backwards, the drops splashed relentlessly on his face, pit-a-pat. In a quarter of an hour he was soaked through, what with his own sweat as well, and steaming like a wash-tub. On this particular morning he was swearing because a drop was determined to go in his eye. He would not stop cutting, and the violent blows of his pick shook him, as he lay between the two rocks like a fly caught between the pages of a book, in danger of being flattened out.

* 35° Centigrade in French text.

50

Not a word was exchanged. They all hacked away, and all that could be heard was their irregular tapping, which sounded distant and muffled, for in this dead air sounds raised no echo but took on a harsh sonority. The darkness was mysterious in its blackness, thick with flying coal-dust and heavy with gases which pressed down upon the eyes. Only reddish points of light could be seen through the gauze covers of the lamps. The coal face was scarcely discernible; it went up slantwise like a broad, flat, sloping chimney, blackened with the impenetrable night of ten winters of soot, and in it ghostly forms moved about and an occasional gleam threw into momentary relief the shape of a man's haunch, a sinewy arm, a wild, dirty, criminal-looking face. Now and then blocks of coal shimmered as they came loose, their surfaces or edges glinted suddenly like crystal, and then all went black again, the picks tapped on dully, and the only other sounds were panting breath and groans of discomfort and fatigue in the heavy air and dripping water.

Zacharie had been out on the spree the day before and was not feeling strong in the arm. He soon gave up work, finding the excuse that some timbering needed doing. This gave him a chance to go off into a dream, whistling to himself and staring vaguely into space. Nearly three metres of the seam were cut away behind them, and they had not taken the precaution to prop up the rock. Fear of losing precious time made them heedless of danger.

'Here, you, the toff!' he called to Étienne. 'Pass me some wood.'

Étienne was being taught by Catherine how to wield his shovel, but he had to take some wood along. There was a little store left over from the previous day. Usually pieces of wood ready cut to the size of the seam were sent down every morning.

'Look sharp, you lazy devil!' Zacharie went on, watching the new haulage man clumsily hoisting himself up amid the coal, with his arms encumbered by four pieces of oak.

With his pick he nicked a hole in the roof and another in the wall, ramming in the ends of the wood which thus propped up the rock. Every afternoon the rippers cleared away the

51

waste after the colliers and filled in the cavities in the seam, leaving the timbering covered in. Only the top and bottom galleries were left intact for haulage.

Maheu stopped groaning. He had got his block loose. Wiping his streaming face on his sleeve, he turned to find out what Zacharie had come up to do behind him.

'Leave that alone,' he said; 'we'll see about it after lunch. Better go on cutting if we want to make our right number of tubs.'

'Yes, but it's getting lower,' answered his son. 'Look! There's a crack here. I'm afraid it'll come down.'

His father only shrugged his shoulders. Come down! Never! Besides, it wouldn't be the first time; they'd get out of it somehow. He finished up by losing his temper and sending his son back to the cutting face.

As a matter of fact, they were all taking a bit of a rest. Levaque, still on his back, was cursing as he looked at his left thumb, which had been grazed by a fall of sandstone and was bleeding. Chaval was tearing off his shirt, stripping to the waist to keep cool. They were already black with coal, coated with fine dust which their sweat turned into a paste that ran in trickles and puddles. Maheu was the first to begin picking again, at a lower level, with his head right down on the rock. And now the drop of water was falling so mercilessly on his forehead that it seemed to be boring a hole through his skull.

'Don't take any notice,' explained Catherine. 'They always holler like that.'

She took up the lesson again like a kindly soul: each loaded tub reached pit-top exactly as it left the face, marked with a special counter so that the checker could credit it to the team. That was why you had to be so careful to fill it, and fill it with clean coal; otherwise it would be rejected.

The young man's eyes were now accustomed to the gloom, and he looked at her. Her skin still had a chlorotic pallor, and he could not have guessed her age, but put it at twelve because she seemed so small. And yet he felt that she must be older, with her boyish freedom of manner and candid cheekiness which he found a little disconcerting; no, he did not like her – her white Pierrot's face with the skull-cap effect of her headgear struck him as too roguish. But he was amazed at the child's strength, a nervous strength with much skill in it. She filled her tub quicker than he did, with fast, regular little movements of her shovel, then pushed it to the incline with a long, slow push without any hitch, passing easily under the low rocks. He, on the other hand, tore himself to shreds, ran off the rails and soon got stuck.

It certainly was not an easy road. From the coal face to the incline was about sixty metres, and the rippers had not yet widened the tunnel, which was a mere pipe with a very uneven roof, bulging at every moment. At some points a loaded tub would only just go through, and the haulage man had to flatten himself and push kneeling down so as not to smash his head. What was more, the timbers were already giving and snapping, and long, pale rents appeared as they gave in the middle, like crutches too weak for their job. You had to be careful not to scrape your skin off on this splintered wood, and as you crawled on your belly under the slowly sinking roof, which could snap oak props as thick as a man's thigh, you felt a haunting fear that suddenly you would hear your own spine crack.

'What, again?' laughed Catherine.

Étienne's tub had gone off the rails at the most awkward spot. He could not manage to steer a straight course on these rails which twisted and turned in the mud, and he cursed and swore as he struggled with the wheels which he could not set back in their place, try as he might.

'Wait a minute,' said the girl; 'if you lose your temper it will never work.'

With a deft backward movement, she inserted her behind under the tub, and using her back as a lever, lifted it and replaced it on the rails. It weighed seven hundred kilogrammes. He was overcome with surprise and stammered excuses.

She had to show him how to get a firm position by straddling the legs and planting the feet against the timbering on either side of the gallery. The body had to be bent forward and the arms kept stiff, so that one could push with all the muscles of the shoulders and haunches. For one journey he followed her and watched; she ran along with her behind so high and her hands so low that she seemed to be trotting on all fours, like one of those dwarf animals in a circus. She sweated and panted and her joints cracked, but she never complained, for familiarity had brought apathy, and you would have thought that being doubled up like that was part of the normal course of human suffering. But he could not do as much himself, and when he walked upside down in this way, his shoes hurt him and his body was in agony. After a few minutes the position became a torture, an intolerable anguish so painful that he sank on to his knees for a moment to straighten up and get his breath.

Then at the incline a new ordeal began. She taught him how to dispatch his tub quickly. At each end of this incline, which served all the cutting faces between two levels, was stationed a pit-boy, the one at the top operating the brakes and the other receiving the tubs. These young monkeys, twelve to fifteen years of age, shouted foul language at each other, and to make them hear you had to shout fouler language louder still. When an empty tub was ready to go up, the receiver signalled and the haulage girl let go a full one, the weight of which pulled up the other one when the brakesman released his brake. Trains were made up at the bottom, and drawn by horses to the shaft.

'Hi! you bloody bastards,' bellowed Catherine down the incline which, being a hundred metres long and completely timbered, boomed like a huge megaphone.

The boys must have been taking a rest, for not a sound came from either. Work stopped on all levels. In the end, the shrill voice of a little girl piped up:

'I bet one of them's on top of Mouquette.'

Stentorian laughter re-echoed; all the haulage girls shook with giggles.

'Who said that?' Étienne asked Catherine.

She named young Lydie, a little hussy who knew a thing or two, and moved her tub as well as a grown woman, in spite of her doll-like arms. As for Mouquette, she was quite capable of taking on both pit-boys together.

But the voice of the receiver shouted up orders to dispatch – doubtless some deputy was on the prowl down there. Movement began again at all nine levels, and nothing could be heard

54

but the regular calls of the boys and the snorting of the haulage girls as they reached the incline, all steaming like overloaded mares. It was at times like this that one of those waves of bestiality ran through the mine, the sudden lust of the male that came over a miner when he met one of these girls on all fours, with her rear in the air and her buttocks bursting out of her breeches.

With each journey back to the coal face, Étienne found the same stifling heat, the soft, regular taps of the picks and the painful gaspings of the miners as they obstinately pushed on with the job. All four had now stripped, and were covered with black mud up to their caps, so that they were indistinguishable from the coal. At one stage Maheu had had to be extricated as he lay gasping for breath – planks had to be taken away to let the coal fall down on to the road. Zacharie and Levaque were furious with the seam for getting hard, as they said, which would upset all their contract arrangements. Chaval turned over on to his back for a moment to curse Étienne, whose presence was decidedly getting on his nerves.

'The miserable worm! Not got the strength of a girl! Are you going to fill your tub, eh? No! you don't want to tire your arms. . . . God Almighty! If you get one of them rejected, I'll stop your ten sous.'

Étienne avoided answering, for so far he was only too glad to have found this galley-slave job, and he accepted the brutal rule of the skilled over the unskilled. But he could hardly keep going, for his feet were bleeding, his limbs twisted with terrible cramps and his stomach squeezed as in an iron belt. Fortunately, it was ten o'clock and the team decided to knock off for lunch.

Maheu had a watch, but he did not even look at it. Down in this starless night he was never five minutes out. They all pulled on their shirts and coats, came down from the face and squatted on their heels, elbows close in to their sides, in the posture that is so natural to miners that they use it even outside the mine, and need neither stone nor beam to sit on. Each one took out his *briquet*, and solemnly began to bite into the thick slice, with only a word now and then about the morning's work. Catherine remained standing, and finally went over to join Étienne, who had lain down across the rails with his back against the timbers. It was more or less dry just there.

'Aren't you eating?' she asked, with her mouth full, holding her sandwich in her hand.

Then, remembering how this fellow was wandering in the night, penniless and probably without a crust of bread:

'Won't you share with me?'

And as he refused, protesting that he was not hungry in a voice shaking with the gnawing pains in his stomach, she gaily went on:

'Oh, well! Of course, if you don't like the look of it. . . . Look here, I've only bitten this side; I'll give you the other.'

No sooner said than done; she had divided the slices in two. He took his half, managed to prevent himself from swallowing it whole, and placed his arms firmly on his thighs so that she should not see how he was trembling. With her unembarrassed air of good comradeship she had stretched herself on the ground beside him, lying on her front with her chin in one hand and slowly eating with the other. Their lamps stood between them and lit them up.

For a moment Catherine silently contemplated him. She evidently found him nice-looking, with his delicate features and black moustache, for she smiled happily to herself.

'So you are a mechanic, and your railway sacked you. Why?'

'Because I hit my chief.'

All her inherited ideas of subordination and passive obedience were turned upside down, and she remained speechless.

'Mind you, I had been drinking,' he went on, 'and when I drink I go mad, fit to do myself in and everybody else too. . . . Yes, I can't swallow two little nips without wanting to go for somebody. . . . And afterwards I'm ill for two days.'

'Then you mustn't drink,' she said gravely.

'Oh, don't be afraid. I know myself.'

And he shook his head. He hated spirits with the hatred of the last child of a race of drunkards, and his flesh was so vitiated by an ancestry sodden and maddened by alchohol, that the least drop had become poison to him.

'It's because of Mother that I'm so fed up at being on

the tramp,' he said after swallowing a mouthful. 'She's down on her luck and I used to send her a five-franc piece now and then.'

'Where is your mother, then?'

'Paris. . . . Laundress, Rue de la Goutte d'Or.'

There was a pause. Whenever he thought about these things a pale flicker came into his dark eyes, as he glimpsed the terrifying hidden flaw in his fine youthful vigour. For a moment he gazed unseeing into the darkness of the mine, and there, in these depths, under the suffocating weight of earth, he saw his childhood again – his mother, still pretty and stout-hearted, abandoned by his father, and then taken up again after marrying another man; living between the two of them who both preyed on her, and finally rolling with them in drink and filth down to the gutter. It was away yonder. . . . Yes, the street and all the details came back to him now – the dirty linen lying all over the shop, the drunken orgies stinking all over the house, the jaw-breaking blows.

'But now,' his voice went on slowly, 'on thirty sous I shan't be able to send her presents. She'll die of want, for certain.' He mournfully shrugged his shoulders and took another bite of sandwich.

'Want a drink?' asked Catherine, uncorking her flask. 'Oh, it's only coffee; won't do you any harm. . . . You'll choke if you swallow dry like that.'

But he refused, thinking it was quite enough to have taken half her bread. She good-naturedly insisted, and finally said:

'All right, as you are so polite I'll drink first. Only you can't refuse now, it would be rude.'

She held out her flask to him. She had got on to her knees and he saw her quite close in the light of the two lamps. How could he have thought she was ugly? Now that she was black, with her face powdered with coal dust, she looked strangely attractive. In her dusky face, with its large mouth, her teeth shone dazzlingly white, and her eyes gleamed large with a greenish light, like a cat's. A wisp of reddish hair, escaping from her cap, was tickling her ear and making her laugh.

'Well, just to oblige,' he said, taking a swig and handing back the flask.

She had another drink and made him do the same, saying she wanted them to share, and they laughed at the way the narrow neck of the flask passed from mouth to mouth. Suddenly he wondered whether he should seize her in his arms and kiss her. Her full, pale pink lips, set off by coal, teased him with a growing desire. But he did not dare – she made him feel shy. At Lille he had only had street-walkers, and the cheapest ones at that, and he did not know how to set about a working girl still living at home. He attacked his bread again.

'You must be about fourteen?'

She was surprised, almost annoyed.

'What, fourteen? No, I'm fifteen. I'm not very big, I know. Girls don't grow very fast hereabouts.'

He went on asking questions, and she told him everything without being brazen or prudish. Not that there was anything she did not know about men and women, but he sensed that she was still virgin in body, with the virginity of a child whose puberty had been retarded by the conditions of bad air and fatigue in which she lived. When he tried to embarrass her by coming back to the subject of Mouquette, she told him hair-raising stories in a calm voice and with much relish. Oh! she got up to some fine larks, did Mouquette! And when he wanted to know whether she had any boys herself, she jokingly answered that she did not want to upset her mother, but that it was bound to happen one of these days. She had hunched up her shoulders and was shivering a little in her sweat-soaked clothes. Her face bore a look of gentle resignation, ready to submit to things and men.

'When you all live mixed up together, lovers can easily be found, can't they?'

'Of course.'

'And besides, it doesn't hurt anybody. There's no need to tell the priest.'

'Oh, the priest! I don't care a damn about him. But there's the Black Man.'

'The Black Man?'

'The old miner who comes back down the mine, and wrings bad girls' necks.'

He looked at her, afraid that she was making fun of him.

'You believe in fairy-tales like that? Don't you know anything, then?'

'Oh yes, I do. I can read and write. It is useful for us at home, for in Dad and Mum's time they never taught them anything.'

She really was rather nice. He made up his mind to take her and kiss her full pink lips when she had finished her bread. It was the resolution of a timid man, an idea of violence which choked his voice. These boy's clothes, this jacket and breeches on a girl's body, excited and troubled him. He had swallowed his last mouthful, drunk out of the flask and handed it back for her to empty. The moment for action had come; he was taking a nervous look at the miners up the passage, when the view was cut off by a dark form.

Chaval had been standing there for a minute, watching them. Now he came forward, made sure that Maheu could not see him, and as Catherine was still sitting on the ground, he seized her by the shoulders, bent her head back and crushed her mouth with a brutal kiss. He did it quite calmly, pretending not to bother about Étienne. In that kiss there was the staking out of a claim, a sort of jealous resolution.

But she had resisted.

'Leave me alone, will you?'

He kept hold of her head and looked into her eyes, his moustache and billy-goat beard flaming red in his black face, with its big aquiline nose. Then he released her and went off without a word.

A cold shudder had run through Étienne. What a fool he was to have waited! But now he certainly would not kiss her, for it would probably look as though he wanted to do the same as the other fellow.

'Why did you tell me a lie?' he whispered. 'He's your lover.' In his wounded vanity he felt a positive despair.

'No! No! I swear he isn't; there's none of that between us. . . . He fools about sometimes. . . . He doesn't even belong here, he came from the Pas-de-Calais six months ago.'

They both got to their feet, as it was time to start work again. She seemed upset to see him so cool. Perhaps she found him nicer-looking than the other and would have preferred

59

him, for she felt an urge to do him some kindness or console him in some way. As the young man was looking at his lamp, which was burning blue with a large pale ring, she made an attempt to occupy his mind, at any rate.

'Come along, and I'll show you something,' she murmured gaily.

She led him to the end of the coal-face, and showed him a fissure from which was coming a sort of soft bubbling sound, like the chirping of a bird.

'Hold your hand there, you can feel the draught. That's fire-damp.'

He was amazed. Was that all there was to it? So this was the terrible stuff that blew everything sky-high? She laughed, and said that there was a lot of it about today to make the lamps burn so blue.

'When you've done chattering, you lazy devils!' broke in the rough voice of Maheu.

Catherine and Étienne hastily filled their tubs and pushed them to the incline, crawling stiff-backed under the bulging roof. By the time they had done two journeys they were soaked in sweat and the bones were cracking again.

The colliers had again started work at the coal-face, for they usually cut down their lunch time so as not to get cold. Far from the light of day they gulped down their food without a word, and now the sandwiches lay in their stomachs as heavy as lead. Stretched out on their sides, they were picking away harder than ever, with only one idea in their heads: to make up a large total of tubs. In this desperate fight for such hard-earned gain, everything else faded into insignificance. They no longer noticed the water running down them and making their limbs swell, the cramps from unnatural postures, the stifling darkness in which they were blanched like plants in a cellar. And yet, as the day wore on, the air became more and more foul, what with the heat and smoke from the lamps, the bad breath, the asphyxiating gas, which clung to their eyes like cobwebs and would only be cleared away by the night's ventilation. Like moles burrowing under the weight of the earth, without a breath of air in their burning lungs, they went on picking away.

W𝗜𝗧𝗛𝗢𝗨𝗧 looking at his watch, which he did not even take out of his coat, Maheu stopped and said:

'Just on one. Finished yet, Zacharie?'

The young man had been timbering for a minute or two, but had stopped in the middle of the job, and lay on his back, dreaming with unseeing eyes about yesterday's game of *crosse*. He woke up and answered:

'Yes, it'll do; we'll see about it tomorrow.'

And back he went to his place at the cutting face. Levaque and Chaval were also getting tired of their picks, and there was a general pause while they all wiped their faces on their bare arms and looked at the cracks running in all directions on the shaly roof. They hardly ever talked except about their work.

'Just like our luck to run into loose earth,' muttered Chaval; 'they didn't count that in the bargain.'

'The sharks!' growled Levaque. 'All they bloody well want is to bury us down here.'

Zacharie began to laugh. He didn't care a damn about the work, but it amused him to hear the Company abused. Maheu pointed out in his quiet way that the nature of the earth changed every twenty metres. You had to be fair; they couldn't foresee everything. But as the other two went on running down the bosses, he began glancing round uneasily.

'Sh! That'll do.'

'Yes, you're right, mate,' said Levaque, also lowering his voice, 'it isn't healthy.'

Even at this depth they were haunted by the fear of informers, as though the shareholders' coal had ears while still in the seam.

'That won't prevent me,' said Chaval, 'from chucking a brick into that swine Dansaert's belly if he talks to me again like he did the other day.' His tone of voice was loud and provocative. 'It isn't as though I stopped him treating himself to beautiful blondes.'

That made Zacharie burst right out laughing, for the affair

between the overman and Pierron's wife was the standing joke of the mine. Even Catherine stood leaning on her shovel at the bottom of the face and held her sides, as she let Étienne into the joke with a word or two. But Maheu could no longer hide his nervousness, and lost his temper:

'Shut up, will you? Wait till you're alone if you want to get into trouble.'

Before he had finished speaking, footsteps could be heard in the gallery above, and almost at once the engineer – little Négrel, as the miners called him amongst themselves – appeared at the top of the face with Dansaert, the overman.

'What did I tell you?' muttered Maheu. 'They're always there; they come up out of the ground.'

Paul Négrel, nephew of Monsieur Hennebeau, was a young fellow of twenty-six, slim and handsome, with dark curly hair and a moustache. His pointed nose and keen eyes made him look like an amiable weasel, sceptical and intelligent, but he changed to an abrupt, authoritative manner in his dealings with the workmen. He was dressed like the men, and like them was smeared with coal, and he tried to win their respect by displaying daredevil courage, getting through the most difficult places, always first on the scene at landslides or firedamp explosions.

'This is the place, isn't it, Dansaert?' he asked.

The overman, a coarse-faced Belgian with a fleshy, sensual nose, answered with overdone politeness:

'Yes, Monsieur Négrel. . . . This is the man who was taken on this morning.'

They both slid down to the middle of the coal-face. Étienne was called up. The engineer raised his lamp and peered at him, but did not ask any questions.

'All right. But I don't much like taking on unknown men off the road. Mind you don't do it again.'

He did not listen to the explanation put forward – the exigencies of the work, the policy of replacing women by men for haulage. Whilst the cutters were taking up their picks again, he had begun to examine the roof. Suddenly he exclaimed:

'I say, Maheu, don't you give a damn for anybody? Good God! You'll all end up by being buried alive down here.'

'Oh, its quite strong,' the workman answered quietly.

'What? Strong? Look, the rock is bulging already, and you stick in props more than two metres apart as though you begrudged them. . . . Oh! You're all the same; you would rather have your skulls smashed in than come off the seam to put in the proper time at timbering. Be so good as to prop that at once. Twice as many props – do you understand?'

The surliness of the miners, who began arguing and saying that they were the best judges of their own safety, made him really angry:

'Get along with you! When your heads are smashed in, will you be the ones to stand the consequences? Oh, no! it will be the Company that will have to find pensions for you or your wives. Once again let me tell you that we know all about you. You would give your dead bodies to have two tubs more by the evening!'

Maheu was feeling more and more angry, but he managed to say calmly:

'If we were properly paid we should do the propping better.'

The engineer shrugged his shoulders and said nothing. He had completed his inspection of the face, and from the bottom threw back his final word:

'You have got one hour left. You must all get down to it, and I give notice that the team is fined three francs.'

These words produced a muffled growl from the colliers, who were only held in check by the strength of the hierarchy – the military system which held them down, from pit-boy to overman, by putting each in the power of another. But Chaval and Levaque gave vent to impulsive movements of fury, which Maheu curbed with a look, whilst Zacharie mockingly shrugged his shoulders. Étienne was perhaps the most deeply moved. A feeling of revolt had been steadily mounting in him ever since he had been in this inferno. He looked at Catherine, her back bent in resignation. Was it possible that these people were killing themselves at such a cruel job in this deadly darkness without even making enough for their daily bread?

Meanwhile Négrel was moving off with Dansaert, whose part had simply been to nod agreement all the time. And then their voices rose again, for they had stopped and were inspecting the timbering of the gallery, which was the responsibility of the collier for ten metres back from the coal-face.

'Didn't I tell you they don't care a damn?' shouted the engineer. 'And what about you? Why the hell don't you keep your eye on them?'

'Oh! but I do, I do,' stammered the overman. 'We all get sick and tired of telling them the same thing.'

'Maheu! Maheu!' bellowed Négrel.

They all came down. He went on:

'Look at that! Do you think it's going to hold? A real piece of jerry-building! Look at that capping stuck on in such a hurry that already it isn't resting on the uprights! Yes, I can understand why repairs cost so much. So long as it lasts out while you are responsible, that's all you care, isn't it? And then it all goes phut, and the Company has to have an army of repairers. Take a look at that and see the hash you've made of it.'

Chaval made as if to speak, but he cut him short.

'No! I know what you are going to say. Higher pay, eh? Very good! I warn you that you are forcing the Company to do one thing, and that is to pay you separately for timbering and reduce the rate per tub in proportion. And then we'll see whether you are better off! Meanwhile, re-timber all that at once, will you? I'll be round again tomorrow.'

During the sensation caused by this threat, he took himself off. Dansaert, who was so humble in his presence, stayed behind a few moments to say brutally to the men:

'You are getting me into a row, you lot! You'll get something more than three francs fine from me. Just you look out!'

When he had gone it was Maheu's turn to blow up:

'God! What isn't fair isn't fair! I'm all for calmness, because it is the only way of getting along, but in the end they drive you mad. Did you hear? The rate per tub down and timbering separate! Another way of paying us less! Christ Almighty!'

He looked round for somebody to vent his rage on, and saw Catherine and Étienne standing with their arms dangling.

'Just give me some wood, will you! You think its nothing to do with you? You'll feel my boot somewhere!'

Étienne went and took up a load, feeling no resentment at this bullying; indeed, he was so angry with the bosses himself that he thought the miners were too good-natured. Levaque and Chaval had relieved their feelings with oaths. They were all timbering for dear life, even Zacharie, and for nearly half an hour nothing could be heard but the creaking sound of the beetles driving home pieces of wood. Not another word did they utter, but snorted furiously as they struggled with the rock, which they would have rough-handled and shoved back with their shoulders if they had been able.

'That'll do,' said Maheu at length, worn out with fatigue and anger. 'Half past one! This is a nice day, this is! We shan't make fifty sous. I'm off. I'm fed up with it.'

Although there was another half hour to go, he put on his things and the others did the same. The very sight of the coal-face made them boil with rage. As Catherine had gone on with her trimming, they called her back, for her zeal annoyed them: let the coal come out on its own feet, if it had any! And all six set off with their tools under their arms, to face the two-kilo-metre walk back to the shaft by the road they had taken in the morning.

When they reached the chimney, Catherine and Étienne held back while the others slid down. They met little Lydie, who had stopped in the middle of the gallery to let them pass, and she told them about one of Mouquette's disappearances. She had had such an attack of nose-bleeding that she had gone off an hour since to bathe her face somewhere or other. When they left her, the child pushed her tub on again, weary and covered with mud, stiffening her spindly arms and legs like a thin black ant, struggling with too heavy a burden. They slid down on their backs, keeping their shoulders well back so as not to graze the skin off their foreheads; and so fast did they slip over the rock, polished smooth by the behinds of all the miners, that now and then they had to grab hold of the timbering so that their backsides should not catch fire, as they jokingly put it.

At the lower end they found themselves alone. Red dots of light were vanishing in the distance round a bend in the gallery. Their mirth subsided, and they set out with heavy, tired

65

steps, she first, he following. The lamps were sooty and he could hardly see her, lost as she was in a sort of smoky haze. He was disturbed by the knowledge that she was a girl, for he felt he was foolish not to kiss her, but the thought of the other man stopped him. Of course she must have lied to him; the other chap was her lover, they did it together on those heaps of slack, for she already had the swinging walk of a tart. He sulked quite unreasonably, as though she had deceived him. But she, on her side, seemed to be inviting him to be friendly, for every moment she turned round to warn him about some obstacle. They were so cut off – it would have been so easy to have a bit of fun! At last they came out into the main haulage road, which put a welcome end to his painful indecision, but she gave him a last sad glance, full of regret for a bit of happiness that would not come their way again.

The life of the underworld was now rumbling round them, with deputies continually running to and fro, trains going up and down, drawn by trotting horses. The darkness was starred by countless lamps. They had to flatten themselves against the rocky walls to let shadowy men and beasts go by, so close that they could feel their breath. Jeanlin, running barefoot behind his train, shouted some foul remark at them, but they could not hear it for the rumbling of wheels. On they went, she now silent and he unable to recognize the roads and junctions of the morning, and imagining that she was taking him further and further away underground. What worried him most was the cold. He had noticed it on leaving the coal-face, and it was getting worse; and the nearer they came to the shaft the more he shivered. Once again, the air was blowing like a hurricane between the narrow walls. He was beginning to despair of ever reaching their destination, when suddenly they found themselves at pit-bottom.

Chaval threw a sidelong glance at them, and his lips were pursed with suspicion. The others were there, sweating in the icy draught, and like him they were silently swallowing their resentment. They were too early and would not be allowed up for another half hour, especially as the complicated business of bringing down a horse was going on. Onsetters were still sending up tubs with the deafening clang of old iron, and the cages flew away up into the sheets of rain pouring down the black hole. Down below, the sump, a ten-metre well full of this streaming water, gave forth its own dank and slimy smell. All the time, men were busying themselves round the shaft, pulling signal ropes, pressing on levers, in the middle of this drenching spray. The reddish glare of the three open lamps threw up their great moving shadows, and made this underground hall look like some criminals' den or bandits' forge beside a torrent.

Maheu made one last attempt. He went up to Pierron, who had come on duty at six.

'Look here, you might just as well let us up.'

The onsetter was a handsome fellow with strong limbs and a gentle face. But he refused with a scared gesture.

'Can't be done. Ask the deputy. I'd be fined.'

There was a fresh burst of grumbling, but it died down. Catherine bent over and whispered into Étienne's ear:

'Come along and see the stables. It's nice there.'

They had to slip off unnoticed, for it was against the rules. The stables were along a short gallery running off to the left. They were in a chamber hewn out of the rock and roofed with brick, twenty-five metres long and four in height, with accommodation for twenty ponies. It certainly was nice there, with the comfortable warmth of living creatures and a good smell of fresh straw kept clean. The single lamp shone softly like a nightlight. Resting ponies looked round with their big child-like eyes, and then went on with their oats again, stolidly, like healthy, well-fed workers, popular with everybody.

Catherine was reading out the names on the zinc plates over the mangers, when she uttered a little scream as a body suddenly rose up in front of her. It was Mouquette, jumping up in a fright out of a heap of straw in which she had been sleeping. Every Monday, being worn out after Sunday's goings-on, she would give herself a good punch on the nose, leave the coal-face with the excuse that she had to get some water, and then come and snuggle down here in the warm straw with the ponies. Old Mouque, her father, was very indulgent and let her do it, at the risk of getting himself into trouble.

He happened to come in just then. He was short, bald, and

67

looked worn out, but he was still fat, which is unusual for an ex-miner of fifty. Since he had been made a ponyman, he chewed so incessantly that his gums bled in his black mouth. He was annoyed when he saw the other two with his daughter.

'What are you all up to in here? Come on, out you get! You little hussies, bringing a man in here! A nice thing, coming to do your dirty tricks in my straw!'

Mouquette held her sides with mirth, but Étienne went off feeling awkward, while Catherine smiled at him. As the three of them came back to pit-bottom, Bébert and Jeanlin reached there with a train of tubs. During the pause for manoeuvring the cages, the girl went up to their pony, stroked him and told her new friend all about him. He was Bataille, the *doyen* of the mine, a white pony who had been ten years below ground. For ten years he had lived in this hole and occupied the same corner of the stable, performing the same task along the black galleries without ever seeing daylight. Sleek, with shining coat, he had a good-natured look, and seemed to live the life of a sage, sheltered from the trials of the upper world. Moreover, in this shadowy underworld he had become extremely crafty. The road along which he worked had become so familiar, that he pushed open the ventilation doors with his head and dipped so as not to bang his head when the roof was low. Most likely he kept count of his journeys, too, for when he had done the regulation number, he refused to start another and had to be taken back to his manger. Now, with advancing years, his cat-like eyes sometimes took on a far-away wistful look. Perhaps in his misty dreams he could dimly see the mill near Marchiennes where he was born, by the banks of the Scarpe amidst broad, wind-swept meadows. Something used to burn high up in the air, a sort of huge lamp, but his animal memory could not quite recollect what it was like. And there he stood shakily on his old legs, vainly trying to remember the sun.

Meanwhile, the manoeuvres were still going on in the shaft. Four clangs from the signal hammer meant that the pony was being sent down. This was always a sensation, for it sometimes happened that the animal was so terrified that it was brought out dead. At pit-top it fought frantically when put into a net, but as soon as it felt the ground give way, it was petrified and disappeared with quivering skin and wide, staring eyes. This one was too big to pass down between the guides, and had to be suspended beneath the cage, its head turned round and lashed to its side. The descent lasted nearly three minutes, the engine being slowed down as a safety measure. At the bottom the excitement grew and grew. What? Was it going to be left half-way, stuck in the dark? But in the end it did arrive, still motionless as stone, its staring eyes dilated with terror. It was a bay, scarcely three years old, called Trompette.

'Mind!' shouted old Mouque who had the job of receiving the pony. 'Bring him along here, but don't untie him yet.'

Soon Trompette was lying on the iron flooring, an inert mass. Still he did not move, but seemed lost in the nightmare of this black and endless cavern, this vast chamber full of noises. As they were setting about untying him, up came Bataille, who had just been unharnessed. He stretched his neck and sniffed at this new pal who had dropped down from the earth. The miners laughingly made room for him in the circle. Well, now – what did he think of this nice new smell? But Bataille did not let their gibes damp his enthusiasm. Perhaps he found in his new friend the good smell of the open air, the long-forgotten smell of the sun-kissed grass, for all of a sudden he burst into a resounding whinny, a song of joy with a sob of wistfulness running through it. This was his act of welcome, made up of delight in this fragrance of the old, far-off things and sadness that here was one more prisoner who would never go back alive.

'Ah, old Bataille is a one!' said the workmen, tickled by their favourite's tricks. 'Look at him talking to his mate!'

But Trompette still did not budge, although he was now untied. There he lay on his side, garrotted by fear, as though he could still feel the net round him. In the end, he was put on his feet with a flick of the whip and stood there bewildered, shuddering in all his limbs. Old Mouque led the two animals away, fraternizing.

'Well, are we ready now?' asked Maheu.

The cages had to be cleared, and in any case there were still ten minutes to go before it was time for the ascent. Gradually the coal-faces were emptying, and men were returning from all the galleries. Already some fifty of them were standing there, wet and shivering in draughts that were enough to give anybody pneumonia. Pierron, for all his smooth and smarmy manner, cuffed his daughter Lydie because she had left work early. Zacharie was slyly pinching Mouquette, just to keep warm. But they were all getting more and more annoyed; Chaval and Levaque were telling everybody about the engineer's threat to cut the price per tub and pay for timbering separately, and this news was greeted with exclamations. A rebellion was germinating in this narrow hole nearly six hundred metres below ground. Soon the voices rose in anger, and these men, blackened with coal and frozen with waiting, accused the Company of killing half its employees underground and letting the other half die of hunger. Étienne listened and was deeply impressed.

'Hurry up, hurry up!' Richomme the deputy kept saying to the onsetters.

He was anxious to speed up the ascent, and, not wanting to have to reprimand them, pretended not to hear. But the protests became so violent that he had to interfere. Behind him they were saying that things would not go on like this for ever, and that one fine day the whole show would blow up.

'You are a reasonable chap,' he said to Maheu; 'tell them to shut up. When you haven't got strength on your side, you have to have prudence.'

But Maheu, who was calming down and feeling nervous himself, did not have to intervene, for the voices suddenly stopped. Négrel and Dansaert, back from their tour of inspection, were coming out of a gallery, both dripping with sweat like everybody else. An age-old habit of discipline made the men stand back while the engineer walked through the crowd without a word. He got into one tub and the overman into another, the signal rope was pulled five times – the special meat-call, as they called it for the bosses – and the cage flew upwards amid sullen silence.

[6]

As he was going up in the cage, into which he had piled with four others, Étienne made up his mind to resume his hungry tramp on the road. He might just as well die at once, as go down again into that hell where you could not even earn your keep. Catherine was in the load above, and no longer at his side to warm him and lull his misgivings. Besides, it was wiser to clear out and not let his mind run along silly lines like that, for with his better education he could not share the herd-like resignation of these people, and knew he would end up by throttling one of the chiefs.

Suddenly he was blinded. The ascent had been so rapid that the broad daylight quite dazed him, and he stood blinking in a glare to which he was already unaccustomed. All the same, he was relieved to feel the cage settle back on its catches. A banksman, young Mouquet, opened the gates, and the miners poured out of the tubs.

'I say, Mouquet,' Zacharie whispered in his ear, 'what about going to the Volcan tonight?'

The Volcan was a pub (licensed for music and dancing) at Montsou. Mouquet winked his left eye, and his lips parted in a silent grin. He was short and stocky, like his father, with the saucy look of the spendthrift who takes no thought for the morrow. Mouquette came out just then, and he dealt her a re-sounding whack on the behind, to show his brotherly love.

Étienne hardly recognized the lofty nave of the pit-head, which he had last seen looking terrifying in the uncertain glimmer of the lanterns. Now it was merely bare and dirty, with a grey light filtering through the dusty windows. The only bright thing about it was the shining copper-work of the engine, up at the other end; the greasy steel cables flying through the air like inked ribbons, the winding-pulleys high upon their huge scaffolding, the cages and tubs, all this mass of metal, darkened the shed with the hard, grey tones of old iron. Wheels ceaselessly rumbled over the sheet-iron flooring, whilst from the quantities of coal being moved about, there

71

arose a fine dust which blackened ground, walls and even the joists of the headgear.

Meanwhile, Chaval had gone into the checkweighman's little glass office to look at the tokens-indicator, and now he came back furious. He had seen that two of their tubs had been refused, one for not containing the regulation amount, the other for dirty coal.

'The end of a perfect day!' he stormed. 'Another twenty sous down! That's what comes of taking on slackers whose arms are about as much good as a pig's tail!'

And a sidelong glance at Étienne completed his thought. Étienne felt like answering him with his fists, but then he asked himself what was the use, as he was leaving anyway. This finally settled it for him.

'You can't do well the first day,' said Maheu, trying to keep the peace; 'he'll be better tomorrow.'

Nevertheless, they were all on edge and spoiling for a quarrel. As they went through the lamp-room to give in their lamps, Levaque fell out with the lamp-man, accusing him of not having cleaned his lamp properly. They only began to calm down a little when they reached the locker-room, where the fire was still burning. Indeed, it must have been made up too well, for the stove was red hot, and its blood-red reflection on the walls made the great windowless room seem all ablaze. There were grunts of pleasure as all these backsides stood roasting themselves at a respectful distance, steaming like soup. When it was too hot behind, you toasted your front. Mouquette had calmly let down her breeches to dry her shirt. Some of the boys were facetious about it, and there was a roar of laughter when she suddenly showed them her bum. This, from her, was the supreme expression of contempt.

'I'm off,' said Chaval, having put away his tools in his locker.

Nobody else moved except Mouquette, who hurried off after him because, it was alleged, they both went in the Montsou direction. But nobody took that seriously, as they knew full well that he had finished with her.

Meanwhile, Catherine had been looking thoughtful and had just whispered something to her father. He first looked surprised and then nodded his approval. Calling Étienne to give him back his bundle, he said:

'Look here, you haven't a sou, and by the time pay-day comes you'll have pegged out. Would you like me to try and get you credit somewhere?'

For a minute the young man was embarrassed, as he was just about to claim his thirty sous and go. But the girl's presence shamed him. She was looking very hard at him and perhaps thinking he was work-shy.

'I can't promise anything, you know,' Maheu went on, 'but they can only refuse.'

Then Étienne gave in. He told himself that they would refuse, and that anyhow he had made no promise and could still move on after having something to eat. But then he saw Catherine's pleasure, how prettily she laughed and how friendly she looked, how glad to have come to the rescue, and he was vexed with himself for not having said no. For what was the use of going on with all that?

Having put on their clogs and shut up their lockers, the Maheu family left the shed, following their mates who were going off one by one after having a good warm. Étienne brought up the rear, and Levaque and his brat joined the party. But on the way past the screens they were halted by a violent scene.

The screening took place in a huge shed, with beams black with the flying dust and large shutters through which blew a continual draught. The tubs of coal came there straight from pit-top, and were emptied by tips into hoppers, long iron shoots; and on each side of these shoots the screeners, standing on steps and armed with shovels and rakes, took out the stones and pushed on the good coal, straight down through funnels into the railway trucks which ran in under the shed.

Philomène Levaque was there, thin and pale, with the sheep-like face of a consumptive girl. She had a bit of blue woollen material round her head by way of protection, and her hands and arms were black up to the elbows. She was sorting immediately below an aged crone, the mother of Pierronne – Ma Brûlé, as she was called – terrifying-looking with her owl's eyes and mouth as tight as a miner's purse. They were going for each other hammer and tongs, the younger one accusing the old woman of raking away her stones, so that she could not fill a basket in ten minutes. They were paid by the basket, which gave rise to quarrels without end. Hair was flying, and the marks of black hands stood out on red faces.

'That's it! Bash her bloody head in!' Zacharie shouted down to his mistress from above.

The screeners all shrieked with laughter. But Ma Brûlé turned on the young man and snarled:

'Now then, you dirty bastard! The best thing you can do is to own up to the two kids you've got her with! Did you ever! A slip of an eighteen-year-old who can't even hold herself up!'

Maheu had to prevent his son from going down to have a look at the colour of that old carcase's skin, as he put it. But a foreman was on the way, and all rakes suddenly began scrabbling at the coal again. All that could be seen along the whole length of the shoot, was the rounded backs of women fiercely squabbling over stones.

Outside, the wind had suddenly dropped, and a cold dampness was coming down from the grey sky. The miners squared their shoulders, folded their arms, and set off in a straggling line, with a rolling gait that made their big bones stand out through their thin clothes. As they went along in broad daylight, they looked like a band of Negroes who had fallen into the mud. Some of them had not finished their sandwiches, and the remainder of their bread, carried home between their shirt and jacket, gave them a humpbacked appearance.

'Look, there's Bouteloup,' said Zacharie with a sneer.

Without stopping, Levaque exchanged a word or two with his lodger, a big, dark fellow of thirty-five, with a placid, open face.

'Soup ready, Louis?'

'I think so.'

'Then the missus is in a good mood today?'

'Yes, quite all right, I think.'

Other rippers were coming along in new groups which disappeared one by one into the mine. It was the three o'clock shift going down, more men devoured by the pit to replace the teams of colliers at the far ends of the galleries. The pit was never idle; night and day human insects picked away at the rock six hundred metres below the fields of beet.

The youngsters were going on ahead. Jeanlin was confiding to Bébert a complicated plan for getting four sous' worth of tobacco on tick, whilst Lydie followed them at a respectful distance. Next came Catherine with Zacharie and Étienne. It was only when they reached a pub, the Avantage, that Maheu and Levaque caught them up.

'Here we are,' Maheu said to Étienne. 'Would you like to go in?'

The party broke up. Catherine stood still for a moment, having a last look at the young man with her big eyes, limpid like spring-water, their crystalline depths made deeper still by the blackness of her face. Then she smiled, and disappeared with the others up the steep road to the village.

The pub stood at the crossroads, midway between the village and the pit. It was a two-storeyed brick house, white-washed all over and enlivened by a broad band of sky blue round the windows. On a square sign nailed over the door was the legend, painted in yellow: '*À l'Avantage*. Rasseneur, Licensee.' Behind the house was a skittle-alley surrounded by a hedge. The Company had done everything in its power to buy up this small enclave of land within its own huge properties, and was very sore about this inn that had sprung up in the middle of the fields at the very gates of Le Voreux.

'Come in,' repeated Maheu.

The parlour was small, bare, and light with its white walls, three tables, a dozen chairs, and deal counter the size of a kitchen dresser. There were ten glasses on it at the most, with three bottles of spirits, a decanter, and a little zinc tank with pewter tap, for the beer. And nothing else – not a picture, not a shelf, not a single game. In the iron fireplace, all shining with blacklead, a coal block was gently burning. A thin layer of white sand on the flagstones soaked up the everlasting moisture of this waterlogged district.

'One small,' ordered Maheu, addressing a buxom blonde, a neighbour's daughter who sometimes obliged in the bar. 'Rasseneur at home?'

The girl turned the tap, answering that the boss would soon be back. The miner emptied half the glass in a slow, single gulp, to rinse away the dust clogging his throat. He did not offer anything to his companion. One other customer, another damp and grimy miner, was sitting at a table drinking his beer in silence, with an air of profound meditation. A third came in, made a sign, was served, paid, and took himself off without uttering a word.

Then a heavily built man of thirty-eight came in. He had a round, clean-shaven face, good-natured and smiling. It was Rasseneur, an ex-miner whom the Company had dismissed three years before, following a strike. Being a first-rate workman and able to speak well, he had taken the lead when any complaints had been voiced, and had ended by being the centre of disaffection. His wife already kept a bar, like so many miner's wives, and when he was thrown out on the streets he became a publican himself, raised some money, and planted his pub right opposite Le Voreux as a gesture of defiance to the Company. Now his house was prosperous and he was becoming a rallying-point, thriving on the resentments he had slowly kindled in the hearts of his former mates.

'This is the chap I took on this morning,' Maheu hastened to explain. 'Have you got one or other of your rooms free, and will you give him a fortnight's credit?'

Suddenly a look of extreme wariness came over Rasseneur's broad face. He glanced critically at Étienne, and without bothering to express any regret answered:

'Both my rooms are taken. Can't be done.'

The young man was expecting such a refusal, and yet it hurt him, and he was surprised to find how loth he was all of a sudden to go away. Still, go he would as soon as he got his thirty sous. The miner who had been drinking at the table had gone. Others kept coming in one by one to clear their throats, and then went on again with the same ambling gait. It was just a rinse, with no joy or emotion in it – the silent satisfaction of a need.

Maheu was sipping the rest of his beer. 'So there's nothing doing?' Rasseneur asked him in a tone full of meaning.

Maheu looked round and saw that only Étienne was there.

'Well, there's been another shemozzle. . . . Yes, about timbering.'

He told his story, and the publican's face reddened and swelled as though some sanguine emotion were burning through his skin and flaming through his eyes. Then he burst out:

'Very well! If they decide to cut the rate they are sunk.'

He found Étienne embarrassing, but he went on, casting sidelong glances at him and using indirect expressions and allusions, referring to the manager, Monsieur Hennebeau, his wife, his nephew, little Négrel, without mentioning any names, repeating that things could not go on like this and that there was bound to be a blow-up one of these fine days. The poverty was too cruel – he named factories that were closing down and the workmen leaving the district. He had been giving away more than six pounds of bread every day for the last month. Only yesterday he had been told that Monsieur Deneulin, the owner of a neighbouring pit, did not know how he was to keep going. Moreover, he had just had a letter from Lille full of disquieting details.

'You know,' he murmured, '– from the person you saw here one evening.'

He was cut short by his wife who now came in. She was a tall, gaunt firebrand of a woman, with a long nose and cheeks of a violet hue. In politics she was much more radical than her husband.

'Pluchart's letter?' she said. 'Ah! now if he were the master, things would soon look up!'

Étienne had been listening for a minute, and he began to grasp these notions of suffering and revenge, and they stirred him deeply. The sudden mention of that name made him start, and involuntarily he said aloud:

'Pluchart! I know him.'

Feeling their eyes turned on him, he had to go on:

'Yes, I'm a mechanic, and he was my foreman at Lille. . . . He's an able fellow. I've often had talks with him.'

Rasseneur examined him afresh, and a rapid change came over his face, a sudden look of sympathy. Then he spoke to his wife:

77

'Maheu has brought this gentleman, one of his haulage men, to see if there is a room upstairs and whether we can give him a fortnight's credit.'

Thereupon the matter was settled in four words. Yes, there *was* a room, the tenant had left that very morning. The publican, warming to his subject, became very expansive, repeating that he was not asking of the owners any more than they could manage, he was not demanding things that could not be done, as some others did. His wife merely shrugged her shoulders. She wanted her pound of flesh, and no compromise.

'Well, good night,' Maheu broke in. 'That's all very fine and large, but it won't prevent men going down there, and so long as men go down, men will die at it. . . . Now look at yourself; you have been the picture of health for the past three years, since you got out of it.'

'Yes, I feel much better,' declared Rasseneur complacently.

Étienne followed the miner to the door to thank him, but he shook his head without a word, and the young man watched him plod wearily up towards the village. Madame Rasseneur was in the middle of serving customers, and asked him to wait a minute until she could take him up to his room for a wash. Should he stay? His doubts had seized him again, and an uneasy longing for the freedom of the open road, hunger in the sunshine gladly endured for the sake of being one's own master. Since he had climbed up that slag-heap, buffeted by the gale, he seemed to have lived long years underground, crawling on his belly along those black passages. He dreaded beginning it all over again, it was unjust and altogether too hard; the thought of being a beast of burden, to be blinded and crushed, outraged his pride as a man.

While he was turning all this over in his mind, his eyes wandered out over the wide plain and gradually took in what they saw. And it surprised him, for he had not imagined that the horizon was like this, when old Bonnemort had pointed it out in the darkness with a wave of the hand. True, he recognized Le Voreux in front of him, lying in a hollow with its timber and brick buildings, the tarred screening shed, the slated headgear, the winding-house and the tall, pale red chimney. There it all was, squat and evil-looking. But the

78

yards round the buildings were much more extensive than he had imagined, like a lake of ink with heaps of coal for waves, bristling with high trestles supporting the rails of the elevated tracks, cluttered up at one end with the stock of timber, looking like a forest that had been mown down and gathered in. The view to the right was blocked by the slag-heap, rising colossal like a giant's earthwork; it was already grass-covered on its older parts, but at the other end it was being consumed by an inner fire, which had been burning for a year with dense smoke, and as it burned had left long trails of bloody rust on the surface of dull grey shale and sandstone. Further away stretched fields, endless fields of corn and beet, all bare at this time of the year, marshes with coarse vegetation and here and there a stunted willow, distant meadows cut up by slender rows of poplar. In the far distance, towns showed like small white patches – Marchiennes to the north, Montsou to the south – whilst eastwards the forest of Vandame, with its leafless trees, made a purplish line on the horizon. And on this dull winter afternoon, beneath the colourless sky, it seemed as if all the blackness of Le Voreux and all the flying coal-dust had settled on the plain, powdering the trees, sanding the roads, sowing seed in the ground.

But what surprised Étienne most of all, as he stood there looking, was the canal, or rather the canalized river Scarpe, which he had not seen during the night. It ran in a straight line from Le Voreux to Marchiennes, like a dull silver ribbon two leagues long, an avenue bordered with tall trees, raised above the low-lying surroundings and running on and on between its green banks, its pale water broken by the moving, red-painted sterns of barges. There were boats tied up at a landing-stage near the pit, and they were being loaded directly from tubs running on trestle railways. Then came a bend in the canal, which slanted off across the marshes; and the whole soul of this flat plain seemed to be concentrated in this geometrical water, which crossed it like a highroad, bearing along coal and iron.

Étienne's gaze travelled up from the canal to the village perched on the plateau, but all he could make out was the red-tiled roofs. Then down again to Le Voreux, pausing at the foot of the clayey slope to notice two enormous stacks of bricks, made and baked on the premises. A branch of the Company's railway ran along behind a fence, serving the pit. The last batch of rippers must be going down now. A single truck being pushed by some men gave forth a piercing screech. Gone were the mysteries of darkness, the inexplicable thunderings, the flaring of unknown stars in the sky. The distant blast-furnaces and coke-ovens had paled with the light of day. There only remained the untiring exhaust of the pump, still panting with the same slow and heavy breath; he could now see it, like the breath of an insatiable ogre, in puffs of grey steam.

Suddenly Étienne made up his mind. Maybe he thought he saw Catherine's pale eyes up yonder, where the village began. Or perhaps it was some wind of revolt blowing from Le Voreux. He could not tell. But he wanted to go down the mine again to suffer and to fight. And his thoughts turned fiercely towards those folk Bonnemort had been talking about, and towards this god, crouching and replete, to whom ten thousand starving men were offering up their flesh, though they did not even know him.

Part Two

<hr>

[1]

LA PIOLAINE, the Grégoires' property, was two kilometres east of Montsou, along the Joiselle road. It was a big square house, without any particular style, built at the beginning of last century. All that remained of the great estates originally belonging to it was some thirty hectares, walled in and easy of upkeep. The orchard and kitchen-garden, in particular, were much admired for some of the finest fruit and vegetables in the district. For the rest, there was no park but only a little wood. The avenue of old limes, a leafy cathedral three hundred metres long, stretching from the railings to the steps of the house was one of the sights of this bare plain, where the large trees between Marchiennes and Beaugnies could easily be counted.

On this particular morning the Grégoires had risen at eight, though as a rule they did not stir till up to an hour later, for they were heavy and determined sleepers, but they had had a disturbed night owing to the storm. While her husband went off at once to see whether the wind had done any damage, Madame Grégoire had gone down to the kitchen in her slippers and flannel dressing-gown. She was short and dumpy, and at fifty-eight her face was still round, doll-like, and wide-eyed, beneath hair of a dazzling whiteness.

'Mélanie,' she said to the cook, 'suppose you make a brioche this morning? The dough is all ready mixed. Mademoiselle will not be up for another half-an-hour and she could have some with her chocolate. .... It would be a nice surprise, wouldn't it?'

Cook, a skinny old woman who had been in their service for thirty years, began to laugh.

'Yes, that's true, it would be a lovely surprise. My stove is alight and the oven must be hot . . . and besides, Honorine can give me a hand.'

Honorine was a girl of twenty who had been taken in as a child and trained in the house. She was now housemaid. Apart from these two women, the only staff employed was François the coachman who also did heavy jobs. A gardener and his wife looked after the fruit, vegetables, flowers, and chickens. And as the establishment was run on patriarchal lines, without formality, this little society lived together on friendly terms.

Madame Grégoire, who had thought out the surprise of the brioche while still in bed, stayed to see the dough put in the oven. The kitchen was vast, and by its scrupulous cleanliness and the arsenal of saucepans, pots and utensils which filled it, you could tell that it was the most important room in the house. It had a goodly smell of food. Racks and cupboards were overflowing with provisions.

'And mind it's a nice golden brown!' Madame Grégoire reminded them as she went into the dining-room.

Although the whole house was centrally heated, there was a coal fire to brighten up the room. Otherwise it was very simply furnished: just a dining-table and chairs and a sideboard, all of mahogany. But two capacious armchairs spoke of love of comfort, of long, happy hours given to digestion. They never used the drawing-room, but stayed here in a family circle.

Just then Monsieur Grégoire came in, clad in a thick fustian jacket; he too was pink and young-looking for his sixty years, with large, kindly features and snow-white curls. He had seen the coachman and the gardener: no real damage except one chimney-pot down. He loved to have a look round La Piolaine every morning, for as it was not large enough to be a worry, it gave him all the pleasures of ownership.

'And Cécile?' he asked; 'isn't she going to get up today?'

'I can't make it out,' answered his wife, 'I thought I heard her moving about.'

The table was laid with three bowls on the white cloth.

Honorine was sent up to see what Mademoiselle was doing. But she came straight down again. stifling giggles. and speaking in a whisper as though she were still in the room upstairs.

'Oh if Monsieur and Madame could only see Mademoiselle! She is sleeping like. . . . oh! like a picture of Jesus. You can't imagine! It's a joy to look at her.'

The father and mother glanced at each other with looks of tender indulgence.

'Coming up to have a look?' he smiled.

'Poor little darling! Yes I'm coming.'

And up they went together The room was the only luxurious one in the house· it had blue silk hangings and white lacquer furniture picked out with blue lines, the whim of a spoilt child indulged by her parents. In the half-light coming between the curtains, in the vague whiteness of the bed, the girl was sleeping with her cheek on her bare arm. She was not pretty, being too heavy and full-blooded and quite mature at eighteen, but her perfect flesh was as white as milk; she had dark hair, a round face and an obstinate little nose peeping out between her cheeks. The coverlet had slipped down, and she was breathing so gently that her already ample bosom scarcely rose and fell.

'She can't have had a wink of sleep with that dreadful wind,' whispered her mother.

Father signalled to her to be quiet. Together they leaned over and gazed in adoration at this daughter for whom they had longed for so many years, whom they had had late in life when they had given up hope. There she lay in her virgin nudity, and to them she was perfection – not too fat, never well enough fed. She slept on, unaware that they were so near that their faces touched hers. But a slight movement passed like a wave over her motionless features. Trembling lest she might wake, they tiptoed away.

'Sh!' whispered Monsieur Grégoire when he reached the door, 'if she has had a bad night we must let her sleep on.'

'As long as she likes, the pet!' agreed Madame Grégoire. 'We'll wait.'

They went downstairs and took up their positions in the

dining-room armchairs, and the maids, amused at Mademoiselle's heavy sleep, did not mind keeping the chocolate warm on the stove. He took up a paper and she knitted away at a large bedspread. Not a sound was heard in the house, which was very warm.

The Grégoire fortune, worth some forty thousand francs a year, was all invested in shares in the Montsou mines. They loved telling people about its origins, which went back to the very formation of the Company.

About the beginning of the last century there had been a mad boom in coal between Lille and Valenciennes. All heads had been turned by the success of the holders of the concessions who were later to form the Anzin Company. Soundings were taken in every parish, companies were floated and concessions sprang up overnight. But of all the indomitable fighters of that period, the one who left behind the greatest reputation for tenacious intelligence was without doubt Baron Desrumaux. For forty years he had fought on untiringly against continual odds: fruitless early investigations, new pits abandoned after months of toil, borings filled in by landslides, workmen drowned by sudden floodings, hundreds of thousands of francs thrown into the earth; to say nothing of administrative bothers, shareholders' panics, fights with landlords who refused to recognize royal concessions unless they had been approached first. When at length he had founded Desrumaux, Fauquenoix and Co. to work the Montsou concessions, and the mines were beginning to show a slight profit, two neighbouring concessions – Cougny, belonging to Count Cougny, and Joiselle, belonging to Cornille and Jernard – nearly smashed him with their cut-throat competition. Fortunately, on the 25th August, 1760, a settlement was reached between the three concessions and they amalgamated, forming the Montsou Mining Company as it still exists today. For the apportionment of shares the total property was divided, according to the financial system of the time, into twenty-four *sous*, each one of which was subdivided into twelve *deniers*, making two hundred and eighty-eight *deniers* in all; and as the *denier* was worth ten thousand francs, the capital represented a sum of nearly three millions. Desrumaux, at the point of death but triumphant, received as his share six *sous* and three *deniers*.

In those days the Baron owned La Piolaine, together with three hundred hectares of land, and he had in his employ a steward named Honoré Grégoire, a fellow from Picardy and great-grandfather of Léon Grégoire, Cécile's father. At the time of the Montsou amalgamation Honoré, who had some fifty thousand francs of savings hoarded in a stocking, yielded in fear and trembling to his master's burning faith, brought out ten thousand in hard cash, took one *denier*, and lived in terror of having robbed his children of that amount. It is true that his son Eugène's dividends were very slender, and as he had set himself up as an independent gentleman and been foolish enough to lose the other forty thousand francs of his paternal heritage in a disastrous partnership, he led a very penurious existence. But the rate of interest on the *denier* went on steadily rising, and the family fortune began with Félicien, who was able to realize the dream on which his grandfather, the former steward, had brought him up: he bought La Piolaine for a mere song when the property was broken up and sold as nationalized land. But some very lean years followed, until the Revolution had run its violent course and Napoleon had crashed in bloodshed. And so it was Léon Grégoire who really reaped the immensely multiplied harvest from the timid and anxious little investment of his great-grandfather. That humble ten thousand francs grew and grew with the prosperity of the Company. By 1820 it was yielding a hundred per cent – another ten thousand. In 1844 it was twenty thousand, by 1850 it was forty. Finally, two years previously, the dividend had gone up to the staggering figure of fifty thousand francs; that is to say that in a century the value of the *denier*, quoted at one million on the stock exchange at Lille, had multiplied a hundredfold.

When the million rate had been touched, Monsieur Grégoire was advised to sell, but he refused with a superior smile. Six months later there came an industrial crisis, and the *denier* fell to six hundred thousand. But he went on smiling and had no regrets, for the Grégoires had an unshakeable faith in their mine. It would go up again; why! God Himself was not more reliable. And this religious faith was mingled with a profound gratitude for an investment which had kept the family in idleness for a century. It was their private deity, whom they, in their egotism, extolled with sacred rites as the divine benefactor of their home, who gently rocked their slothful bed and fattened them at their groaning table. This had gone on from father to son – why risk offending destiny by harbouring doubts? Behind their faith there lurked a superstitious dread: the frightening thought that their million might have melted away if they had cashed it and put it away in a drawer. It seemed more secure to them buried in the earth, from which a race of miners, generations of starving men, would continue to dig it out for them, little by little, day by day, according to their needs.

Moreover, blessings rained on this house. Monsieur Grégoire, while still very young, had married the plain and penniless daughter of a chemist in Marchiennes; but he worshipped her, and she repaid him with happiness in full measure. She had always been engrossed in her home, adored her husband and had no wish but his; no differences of taste ever came between them, their desires were merged in one and the same ideal of comfortable well-being. This well-regulated existence of affection and little kindnesses done to each other, had gone on for forty years; the income of forty thousand was quietly spent and their savings went on Cécile, whose arrival late in their married life had caused a momentary disturbance in their budget. They still satisfied her every whim: a second horse, two more carriages, dresses from Paris. As nothing was too good for their daughter, this outlay was an additional pleasure, though for their own part they so hated display that they kept to the fashions of their youth. Any unprofitable expense was silly, they thought.

The door burst open and a loud voice cried:

'Well! what's going on here? Breakfast without me!'

It was Cécile, straight from bed, her eyes still heavy with sleep. She had simply tied up her hair and slipped on a white woollen dressing-gown.

'Oh no!' said her mother. 'You can see we've waited for you. The wind must have kept you awake, my darling!'

The girl stared at her, quite taken aback.

'Has it been windy? I had no idea. I haven't stirred all night.'

That struck them as funny, and they all three started laughing, and both the servants, who were bringing in the breakfast, burst out laughing as well. Everybody was so amused to think that Mademoiselle had slept the clock round. The sight of the brioche added the final touch to the joy on their faces.

'What, all freshly cooked?' repeated Cécile. 'This must be a special surprise for me. My! won't it be lovely all hot in the chocolate!'

At length they sat down, the chocolate steamed in the bowls and the talk ran on for some time about the brioche. Mélanie and Honorine stayed in the room and supplied details about the cooking, and watched them stuffing themselves, their lips all greasy, saying what a pleasure it was to make a cake when you saw how the master and Madame and Mademoiselle enjoyed eating it.

But the dogs barked loudly, and they thought it must be at the piano mistress who came from Marchiennes on Mondays and Fridays. A professor of literature came, too. All Cécile's education had been carried on in this way at La Piolaine, in carefree ignorance, just as the fancy moved her. As soon as any question bothered her, out went the book through the window.

'It's Monsieur Deneulin,' said Honorine.

Deneulin, Monsieur Grégoire's cousin, followed her in without ceremony. He was loud of voice, quick of movement, and walked like a retired cavalry officer. Although over fifty, his close-cropped hair and heavy moustache were black as ink.

'Yes, it's me. Good morning. Please don't let me disturb you!'

He sat down amid exclamations from the family, who eventually returned to their chocolate.

'Have you anything to tell me?' asked Monsieur Grégoire.

'Oh, no, nothing at all!' Deneulin answered, rather hastily. 'I was out for a ride to loosen the old joints a bit, you know, and as I happened to pass your gate I just came in to say how do you do.'

87

Cécile asked him about his daughters, Jeanne and Lucie. They were quite well, thank you; the former was mad on her painting, whilst the other, the elder, practised singing at the piano from morn till eve. But there was a slight quiver in his voice, a sort of anxiety which he tried to conceal with bursts of gaiety.

'Everything all right at the pit?' went on Monsieur Grégoire.

'Well, as a matter of fact I'm a bit put out over this blasted crisis. Ah! we are paying for the good years now! Too many factories have been built, too many railways, too much capital has been tied up with a view to getting enormous output. And today money is all lying doggo, you can't find enough to keep the show going ... Still, fortunately things aren't desperate yet. I shall get over it.'

Like his cousin, he had inherited a *denier* in the Montsou mines. But being a go-ahead engineer and out to make a huge fortune, he had hastened to sell out as soon as the *denier* had reached the million mark. For months he had been turning a plan over in his mind. His wife had inherited from an uncle the little concession of Vandame, in which there were only two pits working, Jean-Bart and Gaston-Marie, and these were in such a state of disrepair and the plant was so defective that the output hardly covered working costs. His dream was to repair Jean-Bart, modernize the plant and widen the shaft so that it would take more down it, leaving Gaston-Marie for ventilation only. There should be gold down there by the shovelful, he said. The idea was sound, but his whole million had gone into it, and this damned industrial crisis would go and break out at the very moment when his faith was on the point of being justified by huge profits. Moreover, he was a bad manager, kind to his workmen in a gruff sort of way, and since his wife's death he had let people swindle him. Also he had no control over his daughters, the elder of whom talked of going on the stage whilst the younger had already had three landscapes turned down by the Salon. The girls faced disaster with merry laughter, and the threat of poverty was bringing out their real qualities as housekeepers.

'You see, Léon,' he faltered, 'you were wrong not to sell

out when I did. Now everything is going to pot and anything might . . . and, er, if you had entrusted your money to me you would have seen what we could have done with it at Vandame, in our mine!'

Unhurriedly, Monsieur Grégoire was finishing his chocolate. He gently answered:

'Never! You know that I won't speculate. I like a quiet life, and it would be so silly to bother my head with business worries. As for Montsou, it may well go on falling, but it will always yield enough for our needs. We mustn't be greedy, you know! And mark my words, you'll be sorry one of these days, for Montsou will go up again, and Cécile's children's children will still be making a good thing out of it.'

Deneulin listened with an embarrassed smile.

'So if I were to say anything about putting a hundred thousand francs into my show, you would say no?'

But seeing the alarm on the Grégoires' faces, he wished he had not gone so fast, and put off his idea of a loan for another day, keeping it in reserve as a desperate measure.

'Oh! I haven't got as far as that yet! I was only joking. . . . Yes, you are probably right; the money other people earn for you is the best to get fat on.'

They changed the subject. Cécile came back to her cousins, for she found their tastes most interesting, absurd though they were. Madame Grégoire promised to take her daughter to see the darlings on the first sunny day. But Monsieur Grégoire was not following the talk; he seemed lost in a dream. He suddenly broke in:

'If I were in your shoes I wouldn't hold out any longer, I would come to terms with Montsou. They want it badly, and you would get your money back.'

He was referring to the ancient feud between the Montsou and Vandame concessions. Although the latter was only a small concern its powerful neighbour was exasperated to see this square league belonging to somebody else wedged in the middle of its own sixty-seven communes. Having tried in vain to kill it, Montsou was now plotting to buy it up for next to nothing when it was mortally ill. The war went on without quarter, each company stopping its galleries two hundred metres short of those of the other. It was a duel to the last drop of blood, though outwardly the managers and directors were on terms of polite friendship.

Deneulin's eyes blazed.

'Never!' it was his turn to exclaim. 'As long as I'm alive Montsou shall not have Vandame. . . . I dined at Hennebeau's on Thursday and I could see he was crawling round me. As early as last autumn, when the big-wigs came down to the head office, they made me all sorts of overtures. Oh yes! I know these noble lords and dukes, and the generals and ministers as well – a pack of rogues who would strip you, shirt and all, at the edge of a wood!'

And he went on and on. In any case, Monsieur Grégoire held no brief for the Board of Directors of Montsou – the six directors set up by the agreement of 1760, who ruled the Company with a rod of iron. When one of these died, the five survivors chose the new member from amongst the wealthy and influential shareholders. In the opinion of the owner of La Piolaine, who was a man of modest ideas, these gentlemen sometimes overstepped the limits in their lust for money.

Mélanie came in to clear away. The dogs barked again outside, and Honorine was going to open the door when Cécile, gorged with food and stifled with heat, rose from the table.

'No, don't bother. It must be my lesson.'

Deneulin had risen too. He watched the girl go out, and asked with a smile:

'Well, what about this marriage with young Négrel?'

'There is nothing settled yet,' said Madame Grégoire. 'It's just a vague idea . . . it needs thinking out.'

'Of course,' he went on, laughing suggestively. 'I believe that the nephew and his aunt. . . . What simply staggers me is that Madame Hennebeau should be the one to fall on Cécile's neck.'

Monsieur Grégoire was outraged. A lady of such distinction, and fourteen years older than the young man! It was an appalling idea, and such things should not be joked about. Deneulin, still laughing, shook hands and took his leave.

'No, it isn't the lesson yet,' said Cécile, coming back again.

'It's that woman with the two children – you know, Mummy, the miner's wife we met. Shall we let them in?'

They hesitated. Were they very dirty? No, not too bad, and they could leave their clogs on the steps outside. The Grégoire parents were already recumbent in their armchairs, digesting their food. Fear of a change of atmosphere made up their minds for them.

'Show them in here, Honorine.'

And in came Maheude and her children, frozen, hungry, and panic-stricken at finding themselves in this warm room where there was such a lovely smell of brioche.

[2]

Up in the bedroom, through the closed shutters, dawn had gradually thrown bars of grey light over the ceiling, like a fan, the air was close and heavy and everybody had resumed the night's sleep. Lénore and Henri lay in each other's arms, Alzire was propped up on her hump but her head had lolled over, whilst Grandpa Bonnemort, now in sole possession of Zacharie and Jeanlin's bed, snored away open-mouthed. Not a sound came from the little room, where Maheude had dropped off again in the middle of feeding Estelle, with her breast hanging over to one side and the baby lying across her stomach, gorged with milk and fast asleep as well, half suffocated in the soft cushion of her mother's bosom.

The cuckoo downstairs struck six. Doors could be heard banging along the terraces of the village, and clogs clattered on the paving stones. It was the screeners going on. Silence fell again until seven when shutters flew back and yawns and coughs could be heard through the walls. Somebody's coffee-mill went on squeaking for a long time before anybody woke in the room.

But suddenly a distant sound of blows and shouting made Alzire sit up. Realizing what the time was, she ran barefoot and gave her mother a shake.

'Mummy! Mummy, it's late! You've got to go out. Mind!

You are squashing Estelle.' She rescued the baby, half smothered under its mother's great pendulous breasts.

'Oh, what a hell of a life!' muttered Maheude, rubbing her eyes. 'I'm so knocked up I could sleep all day. You dress Lénore and Henri, and I'll take them with me while you mind Estelle. I don't want to cart her about for fear she'll pick up a cold in this filthy weather.'

She washed hurriedly, slipped on an old blue skirt, her cleanest, and a grey woollen jacket that she had patched in two places the day before.

'And the soup! Oh dear, oh dear, what a life!' And she muttered on while she went downstairs, knocking everything over on her way, whilst Alzire took Estelle back with her into the bedroom. The baby had begun to yell, but she was used to her tantrums, and already, at the age of eight, had recourse to a woman's tender wiles to calm her and distract her attention. She gently laid her in her own warm bed and coaxed her to sleep by giving her a finger to suck. It was high time, too, for a new hubbub was beginning and she had to make peace between Lénore and Henri who were at last waking up. These two scarcely ever got on together, and never put their arms round each other's necks except when they were asleep. As soon as she got up in the morning the girl, who was six, fell upon the boy, two years her junior, and rained blows on him which he could not return. They both had the family head, too big, looking as though it were inflated, and with tousled yellow hair. Alzire had to pull her sister by the legs and threaten to skin her bottom for her. Then there was a stamping scene over washing and each garment she put on them. The blinds were left pulled so as not to disturb Grandpa Bonnemort's sleep. He went on snoring away all through the appalling hullabaloo.

'Ready!' shouted Maheude. 'How are you getting on up there?'

She had pushed back the shutters, given the fire a poke and put some more coal on. She had hoped that the old man would not have swallowed all the soup, but she found the saucepan wiped clean, and so she put a handful of vermicelli on to boil, having kept this in reserve for three days. They would have to eat it plain, without butter, for there could not possibly be any of yesterday's little bit left. To her surprise, she found that Catherine had performed the miracle of making the sandwiches and yet leaving a piece the size of a walnut. But now the cupboard really was bare: not a crust, not a scrap, not a single bone to gnaw, nothing at all. What was to become of them if Maigrat went on refusing credit and if the people at La Piolaine did not give her five francs? When the men and her daughter came home from the pit they would have to eat, though, for unfortunately nobody had yet invented a way of living without food.

'Come down, will you!' she shouted irritably; 'I ought to be gone by now!'

When Alzire and the children were down, she divided the vermicelli out on three plates, saying that she was not hungry herself. Although Catherine had already put water through yesterday's coffee-grounds, she did so again and drank two large glasses of a coffee so pale in colour that it looked like rusty water. But still, it would keep her going.

'Now listen,' she told Alzire; 'let Grandpa sleep on and mind Estelle doesn't bang her head. If she wakes up and hollers too much, look, here is some sugar you can melt and give her in a spoon. I know you are a good girl and won't eat it yourself.'

'What about school, Mummy?'

'School? Well, that will have to wait for another day. Today I want you.'

'What about the soup? Do you want me to make it if you are late getting back?'

'The soup? Let me see . . . no, wait till I come.'

Alzire evidently understood, for she asked no more questions. She knew all about soup-making; she had the precocious intelligence of the invalid child. By now the whole village was agog, and children were going off to school in twos and threes, shuffling along in their clogs. It struck eight, and from the Levaques' on the left the chatter of tongues grew louder and louder. The women's day was starting: they stood round the coffee-pots, hands on hips, tongues going round and round like millstones. An over-blown face, with thick lips and flat nose, was pressed against the window-pane and calling:

'Just a minute! I've got some news.'

'No, no, see you later,' replied Maheude; 'I've got to go out.'

And she hustled off Lénore and Henri, for fear of yielding to a proffered glass of hot coffee. Grandpa Bonnemort was still snoring upstairs, with a regular snore that rocked the house.

When she was out in the street she was surprised to find that the wind had dropped. There had been a sudden thaw, the sky was the colour of the earth, the walls were sticky with greenish condensation and the streets thick with mud – a special mud peculiar to the coal country, as black as a solution of soot, but so thick and viscous that it nearly pulled her shoes off. She suddenly had to clout Lénore because the child was having a game with her clogs, using them like spades to dig up the mud. On leaving the village, she first skirted the slag-heap and then followed the canal road, taking short cuts along abandoned roads, across tracts of waste ground marked off by moss-covered fences. Shed followed shed, and long factory buildings, with tall chimneys belching forth soot and blackening these desolate outskirts of an industrial town. Behind a clump of poplars rose the crumbling headgear of the Réquillart pit, with only its skeleton still standing. Turning to the right, she came out on the main road.

'Just you wait, you dirty little pig! I'll give you mud-pies, I will!'

This time it was Henri; he had picked up a handful of mud and was kneading it into a ball. The two children were cuffed indiscriminately and resumed an orderly progress, squinting down at the holes their feet made in the heaps of mud. They were already too tired to keep on pulling their feet out at each stride, and just paddled through it.

The road stretched ahead towards Marchiennes with its two leagues of cobblestones, running dead straight through the reddish earth like a greasy ribbon. But in the opposite direction it zigzagged down through Montsou, which was built on a slope of the great rolling plain. These roads in the

Nord, running straight as a die from one manufacturing town to another, or with slight curves and gentle gradients, are gradually being built up, and the whole Department is turning into a single industrial city. The little brick houses, colour-washed to make up for the climate, some yellow, some blue, but others black (perhaps so as to reach the ultimate black with the least delay), ran down hill, twisting to right and left. Here and there the line of little huddled façades was broken by a large two-storeyed house, the home of some manager. A church, built of brick like everything else, looked like some new type of blast furnace, with its square tower already black with coal-dust. But what stood out most of all among the sugar refineries, rope-works and sawmills, was the immense number of dance-halls, bars, and pubs – there were over five hundred of them to a thousand houses.

On nearing the Company's yards, a vast series of workshops and sheds, Maheude decided to take Lénore and Henri by the hand, one on each side. Just beyond was the house of the managing director, Monsieur Hennebeau, a large chalet-like building standing back behind iron gates and a garden containing some scraggy trees. A carriage happened to be drawn up at the gate, setting down a gentleman wearing a ribbon in his buttonhole, and a lady in a fur coat, evidently guests from Paris who had come from Marchiennes station, for Madame Hennebeau, dimly visible in the doorway, was uttering a little scream of surprise and joy.

'Come on, lazybones!' growled their mother as she hauled along the two children who were just standing about in the mud.

She had reached Maigrat's and was feeling very apprehensive. Maigrat lived next door to the manager, from whose home his little house was separated only by a wall, and he kept a store, a long building, opening on to the road, like a shop without windows. He stocked everything: grocery, provisions, greengrocery; he sold bread, beer, and pots and pans. Formerly an inspector at Le Voreux, he had set up in business with a small canteen, and then, thanks to official protection, his trade had grown and grown until it had killed the small shops in Montsou. He combined everything under one roof, and his large number of customers from the industrial villages enabled him to undercut and give more credit. Incidentally he was still in the Company's power, for they had built his little house and shop for him.

'Here I am again, Monsieur Maigrat,' said Maheude humbly, finding him standing at his shop door.

He looked at her without speaking. He was a fat man, coldly polite in manner, and he prided himself on never going back on a decision.

'You won't turn me away like you did yesterday, will you? We must eat between now and Saturday. . . . I know we have owed you sixty francs for two years now. . . .'

And she tried to explain in awkward, short sentences. It was a long-standing debt that went back to the last strike. They had promised to pay it off a score of times, but could never manage to let him have his forty sous per fortnight. And then she had had more trouble the day before yesterday, when she had had to pay a cobbler twenty francs because he was threatening to put the bailiffs in. And that was why they hadn't a penny. Otherwise they would have managed until Saturday, same as the others.

But Maigrat stood there, arms folded over distended belly, answering each supplication with a shake of the head.

'Only two loaves, Monsieur Maigrat. I don't expect a lot, I am not asking for coffee. . . . Just two three-pound loaves a day!'

'No!' he shouted at the top of his voice.

His wife had appeared; she was a sickly creature, who spent the whole day poring over a ledger and not even daring to raise her head. The sight of this poor woman's pleading eyes terrified her, and she fled. It was said that she gave up her place in her husband's bed to haulage girls among the customers. It was a known fact that when a miner wanted more credit, all he had to do was to send along his daughter or wife, no matter whether she was pretty or plain so long as she was willing.

Maheude was still looking at Maigrat imploringly, but the lecherous flicker in his little eyes as he looked her up and down made her feel naked and ashamed. It angered her, too –

there might have been some excuse for it when she was young, before she had had seven children. She dragged away Lénore and Henri, who were picking nutshells up from the gutter and examining them, and set off again.

'This won't do you any good, Monsieur Maigrat, you mark my words!'

The only thing left now was the people at La Piolaine. If they did not cough up five francs, then they could all go to bed and die. She had now turned left along the Joiselle road. The Offices were along there on a corner, a real palace of bricks and mortar where the big-wigs from Paris, generals and government gentlemen, came and had grand dinners every autumn. As she walked on, she was already laying out the five francs in her mind: first bread and coffee, then a quarter of butter, a bushel of potatoes for the morning soup and evening stew, and then perhaps a little brawn because Dad needed some meat.

The parish priest of Montsou, abbé Joire, came along, holding up his cassock like a dainty and well-fed cat, afraid of dirtying his frock. He was a gentle little man who affected to take no part in anything so as not to upset either workers or employers.

'Good morning, Monsieur le Curé.'

He hurried on without stopping, throwing a smile at the children and leaving her standing in the middle of the road. She was no churchgoer, but she had suddenly imagined that this priest was going to do something for her.

The tramp through the black, sticky mud began again. There were still two kilometres to be done and the children were not finding things so funny now, but were scared and dragging behind more and more. On either side, the same waste ground stretched on and on with its moss-covered fences, the same black and grimy factory buildings bristling with tall chimneys. Further away the land spread out in open fields, endlessly flat like a sea of brown clods with never a tree for a mast, on and on to the purple line of the forest of Vandame.

'Mummy, I want to be carried.'

She carried them in turns. The pot-holes were full of water, and she held up her skirt for fear of being too dirty when she got there. Three times she all but fell down, so slippery were the dratted cobblestones. When at long last they came out in front of the steps, two huge dogs leaped out, barking so loud that the children screamed in terror. The coachman had to take a whip to them.

'Leave your clogs here and come in,' said Honorine.

Mother and children stood motionless in the dining-room, dazed by the sudden warmth and overawed by this elderly gentleman and lady staring at them from the depths of their armchairs.

'My dear,' said the lady to her daughter, 'give your little presents.'

The Grégoires made Cécile distribute their charities; it was part of a ladylike education, they thought. One must be charitable, and they used to say that their house was the Lord's dwelling. But they flattered themselves that their charity was discriminating, and were continually haunted by the fear of being hoodwinked and so encouraging wickedness. Therefore they never gave money, never! – not ten sous, not even two sous, for it was a known fact that as soon as the poor had two sous they drank them. No, their charity was always in kind, especially warm clothing, distributed in the winter to necessitous children.

'Oh, poor little things!' cried Cécile. 'How peaky they look after that walk in the cold. . . . Honorine, go and fetch the parcel from the cupboard.'

The maids were also staring at these poor creatures, with that sympathy not unmixed with uneasiness displayed by the well-fed. Whilst the parlourmaid was going upstairs, cook put the remains of the brioche down on the table, and stood there gaping and empty-handed.

'Yes,' Cécile went on, 'I happen to have two woollen frocks and some shawls left. Think how they will keep the poor little things warm!'

At last Maheude found her tongue and managed to say:

'Thank you very much, Mademoiselle. . . . You are all very kind.'

Her eyes filled with tears, and she felt confident of getting

98

the five francs – only she was a bit worried about the best way to ask for them if they were not forthcoming. The maid had not reappeared, and there was an awkward silence. The two children clung to their mother's skirts and stared wide-eyed at the brioche.

'You have only these two?' asked Madame Grégoire, by way of breaking the silence.

'Oh, no, Madame! I have seven.'

At this Monsieur Grégoire, who had taken up his paper again, jumped with outraged surprise.

'Seven children! But why, in Heaven's name?'

'Not very prudent,' murmured his wife.

Maheude made a vaguely apologetic gesture. That's how it was, you didn't give it a thought and then they just came along naturally. But then when they grew up they brought in money and kept the home going. Now they, for instance, would have managed all right if it hadn't been for grandfather getting so stiff, and out of the whole bunch of them only the two boys and her eldest girl were old enough to go down the mine. You see, you still had to feed the little ones who did nothing at all.

'So you have been working in the mines a long time?'

Maheude's sallow face lit up in a grin.

'Oh yes, oh yes! I was down there till I was twenty. When I had my second baby, the doctor warned me I would stay down for good because something was misplaced in my innards, it seemed. . . . But in any case, I got married just then and I had enough to do at home. But on my husband's side they've been down for ages. It goes back to grandfather's grandfather, in fact nobody knows when – right to the start, when they first began to sink Réquillart.'

Monsieur Grégoire gazed reflectively at the mother and her pitiful children, at their wax-like flesh, colourless hair, their look of stunted degeneration, wasted by anaemia, and the miserable ugliness of the underfed. There was another silence, only broken by the spurting of gas from the burning coal. The warm room was full of that heavy feeling of well-being in which cosy bourgeois love to settle themselves down to slumber.

'What *is* she up to?' exclaimed Cécile in annoyance. 'Mélanie, go up and tell her that the parcel is at the bottom of the cupboard, on the left.'

Monsieur Grégoire continued aloud the thoughts inspired by the sight of these starving creatures:

'Yes, there is a lot of suffering in this world, it is true; but, my good woman, we must also admit that the workers are not very sensible. Instead of putting a little on one side as the peasants do, the miners drink, run into debt, and end up by being unable to support their families.'

'You are quite right, Sir,' answered Maheude, smugly serious; 'they don't always keep to the right path. That's what I always say to ne'er-do-wells when they complain. Now I am fortunate, my husband doesn't drink. Of course, he does sometimes have a little too much on holiday Sundays, but it never goes beyond that. And that is all the nicer of him because before we were married he drank like a swine, begging your pardon. And yet, you see, his being so moderate doesn't seem to do us much good. There are days like today when you could turn out all the drawers in the house and never find a brass farthing.'

She was trying to convey the idea of a five-franc piece to them, and went on in her soft voice to explain the fatal debt, modest at first, but soon swelling to overwhelming proportions. You paid up regularly for fortnights on end, but one day you got late and that was that; you never caught up again. The gap got wider and the men couldn't see the point of working if they couldn't ever pay their way. Then, God help you, you were in the soup until Kingdom come. Besides, you had to try and understand: a miner needed a half-pint to wash the dust out of his tubes. That's how it began, and then when things got difficult, he sat in the pub all day. Perhaps, without complaining about anybody in particular, it might be that the workers really did not earn enough.

'But I thought the Company gave you accommodation and fuel?' said Madame Grégoire.

Maheude gave a sidelong glance at the coal blazing in the grate.

'Oh, yes, we are given coal of a sort, though it does burn, I suppose. . . . As for the rent, it is only six francs a month, which doesn't sound anything at all, but it's often jolly hard to find. Now look at me today – you could cut me up into little pieces and never find a halfpenny. Where there's nothing, there's nothing.'

The lady and gentleman sat silent in their comfortable armchairs, for this exhibition of poverty was beginning to upset them and get on their nerves. Maheude was afraid she had offended them, and so went on in her calm, fair, and practical way:

'Oh, I don't mean to complain. That's how things are and we have to accept them, especially as however much we struggled we probably shouldn't be able to alter anything. So the best thing, Monsieur and Madame, is to try to do your job properly in the place God has put you, isn't it?'

Monsieur Grégoire emphatically agreed:

'With such sentiments, my good woman, one is proof against misfortune.'

At last Honorine and Mélanie came in with the parcel. Cécile undid it and took out the two frocks, to which she added shawls and even stockings and mittens. Yes, they would all fit beautifully, and she made haste to get the servants to pack them up; for her music-mistress had just arrived, and she bundled mother and children towards the door.

'We are very hard up,' stammered Maheude; 'if only we had a five-franc piece. . . .'

The words stuck in her throat, for the Maheus were proud and did not beg. Cécile glanced anxiously at her father, but he refused point-blank with the air of doing a painful duty.

'No, it is not our custom. It can't be done.'

Cécile was touched by the mother's tragic face and wished to do all she could for the children. They were still staring at the brioche. She cut two pieces and gave them one each.

'Look! this is for you.'

Then she took them back and asked for an old newspaper.

'Wait a minute, you can share them with your brothers and sisters.'

She managed to push them out of the room, while her parents fondly looked on. The poor, starving brats went off,

101

respectfully holding the pieces of brioche in their numbed little fists.

Maheude dragged the children along the road, and now she never noticed the deserted fields, the black mud, or the lowering grey sky. On her way back through Montsou, she boldly went into Maigrat's and begged so hard that in the end she came away with two loaves, coffee, butter and even her five-franc piece, for he also lent money by the week. It was not her he wanted, it was Catherine, as she realized when he suggested that she should send her daughter up for the groceries. Well, she thought, we shall see. If he comes breathing too near she will give him a box on the ears.

[3]

It was striking eleven at the little brick church of Village Two Hundred and Forty, where Father Joire came over on Sundays to say Mass. You could hear the children's sing-song voices coming from the school next door, although the windows were shut to keep out the cold. The open spaces between the four long rows of uniform houses, divided into little gardens that backed on to each other, were all deserted. These gardens were devastated by winter, and their wretched marly soil was bare but for a few clumps of decaying vegetables. It was soup-making time, chimneys were smoking and every now and again, somewhere along the rows, a woman appeared, opened a door and disappeared again. Although it was not actually raining, the heavy grey air was so damp that drain-pipes dripped steadily into the water-butts standing all along the cobbled pavements. This village, thrown up all in one go in the middle of the endless plain, with its black roads all round like a mourning border, had but one bright thing about it – the regular strips of red-tiled roofing, washed clean by the incessant rains.

On her way home Maheude made a detour to buy some potatoes from an inspector's wife who had some of last year's crop left. Screened by a row of scraggy poplars, the only trees that will grow in these flat expanses, there stood a group of isolated buildings, houses in blocks of four with gardens all round. As this new venture was set aside by the Company for deputies, the workmen had dubbed this part of the village Silk Stocking Estate, just as they called their own part Pay Up, with the wry humour of the poor.

'Well, here we are,' said Maheude, all laden with shopping and pushing in Lénore and Henri, both covered with mud and dead beat.

By the fire Estelle was bawling in Alzire's arms. Having run out of sugar and not knowing how to stop the baby, she had pretended in the end to give her the breast. This trick had often worked before, but this time it was all to no purpose; she had opened her dress and pressed the baby's mouth to her eight-year-old chest but, finding nothing there but skin and bone, the baby was screaming with rage.

'Here, give her to me,' said her mother, as soon as she had put down her shopping. 'She'll never let us get a word in edgeways.'

She took one of her breasts, as swollen as a wineskin, and when she had put the baby to the nipple, the crying stopped abruptly and they were able to talk. Everything was in good shape, for the little housewife had kept the fire in, swept up and tidied the room. In the sudden silence you could hear Grandpa snoring upstairs, with the same regular snore that never let up for a moment.

'What a lot of things!' murmured Alzire, smiling at the sight of all the groceries. 'I'll make the soup for you if you like, Mummy.'

The table was all cluttered up, with a parcel of clothes, two loaves, potatoes, butter, coffee, chicory, and half a pound of pork brawn.

'Oh, the soup!' said Maheude wearily, 'that means picking sorrel and pulling some leeks. . . . No, I'll do some later on for the men. Put some potatoes on to boil, and we'll have them with a bit of butter. And coffee, eh? don't forget the coffee!'

Then she suddenly thought of the brioche again, and saw the empty hands of Lénore and Henri, who had now got over their tiredness and were quite perky, fighting on the floor.

Blow me if the artful little pigs hadn't quietly eaten the brioche on the way! She clouted them, but Alzire, who was busy putting the saucepan on the fire, tried to calm her down:

'Leave them alone, Mummy. If it was for me, you know I don't mind about brioche. They were hungry with all that walking.'

It struck twelve, and you could hear the children's clogs as they were coming out of school. The potatoes were done, and the coffee, quite half of it chicory by way of thickening, was dripping through the strainer with a tinkling sound. One corner of the table was cleared, but the mother was the only one who used it for eating – the three children managed on their knees. All the time the boy, one of those quiet wolfers, never took his eyes off the brawn in its exciting greasy paper, and never uttered a sound.

Maheude was sipping her coffee, holding the glass in both hands so as to warm them, when old Bonnemort came down. As a rule he got up later than this and his dinner was kept on the hob. But today he began grumbling because there was no soup. However, when his daughter-in-law had pointed out that you couldn't always do what you wanted, he ate his potatoes without a word. Now and again he got up and spat into the embers, out of decency, and then, slumped in a heap in his chair, he went on chewing the cud, head down, eyes unseeing.

'Oh, I forgot, Mummy,' said Alzire, 'next door came in. . . .'

Her mother cut her short.

'Blast her!'

She harboured a smouldering resentment against la Levaque who only the day before had been whining poverty so as not to have to lend her anything; and she knew that at that very moment she must be well off, as the lodger Bouteloup had paid his fortnight in advance. There was precious little lending between families in the village.

'Oh, that reminds me,' she went on. 'Put a millful of coffee into a bit of paper. I'll take it back to Pierronne. It's been owing since the day before yesterday.'

When her daughter had done up the packet, she added that

104

she would be back straight away to put the soup on for the men. Then she went off, carrying Estelle and leaving old Bonnemort slowly chewing his potatoes, while Lénore and Henri squabbled as to who should eat the skins he dropped on the floor.

Instead of going round by the road Maheude cut straight across the gardens, for fear of being caught by la Levaque. Her garden happened to back on the Pierrons' and there was a gap in the fence through which everybody fraternized, for the well was there which served four houses. Behind some stunted lilac bushes, just to one side, was the low shed, full of old tools, where rabbits were fattened up for holidays. It struck one – coffee time – and not a soul was to be seen at any door or window. One solitary man was bent over his cabbage-patch; he was a ripper, getting in some digging before the time to go down. As Maheude reached the opposite block, she was surprised to see a gentleman and two ladies coming round by the church. She stopped a second and then recognized them: it was Madame Hennebeau showing two visitors round the village. The gentleman wore the ribbon of the Legion of Honour, the lady a fur coat.

'Oh, why did you bother?' said Pierronne, when Maheude had returned her coffee. 'There was no hurry.'

She was twenty-eight and looked upon as the belle of the village, with her dark hair, low forehead, big eyes and little mouth, and she was smartly turned out, too, as dainty as a kitten. She had kept her lovely figure, for she had had no children. Her mother, Ma Brûlé, widow of a collier killed in the mine, had sworn that her daughter should never marry a miner, and sent her to work in a factory. And now she could not get over her anger that this daughter of hers had married, rather late in the day, Pierron, who was a widower into the bargain, with a girl of eight.

And yet the couple got along quite happily amid all the gossip. Stories went round about the husband's complaisance and the wife's lovers: nothing owing, meat twice a week, and with it all the house so perfectly kept that you could see your face in the saucepans. To add to their good fortune, thanks to some wire-pulling the Company had granted her a concession to sell sweets and biscuits. She displayed the jars on two shelves in her window. This brought in six or seven sous' profit per day, and sometimes twelve on Sundays. The only flies in the ointment were old mother Brûlé, who went on bellowing her revolutionary fury, demanding vengeance on the bosses for her man's death, and little Lydie, who caught rather too many boxes on the ears from the excitable family.

'Isn't she getting a big girl!' cooed Pierronne at Estelle.

'Oh, don't talk to me about kids. You've no idea what a lot of trouble they are. You're lucky not to have any; you can at least keep the place clean.'

In her own house, to be sure, everything was in good order and she washed every Saturday, but all the same she was envious as she cast a housewife's eye round the spotless room, where there was even a certain amount of luxury – gilt vases on the sideboard, a mirror, three framed pictures.

Pierronne was drinking coffee on her own as all her folk were down the mine.

'Have a glass with me, dear,' she said.

'No, thanks, I've just this minute had mine.'

'Well, what of it?'

What of it, indeed? And as they slowly drank, their gaze wandered out between the jars of biscuits and sweets and rested on the row of houses opposite. The whiteness or otherwise of the little curtains at the windows proclaimed the virtues of the housewives. The Levaques' curtains were very dirty, real rags that looked as if they had been used on the bottoms of saucepans.

'How could anyone live in such filth!' murmured Pierronne.

That set off Maheude, and there was no stopping her. Oh! now if she had a lodger like Bouteloup she could have made both ends meet all right! If you knew how to set about it, a lodger was a very paying proposition. Only you shouldn't sleep with him. And then there was her husband who drank and beat her, and ran after the singing-girls in the pubs at Montsou.

Pierronne assumed an expression of profound disgust. Those singers! They spread all the diseases. There was one at Joiselle who had infected a whole mine.

'What I can't understand is how you can let that son of yours go with their girl.'

'Oh, can't you? Just you try to stop them. Their garden is next to ours. In the summer Zacharie was always hanging round with Philomène behind those lilac bushes, and they didn't care what they got up to on the shed. You can't draw water from the well without catching them at it.'

Such was the regular story of the village promiscuities. As soon as it was dark, the boys and girls began their dirty tricks – up-ending themselves, they called it – on the low, sloping roofs of the sheds. That was where every haulage girl picked up her first baby, unless she took the trouble to go as far as Réquillart for it, or got it in the cornfields. It didn't make much odds, anyway, as they got married in due course, and the only ones to be annoyed were the mothers when their boys began too soon, because a boy who got married brought no more in.

'If I were you I'd rather get it over,' observed Pierronne sagely. 'Your Zacharie has already planted two on her, and they will go and set themselves up somewhere else. . . . In any case the money has gone up the spout.'

Maheude gesticulated furiously and cried:

'Look here, if they do that I shall curse them. Shouldn't Zacharie show us some consideration? He has cost us money, hasn't he? Well, he's got to pay some of it back, before saddling himself with a woman. . . . What would become of us all, I'd like to know, if our children started straight away working for somebody else? Might as well kick the bucket!'

But she pulled herself together.

'I'm just talking in a general way, we'll see later on. . . . Your coffee is jolly strong. You know what to put in the pot!'

And after a quarter of an hour of further gossip she made off, saying that the men's soup was still to be made. Outside, the children were going back to school, and a few women were on the doorsteps looking at Madame Hennebeau, who was going along one of the blocks, pointing out things to her guests. This inspection was beginning to make a stir in the village. The ripper stopped his digging for a moment, and two frightened hens squawked in the gardens.

107

On her way back Maheude ran into la Levaque, who had come out to pounce on the Company's doctor, Dr Vanderhaghen, as he went by. Overworked, always in a hurry, the poor little devil gave consultations while on the wing.

'Oh, Doctor,' she said, 'I can't get any sleep. I ache all over . . . you might at least tell me something. . . .'

'Buzz off! You drink too much coffee,' he said, without stopping.

'What about my husband, Doctor?' said Maheude, getting her word in. 'You were coming to see him. . . . He has still got those pains in his legs.'

'That's because you wear him out, buzz off!'

The two women stood rooted to the spot, watching the doctor's receding back. They exchanged despairing shrugs of the shoulders.

'Why not come in?' said la Levaque. 'I must tell you the latest. . . . And you'll have a cup of coffee, won't you? It's just made.'

Maheude tried to resist, but hadn't the energy. Oh, well! just a drop so as not to offend. In she went.

The room was black with dirt, with greasy stains on the floor and walls, the dresser and table coated with grime. A stench of slatternly neglect caught your throat. Bouteloup was finishing up some stew by the fire, elbows on table and nose in plate. Big, broad-shouldered, and easy-going, he looked young for thirty-five. Little Achille, Philomène's eldest, already over two, was standing propped up against him, looking up with the mute appeal of a famished animal. Every now and again the lodger, who had a kind heart in spite of his ferocious black beard, poked a bit of meat down the child's throat.

'Just a minute while I put the sugar in,' said la Levaque, putting the sugar straight into the coffee-pot.

She was six years older than Bouteloup, worn out and frightful to behold. Her bosom hung over her stomach and her stomach touched her thighs. Her flat face had greyish whiskers and her hair was all over the place. He had taken her as a matter of course, without cleaning her up any more than the soup, where he found hairs, or than his bed, where

108

the sheets had to do for three months. She was included in the board and lodging, and her husband was fond of repeating that satisfied customers make the best friends.

'Well, this is what I wanted to tell you,' she went on. 'Yesterday Pierronne was seen going off on the Silk Stocking crawl. Mr You-Know-Who was waiting behind Rasseneur's, and off they went together along the canal. Nice goings-on for a married woman, eh?'

'What else do you expect?' said Maheude. 'Before he was married Pierron used to give the deputy rabbits, now it is cheaper to lend him his wife.'

Bouteloup burst into a thunderous guffaw and chucked a bit of gravy-soaked bread down Achille's throat. The two women finished venting their spleen on Pierronne – a bitch, that's what she was, and no prettier than anybody else, but always busy going over every pore in her skin, what with her lotions and face-creams. Oh, well! It was her husband's business, if he liked that sort of thing. Some men were so ambitious that they would wipe the bosses' backsides, just to hear them say thank-you. And on they went, until they were interrupted by the arrival of a neighbour bringing back a nine-month-old baby, Désirée, Philomène's latest. The latter, who had her lunch at the screening shed, arranged for her baby to be taken there, and fed it while she sat down for a minute on the coal.

'I can't leave mine a single minute, she starts screaming at once,' said Maheude, looking at Estelle who had gone off to sleep in her arms.

But it was no use trying to dodge what had been clearly written for the past few moments on La Levaque's face – a grand showdown.

'You know, it's nearly time we thought about settling this business.'

At first, without a word having been said on either side, the two mothers had agreed not to conclude the marriage. Zacharie's mother was just as anxious to have her son's wages as Philomène's was furious at the idea of losing her daughter's. There was no hurry, and the latter had even preferred to look after the baby, so long as there was only one; but now that one was growing up and eating food and another had come along, she found herself out of pocket, and, unwilling to do things at a loss, she was all for the marriage.

'Zacharie has drawn his number,' she continued; 'nothing else to wait for. . . . Look here, when shall it be?'

Maheude was embarrassed. 'Let's put it off till the fine weather,' she said. 'What a nuisance these things are! Just as though they couldn't have waited till they were married before going together. Upon my word, I tell you I'd throttle my Catherine if I found out she'd been acting the fool!'

La Levaque shrugged her shoulders.

'Oh, come off it! She'll go the same way as everybody else.'

Bouteloup, perfectly at home, went and rummaged in the dresser for the loaf. Some vegetables for Levaque's soup, potatoes and leeks, were hanging about half peeled on a corner of the table; they had been taken up and put down ten times in the midst of ceaseless gossip. She had just gone back to them yet again when she dropped them so as to go and stare out of the window.

'What's going on over there? Well I never! It's Madame Hennebeau with some visitors. There they go into Pierronne's.'

That started them off on Pierronne again. Oh, yes! sure as fate, every time the Company showed visitors round the village, they were taken straight there because it was clean. Presumably they were not told of the goings-on with the overman. Of course you can be nice and clean when you have got lovers earning three thousand, plus free lodging and coal, to say nothing of other perks. It might be clean on top, but it was anything but clean underneath. And so they rattled on all the time the visitors stayed there.

'They're coming out now,' said la Levaque at length. 'Doing the grand tour. Oh, look! I think they are going to you, dear!'

Maheude was seized with panic. Had Alzire wiped over the table? And her own soup wasn't ready any the more! Muttering a word of farewell, she fled at top speed, looking neither to right nor left.

But everything was bright and shining. When she realized that her mother was not coming back, Alzire had solemnly put on a duster for an apron and set about doing the soup. She had pulled up the last of the leeks in the garden, picked some sorrel, and was now cleaning the vegetables, while a big cauldron of water was warming on the fire for the men's baths when they came. Henri and Lénore were good, for once, busily tearing up an old calendar on the floor. Grandpa Bonnemort was quietly smoking his pipe.

Maheude was still recovering her breath when Madame Hennebeau knocked.

'You don't mind, do you, my good woman?'

She was tall, fair, about forty, and her stately maturity was inclining towards heaviness. She was smiling with forced affability and disguising tolerably well her fear of dirtying her bronze silk dress and black velvet wrap.

'Come in, do come in,' she repeated to her guests. 'We are not putting anybody out. . . . Once again, isn't it clean? And this good woman has seven children! All our families are like this. . . . As I was explaining to you, the Company rents them the house at six francs a month. A large room on the ground floor, two rooms upstairs, cellar and garden.'

The dazed expression and vaguely staring eyes of the decorated gentleman and the lady in the fur coat showed that they had dropped only that morning from the Paris train into a new world which had thrown them off their balance.

'And garden,' echoed the lady. 'One really could live here oneself. Quite delightful!'

'We give them more coal than they can burn,' went on Madame Hennebeau. 'A doctor sees them twice a week, and when they are old they are given a pension although no deduction is made from their wages.'

'Arcadia!' murmured the gentleman in ecstasy. 'A land flowing with milk and honey!'

Maheude had hastened to offer them chairs, but the ladies declined. Madame Hennebeau had already had enough. The role of circus showman gave her a few minutes' amusement and took her mind off her isolation and boredom, but in spite of the carefully selected houses she ventured into, she was

111

quickly nauseated by the stale reek of poverty. In any case, she only repeated catch-words, and never lost any sleep over these working people toiling and suffering at her gates.

'What sweet children!' murmured the lady, thinking how hideous they were, with their big heads and shocks of straw-coloured hair.

And their mother had to give their ages and answer the questions about Estelle which they asked out of politeness. Grandpa Bonnemort had respectfully taken his pipe out of his mouth, but all the same he was a constant source of anxiety – he was so shattered by his forty years underground, his legs were stiff, his body worn out and his face ashen. As he felt one of his violent coughing fits coming on, he thought it better to go and spit outside, thinking that his black spittle might upset people.

Alzire was the star turn. Such a pretty little housewife with her duster! Her mother was complimented on having such a clever little girl for her age. But nobody mentioned her hump, though some pitying and uneasy glances were cast at the poor, infirm creature.

'So now,' concluded Madame Hennebeau, 'if they ask you in Paris about our mining villages, you will be in a position to reply. . . . Never any more noise than this, perfect morality, everybody happy and well as you can observe. In fact, you ought to come to a spot like this to set yourself up in pure air and peaceful surroundings.'

'Wonderful, wonderful!' cried the gentleman in a final burst of enthusiasm.

They went out wearing the rapt expression of people emerging from a booth at a fair. Maheude saw them off and stood on the step while they slowly moved away, conversing in loud tones. The streets had filled, and they had to pass through groups of women whom the report of the visit had brought out from their houses.

Pierronne had just come out to have a look and had been caught by la Levaque just outside the latter's house. The two women affected a shocked astonishment. Well, did you ever? Were these people going to sleep the night at the Maheus' then? Not all that exciting, I should think!

'Always broke, and think of what they earn! Of course, if you go in for certain sorts of things. . . .'

'I've just heard that this morning she went begging to the gentry at La Piolaine, and Maigrat, who had refused to let them have any more food, gave her some. . . . We all know how Maigrat takes his payment!'

'On her? Oh, no! That would need some courage! He takes his payment on Catherine.'

'Oh, I like that! And she had the sauce to tell me just now that she would throttle Catherine if she acted the fool! Just as though that lanky Chaval hadn't thrown her on her backside on the shed ages ago!'

'Sh! Here they come.'

And the two women, standing innocently by, without any disrespectful curiosity, looked out of the corner of their eyes as the visitors came out. Then they quickly beckoned Maheude, who still had Estelle in her arms, and the three of them stood there watching the well-clad backs of Madame Hennebeau and her visitors receding into the distance. When they were some thirty paces off, the chatter started up again with renewed violence.

'They've got some money's worth on their backs. More than they're worth themselves, I should think!'

'Yes, that's a fact. . . . I don't know the other one, but I wouldn't give twopence for the one from here, fat and all. There are stories going round. . . .'

'Oh? What stories?'

'She's supposed to have men, of course. First of all, there's the engineer. . . .'

'What! that skinny little shrimp? Oh, no! he's too small; she'd lose him in the bedclothes.'

'Well, what does that matter if that's how she likes it? I don't trust the look of a dame who puts on high and mighty airs and never looks pleased wherever she is. Look how she is swinging her behind just to show what she thinks of us all. Not very nice, if you ask me!'

The visitors were walking on at the same leisurely pace, still chatting, when a barouche drew up in front of the church. There got out a gentleman of about forty-eight, in a tight-fitting black coat. He was very dark, and his face wore a formal and authoritative expression.

'The husband!' whispered la Levaque, lowering her voice as if he could have heard. She was overcome by the hierarchical awe which the managing director inspired in his ten thousand employees. 'But all the same, you can see by the look of him that his wife plays him up.'

By now the whole village was out in the streets. As the women's curiosity grew, groups closed together and fused into a crowd, whilst gangs of dirty-nosed brats stood gaping about on the pavements. For one moment even the pale face of the schoolmaster could be seen peeping over the school fence, and the man digging in the gardens stopped with his foot on his spade and stared. And the talk grew and grew into a continuous shushing sound, like dry leaves stirred by a gust of wind.

The crowd was thickest in front of la Levaque's door, where two, ten, and then twenty women had appeared. Now that there were too many listening ears, Pierronne kept discreetly silent. Maheude, who was one of the more sensible ones, was also content to be an onlooker. Estelle had woken and was yelling, and to shut her up she had calmly taken out her breast in broad daylight, and there it hung like the udder of a good milch cow, swollen with its unfailing supply of milk. When Monsieur Hennebeau had settled the ladies in the back seats and the carriage had set off in the direction of Marchiennes, there was a final explosion of chattering voices, everybody gesticulating and shouting in each other's faces. It was like an ant-hill in full revolutionary upheaval.

And then it struck three. The rippers had all gone off to work, Bouteloup and the rest, and the first returning colliers appeared round the corner of the church, black-faced, soaking wet, arms folded and backs bent. That precipitated a wild scurry among the women. They were caught napping through too much coffee and talk, and now they all rushed home in a fluster. Nothing could be heard but this one anxious cry, pregnant with domestic scenes:

'Oh, Lord! The soup! My soup isn't ready!'

[4]

WHEN Maheu came in after leaving Étienne at Rasseneur's, he found Catherine, Zacharie, and Jeanlin sitting down and finishing their soup. When you got home from the pit you were so famished that you ate in your wet clothes without even stopping to wash; nobody waited for anybody else, and the table was laid from morn till night, for there was always somebody gulping down his meal, according to the shift he was working on.

As soon as he opened the door, Maheu saw the food. He said nothing, but the worried look went from his face. All the morning, as he had hacked away at the seam in the stifling depths of the coal face, he had been haunted by the empty cupboard and the house without coffee or butter, and the memory had kept on jerking itself back into his mind in painful stabs. How would his wife have managed? And what was to become of them if she came back empty-handed? And now, lo and behold! here was everything. She could tell him all about it later on. He laughed with relief.

Catherine and Jeanlin had already left the table and were drinking their coffee standing up. But Zacharie, whose soup had not filled him up, was cutting a thick slice of bread and spreading it with butter. He noticed the brawn on a plate, but did not touch it, for when there was only enough meat for one it was for father. They had all washed their soup down with a good swig of cold water, the fine, clear drink of the end of the fortnight.

'I haven't got any beer,' said Maheude, when father had sat down. 'I wanted to hang on to a little money. . . . But if you would like some, the girl can run and get you a pint.'

His face was radiant. What? She had money as well!

'No, no,' he said. 'It's all right. I've had some already.'

And he began to put away steadily, spoonful by spoonful, the mash of bread, potatoes, leeks, and sorrel piled up in the basin which he used as a plate. His wife, without letting go of Estelle, helped Alzire to see that he had everything he

115

wanted, passing him the butter and brawn, putting his coffee back on the fire to keep it nice and hot.

Meanwhile, bathing was beginning in front of the fire in a half-barrel turned into a wash-tub. Catherine, who had first turn, had filled it with warm water and was calmly undressing, taking off her cap, jacket, trousers, and vest as she had been in the habit of doing since she was eight, without seeing anything wrong in it. But she did turn to face the fire and then rubbed herself vigorously with soft soap. Nobody took any notice of her, even Lénore and Henri had long since got over their curiosity to know how she was made. When she was clean, she ran up the stairs quite naked, leaving her damp vest and the rest of her clothes in a heap on the floor. Then a row began between the two brothers. Jeanlin had hurriedly jumped into the tub, on the pretext that Zacharie was still eating, and Zacharie shoved him out of the way and demanded his turn, declaring that if he was kind enough to let Catherine have the first dip, it did not mean that he wanted kids' bathwater, especially as when Jeanlin had been through you could fill the school inkwells with it. In the end they had their bath together, facing the fire also, and even helped to rub each other's backs. Then they disappeared upstairs, naked like their sister.

'What a mess they do make!' said Maheude, picking the clothes up from the floor to put them to dry. 'Alzire, give it a bit of a sponge round, will you?'

But she was interrupted by a commotion on the other side of the wall – a man's voice swearing, a woman wailing, a noise of fighting and running feet, with muffled blows sounding like thuds on an empty pumpkin.

'La Levaque having her trouncing,' Maheu calmly observed, scraping the bottom of his basin with his spoon. 'Funny, though – Bouteloup made out that the soup was ready.'

'Ready? I should say so!' chimed in Maheude. 'I saw the vegetables on the table not even peeled!'

The shouts redoubled and culminated in a terrible thump which shook the wall, and then there was silence. Swallowing his last spoonful, the miner concluded with an air of dispassionate justice:

'Oh, well! – if the soup isn't ready you can understand.'

He drank off a glass of water and then fell to on the brawn. He cut off square chunks, spiked them on the end of his knife and ate them on his bread, without a fork. Nobody talked while father was eating. This did not seem like Maigrat's usual potted meat, it must have come from somewhere else; but he did not ask his wife any questions, and ate on in silence. He only wanted to know whether the old chap was still asleep upstairs. No, Grandpa had already gone out for his usual walk. A fresh silence fell.

But the smell of meat had made Lénore and Henri look up from their game of guiding the spilt bath-water into little streams. They both came and took up their positions by their father, the little boy in front. They followed each piece with their eyes, full of hope as it left the plate, but of consternation as it disappeared into his mouth. At length he noticed how their faces grew pale and their lips moist with ravenous desire.

'Have the children had any?' he asked.

And as his wife hesitated, he went on:

'You know, I hate this unfairness. It takes my appetite away to see them hanging round begging for scraps.'

'But of course they have!' she angrily exclaimed. 'If you listen to what they say, you can give them your share and everybody else's, and they'll go on stuffing until they bust. Alzire, we have all had some brawn, haven't we?'

'Oh yes, Mummy!' answered the little cripple, who in such circumstances could lie as coolly as any grown-up.

Lénore and Henri, who were whipped for not telling the truth, were struck speechless by such a barefaced fib. Their little hearts were full to overflowing, and they wanted to protest that they were not there when the others had had theirs.

'Get along with you!' said their mother, driving them to the other end of the room. 'You ought to be ashamed of yourselves, always sticking your noses in your Dad's plate! And suppose he was the only one to have any; doesn't he do the work? But all you lot of good-for-nothings, all you do is cost money. Yes, and more than your size is worth!'

Maheu called them back and sat Lénore on his left thigh and Henri on the other, and they finished the brawn between them. Each one had his share and he cut theirs up into little pieces. The children gobbled them up in high glee.

When he had finished he said to his wife:

'No, don't pour out my coffee yet. I'll wash first. Give me a hand with the dirty water.'

They took the tub by the handles and were emptying it out into the gutter in front, when Jeanlin came down in dry clothes – trousers and a woollen overall, an old one of his brother's, too big for him and already faded and tired-looking. Seeing him slinking out through the open door, his mother stopped him.

'Where are you off to?'

'Down there.'

'Down where? Just listen – you go and pick a dandelion salad for this evening. You understand, eh? If you don't bring some salad back you'll have me to deal with.'

'All right, all right.'

Jeanlin departed, hands in pockets, slopping along in his clogs, a ten-year-old swinging his skinny little hips like a seasoned miner. Zacharie came down next, more spruced up, with his figure set off in a black jersey with blue stripes. His father told him not to be late back and he sallied forth without a word, shaking his head and holding his pipe between his teeth.

The tub was refilled with warm water and father was beginning to take off his jacket. A warning glance was the signal for Alzire to take Lénore and Henri to play outside. Dad did not like bathing in front of the family, as they did in many other homes in the village. Not that he was criticizing anybody; he only meant that dabbling about together was all right for children.

'What are you doing up there?' Maheude called up the stairs.

'Mending my dress that I tore yesterday,' Catherine called back.

'All right, but don't come down; your father's washing.'

Maheu and his wife were alone. She had made up her mind

to put Estelle down in a chair as, for a wonder, she was not yelling, being near the fire. She gazed at her parents with the expressionless eyes of a tiny creature without intelligence. He crouched naked in front of the tub and began by dipping his head in, well lathered with soft soap. The use of this soap for generations past had discoloured the hair of all these people and turned it yellow. Then he stepped into the water, soaped his chest, belly, arms, and legs and rubbed them hard with his fists. His wife stood looking on.

'Well,' she began, 'I saw the look on your face when you came in. You were feeling pretty worried, weren't you? And the sight of the food cheered you up no end. Just fancy, those gentry up at La Piolaine never coughed up a sou. Of course, they were very nice – they gave the kids some clothes and I was ashamed to beg. It sticks in my throat when I have to cadge.'

She broke off to settle Estelle firmly in the chair, for fear she might topple over. Father went on pummelling his skin, without trying to hurry the story by asking questions. It interested him, but he patiently waited for things to be made plain.

'I must tell you that Maigrat had turned me down flat, like turning a dog out. You can imagine what a nice time I had. Woollen clothes may be all right for keeping you warm, but they don't fill your stomach, do they?'

He looked up, but still said nothing. Nothing from La Piolaine, nothing from Maigrat: well, what? But she was going on with the usual routine, having rolled her sleeves up so as to do his back and the places that are hard to get at. Anyway, he loved her to soap him and rub him all over fit to break her wrists. She took some soap and worked away at his shoulders, while he stiffened his body to withstand the attack.

'So back I went to Maigrat's and told him the tale. Oh, I didn't half tell him the tale! Said he couldn't have any heart, that he would come to a bad end if there was any justice in the world. He didn't like that at all, and he rolled his eyes round and would have liked to skedaddle. . . .'

She had gone down from his back to his buttocks and, warming up to the job, she pushed ahead into the cracks and did not leave a single part of his body untouched, making it shine like her three saucepans on spring-cleaning Saturdays. But the terrible arm-work made her sweat, shook her and took her breath away, so that her words came in gasps.

'Anyway, he called me an old limpet. . . . We've got enough bread till Saturday, and the best of it is that he lent me five francs. What's more, I got the butter, coffee, and chicory from him and was going to buy the meat and potatoes, but I saw he was beginning to jib. . . . Seven sous for the brawn, eighteen for the potatoes, that leaves me three francs seventy-five for a stew and some boiled beef. I haven't wasted my morning, have I, eh?'

She was now drying him, dabbing with a towel at the places that were difficult to dry. He, happy and carefree about the morrow's debts, laughed out loud and threw his arms round her.

'Don't be silly! You have made me all wet! Only. . . . I'm afraid Maigrat had got something in mind. . . .'

She was on the point of mentioning Catherine, but checked herself. Why upset father? It would start off an endless fuss.

'Got what in mind?'

'Oh, only how to swindle us. Catherine will have to go over the bill carefully.'

He seized her again, and this time did not leave go. The bath always ended up like this – she made him excited by rubbing so hard and then towelling him everywhere, tickling the hairs on his arms and chest. It was the time when all the chaps in the village took their fun and more children were planted than anybody wanted. At night they had their families in the way. He pushed her to the table, cracking jokes to celebrate the one good moment a chap can enjoy during the whole day, calling it taking his dessert – and free of charge, what's more! She, with her flabby body and breasts hanging all over the place, put up a bit of resistance, just for fun.

'You silly, you! Oh, you are a one! And there's Estelle looking at us! Wait a minute while I turn her head the other way.'

'Oh, rubbish! What does she understand at three months?'

When it was over, he put on just a dry pair of trousers.

120

After his bath and when he had had his fun with his wife, he liked to stay a little while stripped to the waist. His skin, as white as that of an anaemic girl, was tattooed with scratches and grazes made by the coal – grafts, the miners called them – and he took a pride in them, stretching his brawny arms and puffing out his broad chest which shone like blue-veined marble. In summer time all the miners could be seen on their doorsteps like this. Even now, despite the wet weather, he went out for a moment and shouted a coarse joke to one of his mates who was standing, also stripped to the waist, on the other side of the gardens. Others came out, and the children playing on the pavement looked up and grinned for joy at all this weary labouring flesh out for an airing.

While he was drinking his coffee, still without his shirt, Maheu told his wife how wild the engineer had been about the timbering. He now felt relaxed and calmer, and nodded approval at his wife's sensible advice, for she was very wise over such matters. She always said there was nothing to be gained by running your head up against the Company. Then she told him about Madame Hennebeau's visit. Though they did not say so, they were both proud of this.

'Can I come down now?' Catherine called from the top of the stairs.

'Yes, yes, Dad's drying himself.'

She had put on her Sunday dress, an old dark-blue poplin one, faded and worn at the pleats, and was wearing a simple little black tulle bonnet.

'Oh, you're all dressed up! Where are you off to?'

'Montsou, to buy a ribbon for my bonnet. I've taken the old one off because it was too dirty.'

'You've got some money, then?'

'No, Mouquette has promised to lend me ten sous.'

'Look here, don't you go buying it at Maigrat's. He'll diddle you, and he might think we're rolling in money.'

Her father, squatting by the fire to dry his neck and arm-pits quickly, merely added:

'And try not to hang about the streets after dark!'

Maheu spent the afternoon working in his garden. He had already planted potatoes, beans, and peas, and now he began to plant out cabbage and lettuce seedlings which he had heeled in the day before. This bit of garden kept them in vegetables, except potatoes, of which they never had enough. He was very good at gardening and even raised artichokes, which the neighbours regarded as mere showing-off. As he was preparing his row, Levaque came along to smoke a pipe on his plot and have a look at some cos lettuce that Bouteloup had planted that morning, for if it had not been for the lodger's hard digging, nothing would have grown there but nettles. A conversation sprang up over the fence. Levaque, refreshed and revived by having given his wife a thrashing, tried to make Maheu go along with him to Rasseneur's, but in vain. Oh, come on! He wasn't afraid of half a pint, was he? They could have a game of skittles, see some of the chaps for a few minutes and get back for dinner – that was the thing to do after coming off the shift. No doubt there was no harm in it, but Maheu stuck to his point: if he did not plant out his lettuces they would be dead by the next day. But really it was caution that held him back, for he did not want to ask his wife for a sou of the rest of the five francs.

It was striking five when Pierronne came to ask whether her Lydie had gone off with Jeanlin. Levaque answered that it must be something like that, for his Bébert had disappeared too, and these kids always buggered about together. Maheu reassured them by mentioning the dandelion salad, and then he and his mate began chaffing the young woman with good-natured coarseness. She pretended to take offence, but did not move off, for she was really tickled by the crude words which made her scream with her hands on her sides. A skinny woman came to her rescue, stuttering with rage like a clucking hen. Others, on their doorsteps up the street, screamed in sympathy, without knowing why. School was now over, and all the kids were about, swarms of little creatures howling, rolling over and fighting, whilst those fathers who had not gone to the pub were squatting on their heels in twos and threes in the shelter of the wall, taking up the normal posture as though down the mine, and smoking their pipes and exchanging a word or two now and then. When Levaque tried to feel whether her thighs were nice and firm, Pierronne flounced off in high dudgeon, and he made up his mind to go to Rasseneur's on his own, while Maheu went on with his planting.

Twilight came suddenly and Maheude lit the lamp, vexed that neither her daughter nor the boys were back. She could have laid a bet on it: they were never all there for the one meal when they could have sat down together. And then she was still waiting for the dandelion salad. What could that dratted child be picking at this hour, when it was as black as your hat? A salad would go so well with the stew she was simmering on the fire, potatoes, leeks and sorrel chopped up with fried onions! The whole house smelt of fried onion, that goodly smell which gets stale so soon, and fills the very bricks of these mining villages with such a reek that you can tell them from far away in the country by the strong scent of Poor Man's Cookery.

Night fell and Maheu came in from the garden, and at once dropped off to sleep on a chair with his head against the wall. As soon as he sat down in the evening he was asleep. The cuckoo struck seven, Henri and Lénore had just smashed a plate through insisting on helping Alzire lay the table, when Grandpa Bonnemort came in first, in a hurry to have his dinner before going on his shift. Then Maheude woke her husband.

'Oh, well, let's start! They're big enough to find the way home. But its a nuisance about the salad!'

[5]

At Rasseneur's Étienne had some soup, then went up to the tiny attic facing Le Voreux which he was to occupy, and fell exhausted on his bed, fully dressed. He had not had four hours' sleep in two days. It was nearly dark when he awoke, and for a moment he was quite dazed and did not know where he was. He felt so stiff and his head was so heavy that he found it hard to get on to his feet, thinking he ought to breathe some fresh air before having dinner and turning in for the night.

Outside it was becoming much milder, the grimy sky was taking on a coppery hue, betokening one of those long northern rains which give warning of their approach by the sultry humidity of the air. Night was coming down like a pall of smoke, obscuring the more distant parts of the plain. Over this measureless sea of red earth the low sky seemed to be melting into black dust, and not a breath of air stirred the shadows. It was like the pallid, deathly melancholy of the tomb.

Étienne wandered on, with no other object than to shake off his throbbing headache. As he passed Le Voreux, already dark in its lair, for no lamps were yet lit, he paused to watch the day shift coming off. It must be six o'clock, for labourers, onsetters and ponymen were going off in groups with the screening girls, laughing and dimly visible in the darkness.

First he recognized Ma Brûlé and her son-in-law Pierron. She was giving him a piece of her mind for not having backed her up in a dispute with a foreman about pay for her baskets of stones.

'Oh, get along with you, you ninny! Call yourself a man and grovel like that in front of these blood-sucking swine!'

Pierron calmly let her go on and did not answer. But at length he said:

'I suppose you expected me to go for the boss? I've quite enough trouble without that, thank you!'

'Why don't you offer him your backside, then?' she shouted. 'My God, if only that girl of mine had listened to me! . . . It isn't enough that they killed her father, perhaps you would like me to say thank-you as well. No, I tell you, I'll get them yet!'

Their voices died away. Étienne watched her disappearing, with her eagle beak, white hair flying and long skinny arms waving furiously. But the voice of two young men behind him made him prick up his ears. He recognized Zacharie, who was waiting there and had just been joined by his friend Mouquet.

'Are you ready?' asked Mouquet. 'We'll have something to eat and bunk off to the Volcan.'

'Later on, I'm busy now.'

'Why? What's up?' He looked round and saw Philomène coming out from the screening shed, and thought he understood.

'Oh yes, I see,' he said. 'All right, I'll go on ahead.'

'Right-oh, I'll catch you up.'

As he went off, Mouquet ran into his father, old Mouque, who was also leaving Le Voreux. The two men simply exchanged a goodnight, and the son took the main road while the father went along the canal.

Zacharie was already pushing Philomène along the same lonely path, in spite of some resistance on her part. No, she was in a hurry – some other time. And they argued like an old married couple. It was no joke only meeting out of doors, especially in the winter when the ground was wet and there was no corn to lie in.

'No, no, it isn't for that,' he muttered impatiently. 'I've got something to say to you.'

He put his arm round her waist and gently led her away. Then, when they were in the shadow of the slag-heap, he wanted to know whether she had any money on her.

'What for?' she asked.

Then he lost his head and said something about owing two francs and how upset his family would be about it.

'Don't tell me the tale! I saw Mouquet, you're going to the Volcan again where those filthy tarts are.'

He denied it, laid his hand on his heart, gave his word of honour. But, as she merely shrugged her shoulders, he suddenly changed his tune:

'All right, come along with us if you are interested. You see I don't want to get rid of you. What should I want with those bitches? Are you coming?'

'What about the kid?' she replied. 'How can anybody go about with a baby always crying? . . . Let me go home, I bet there's a shindy going on there.'

But he would not let her go, implored her not to, in fact. Look, it was only so as not to look silly in front of Mouquet, because he had promised. A chap couldn't go to roost like the fowls every night, could he? Her resistance was soon worn down, and she turned up the hem of her jacket, cut a thread with her nail and took out some ten-sou pieces from a corner of the lining. For fear of being robbed by her mother, she had hidden there what she made from overtime at the pit.

'You see I've got five. I don't mind letting you have three. Only you must swear to me that you will make your mother agree to our being married. I'm fed up with life in the open air! And Mum begrudges every mouthful I eat. Swear . . . go on, swear first.'

Her voice was soft, it was the voice of a sickly, overgrown girl, without passion, just tired of living. He swore that it was a sacred promise, and then when he had the three coins in his possession, he kissed her, fondled her and made her laugh, and he might have taken things to their conclusion in this corner of the slag-heap which was the winter bedroom of their old-established life together, but she repeatedly refused, saying it would not give her any pleasure. She went back to the village alone, while he cut across the fields to join his pal.

Étienne had watched them from a distance, automatically, without taking it in, thinking it was just a lovers' meeting. The girls developed early in the coalfields, and he called to mind the Lille work-girls he used to wait for behind the factories, gangs of fourteen-year-olds already corrupted in the promiscuity of poverty. But a fresh meeting was more surprising and made him stop short.

There was a hollow at the base of the slag-tip, formed by some fallen stones, and here Jeanlin was loudly giving a piece of his mind to Lydie and Bébert, sitting one on each side of him.

'Eh? What d'you say? . . . I'll give you both a good hiding if you grumble. . . . Whose idea was it, anyway?'

Jeanlin certainly had had an idea. After he had roamed about for an hour in the fields along the canal picking dandelions with the two others, he had bethought himself, confronted with the heap of leaves, that they would never eat all that lot at home. So instead of going back to the village, he had gone to Montsou where, with Bébert posted on the look-out, he had made Lydie ring at grand people's doors and offer the dandelions for sale. He already knew all about life, and said that girls could sell anything they wanted to. In the excitement of doing business the whole pile had disappeared but she had made eleven sous. And now, empty-handed, they were sharing out the takings.

'It isn't fair!' declared Bébert. 'You must divide by three. . . . If you keep seven, we shall only get two each.'

'Not fair, why?' answered Jeanlin angrily. 'To begin with, I picked more!'

Usually the other boy gave in with timid admiration, and his credulity made him the perpetual dope. Although he was older and bigger, he would even let himself be punched. But this time the thought of all that money stirred him to rebellion.

'He's swindling us, isn't he, Lydie? If he won't share, we'll tell his mother.'

Instantly Jeanlin put a fist under his nose.

'You say that again and I'll go and tell yours that you sold my Mum's salad. And in any case, you silly fool, how can I divide eleven by three? You try it yourself as you're so clever. Here's your two sous each. Buck up and take them or I'll stick them back in my pocket.'

Bébert, now completely cowed, accepted the two sous. Lydie had trembled and said nothing, for she loved and feared Jeanlin like a bullied little wife. He held out the two sous and she put out her hand with a submissive smile. But he suddenly changed his mind.

'But what the hell can you do with all that? Your mother's sure to pinch it if you can't hide it. I'd better keep it for you. When you want some money, ask me.'

The nine sous disappeared. To shut her mouth he laughingly seized her and rolled over with her on the tip. She was his little wife, and together in holes and corners they used to try out the love-making that they saw and heard at home, behind partitions, through cracks in doors. They knew everything but could not do much, they were too young; but they spent hours feeling round, playing about, like vicious little puppies. He called it 'playing mothers and fathers', and she rushed with him wherever he took her and let him have her with the delicious thrill of instinct, often angry but always yielding in the hope of something which never came.

As Bébert was not allowed to take part in these games but was shooed off if he tried to touch Lydie, he always stood by sullenly, torn between anger and embarrassment, while the others had their fun, which they did not in the least mind doing in his presence. And so his one idea was to scare them off it by shouting that somebody was looking.

'It's no good! There's a man watching.'

This time it was true; it was Étienne, who had decided to walk on again. The children jumped up and ran off, and he went on round the tip, following the canal, laughing at the scare he had given these varmints. Perhaps it really was too early at their age; but still, they saw so much of it going on and heard such filthy talk, that to stop them you would have had to tie them up. Nevertheless it saddened him.

A hundred paces further on he came across more couples. He was now at Réquillart, where all the Montsou girls used to prowl round with their lovers in the ruins of the disused mine. This lonely, remote spot was the common meeting-place where haulage girls picked up their first baby when they did not dare to do so on the shed roof at home. The broken fences left the way open for everybody to go into the old yard, now a piece of waste land cluttered with the remains of two workshops that had fallen in and the skeletons of headgears still standing. Disused trucks were lying about and stacks of rotting timber. This bit of land was reverting to dense thicket, luxuriant grass had spread everywhere and young trees were growing vigorously. Every girl could make a little home here, for there were nooks and crannies for all, and young fellows up-ended them on beams, behind wood-piles or in trucks. Here they all made themselves at home cheek by jowl, without bothering about their neighbours. It was as though round this dead machine, by this pit worn out with bringing forth coal, the life-force was taking its revenge in the untrammelled love which used the lash of instinct, and planted children in the wombs of those who were scarcely more than children themselves.

And yet there was a caretaker on the premises, old Mouque, whom the Company allowed to occupy two rooms almost underneath the dismantled frame of the headgear, continually

threatened by the last remaining timbers which were bound
to fall sometime. He had even had to shore up part of his
ceiling, but he had made a very comfortable home for himself
and his family: himself and Mouquet in one room and
Mouquette in the other. As there was not a single pane of
glass left, he had boarded up the windows, but it was warm
even if you could not see very well. In any case this caretaker
took care of nothing, but went to look after his ponies in
Le Voreux and never bothered about the ruins of Réquillart,
the only part to be preserved being the shaft, which acted as a
chimney for a fire ventilating the neighbouring pit.

Thus Daddy Mouque was slipping into old age, surrounded
by young love. Ever since she was ten, Mouquette had been
at it in every corner of the ruins, not as a scared and green
little scamp like Lydie, but as a plump and fully formed girl,
already ripe for bearded youths. Her father made no objection,
because she was considerate and never brought a man home.
Besides, he was used to such accidents. Whenever he went
to work at Le Voreux, or came home, in fact each time he
ventured forth from his lair, he could not put a foot forward
without treading on some couple in the grass, and it was
worse still if he was gathering wood to heat the soup or
looking for burdock for his rabbits at the far end of the enclosure; for then he saw the sensual noses of all the Montsou
girls popping up one by one, and had to be careful not to trip
over legs stretched out across the paths. But gradually these
encounters had ceased to upset anybody, neither him – for he
was only concerned with not tripping up – nor the girls, whom
he tactfully left to get on with their business, moving off on
tip-toe like a good fellow who just accepted the facts of
nature. Just as by now they knew him, so he eventually knew
them, in the same way as you recognize the magpies who
wantonly carry on their amours in the pear-trees in your
garden. Ah! youth, youth, how greedily it took its fill! But
at times the sight of these wenches noisily panting in the
shadows made him turn away, shaking his head with silent
regrets. Only one thing used to annoy him: two young things
had got into the bad habit of doing their love-making against
the wall of his shack. It was not so much that they prevented

him sleeping, but they pushed so hard that in the end they were damaging the wall.

Every evening old Mouque was visited by his friend Grandpa Bonnemort, who took the same stroll regularly before dinner. The two old boys hardly spoke at all and rarely exchanged more than ten words in the half-hour they spent together. But it cheered them up to be there, dreaming of the good old days and ruminating together without needing to talk. At Réquillart they would sit on a baulk of timber side by side, and a word would start them off on a journey to dreamland while their heads stayed bent towards the earth. They felt young again, perhaps, while these young fellows all round them embraced their sweethearts, and there was a whispering sound of laughter and kisses and a warm scent of woman's flesh mingled with the cool smell of crushed grass. It was now forty-three years since old Bonnemort had taken his wife over yonder behind the pit; she was a haulage girl, and such a little scrap that he used to set her on a truck so as to kiss her more easily. Ah! those were the days, long ago! And the two old men would shake their heads and part, often without even saying goodnight.

But on this particular evening, as Étienne came up, old Bonnemort was rising from the baulk to go back home to the village and was saying to Mouque:

'Good night, mate! I say, did you know that girl Roussie?'

Mouque said nothing for a minute, but stood shrugging his shoulders; then, as he walked off into his shack:

'Good night, good night, mate!'

Étienne sat down on the same beam. Without quite knowing why, he felt more and more depressed. The disappearing back of that old man reminded him of his arrival that morning, and of the torrent of words torn from this usually silent man by the infuriating wind. What misery! and all these girls, broken by fatigue, were silly enough to come here at night and make babies, more flesh to toil and suffer! It would never end while they went on getting themselves filled with starvelings. Ought they not rather to stop up their wombs and close their thighs tight against approaching disaster? But then, perhaps he was only harbouring these dismal thoughts because he resented being alone when all the others were pairing off to take their pleasure. He was oppressed by the sultry weather, and a few drops of rain fell upon his hot hands. Yes, all the girls came to it, it was stronger than reason. Just then, while he was sitting there motionless in the dark a couple coming from Montsou almost touched him, without seeing him, and went on into the waste ground of Réquillart. The girl – she must be a virgin, he thought – was struggling and resisting with whispered supplications, but the man was silently edging her towards the dark corner of a shed, still left standing, in which there were piles of old mildewed rope. It was Catherine and that lanky Chaval. But Étienne had not recognized them as they passed, and now he watched, waiting for the end of the story, with a sensual interest which changed the course of his reflections. After all, why should he interfere? When girls say no it means that they want to be forced first.

On leaving the village Catherine had gone to Montsou by the main road. Since she was ten and had been earning her living in the pit, she had gone everywhere on her own with the complete freedom of mining families, and if she had reached the age of fifteen untouched by man, it was because she was late in developing, and indeed the decisive change into womanhood was yet to come. When she was opposite the Company's works, she crossed the road and went into a laundry, where she was sure she would find Mouquette who almost lived there, with a lot of women who treated each other to rounds of coffee from morn till night. But here Catherine had a setback, for Mouquette had just paid for her round and so could not lend her the promised ten sous. The women vainly tried to console her with a piping hot glass of coffee. She would not even let her friend borrow from another woman, for a sudden fit of economy seized her, a sort of superstitious fear amounting to a certainty that if she bought the ribbon now it would bring her bad luck.

She hurried off along the road home and had reached the last houses in Montsou, when a man standing at the door of Piquette's bar called out:

'Hi, Catherine, where are you running off to?'

It was Chaval. She was taken aback, not because she did not like him but because just then she was in no mood for pleasantries.

'Come in and have a drink. . . . Just a little glass of something sweet, won't you?'

She politely refused: it was nearly dark and she was expected at home. But he came out into the middle of the road and whispered earnest entreaties. For a long time he had been trying to coax her up into the room he occupied on the first floor of Piquette's, a nice room with a big double bed. What, was she afraid of him, that she kept on refusing? She jokingly said that she would go up there the week children didn't come. The talk drifted on from one thing to another and, without quite knowing how, she found herself mentioning the blue ribbon, she had been unable to buy.

'Let me treat you to one,' he exclaimed.

She blushed, feeling that it would be wise to refuse, but inwardly coveting the ribbon. She came back to the idea of a loan and finally accepted on condition that she paid him back later. This struck them as funny again, and they laughingly agreed that he would have his money back if she did not sleep with him. But when he suggested going to Maigrat's, that raised another difficulty.

'No, not Maigrat's, Mum told me not to.'

'Oh, don't be silly! Have you got to say where you got it? He stocks the best ribbons in Montsou.'

When he saw Chaval and Catherine coming into his shop like a couple of sweethearts buying their wedding-present, Maigrat went very red and brought out his pieces of ribbon in a furious temper, as though he had been laughed at. After they had made their purchase, he stood in the doorway watching them go off into the dusk, and when his wife came and nervously asked him for something, he fell upon her with oaths and swore that some day he would see to it that these damned ungrateful people were sorry. They all ought to be grovelling on the ground licking his boots.

Chaval walked along the road with Catherine, keeping very close to her but with his arms dangling at his sides. All the same he pressed his hip against her and guided her without seeming to do so. She suddenly realized that he had made her leave the main road and that they were going along the narrow lane leading to Réquillart. She had no time to remonstrate, however, for his arm was already round her waist and he was intoxicating her with a ceaseless flow of endearing words. How silly of her to be afraid! As though he could wish any harm to a little darling like her, for she was as soft as silk and so tender he could eat her! His breath caressed her behind the ear and sent a quiver all through her body. She was too flustered to say anything. He really did seem to love her. Only last Saturday night, after blowing out the candle, she had wondered what would happen if he took her like this, and as she was dropping off to sleep she had dreamed that she was overcome by pleasure and could not go on saying no. Then why today should the very same thought fill her with repugnance and a sort of regret? While his moustache was tickling the back of her neck so gently that she shut her eyes, the form of another man passed across the blackness of her closed lids, the fellow she had seen that morning.

Suddenly she looked around. Chaval had brought her into the Réquillart ruins, and she backed shudderingly away from the darkness of the broken-down shed.

'Oh no! oh no! Let me go, please!'

She was seized by terror of the male, that fear which makes a girl instinctively tense her muscles in self-protection, even though she is willing, when she feels the all-conquering approach of man. Her virginity had nothing to learn, but yet it was terrified as at the threat of some blow, some wound the unknown pain of which filled her with dread.

'No, no, I don't want to! I'm too young, I tell you! Yes, I am – later on, perhaps, when I'm properly grown up.'

'Don't be silly,' he said in a low voice. 'In that case there's nothing to be afraid of. What difference does it make?'

He said no more, but seized her in his strong arms and threw her into the shed. She fell back on the coils of rope and gave up the struggle, passively receiving the male, immature though she was, with the same inherited submissiveness which laid low the girls of her race while still children. Her frightened stammerings died away, and only the man's panting breath could be heard.

All through this Étienne had sat motionless, listening. Yet another of them taking the leap! Now that he had seen the performance he rose to leave, feeling ill at ease, with a sort of jealous excitement mingled with anger. He gave up trying to be quiet and strode over the beams, for these two were now far too busy to mind. He was therefore surprised when, after walking a hundred paces or so along the road, he turned round and saw them already standing up and apparently returning to the village, like himself. The man had put his arm round the girl again and was holding her tight with an air of gratitude, still whispering into her ear, while she seemed in a hurry to get home and looked vexed at the delay.

Étienne was seized with a desire to see their faces. It was stupid, and he quickened his pace so as not to give in to it. But his steps slowed down of their own accord, and when he reached the first lamp-post he hid in the shadows. He stood rooted to the spot with astonishment when he recognized Catherine and Chaval. At first he could not believe it: could this girl in the dark blue frock and bonnet really be the same young scamp he had seen in trousers with her hair screwed up under a cloth cap? That was why she had passed right by him without his seeing through the disguise. But there was no doubt now, for he had seen her eyes again, those limpid green eyes, as clear and deep as spring water. What a bitch! He felt a sudden and quite unjustified desire to be revenged on her and scorn her. Anyhow, girl's clothes did not suit her; she looked hideous.

Catherine and Chaval had slowly passed on, all unaware that they were being watched. He stopped to kiss her behind the ear, and she was beginning to slow down and enjoy his caresses, which made her laugh. As he was now behind, Étienne had perforce to follow them, and he resented their being in front where he had to witness things that exasperated him. So what she had sworn that morning was true: she did not yet belong to anybody; and to think that he had not believed her, but had resisted the temptation to touch her so as not to behave like that other fellow! And now he had let her

134

be taken under his very nose, and had carried his stupidity to the point of enjoying the dirty fun of watching them! It drove him mad, and he clenched his fists and wished he could slay the man, in one of those murderous moods when he saw red.

The walk went on for half an hour. When they came near Le Voreux, Catherine and Chaval went even slower; twice they stood still by the canal and three times as they rounded the slag-heap, for by now they were very happy and indulging in the tender playfulness of lovers. For fear of being seen Étienne had to stop too at the same places. He tried to have only one regret, and that a brutal one; this would teach him to go carefully with girls out of good manners! After passing Le Voreux, although it was now possible to go and have his dinner at Rasseneur's, he went on following them as far as the village, and there he stood in the dark for a quarter of an hour waiting for Chaval to let Catherine go indoors. When he was quite sure that they had separated, he started walking again, and went a long way along the Marchiennes road for the sake of walking, not thinking what he was doing, too indignant and upset to shut himself up in a room.

It was an hour later, and nearly nine o'clock, before Étienne came back through the village, telling himself that he must have something to eat and go to bed if he expected to be up at four in the morning. The village was already in darkness and asleep; not a single gleam of light showed through the closed shutters, and the long rows stretched on, wrapped in the heavy slumber of a barracks. A solitary cat sped across the empty gardens. It was the end of another day, the toilers had staggered from table to bed, overcome by exhaustion and food.

At Rasseneur's there was still a light in the bar and a mechanic and two men on day shift were drinking their half-pints. Before going in Étienne paused and took a last look at the darkness. Here he was again in the same measureless blackness as he had been when he arrived in the howling wind that morning. There in front of him Le Voreux was crouching like an evil beast, only dimly visible, with here and there the gleam of a lantern. The three braziers on the slag-tip were still flaring high in the air like bloody moons, showing up now and then the gigantic silhouettes of old Bonnemort and his cream horse. Darkness had submerged everything in the plain beyond, Montsou, Marchiennes, the forest of Vandame, the vast sea of beet and corn, unrelieved now except by far-off beacons – the blue flames of blast-furnaces and the red glare of coke-ovens. It was raining now and the darkness was thickening, as the steady continuous downpour engulfed everything in its monotonous stream. Only one voice could still be heard, the slow, heavy breathing of the drainage pump, ceaselessly panting day and night.

Part Three

[1]

NEXT day and the following days Étienne went on with his work in the pit. He gradually became accustomed to it, and his existence adjusted itself to the new work and new habits which had seemed so hard at first. The monotony of the first fortnight was broken by a bout of feverishness, which kept him in bed for forty-eight hours with aching limbs and a throbbing head, dreaming in a sort of delirium that he was pushing his tub along a tunnel too narrow to get through. But this was merely beginner's stiffness and an over-tiredness from which he soon recovered.

Days followed days, and weeks and months passed. He now rose at three like his mates, drank the coffee and took the double sandwich prepared for him overnight by Madame Rasseneur. Regularly on his way to the pit in the morning he met old Bonnemort going home to bed, and on coming out in the afternoon he passed Bouteloup going on duty. He had his cap, breeches, and cloth coat, he shivered and warmed his back at the big fire in the locker-room. Then there was the wait, barefoot, on the top landing, with its piercing draughts. But he no longer noticed the engine with its powerful steel limbs and copper-work gleaming in the darkness above, nor the cables winging their black and silent course like birds of the night, nor the cages for ever rising and plunging amid the din of clanging signals, shouted orders and tubs rumbling on the iron floor. His lamp did not burn properly – that blasted lamp-man couldn't have cleaned it – and he only began to thaw when Mouquet packed them all into their cages with playful resounding slaps on the girls' behinds. The cage took off and fell like a stone into a well, but nowadays he did not even look round to see the daylight vanish. He never even contemplated the possibility of a fall, and as he descended into the darkness and streaming water, he felt more and more at home. At pit-bottom, when Pierron had let them out with his meek and sanctimonious air, it was always the same trampling herd, each team branching off and slouching along to its coal-face. By now he knew the galleries in the mine better than the streets of Montsou, he knew you had to turn here, stoop a little further on, avoid a puddle somewhere else. He had so got into the way of these two kilometres underground, that he could have done them without a lamp, keeping his hands in his pockets. And each time there were the same encounters: a deputy shining his light in their faces as they passed, old Mouque fetching a pony, Bébert leading the snorting Bataille, Jeanlin bringing up the rear of the train so as to shut the ventilation doors after it, and fat Mouquette and thin Lydie pushing their tubs.

Moreover, in due course Étienne found the damp stuffiness of the coal-face much less irksome. The chimney now seemed a very handy way up, as though he had found out how to melt and trickle through cracks where formerly he would not have risked putting one hand. He could breathe coal dust without discomfort, see in the dark and sweat at his ease, being now quite inured to the sensation of having his clothes soaking wet from morning till night. Neither did he now waste his strength in clumsy movements, but had acquired a skill and rapidity that amazed the whole team. After two weeks he passed for one of the good haulage men – nobody pushed his tub to the incline at a quicker pace or dispatched it more neatly. Thanks to his slender figure he could slip through anywhere, and girlishly thin and white though his arms might be, they seemed to be made of steel under their delicate skin, so energetically did they do the job. He never complained even when he was gasping with fatigue; he was probably too proud. The only fault that could be found with him was that he could not see a joke, because he flared up at once if he was criticized. In fact he was accepted and looked upon as a real miner, as the crushing mould of habit pressed him a little more each day into the likeness of an automaton.

Maheu in particular took to Étienne, for he respected good workmanship; and besides, he felt like the others that this chap was better educated than himself: he saw him read, write, sketch plans, and heard him discuss things which he did not even know existed. That did not surprise him, for colliers are rough and ready men with harder heads than mechanics, but what did surprise him was the little fellow's courage and the cheerful way he had dug himself into coal rather than die of hunger. He was the first casual labourer to get the hang of things so promptly. And so when coal-getting was urgent and he did not want to take a collier off the job, he would entrust timbering to the young man in the knowledge that it would be done properly and hold firm. The bosses were always hounding him over this accursed business of timbering, and at any moment he was afraid of seeing Négrel appear, with Dansaert in his wake, shouting and arguing and having everything done again. Now he had noticed that his new man's timbering was more satisfactory to these gentlemen, in spite of their appearance of never being pleased and their repeating that sooner or later the Company would have to take desperate measures. Things dragged on and the whole mine was seething with discontent; even Maheu himself, normally so placid, used to come to the point of clenching his fists.

At first there had been some rivalry between Zacharie and Étienne, and one evening they had almost come to blows. But Zacharie, good-natured and not interested in anything except his pleasure, had been won over at once by a friendly glass of beer and had soon had to acknowledge the newcomer's superiority. Levaque was now quite pleasant too, and talked politics with this haulage man who had ideas, he said. In fact, Étienne was not conscious of hidden resentment from any of the team except Chaval; not that they were openly hostile – on the contrary they had become comrades – but still, even when they were joking together, their eyes betrayed their dislike. Between the two of them Catherine had continued her weary and resigned existence, bending her back, pushing her tub, always kind to her fellow worker who now in his turn sometimes gave her a helping hand, but at the same time submitting to the will of her lover, whose caresses she openly underwent. The situation was now accepted; they were an acknowledged couple, and even her family turned a blind eye when Chaval took her behind the tip every night and brought her back to her parents' doorstep, where he kissed her goodnight in front of the whole village. Étienne, who thought he had faced up to the position, often teased her about these walks, using coarse words of the kind that are used between men and girls down in the pits; and she answered in the same tone, and out of bravado would tell him what her lover had done, but when the young man's eyes met hers she paled and looked confused. Then they would both look away and not say another word for an hour or two, as though they hated each other for things deep down inside which they could not put into words.

Spring had come. One day, as he came off work, Étienne felt the warm, moist April breeze on his face, and smelt the goodly smell of brown earth, new grass, and fresh open air; and now each time he came up, spring smelt better and warmed him more after his ten hours of work in the eternal winter below, with its damp shadows that no summer ever dispelled. The days grew longer and longer, and by May he was going down at sunrise, as the crimson sky bathed Le Voreux in the dusty mist of dawn and the white steam from the exhaust pipes rose up in crests of pink. No more shivering, a soft breeze blew from the distant expanses of the plain and larks sang high in the heavens. Then every afternoon at three he was dazzled by the blazing sun, which lit up the far horizon and reddened the bricks beneath their grimy coat of coal. By June the corn already stood high, and its bluish green contrasted with the almost black beet. As day followed day, this boundless sea, rippling with every breath of wind, spread and grew before his very eyes, and he was sometimes as amazed as though he had seen the green flood rise between morning and evening. Along the canal the poplars wore their leafy crests. Weeds spread over the slag-heap, the meadows were covered with flowers, and while he was groaning with suffering and fatigue down below, the ground above him quickened with life springing up anew.

Now, on his evening walk, Étienne no longer surprised

pairs of lovers behind the slag-tip. He followed their tracks into the cornfields, and guessed where their love-nests were by the movements of the yellowing corn and the great red poppies. Zacharie and Philomène went back there out of force of habit; old mother Brûlé, always hunting down Lydie, was continually running her to earth with Jeanlin – the two of them would be so dug in that you had to tread right on them before they would budge; while as for Mouquette, she lay about everywhere, you could not cross a field without seeing her head bob down and her legs fly up in one of her somersaults. But they were all free to do as they chose, and the young man only found it offensive on the evenings when he came across Catherine and Chaval. Twice, as he came near, he saw them drop down in the middle of a field and the cornstalks go deathly still. Another time, as he was going along a narrow path, he caught a momentary glimpse of Catherine's eyes level with the corn, then they disappeared. Then the vast plain seemed too small for him, and he preferred to spend the evening at Rasseneur's pub, the Avantage.

'Madame Rasseneur, give me half a pint. . . . No, I shan't go out tonight, I'm dead beat.'

And he turned to one of his mates who usually sat at the end table, his head leaning against the wall.

'One for you, Souvarine?'

'No, thanks, I won't have anything.'

Through living side by side Étienne and Souvarine had struck up a friendship. He was an engineman at Le Voreux, and had the furnished room next to his own on the top landing. He looked about thirty, was slim and fair with an intelligent face framed by long hair and a slight beard. With his white pointed teeth, small mouth, thin nose, and pink complexion he had a girlish look about him, but his air of gentle obstinacy could harden when his steely eyes flashed. The only possessions he had in his poor working-man's room were papers and books in a trunk. He was Russian and never talked about himself, but let tales go round. The miners, always very suspicious of strangers, felt that he belonged to some other class because of his genteel little hands, and had at first credited him with some adventure – perhaps he was a murderer fleeing

141

from justice. But then he had shown himself so friendly with them all, and not at all proud, giving all his spare coins to the village children, that they now accepted him as one of themselves, reassured by the term 'political refugee' which was bandied about. This vague term seemed to them a sufficient excuse even for crime, and it made him a sort of comrade in suffering.

During the first weeks Étienne found him reserved to the point of surliness, and he had only found out his story later. Souvarine was the youngest child of a noble family in the province of Tula. While he was a medical student in St Petersburg, the wave of socialist enthusiasm, which at that time was sweeping all the youth of Russia off its feet, had decided him to learn a manual skill, that of mechanic, so that he might mingle with the people, understand them and help them like a brother. And this was what he lived on now, having fled after an unsuccessful attempt on the life of the emperor: he had lived for a month in a greengrocer's cellar, hollowing out a tunnel under the roadway, charging his bombs in constant danger of being blown up with the house. Cast off by his family, penniless and blacklisted from French workshops because he was a foreigner and therefore regarded as a spy, he was on the point of starvation when the Montsou Company had taken him on during a labour shortage. He had been working there for a year now, conscientiously, soberly and silently, one week on the day shift and the next on nights, and was so reliable that his employers quoted him as an example.

'Aren't you ever thirsty?' Étienne jokingly asked.

He answered in his gentle voice and with scarcely a trace of foreign accent:

'I am thirsty when I eat.'

His friend chaffed him about women and swore he had seen him with a haulage girl in the cornfields over by the Silk Stockings. But he shrugged his shoulders with calm indifference. What should he want with a haulage girl? To him a woman was just another fellow, a chum, so long as she had a man's friendliness and courage. And if she had not, well, why run the risk of doing something you would regret? No, he did not want any ties, whether women or friends, and then he was free to do what he liked with his own blood and the blood of others.

Every night at about nine, when the bar emptied, Étienne stayed on talking to Souvarine. He sipped his beer while the mechanic smoked interminable cigarettes which had stained his delicate fingers. He would dreamily watch the smoke with the rapt gaze of a mystic, while his left hand would nervously grope about in space feeling for something to do. He usually finished by taking up on his lap a tame rabbit who wandered freely about the house, always in an advanced state of pregnancy. This rabbit, whom he had christened Poland, had become passionately attached to him, and she would sniff at his trousers and scratch him with her fore-paws until he took her up like a child. Then she nestled up against him, put back her ears and shut her eyes, whilst he untiringly and unconsciously stroked her grey silky coat, finding peace in this soft, warm, living thing.

'You know,' Étienne told him one evening, 'I have had a letter from Pluchart.'

They were alone but for Rasseneur. The last customer had gone home to the village and to bed.

'Oh, have you?' said the publican, coming over and standing in front of his two lodgers. 'What's he doing now?'

For two months Étienne had kept up a regular correspondence with the mechanic at Lille, whom he had told about the job he had got at Montsou, and who was now training him in political doctrine, realizing how valuable he might be as a propagandist among the miners.

'The association in question is going on very well. It seems there are recruits coming in from all sides.'

'What do you think of their society?' Rasseneur asked Souvarine.

Souvarine tenderly scratched Poland's head, blew out a cloud of smoke and murmured in his soft voice:

'Another lot of balderdash!'

Nothing daunted, Étienne warmed up to his subject. All his rebellious instincts threw him into the struggle of labour against capital, for he was still in the first illusions of ignorance. He had been referring to the Workers' International,

143

the famous International which had just been founded in London. Was it not a superb effort, a campaign in which justice must at length prevail? No more frontiers, the workers of the whole world rising up united to guarantee the working man the bread he earns. And what simple and impressive organization: at the bottom the section, representing the commune; then the federation, grouping together the sections of a province; then the nation, and over and above all humanity, in the form of a General Council, in which each nation was represented by a corresponding member. Before six months were up they would have conquered the world, and dictated terms to the employers if they tried to be nasty!

'Balderdash!' said Souvarine agáin. 'Your friend Karl Marx is still at the stage of wanting to leave things to natural evolution. No politics, no conspiracies, isn't that the idea? – everything in broad daylight and the sole aim a rise in wages. Don't talk to me about evolution! Raise fires in the four corners of cities, mow people down, wipe everything out, and when nothing whatever is left of this rotten world perhaps a better one will spring up.'

Étienne began to laugh. He did not always understand his friend's words, and this theory of destruction sounded to him like a pose. Rasseneur was still more matter-of-fact, with the commonsense of a man well established in the world, and he did not bother to lose his temper, but simply asked for precise information.

'So you are going to try to form a section at Montsou?'

That was what Pluchart wanted, for he was secretary of the Federation for the Nord. He called particular attention to the help the association might give the miners some day if they went on strike. Now Étienne thought that a strike was imminent: the timbering dispute was bound to lead to trouble, and one more turn of the screw on the Company's part would bring all the pits to revolt.

'The snag is the subscriptions,' Rasseneur declared sagely. 'Fifty centimes a year for the central fund and two francs for the section doesn't sound much, but I bet lots of them will refuse to pay it.'

'Particularly,' added Étienne, 'as we ought to start by

144

having a provident fund which we could turn into a fighting fund if need arose. . . . Still, it's time we began to think about it. I'm ready, if others are.'

There was a pause. The oil lamp smoked away on the counter. Through the open door you could distinctly hear the shovel of one of the stokers at Le Voreux feeding a furnace.

'Everything is so dear!' Madame Rasseneur chimed in, for she had come into the bar and had been listening sullenly, looking larger than life in her everlasting black dress. 'When I tell you that I paid twenty-two sous for eggs. . . . There will have to be a bust-up.'

This time the three men were in agreement. One after another in doleful tones they poured forth the tale of woe. The worker could not carry on any longer; the revolution had only landed him in a worse plight than ever – since 1789 the bourgeois had been living on the fat of the land, and so greedily that they didn't leave the working man even the plates to lick. Now who could pretend that the worker had had his fair share of the extraordinary advance in wealth and living standards during the last hundred years? It was a mockery to call them free – yes, they were free to die, and they did that all right! It didn't put any more bread into the bin to vote for blokes who went and did themselves well, not bothering any more about the poor than about their old boots! No, a stop would have to be put to it somehow or other; either nicely, through laws and a friendly understanding, or brutally, by general fire and slaughter. The children would surely live to see it, even if the old men didn't, for before the century was out there would have to be another revolution, and this time it would be the workers' revolution – a grand show-down that would clean up society from top to bottom, and then rebuild it with more decency and justice.

'There will have to be a bust-up,' repeated Madame Rasseneur forcefully.

'Yes, yes,' they all agreed, 'there will have to be a bust-up.'

Souvarine was now tickling Poland's ears, and her nose was quivering with pleasure. He murmured softly, as though to himself, with a far-away look in his eyes:

'Raise wages? Can it be done? They are fixed by cast-iron

laws at the lowest indispensable figure – just the bare minimum so that workers can feed on dry bread and produce children. If wages drop too low the workers die, and the demand for more men raises them again. If they go too high there's too much labour available, and down they come again. It is an equilibrium of empty bellies, a life-sentence in the prison of hunger.'

When he forgot himself like this and embarked on intellectual socialist theory, Étienne and Rasseneur felt uncomfortable, for his depressing statements disturbed them because they could not find an answer to them.

'Don't you see?' he went on in his usual calm voice, 'everything must be destroyed or else hunger will start up again. Yes, anarchy, the end of everything, the whole world bathed in blood and purified by fire. . . . Then we shall see.'

'The gentleman is quite right,' declared Madame Rasseneur, who was always most polite, even in her revolutionary outbursts.

Étienne, feeling hopelessly ignorant, would not go on arguing. He stood up, saying:

'Let's go to bed. None of this will prevent my having to get up at three.'

Having put out the cigarette that was stuck to his lips, Souvarine was already delicately inserting his hand under the fat rabbit's belly in order to put her down. Rasseneur was locking up. They separated in silence, ears buzzing and heads bursting with the weighty questions they had discussed.

Every evening there were similar conversations in the bare room, over the single half-pint that took Étienne an hour to drink. A whole crowd of obscure, slumbering ideas were beginning to stir and grow within him. First and foremost, he was obsessed by his lack of knowledge. For a long time he had hesitated to borrow books from his fellow lodger, who unfortunately possessed very few apart from German and Russian ones. Finally, however, he had got Souvarine to lend him a French book on co-operative societies – just a lot more balderdash, Souvarine called it – and he also regularly read a paper the latter took called *Le Combat*, an anarchist sheet published in Geneva. For the rest, although they were together every day, he still found him just as reserved, appearing to be camping-out in life, with no interests, no emotions, and on possessions of any kind.

Early in July Étienne's position improved. An accident had broken the monotonous existence in the mine, with its sequence of identical days: the teams working in the Guillaume seam had come across a disturbance in the stratum which probably meant that they were coming to a fault; and in due course the fault had appeared, a feature unsuspected by the engineers in spite of their detailed knowledge of the terrain. The whole pit was thrown out of gear, and the sole topic of conversation was the seam that had vanished, having presumably subsided on the other side of the fault. The old hands began to sniff round, like a pack of good coal-hounds when the quarry has gone. But meanwhile the teams could not stand about with idle hands, and notices were put up that the Company would auction new contracts.

One day, as they were knocking off, Maheu walked along with Étienne and offered him a place in his team as a collier, instead of Levaque who had joined another. He had already fixed it up with the overman and the engineer, who were very pleased with the young man. And so all Étienne had to do was to accept this rapid promotion, feeling very gratified at Maheu's increasingly good opinion of him.

That very evening they went back to the pit together to study the notices. The working faces up for auction were in the Filonnière seam, in the northern gallery of Le Voreux. They did not look very profitable ones, and Maheu shook his head as Étienne read out the conditions to him. And, sure enough, next day, when they were below ground and he had taken him to look at the seam, he pointed out to Étienne the distance from pit-bottom, the shifty nature of the rock, the narrowness and the hardness of the coal. But still, if you wanted to eat you had to work. And so on the following Sunday they went to the auction in the locker-room, presided over, in the absence of the divisional engineer, by the engineer of the pit, assisted by the overman. Five or six hundred colliers were there facing the little platform in the corner, and the bidding went on so fast that nothing could be heard but a babble of voices calling out figures which were cancelled by other figures.

At one moment Maheu was afraid of not securing one of the forty lots offered by the Company. The competing bidders went lower and lower, being nervous about rumours of a crisis and terrified of unemployment. This cut-throat competition encouraged Négrel to take his time, and he let the bids sink to the lowest possible figures, whilst Dansaert, on the contrary, anxious to speed things up, told barefaced lies about the excellent bargains. In order to get his fifty-metre heading, Maheu had to fight a comrade who was equally determined; each in turn knocked another centime off the rate per tub, and he only won in the end by dint of cutting down the wage so low that Richomme the deputy, who was standing behind him, swore under his breath and nudged him with his elbow, angrily muttering that he would never make anything out of it at that price.

Étienne was swearing too as they came out, and on seeing Chaval coming back from the fields with Catherine, having had his fun whilst his father-in-law was engaged in serious business, he blew up altogether.

'God Almighty! what a massacre! It's come to this now, that workers have to fight their fellow workers.'

Chaval stormed – he would never have lowered his price, not he! Zacharie, who had come out of curiosity, declared that it was disgusting. But Étienne stopped them with an angry wave of the hand:

'It won't go on like this for ever. We'll be the masters, some day!'

Maheu had not said a word since the auction, but now, as though waking out of a dream, he repeated:

'The masters . . . it's bloody well time, too!'

[2]

It was the last Sunday in July, Montsou fair-day. On the Saturday night the good housewives of the village had swilled down their living-rooms – a real deluge, pailfuls of water thrown over the stone floors and against the walls – and the floors were not yet dry, although they had been spread with white sand, quite an expensive luxury for slender purses. The day looked like being very hot, with one of those heavy, thundery skies beneath which the endlessly flat, bare plains of the Nord swelter in summer.

On Sundays, in the Maheu household, times of getting up were all at sixes and sevens. From five o'clock in the morning Dad fumed in bed and had to get up and dress, but the children had a late lie-in until nine. On this particular day Maheu went and smoked a pipe in the garden, and eventually came in and ate a slice of bread alone while waiting. He pottered about all the morning at something or other: he mended a leak in the wash-tub and stuck up under the cuckoo clock a portrait of the Prince Imperial that had been given to the children. The others came down one by one, Grandpa Bonnemort took a chair outside to sit in the sun, Mother and Alzire at once set about cooking the dinner, Catherine appeared bringing down Lénore and Henri whom she had dressed; and it was striking eleven and the smell of stewed rabbit and potatoes was filling the house by the time Zacharie and Jeanlin came down, last of all, still yawning and heavy-eyed.

The village was all agog over the fair, hurrying on with the dinner so that everybody could go off in parties to Montsou. Swarms of children ran about, and men in shirtsleeves shuffled along in slippers with the lazy slouch of the day off. Through windows and doors, all wide open in the fine weather, you could see into one living-room after another, and they were all crammed to bursting point with shouting and gesticulating family parties. And from one end of the rows to the other the rich smell of stewed rabbit vied with the permanent one of fried onions.

149

The Maheus dined at exactly twelve. They made very little noise compared with the gossiping from door to door, the continual racket of women calling to their neighbours, answering, borrowing and lending things, running after children, hitting them and bringing them back. As it happened they had been estranged for the past three weeks from their neighbours the Levaques over the question of the marriage of Zacharie and Philomène. The men saw each other, but the women pretended to be complete strangers. The quarrel had brought them into friendlier relations with Pierronne. But today Pierronne, leaving her husband and Lydie to her mother's tender care, had gone off early in the morning to spend the day with a lady cousin at Marchiennes, to everybody's amusement, for they all knew who this cousin was – she had a moustache and was overman at Le Voreux. Maheude gave it as her opinion that it was a bit thick to leave your family on fair-day.

As well as the rabbit and potatoes – the rabbit had been fattening up in the shed for a month – the Maheus had meat soup and beef. The fortnightly pay-day had fallen the day before and they never remembered such a feast. Even last Sainte-Barbe, the miners' holiday when nobody does anything for three days, the rabbit had not been so fat and tender, and the ten pairs of jaws, from little Estelle's, whose teeth were just coming through, to old Bonnemort's, who was losing his, were working with such vim that even the bones were disappearing. What good stuff meat was! But they did not digest it very well because they saw it so seldom. Everything was gobbled up except a bit of boiled beef for the evening. If they were hungry then they would have to have bread with it.

Jeanlin was the first to go out. Bébert was waiting for him behind the school, and for a long time they prowled about before being able to lead Lydie astray, because Ma Brûlé did not want to go out herself and tried to keep her in. When she found out that the child had run off, she bawled and waved her skinny arms, whilst Pierron, sick of all this row, sloped off quietly for a stroll with the air of a husband enjoying himself with a clear conscience, in the knowledge that his wife was having her fun too.

150

Old Bonnemort went off next, and Maheu decided to take the air after asking his wife if she would join him down there. No, she didn't quite see how she could, it was a perfect nuisance with the children; well, yes, perhaps she would all the same, she would think about it, they would find each other all right. When he was in the street he hesitated a moment, and then called next door to see if Levaque was ready. But there he found Zacharie waiting for Philomène; and then la Levaque brought up the everlasting topic of the marriage, shouting that nobody cared a damn about her, that she was going to have it out with Maheude once and for all. What sort of a life was it for her, minding her daughter's fatherless children while she wallowed about with her lover? Philomène took no notice, but finished putting on her bonnet, and Zacharie took her off saying that he was quite willing whenever his mother was. In any case, Levaque had already gone and Maheu hurriedly took himself off, referring la Levaque to his wife. Bouteloup was finishing a piece of cheese, with his elbows on the table, and steadily refused to come out and have a friendly drink. He was staying at home, like a good husband.

The village was now gradually emptying, all the men were going off one after the other, while the girls, watching at the front doors, went in the opposite direction on their young men's arms. As her father disappeared round the church, Catherine, seeing Chaval, hurried over to him and went along the Montsou road. Her mother, left alone with the rabble of children, had not the strength to get up from her chair, but poured herself out another glass of boiling coffee and sat sipping it. Only the wives were now left in the village, and they invited each other in and drained the coffee-pots round tables still warm and greasy with dinner.

Maheu had a feeling that Levaque would be at the Avantage, and he walked slowly down to Rasseneur's. Yes, there he was behind the pub, in the little hedged garden, playing a game of skittles with some of the chaps. Grandpa Bonnemort and old Mouque were looking on and were so engrossed in watching the ball that they even forgot to nudge each other. The blazing sun was beating straight down and there was only one strip of shade along the pub side, and there Étienne was sitting drinking his beer at a table, vexed because Souvarine had left him to go up to his room. Almost every Sunday he shut himself in to read and write.

'Having a game, mate?' Levaque asked Maheu.

Maheu refused, saying he was too hot and already dying with thirst.

'Rasseneur!' called Étienne, 'bring half a pint.' And, turning to Maheu:

'This is on me, mate.'

They all 'mated' each other now. Rasseneur was in no hurry and had to be called three times; eventually it was Madame Rasseneur who came out with some lukewarm beer. The young man dropped his voice and grumbled about the place: they were good folk, of course, folk with the right ideas, only the beer was no good and the soup beastly! He would have changed his lodgings ten times over if he had not been put off by the walk from Montsou. But one of these days he would look for lodgings with a family in the village.

'Yes, of course,' said Maheu in his slow way; 'yes, I'm sure you would be better off in a family.'

There was a burst of shouting. Levaque had knocked over all the skittles with one ball. In the midst of the hubbub Mouque and Bonnemort kept their eyes glued to the ground in deeply appreciative silence. The general delight at such a feat gave rise to much joking, especially when the players saw the radiant face of Mouquette looking over the hedge. She had been lurking about for an hour, and hearing the laughter had ventured to come nearer.

'What, alone?' called out Levaque. 'What have you done with your boy friends?'

'My boy friends? I've left them in the stable,' she answered with a fine impudent gaiety. 'I'm looking for one now!'

They all offered themselves, warming her up with spicy words. She shook her head and laughed louder than ever, pretending to be coy. Her father, incidentally, heard all this banter but did not even raise his eyes from the fallen skittles.

'Go on!' continued Levaque, glancing at Étienne; 'we all know the one you've got your eye on, my girl! You'll have to take him by main force.'

152

This made Étienne laugh too. She certainly was sniffing round him. He turned down the offer, but in a good-natured way. She did not tempt him in the least. She stayed a few minutes longer planted behind the hedge, staring at him wide-eyed, then slowly walked away, and her face had suddenly become serious, as though she were overcome by the hot sun.

Étienne had resumed his whispered explanations to Maheu on the importance of setting up a provident fund for the Montsou miners:

'What is there to be afraid of, since the Company claims to leave us free? All we've got is the pensions they give us, and as they don't make any deductions from our pay, they award them as they see fit. Well, then, it would be wise to start off a mutual aid society that would be independent of their good pleasure, and at least we could rely on that for cases of urgent need.'

And he went into details, discussed organization, and promised to do all the work himself.

'I'm willing,' said Maheu, now convinced. 'Only there are the others. . . . Try to persuade them.'

Levaque had won the game, and skittles were abandoned in favour of beer. But Maheu would not have another: later on he would see, the day was still young. He had just thought of Pierron – where could Pierron be? At Lenfant's, probably. He got Étienne and Levaque to join him, and the three of them set out for Montsou, as a fresh group took possession of the skittle-alley at the Avantage.

As they went along the main road they had to call in at Casimir's bar and then at the Progrès. Various mates called out to them through the open doors and they could not refuse. Each time meant a beer, two if they politely stood one in return. They stayed about ten minutes, exchanged a few words and began again further on. But they ran no risk, knowing the beer of old; you could fill yourself up with it, the only nuisance being that you pissed it out again immediately in exactly the same quantity, clear as the crystal spring. At Lenfant's they ran straight into Pierron finishing his second glass, and so as not to refuse to clink glasses he had a third. Naturally they had one as well. The four of them now set out to see if

153

Zacharie was at Tison's. But the bar was empty, and so they called for half-pints while waiting. Then they thought of the Saint-Éloi, where they accepted a round from the deputy Richomme, and from there wandered from pub to pub just for the sake of the walk.

'Let's go to the Volcan,' Levaque suddenly said. He was getting lit up.

The others laughed, hesitated, and then made their way with their mate through the growing crowds at the fair. In the long narrow room at the Volcan there was a wooden platform at one end across which five 'singers', the dregs of the Lille prostitutes, strutted and postured in low-cut dresses and with monstrously obscene gestures. Customers paid ten sous when they wanted to have one behind the stage. Most of these were haulage men and trammers, and even pit-boys of fourteen – in fact all the young idea of the mines, who also drank more gin than beer. A few older men had a go as well, but they were the dirty husbands of the villages, the ones whose homes were going to pieces.

As soon as their group was seated round a little table, Étienne got hold of Levaque in order to explain his idea about a provident fund. Like all recent converts who believe they have a mission, he was an untiring propagandist.

'Each member,' he was saying, 'could easily give twenty sous a month. With these twenty sous accumulated over four or five years we should have a nest-egg, and when you have money behind you you are strong, aren't you, whatever happens. . . . Well, what do you think?'

'Well, I don't say no,' answered Levaque in far-away tones; 'we'll talk it over some time.'

His attention was taken up by an enormous blonde, and when Maheu and Pierron, having finished their drinks, wanted to go without waiting for the next musical turn, he insisted on staying behind.

Étienne went with them and came across Mouquette again outside. She seemed to be following them round, for there she still was, gazing at him with her big, staring eyes and laughing her good-natured laugh, as if to say: 'Do you want me?' The young man made a joking remark and shrugged his shoulders. With an angry gesture she disappeared into the crowd.

'Where has Chaval got to?' asked Pierron.

'Yes, that's an idea,' said Maheu; 'he must be at Piquette's. Let's go to Piquette's.'

But as the three of them reached Piquette's bar they were pulled up short by the sound of fighting at the door. Zacharie was shaking his fist at a thickset and stolid-looking Walloon nailmaker, whilst Chaval was looking on with his hands in his pockets.

'Look, there's Chaval,' said Maheu calmly, 'he's with Catherine.'

She and her lover had been walking about the fair for five long hours. All along the Montsou road, from the wide street with its low, colour-washed houses, down the zigzag bends, a stream of humanity was flowing along in the sunshine, like a trail of ants, and losing itself in the flat, bare plain below. The ubiquitous black mud had dried, and black dust was rising like the haze before a storm. On either side the pubs were crammed, and the tables had been extended as far as the roadway, in which stood a double row of stalls, open-air bazaars with scarves and mirrors for the girls, knives and caps for the lads, to say nothing of sweets, dragees and biscuits. There was archery going on in front of the church and bowls opposite the works. At the corner of the Joiselle road, by the Company's offices, a great attraction was a cockpit in a wooden enclosure, where there was a fight going on between two huge red cocks with metal spurs and bleeding breasts. Further on, at Maigrat's, aprons and breeches could be won as prizes in a billiards contest. There were long intervals of silence while the crowds drank and gorged without uttering a word, and the stifling heat, made hotter still by the open-air fish and chip bars, witnessed titanic if silent efforts to digest beer and fried potatoes.

Chaval bought Catherine a mirror for nineteen sous and a scarf for three francs. Each time they went round they met Mouque and Bonnemort who had come to the fair and were pensively waddling along on their bad legs. But another encounter made them very angry: they saw Jeanlin in the act of inciting Bébert and Lydie to steal bottles of gin from a booth set up at the edge of some waste ground. All Catherine could do was box her brother's ears, for the small girl was already running off with a bottle. These diabolical kids would end up in prison.

When they came to the Tête Coupée, it occurred to Chaval to take his girl in to see a chaffinch contest which had been advertised outside for a week. Fifteen nailmakers from the Marchiennes nailworks had entered, each with a dozen cages; and the little darkened cages, containing the motionless and blinded finches, were already hanging up on a fence in the yard. The point of the contest was to decide which one would repeat his particular song the most times in an hour. Each nailmaker stood behind the cages with a slate, marking, checking his neighbours and being checked by them. Off went the finches, the *chichouïeux* with a deeper note, and the more high-pitched *batisecouics*, timid at first and only venturing an occasional phrase, but working each other up and quickening their pace, and finally carried away by such furious rivalry that some even collapsed and died. The nailmakers frantically urged them on, shouting to them in Walloon to sing more, more, just a little more; whilst a hundred or so onlookers were breathless and silent in the midst of this infernal music of a hundred and eighty chaffinches all repeating the same song at different speeds. The first prize, a metal coffee-pot, was awarded to a *batisecouic*.

While Catherine and Chaval were there, Zacharie and Philomène came in. They all shook hands and stayed together. But Zacharie suddenly flared up when he saw a nailmaker, who had come just to be with his friends, pinching his sister's thigh. She went very red but made him keep quiet, dreading a free fight in which all the nailmakers might go for Chaval if he resented her being pinched. Of course she had felt the man, but she had wisely taken no notice. But Chaval only sneered, all four went out, and the matter seemed closed. Scarcely had they gone into Piquette's for a drink, however, when the nailmaker came in, deliberately flouting them, breathing in their faces in a provocative way. Zacharie's family feelings were outraged and he went for the insolent devil.

'That's my sister, you swine! Just you wait! By God, I'll make you respect her!'

Several people rushed to separate the two men, but Chaval calmly repeated:

'Leave off, this is my business. . . . And I say I don't bloody well care what he does.'

Maheu and his friends arrived, and he consoled Catherine and Philomène, who were already in tears. By now there was laughter in the crowd, but the nailmaker had vanished. Chaval, who was in his own home at Piquette's, stood beers all round to dispel the gloom. Étienne had to raise his glass to Catherine and everybody drank together: the father, his daughter and her lover, his son and his mistress, all politely wished good health to all. Then Pierron insisted on paying for another round, and general harmony prevailed, when Zacharie, catching sight of his crony Mouquet, flew into a rage again. He called on him to come and help him deal with the nailmaker.

'I must have a bash at him! Look here, Chaval, you keep Philomène with Catherine. I'll soon be back.'

It was now Maheu's turn to stand beers. After all, if the lad wanted to stick up for his sister, it was not a bad thing. But the sight of Mouquet had put Philomène's mind at rest on that score, and she shook her head. Those two buggers had gone off to the Volcan, she was quite sure.

On fair nights the day's celebrations ended up at the Bon Joyeux dance. This was run by widow Désir, a stout matron of fifty, round as a barrel but still so fresh that she had six lovers, one for each weekday, as she put it, and all six together on Sundays. She called all the miners her boys, and grew quite sentimental at the thought of all the rivers of beer she had poured out for them these thirty years. It was also her boast that not a single haulage girl became pregnant without first having lost her virtue at her establishment. There were two rooms at the Bon Joyeux: the bar, containing the counter and tables, and, leading out of it on the same level through a wide archway, the dance-hall, a huge room with a wooden floor in the centre only and a brick surround. It was adorned with two chains of paper flowers crossing the ceiling from corner to corner, and caught up at the intersection by a wreath

of the same flowers. Round the walls ran a row of gilt shields
bearing saints' names: Saint Éloi, patron of iron-workers,
Saint Crispin, patron of shoemakers, Sainte Barbe, patroness
of miners and, in fact, the calendar of all the trades. The ceiling was so low that the three musicians on their platform the
size of a pulpit could touch it with their heads. At night illumi-
nation was supplied by four oil-lamps hung at each corner of
the hall.

On this particular Sunday dancing was in full swing by five
o'clock, with broad daylight coming through the windows.
But it was about seven before the place filled up. A stormy
wind had sprung up outside, raising clouds of black dust which
blinded people and sizzled in the pans of frying-fat. Maheu,
Étienne, and Pierron had come into the Bon Joyeux for a sit
down, and found Chaval dancing with Catherine while Philomène stood by watching. There was no sign of Levaque or
Zacharie. As there were no seats round the dance floor,
Catherine came after each dance to her father's table for a rest.
Philomène was invited, but she preferred to stand. As darkness fell, the musicians played like mad, and nothing could be
seen but jigging haunches and bosoms in a confusion of waving arms. A great shout greeted the appearance of the four
lamps, and everything was suddenly lit up – red faces, hair
coming down and sticking to the skin, skirts flying and waft-
ing a strong smell of sweating couples. Maheu called Étienne's
attention to Mouquette: round and fat like a bladder of lard,
she was gyrating dizzily in the arms of a tall, thin trammer.
Evidently she had consoled herself by picking up a man.

It was eight o'clock when eventually Maheude appeared,
with Estelle at her breast and her troop of brats following on,
Alzire, Henri and Lénore. She had come straight there to find
her husband, with no fear of making a mistake. They could
have supper later on, nobody was hungry, for their stomachs
were all swimming with coffee and blown out with beer. Other
women came in, and there was some whispered comment when
la Levaque was seen following Maheude and accompanied by
Bouteloup, who was holding by the hand Philomène's children, Achille and Désirée. The two neighbours seemed on the
best of terms, for one was turning round and chatting to the

other. They had had a heart-to-heart talk on the way along, and Maheude had resigned herself to Zacharie's marriage, grief-stricken at losing her firstborn's money but convinced by the argument that she could not keep it any longer without injustice. So she was trying to put a bold face on it, though as a housewife she was wondering how she would make both ends meet now that the best item in her budget was about to fade away.

'Sit down there, dear,' she said, pointing out the table next to the one where Maheu was drinking with Étienne and Pierron.

'Isn't my husband with you?' asked la Levaque.

His mates told her that he would be back soon. They all squeezed up close, including Bouteloup and the babies, and were so hemmed in by masses of drinkers that their two tables ran together into one. Drinks were ordered. Seeing her mother and her children, Philomène made up her mind to join in. She accepted a chair and seemed pleased to hear that she was at last to be a bride. As somebody was wondering where Zacharie was, she said in her gentle voice:

'I'm expecting him, he's over there.'

Maheu had exchanged glances with his wife. So she had agreed? He became pensive and smoked on in silence, for he also was filled with anxiety for the morrow in view of the ingratitude of these children who would get married one after the other, leaving their parents destitute.

They were still dancing; a quadrille was ending in a cloud of reddish dust, the walls were splitting, a cornet was giving vent to high-pitched whistlings like a railway engine in distress, and when the dancers stopped they were steaming like horses.

'Do you remember, my dear,' la Levaque whispered in Maheude's ear, 'how you said you would throttle Catherine if she acted the fool?'

Chaval was bringing Catherine back to the family table, and they stood behind Maheu finishing their beer.

'Oh well,' murmured Maheude, looking resigned, 'you say these things! But what comforts me is that she can't have a baby. . . . Oh yes, I'm quite sure about that. Just think where we should be if she did, and I were forced to marry her as well. What should we have to live on then?'

The cornet was now blowing a polka, and when the hubbub had started again Maheu softly told his wife about his idea. Why not take a lodger, Étienne for example, who wanted somewhere to live? They would have room as Zacharie was going, and what they lost through that they could make up from the other, or partly. Maheude's face brightened: yes, perhaps, good idea, must be arranged. Once again it looked as though she had been saved from famine, and her spirits revived so noticeably that she ordered another round of drinks for everybody.

Meanwhile Étienne had been trying to preach the gospel to Pierron, explaining his scheme for a provident fund. He had got him to promise his support when he unwisely gave away his real aim:

'And if we go on strike you can see how useful this fund will be. We can afford to snap our fingers at the Company, for there is our fighting fund. . . . Well, that's settled, you'll join?'

Pierron had turned pale and was looking down his nose:

'Er . . . I'll think it over. . . . Good behaviour is the best savings-bank.'

Then Maheu claimed Étienne's attention, and in his blunt and friendly way offered to take him as a lodger. The young man accepted in the same spirit, as he was anxious to live in the village so as to mix more with his fellow workers. The matter was settled in a few words, Maheude declaring that they would wait until the children were married.

Just then Zacharie at last came in with Mouquet and Levaque, all three bringing with them aromas of the Volcan, ginny breath and the sharp musky smell of slatternly whores. They were very drunk and looking extremely pleased with themselves, nudging each other and giggling. When he heard that he was at last to be married Zacharie laughed so loud that he nearly choked, and Philomène observed philosophically that she would much rather see him laugh than cry. As there were no chairs left, Bouteloup squeezed up to give half his to Levaque who, coming over all sentimental at seeing them all together like one family, called for yet another round of beers.

'Christ Almighty! we don't enjoy ourselves as often as all that!' he bawled.

They stayed until ten. Women kept coming in to find their men folk and take them home; droves of children tagged on behind, and mothers, giving up any pretence of delicacy, took out breasts that hung down like long, yellow sacks of oats, and smeared their chubby offspring with milk; whilst the children who could already walk, blown out with beer, crawled about on all fours under the tables and shamelessly relieved themselves. All round there was a rising tide of beer, widow Désir's barrels had all been broached, beer had rounded all paunches and was overflowing in all directions, from noses, eyes – and elsewhere. People were so blown out and higgledy-piggledy, that everybody's elbows or knees were sticking into his neighbour and everybody thought it great fun to feel his neighbour's elbows. All mouths were grinning from ear to ear in continuous laughter. The heat was like an oven and everybody was roasting, so they made themselves comfortable by laying bare their flesh, which appeared golden in the thick clouds of pipe smoke. The only nuisance was when you had to go outside; now and again a girl would get up, go to the other end, lift her skirt by the pump and come back. Underneath the paper chains the dancers could no longer see each other for sweat, and this encouraged pit-boys to catch hold of backsides at random and throw haulage girls on their backs. But when a girl fell down with a man on top of her, the cornet drowned their fall with its frenzied tootlings and feet trampled all over them as though the dance itself had buried them alive.

Somebody came by and told Pierron that his daughter Lydie was lying asleep across the pavement just outside. She had swallowed her share of the stolen bottle of gin and was dead drunk, and he had to carry her off on his shoulder, while Jean-lin and Bébert, who were stronger in the head, followed at a safe distance thinking it was a scream. This was the signal for a general exodus and families were beginning to leave the Bon Joyeux, so the Maheus and Levaques decided to make their way back to the village. At the same time old Bonnemort and Mouque were also leaving Montsou at their usual sleep-walking pace, wrapped in the impenetrable silence of their

161

memories. So they all went back together, passing for the last time the fair, the pans of congealing fish and chips, the pubs from which the last glasses of beer were flowing out into the middle of the road in streams. The storm was still threatening, and as soon as they had left behind the lighted houses of Montsou and began walking along the pitch black country road, the laughter became louder and louder. From the ripe corn there was arising a breath of passion; a good many children must have been made that night. They reached the estate strung out in twos and threes. Neither the Levaques nor the Maheus enjoyed their supper, and the latter dropped off to sleep in the middle of eating their boiled beef left over from the morning.

Étienne had taken Chaval for another drink at Rasseneur's.

'Count me in!' said Chaval, after his mate had told him about the provident fund. 'Put it there, you're one of the best!'

Étienne's eyes were gleaming with incipient drunkenness as he cried:

'Yes, let's be friends. You see, I would give everything up, women and drink and everything, for the sake of justice. There's only one thing that warms my heart, and that is that we are going to sweep away these bourgeois!'

[3]

ÉTIENNE moved in to the Maheus' about the middle of August when Zacharie, as a married man, was granted a vacant house in the village for Philomène and the two children, and at first he felt awkward in front of Catherine.

They lived in constant intimacy, for he replaced her elder brother in all respects, sharing Jeanlin's bed beside his big sister's. At bedtime and in the morning he had to undress and dress in front of her and saw her do the same. When the last garment came off she showed the pale whiteness of her flesh, which had the transparent snowy look of the anaemic fair type; and he felt disturbed every time by the contrast between this whiteness and the ravaged skin of her hands and face. It was as though she had been dipped in milk from her heels to

162

her neck, where the roughened skin made a sharp line like an amber necklace. He pretended to look away, but his knowledge of her gradually grew, beginning with her feet, which he saw with his lowered eyes, then a glimpse of a knee as she slipped under the coverlet, and later her bosom with its rigid little breasts as she stooped over the wash-basin in the morning. She did not look at him, but made as much haste as she could, and it took her no more than ten seconds to undress and lie down beside Alzire as quickly and nimbly as a snake, so that he had hardly taken off his shoes before she had disappeared, turning her back on him and only showing her heavy knot of hair.

She never had any cause for complaint. Even though a sort of uncontrollable obsession made him watch out for the moment when she got into bed, he avoided any pleasantries and kept his hands out of danger. Not only were her parents close by, but he regarded her with a feeling of mingled comradeship and resentment which prevented his treating her as a girl to be desired, even in the promiscuity of this new life together, whether it were at washing, mealtimes, work or, since nothing could be kept private, even intimate personal needs. The last remaining stronghold of the family modesty was the daily bath, which she now took on her own upstairs while the men washed downstairs, one after the other.

And by the time the first month had elapsed Étienne and Catherine seemed to have ceased to notice each other, and they moved about the room undressed before blowing out the candle. She no longer hurried over her undressing, but went back to her former habit of tying up her hair while sitting on the bed with her arms raised and her chemise up to her thighs, whilst he, without his trousers, sometimes helped her look for lost hairpins. Custom had put an end to the self-consciousness of being naked, and they thought it perfectly natural to be like that, for they were not doing anything wrong and it was not their fault that there was only one room for so many people. And yet sometimes, when nothing was further from their minds than guilty thoughts, they would suddenly become embarrassed. He might not even have noticed her pale body for nights on end, and then all of a sudden he would realize how white it was, and its whiteness would send a quiver through his body and he would turn away for fear of giving in to an impulse to take her in his arms. Or, on other evenings, it would be she who would have an access of modesty for no apparent reason, and rush and hide between the sheets as though she had felt this man's hands grasp her. Then, having blown out the candle, they both realized that, tired as they were, they would never get to sleep but were thinking of each other. That left them touchy and moody all the next day; they preferred the quiet nights when they were just straightforward with each other, like chums.

Étienne's only cause for complaint was Jeanlin, who slept all curled up in a ball. Alzire's breathing was gentle, and Lénore and Henri were always found in the morning locked in each other's arms, just as they had been put to bed. The only sound in the dark house was the snoring of Maheu and his wife, regular and rhythmical like the bellows of a smithy. Taking it all round he was better off than at Rasseneur's, the bed was not bad and the sheets were changed once a month. He ate better soup, too, only he found the scarcity of meat trying. But everybody was in that position, and he could hardly demand rabbit at every meal for forty-five francs. These forty-five francs helped the family, and they managed to make both ends meet by leaving some small debts unpaid; and the Maheus showed their gratitude to their lodger by washing and mending his clothes, sewing on buttons and generally looking after him; in fact, he was conscious of being surrounded by a woman's kindly care and attention.

It was at this time that Étienne began to understand the ideas that had been vaguely buzzing round in his head. Until then all he had had was an instinct to rebel, in the midst of the inarticulate discontent of his comrades. All sorts of questions had occurred to him: why poverty for some and wealth for others? why should the former be ground under the heel of the latter, without any hope of ever taking their place? The first step forward had been the realization of his own ignorance. From then onwards he had been a prey to secret shame, a hidden sorrow; knowing nothing he dared not talk about the things most on his mind, such as the fact that all men are equal, and equity demands a fair share for all of the things of this world. He therefore cultivated a taste for study, but it was the uncoordinated study of the ignorant with a mania for science. He was now regularly corresponding with Pluchart, who was better informed and deeply involved in the socialist movement. He sent for books and swallowed them whole, which threw him into a frenzy of enthusiasm; in particular a medical book *L'Hygiène du mineur*, in which a Belgian doctor discussed the diseases that are killing mining communities, and of course treatises on political economy of incomprehensible technical aridity, anarchist pamphlets that left him gasping, and old numbers of periodicals which he put by as irrefutable arguments for use in some future discussion. Souvarine also lent him books, and one on co-operative societies had set him dreaming for a month about a universal exchange system whereby money would be abolished and the whole of social life be based on work. He was losing his feeling of shamefaced ignorance, and a new pride possessed him now that he knew he was thinking.

During these first months Étienne got no further than the excitement of the new convert; his heart overflowed with noble indignation against the oppressors, and leaped up in hope for the coming triumph of the oppressed. He had not yet reached the stage of constructing a system out of the odds and ends picked up from reading. In him there was a mixture of Rasseneur's practical demands and Souvarine's violent destructiveness, and almost every day on leaving the Avantage, where he joined them in violent denunciations of the Company, he would walk in a dream and see visions of the peoples of the world wholly transformed without so much as one window broken or one drop of blood spilt. Of course methods of achieving all this remained undefined, he preferred to believe that things would work themselves out quite well on their own, for as soon as he tried to formulate a programme of reconstruction his mind went round in a whirl. He was even full of illogical moderation, sometimes saying that politics should be kept apart from the social problem – a phrase he had read somewhere and which seemed a useful one to repeat in the phlegmatic mining circles in which he moved.

At Maheu's every evening now they would stay talking for

half an hour before going up to bed, and Étienne always went on with the same subject. Now that his own nature was becoming steadily more refined, he was increasingly disgusted by the promiscuity of life in the village. Were they just cattle, then, to be herded together like this in the fields, so on top of each other that nobody could change his shirt without showing his behind to his neighbours! How wonderful it was for health, and how inevitably the boys and girls grew up together in filth and corruption!

'Lord bless you!' Maheu replied, 'of course if there were more money there would be more comfort. All the same, it's quite true that it doesn't do people any good to live all on top of each other. It always ends up with the men tight and the girls in the family way.'

That started them all off, and each threw in his word, while the fumes of the oil lamp mingled with the reek of fried onions. You worked like a beast of burden at a job that used in the olden days to be a punishment for convicts, more often than not you died in harness, and with all that you could not even have meat on the table at night. Of course you had food of a kind, you did eat, but so little that it was just enough to keep you suffering without dying outright, weighed down by debts and hounded as though you had stolen the bread you ate. When Sunday came round you were only fit to sleep. The only pleasures in life were to get drunk or get your wife with a baby, and even then the beer made you too fat in the paunch, and when the child grew up he didn't care a bugger about you. No, life wasn't funny at all.

Then Maheude chimed in:

'You see, the worst of it is when you have to admit that it can't ever change. When you are young you think happiness will come later on, and you hope for things; and then the same old poverty gets hold of you and you are caught up in it. . . . Now I don't wish anybody any harm, but there are times when the injustice of it makes me mad.'

In the ensuing silence they all breathed hard, with the uneasy feeling of being hemmed in. Only Grandpa Bonnemort, if he was there, raised his eyebrows in surprise, for in his day people used not to make such a fuss: you were born in coal,

166

you hacked away at the seam and didn't ask questions, but now there was something in the air that gave miners high and mighty ideas.

'Mustn't turn your nose up at anything,' he would murmur. 'A good beer is a good beer. The bosses are often swine, but there'll always be bosses, won't there? What's the good of racking your brains to try and make sense out of it?'

That would start Étienne off. What! wasn't the worker allowed to think for himself? That was exactly why things were going to change soon, because the worker was beginning to think now! In the old chap's day the miner lived in the mine like an animal, like a coal-extracting machine, and being underground, his ears and eyes were closed to events outside. And the wealthy ruling classes found it quite simple to agree among themselves to buy and sell him and live on his flesh, while he himself didn't even know what they were up to. But now the miner was waking up under the ground, germinating in the earth like good seed, and one fine morning you would see him springing up like corn in the fields; yes, men would spring up, an army of men to bring justice back into the world. Had not all citizens been equal since the Revolution? Since they all voted together, why should the worker remain the slave of the employer who paid him? The big Companies now crushed everything down with the weight of their machines; and now you hadn't even got safeguards against them as they used to have in the old days, when folk in the same trade banded together in guilds for self-defence. And, by God! that, among other things, was why the whole show would blow up one of these days, thanks to education. You only had to look round the village: the grandfathers could not have signed their names, the fathers could already do that much, and as for their sons, why! they could read and write like professors! Ah, things were beginning to move little by little, and a great harvest of men was ripening in the sun! Now that everybody was no longer tied to the same thing for the whole of his existence, but could aspire to his neighbour's place, why shouldn't we use our fists and try to be the masters?

Maheu was deeply moved, but remained sceptical: 'But as soon as you stir they hand you back your card. The old man's right; the miner will always suffer, without even the chance of a leg of mutton now and again as a reward.'

Maheude had been silent for a time, but now seemed to wake up from a dream:

'And then, if only there were some truth in what the priests say, if only the poor of this world were rich in the next!'

These words were greeted with a burst of laughter, and even the children shrugged their shoulders, for the hard wind blowing from the outer world had taken away all their belief. They harboured a secret fear of ghosts down in the mine, but scoffed at the empty heavens.

'Pooh, the priests!' cried Maheu. 'If they believed in it themselves they would eat less and do a little more work, if only so as to book themselves a nice place up there. No, when you're dead you're dead.'

Maheude fetched a deep sigh.

'Oh dear, oh dear!'

She dropped her hands on her lap and said with utter weariness:

'So there it is, we're done for.'

They all sat and looked at each other. Grandpa Bonnemort spat into his handkerchief and Maheu forgot that his pipe had gone out in his mouth. Alzire sat at the table listening, between Lénore and Henri who had dropped off to sleep. But Catherine sat with her chin resting on her hands and her great pale eyes fixed on Étienne, while he protested and declared his faith, opening up the magic vista of his social dreams. All round them the village was settling down for the night, and the only sounds to be heard were a baby crying or the grumbling of a belated drunk. The cuckoo slowly ticked in the room where, despite the stifling heat, a cool dampness rose from the sanded floor.

'*There's* a lot of silly ideas for you,' said Étienne; 'why do you need a God and a paradise to be happy? Can't you make your own happiness in this world?'

He talked on and on, like one possessed. Suddenly the closed horizon burst asunder as he spoke, and there opened a gap of light in the dark existence of these poor folk. The never-ending round of poverty and bestial toil, the destiny of the

168

animal slaughtered for its wool, all this misery vanished as though swept away by a great beam of sunlight, and justice came down from heaven like a dazzling fairy vision. Since God was no more, it was the turn of justice to bestow happiness upon mankind and usher in the kingdom of equality and brotherhood. As happens in dreams, there grew up a new society in a single day and, shining like a mirage, a great city, in which each citizen lived by his own appointed task and shared in the joys of all. The old decaying world had crumbled into dust; humanity, made young again and cleansed of its crimes, was but a single nation of workers having for its motto: To each according to his worth, and each man's worth determined by his works. And the dream grew ever grander, ever more beautiful, ever more enchanting, as it soared higher and higher into the impossible.

At first Maheude refused to listen, for she was filled with inexpressible dread. No, no! it was too beautiful – such ideas should not be allowed to get a hold on you because they made real life look so abominable afterwards, and you felt like smashing everything up in order to find happiness. When she saw her husband wavering and then won over, starry-eyed, she took fright and cut Étienne short, shouting:

'Don't you listen to him, man. You can see he's only telling fairy-tales. As though the bourgeois will ever be willing to work like we do!'

But gradually the spell worked on her too. After a time her imagination was aroused, and she smiled as she too entered this enchanted land of hope. It was so lovely to forget miserable reality for a brief hour! When you live like beasts, with your nose to the earth, you must have a little corner for illusions, where you can go and enjoy feasting on things you will never possess. But what excited her and drew her towards the young man was the idea of justice.

'You are right there!' she said. 'When a thing is right I would let myself be cut in pieces. . . . And it's . fact that it would be justice for us to have a turn at enjoying things.'

That encouraged Maheu to let himself go:

'God's truth! I'm not a rich man, but I would gladly give a hundred sous so as not to die before seeing it! What a grand shemozzle, eh? Will it come soon, and how shall we set about it?'

Étienne began talking again. The old order was breaking up and could not last longer than a few months, he confidently affirmed. When it came to ways and means he was vaguer, jumbling up his odd bits of reading; and, with such an ignorant audience, not hesitating to embark on explanations that he could not follow himself, into which he threw all the different systems, tempered by his certain knowledge of an easy triumph, a universal kiss of peace that would put an end to class misunderstandings. He took no account of recalcitrant employers and bourgeois, who might have to be forced into the right path. The Maheus looked as though they were following, they approved of these miraculous solutions and accepted them with the blind faith of new believers, like the earliest Christians who expected a perfect society to spring up out of the dunghill of the ancient world. Little Alzire caught a word here and there, and visualized bliss in the form of a warm house where children could play and eat as much as they liked. Catherine stayed motionless, with her chin still in her cupped hands, gazing at Étienne, and when he stopped speaking she looked quite pale and a slight shudder ran through her as though she felt cold.

But Maheude looked at the cuckoo clock.

'Past nine – well, did you ever! We shall never get up in the morning!'

And the Maheus stood up from the table, feeling hopeless and sick at heart. It seemed as though they had been rich and then had suddenly fallen back into the mire. Old Bonnemort, setting off for the pit, growled that all this talk wouldn't make the soup any better, while the rest went upstairs one by one, suddenly becoming aware of the damp walls and hot, stinking air. Upstairs, when the rest of the village was wrapped in heavy slumber and Catherine was last into bed and had blown out the candle, Étienne listened to her turning over restlessly before going to sleep.

Neighbours often came in for these talks – Levaque, very enthusiastic at the thought of a share-out, Pierron, who prudently went home to bed as soon as they began to criticize the

Company. Occasionally Zacharie dropped in for a minute, but politics bored him to death and he preferred to go down to the Avantage for a beer. As for Chaval, he went one better than everybody else and called for blood. He spent an hour at the Maheus' almost every evening, and this assiduity sprang from unconfessed jealousy and fear of being robbed of Catherine. He was already tiring of her, but found that she was precious to him now that a man slept near her and might take her in the night.

Étienne's influence spread far and wide and gradually he was revolutionizing the village. His unobtrusive propaganda was made all the more telling by his increasing popularity. In spite of her cautious housewifely instincts, Maheude treated him with consideration as a young man who paid regularly, did not drink or gamble, but had his nose always buried in a book; and thanks to her he acquired a reputation for wisdom among the women of the neighbourhood, who took advantage of it and made him write their letters for them. He became a sort of business and legal adviser, whom families entrusted with their correspondence and consulted over delicate questions. By September he had really established his beloved provident fund, in a very small way at first, with a membership only extending to the residents in the village; but he hoped to secure the support of miners from all the pits, especially if the Company continued to be inactive and not stand in his way. He had been nominated secretary of the association and even had a small fee for the writing involved, which made him almost wealthy. A married collier may not be able to make both ends meet, but a steady, single man without dependants can even save.

From this time a slow transformation began to come over Étienne. A certain instinctive care for his appearance and for the refinements of life, which had been overlaid by poverty, now came to the surface, and he bought some good-quality clothes and smart shoes. This at once put him in a leading position, and all the village looked up to him. He tasted the joys of satisfied vanity and drank the heady wine of growing popularity – it filled him with pride to think that, young as he was, and so recently only an unskilled labourer, he was now at the head of the others and in a position to command, and this encouraged still more his dreams of the coming revolution in which he was destined to play a part. His face changed its expression and assumed a look of preoccupation with weighty affairs, he liked the sound of his own voice, and his growing ambition inflamed his theories and inspired him with militant ideas.

But autumn was now well advanced and the October frosts had turned the little gardens brown. No longer did pit-boys lay girls on shed roofs behind the scraggy lilac bushes; nothing was left now but winter vegetables – cabbages jewelled with hoar-frost, leeks, and pickling vegetables. Once again the rains lashed the red tiles, filled the water-butts, swished like torrents down the gutters. Stoves were never let out in the houses and, piled up with coal, filled the rooms with acrid fumes. Another season of grinding poverty was at hand.

On one of the first frosty nights in October Étienne, his mind still over-active from the talk downstairs, could not get to sleep. He had watched Catherine slip into bed and blow out the candle. She seemed very worked up too, and had one of her fits of modesty when she hurried so clumsily that she showed more than usual. She lay still as death in the darkness, but he could tell that she was not asleep any more than he was, and thinking of him just as he was thinking of her, and this silent communication between them had never been so disquieting. Minutes went by without the slightest movement from either, until their breathing became awkward despite their efforts to hold it in. Twice he was on the point of getting up and taking her. It was ridiculous for them both to be wanting each other so much and not to satisfy that want. Then why should they go on sulking in spite of themselves? The children were asleep and she was willing now, at once: he was certain she was expecting him, choking with desire, that she would crush him in her arms, silently, with teeth clenched. Nearly an hour went by. He did not go and take her, she did not turn over for fear of calling him. The longer they lived side by side, the higher there arose between them a barrier of modest feelings, repugnancies, and delicate sentiments of friendship which they could not have explained even to themselves.

172

[4]

'OH, by the way,' said Maheude to her man, 'as you are going into Montsou for your wages, bring me back a pound of coffee and a kilo of sugar, will you?'

He was sewing up one of his shoes to save taking it to the cobbler's.

'All right,' he said, without looking up.

'I should like to ask you to go to the butcher's as well. . . . What about a bit of veal? We haven't seen any for such a long time.'

This time he did look up.

'You must think I'm going to draw hundreds and thousands. . . . It's a short fortnight, with their bloody idea of constantly stopping work.'

They both fell silent. It was after lunch on a Saturday at the end of October. Alleging that pay-day disorganized work, the Company had once again held up output in all the pits. Panic-stricken at the growing industrial crisis and anxious not to increase its already heavy stock, it seized the slightest pretext for forcing its ten thousand employees into idleness.

'You know Étienne will be expecting you at Rasseneur's,' went on Maheude. 'Take him along with you, he will be sharper than you at figuring it all out if they dock some of your hours.'

He nodded.

'And have a word with those gentlemen about your father. The doctor is hand in glove with the manager. The doctor's wrong, isn't he, Grandad, and you can still work, can't you?'

For ten days old Bonnemort had been tied to his chair, being numb in the paws, as he put it. She had to repeat her question and he growled back:

'Of course I shall work. You aren't finished because you've got gammy legs. It's all a tale they've made up so as to do me out of my hundred and eighty franc pension.'

Maheude thought of the old man's forty sous that he might never bring in again, and uttered a cry of distress:

'God! we shall all be dead soon if it goes on like this.'

'When you're dead you aren't hungry,' said Maheu.

He put some nails in his shoes and made up his mind to set off. Village Two Hundred and Forty would not be paid before about four, the men were in no hurry, but hung about and dawdled off one by one, followed by their wives begging them to come straight back. Many of them asked them to do errands on purpose to prevent their dallying about in pubs.

Étienne was at Rasseneur's because of the news. There were disturbing rumours abroad, the Company was said to be more and more dissatisfied with the timbering. Workmen were being crushingly fined and a conflict seemed inevitable. But in reality all that was only the surface dispute, and under the surface there were other more complicated issues, hidden and serious ones.

Just as Étienne came in, one of his mates, who had come in for a drink on his way back from Montsou, was saying that a notice had been put up in the cashier's office, but he was not quite sure what it was all about. Another came in, and then a third, and each one told a different story. But clearly the Company had come to some decision.

'What do you think about it?' Étienne asked Souvarine, joining him at a table at which the sole 'drink' was a packet of tobacco.

Souvarine took his time and finished rolling a cigarette.

'I'd say it was easy to foresee. They mean to drive you to desperation.'

He was the only one with a clear enough intelligence to analyse the situation, which he explained in his quiet way. The Company had been hit by the crisis and had to cut expenses or go under; and of course it was the workers who would have to tighten their belts. The Company would knock bits off their wages on some pretext or other. Since most of the factories were idle, coal had been piling up in the yards for two months now, and as the Company had not shut down as well for fear of the terrible effect on the plant, it was thinking out a middle course – a strike, perhaps – from which its miners would emerge beaten and lower paid. And finally it was worried about the new provident fund, which was regarded as a threat

174

that a strike would remove, because it would be used up while it was still small.

Rasseneur had sat down by Étienne, and the two of them listened with a horrified expression. As there was nobody now but Madame Rasseneur sitting at the counter, they could talk openly.

'How ridiculous!' said the publican. 'What would be the point of all that? The Company has nothing to gain from a strike, nor have the men. Much better come to an understanding.'

It was very prudent. Rasseneur was always for reasonable claims. Now that his former lodger's popularity had grown so fast, he even overdid his theory of progress through the strictly possible, saying that if you wanted everything at once you got nothing at all. His fat, jolly, beery-looking exterior concealed a growing jealousy, aggravated by the falling off of his trade, for the miners of Le Voreux were not coming in so often now to drink and listen to him. Sometimes he even went so far as to stand up for the Company, forgetting his resentment at having been sacked.

'So you're against a strike?' Madame Rasseneur said to him from the counter.

And as he was answering yes with considerable energy, she cut him short.

'Well, you've got no guts. Let these gentlemen speak.'

Étienne looked thoughtfully into the beer she had served him, and then raised his head.

'No, everything our friend has said is quite possible, and we shall have to make up our minds to have this strike if we are forced into it. . . . Pluchart has written some sound sense about it. He is opposed to a strike, too, because the worker suffers as much as the employer and nothing definite comes out of it. Only he thinks it is an excellent chance to make our men decide to go into this affair of his. Here is his letter.'

The truth was that Pluchart, bitterly disappointed by the suspicious attitude of the Montsou miners towards the International, hoped that they would join in a body if they were forced by a dispute to fight the Company. In spite of his efforts, Étienne had not succeeded in disposing of a single membership card, though it was true that he had put the best of his canvassing into his provident fund, which was much better supported. But this fund was still so small that it would soon be exhausted, as Souvarine said, and then the strikers would inevitably join the Workers' Association so that their brothers in all countries could come to their rescue.

'How much have you got?' asked Rasseneur.

'Barely three thousand francs,' answered Étienne, 'and you know the Administration sent for me the day before yesterday. Oh yes, they are always very polite; they repeated that they do not seek to prevent their workmen from setting up a reserve fund. But I gathered that they wanted to control it themselves. In any case we shall have a pitched battle over that.'

The publican had begun walking up and down, whistling scornfully. Three thousand francs! What the hell do you think anyone can do with that? It wouldn't provide bread for six days, and as for relying on foreigners, people living in England, you might just as well lie down and swallow your own tongue. No, this idea of a strike was just too silly.

Then for the first time bitter words were exchanged between these two men who, in their common hatred of capitalism, usually ended up in agreement.

'Well, and what do you say?' Étienne again asked Souvarine.

He answered with his usual scornful term:

'Strikes? Balderdash!'

An angry silence followed, and then he went on softly:

'If it amuses you, I don't really say no. A strike ruins some and kills off others, and that is always so much cleared away. Only, at that rate it would take a good thousand years to renew the world. Why don't you begin by blowing up this prison in which you are all dying?'

He waved his delicate hand towards the open door through which the buildings of Le Voreux could be seen. Then he was interrupted by an unforeseen sensation: Poland, the fat tame rabbit, who had ventured abroad, came hurtling back, chased with stones by a gang of pit-boys. She was mad with fright and came for refuge against his legs, ears down and tail up,

176

and scratched him, imploring him to pick her up. He laid her on his lap, covered her with both hands, and fell into the kind of reverie that always came over him when stroking her soft, warm fur.

Almost at the same time Maheu came in. He would not have anything to drink, despite polite solicitations from Madame Rasseneur, who sold her beer as though she were graciously presenting it. Étienne had already jumped to his feet and they went off together to Montsou.

On the Company's pay-days Montsou wore a bank-holiday look, like fine Sundays when there was a fair. A multitude of miners came in from all the villages. As the cashier's office was very small, they preferred to stand about in groups on the pavement outside, and the constantly changing queue blocked the roadway. Hawkers took advantage of such a chance and set up their stalls, even displaying pottery and cooked meats. But it was more particularly the pubs and cafés that made a good thing of it: before being paid the miners drowned their impatience at the counters, and they went back to christen their pay as soon as it was in their pockets. And it was only the sensible ones who did not go on and finish the good work at the Volcan.

As Maheu and Étienne threaded their way through the groups, they were conscious of an atmosphere of growing resentment. There was none of the usual carefree drawing of money and spending at pubs. Fists were being clenched and violent language was flying from mouth to mouth.

'So it's true, then?' Maheu asked Chaval whom he met in front of Piquette's. 'They've done the dirty on us?'

But Chaval merely growled with rage, casting a sidelong glance at Étienne. Since the new contracts he had joined up with another team, and was more and more jealous of the new man, this stranger who set himself up as a leader and whose boots the whole village was now licking, so he said. It was all intensified by a lovers' quarrel, for now he never took Catherine behind the slag-heap at Réquillart without accusing her in disgusting language of sleeping with her mother's lodger and then, in a new burst of desire, he would half kill her with caresses.

Maheu asked him another question.

'Is it the turn for Le Voreux now?'

He nodded and turned away, and the two men decided to go into the yard.

The cashier's office was a small rectangular room divided into two by a grille. Five or six miners were waiting on benches along the walls, while the cashier and his clerk were paying another who was standing, cap in hand, at the window. A yellow notice had been put up over the left-hand bench and it stood out fresh against the smoke-grimed plaster wall. Since first thing in the morning a continuous line of men had been moving past it. They came in in twos and threes, stood there and then went out without a word, shrugging their shoulders as though a new burden had been laid on their backs.

Two men were standing in front of the notice, a young one with a square, pugnacious head, and a very lean old man whose face was expressionless with age. Neither could read, but the young one's lips were spelling out the words, while the old one stared blankly. Many of them came in like this just to look, without understanding.

'You read us that,' said Maheu, who was not very good at reading either.

So Étienne began to read out the poster. It was a notice from the Company to the miners in all pits, informing them that, in view of the lack of attention paid to timbering and as it was tired of inflicting useless fines, it had decided to introduce a new system of payment for coal-getting. Henceforth timbering would be paid for separately, by the cubic metre of wood taken down and used, with due regard to the quantity necessary for good work. The price per tub of coal extracted would of course be lowered from fifty to forty centimes, but taking into account the character of the seam and the distance from pit-bottom. Then followed a very obscure calculation intended to establish that this cut of ten centimes would be exactly balanced by the payment for timbering. Furthermore, the Company pointed out that in order to give everybody time to work out for himself the advantages of this new method of payment, it did not propose to apply it until Monday, 1st December.

'Must you read so loud over there?' shouted the cashier. 'We can't hear ourselves speak!'

Étienne ignored the observation and went on with his reading. But his voice was shaking, and when he had finished they all went on staring at the notice. The old man and the young one still seemed to be waiting for something, but in the end they went off, looking crushed.

'God Almighty!' muttered Maheu.

He and Étienne had sat down. While the procession went on filing past the yellow notice, they lowered their heads and concentrated on arithmetic. What did the Company take them for? The timbering would never make up the ten centimes cut per tub. The most they could make would be eight centimes, and that meant that the Company was doing them out of two, apart from the time careful work would take. So that was what the Company was up to, a disguised wage-cut! They were economizing out of the miners' pockets.

'God Almighty!' repeated Maheu, looking up, 'if we accept this we are bloody fools!'

By now the window was free and he went up to be paid. Only the contractors went to get the money, and then they shared it out amongst their men, which saved time.

'Maheu and team,' said the clerk, 'Filonnière seam, number seven face.'

He consulted the lists, which were made up from the books in which the deputies entered the number of tubs per team per day. Then he repeated:

'Maheu and team, Filonnière seam, number seven face. A hundred and thirty-five francs.'

The cashier paid it out.

'Excuse me, sir,' stammered the collier, aghast, 'are you sure there isn't some mistake?'

He stood looking at the paltry sum, without picking it up, and he felt a shudder run down to his heart. He certainly had expected a bad fortnight's pay, but it could not be as low as this unless he had miscalculated. When he had paid out their shares to Zacharie and Étienne and the other man who had replaced Chaval, he would have at the most fifty francs left for himself, his father, Catherine and Jeanlin.

179

'No, no, there's no mistake,' answered the cashier. 'You have to deduct two Sundays and four rest days. That leaves you nine working days.'

Maheu followed this calculation and totted up under his breath: nine days gave him about thirty francs, eighteen for Catherine, nine for Jeanlin. It was true that old Bonnemort had only put in three days. But all the same if you added ninety for Zacharie and the two others, it surely made more than that.

'And don't forget the fines,' went on the clerk. 'Twenty francs fine for defective timbering.'

Maheu raised his hands in despair. Twenty francs fine and four days idle! That made it right, then. To think that he had taken as much as a hundred and fifty for a fortnight when old Bonnemort was working and Zacharie had not yet set up house!

'Are you going to take it or not? Make up your mind!' shouted the cashier impatiently. 'Can't you see there's somebody else waiting? If you don't want it you've only got to say!'

As Maheu was preparing to take up the money in his big, trembling hand, the clerk called him back.

'Just a minute, I've got your name here. Toussaint Maheu, aren't you? The secretary wants to see you. Go in, he's alone.'

The dazed workman found himself in an office furnished in old mahogany and faded green rep. For five minutes he listened while the secretary, a tall, pale-faced gentleman, talked to him over the papers on his desk, without getting up. But the buzzing in his ears prevented his taking in what was said. He gathered that it was about his father, whose retirement was to be considered at a pension of a hundred and fifty francs . . . fifty-eight years of age with fifty years' service.* Then he thought the secretary's voice hardened. It was a reprimand. He was accused of taking part in politics, there was a reference to his lodger and the provident fund, and finally he was advised not to get himself mixed up in such nonsense, for he was one of the best workmen in the mine. He wanted to protest, but could only find disconnected words,

* Zola's French text gives *fifty* and *forty* respectively. Clearly this is a mistake. In Ch. 1 he is fifty-eight. His son, Maheu, is forty-two.

feverishly twisted his cap in his fingers and beat a retreat, stammering:

'Certainly sir. . . . I assure you, sir . . .'

Back outside with Étienne, who was waiting, he exploded.

'What a bloody coward I am, I should have answered him back! Not enough money to buy bread, and insults thrown in! Yes, you're the one he's got his knife into. He said the village was being poisoned. For Christ's sake, what's to be done? Bow down under it and say thank you, I suppose. He's right, it's the wisest thing.'

Maheu relapsed into silence, torn between rage and fear. Étienne was lost in gloomy thought. Once again they were threading their way between groups of men blocking the road. The general exasperation was growing, the exasperation of normally placid folk with no violent gestures, like the muttering of distant thunder brooding and terrible over this sullen mass. Some of those who could count had worked it out, and the news about the two centimes made by the Company on timbering was flying round and turning the heads of the most stolid. But above all there was general fury at this disastrous pay-day, the revolt of the hungry against unemployment and fines. Already there was nothing to eat, what was to become of them if wages went down again? There were loud recriminations in the pubs, and men's throats were so parched with anger that the little money they had been paid was left on the counters.

All the way home Étienne and Maheu never said a word. When the latter came in, Maheude, who was alone with the children, saw at once that he was empty-handed.

'Well, you're a nice one!' she said. 'What about my coffee and sugar and meat? A bit of veal wouldn't have ruined you!'

He made no reply, trying to fight down his emotion. Then the heavy face of this man, hardened by toil in the pits, suddenly twisted up in despair, big tears filled his eyes and ran down in a hot stream. He fell in a heap on to a chair and cried like a child, flinging the fifty francs on the table.

'Look,' he sobbed, 'that's what I've brought you. . . . That, for all our work!'

Maheude looked at Étienne who was plunged in gloomy

silence; and then she also began to weep. How can you feed nine for a fortnight on fifty francs? Her eldest had left them and the old man had lost the use of his legs: it would soon mean death for them all. Alzire flung herself on her mother's neck, terrified at seeing her cry. Estelle was yelling, Lénore and Henri sobbing.

And soon the same cry of distress was going up from the whole village. The men had come back and every home was bewailing this disastrous fortnight's pay. Doors opened and women came out, shouting as though the cramped space indoors were too confined for their lamentations. It was drizzling, but they did not even feel that as they held out their hands and showed each other their money.

'Look, that's what they gave him. A bleeding mockery, that's what it is!'

'But what about me? I can't even pay for the fortnight's bread, let alone anything else.'

'And me! Just you work it out. I shall have to sell my underclothes.'

Maheude had come out like the others. A group formed round la Levaque who was bellowing loudest of all, for her drunkard of a husband had not come back at all, and she guessed that his wages, big or little, would melt away at the Volcan. Philomène was lying in wait for Maheu before Zacharie could have a chance to break into his. The only one who remained fairly calm was Pierronne, but then that sneak of a Pierron always managed, God knows how, to get more hours entered in the deputy's book than any of his mates. But Ma Brûlé thought this a mean trick on her son-in-law's part and she was with the demonstrators, standing lean and erect in the middle of the group, brandishing her fist towards Montsou.

'And to think,' she screamed, without naming the Hennebeaus, 'that this morning I saw their maid sail by in a carriage! Yes, their cook in a carriage and pair, off to Marchiennes to buy some fish, I bet!'

A clamour arose, and a fresh burst of oaths. The idea of the servant in her white apron taken to the market of the neighbouring town in her employers' carriage filled them with indignation. When the workers were dying of starvation they had to have fish just the same? Perhaps they wouldn't always be eating fish, for the turn of the poor would come. And in this cry of revolt the ideas sown by Étienne sprang up and flowered. They were impatient to see the promised golden age, in a hurry for their share of happiness beyond this horizon of poverty hemming them in like a tomb. The injustice of it all was getting too great, and now that the bread was being taken out of their mouths they would end up by demanding their rights. The women especially would have liked to batter their way at once into the dream city of progress where there would be no more poor. It was now nearly dark and raining hard, but still they filled the village with their wailing, in the midst of crowds of screaming children.

In the Avantage that night they took the decision to strike. Rasseneur had given up resisting and Souvarine accepted it as a first step. Étienne summed up the situation in a word: if the Company really wanted a strike, the Company would get a strike.

[5]

A week passed, and work went on in gloom and suspicion as the expected conflict drew nearer.

The next fortnight's money for the Maheus looked like being smaller still, and for all her moderation and common-sense Maheude was becoming more embittered. And now her daughter Catherine had taken it into her head to stay out all one night! The next day she had come back from this escapade so knocked up and ill that she had not been able to go to work, but cried and said it wasn't her fault but that Chaval had kept her, threatening to beat her if she ran away. Chaval was now mad with jealousy, and wanted to prevent her from going back into Étienne's bed where, he declared, he knew her family put her. Maheude was furious, forbade her daughter ever to see such a brute again and talked of going into Montsou herself to box his ears. But in any case it was a day lost, and now that she had a lover the girl did not want a change.

Two days later there was another fuss. On Monday and Tuesday Jeanlin, who they supposed was quietly working in Le Voreux, ran off and went on a spree in the marshes and in the forest of Vandame, with Bébert and Lydie. It was he who was the instigator, and nobody ever knew what robberies they had committed or what precocious vice they had been up to. He received a heavy punishment; his mother thrashed him out on the pavement in the presence of all the terrified children of the village. The idea of such a thing! Children of hers, who had cost money ever since they were born, and ought now to be bringing some in! In this outburst lurked the memory of her own hard childhood, hereditary poverty making of each child in the litter a future breadwinner.

That morning, when the men and the girl set off for the pit, Maheude sat up in bed and called to Jeanlin:

'And mind, if you start that again, you little demon, I'll take the skin off your bottom.'

The work was difficult at Maheu's new pitch. At this point the Filonnière seam narrowed down so much that the colliers were wedged between wall and roof and grazed their elbows while working. In addition to that it was very wet, and every hour they were afraid of a rush of water, one of those sudden torrents that burst rocks asunder and sweep men away. On the previous day Étienne, pulling his pick out after a heavy blow, had received a jet of water in the face, from a spring; but it had been a false alarm and had merely made the work wetter and more unhealthy. He hardly ever thought now about possible accidents, but worked on with his mates, oblivious of danger. They lived in fire-damp without even noticing the weight pressing on their eyelids and the cobwebby veil it left on the lashes. Sometimes they thought about it when the lamps burned pale and blue, and then a miner would put his ear to the seam and listen to the little noise of the gas, a noise like air-bubbles sizzling through each crack. But the constant threat was falls of rock, for apart from inadequate timbering (always bodged up in a hurry), the earth itself was unstable, being saturated with water.

Three times in one day Maheu had to make them strengthen the timbering. It was half past two and they were on the point

184

of knocking off. Étienne was lying on his side, finishing the loosening of a block, when a distant roar of thunder shook the whole mine.

'What's up?' he called, leaving his pick so as to listen.

He thought the whole gallery had fallen in behind him.

But already Maheu was sliding down the sloping coal-face, saying:

'A fall! Quick, quick!'

They all tumbled down as fast as they could, moved by a common impulse to help their brothers. In the deathly silence that had ensued, their lamps bobbed up and down as they ran in single file along the passages with their backs bent double as though they were galloping on all fours. Without slackening speed they exchanged rapid questions and answers: where? at the cutting face, perhaps? no, it came from lower down! more likely the haulage. When they reached the chimney they plunged down one on top of the other, heedless of bruises.

Jeanlin, with his skin still smarting from yesterday's hiding, had not dodged the pit that day. He trotted along barefoot behind his train, shutting the ventilation doors one by one, and sometimes, when he felt there was no danger of meeting a deputy, he clambered up on the last tub, which was prohibited for fear of his going to sleep. But the best fun came every time the train pulled up on a loop to let another pass, when he would go up to the front and join Bébert, who held the reins. He would steal up softly without his lamp and give his chum a good pinch or think out some evil monkey tricks, his yellow hair, big ears, and pointed face lit up by little green eyes that shone in the dark. Unhealthily precocious, he seemed to have the mysterious intelligence and bodily skill of a human foetus reverting to its animal origins.

In the afternoon Mouque brought Bataille along to do his turn with the pit-boys, and as the horse was blowing hard in a siding Jeanlin, who had slipped up to Bébert, asked:

'What's up with the old crock, stopping short like that? He'll make me break my legs.'

Bébert could not answer, for he had to hold in Bataille who was getting lively as another train was coming. The horse had recognized from far off the scent of his friend Trompette, for

185

whom he had felt great affection ever since he had seen him unloaded at pit-bottom. It was like the tender pity of an aged philosopher anxious to comfort a young friend by instilling into him some of his own patient resignation; for Trompette could not get used to it, and pulled his train unwillingly with lowered head, still blinded by the darkness and always fretting for the sunlight. So every time Bataille met him he stretched out his neck, snorted and gave him an encouraging lick.

'God's truth!' swore Bébert, 'they're at it again, sucking each other's skins!'

Then, when Trompette had gone, he answered the question about Bataille:

'He's a knowing old devil. . . . When he stops like that it is because he can sense trouble ahead, some stones or a hole. And doesn't he look after himself! He doesn't mean to break any bones. I don't know what's come over him today when he passes that door. He keeps pushing it and standing stock still. . . . Have you noticed anything?'

'No,' said Jeanlin, 'except that there's plenty of water. It's up to my knees.'

The train moved off again. But on the next journey Bataille, having pushed open the ventilation door with his head, once again refused to go on and stood whinnying and trembling. When he did make up his mind he dashed off like lightning.

Jeanlin had stayed behind to shut the door. He stooped down to look at the pool in which he was standing, then raised his lamp and saw that the timbers had shifted because of the continual dripping of a spring. Just at that moment a collier, called Berloque but nicknamed Chicot, was coming back from the coal-face, being in a hurry to go home to his wife who was having a baby. He stopped as well to look at the timbering. Suddenly, just as the boy was going to run on to catch up his train, there was an appalling crash and the fall buried man and boy.

There was a long silence. The draught caused by the fall raised a cloud of dust in the galleries which blinded and choked the miners who were rushing down in all directions from the most distant workings, and their bobbing lamps dimly lit a stampede of black figures like moles in their runs. Another lot of men from the further coal-faces were on the other side of the fall, which had completely stopped up the gallery. It was at once clear that the roof had collapsed for a dozen metres at the most. The damage was not serious at all. But then a dying groan came from beneath the heap of rubble, and pang of grief gripped their hearts.

Bébert had left his train and rushed up shouting:

'Jeanlin is under there! Jeanlin is under there!'

At the very same moment Maheu tumbled out of the chimney with Zacharie and Étienne. In his wild despair he could only utter a stream of oaths:

'Christ Almighty! Christ Almighty! Christ Almighty!'

Catherine, Lydie, and Mouquette had rushed up too, and began to sob and howl with terror in this awful scene of destruction, made even worse by the darkness. The men tried to stop them, but they were hysterical by now, and each groan from the victims made them scream louder.

Richomme, the deputy, had come at full speed but was very upset that neither Négrel, the engineer, nor Dansaert was in the pit. He put his ear to the fallen rocks and listened, then said that the sounds could not come from a child. There was a man under there, for certain. Maheu had already called Jeanlin a score of times, but there was not a sound. The child must have been crushed to death.

But the monotonous groaning went on and on. They called to the dying man, asking him his name, but the only answer was the same groan.

Richomme had already organized the rescue work. 'Make haste,' he kept on saying; 'we can talk afterwards.'

The miners attacked the fall from both ends with picks and shovels. Chaval worked without a word beside Maheu and Étienne, while Zacharie saw to clearing away the earth. The time for knocking off had come and gone, nobody had had any food, but you didn't go off to have your supper when comrades were in peril. It did occur to them, however, that they would be worried in the village if nobody came up, and it was suggested that the women should be sent home. Neither Catherine nor Mouquette, nor even Lydie, would budge, however, for the need to know kept them rooted there, and they helped with the clearing. And so Levaque undertook to take the news of the landslip and explain that it was just an accident that was being put right. It was nearly four o'clock; in less than an hour the miners had done a day's work, and already half of the fallen earth would have been cleared away had there not been a fresh fall from the roof. Maheu worked on in such a frenzy of determination that he refused with a terrible gesture when somebody offered to relieve him for a moment.

'Mind how you go!' said Richomme. 'We're nearly through . . . you might finish them off!'

Yes, the groaning was becoming more and more distinct. It was this continuous groaning that guided the men in their work, and now it seemed to come from right under their picks. It suddenly stopped.

They all felt the icy touch of death pass by in the darkness, and silently looked at each other and shivered. Then again they dug away, soaked in sweat and their muscles strained to breaking-point. A foot came into sight, and then they cleared the debris away with their hands, freeing the other limbs one by one. The head had not been damaged. The light of the lamps fell on it and the name of Chicot was passed back. He was still warm. His spine had been broken by a rock.

'Wrap him up and put him on a tub,' ordered the deputy. 'And now for the kid, and look sharp about it!'

Maheu struck one last blow and a hole appeared; they were through to the men digging from the other end. They called out that they had just found Jeanlin unconscious, with both legs broken, but still breathing. His father carried him in his arms, and through clenched teeth all he could mutter was 'Christ Almighty!' to express his grief, whilst Catherine and the other girls began moaning again.

A procession soon formed. Bébert had brought back Bataille and harnessed him to two tubs: in the first lay the body of Chicot, held steady by Étienne, and in the second sat Maheu with Jeanlin lying unconscious in his lap, wrapped in a bit of cloth from a ventilation door. They set off at a walking pace. On each tub a lamp was burning like a red star. There followed a long line of miners, some fifty shadowy forms in single file. They had now given in to fatigue and were dragging themselves along, slipping in the mud, like a mournful herd of cattle stricken with the murrain. It took nearly half an hour to reach pit-bottom, for this underground funeral procession seemed to wind on for ever through wandering, branching, twisting galleries.

At pit-bottom Richomme, who had gone on ahead, had ordered an empty cage to be kept ready. Pierron at once packed in the two tubs, Maheu in one with his injured child on his knees, whilst in the other Étienne had to hold Chicot's body in his arms to keep it steady. The rest piled into the other decks and the cage went up. It took two minutes. The water streaming from the lining felt icy cold and they all looked up impatiently for daylight to appear.

Fortunately the boy who had been sent for Dr Vanderhaghen had found him and brought him at once. Jeanlin and the dead man were carried into the deputies' room, where there was always a big fire burning from one end of the year to the other. A row of pails full of warm water for foot-washing was put on one side, two mattresses were spread on the floor, and the man and child laid on them. Only Maheu and Étienne went in. Outside stood a crowd of haulage girls, colliers and boys, talking in hushed voices.

The doctor took one look at Chicot and said:

'He's done for! You can wash him.'

Two chargehands stripped and sponged down this coal-black corpse, filthy with the sweat of toil.

'Nothing wrong with his head,' went on the doctor, kneeling on Jeanlin's mattress. 'Chest's all right, too. . . . Ah, it's his legs that have caught it.'

He undressed the child himself, unfastening his cap, pulling down his trousers and lifting off his shirt with the skill of a nurse. And the pathetic little body came into view, as thin as an insect's, soiled with black dust and yellow earth and mottled with bloody stains. It was impossible to see anything; he had to be washed as well. The sponging seemed to make him thinner than ever, his flesh was so pallid and transparent that the bones showed through. It was pitiful to see this last decadent specimen of a race of starving toilers, this mere wisp of suffering, half crushed by the rocks. When he had been cleaned, the bruises on his thighs showed: two red patches on the white skin.

Jeanlin came out of his faint and moaned. Maheu stood at the foot of the mattress, with his arms hanging loose, looking at him, the tears running down his cheeks.

'Are you the father?' said the doctor, looking up. 'There's no need to cry, you can see he's not dead. Give me a hand instead.'

He diagnosed two simple fractures. But the right leg was disquieting: it might have to be amputated.

At that moment Négrel, the engineer, and Dansaert, who had at last been told, came in with Richomme. The former listened to the deputy's tale and then burst out in exasperation: always this blasted timbering! hadn't he repeated a hundred times that men would be left down there dead? and then these brutes talked about going on strike if they were forced to make their timbering a bit more safe! And the worst of it was that the Company would now have to pay for the damage. Monsieur Hennebeau would be pleased!

'Who is it?' he asked Dansaert, who was standing silently by the body, which was being wrapped in a sheet.

'Chicot, one of our best workmen,' answered the overman. 'He has three children. . . . Poor devil!'

Dr Vanderhaghen stipulated that Jeanlin should be transported home at once. It was striking six and already getting dark, and it would be a good idea to take the corpse as well; the engineer gave orders for horses to be put to the van and a stretcher to be brought. The injured child was put on the stretcher and the dead man, on his mattress, was packed into the van.

The girls were still waiting outside the door, talking to some of the miners who had stayed behind to see. When the door of the deputies' room opened again, they were all silent. A new procession was formed, first the van, then the stretcher, with the onlookers bringing up the rear. They moved out of the yard and slowly climbed the steep road up to the village. The first chilly days of November had stripped the vast plain, and night was slowly covering it like a shroud falling from the ashen sky.

Étienne suggested in a whisper to Maheu that Catherine should be sent on ahead to warn Maheude and soften the blow, and the grief-stricken father, following the stretcher, nodded his agreement. The girl ran on as fast as she could, for they were nearly there. But already the van, that dreaded black box, had been sighted, and women were rushing out into the street, three or four of them running about distraught and bare-headed. Soon there were thirty, then fifty, all gripped by the same terror. So there was somebody killed? Who? Levaque's story had reassured them at first, but it had now thrown them into an exaggerated nightmare of dread: it was no longer one man who had perished, but ten, and the van was going to bring them back one by one.

Catherine had found her mother tortured by forebodings, and before she could stammer out more than a word the former said:

'Dad is dead!'

The girl protested in vain, mentioning Jeanlin, but Ma-heude had rushed off without listening. Seeing the van come out opposite the church, she grew pale and faint. Women stood on their doorsteps craning their necks in speechless horror, whilst others ran after the procession trembling with anxiety to see at which house it would stop.

The van went by, and Maheude saw Maheu walking behind with the stretcher. When they set the stretcher down outside her door and she saw Jeanlin alive but with broken legs, she had such a violent reaction that she nearly choked with rage, and stammered dry-eyed:

'That's how it is! They cripple our children now! Both legs, my God! What do they think I can do with him?'

'Now, now, shut up!' said Dr Vanderhaghen, who had come to bandage Jeanlin. 'Would you rather he had stayed down there?'

But Maheude grew more and more frenzied, while Alzire, Lénore, and Henri wailed. While helping to take the patient upstairs and giving the doctor what he needed, she cursed her fate, asking where they expected her to find the money to feed invalids. As if the old man wasn't enough, now the kid had lost his legs as well! And she went on and on, while other cries

191

and lamentations came from a nearby house: Chicot's wife and children were weeping over his body. It was now quite dark, and gloomy stillness had fallen over the village, only broken by these bitter wailings. The exhausted miners were at last eating their supper.

Three weeks went by. They had been able to avoid amputation. Jeanlin would keep both his legs, but would always be lame. After an enquiry the Company had resigned itself to an award of fifty francs. It had also promised to find the little cripple a surface job as soon as he was fit again. Nevertheless it meant that they were poorer than ever, for the shock had laid the father low with a severe attack of fever.

Maheu had been back at work since Thursday, and it was now Sunday. That evening Étienne talked about the approaching date of the 1st December, and was anxious to see whether the Company would carry out its threat. They sat up until ten waiting for Catherine, who must be dallying with Chaval. But she did not come home. Without saying a word Maheude furiously bolted the door. Étienne lay awake for a long time, upset by the thought of the empty bed in which Alzire was taking up so little space.

The following day, still no sign of her. It was only in the afternoon, after work, that the Maheus learned that Chaval was keeping Catherine. He nagged her so abominably that she had made up her mind to live with him. To avoid recriminations he had suddenly left Le Voreux and taken a job at Jean-Bart, Monsieur Deneulin's pit, and she had gone there with him as a haulage girl. But the couple was still living in Montsou, at Piquette's.

At first Maheu talked of going and giving the man a thick ear and bringing his daughter home with a kick up the backside. But then he threw up his arms in resignation: what was the use? it always went that way and you couldn't prevent girls picking up men if they wanted to. Better quietly wait for them to get married. But his wife did not take things so calmly:

'Now did I hit her when she went with this chap Chaval?' she asked Étienne, who listened in awkward silence. 'Tell me, you are a man of the world . . . we left her quite free, didn't we?

because, after all, they all go the same way. Take me, for example – I was in the family way when Dad married me. But I didn't leave my parents in the lurch for all that; I would never have done the dirty trick of taking my wages, at that age, to a man who didn't need them. . . . It's disgusting, I tell you! It's enough to make people give up having children.'

As Étienne made no answer except to nod his head, she returned to the charge:

'A girl who went out every evening wherever she wanted to! What's come over her? Fancy not being able to wait until she had helped us over the hard times and I let her marry! You have a daughter so that she can work – that's natural, isn't it? But there you are, we've been too kind, we ought not to have let her go about with a man. Give them an inch and they take an ell.'

Alzire nodded in agreement. Lénore and Henri, cowed by the storm, whimpered quietly, while their mother proceeded to enumerate their woes: first there was Zacharie – they had had to let him get married – then old Bonnemort stuck there in his chair with twisted feet, then Jeanlin who wouldn't be able to leave his room for ten more days because his bones hadn't set properly, and then this as a last straw, this little bitch of a Catherine, gone off with a man! The family was going to pieces. Only Dad left at work! How could she feed seven people on his three francs, to say nothing of Estelle? They might as well go in a body and throw themselves into the canal.

'It doesn't do a bit of good fretting like that,' murmured Maheu. 'We may not be at the end of it yet.'

Étienne had kept his eyes down on the floor, but he now looked up, as though at a vision of the future, and said:

'Ah, it's about time! it's about time!'

Part Four

▪▪

[1]

ON that Monday the Hennebeaus had invited the Grégoires
and their daughter Cécile to lunch. They had planned quite an
outing: immediately after the meal Paul Négrel was to take
the ladies round a mine, Saint-Thomas, which was being
fitted up as a show place. But all that was really a polite
fiction, for the excursion had been thought out by Madame
Hennebeau as a way of bringing nearer the marriage of
Cécile and Paul.

And then on that very Monday, at four o'clock in the morning, the strike had broken out. When the Company had put
into effect its new wage system on the 1st December, the miners
had shown no excitement. Not one had made the slightest
complaint on pay-day at the end of the fortnight. The whole
staff, from the manager down to the most junior chargehand,
thought that the scale had been accepted, and great was everybody's surprise that morning at this declaration of war which
had been carried through with a tactical skill and solidarity
that suggested energetic leadership.

At five Dansaert awoke Monsieur Hennebeau and told
him that not a single man had gone down into Le Voreux. He
had just come through Village Two Hundred and Forty and it
was still fast asleep, with doors and windows shut tight.
From the moment the manager had got out of bed, his eyes
still heavy with sleep, he was overwhelmed with news:
messengers appeared every quarter of an hour and dispatches
fell on to his desk thick as hailstones. At first he hoped that
the revolt was confined to Le Voreux, but each minute the
news was more serious: Mirou and Crèvecœur were
affected, and only ponymen had turned up at Madeleine; in

La Victorie and Feutry-Cantel, the most law-abiding pits, only a third of the men had gone down; Saint-Thomas alone had its full complement and seemed to be unaffected by the movement. Until nine o'clock he dictated dispatches and telegraphed in all directions, to the Prefect at Lille, the directors of the Company, warning the authorities, asking for orders. He had sent Négrel on a tour of the neighbouring pits to get exact information.

Suddenly Monsieur Hennebeau remembered about the luncheon party, and he was on the point of sending the coachman to tell the Grégoires that it was postponed. And then this man, who had just prepared for battle in clipped, military phrases, hesitated and paused in a fit of indecision. He went upstairs to find his wife, who had just had her hair done by her maid in her dressing-room.

'Oh, so they're on strike,' she said, nonchalantly, when he had asked her about the lunch; 'well, what difference does that make to us? We aren't going to give up eating, I take it?'

In vain he pointed out that the lunch would be very disturbed and that the visit to Saint-Thomas could not take place; she insisted and had an answer ready for everything. Why throw away a lunch already being cooked? And as to visiting the mine, well, they could give that up later if it really proved unwise to go.

'Besides,' she went on, after her maid had gone, 'you know why I particularly want to have these good folk. You must surely be more interested in this marriage than in this silly nonsense of your workmen. . . . Anyway, I want it, so don't go against me.'

As he looked at her a slight tremor ran through him, and his hard, inscrutable face, the face of a disciplinarian, betrayed the hidden grief of a heartbroken man. Her shoulders had remained uncovered, she was already over-mature, but still lovely and desirable, with a bosom like Ceres gilded by autumn. For a moment he felt a brutal desire to seize her and bury his head between the breasts she was displaying, in this warm room with all the intimate luxury of a sensual woman, where there lingered an exciting scent of musk; but

196

he drew back – for ten years now they had occupied separate rooms.

'All right,' he said, going out, 'we'll let the arrangement stand.'

Monsieur Hennebeau was a native of the Ardennes. In his early career he had known the difficulties of a penniless young man thrown as an orphan on the streets of Paris. After a hard grind at the School of Mines, he had gone at twenty-four to the Grand'Combe as engineer in the Sainte-Barbe pit. Three years later he had become divisional engineer in the Pas-de-Calais at the Marles mines, and there, by one of those strokes of luck which seem to be the rule among mining engineers, he had married the daughter of a rich Arras spinner. For fifteen years they had lived in the same small provincial town, without any event to break the monotony of their existence, not even the birth of a child. Madame Hennebeau, brought up to worship money and looking down on this husband who worked hard to earn a moderate salary which satisfied none of her extravagant schoolgirl dreams, had gradually drifted away from him in growing irritation. He was strictly honest, never speculated, and stuck to his post like a soldier. Their estrangement had gone on growing, made more marked by one of those curious incompatibilities of the flesh which can cool even the most hot-blooded; he worshipped his wife, and she had the voluptuous nature of a sensual blonde, and yet already they slept apart, unable to adjust themselves and quick to hurt each other. Unknown to him she had taken a lover. Finally he left the Pas-de-Calais for a secretarial position in Paris, hoping that she would be grateful. But Paris was to complete their separation – Paris, that she had been dreaming about ever since she had her first doll – for it took her just one week to shake off every trace of provincialism and become elegant, throwing herself into all the expensive crazes of the moment. The ten years she had spent there were filled by a great passion, a public liaison with a man who had nearly killed her with grief when he left her. This time the husband could not remain in ignorance, and he had accepted the situation after many appalling scenes, powerless in the face of this woman's tranquil amorality, for she simply took her pleasure where she found it. It was after the break-up of this affair, when he saw she was ill with grief, that he had accepted the management of the Montsou mines, in the hope that he might be able to reform her in the wilderness of the coal country.

Since they had been at Montsou, the Hennebeaus had gone back to the bored irritation of the early days of their marriage. At first the quiet regularity of the life had seemed to do her good; she found peace in the flat monotony of the endless plain, and buried herself like a woman whose life is finished, affecting to be dead to love and so indifferent to worldly affairs that she did not even mind getting stout. Then beneath this apparent indifference a last burst of passion had flamed up, a desire to live once more, which she had kept at bay for six months by furnishing and fitting out the manager's small house to her own taste. She said it was hideous, and filled it with tapestries, antiques, and all sorts of artistic luxuries which were commented on as far away as Lille. But now she found the country exasperating, with its silly fields going on and on for ever, its endless black roads with never a tree, peopled by horrible creatures who filled her with disgust and fear. She began complaining of being exiled, and accused her husband of having sacrificed her for the sake of the salary of forty thousand francs – a mere pittance that was hardly sufficient to run the house. Couldn't he have done what others had done and demanded a partnership, bought shares, in fact made a success of something? She nagged about this with all the cruelty of an heiress who had brought the money with her. As for him, behind the deceptively correct and cold exterior of an administrator, he was ravaged by one of those violent passions which develop in middle life. He had never possessed her as a favoured lover, and now he was obsessed by an inescapable vision: to have her just once for himself as she had given herself to another. Every morning he dreamed of winning her that night, and then, when she turned her cold eyes on him and he felt that everything in her was repelled by him, he avoided even touching her with his hand. It was a relentless torture without hope of a cure, concealed beneath the stiffness of his normal behaviour, the suffering of an

198

affectionate nature secretly heartbroken at not having found happiness in his home. When the six months were over and the house was completely refurbished and no longer interested her, Madame Hennebeau relapsed into languid boredom, like a victim doomed to be killed by exile and who would be glad to die.

Just then Paul Négrel came on the scene at Montsou. His mother, the widow of a captain in Provence, living at Avignon on a small pension, had gone without everything in order to send him to the École Polytechnique. He had passed out with very low marks and his uncle, Monsieur Hennebeau, had given him a chance to leave by offering to take him as engineer at Le Voreux. From then on he had been treated as one of the family, he had his own room and lived with them, and this enabled him to send his mother half his salary of three thousand francs. Monsieur Hennebeau disguised this charity by saying how awkward it was for a single young man to set up house on his own in one of the little huts allocated to engineers. Madame Hennebeau had at once cast herself in the role of affectionate aunt, treating him with familiarity and looking after his comfort. During the first months, especially, she was full of maternal solicitude and good advice about everything. But she was still a woman, and soon slipped into personal confidences. This boy was so young and yet so sensible, with his hard-headed intelligence; he professed philosophical theories about love, and amused her with the keen pessimism that had left its mark on his thin face and pointed nose. Of course one evening he found himself in her arms; she seemed to give herself out of kindness of heart, protesting the while that she was dead to love and only wanted to be his friend. And certainly she was not jealous, but teased him about haulage girls, whom he declared to be horrible, and almost reproached him for having no spicy youthful exploits to tell her about. Then she threw herself into plans for finding him a wife, fancying herself as a martyr voluntarily giving him up to some rich girl. Not that their physical relationship ceased, but that was just an amusement into which she put the last flickers of passion of an idle woman who had really finished with such things.

Two years had passed. One night, hearing somebody going barefoot past his door, Monsieur Hennebeau had his suspicions. Really, this latest adventure was disgusting, here, in his own house, and as it were between mother and son! But the very next day his wife spoke to him about the choice she had made of Cécile Grégoire for their nephew, and she was so enthusiastic about this marriage that he blushed at his own monstrous imaginings. And so he merely remained grateful to the young man for having made his home a little less gloomy.

On coming down from his wife's dressing-room, Monsieur Hennebeau met Paul coming in. He seemed quite amused by all this strike business.

'Well?' asked his uncle.

'Well, I have been round the villages, and they all seem very subdued. . . . But I think they are going to send you a deputation.'

At that moment Madame Hennebeau's voice called from upstairs.

'Is that you, Paul? Come up and tell me all about it. Isn't it funny that these people should be so unpleasant when they are so well off!'

The manager had to give up hopes of learning anything else since his wife had stolen his messenger. He returned to his desk, on which still more dispatches had piled up.

When the Grégoires arrived at eleven they were surprised to find Hippolyte, the footman, standing on guard, and to be hurried inside without ceremony after he had looked anxiously up and down the street. The drawing-room curtains were pulled across, and they were shown straight into Monsieur Hennebeau's office, where he apologized for receiving them in this fashion but explained that the drawing-room looked on to the street, and there was no point in appearing deliberately provocative, was there?

'What, didn't you know?' he went on, seeing their amazement.

When Monsieur Grégoire heard that the strike had at last broken out, he shrugged his shoulders in his placid way. Bah! it wouldn't be anything much, these people were really quite nice. Madame Grégoire nodded in agreement to show that she shared his confidence in the age-old resignation of the miners; whilst Cécile, who was in very high spirits that day and looking radiant in a flame-coloured dress, smiled when she heard the word 'strike,' which conjured up visions of trips to the village to distribute gifts.

Madame Hennebeau appeared, in black silk, followed by Négrel.

'Isn't it tiresome!' she said, coming through the doorway, 'just as though these people couldn't have waited! Paul simply won't take us to Saint-Thomas, you know.'

'Then we'll stay here,' said Monsieur Grégoire obligingly; 'it will all be delightful, I'm sure!'

Paul had merely bowed to Cécile and her mother. Vexed to see him so undemonstrative, his aunt signalled with her eyes that he was to attend to the young lady, and when she heard them laughing together she enveloped them in a look of motherly affection.

Meanwhile Monsieur Hennebeau finished reading through the dispatches and wrote several replies, while the chatter went on all round him. His wife was explaining that she had not done anything about the office, which still had its old faded red wallpaper, heavy mahogany furniture, and worn-out cardboard files. After three-quarters of an hour they were about to go in to lunch, when the footman announced Monsieur Deneulin, who came in looking very disturbed and bowed to Madame Hennebeau.

'Oh, are you here?' he said when he saw the Grégoires, and then at once began speaking to the manager.

'It has come, then? I have just heard from my engineer. . . . All my men went down all right this morning, but it may well spread. I am not too happy about it. How are things with you?'

He had come over on horseback, and his anxiety was perceptible in his loud voice and abrupt gestures, which made him look like a retired cavalry officer.

Monsieur Hennebeau was beginning to explain the exact situation when Hippolyte threw open the dining-room door. So he broke off and said:

'Have lunch with us. I'll tell you all the rest over dessert.'

'Yes, just as you like,' said Deneulin, whose mind was so preoccupied that he accepted without further formality.

But then he realized how discourteous he was and turned to apologize to Madame Hennebeau, who was at her most charming. When she had had a seventh place laid, she arranged her guests thus: Madame Grégoire and Cécile on each side of her husband, Monsieur Grégoire and Deneulin on her own right and left. Paul was placed between the young lady and her father. As they attacked the hors d'œuvres she said with a smile:

'Do forgive me, I meant to give you oysters. On Mondays, you know, they have a delivery of Ostend oysters at Marchiennes, and I had intended to send cook in the carriage. . . . But she was afraid they might throw stones at her.'

There was a roar of laughter. They all thought this most amusing.

'Sh!' said Monsieur Hennebeau, with an uneasy glance at the windows, through which the road could be seen. 'There's no need to let everybody know we have company this morning.'

'Well anyhow, here's a slice of sausage they won't get,' declared Monsieur Grégoire.

There was another laugh, but more subdued this time. The guests all had a feeling of well-being in this room, hung with Flemish tapestries and furnished with antique oak court-cupboards. Silver plate gleamed through the glass doors of the cabinets, and there was a large copper chandelier, in the burnished globes of which were reflected a palm and an aspidistra, growing in majolica pots. Outside there was a freezing December day with a keen north-east wind blowing. Not a breath of this came indoors, however, where the hot-house warmth brought out the scent of a sliced pineapple in a cut-glass bowl.

'Suppose we draw the curtains?' suggested Négrel, tickled by the idea of frightening the Grégoires.

The maid, who was helping the footman to serve, thought this was an order and went and pulled them across. From then onwards there were jokes without end; every fork and glass was put down with infinite precaution, and each new dish was greeted like a piece of salvage rescued from a sacked town. Underlying this forced merriment, however, there was an unspoken fear, betrayed by involuntary glances in the direction of the road, as though a famished army were watching the table from outside.

After scrambled eggs with truffles came river trout. The conversation had turned to the industrial crisis which had been steadily worsening for eighteen months.

'It was inevitable,' said Deneulin, 'that too much prosperity during recent years should land us into this. Think of the enormous amount of capital immobilized in railways, docks, and canals, and all the money buried in ridiculous speculation. In our neighbourhood alone they have set up enough sugar refineries for three times the beet harvest of the Department. And of course the result is that money has now become scarce and the people have got to wait for the interest to come in from the millions that have been laid out. All this has led to a fatal glut and complete business stagnation.'

Monsieur Hennebeau disagreed with the theory, but admitted that the workers had been spoiled by years of prosperity.

'When I think that in our pits these chaps could make as much as six francs a day, double what they earn nowadays! And they lived well, too, and developed a taste for luxuries. Now of course they think it hard to go back to their former frugality.'

'Monsieur Grégoire,' broke in Madame Hennebeau, 'do have a little more trout. They are delicious, aren't they?'

The manager would not be deflected.

'But is it really our fault?' he went on. 'We are very hard hit as well. . . . Since the factories have been closing down one by one we have been having the devil of a job to get rid of our stocks, and in view of the decreasing demand we are obliged to lower our prices. That's what the workers simply refuse to understand.'

There was a pause. The footman served roast partridges while the maid began filling glasses with Chambertin.

'There has been a famine in India,' Deneulin went on in a

low voice, as though speaking to himself. 'The Americans have stopped ordering iron and cast-iron, and that has dealt a heavy blow to our smelting works. Everything hangs together, and a distant shock is enough to shake the whole world. And to think that the Empire was so proud of the industrial boom!'

He attacked his wing of partridge, then raised his voice:

'The worst of it is that in order to cut our selling price we ought logically to increase production; otherwise the cut must come from wages, and then the worker is quite right to say that he always pays for the damage.'

This admission, which he made in all honesty, led to an argument. The ladies were finding things very dull. Incidentally everyone was in the first flush of appetite and busy eating. The footman came in just then, looking as though he had something to say but hesitating to say it.

'Well, what is it?' asked Monsieur Hennebeau. 'If it is more dispatches, let me have them. I am expecting some answers.'

'No, sir, it is Monsieur Dansaert, in the hall. But he does not want to intrude.'

The manager apologized and had the overman shown in. He remained standing a few feet away from the table, and they all turned round to look at this great big man, breathless with the news he was bringing. All was quiet in the villages, but they had made up their minds to send a deputation, which would probably arrive in a few minutes.

'That's all right, thank you!' said Monsieur Hennebeau. 'I shall want a report night and morning, you understand.'

As soon as Dansaert had gone, the joking began again, and they fell to on the Russian salad, saying that there was not a second to be lost if they ever hoped to finish it. But the fun reached its height when Négrel asked the maid for some bread and she answered with such a whispered and terrified 'Yessir!' that she might have had a band of murderers and ravishers behind her back.

'You can speak up,' said Madame Hennebeau sweetly, 'they are not here yet.'

Another packet of letters and dispatches had been brought

to the manager, who asked to be allowed to read one out. It was from Pierron, pointing out in respectful phraseology that he was obliged to go out on strike with his fellow workers for fear of being rough-handled, and adding that he had not been able to refuse to take part in the deputation, much as he deplored this move.

'And that's what they call freedom to work!' exclaimed Monsieur Hennebeau.

The talk came back to the strike, and he was asked his opinion.

'Oh,' he answered, 'we have seen plenty of them before. It will mean a week of idleness, or a fortnight at the most, like last time. They will hang about in the pubs and then go back to the pits when hunger begins to pinch.'

Monsieur Deneulin shook his head.

'I'm not so sure. They seem better organized this time. They've got a provident fund, haven't they?'

'Yes, but hardly three thousand francs. What can they do with that? I suspect that a fellow called Étienne Lantier is the ringleader. He is a good worker, and I should be sorry to have to sack him as I did the famous Rasseneur, who is still poisoning Le Voreux with his ideas and his beer. Never mind, half of them will have gone back at the end of a week, and the whole ten thousand of them will be down below in a fortnight.'

He was sure of it. His only worry was the chance of his getting into trouble if the Board held him responsible for the strike. For some time he had felt that he was losing favour. And so, abandoning the spoonful of Russian salad he had taken, he re-read the instructions from Paris, trying to see hidden meanings behind each word. He had to be excused if the meal was turning into a soldier's lunch, snatched on the battlefield before opening fire.

The ladies joined in the conversation. Madame Grégoire pitied the poor folk who were going to suffer hunger, and already Cécile could see herself distributing bread and meat coupons. But Madame Hennebeau was astonished at the talk of sufferings on the part of the Montsou miners. Were they not very fortunate? Why, they had lodging, fuel and medical attention at the Company's expense! In her indifference to this herd of cattle, all she knew about them was the lesson she had learned by heart and which she recited for the delight of visitors from Paris; and in the end she had come to believe it herself and was indignant at the people's ingratitude.

All this time Négrel went on scaring Monsieur Grégoire. Cécile did not displease him, and he was not averse to marrying her if it would please his aunt, but there was no passionate ardour about it, for, as he said to himself, he was an experienced man of the world who had grown out of losing his head. He called himself a republican, but that did not prevent his treating the workers with the utmost severity, and making fun of them in the presence of the ladies.

'I do not share my uncle's optimism either,' he said. 'I fear serious troubles. So, Monsieur Grégoire, I advise you to lock up La Piolaine. It might be looted.'

Just then, with the smile that always lit his kindly face, Monsieur Grégoire was vying with his wife in expressing paternal sentiments towards the miners.

'Looted? my house!' he cried, aghast. 'And why should they want to rob me?'

'Aren't you a shareholder in Montsou? You do no work, you live on the work of others – in fact, you are the accursed capitalist, and that is enough. You can be certain that if the revolution were to win it would force you to make restitution of your fortune as stolen money.'

Monsieur Grégoire suddenly lost the childlike tranquillity and serene indifference in which he lived. He stammered out:

'Stolen money! my fortune! But didn't my great-grandfather earn it, and with the sweat of his brow, this money he invested? Haven't we borne all the risks of the enterprise? Am I putting my money to bad use now?'

Madame Hennebeau, alarmed at seeing mother and daughter white with fear as well, hastened to intervene.

'Paul is joking, my dear sir.'

But Monsieur Grégoire was by now beside himself. As the servant was passing round a dish of crayfish, he took three without realizing what he was doing, and began breaking their claws with his teeth.

'Ah, I don't say that there aren't shareholders who abuse

their position. For instance, I have heard tales about Ministers receiving *deniers* in Montsou by way of bribes for services rendered to the Company. Or like the noble peer whose name I won't mention, a duke and the biggest of our shareholders, whose life is a scandal of extravagance – millions thrown away on women, orgies and useless luxury. . . . But people like us who live without any display, just as ordinary, decent people! We don't speculate, we are content to live sensibly with what we've got, sharing it with the poor! . . . Come, come, the workers would have to be proper rogues to rob us of a pin!'

Négrel himself had to reassure him, inwardly very amused at his panic. The crayfish were still going round, and the conversation moved on to politics to the accompaniment of the cracking of shells. Despite everything, and although he was still shuddering, Monsieur Grégoire declared himself a liberal and sighed for the days of Louis-Philippe. Deneulin was for a strong government, and in his opinion the Emperor was on the slippery slope of dangerous concessions.

'Remember '89,' he said. 'It was the aristocracy that made the revolution possible by its complicity, by flirting with philosophical novelties. Well, today it is the middle class playing the same foolish game, with its mania for liberalism, its insensate destructiveness and toadying to the people. . . . Yes, yes, you are sharpening the teeth of the monster so that it can devour us. And devour us it will, you mark my words!'

The ladies made him stop and tried to change the subject by asking for news of his daughters. Lucie was at Marchiennes, singing with a friend, Jeanne was painting the head of an old beggar. But he said all this absent-mindedly, keeping his eye on the manager who was absorbed in his dispatches and quite oblivious of his guests. Behind these sheets of paper was Paris and the Board of Directors, whose orders would decide the course of the strike, and Monsieur Deneulin could not help coming back to the subject on his mind.

'Well, what are you going to do?' he suddenly asked.

Monsieur Hennebeau started, then avoided the issue with a non-committal: 'We shall see.'

Deneulin went on thinking aloud 'No doubt; you are strong

and you can wait. But if the strike reaches Vandame I shall never recover. I have thoroughly modernized Jean-Bart, I know, but with only one pit I must have constant production in order to keep going. Oh, I'm not in for a very jolly time, I can assure you.'

This involuntary confession seemed to start Monsieur Hennebeau on a new train of thought. As he listened a new plan took shape in his mind: supposing the strike were to become more serious, why not utilize it and let things go from bad to worse until his neighbour was ruined, and then buy him up for a song? It was the most certain way of winning back favour with the directors, who had been dreaming of laying their hands on Vandame for years past.

'If Jean-Bart worries you to that extent,' he said with a smile, 'why not let us have it?'

Already Deneulin was sorry to have betrayed his fears:

'Never on your life!'

His violence made everybody laugh, and by the time dessert appeared the strike was at last forgotten. An apple charlotte meringue received the highest praise. The ladies then discussed a recipe in connexion with the pineapple, which was also declared to be exquisite. That feeling of mellow contentment at the end of a copious meal was rounded off by fruit, grapes and pears, and they were all merrily talking at once and the footman was pouring out a Rhenish wine instead of champagne, which was deemed commonplace.

In this mellow mood of dessert the marriage of Paul and Cécile certainly came a good step nearer. His aunt threw such meaning glances at the young man that he put on his most charming manner, and his honeyed attentions quite won back the Grégoires, who had been very depressed by his tales of plunder. Seeing the close understanding between his wife and nephew, Monsieur Hennebeau gave way for a moment to his horrible suspicion, as though he had surprised some guilty physical contact behind the glances they exchanged. But once again he was reassured by the sight of this marriage being settled here in front of his very eyes.

Hippolyte was serving coffee when the maid rushed in panic-stricken.

'Sir, sir! Here they are!'

It was the deputation. Doors banged and a cold breath of fear could almost be heard coming through the rooms.

'Show them into the drawing-room,' said Monsieur Hennebeau.

The guests sat round the table in silence, nervously looking at each other. Then they tried to resume their joking, pretending to put the rest of the sugar into their pockets and talking of hiding the cutlery. But the manager looked very grave and the laughter died down to a whisper as the heavy footsteps of the delegates could be heard on the drawing-room carpet next door.

Madame Hennebeau said softly to her husband:

'You are going to drink your coffee, I presume.'

'Of course. Let them wait.'

He was fidgety, listening to every sound, though apparently only concerned with his cup.

Paul and Cécile had risen from the table and he had made her peep through the keyhole. They whispered to each other, stifling their giggles.

'Can you see them?'

'Yes, a fat one, with two little ones behind.'

'Haven't they got frightful faces?'

'Oh no, they're very nice.'

Monsieur Hennebeau suddenly left his chair, saying that the coffee was too hot and that he would drink it afterwards. As he went out he put a finger on his lips to enjoin prudence. They all sat down again and stayed round the table, silent and not daring to move, straining their ears to catch the meaning of these loud, frightening male voices.

[2]

At a meeting held at Rasseneur's on the previous day Étienne and some of his mates had chosen the delegates to go next day to see the manager. On hearing that evening that her husband was a delegate, Maheude was very upset, asking whether he wanted to have them all thrown out on the street. Maheu himself had consented very reluctantly. However unjust their sufferings might be, when it came to action they both relapsed into the traditional resignation of their race, trembling for the morrow and preferring to bend their necks to the yoke. Usually Maheu relied on his wife's judgement in matters of practical behaviour, for she gave sound advice. But this time he resented it, especially as he secretly shared her misgivings.

'Oh, shut up, do!' he said, getting into bed and turning his back on her. 'A nice thing it would be to leave my mates in the lurch! I'm doing my duty.'

She got into bed too, and for a long time not a word was said. Then she answered:

'You are right, you must go. But you know, old boy, we're done for!'

They had a meal at noon because the meeting-place was the Avantage at one o'clock, and they were going on from there to Monsieur Hennebeau's house. There were potatoes, but as there was only a small piece of butter left, nobody touched it. It would go with the bread in the evening.

'You know we are relying on you to speak,' Étienne suddenly said to Maheu.

The latter was quite overcome; his emotion had taken away his voice.

'Oh no, that's too much!' said his wife. 'I don't mind his going, but I won't let him be the ringleader. Why him rather than anybody else?'

So Étienne explained with his eloquent enthusiasm. Maheu was the best collier in the pit, the most popular, the most respected, the one everybody quoted as an example of good sense. The miners' demands would carry weight if voiced by him. At first Étienne was to speak, but he had not been at Montsou long enough, and they would be more likely to listen to an old hand who had always lived there. In fact, the chaps were entrusting their interests to the best man, and he could not refuse; it would be cowardly.

Maheude waved her arm in despair.

'All right, you go, my man, and let yourself be done in for the sake of the others. I'm not stopping you!'

'But I could never do it,' stammered Maheu. 'I should say something silly.'

Étienne patted him on the shoulder, glad to have made him accept.

'Just say what you feel, it'll be all right!'

Grandpa Bonnemort, whose swollen legs were getting better, listened with his mouth full, shaking his head. There was a pause. Whenever there were potatoes for dinner, the children stuffed themselves to choking point and were very subdued. Having swallowed his mouthful the old man slowly murmured:

'Say what you like, it'll be the same as though you hadn't said anything. Oh, I've seen plenty of it, plenty of it I've seen, just like this! Forty years ago they chucked us out of the manager's door, and with swords, too! Today they'll most likely let you in, but they won't answer you, no more than that wall. Well, anyway, what do you expect? They've got the money, it doesn't matter to them!'

Another silence. Maheu and Étienne rose and left the family sitting gloomily in front of their empty plates. As they went out, they picked up Pierron and Levaque, and all four went together to Rasseneur's, where the delegates from the other villages were coming in twos and threes. When the twenty members of the deputation were all met, they drew up the counter-proposals they would make to the Company's conditions, and set out for Montsou. The keen north-east wind was sweeping the cobbled road. They arrived as it was striking two.

At first the footman told them to wait, and shut the door on them. Then he came back and led them into the drawing-room, pulling back the curtains. A soft light filtered through the lace. Left alone, the miners were afraid to sit down, but stood about awkwardly, all in their Sunday best and carefully shaved, with fair hair and moustaches, twisting their caps in their hands and throwing sidelong glances at the furniture, which was in that jumble of all the styles made fashionable by the craze for the antique: Henri II armchairs, Louis XV occasional chairs, a seventeenth-century Italian cabinet, a fifteenth-century Spanish *contador*, an altar-front draping the mantel-shelf, and old chasuble embroideries cut out and sewn on to the portières. The display of old gold, the tawny hues of old silks, and all this ecclesiastical splendour filled them with respectful awe. The deep pile of the oriental carpets seemed to cling to their feet. But the heat, above all, overwhelmed them: they could not understand this uniform heat given by the stoves, especially as their cheeks were stinging from the icy wind outside. Five minutes went by, and this discomfort increased in this sumptuous room so snugly closed to the outer world.

Monsieur Hennebeau came in at last, with his frock coat buttoned up in military fashion, and wearing on his lapel the little rosette of his decoration. He was the first to speak.

'Ah! – here you are! This is a revolt, it seems.'

He broke off to add with stiff politeness:

'Sit down. I am only too delighted to have a chat.'

The miners turned round looking for seats. A few ventured to sit on chairs, but most of them took fright at the look of the silken embroideries, and preferred to stand.

Another pause. Monsieur Hennebeau had moved an arm-chair in front of the chimney-piece and was now looking them rapidly up and down to try to place their faces. He recognized Pierron hiding in the back row, and his eyes came to rest on Étienne, seated in front of him.

'Well,' he said, 'what have you to say to me?'

He expected the young man to speak, and when Maheu came forward was so surprised that he could not help adding:

'What, you? One of the best workmen, who have always been so reasonable, an old inhabitant of Montsou whose family has been working here ever since the first blow was struck! Oh, I am sorry, I really am sorry to see you at the head of these malcontents.'

Maheu stood listening, looking at the floor. Then he began in low, diffident tones:

'Sir, it's just because I am a quiet man and nobody has anything against me that my mates have chosen me. That is enough to show you that this is not the work of a few agitators or bad lots trying to make trouble. We only want justice: we

212

are getting tired of dying of hunger, and it seems to us high time to come to some arrangement so that at any rate we get bread to eat every day.'

His voice gained strength, and he raised his eyes and looked straight at the manager:

'You know quite well that we cannot accept your new system. We are accused of not timbering properly, and it is quite true that we don't put in the necessary time on the work. But if we did, our day would be cut down still more, and as it doesn't give us enough to eat as it is, that would be the end of everything, the clean sweep that would finish all your men off. Pay us better and we shall timber better, and we shall put in the right number of hours at it instead of concentrating all the time on coal-getting, which is the only job that pays. There is no other possible way: if the work is to be done it must be paid for. . . . And what have you hit on instead? Something we can't possibly entertain, sir, don't you see? You cut down the price per tub and then pretend to make up for the cut by paying for timbering separately. Even if that were true, we should still be the losers because timbering always takes more time. But what makes us so angry is that it isn't even true: the Company doesn't compensate us at all, but simply pockets two centimes on every tub. So there you are!'

'Yes, yes, that's right,' chimed in the other delegates, seeing Monsieur Hennebeau trying to cut him short with a violent wave of the hand.

But it was Maheu who did the cutting short. Now that he was well launched the words came of themselves. At times he was surprised at the sound of his own voice, as though it were a stranger speaking inside him. Things stored up in his heart, that he did not even know were there, now came tumbling forth in a great outpouring of emotion. He spoke of their universal poverty, of the hard toil and brutish life, women and children crying out with hunger in their homes. He quoted the recent disastrous pay-days, the ridiculous wages of some of the fortnights, eaten into by fines and stoppages of work, and taken home to families in tears. Were they determined to kill all the miners off?

'And so, sir,' he concluded, 'we have come to say that,

death for death, we prefer to die in idleness. At any rate it is not so tiring. We have left the pits, and we shall not go down again unless the Company accepts our conditions. You want to cut the price per tub and pay separately for timbering. We want things to stay as they were, and moreover we want five centimes more per tub. Now it's up to you to show whether you are on the side of justice and the workers.'

The miners' voices rose in chorus:

'That's right. . . . He has said what we all feel. . . . We are only asking for what is right.'

Those who did not speak nodded in agreement. The sumptuous room with its gold and embroideries and its strange collection of antiques had disappeared, and they were no longer even conscious of the carpet beneath their heavy boots.

'Give me a chance to answer,' shouted Monsieur Hennebeau, who was beginning to lose his temper. 'To begin with, it is not true that the Company is making two centimes on each tub. Let's look at the figures.'

That led to a confused argument. In an attempt to divide them against themselves, the manager called upon Pierron, who muttered something non-committal. Levaque, on the other hand, voiced the sentiments of the most aggressive elements, and confused the issue by affirming facts that he knew nothing about. In this hot-house atmosphere the shouting was muffled by the rich hangings.

'If you all talk at once,' said Monsieur Hennebeau, 'we shall never get anywhere.'

He had now recovered his brusque politeness and calm, with no trace of bitterness; in fact, the manner of the administrator who has his instructions and means to have them respected. From the outset he had never taken his eyes off Étienne, and he was manoeuvring to draw him out of his self-imposed silence. To this end he now dropped the question of the two centimes and suddenly widened the basis of the discussion.

'No, why don't you own up to the truth – you are being led on by detestable agitators. It is a plague infecting all workers nowadays and corrupting even the best. . . . Oh, I am not asking anybody to admit anything, but I can see that you have been

214

changed; you used to be so contented. You have been promised more butter than bread, haven't you? And you have been told that it is your turn to be masters. . . . In fact, you have been recruited into this famous International, this band of criminals whose dream is the destruction of society.'

Then Étienne did break in:

'You are mistaken, sir. Not a single Montsou miner has yet joined. But if they are forced into it, every pit will join. It depends on the Company.'

From then onwards the struggle was between Monsieur Hennebeau and Étienne, as though the other miners were no longer there.

'The Company watches over its men like Providence, and you are very wrong to threaten it. This year it has spent three hundred thousand francs on building new housing estates, and that does not bring in two per cent, and I am not counting the pensions it pays out, nor the free coal and free medical attention. You seem to be intelligent and in a few months you have become one of our most highly-skilled men, but wouldn't you be better employed in spreading truths like that than in ruining your prospects by getting mixed up with notoriously bad characters? Yes, I am referring to Rasseneur, whom we had to get rid of to save our pits from socialist corruption. You are always at his place, and no doubt it is he who has urged you to start up this provident fund, which we were perfectly willing to allow if it was simply a means of saving. But as we see it, this fund is a weapon against us, a reserve fund in anticipation of the costs of war. And while we are on the subject, I must add that the Company means to exercise some sort of check on that fund.'

Étienne let him talk on, looking him straight in the eyes, but his mouth was twitching nervously. The last phrase made him smile, and he answered:

'That, sir, is a fresh imposition, for up to now you have omitted to ask for any such check. Unfortunately, our wish is that the Company should look after us a little less. Instead of playing the part of Providence, we simply want it to play fair by giving us our due, the profits we make which at present it is sharing out for itself. Is it right, whenever a crisis comes, to let the workers die of starvation so as to keep the shareholders' dividends intact? However you put it, sir, the new system is a disguised wage-cut, and that is what we are up against, for if the Company must economize, it is quite wrong for it to do so wholly at the workers' expense.'

'Ah, here it comes!' exclaimed Monsieur Hennebeau. 'I was expecting this accusation of starving the people and living on their toil and sweat! How can you say such stupid things when you ought to realize what enormous risks capital runs in industry, for example in the mines? Today a properly equipped pit costs anything from fifteen hundred thousand to two millions, to say nothing of all the trouble and anxiety before a meagre return comes in from all that money sunk! Nearly half the mining companies in France are bankrupt. Besides it is foolish to accuse the successful ones of cruelty. If their workmen suffer they suffer themselves. Do you think that the Company hasn't as much to lose in the present crisis as you have? It cannot fix wages as it likes, it must be competitive or go under. Why don't you blame the facts instead of the Company? But you won't listen, you refuse to understand.'

'On the contrary, we understand perfectly that there is no chance of improvement for us as long as things go on as they are now. Indeed, it is for that very reason that sooner or later the workers will see to it that things are managed differently.'

This remark, so moderate in form, was said in a low voice, trembling with such conviction and implied threats that everybody was reduced to silence, and a wave of embarrassment and fear could be felt in the quiet room. The other delegates had not followed very well, but sensed that their comrade had asked for their share of all this comfort, and once again they cast sidelong glances at the warm hangings, the comfortable chairs, and all this luxury, the most trifling knick-knack of which would have kept them in soup for a month.

Monsieur Hennebeau, after sitting for some moments in thought, rose to show them out. They all stood up. But Étienne had gently nudged Maheu in the elbow, and the latter began in a tongue-tied and awkward manner:

'So that's all you have to answer, sir. . . . We shall have to tell the others that you reject our terms.'

'But my dear fellow,' exclaimed the manager, 'it isn't me! I am not rejecting anything. I am just a paid servant like you and I have no more say in all this than the youngest of your pit-boys. I am given my orders, and my job is to see them properly carried out. I have told you what I felt I ought to say, but the decision is not in my hands. . . . You bring me your demands, I shall pass them on to the Board of Directors and then I shall let you know their answer.'

He was now using his correct administrative manner, avoiding personal emotion, with the curt politeness of a mere instrument of authority. And by now the miners were looking suspiciously at him, wondering what he was up to and what interest he could have in lying to them, what he was making out of standing between them and the real masters. He must be some sort of intriguer, presumably, to be paid like a workman but to live so well!

Étienne made bold to intervene once more:

'You see, sir, what a pity it is that we cannot plead our cause in person. We could explain many things and use arguments which naturally mean nothing to you. If only we knew whom we ought to see!'

Monsieur Hennebeau did not take offence. He even smiled.

'Oh, well, it gets awkward if you have no confidence in me. . . . You will have to go down there.'

The delegates looked at his hand pointing vaguely to one of the windows. Where was 'down there'? Paris, presumably. But they could not say for sure; the whole question was receding into some distant and terrifying place, some far off, metaphysical region where the unknown god was crouching on his throne in the depths of the tabernacle. They would never see this god, but they felt him as a power, weighing down from afar on the ten thousand miners of Montsou. And when the manager spoke, he had this hidden power behind him and pronounced its oracles.

They were profoundly discouraged, and even Étienne shrugged his shoulders as if to say that the best thing to do was to go. Monsieur Hennebeau was tapping Maheu's arm in a friendly way and asking about Jeanlin.

'Now there's a terrible lesson for you, and yet you defend

faulty timbering! . . . Think it over, my friends, and you will realize that a strike would be a disaster for all concerned. You will be dying with hunger before a week is out, and then how will you manage? However, I rely on your good sense, and am convinced that you will go back into the pits by Monday at the latest.'

They all made their way out, leaving the room with bowed heads like a herd of animals, saying not a word in answer to this hope of their giving in. The manager, as he saw them out, had to wind up the discussion himself: the Company on the one hand with its new wage-scheme, the men on the other with their demand for an increase of five centimes per tub. So as to leave them under no misapprehension, he felt it his duty to warn them that their terms would certainly be rejected by the Board.

'Think it out before doing anything rash,' he repeated, for their silence worried him.

In the hall Pierron bowed obsequiously, but Levaque deliberately put on his cap. Maheu was trying to find some parting word, but once again Étienne nudged him on. They all went off in ominous silence. The only sound was the bang of the door closing behind them.

Monsieur Hennebeau went back into the dining-room and found his guests sitting glum and silent, with liqueurs in front of them. He explained the position briefly to Deneulin, who looked even more depressed. Then, while he was drinking his cold coffee, they tried to change the subject. But even the Grégoires came back to the strike, expressing their astonishment that there was no law to prevent workpeople from leaving their work. Paul reassured Cécile by saying that they expected the police.

At length Madame Hennebeau summoned the footman:

'Hippolyte, before we go into the drawing-room, open the windows and let in a little air.'

A FORTNIGHT had gone by, and on the Monday of the third week the lists sent up to the manager showed a new decrease in the number of men underground. It had been expected that work would be resumed that morning, but the miners were exasperated by the unyielding obstinacy of the Board. Le Voreux, Crèvecœur, Mirou and Madeleine were not the only idle pits; by now scarcely a quarter of the men had gone down into La Victoire and Feutry-Cantel, and even Saint-Thomas was affected. The strike was steadily spreading.

At Le Voreux the yard was wrapped in heavy silence. It was like a dead factory; the great workings were empty and abandoned and everything was at a standstill. Beneath the grey December sky three or four forgotten tubs were standing on the raised track with the mute sadness of inanimate objects. Lower down, between the slender uprights of the trestles, the stock of coal was running out, leaving the earth bare and black, whilst the stack of pit-props was rotting in the rain. A half-loaded barge by the canal wharf looked asleep in the dirty water, and on the deserted pit-bank, where decomposing sulphide was smoking despite the rain, a cart thrust its shafts up into the air drearily. But it was above all the buildings that seemed frozen in torpor; the screening-shed with its shutters closed, the headgear which no longer heard the rumbling sounds of the pithead, the cold boiler-house and the great chimney now too large for the occasional wisps of smoke. The winding-engine only worked in the morning, for the ponymen had to go down with fodder for their beasts, and deputies, who were the only men now working underground, had to act as ordinary labourers and keep an eye open for accidents that might damage the roads now that they were not being regularly looked after. From nine o'clock onwards any other journeys had to be made by ladder. Above these dead buildings, shrouded in black dust, the only sound was the slow heavy panting of the exhaust of the pump, all that remained of the life of the pit, which would be destroyed by water if the panting stopped.

On the high ground opposite, Village Two Hundred and Forty seemed dead, too. The Prefect had come from Lille, police had patrolled the roads, but in view of the quietness of the strikers Prefect and police had gone back home. Never had the village set such a good example in the great plain. The men slept all day so as not to go to the pubs, and the women, through having had to ration themselves with coffee, had become much more sensible and less furiously talkative and quarrelsome. Even the gangs of children seemed to understand, and behaved so well that they ran about barefoot and hit each other with the minimum of noise. The word of command had been repeated and sent round: exemplary behaviour.

However, the Maheus' house was always full of people coming and going. Étienne, as secretary, had used it as headquarters for sharing out the three thousand francs of the fund amongst necessitous families, and a few hundred francs more had come in from various sources like subscriptions and collections. But now all resources were drying up; the men had no money left to carry on the strike, and hunger was staring them in the face. Maigrat had promised everybody a fortnight's credit, but had changed his mind at the end of a week and cut off supplies. He usually took his orders from the Company, which probably wanted to make a speedy end of it all by starving the villages. Moreover he acted like a capricious tyrant, giving bread or withholding it according to the face of the girl sent by her parents for provisions; and he shut his door on Maheude in particular, full of resentment and determined to take it out of her because he had not had Catherine. And as the last straw, it was freezing hard, and the women watched their shrinking coal supplies with the anxious thought that they would not be renewed so long as the men did not go to work. It wasn't enough to die of hunger, they were going to freeze to death as well.

Already everything had run short at the Maheus'. The Levaques still had something to eat thanks to a twenty-franc piece lent by Bouteloup. The Pierrons still had money, of course, but fearing they might be called upon for loans they put on outward appearances of being as hard up as everybody else and bought food on credit from Maigrat, who would have thrown all his shop at Pierronne if she had shown him a bit of her skirt. By Saturday many families had gone to bed supperless. But although they could see terrible days setting in, not a single person uttered a complaint; everybody obeyed orders quietly and courageously. Despite all, there was absolute confidence, religious faith, the blind self-dedication of a community of believers. Since they had been promised the new era of justice, they were prepared to suffer for the conquest of happiness for all. Hunger filled their souls with mystic elation; never before had the closed-in horizon opened out a broader vision of the beyond before these poor people, now light-headed from misery. Though their eyes were dim with weakness they perceived over yonder the ideal city of their dreams, now drawing near and almost real, where all men were brothers, a golden age when work and food would be shared by all. Nothing could shake their conviction that they were at last on the threshold. The fund was exhausted, the Company would never budge, each day could only make the situation worse; and still they kept their hope and smiled scornfully at hard facts. If the earth were to open beneath their feet they would be saved by a miracle. Their faith was bread and warmth enough. When the Maheus and the rest had gulped down their clear water soup too fast, they floated away into a kind of trance, the same ecstatic vision of the promised land which threw the martyrs of old to the wild beasts.

From now on Étienne was the undisputed leader. As study sharpened his intellect and enabled him to speak on all subjects with authority, the evening conversations became oracles which he delivered. He spent his nights reading and received more and more letters; he had even begun subscribing to *Le Vengeur*, a Belgian socialist paper, and this, the first paper of its kind to be seen in the village, had earned him a position of extraordinary prestige among his mates. Every day his popularity grew, and every day he felt more elated. To be carrying on an extensive correspondence, discussing the fate of workers in the four corners of the province, giving consultations to the miners of Le Voreux, above all to be a centre and feel the

221

world pivoting on oneself, a mere ex-mechanic and collier with black, greasy hands, all this naturally flattered his vanity. In reality he was climbing a rung of the social ladder into the ranks of the detested bourgeoisie, with an intellectual satisfaction and feeling of well-being which he dared not admit to himself. He still had one cause for uneasiness, his lack of education, consciousness of which made him awkward and nervous as soon as he was with a gentleman in a black coat. He went on studying voraciously, but his lack of method made real learning slow, and his mind was becoming so muddled that he found that he knew things by heart that he had not understood. And so in his more self-critical moments had had doubts about his mission and feared that he might not after all be the man the world was waiting for. Perhaps that man ought to be a lawyer, a learned man able to speak and act without compromising his fellow workers? But then a reaction soon restored his self-esteem. No, no, they didn't want lawyers! All lawyers were rogues using their knowledge to enrich themselves at the people's expense. Come what may, the workers must manage their own affairs. Thereupon he found renewed delight in his dream of becoming a popular leader: Montsou at his feet, Paris in the mists of the future, who could tell? member of parliament some day, the dais of some great hall where he visualized himself castigating the bourgeois in the first speech made in parliament by a working man.

During the past few days Étienne had been perplexed. Pluchart had written letter after letter, offering to come to Montsou and inspire the strikers with new zeal. He suggested that a private meeting might be arranged, with Étienne in the chair. His underlying idea was to exploit the strike and win the men over to the International, towards which so far they had shown themselves very lukewarm. Étienne was afraid of a disturbance, but all the same he would have let Pluchart come had not this move been violently criticized by Rasseneur. Strong though his position was, the young man had to reckon with the publican, whose services to the cause dated back further than his own, and who still had his supporters among his customers. So he still hesitated, not knowing what to reply.

On this particular Monday, at about four, another letter

came from Lille while Étienne was alone in the downstairs room with Maheude. Her husband, chafing at the inactivity, had gone off fishing, for if he was lucky enough to catch a good fish below the canal lock he could sell it and buy bread. Old Bonnemort and young Jeanlin had sallied forth to try out their newly restored legs, whilst the children were with Alzire, who spent hours and hours on the pit-bank, gleaning for cinders. By the tiny fire, which they dare not attempt to mend, Maheude was sitting with her dress unbuttoned, one breast hanging down to her stomach, feeding Estelle.

When Étienne had folded up the letter she asked:

'Good news? Are they sending us any money?'

He shook his head, and she went on:

'I don't know how we are going to get through this week. . . . . Still, we'll hold out somehow. When you have right on your side it gives you strength, doesn't it? And you are bound to win in the end.'

By now she was more or less in favour of the strike. It would have been better still if they could have stayed at work and yet forced the Company to be fair. But since they had stopped, they should not start again before seeing justice done. On this point she was quite uncompromising. Better die than appear to have been wrong when you were right!

'Ah,' exclaimed Étienne, 'if only a nice outbreak of cholera would rid us of all these slave-driving Directors!'

'No, no,' she replied, 'we mustn't wish for anybody's death. It wouldn't get us anywhere, either, for some more would spring up in their place. All I ask is that they come round to a more sensible way of thinking, and that's what I expect will happen, because there are decent people in all walks of life. . . . You know I don't hold at all with your politics.'

In fact, she always blamed his violent language and thought he was aggressive. To get one's work paid for at a proper rate, well and good, but why concern oneself with all sorts of other questions – the bourgeois, the government? Why interfere with other people's business when you could only bring harm on yourself? But she respected him, nevertheless, because he did not drink and paid his forty-five francs regularly. When a man was steady you could overlook a lot of other things.

Then Étienne talked about a republic, which would guarantee a living wage for everybody. But Maheude shook her head, for she could remember 1848, the hell of a year that had left her and her husband stripped naked as worms in the early days of their married life. She talked on, telling him about those troubled days in a mournful voice, gazing into space and her breast still bare, whilst Estelle was falling asleep on her lap, still sucking. Étienne could not take his eyes off this huge breast, which contrasted with the worn and yellow skin of her face.

'We hadn't a farthing,' she murmured, 'nothing to eat and work stopped in all the pits. It was just death for poor people, same as now!'

But at that moment the door opened and they were speechless with surprise to see Catherine come in. She had never been back to the village since the day she ran off with Chaval. She was so overcome with emotion that she forgot to shut the door behind her, but stood there mute and trembling, for she had expected to find her mother alone, and the sight of the young man had driven the carefully prepared speech right out of her head.

'What have you come here for?' said Maheude, without even getting up. 'I've done with you, clear out!'

Catherine tried to remember her speech:

'Mother, here's some coffee and sugar. . . . Yes, for the children. . . . I've made something on overtime, and I thought that they . . .'

She took out of her pocket a pound of coffee and a pound of sugar, and ventured to put them on the table. It worried her very much that there was a strike at Le Voreux whereas she was working at Jean-Bart, and this was the only way she could think of to help her parents while pretending to think of the children. But her kindness did not disarm her mother, who countered:

'Instead of bringing us presents you would have done better to stay at home and earn us some bread.'

Then she relieved her pent-up feelings by heaping abuse upon her daughter, and saying to her face all the things she had been saying about her for the past month. The idea of running off with a man and getting tied up at sixteen when you have a family in want! Only the most unnatural child could think of such a thing! You could forgive one piece of silliness, but no mother could ever forget a trick like this. You could have understood if she had been kept on a lead! But no, not a bit of it! She had been free as air, the only thing she had been asked to do was come home to sleep.

'Tell me, what's come over you, at your age?'

Catherine stood by the table and listened, hanging her head. A shudder ran through her thin, undeveloped body, and she tried to answer in disjointed words:

'Oh, if it was only me . . . what fun do you think I get out of it? It's him. What he wants I have to want as well, don't I? Because he's the strongest, you see. . . . How can you tell how things turn out? Anyhow it's done now and can't be undone. Just as soon him as anybody else, now. He'll have to marry me.'

She went on trying to justify herself, without bitterness, with the passive resignation of the girl who has to submit to the male at an early age. It was the usual thing, wasn't it? She had never imagined it would be anything else – raped behind the slag-heap, a baby at sixteen and then a poverty-stricken home if her lover married her. And the only reason why she was blushing with shame and trembling was that she was being treated like a whore in front of this young man, whose presence filled her with hopeless misery.

Meanwhile Étienne had risen and was busying himself trying to mend the remainder of the fire so as not to embarrass her in her explanations. But their eyes met, and he thought how pale she looked, and worn out, and yet pretty, with her eyes looking so bright in her tanned face; and he felt a strange emotion from which all bitterness had gone, and only a wish to see her happy with the man she had preferred to him. He still wanted to look after her, to go to Montsou and force the other fellow to be kind to her. But all she could see in the affection he was still offering her was pity – how he must despise her to look at her like that! Her heart was so full that her voice failed her and she could find no other excuses to stammer out.

225

'That's right, you'd much better keep your mouth shut,' went on her mother implacably. 'If you have come back for good, well, come in; if not, then clear off at once and think yourself lucky that I'm taken up with the baby, otherwise I would have put my foot somewhere before this!'

As though this threat had suddenly been realized, Catherine received a flying kick in the behind; so violent that she was stunned with surprise and pain. It was Chaval, who had leapt in through the open door and charged at her like a wild beast. He had been watching outside for the last minute or two.

'You bitch!' he bawled, 'I've followed you. I knew you came back here to get him to fill you up. And you pay him to do it, do you? You pour coffee down him out of my money!'

Maheude and Étienne were too thunderstruck to move. Chaval was furiously driving Catherine towards the door.

'Will you get out, blast your eyes!'

As she went and cowered in a corner he turned on the mother: 'A nice business, keeping watch while your bitch of a daughter has her legs in the air upstairs!'

He seized Catherine by the wrist and jerked her towards the door. In the doorway he turned again on Maheude, who was still rooted to her chair and had forgotten to put back her breast. Estelle had fallen forward in her sleep and buried her face in her mother's woollen skirt. The great bare breast was hanging free like the udder of a huge cow.

'When the daughter's not at it the mother gets herself plugged!' he shouted. 'Go on, show him all you've got! He's not particular, is your filthy lodger!'

Étienne rushed to hit him. Only the fear of rousing the whole village by a fight had prevented his snatching Catherine out of this man's hands. But it was now his turn to fly into a rage, and the two men stood face to face with eyes blazing. Their old hatred and repressed jealousy now flared up. It was clear that one of them would have to kill the other.

'Take care,' Étienne muttered through clenched teeth, 'I'll do you in!'

'Just you try!' answered Chaval.

For several seconds they stood glaring at each other, so close that each could feel the other's hot breath. Catherine

226

seized her lover's hand in mute supplication and dragged him outside and away from the village, without a glance behind.

'What a brute!' said Étienne, slamming the door. He was so angry that he had to drop into a chair.

Maheude was still motionless in front of him. She waved her arm in a sweeping gesture and there fell one of those painful silences, heavy with unspoken thoughts. Try as they might to avoid it, his eyes kept coming back to her breast, that expanse of flesh the dazzling whiteness of which embarrassed him. She might well be forty and shapeless from having too many children, but many still admired her with her firm, strong-looking body and large, long face that had once been beautiful. She had slowly and calmly taken her breast in both hands and put it back into her dress. A pink corner refused to go in, and she pushed it with her finger and buttoned herself up, and was now black and sloppy again in her old jacket.

'He's a swine,' she said at last. 'Only a dirty swine could have such filthy ideas. Not that I care! It wasn't worth answering.'

Without taking her eyes off the young man she went on in a straightforward tone:

'Not that I haven't my faults, of course, but not that one. . . . Only two men have ever touched me: a trammer years ago when I was fifteen, and then Maheu. If he had left me in the lurch like the other one, well, I don't know what might have happened. And I'm not all that proud of having been loyal to him since we were married, because when you've done no wrong the reason often is that you've never had the chance. I'm only saying how it is, and I know some of our neighbours who couldn't say as much, could they?'

'Yes, that's true,' said Étienne, getting up to go.

And out he went, while she made up her mind to light the fire again, having put down the sleeping Estelle on two chairs. If Dad had caught and sold a fish they might be able to have some soup after all.

Outside night was already falling, a freezing night, and Étienne walked on with his head down, feeling desperately sad. It was no longer just anger with the man and pity for the poor, ill-treated girl. The brutal scene itself faded into insignificance, but it forced his mind back to the sufferings of all of them, the abomination of poverty. In his mind's eye he saw the village without food and these women and children who would have nothing to eat that night, all these starving people fighting on. And in the horrible, gloomy twilight the doubts that he had already felt at times rose again within him and tortured him with misgivings he had never had so strongly before. What a terrible responsibility he had shouldered! Was he to urge them on to still more obstinate resistance, now that there was no money and no credit left? And what would be the end of it all if no help were forthcoming and hunger got the better of their courage? Suddenly he saw a vision of disaster: children dying, weeping mothers, and the men, thin and haggard, going back to the pits. On and on he walked, stumbling over stones, and the thought that the Company would prevail and that he would have brought about the misfortune of his mates filled him with unbearable anguish.

He looked up and found himself in front of Le Voreux. Its buildings rose in a dark mass in the deepening gloom. The deserted yard, in the middle of which stood great motionless shadows, looked like the corner of an abandoned fortress. As soon as the winding engine stopped, these walls lost their soul. At this hour of the night there was nothing left alive, not a single lamp or voice; the very exhaust of the pump sounded like the gasps of the dying, coming from some far-off part of the emptiness that was once a pit.

As he looked, Étienne's spirits rose again. The worker might be dying of hunger, but the Company also was eating into its millions. Was it inevitable that it should be the stronger in this war of labour against money? At all events, its victory would cost it dear and it would have its casualties, too. Once again he felt the fury of battle, the fierce desire to have done with suffering for good, even if the price were death. The village might just as well die straight away as die little by little of starvation and injustice. His ill-digested reading came back into his mind, with examples of people burning their own towns to halt the enemy, vague stories of mothers saving their children from slavery by dashing their brains out on the pavements, or of men deliberately starving to death rather than eat the bread of tyrants. How inspiring they were! A red gaiety succeeded his black melancholy, casting out doubt and making him ashamed of his momentary weakness. And in this revival of his faith, gusts of pride wafted him higher and higher, carried aloft by the joy of leadership, of being obeyed to the point of sacrifice, and his dream broadened out to a vision of his own power on the night of triumph. Already he saw in his mind's eye a scene of simple grandeur: himself as a triumphant leader renouncing power and placing all authority in the hands of the people.

Then he was rudely awakened by the voice of Maheu recounting his good luck; he had caught a wonderful trout and sold it for three francs. There would be some supper after all. He let his friend go back to the village, saying he would follow on later, and went and sat down in the Avantage. After a customer had gone he told Rasseneur, without any beating about the bush, that he was going to write and ask Pluchart to come at once. He had made up his mind to organize a private meeting, for victory seemed assured if only the miners of Montsou would solidly join the International.

[4]

THE meeting was fixed for the following Thursday at two o'clock at the Bon Joyeux, widow Désir's place. The widow was outraged at the sufferings inflicted upon her children the miners and, especially since her custom had fallen off, her anger had never cooled. Never had a strike been less thirsty; even the drunkards shut themselves up at home for fear of disobeying the command to keep sober. Montsou, packed solid on fair-days, was now silent and dismal with its broad street stretching on in endless desolation. No more beer pouring from counters and bellies, the gutters had dried up. From the pavement outside Casimir's and the Progrès, all that could be seen was the pale faces of the barmaids hopefully looking out at the street. In Montsou itself the whole line of pubs was empty, from Lenfant's to Tison's, passing by Piquette's and the Tête-Coupée. It was only at Saint-Éloi, where the deputies forgathered, that a few glasses were still being served. The solitude even extended to the Volcan, the ladies of which were resting for want of gentlemen admirers, although they would willingly have lowered their fee from ten sous to five in view of the hard times. The whole neighbourhood was sunk in blackest despair.

'My God!' widow Désir had exclaimed, slapping her thighs with both hands, 'it's all the fault of the police! They can bung me in prison if they want to, but I must go for them all the same.'

To her all authorities, all employers were policemen, a term of general contempt which covered all enemies of the people. So she had welcomed Étienne's proposition with delight: her whole house belonged to the miners, she would let them have her ballroom free of charge, she would issue invitations herself since that was the law. And if the law took exception, well, so much the better, she would give the law a bit of her mind. The next day Étienne brought her fifty letters to sign, having had them copied by those neighbours in the village who could write, and these letters were sent off to the delegates and some other safe men in the pits. Ostensibly the agenda was to discuss the continuation of the strike, but in reality Pluchart was expected, and it was hoped that a speech from him would produce a mass recruitment to the International.

On Thursday morning Étienne was very worried because his old foreman had not come, for he had telegraphed to say that he would be there on Wednesday. What could be the matter? He was very disappointed not to be able to talk things over with him before the meeting. By nine o'clock he was in Montsou, thinking that Pluchart had perhaps gone there direct without calling at Le Voreux.

'No, I've not seen your friend,' answered widow Désir. 'But everything is ready, come and have a look.'

She led him into the dance-hall. The decorations were still the same: paper chains meeting in a wreath of artificial flowers in the middle of the ceiling, gold cardboard shields round the walls, with saints' names. But instead of the musicians' platform a table and three chairs had been put in a corner and rows of seats faced them, crossing the hall obliquely.

'Perfect,' declared Étienne.

'And you know you are quite at home,' she went on; 'you can bawl your heads off if you like, and if the police come they will have to pass over my dead body.'

Anxious as he was, he could not help smiling at the look of her; she seemed so vast, with a pair of breasts each one of which required a man to embrace it. Rumour had it that nowadays she had to have two of her weekday lovers each night to cope with the job.

But to his surprise Rasseneur and Souvarine came in, and as the widow was going out to leave the three of them together in the hall, he exclaimed:

'What, you already!'

Souvarine, who had been on the night shift at Le Voreux as the engineman were not on strike, had simply come out of curiosity. But Rasseneur had been looking ill at ease for two days past, and his fat round face had lost its good-natured smile.

'Pluchart hasn't turned up and I am very worried,' Étienne went on.

The publican looked away and muttered awkwardly:

'I'm not surprised. I am not expecting him now.'

'What?'

Then Rasseneur took the plunge, looked Étienne squarely in the face and said jauntily:

'You see, I sent him a letter, too, if you want to know, and urged him not to come. . . . Yes, I think we ought to settle our own affairs and not drag strangers in.'

Étienne, trembling and beside himself with rage, looked his companion in the eyes and all he could find to say was:

'You have done that! You have done that!'

'Yes, I've done that! And yet, you know, I've every confidence in Pluchart. He's clever and reliable and a man you can work with. But then, you see, I don't give a damn for your ideas – politics, government and all that – not a damn! What I want is to see the miners better treated. I worked underground myself for twenty years, and I sweated so much with

231

poverty and fatigue that I have sworn I'll get some of the pleasures of life for the poor buggers who are down there still; and I am quite sure that you will never get anything with all your talk, you will only make the miner's lot even worse. When he is forced down again by starvation the Company will bleed him still more, and thrash him like a cur that has escaped and is being driven back to his kennel. And that's what I mean to prevent, do you understand?'

He stood there foursquare on his thick legs, belly thrust forward and shouting at the top of his voice. And all the reasonable and patient nature of the man poured itself forth in clear, effortless phrases as he made his confession of faith. Surely it was stupid to think that the world could be changed at one blow, the workers put in the place of the employers and money shared out like dividing up an apple? It would need perhaps thousands and thousands of years for that to come about. So don't let anyone talk to him about miracles! The wisest course, if you didn't want to come a cropper, was to go straight ahead with demanding feasible reforms and bettering the workers' conditions as and when the chances arose. So he was making it his business to bring the Company round to better conditions, whereas, if they were pig-headed about it – well, they would all go under!

Étienne had let him talk on, too indignant to utter a sound. At last he cried:

'God Almighty! haven't you got any blood in your veins?'

For a moment he was on the point of striking him, and to resist the temptation he worked off his fury on the seats, striding down the hall and knocking them out of the way.

'You might at least shut the door,' said Souvarine. 'There's no need for everybody to hear.'

He went and shut it himself and then calmly sat on one of the platform seats. He rolled a cigarette and sat watching the others with his gentle, intelligent eyes, and his lips were pursed in a wry smile.

'You can lose your temper as much as you like, but it doesn't get us anywhere,' observed Rasseneur judiciously. 'At first I thought you had some sense. You did well to urge the chaps to keep calm and not leave their own houses, in fact to

232

use your influence to maintain order. But now you are going to land them in the soup!'

In the intervals of careering up and down between the seats Étienne came up to the publican, took him by the shoulders and shook him, shouting answers in his face.

'But damn it all, I *am* for being calm! Yes, I have imposed discipline on them and I am still advising them to lie low. But we can't just let those people snap their bloody fingers at us. You are fortunate enough to keep cool, but as for me there are times when I feel I'm going off my head.'

It was now his turn to make a confession. He made fun of his own early illusions, his religious dream of universal compassion when justice would speedily come and reign over the brotherhood of mankind. A fine method, indeed, to wait with folded arms if you wanted to see men devour each other like wolves for ever and ever! No, you had to take a hand in it yourself or else injustice would never end and the rich would always suck the blood of the poor. That was why he could not forgive himself for having once been so silly as to say that politics should be banished from the social question. He was ignorant then, but since that time he had read books and studied. Now his ideas were mature, and he flattered himself that he had a system. But he expressed it badly, in confused phrases which kept bits of all the theories he had worked through and abandoned. At the summit stood unshakeable the idea of Karl Marx: capital was the result of theft, and labour had the duty and the right to recover its stolen wealth. In practice, like Proudhon, he had first of all been taken in by the dream of mutual credit – a vast bank of exchange which would cut out middlemen. But later he had been enthralled by the co-operative societies of Lassalle, subsidized by the state and gradually transforming the world into one great industrial city – until one day he had lost his taste for them on realizing the difficulty of control – and more recently still he had reached the stage of collectivism and demanded that all instruments of work be handed over to collective ownership. But all that remained very vague, and he could not see how to realize this new dream, for he was still held back by scruples of human feeling and commonsense and did not dare to advance the uncompromising affirmations of the fanatics. He was therefore still at the stage of saying that first of all the government must be taken over. After that they would see.

'But what has come over you? Why have you gone over to the bourgeois?' he went on violently, coming back and holding forth at Rasseneur. 'You yourself used to say that it would have to come to a show-down!'

Rasseneur coloured slightly.

'Yes, I did say that once. And if it does come to a show-down you will see that I am no more of a coward than anybody else. Only I will not side with people who trouble the waters still more so as to fish themselves a position. . . .'

It was Étienne's turn to colour. The two men had now given up shouting at each other and were coldly bitter and spiteful in their open rivalry. In fact it was what always lies at the bottom of exaggerated dogmas: one man runs to revolutionary violence and the other, by way of reaction, to insincere moderation, and both get carried far beyond their genuine convictions simply because they find themselves cast for parts not of their own choosing. On the fair, girlish face of Souvarine, watching these two, appeared an expression of silent scorn, the crushing scorn of the man prepared to sacrifice his own life in obscurity without even the glory of a martyr's crown.

'That's meant for me I suppose?' said Étienne. 'Are you jealous?'

'Jealous of what?' answered Rasseneur. 'I don't set myself up as a great man, I'm not trying to found a section at Montsou so as to be the secretary!'

Ignoring the other's attempts to interrupt him he went on:

'Why don't you be honest? You don't care a damn about the International, all you are longing for is to be our leader and play the gentleman writing letters to the famous Conseil Fédéral du Nord!'

After a pause Étienne replied, trembling with passion:

'All right. . . . I thought I had nothing to reproach myself with. I always consulted you because I knew you had been struggling here long before me. But as you can't bear anyone else on the stage with you, from now on I shall act on my own. And to start with, I am telling you now that this meeting is going on, even if Pluchart doesn't turn up, and that the comrades will join in spite of you.'

'Join!' murmured the publican; 'easier said than done – you've got to get their subscriptions out of them!'

'Oh no, I haven't! The International grants time to workers on strike. We can pay later, but it will come to our help at once.'

This made Rasseneur lose his temper altogether.

'Very well, we'll see. . . . I'm part of this meeting of yours, and I'm going to speak. Yes, I'm not going to let all our friends have their heads turned by you! I'm going to show them where their real interests lie. We shall see which one they mean to follow – me, whom they've known for thirty years, or you who have turned everything upside down in less than one. No, no, that be damned for a tale! We are going to see which of us will smash the other!'

He went out, banging the door, making the paper chains tremble under the ceiling and the gilt shields jump on the walls. And the big hall was once again wrapped in heavy silence.

Sitting at the table Souvarine was smoking peacefully. After striding up and down for a minute or two in silence, Étienne relieved his feelings in a torrent of words. Was it his fault that people deserted that fat lazy devil and turned to him? He denied that he had hunted for popularity, he didn't even know how it had come about – the friendship of everybody in the village, the miners' confidence in him and his present power over them. He was indignant that anyone should accuse him of wanting to stir up trouble to satisfy his own ambitions, and thumped his chest, protesting sentiments of fraternity.

Suddenly he stood still in front of Souvarine and said:

'Don't you see, if I were capable of causing any friend of mine to lose a single drop of blood I would run off to America straight away!'

The engineman shrugged his shoulders and once again smiled his thin smile.

'Oh, blood,' he said, 'what does blood matter? The earth needs some blood.'

Étienne calmed down at once, took a chair and sat opposite him with his elbows on the table. This fair face, with the dreamy eyes that sometimes lit up with fierce red glints, frightened him and at the same time exercised some strange fascination over his will-power. His friend did not even need to speak, for his very silence seemed gradually to dominate Étienne.

'Look here,' he asked, 'what would you do in my place? I am right to want to do something, aren't I? Surely the best thing is for us to join the Association?'

Souvarine slowly blew out a cloud of smoke and answered with his favourite word:

'Balderdash! but in the meantime it's something. What's more, their International will soon begin to work. He is interested in it.'

'Who?'

'He.'

Souvarine had pronounced this word in a hushed voice, full of religious awe, turning his eyes towards the east. He was referring to the Master, Bakunin the Destroyer.

'He is the only one who can deal the knock-out blow. All your intellectuals are cowards with their talk of evolution. Before three years are out the International under his command is bound to wipe out the old world.'

Étienne listened attentively, longing to learn and understand this religion of destruction, about which the engineman only dropped an occasional dark hint, as though he kept its mysteries to himself.

'But why don't you explain? What's your object?'

'To destroy everything. No more nations, no more governments, no more property, no more God or religion.'

'Yes, I gather that. Only where is it going to lead you?'

'To the primitive and formless community, to a new world, a fresh start.'

'And how are you going to carry it out? How do you propose to set about it?'

'By fire, poison, and the dagger. The real hero is the murderer, for he is the avenger of the people, the revolutionary in action, not someone just trotting out phrases out of books. We must have a series of appalling cataclysms to horrify the rulers and awaken the people.'

As he spoke Souvarine became terrible. He rose up in his chair in ecstasy, a mystic flame darted from his pale eyes and his delicate hands gripped the edge of the table so tightly that they almost broke it. The other man watched him in terror, thinking of the stories his friend had half confided in him – mines laid under the Tsar's palaces, police chiefs struck down with knives like wild boars, a mistress of his, the only woman he had ever loved, hanged one rainy morning in Moscow while he, standing in the crowd, kissed her with his eyes for the last time.

'No, no!' cried Étienne, waving away this hateful vision, 'we haven't got to that stage here. Murder, fire, never! It's monstrous and unjust, and all our comrades would rise up and strangle the assassin!'

He still could not understand, for all his racial instincts recoiled from this dark vision of world extermination, of the world mown to the ground like a field of rye. What could they do after that? How would the nations rise again? He demanded an answer.

'Tell me what your programme is. We want to know where we are going.'

Then Souvarine, gazing with misty eyes into space, peacefully concluded:

'Any reasoning about the future is criminal, for it prevents pure destruction and holds up the march of the revolution.'

In spite of the cold chill this answer sent down his spine, Étienne had to laugh. Yet he freely admitted that there was some sense in these ideas, which attracted him by their terrible simplicity. But it would be playing right into Rasseneur's hands if such things were spread among their mates. They had to be practical.

Widow Désir then came in and suggested they had some lunch. They accepted and went into the bar, which on weekdays was separated from the dance-hall by a movable partition. When they had finished their omelette and cheese Souvarine wanted to go; and as Étienne tried to make him stay he said:

'What for, to hear you all talking a lot of useless nonsense? I've seen enough. So long!'

And off he went in his gentle, obstinate way, a cigarette in his mouth.

Étienne felt increasingly anxious. It was one o'clock, and Pluchart was certainly going to let him down. By half past one the delegates began to appear and he had to receive them because he wanted to check them as they came in, for fear of the Company's sending its usual spies. He examined every invitation and scrutinized the bearers, though of course many of them did come in without showing their invitations: if they were known to him it was good enough and they were admitted. As it was striking two he saw Rasseneur come, who, however, finished a pipe at the counter and stood there chatting without hurrying himself. This cool and mocking attitude still further irritated him, especially as the wags had come in full force just to lark about – Zacharie, Mouquet, and plenty of others – people who would not take the strike seriously but thought it fun to be leading a life of idleness. There they all were, sitting at the tables and spending their last penny on a glass of beer, grinning away, pulling the legs of their more serious companions who, they said, had come to make fools of themselves.

Another quarter of an hour went by and the hall was getting restive. In despair Étienne was just making up his mind to go in and begin when widow Désir, who was looking down the street, called out:

'Here comes your gentleman!'

It really was Pluchart. He arrived in a carriage drawn by a broken-winded old hack. He leaped down, slim and dandified, with a square head too big for his body, and in his black frock coat he looked like a well-to-do artisan in his Sunday best. For five years now he had never so much as used a file, and he dolled himself up, taking particular care of his hair, very proud of his success as an orator. But he was still awkward in his movements, and the nails on his broad fingers had not grown for they were permanently eaten away by iron. He served his own ambition very actively, constantly running round the province and airing his views.

'Now you mustn't be angry with me,' he said, forestalling questions and reproaches. 'Yesterday, conference at Preuilly

238

in the morning and an evening meeting at Valençay. To-day, lunch at Marchiennes with Sauvagnat. . . . However, I managed to get a cab. I am quite worn out, just listen to my voice! But never mind, I'll speak to them just the same.'

On the doorstep of the Bon Joyeux he stopped short.

'Gosh! I'm forgetting the cards. That'd be a nice thing!'

He went back to the cab, which the cabby was just going to take home, and pulled out of the box a little black wooden case which he brought in under his arm.

Étienne followed him, radiant, while Rasseneur, covered with confusion, dared not shake hands with him. But Pluchart had already seized his and said a word or two about his letter: what a funny idea! Why not hold this meeting? You should always hold a meeting when you could. Widow Désir said would he take something, but he refused – no point in it, he could speak without drink. But he had very little time, as he hoped to be able to push on as far as Joiselle that evening, be-cause he must have a talk to Legoujeux. So they all went into the hall in a body. Maheu and Levaque, who were arriving late, followed them in. The door was then locked so that they could be undisturbed, which made the gigglers sneer louder than ever, Zacharie calling to Mouquet that perhaps they were all going to be got with child in there.

Some hundred miners were waiting on the benches in the stuffy hall where the hot smells of the last dance seemed to be coming up from the floor. There was some whispering and heads were turned as the newcomers took their places in the empty seats. They stared at the gent from Lille, whose black coat caused some surprise and apprehension.

Étienne began by moving that a proper committee be elected. He suggested names and the floor approved by raising hands. Pluchart was made chairman, with Maheu and Étienne himself as committee members. There was a shifting round of chairs and the committee took its place. For a moment the chairman was lost to sight behind the table, under which he was slipping his box which so far he had been holding tight. When he reappeared, he tapped on the table with his fist to call for attention and then began in a hoarse voice:

'Citizens!'

But at that moment a little door opened and he had to stop. It was widow Désir, who had gone round by the kitchen and was carrying a tray with six glasses of beer on it.

'Don't let me disturb you,' she said. 'Talking is thirsty work.'

Maheu took the tray from her and Pluchart was able to go on. He said he was very touched by the kind reception he had had from the workers of Montsou, apologized for his lateness and mentioned how tired he was, and his sore throat. Then he called upon citizen Rasseneur, who had asked if he could speak.

Rasseneur was already at the table, near the beer. He had turned a chair round and was using it as a sort of rostrum. He seemed deeply moved, and after a preliminary cough shouted at the top of his voice:

'Comrades!'

His influence over the miners was due to his verbal facility, the good-natured way he could go on addressing them for hours without ever tiring. He did not venture on any gestures, but stood stolidly smiling, drowning them with words and hypnotizing them until they shouted as one man: 'Yes, yes, quite true, you're quite right!' But today he felt a hostile undercurrent as soon as he opened his mouth, and therefore he proceeded warily. He confined his remarks to the continuation of the strike, and counted on winning applause before opening the attack on the International. Of course, honour forbade their giving in to the Company's demands; but what a terrible prospect if they had to hold out much longer! And without actually advocating surrender he weakened their courage, painted a picture of the villages dying of starvation, asked what resources the advocates of resistance could count on. Three or four of his friends tried to back him up, which only accentuated the coolness of the majority and their increasing irritation and disapproval of his eloquence. Then, despairing of winning them over, he lost his temper and prophesied woe if they let their heads be turned by agitators from outside. By now two-thirds of the audience were on their feet, angrily trying to prevent him from saying any more since he was insulting them and treating them like children who didn't know how to behave. He stood there, taking gulp after gulp of beer, and went on talking through the din, shouting that the man wasn't yet born who could stop him doing his duty!

Pluchart stood up. As he had no bell, he banged on the table and repeated in his raucous voice:

'Citizens! Citizens!'

He finally obtained some calm, submitted the matter to the meeting, which took away Rasseneur's right to speak. The delegates who had represented the pits at the interview with the manager carried the others with them, for they were all maddened with hunger and their heads were full of the new ideas. The vote was a foregone conclusion.

'You couldn't bloody well care less! You've got plenty to eat!' yelled Levaque, brandishing his fist at Rasseneur.

Étienne had to lean over behind the chairman's back to calm Maheu, who was red in the face with fury at this hypocritical speech.

'Citizens,' said Pluchart, 'may I speak now?'

Silence fell at once. He spoke. His voice was hoarse and painful to listen to, but he was used to that, as he was always on the move and took his laryngitis with him as part of his performance. He strengthened his voice in a gradual crescendo, which produced effects of pathos. He stood with arms open and punctuated his periods with a swing of the shoulders, giving his eloquence some of the character of the sermon, dropping his voice at the end of each sentence in a religious way which carried conviction by its very monotony.

He worked in his set speech on the greatness and benefits of the International, the one he always trotted out at the beginning in localities where he was not known. He explained its object: the emancipation of the workers; he demonstrated its imposing structure: at the base the commune, higher up the province, still higher the nation and at the summit humanity. His arms waved slowly, indicating the successive levels and building the immense cathedral of the world of the future. Next he turned to the internal organization; he read out the statutes and spoke about the congresses, pointing out the growing importance of the aims and objects, the broadening programme which, having begun with discussion of wages, was now working towards the liquidation of society and the

241

abolition of the wage system itself. No more nationalities! the workers of the whole world united by a common hunger for justice, sweeping away the rotten bourgeoisie, establishing at long last the free society in which he who does not work does not reap! He was now bellowing and his breath startled the coloured-paper flowers hanging from the low, blackened ceiling which echoed with the sound of his voice.

A tidal wave ran along the sea of faces. Some voices called out:

'That's right! We're with you!'

He went on. The whole world would be conquered in three years – he enumerated the conquered peoples. New support was coming in from all sides. Never had a new religion made so many converts. And when they were the masters they would dictate the laws to the employers, whose turn it would be to have a hand on their throats.

'Yes, yes! It'll be their turn to go down the mine!'

He enjoined silence with a wave of the hand. Now he came to the question of strikes. In principle he disapproved of strikes, they were too slow and tended to aggravate the troubles of the worker. But until better means could be found, when they became inevitable you just had to make up your mind to have them, for they had the advantage of disorganizing capital. And he showed how, if it came to such a pass, the International would be providential for the strikers and gave examples: in Paris at the time of the bronze-workers' strike the employers had conceded everything immediately, terrified by the news that the International was sending help; in London it had saved some mine-workers by sending back at its own expense a party of Belgians called in by the owners. You only had to join and the Companies trembled, the workers were enrolling in the great army of labour, ready to die for each other rather than remain slaves in a capitalist society.

He was interrupted by a burst of applause. He mopped his brow with a handkerchief, refusing the glass proffered by Maheu. When he tried to start again he was prevented by renewed cheering.

'That's got 'em!' he hissed, quickly to Étienne. 'They're ready now. . . . The cards – quick!'

He dived under the table and reappeared with the little black box.

'Citizens!' he cried, dominating the uproar, 'here are membership cards. If your delegates will come up I will give them some to hand round. . . . We can settle later.'

Rasseneur leaped to his feet and protested again. Étienne was getting excited, as he also had to make a speech. There ensued a moment of extreme confusion. Levaque was punching the air as though he were going into battle. Maheu was on his feet and holding forth, but nobody could hear a word he was saying. In the growing tumult the dust rose from the floor, the floating dust of former dances, filling the air with the strong reek of haulage girls and pit-boys.

The little door suddenly opened and widow Désir, filling the aperture with her stomach and bust, said in stentorian tones:

'Shut up, for God's sake! The police are here!'

The local superintendent had arrived, rather late in the day, to make a report and suspend the meeting. He had four officers with him. For five minutes the widow had been keeping them at bay at the door, telling them that she was in her own home and had a perfect right to have a few friends in. But they had pushed their way in and so she had rushed on ahead to warn her children.

'You'll have to come out this way,' she said, 'there's a dirty policeman guarding the yard. But that doesn't matter, as my little woodshed opens on to the back alley. Look sharp!'

The superintendent was already thumping on the door, and as it did not open he was threatening to smash it in. Some spy must have given them away, for he was shouting that the meeting was illegal as a large number of miners were there without invitations.

In the dance-hall the confusion became even greater. They could not run away like this; no vote had been taken either for joining the International or for going on with the strike. Everybody insisted on talking at once. Then the chairman had the idea of a vote by acclamation. Hands were put up and delegates hurriedly declared that they were joining on behalf of absent comrades. And thus it came about that the ten thousand miners of Montsou became members of the International.

The rout was now setting in. To cover their retreat widow Désir went and stood against the door which the butts of the gendarmes' rifles were already battering down behind her. The miners jumped over benches and made their escape one by one through the kitchen and woodshed. Rasseneur was one of the first to disappear, followed by Levaque who had quite forgotten how he had cursed him and was wondering whether he could cadge a glass to pull himself round. Étienne made sure of the little box and then waited with Pluchart and Maheu, who made it a point of honour to be last out. As they were going the lock was forced, and the superintendent found himself in the presence of the widow, whose bust and stomach still presented a serious obstacle.

'A lot of good it has done you, smashing my place up!' she said. 'You can see there's nobody here!'

The superintendent, a slow-moving person who disliked scenes, merely threatened to take her to the lock-up, and off he went to report, taking his four men and followed by the jeers of Zacharie and Mouquet, who were filled with admiration for the way their mates had played them up, and didn't care tuppence for armed force.

In the street outside Étienne ran along, hampered by the box, with the others at his heels. He suddenly thought of Pierron and asked why he had not been seen, and Maheu, running at his side, answered that he was ill – a diplomatic illness, fear of compromising himself. They wanted to keep Pluchart for a minute but he, still running, declared that he must be off at once to Joiselle where Legoujeux was waiting for instructions. So they shouted good-bye, still without slackening speed, as they ran full pelt through Montsou. A few breathless words were exchanged. Étienne and Maheu now felt sure of triumph and were confidently smiling: when the International had sent help it would be the Company's turn to beg them to go back to work. And in this surging hope, this gallop of big boots clattering on the cobblestones, there was something else, something sombre and fierce, a gust of violence that was to inflame the villages as far as the four corners of the coalfield.

[5]

Aɴᴏᴛʜᴇʀ fortnight went by. It was the beginning of January and cold fogs numbed the immense plain. The misery had worsened, and with every hour the villages suffered greater agonies of famine. Four thousand francs, sent from London by the International, had scarcely provided bread for three days. Since then, nothing. The death of this great hope broke down everybody's courage. Whom could they count on now, since their own brothers were leaving them in the lurch? They felt lost in the cruel winter, cut off from the world.

By Tuesday Village Two Hundred and Forty was at the end of its resources. Étienne and the delegates had redoubled their efforts, opening new subscription lists in the neighbouring towns, and even as far away as Paris; collections were made and conferences organized. All these efforts had little effect, for public opinion, at first deeply stirred, was now getting bored with this strike that dragged monotonously on without any exciting incidents. The few paltry sums collected scarcely sufficed to keep the poorest families. The rest kept themselves alive by pawning clothes and selling up their homes bit by bit. Everything found its way to the dealer's: the wool stuffing from mattresses, kitchen utensils, even furniture. At one stage they thought they were saved, for the small shop-keepers of Montsou, who had been cut out by Maigrat, offered credit to try to entice his customers back, and for a week Verdonck the grocer and the two bakers Carouble and Smelten did keep open shop, but as they could get no more credit themselves, all three stopped. The bailiffs were delighted, and all that came out of it was a burden of debt which would hang over the miners for years. Now, with no more credit anywhere and not a single old saucepan left to sell, all they could do was lie down in a corner and die like mangy dogs.

Étienne would have sold his own flesh if he could. He had given up his fees and pawned his best coat and trousers at Marchiennes, only too glad to be able to keep the pot boiling a little longer for the Maheus. The only thing he kept was his pair of shoes, so as to keep his feet all right, he said. His bitter regret was that the strike had come too early, before the provident fund had had time to accumulate. In his view that was the sole cause of the disaster, for the workers were bound to beat the employers when they could save enough money to resist. And now he remembered that Souvarine had accused the Company of provoking the strike in order to nip the fund in the bud.

The sight of the village and of all these poor people without food or fire depressed him so much that he preferred to go out and tire himself with long walks. One evening, as he was passing Réquillart on his way home, he saw an old woman lying unconscious by the roadside; she was no doubt dying of starvation. After lifting her up, he called out to a girl whom he saw on the other side of the fence.

'Oh, it's you,' he said, recognizing Mouquette. 'Give me a hand – we must make her drink something.'

Mouquette's eyes filled with tears of pity, and she ran home quickly to the rickety hovel her father had fixed up among the ruins, coming back at once with some gin and bread. The gin revived the woman, who greedily gnawed at the bread without saying a word. She was the mother of a miner who lived in a village over Cougny way, and she had collapsed there on her way home from Joiselle where she had vainly tried to borrow ten sous from a sister. When she had eaten the bread she wandered off, still dazed.

Étienne was standing there in the waste ground of Réquillart, with its ruined sheds half buried in brambles.

'Well, won't you come in and have a nip yourself?' asked Mouquette brightly.

And as he hesitated:

'You are still afraid of me, then?'

He followed her in, won over by her merry laughter and touched by her having so freely given the bread. She would not entertain him in her father's room but took him into hers, where she poured out two little glasses of gin. The room was very neat, and he complimented her on it. The family did not seem to be short of anything, for the father was still in his job as ponyman at Le Voreux, and she, saying she could not live with folded arms, had set up as a laundress, which brought in thirty sous a day. Even if you do have fun with men that doesn't mean you're a slacker.

'Tell me,' she suddenly said, coming and putting her arms round his waist, 'why don't you want me?'

He could not help joining in her laughter, for she had said it so winningly.

'Oh, but I do,' he answered.

'No, you don't – not how I want it. . . . You know I'm dying for it. What about it? I should simply love it.'

It was quite true, she had been asking him for six months. He looked down at her as she clung to him, squeezing him with her trembling arms, her face looking up at him with such a supplicating expression that he was quite overcome. There was nothing beautiful about her full round face with its complexion yellowed and mottled by coal, but there was a flame in her eyes, and there emanated from her whole being such a sensual charm, that she seemed very fresh and young. In the face of such a humble and passionate gift of herself he could hardly go on refusing.

'Oh, you will!' she murmured, exultant, 'you will!'

And she gave herself to him with all the swooning clumsiness of a virgin, as though it was the first time and she had never known a man before. When he left her, she was the one to overflow with gratitude, thanking him and kissing his hands.

This piece of good fortune left Étienne a little ashamed of himself. There was nothing to be proud of in having had Mouquette, and on the way home he swore he would not start that again. But still, he looked back on it with friendly gratitude, for she was a good sort.

But the bad news he heard when he reached the village drove the adventure from his mind. There was a rumour that the Company might agree to make a concession if the delegates would make another appeal to the manager. At least, that was the tale the deputies had been spreading round. The truth was that, now that the fight was on, the mine was suffering even more than the miners. On both sides obstinacy was aggravating the trouble: if labour was dying of hunger, capital was being eaten away. Each day's stoppage cost hundreds of thousands of francs. A machine stationary is a machine dead. The plant and material assets were deteriorating and idle money was melting away like water soaking into the sand. Since the small stock of coal on the pit yards had run out, customers were talking of going to Belgium for it; and that constituted a danger for the future. But what worried the Company most of all, and what it was most careful not to disclose, was the ever-increasing damage to the galleries and workings. The deputies could not cope with repairs; props were giving way everywhere and falls were occurring every hour. Soon the accidents became so serious that long months of repair work would be required before production could start again. Stories were already going round: at Crèvecœur three hundred metres of road had subsided in one solid piece, blocking the way to the Cinq-Paumes seam; at Madeleine the Maugrétout seam was flaking away and filling with water. The management would not admit this, but suddenly two accidents occurring one after the other forced an admission. One morning, near La Piolaine, a fissure opened in the ground above the north gallery of Mirou which had fallen in the day before, and the next day there was a subsidence in Le Voreux which shook one corner of the neighbourhood so severely that two houses had almost disappeared.

Étienne and his fellow delegates hesitated to risk another move without knowing the Directors' intentions. They approached Dansaert, but he hedged: of course any misunderstanding was to be deplored, anything possible would be done to bring about an understanding; but he said nothing definite. They finally decided to go to Monsieur Hennebeau, so as to put themselves in the right, for they did not want to be accused later on of not having given the Company a chance to admit it was in the wrong. But they swore they would not give in over any point, but come what might would stand by their terms which were the only fair ones.

The interview took place on Tuesday morning – the day when the village was sinking into black despair. It was less friendly than the first one. Maheu was again the spokesman, explaining that his fellow workers had sent them to enquire whether the gentlemen had anything new to say. At first Monsieur Hennebeau pretended to be surprised: no, no other order had reached him, nothing could be changed as long as the miners persisted in their outrageous revolt. . . . This unbending authoritarianism had the most unfortunate effect – indeed, even if the delegates had been going out of their way to be conciliatory such a reception would have sufficed to stiffen their resistance. Later the manager expressed his willingness to look for a basis for mutual concession: for example, the workers might accept separate payment for timbering whilst the Company on its side might raise this payment by the two centimes it was accused of pocketing. But of course, he added, he was making this offer on his own initiative, for nothing had been decided; he flattered himself, however, that he could bring Paris round to this concession. But the delegates refused, and repeated their terms: the old system to be maintained with a rise of five centimes per tub. Then he admitted that he was in a position to negotiate there and then, and urged them to accept for the sake of their wives and starving little ones. But they remained adamant, and staring at the floor said no, and again no, with savage energy. The talk broke up abruptly, Monsieur Hennebeau slammed the doors and Étienne and the others went off, stamping on the cobblestones with their heavy boots in the mute rage of defeated men at the end of their tether.

At about two o'clock on the same day the women went in a deputation of their own to Maigrat. The only hope left was to touch this man's heart and coax another week's credit out of him. The idea came from Maheude, who often banked too much on people's kindness. She persuaded Ma Brûlé and la Levaque to go with her, but Pierronne begged to be excused, alleging that she could not leave Pierron, whose recovery was exceedingly slow. Other women joined the band, which numbered about twenty. When the good people of Montsou saw them coming, a line of sullen and desperate-looking women stretching right across the road, they anxiously shook their heads. Doors were shut and one lady hid her silver. This was the first time they had been seen acting thus, and there could be no worse augury, for usually the situation had reached breaking point when the women took to the road. At Maigrat's there was a violent scene. He began by letting them in, leering and pretending he thought they had come to pay their bills: it was nice of them to come together and bring the money in a lump sum. Then, as soon as Maheude began to speak, he flew into a simulated rage. What? Were they trying to pull his leg? More credit! Were they thinking of reducing him to beggary? No, not another potato, not a single crumb of bread! He referred them to Verdonck the grocer and Carouble and Smelten the bakers, since they dealt with them now. The women heard him out with an air of frightened humility, and apologized, watching out for any sign of pity in his eyes. He tried to be funny again, offering all his shop to Ma Brûlé if she would have him for her young man. They were all cowardly enough to laugh at this, and la Levaque went one further and said that for her part she was quite willing. But he at once became rough and herded them towards the door. As they went on pitifully pleading, he laid hands on one of them. On the pavement the others shouted that he was in the pay of the Company, and Maheude, raising her arms to heaven in a gesture of avenging indignation, called down death upon him, saying that such a man had no right to eat.

The return to the village was mournful indeed. As the women came back empty-handed, the men looked at them and lowered their eyes. It was all over; the day would end without a single spoonful of soup, and all the other days stretched out ahead in frozen darkness, without any gleam of hope. But they had faced up to this possibility, and nobody spoke of surrender. The very excess of their misery made them all the more quietly determined, like hunted animals prepared to die in their hole rather than come out. Who would have dared to be the first to speak of giving in? They had all sworn with their mates to stand together, and stand together they would, just as they did in the pit when one of them was trapped by a fall. That sort of thing went without saying, for the pit was a good school for resignation, and you could tighten your belt for a week when you had lived on fire and water since the age of twelve. Their loyalty to each other was supplemented by this soldierly pride, the pride in the job of men who in the daily struggle against death have developed a spirit of rivalry in self-sacrifice.

That evening was terrible in the Maheu home. They all sat in silence round the dying fire in which the last cake of damped dust was smouldering. Having emptied the mattress handful by handful, they had resigned themselves two days previously to selling the cuckoo clock for three francs, and the room seemed bare and dead without the familiar tick-tock. The only luxury left was the pink cardboard box on the middle of the dresser, a present from Maheu which his wife clung to like a precious jewel. The only two good chairs having gone, old Bonnemort and the children huddled together on an old mildewed bench brought in from the garden. The grey twilight seemed to intensify the cold.

'What's to be done?' repeated Maheude, crouching in the corner by the oven.

Étienne, who had to stand, looked at the pictures of the Emperor and Empress, stuck up on the wall. He would have torn them down long since, but the family wanted to keep them for ornament. He muttered:

'And to think that those bloody fools who are watching us starve wouldn't fork out two sous!'

'Suppose I took the pink box?' ventured Maheude after some hesitation, looking very pale.

Maheu, sitting on the edge of the table dangling his legs, with his head bowed down in his chest, jumped up:

'No! I won't have it!'

Maheude painfully rose to her feet and walked round the room. Good God! was it possible that they had come down to this? Not a crumb in the cupboard, nothing left to sell and not even an idea how to get a loaf. And the fire going out! She flew into a rage with Alzire, whom she had sent cinder-hunting on the pit-bank that morning, and who had come back empty-handed, saying that the Company wouldn't allow gleaning. Just as though anyone cared a damn about the Company! Was it robbing anybody to pick up a few forgotten bits of coal? The child tearfully explained that a man had threatened to hit her, but she promised to go back next day whether she was hit or not.

251

'And that dratted Jeanlin!' cried her mother. 'Now where's he got to, I'd like to know? He was supposed to bring in some salad; at any rate we could have chewed that like the cows! He won't come back, you mark my words. He stayed out last night as it is. I don't know what he's up to, but the beggar always looks well fed!'

'Perhaps he picks up a few sous on the road,' ventured Étienne.

That made her brandish her fists in a frenzy of rage.

'If I thought that! . . . My children beg! I'd rather kill them and kill myself afterwards.'

Maheu had sunk back on to the table. Lénore and Henri, wondering why there was no supper, began to grizzle, whilst old Bonnemort sat in silence, philosophically rolling his tongue round his mouth to keep hunger at bay. Nobody even spoke now, for they were all stupefied by the accumulation of woes – Grandpa coughing and spitting black, with his old rheumatic complaint turning to dropsy, Father asthmatical, his knees swollen up with water, Mother and the children scarred by scrofula and hereditary anaemia. Of course all that was part of the job, and you didn't complain except when lack of food finished you off; and already in the village they were dropping off like flies. But something had got to be found for supper. What? Where, for God's sake?

Then, as the dismal twilight was making the room darker and darker, Étienne, who for some time had been hesitating, could stand it no longer and came to a decision.

'Wait a bit,' he said, 'I'm going to have a look round.'

He went out. He had thought of Mouquette. She would certainly have a loaf and be only too glad to give it to him. He was vexed at having to go back to Réquillart – she would kiss his hands like a lovesick servant-girl; but still, you couldn't let down friends in trouble, and he would do the necessary with her again if need be.

'I'm going to have a look too,' said Maheude. 'This is too silly!'

She opened the door again after the young man and slammed it behind her, leaving the others silent and motionless in

252

the glimmer of a bit of candle that Alzire had lit. She stopped outside for a moment to consider. Then she went into the Levaques'.

'Look here, I lent you a loaf the other day. Suppose you let me have it back?'

But she said no more, for the sight that met her eyes was anything but encouraging, and the house seemed more poverty-stricken even than her own.

La Levaque was staring at the dead fire, whilst her husband, made dead drunk on an empty stomach by some nailmakers, was asleep on the table. Bouteloup was leaning back mechanically rubbing his shoulders up and down against the wall, utterly bewildered, as a good fellow might well be whose savings have been spent for him and who finds to his surprise that he has to tighten his belt.

'A loaf! oh, my dear!' answered la Levaque. 'And I was just thinking of borrowing another!'

At that moment her husband grunted with pain in his sleep, and she flattened his face against the table.

'Shut up, you swine! A good job too if it burns your guts! Instead of getting yourself treated to drinks, couldn't you have touched some friend for twenty sous?'

She was off, swearing and relieving her feelings, in that filthy house neglected so long already that an unbearable stench arose from the floor. The whole show could go to hell for all she cared! Her son, that little twerp Bébert, had disappeared since the morning, and she bawled that it would be a bloody good riddance if he never came back. Then she said she was going to bed. At least it would be warm. She gave Bouteloup a push.

'Come on, up we go! The fire's out and there's no need to light the candle to look at the empty plates. Are you going to come, Louis? I tell you, we are going to bed; it cheers you up to get together. And let this bleeding drunkard peg out with cold down here on his own!'

Outside once again, Maheude resolutely crossed the gardens and headed for the Pierrons' house. There was laughter inside. She knocked and it stopped dead. They took a full minute to open the door.

'Oh, fancy, it's you!' exclaimed Pierronne, pretending to be most surprised. 'I thought it was the doctor.'

She did not give her a chance to speak, but went straight on, pointing to Pierron who was sitting in front of a big coal fire:

'Oh, he's very poorly, still very poorly. He looks all right in the face, but it affects him in the stomach. So you see he must be kept warm, and we're burning everything we've got.'

Pierron certainly looked bonny, with a good colour and firm flesh. He was trying to act like a sick man by fetching deep sighs, but was not having much success. As soon as she went in, Maheude noticed a strong smell of rabbit: they had whisked away the dish, no doubt! There were crumbs on the table, and right in the middle stood a bottle of wine they had forgotten to hide.

'Mother has gone to Montsou to try to get a loaf,' Pierronne went on, 'and we are just cooling our heels waiting for her.'

But the words stuck in her throat, for she had followed her neighbour's eyes and noticed the bottle. She recovered herself at once, however, and proceeded to tell the story: yes, indeed, it was a bottle of wine, the people from La Piolaine had brought it for her husband, for whom the doctor had prescribed claret. And she overflowed with gratitude – such kind people! especially the young lady, and not a bit proud, coming into working folks' homes and giving her gifts with her own hands!

'Yes, of course,' said Maheude, 'I know them.'

She reflected with a pang that the good things always go to the least poor. It happened invariably, and those La Piolaine people would have carried water to the river. How was it she hadn't seen them about the village? Perhaps she might have got something out of them anyhow.

'Well,' she confessed at length, 'I really came to see if things were a little better with you than with us. Have you got such a thing as a little vermicelli? I shall let you have it back, of course.'

Pierronne noisily expressed her disappointment:

'Nothing whatever, my dear. Not even a grain of

254

semolina. . . . As Mother isn't back that means she has had no luck. We shall go to bed hungry.'

At that moment a sound of crying came from the cellar and she angrily banged on the door with her fist. It was that scamp Lydie, she explained; she had had to lock her in to punish her for not coming home until five after running wild all day. The child was getting quite out of control and always running away.

Maheude went on standing there, unable to tear herself away. The warmth from the big fire went right through her, and was so lovely that it hurt, and the thought that there was food to be had in that house made her stomach feel emptier than ever. Clearly they had got rid of the old woman and shut up the child so as to guzzle rabbit on their own. Ah, well! it was no use denying it, when a woman misbehaved herself it brought good luck to the home.

'Good night,' she said suddenly.

Night had fallen outside, and the moon behind the clouds shed a fitful light. Instead of returning across the gardens, Maheude went round by the road in abject misery, not daring to go in. All along the rows of lifeless houses, the very doors seemed to smell of famine and resound hollowly. What was the use of knocking? It was Poverty & Co. everywhere. Nobody had had a square meal for weeks, and even the smell of onions had gone, the pungent smell that usually heralded the village from far across the countryside. Now the smell was that of old cellars and dank holes where nothing can live. The last sounds were dying away, stifled sobs and muffled oaths, and in the gradually deepening silence you could hear the approach of famished sleep and the thud of people's bodies falling on their beds in nightmare agonies of hunger.

As she passed the church she saw a shadowy figure hurrying along, and a ray of hope made her quicken her step, for she recognized the parish priest of Montsou, abbé Joire, who said Mass on Sundays at the village chapel. Presumably he had come out of the vestry where he had been on business. He was scurrying past, with head bent forward, looking fat and jolly and anxious to live at peace with all the world. He must have chosen to do his errands after dark for fear of being compromised with the miners. It was said that he had just been given a preferment, and he had even brought his successor round, a lean priest with eyes like burning coals.

'Sir, sir,' she stammered.

But he did not stop.

'Good night, good night, my good woman.'

And so she found herself at her own door, scarcely able to stand on her feet. She went in.

Nobody had moved. Maheu was still sitting in a heap on the edge of the table. Old Bonnemort and the children were still huddled together on the bench to keep each other warm. Not a word had been spoken, and the candle had burned down so low that soon there would not even be any light left. Hearing the door open the children looked round, but seeing their mother with nothing in her hands they stared at the floor again, holding back a good cry for fear of being scolded. Maheude sank back into her place by the dead fire, nobody questioned her, and the silence was unbroken. Everybody had understood and they all thought it pointless to tire themselves out by talking, so they settled down to wait, exhausted and utterly downcast, for the last hope – that Étienne might dig something out somewhere. As the minutes went by they gave up counting even on that.

When Étienne did come back he had a dozen cold boiled potatoes wrapped in a rag.

'This is all I could find,' he said.

There was no bread left at Mouquette's either, but she had forced him to take her own dinner which she had put in the rag, kissing him ardently.

'No, thank you,' he said when Maheude offered him his share, 'I had something to eat there.'

It was not true, and he miserably watched the children jump at the food. Their father and mother refrained as well, so as to leave more for them, but the old boy greedily devoured everything. They had to take a potato away from him for Alzire.

Then Étienne said he had heard some news. The Company, in its anger at the obstinacy of the strikers, was talking of handing back cards to compromised miners. Clearly it wanted war. An even more serious rumour was going round that the

Company was boasting that it had persuaded a large number to go down again, and that tomorrow La Victoire and Feutry-Cantel would be back on full time, and even at Madeleine and Mirou there would be a third of the men back. The Maheus were exasperated.

'Good God!' said Maheu, 'if there are traitors they must be dealt with!'

He stood up, carried away by rage and suffering:

'Tomorrow night, then, in the forest. . . . As they won't let us talk it out at the Bon Joyeux, it'll have to be the forest. We shall be on our own there.'

This cry woke old Bonnemort, who was nodding after his gluttony. It was the old rallying-cry, the meeting-place where long ago the miners had plotted defiance to the soldiers of the king.

'Yes, yes, to Vandame! I'm with you if you go there.'

Maheude waved her arms vigorously.

'We'll all go. There must be an end put to these injustices and treacheries!'

Étienne decided that a summons should be sent out to all the villages for the following night. But by now the fire was out, as it was at the Levaques', and the candle suddenly went out too. There was no coal and no oil, so they had to feel their way to bed in the biting cold. The children were crying.

[6]

JEANLIN was better now and able to walk again, but his legs had been so badly set that he limped with both, and it was a sight to see him waddling along like a duck, although he still ran as fast as ever, with the agility of some evil predatory animal.

One evening, just at dusk, Jeanlin, with his two henchmen Bébert and Lydie, was keeping watch on the Réquillart road. He was lying in wait in a piece of waste ground behind a fence, opposite a frowsy little general shop which stood crossways where a path branched off. The shop was kept by an old woman who was nearly blind, and she set outside two or three sacks of lentils and haricot-beans black with dust; but the booty on which he had cast his narrow covetous eyes was an ancient, fly-blown dried cod hanging in the doorway. Twice already he had despatched Bébert to unhook it, but both times somebody had come round the corner. Always nosey-parkers about, you couldn't get on with the job!

A gentleman on horseback appeared, and recognizing Monsieur Hennebeau the children dropped flat on the ground by the fence. Since the beginning of the strike he could often be seen like this on the roads, riding alone through the hostile villages, personally inspecting the lie of the land with quiet courage. No stone had ever whistled past his ears, and all he found was silent men slow to greet him; but more often he came across lovers taking their fill of pleasure in odd corners, heedless of politics. He would trot past on his mare, looking straight ahead so as not to disturb anybody, but his heart ached with unsatisfied longings in the midst of this orgy of free love. He could not help seeing youngsters lying about in heaps, boys on top of girls. So even the kids were already finding fun to drown their sorrows! His eyes grew misty and he rode on, sitting bolt upright in his saddle, buttoned up in his greatcoat like a soldier.

'Bloody rotten luck!' said Jeanlin, 'this is going on for ever. Go on, Bébert, pull it by the tail!'

But now two men were coming, and the boy stifled another oath as he recognized the voice of his brother Zacharie telling Mouquet how he had discovered a forty-sou piece sewn into his wife's skirt. They were both grinning with joy and slapping each other on the shoulder. Mouquet suggested a grand game of *crosse* for the next day: they would set out from the Avantage at two and go on to Montoire, near Marchiennes. Zacharie agreed. Why should anyone bother them with this strike? As there was nothing doing they might just as well enjoy themselves! They were going round the corner when Étienne, coming from the direction of the canal, stopped them and began talking.

'Are they going to sleep there?' asked Jeanlin in exasperation. 'It's nearly dark and the old girl is taking her sacks in!'

Another miner came along, going towards Réquillart. Étienne went with him, and as they were passing the fence Jeanlin heard them mention the forest: the meeting had had to be put off another day for fear of their not being able to let all the villages know in the one day.

'I say,' he whispered to his companions, 'the big show is for tomorrow. We must be there. Shall we bunk off in the afternoon, eh?'

The coast was clear at last. He sent Bébert off.

'At it, boy! Pull its tail! And mind how you go, the old girl's got her broom!'

Fortunately it was quite dark by now. Bébert had taken a flying leap at the cod, hung on to it and broken the string. He made off, waving it like a kite, followed by the other two at full speed. The woman came out of her shop, puzzled and amazed, for she could not make out the band disappearing into the darkness.

The little devils had become the terror of the neighbourhood, which they had progressively ravaged like a horde of barbarians. At first they had been content to roll about in the coal stacked in the yards of Le Voreux, whence they emerged like niggers, or to play hide-and-seek among the stores of timber, where they could get lost as in a virgin forest. Then they had taken the pit-bank by storm, sliding on their behinds down the bare parts which were still hot with hidden fires, lying doggo all day long, busy with quiet little games like mischievous mice. And then they widened their field of conquest; went and fought bloody battles among the piles of bricks, ran wild in the fields, eating all sorts of juicy herbs just as they were, without bread, hunted in the canal banks, caught fish in the mud and swallowed them raw, roamed for miles as far as the tall forest of Vandame, where they gorged on wild strawberries in spring and nuts and bilberries in summer. Soon the whole vast plain had become their territory.

But what sent them prowling with wolfish eyes along the roads between Montsou and Marchiennes was their growing passion for robbery. Jeanlin was always captain of their forays, hurling his troops against all kinds of booty, ravaging fields of onions, pillaging orchards, swooping on things displayed

259

in front of shops. People in the neighbourhood accused the strikers and there was talk of a great organized band. One day he had even forced Lydie to rob her mother, making her bring him dozens of sticks of barley sugar from one of the jars which Pierronne kept on a plank in her window, and although the child had been flayed alive she had not given him away, so terrifying was his authority. The worst of it was that he invariably awarded himself the lion's share. Bébert also had to deliver up his winnings and consider himself lucky if the captain did not hit him and keep the lot.

For some time Jeanlin had been overdoing it. He used to beat Lydie like a real wife, and he exploited Bébert's credulity in order to land him in awkward scrapes, thinking it grand fun to make a fool of this great lout who was stronger that he was and could have knocked him down at one blow. He despised them both and treated them as slaves, telling them he had a princess for his mistress, before whom they were not fit to be seen. And indeed for a week now he had taken to disappearing suddenly, at the end of a street, where a path turned off – anywhere, in fact – after ordering them in a terrible voice back to the village. But never before pocketing the swag.

This was what happened on this particular evening.

'Give it me,' he said, snatching the cod away from his companion, when the three had stopped running at a bend in the road near Réquillart.

Bébert protested.

'I want some, you know. It was me that got it.'

'What!' he shouted, 'you'll get some if I give you any. But it won't be tonight, and that's a fact. Tomorrow, if there's any left.'

He clouted Lydie and stood them side by side in line like soldiers shouldering arms. Then, going behind them:

'Now you are going to stay like that for five minutes without turning round. . . . And, by God, if you do turn round you'll be eaten up by wild beasts. . . . And after that you'll go straight home, and if Bébert touches Lydie on the way I shall know about it and you'll cop it!'

Then he vanished in the darkness so nimbly that they could not even hear the sound of his bare feet. The two children stood still for the five minutes, with never a look behind for fear of a blow from the invisible foe. In their common terror a deep affection had gradually developed between these two. For a long time he had dreamed of taking her and hugging her tight in his arms as he had seen other people do, and she would have liked it too, for it would have been a nice change to be gently caressed. But neither would have dreamed of disobeying. When they moved off they did not even kiss each other, although it was pitch dark, but walked along side by side, despairing of showing their love and certain that, if they touched each other, the captain would hit them from behind.

At the same moment Étienne had reached Réquillart. The day before Mouquette had begged him to come back, and back he had come, feeling ashamed of this desire he would not acknowledge even to himself for a girl who worshipped him like a holy image. But of course he intended to break it off. He would see her and explain that she must not run after him any more because of all their mates. It was no time for fun and games, and it wasn't decent to enjoy pleasures like this when other people were dying of hunger. But not having found her at home he had decided to wait; and so there he was, watching out for passing shadows.

Under the ruined headgear yawned the old shaft, half blocked up. Above the black hole stood one post with a bit of roof on it, looking like a gibbet, and from the broken masonry of the coping grew two trees, a rowan and a plane, as though they were springing up from the depths of the earth. It was a wild and solitary place, the grassy and tufted edge of a chasm, cluttered up with old timbers and overgrown with blackthorn and hawthorn, where hedge-sparrows nested in spring. For the past ten years the Company, wishing to avoid the heavy expense of upkeep, had been meaning to fill in this dead pit, but it was waiting to install a ventilating system in Le Voreux, for the ventilating furnace of the two pits, which were connected, was at the bottom of Réquillart, the old shaft of which acted as a chimney. All that had been done was to hold the lining of the shaft in place by cross-stays, which prevented coal being brought up, and then the upper galleries had been abandoned. Only the bottom one had been kept in order, and there the furnace blazed like the fires of hell, the huge mass of red-hot coal making such a powerful draught that the wind whistled like a hurricane throughout the neighbouring mine. As a measure of prudence an order had been issued to keep the escape-shaft in trim, so that people could go up and down; but as this was nobody's business, the ladders were rotting with damp, and some of the platforms had already collapsed. A clump of brambles blocked the entrance to the shaft, and as the first ladder had lost some of its rungs, you had to hang suspended from a root of the rowan tree and let yourself drop into the darkness, on faith.

Étienne was patiently waiting, hidden behind a bush, when he heard a long swishing sound among the branches. For a moment he thought it was an adder he had disturbed, but to his amazement a match was suddenly struck, and he saw Jeanlin lighting a candle and plunging into the abyss. His curiosity was thoroughly aroused, and he went to the edge of the hole; the boy had disappeared but a faint light was coming from the second platform down. After a moment's hesitation he lowered himself by clinging to the roots, thought he was going to drop sheer down the hundred and twenty-four metres to the bottom, but eventually felt a rung and went softly down. Jeanlin could not be heard. Étienne could still see the light going down and down below him, while the boy's shadow danced about gigantic and frightening with the waddling gait of his poor legs. He was scuttling down as agile as a monkey, catching on by his hands, feet, or chin when there were gaps between the rungs. The seven-metre ladders went on one after the other, some still solid, others shaky and on the point of breaking, the narrow platforms succeeded each other, so green and decayed that you felt as if you were treading on moss, while the lower you went the more stifling the heat became because of the furnace in the shaft. Luckily the fire was very low owing to the strike, for in normal times, when it consumed its five hundred kilogrammes of coal per day, nobody could have ventured down there without being roasted alive.

'Bloody little toad!' swore Étienne between his gasps; 'where the hell is he going?'

Twice he had nearly gone down head first. His feet slipped

on the damp wood. If only he had a candle like the boy! But he banged himself every minute, and his only guide was the faint glimmer always falling away beneath him. It must be the twentieth ladder by now, he thought, and still it went down. Then he began counting: twenty-one, twenty-two, twenty-three, and still down and down. His head felt as though it would explode with the heat, and he thought he was falling into a furnace. At last he struck a level and saw the candle going along a gallery. Thirty ladders – that meant about two hundred and ten metres.

'How long is he going to lead me this dance?' he thought. 'It must be in the stables that he has his hide-out.'

But the road leading to the stables on the left was blocked by a fall. The journey became more and more painful and dangerous. Frightened bats fluttered about and clung to the gallery roof. He had to hurry to keep the light in sight, and threw himself into the same gallery, but where the child slipped through as supple as a serpent, he could only squeeze along, bruising his limbs. Like all disused workings this gallery had narrowed, and was still narrowing every day because of the ceaseless pressure of the earth, and in places it was a mere pipe which must soon disappear altogether. Under this continual squeezing the split and broken props were becoming very dangerous, threatening to saw through his flesh or impale him on their thorn-like points, sharp as swords. He could only make headway by using the greatest care, proceeding on his knees or flat on his belly, feeling in front of him in the darkness. Suddenly a swarm of stampeding rats ran over him from heat to foot.

'Bloody hell! aren't we nearly there?' he growled, gasping for breath, his back breaking.

They were there. After a kilometre of it the passage opened out and they were in a perfectly preserved length of gallery. It was the terminus of the old haulage road, hewn out of the seam like a natural cave. Étienne had to stop, for in the distance he saw the boy had placed his candle between two stones. He was settling himself down, looking happy and relaxed, like a man glad to be back home. He had fitted up this gallery-end and turned it into a comfortable dwelling. In one corner a heap of hay made a soft bed, and on a table made of old pit-props there was everything needful – bread, apples, opened litres of gin – in fact a real robber's den with spoils collected over many weeks, even useless spoils like soap and boot-polish, stolen for the sheer joy of stealing. And the boy was sitting in state, alone with all his plunder, savouring it like a selfish brigand.

'So you don't care a damn about anybody, do you?' said Étienne when he had recovered his breath. 'You come down here and blow yourself out while we are dying of starvation up there!'

Jeanlin was trembling with panic. But when he recognized the young man he recovered at once.

'Won't you have dinner with me?' he said at length. 'What about a piece of grilled cod? You watch.'

He was still clinging on to his dried cod, and now he set about cleaning it up, scraping off the fly-blown bits with a fine new knife, one of those little bone-handled daggers with mottoes carved on them. This one bore the single word: Love.

'You've a nice knife there,' said Étienne.

'A present from Lydie,' answered Jeanlin, omitting to add that she had stolen it under his supervision from a stall in Montsou outside the Tête-Coupée.

And, going on with his scraping, he proudly added:

'I've got a nice place here, haven't I! A bit warmer than up there, and smells much better!'

Étienne had taken a seat, wanting to make the boy talk. His anger had all gone and he was interested in this vicious little devil who was so cheerful and industrious in his crimes. Indeed he was enjoying the comfort of this hole, where it was not too hot and the temperature was constant whatever the season, like a warm bath, while up on the earth the December frost was chapping poor folks' skins. As time passed, the galleries cleared themselves of noxious gases, there was no fire-damp left, and the only smell was that of old, rotten wood, a subtle aroma with the pungency of ether and a dash of cloves. More-over these timbers were interesting to look at; of a pale yellow marble hue, fringed with whitish lace and gossamer-like growths which seemed to drape them with silk and pearl embroidery. Others were spiked with fungi. And white moths flew about, and snowy flies and spiders lived there, a whole colourless population that had never known the sunlight.

'So you aren't afraid?' asked Étienne.

Jeanlin looked surprised.

'Afraid of what? I'm on my own!'

Having at last finished scraping the cod, he lit a small wood fire, spread the embers and grilled it. Then he cut a loaf in two. It made a terribly salt meal, but it was none the less delicious to a strong digestion.

Étienne accepted his helping.

'I'm not surprised that you get fat while we're all getting thin. Don't you think it's a bit thick to blow yourself out like this? Don't you ever think about the others?'

'No. Why are the others so silly?'

'Well, anyway you were right to hide. If your father found out you were stealing he'd give you what for!'

'Just as if the rich didn't steal from us! You're always saying so yourself. When I pinched this loaf from Maigrat I bet it was one he owed us.'

The young man went on chewing in silence. He felt strangely troubled as he contemplated this child who, with his pointed muzzle, green eyes, long ears, resembled some degenerate with the instinctive intelligence and craftiness of a savage, gradually reverting to man's animal origins. The pit had made him what he was, and the pit had finished the job by breaking his legs.

'And what about Lydie?' Étienne began again. 'Do you bring her down here sometimes?'

Jeanlin laughed a sneering laugh.

'That kid? Oh, good Lord, no! Women talk.'

And he went on laughing, full of boundless scorn for Lydie and Bébert. You never saw such soppy kids! The thought of their swallowing all his tales and going off empty-handed while he ate the cod in the warm tickled him to death. Then he concluded with the solemnity of a little philosopher:

'Much better to be on your own, then you never fall out.'

Étienne finished his bread and took a nip of gin. For a moment he had wondered whether to be ungrateful to his host and take him back up there by the ear, letting him know that if he went marauding again he would tell his father. But as he looked round this deep retreat he began thinking: supposing one of these days he needed it for his mates or himself if things got too awkward above ground? So he simply made the child swear not to stay out again all night, as he sometimes did when he dropped off to sleep in the hay, and then, taking a bit of candle, he started off first, leaving Jeanlin methodically putting his house in order.

Mouquette was waiting in desperate anxiety, sitting on a log in spite of the bitter cold. As soon as she saw him she threw herself on his neck; and when he told her he had made up his mind not to see her any more, it was like a stab in the heart. In God's name, why? Didn't she love him enough? Fearing he might succumb to his own desire to go home with her, he drew her away towards the road and explained as kindly as possible that she was compromising him in the eyes of his mates, and therefore jeopardizing their political cause. She was amazed: whatever was this to do with politics? Then it occurred to her that he was ashamed of her – not that she was offended, for it was quite natural – and she offered to let him hit her in public, so as to give the impression that he had broken off the affair. But he could see her just the same, if only for a little while now and then. She implored him almost hysterically, swore to stay in the background; she would not keep him five minutes. He was shaken, but still refused. He had to; but at least he wanted to kiss her good-bye. Step by step they had reached the first houses in Montsou, and they were standing in the light of the full moon with their arms round each other, when a woman passed by and suddenly jumped, as though she had tripped over a stone.

'Who's that?' asked Étienne anxiously.

'Catherine,' answered Mouquette. 'She's on her way back from Jean-Bart.'

The woman was going away with bowed head and stumbling as though she were very tired. The young man watched her go, distressed at having been seen by her and heartbroken with unjustified remorse. Wasn't she living with a man herself? Hadn't she made him suffer the very same pain, here on this very Réquillart road, when she had given herself to this man? But in spite of all that he bitterly regretted having paid her back in the same coin.

'I'll tell you what,' whispered Mouquette as she left him. 'If you don't want me it's because you want somebody else.'

Next day the weather was superb, with a clear frosty sky: one of those lovely winter days when the hard earth rings underfoot like crystal. By one o'clock Jeanlin had made off, but he had to wait for Bébert behind the church, and they almost went without Lydie who had been shut up in the cellar again by her mother. She had just been set free and given a basket, and they had told her that if she did not bring it back full of dandelion leaves she would be shut up yet again, and for the whole night with the rats. And so she was terrified and wanted to go and pick salad at once, but Jeanlin talked her out of it: they would see about that later. For many a long day Poland, Rasseneur's fat rabbit, had been very much on his mind, and just as he was passing the Avantage the rabbit came out into the road. In one swoop he seized her by the ears and stuffed her into the girl's basket, and the three ran for all they were worth. It was going to be great sport making the rabbit run like a dog all the way to the forest.

But they stopped to watch Zacharie and Mouquet who, after a couple of drinks with two friends were beginning the grand *crosse* match. The prize, a new cap and a red silk square, had been deposited with Rasseneur. The four players, in teams of two, were bidding for the first lap, from Le Voreux to Paillot farm, nearly three kilometres, and Zacharie won by bidding to do it in seven against Mouquet's eight. The *cholette*, a little boxwood egg, was placed on the road, point upwards. Each player had a *crosse*, a mallet with an oblique iron head and a long handle tightly bound with string. They began as the clock struck two. Zacharie, whose first drive consisted of three successive strokes, sent the *cholette* in masterly style for more than four hundred metres across fields of beet, for the game was forbidden in villages and on roads, where it had been known to cause fatal accidents. Mouquet, who was also a good player, then drove so vigorously that he brought the *cholette* back a hundred and fifty metres. And so the game went on, one side driving forward and the other back, and always at racing speed over frozen ploughed land that hurt the feet.

At first Jeanlin, Bébert, and Lydie had run behind the players excitedly watching the big drives. Then they remembered Poland, whom they were jogging about in the basket, and abandoning the game in the open country they released the rabbit to see how fast she would run. Off she went, with them in hot pursuit, and the hunt lasted an hour at full pelt, with continual twists and turns, while they yelled to frighten her and then attempted to catch her, only to grasp thin air in their outstretched arms. If she had not been starting another of her pregnancies they would never have got her.

As they were gasping for breath, voices swearing loudly made them look round. They were back in the middle of the *crosse* game, and Zacharie had nearly split open his brother's skull. The players were now in the fourth lap: from Paillot farm they had gone to Quatre-Chemins, then from Quatre-Chemins to Montoire, and now they were on a six-drive lap from Montoire to the Pré-des-Vaches. That made two and a half leagues in an hour, and they had stopped for drinks at Vincent's and at the Trois Sages into the bargain. Mouquet was now leading. Two more strokes and victory was his; but Zacharie, claiming his right with a malicious grin, hit back so skilfully that the *cholette* went into a deep ditch. Mouquet's partner could not get it out, and that meant disaster. All four shouted and got more and more excited, for they were neck and neck, and the whole thing would have to be started again. From the Pré-des-Vaches it was less than two kilometres to the Pointe des Herbes-Rousses, a matter of five strokes. There they could refresh themselves at Lerenard's.

Then Jeanlin had an idea. He let the players go, then produced some string from his pocket, which he tied to Poland's left hind paw. And what fun it was! The rabbit ran along in front of the three little devils, jerking her thigh and limping so pitifully that they had never laughed so much in their lives. Then they tied the string round her neck and made her gallop, and as she got tired they dragged her along on her belly or her back, just like a little carriage. This had been going on for over an hour, and the rabbit was at her last gasp when they popped her back in her basket on hearing the players again near Cruchot's wood. They had stumbled into the game once more.

Zacharie, Mouquet, and the other two were now mopping up the kilometres, only resting long enough to swallow a beer in each of the pubs planned as objectives. From the Herbes-Rousses they had gone to Buchy, then La Croix-de-Pierre, then Chamblay. The earth resounded under their feet as they galloped untiringly after the *cholette* bouncing on the ice. The weather was ideal; there was no fear of sinking into the mud – the only risk was broken legs. The mallet-blows went off like gunshots. Their brawny hands clasped the bound handles and their whole bodies swung forward as though to fell an ox. And this went on for hours, from end to end of the plain, over ditches, hedges, road embankments, and low walls. You needed a good pair of bellows in your chest and iron hinges in your knees. Colliers were passionately fond of this game which loosened their joints after the pit. Some of the young twenty-five-year-old fanatics did their ten leagues. You could not play after forty, you were too heavy.

Five o'clock struck and night was already falling. One lap left, to the forest of Vandame, to decide who should have the cap and silk square; with his sarcastic indifference to politics Zacharie thought it would be fun to fall in with their mates. As for Jeanlin, ever since they had left the village he had been making for the forest, although apparently careering about at random. He intimidated Lydie with a furious gesture when, overcome with remorse and fear, she spoke of returning to Le Voreux to pick dandelions: were they going to cut the meeting? for his part he intended to hear what the old folks had got to say. He egged Bébert on and suggested enlivening the last bit of the journey, as far as the trees, by letting Poland loose and chasing her with stones. His undeclared ambition was to kill her, for he longed to take her down to his lair in Réquillart and eat her. The rabbit ran on with her nose screwed up and her ears back; one stone grazed her back and another cut her tail, and despite the gathering darkness she would have ended her days there if the children had not seen Étienne and Maheu standing in the middle of a clearing. They pounced frantically on the animal and put her back into the basket. Almost at the same moment Zacharie, Mouquet, and the two others with their last drive landed the *cholette* within a few metres of the clearing. They had all dropped pat into the meeting.

Since twilight had set in, there had been a steadily moving stream of silent shadows wending their way singly or in groups from all corners of the countryside, along roads and paths across the plain towards the purple glades of the forest. Every village had emptied, and women and even children had set off under the clear open sky as if for a holiday jaunt. The roads were now nearly dark and this crowd making its way to the same meeting-place could no longer be seen, but its presence could be felt as it tramped obscurely on, led forward by one and the same thought. Between the hedges, among the bushes, there was just a faint rustling sound like the vague murmur of nocturnal voices.

Monsieur Hennebeau, who happened to be on his way home riding his mare, listened to these mysterious sounds. He had passed several couples, quite a slow procession of people out walking in the lovely winter night. Still more lovers going to take their pleasure behind the walls with lips pressed to lips. These were his normal encounters now: girls on their backs in every ditch, penniless louts gorging themselves with the only joy that cost nothing. And these fools grumbled at their life when they had bellyfuls of the one and only happiness of love! How gladly he would have starved like them if he could have begun his life again with a woman who would give herself to him here on the ground with all her body and all her heart. His misfortune was without any possible consolation, and he envied these poor wretches. He rode slowly home with bowed head, tortured by these long-drawn-out sounds in the depths of the black countryside, where he seemed to hear nothing but kisses.

THE Plan-des-Dames was a great clearing recently opened
up by tree-felling. It was on a gentle slope, girt by lofty trees,
magnificent beeches whose straight, regular trunks surrounded it with a white colonnade flecked with green lichens. Some
of the fallen giants still lay on the grass, while to the left a pile
of sawn logs stood in a geometrical cube. With the coming of
evening the cold had sharpened, and the frozen mosses
crackled under foot. At ground level it was quite dark already,
but the higher branches showed up against the pale sky, in
which the rising full moon would soon dim the stars.

Nearly three thousand mining folk had come to the meeting-place, a milling crowd of men, women, and children gradually pouring into the clearing and overflowing into the under-
growth. Latecomers were still arriving, and the sea of faces
wrapped in shadow stretched as far as the nearby beeches. A
hum of conversation rose from it like a stormy wind in the
still, frozen forest.

Étienne stood at the top, looking down the slope, with Rasseneur and Maheu. A dispute had broken out and their voices
could be heard in sudden bursts. Men standing near were
listening, Levaque with clenched fists, Pierron turning his
back to them and very worried because he had not been able
to plead sickness any longer. Grandpa Bonnemort was there
too, and old Mouque, side by side on a log, looking very
philosophical. And behind them were the scoffers, Zacharie,
Mouquet, and others who had come for fun; but the women,
on the contrary, made a very serious group, as solemn as
though they were in church. Maheude silently nodded while
la Levaque swore under her breath. Philomène was coughing,
her bronchitis having returned with the winter. The only one
who frankly laughed was Mouquette, tickled by the way Ma
Brûlé was carrying on about her daughter, calling her an unnatural creature who had got rid of her mother so as to guzzle
rabbit, a creature who sold herself and throve on her husband's
cowardice. Jeanlin had taken up his position on the pile of

271

wood, hoisting up Lydie and making Bébert follow, all three of them up in the air and higher than anybody else.

The dispute had arisen because Rasseneur wanted to proceed constitutionally by electing officers. He was still smarting from his defeat at the Bon Joyeux, and he had sworn to have his revenge, counting on regaining his former prestige with the rank and file of the miners and not merely with the delegates. Étienne thought that a committee was outrageous and ridiculous here in the forest. Since they were hunted down like wolves they must act like revolutionaries and savages.

Seeing that the argument might go on for ever, he took control of the crowd at once by standing on a felled trunk and shouting:

'Comrades! comrades!'

The confused murmur died down like a long-drawn-out sigh. While Maheu silenced Rasseneur's protests, Étienne went on in stentorian tones:

'Comrades, since we are forbidden to speak, since they put the police on to us as though we were thieves, we have come here to thrash the matter out! We are free here, we are at home, and nobody will come and shut us up, any more than you can the birds and animals!'

He was answered by a thunder of cries and exclamations.

'Yes, yes the forest is ours, we've a right to talk here. . . . Go on!'

Étienne stood still for a moment on his log. The moon was still too low on the horizon, and only lit the topmost branches, so that the crowd, which had gradually calmed down into complete silence, was still lost in shadow. He too looked black, and stood out above the crowd at the top of the slope like a dark pillar.

Slowly he raised one arm and began; but his voice no longer thundered, for he had adopted the frigid tones of a simple representative of the people making his report. Now at last he was able to work in the speech which the police had cut short at the Bon Joyeux. He began with a rapid history of the strike, making a point of expressing it with scientific eloquence – facts, nothing but facts. He spoke first of his dislike of strikes; the miners had not wanted this one, the directors had provoked them with their new scale of payment for timbering. Then he reminded them of the first approach made by their delegates to the manager, and of the bad faith of the Administration; and then, later, at the time of their second deputation, the tardy concession, the two centimes* given back after they had tried to steal them. So now here they were: he quoted figures to show that the provident fund was exhausted, gave details of the allocation of the help that had been sent, devoted a few sentences to excusing the International, Pluchart, and the others for not having done more for them in the middle of all their preoccupations in the struggle for world conquest. So the situation was daily going from bad to worse, the Company had given them back their cards and was threatening to take on workers from Belgium, moreover they had intimidated the weaker brethren and had persuaded a number of miners to go back to work. He still spoke in a monotonous tone, as though to drive home the seriousness of his news; he told of the victory of famine and the death of hope, the struggle that had reached the culminating frenzy of courage. Then suddenly, without raising his voice, he concluded:

'It is in these circumstances, mates, that you must come to a decision tonight. Do you want the strike to go on? And if so, what do you propose to do to beat the Company?'

A great silence fell from the starry sky. In the darkness the unseen crowd held its peace at these heartbreaking words, and a sigh of despair was the only sound that could be heard through the trees.

But already Étienne was speaking again, in a different voice. He was no longer the secretary of an Association, but a leader, an apostle bringing the gospel of truth. Were there any cowards among them who would break their word? Why, they would have suffered for a whole month in vain and go back to the pits hanging their heads, back once again to face the never-ending agony! Wouldn't it be better to die at once in an attempt to destroy the tyranny of capital starving the workers? Wasn't it a stupid game that they had had quite

*Zola's text gives *ten* here, but *two* on all other occasions when the dispute is mentioned.

enough of, this business of always submitting under the lash of hunger until it came to the point when once again hunger drove even the meekest of them to revolt? He showed how the miners were exploited and were the only ones to suffer from these disastrous crises, reduced to starvation whenever the exigencies of competition brought down prices. No! the timbering scale was unacceptable, it was only a disguised economy, they meant to rob each man of one hour of his working day. This time it had gone too far, and the time was coming for the downtrodden worms to turn and see justice done.

He paused, with arms outstretched. The word justice shook the crowd, and a burst of applause passed over it like the rustle of dry leaves. Voices shouted:

'Justice! it's high time. . . . Justice!'

Gradually Étienne was warming up. He lacked Rasseneur's facile stream of words. Often he was at a loss, and had to use tortuous sentences from which he emerged with an effort emphasized by a forward lunge of his shoulders. But when he was pulled up in this way he found simple, energetic images which struck home to his audience, whilst his movements, those of a workman on the job, elbows now well back and now thrust forward to strike out with his fists, his jaw suddenly jutting out as though to bite, had an extraordinary effect upon his mates. As they all said, he was not very big but he made you listen.

'The wage system is a new form of slavery,' he went on in a still more ringing voice. 'The mine should belong to the miner, like the sea to the fisherman and the earth to the peasant. . . Do you understand? The mine is yours – yours, for you have all paid for it with a hundred years of blood and misery!'

He faced up squarely to the thorny legal question, and lost his way in the maze of special regulations on mines. The subsoil belonged to the nation just as much as the soil. It was only a hateful privilege that handed over the monopoly to the Companies, and this was all the more shameful in the case of Montsou, where the so-called legality of the concessions was complicated by agreements made ages ago with owners of ancient fiefs according to the old custom of Hainault. The mining folk had only to reconquer their own possessions, he said, as with a wave of the hand he took in the whole country, beyond the forest. Just then the moon rose clear of the topmost branches and lit him up. When the crowd, still in darkness, saw his figure standing out white, distributing fortunes with open hands, they burst out again into prolonged applause.

'Yes, yes, quite right! . . . Bravo!'

Then Étienne trotted out his favourite subject, the collectivization of the means of production, as he said more than once in a phrase the pedantic jargon of which pleased him mightily. His own evolution was now complete. He had started from the sentimental fraternity of the novice, the need to reform the wage system, and now he had reached the political theory of abolishing wages altogether. Since the Bon Joyeux meeting his collectivism, from being vague and humanitarian, had hardened into a complicated programme each point of which he could argue scientifically. As a first point he affirmed that liberty could only be gained by the destruction of the State. Then, when the people had the government in their own hands, reforms could begin: return to the primitive community, substitution of a free and equal family for the morally oppressive one, absolute civil, political, and economic equality individual independence guaranteed thanks to the possession of the tools for work and of the whole output, and finally free technical education paid for out of collective funds. That involved a total recasting of the old corrupt society: he attacked marriage and the right to bequeath property, limited everybody's personal fortune and overthrew the iniquitous monument of dead centuries with the same repeated sweeping gesture of the harvester striking down the ripe corn with his scythe; then with the other hand he built humanity of tomorrow, an edifice of truth and justice rising in the dawn of the twentieth century. Reason tottered before this mental effort and left only the obsession of the fanatic. Gone were the scruples of his human feeling and common sense, and nothing seemed simpler than the realization of this brave new world: he had foreseen everything and he referred to it as though it were a machine he could fix up in a couple of hours, and neither fire nor blood counted.

'It is our turn now,' he yelled in a final crescendo. 'It is our turn to have power and wealth!'

Acclamations roared towards him from the depths of the forest. By now the moon lit up the whole clearing and picked out the isolated points in the sea of heads, far off into the dim recesses of the glades between the tall grey trunks. Here, in the icy winter night, was a whole people in a white heat of passion, with shining eyes and parted lips, famished men, women, and children let loose to pillage the wealth of ages, the wealth of which they had been dispossessed. They no longer felt the cold, for these burning words had warmed them to the vitals. They were uplifted in a religious ecstasy, like the feverish hope of the early Christians expecting the coming reign of justice. Many obscure phrases had baffled them, they were far from understanding these technical and abstract arguments, but their very obscurity and abstract nature broadened still further the field of promises and carried them away into hallucinations. What a wonderful dream! To be the masters and suffer no more! To enjoy life at last!

'That's right, by God! Our turn now! Death to the exploiters!'

The women were hysterical. Maheude forgot her usual calm and yielded to the intoxication of hunger, la Levaque was yelling, Ma Brûlé, beside herself, was waving her witch's arms, Philomène was shaking herself to pieces in a fit of coughing, and Mouquette was so worked up that she was shouting endearments at the speaker. Amongst the men, Maheu was quite won over and had exclaimed with impatience at Pierron trembling on one side of him and Levaque talking too much on the other, whilst the scoffers, Zacharie and Mouquet, feeling ill at ease, tried to raise a giggle by saying how amazed they were that the comrade could say so much without having a drink. But the biggest noise of all came from the wood-pile, on which Jeanlin was shouting and egging on Bébert and Lydie by brandishing the basket containing Poland.

The clamour rose again. Étienne was tasting the heady wine of popularity. This was power that he was holding in his hands, materialized in the three thousand breasts whose hearts were beating at his bidding. Had he deigned to come, Souvarine would have applauded his ideas in so far as he recognized them, and would have been pleased to see his pupil's progress towards anarchy. He would have given his approval to the programme, except in the matter of education, which was a relic of sentimental silliness, for holy, salutary ignorance must be the bath in which men would be tempered anew. As for Rasseneur, he was shrugging his shoulders in angry scorn.

'You are going to let me speak!' he shouted at Étienne.

Étienne jumped down from his tree-trunk.

'Speak away, we'll see if they listen to you!'

Rasseneur had at once jumped up in his place and was already waving his arms for silence. But the noise did not die down, for his name was being passed on from the front rows, who had recognized him, to the back rows away under the beeches; and they refused to give him a hearing, for he was a fallen idol the very sight of whom annoyed his former supporters. His facile elocution and cheery flow of words, which had charmed them so long, was now treated as lukewarm tea fit only for lulling cowards to sleep. He bellowed in vain through the din, trying to bring out once again his stock speech on appeasement: the impossibility of changing the world by acts of parliament, the necessity of allowing social evolution time to come about. But they only laughed and shushed him, and his defeat at the Bon Joyeux now worsened beyond redemption. In the end they threw bits of frozen moss at him, and a woman's shrill voice screamed: 'Down with the traitor!'

He was trying to explain that the mine could never be the miner's property in the way that the loom is the weaver's, and that he preferred profit-sharing, which made the worker an interested party, one of the family, so to speak.

'Down with the traitor!' a thousand voices repeated, and stones began to whistle.

Rasseneur turned pale and his eyes filled with tears of despair. His whole life-work was crumbling, twenty years of ambitious fraternizing crushed by the ingratitude of the mob. He stepped down from the log, cut to the heart and without the strength to go on.

'You think it's funny,' he stammered to the triumphant Étienne. 'All right, I hope it happens to you! And happen it will, make no mistake!'

And as though disclaiming any responsibility for the misfortunes he could foresee, he made one final sweeping gesture and walked off alone into the quiet and silvery countryside.

Some cat-calls were raised, and to everybody's amazement old Bonnemort could be seen standing on a log and holding forth in the midst of the uproar. Until then Mouque and he had stood there absorbed, appearing, as they always did, to be musing on far-off things. Probably he was overcome by one of those garrulous fits which suddenly came and stirred up the past so violently that his memories welled up and poured out of his mouth for hours. A deep silence had fallen, and they listened to this old man, this ghostly spectre in the moonlight and as he was telling things with no obvious bearing on the discussion, long stories that nobody could understand, the amazement grew. He was talking about his own young days, the death of his two uncles who were crushed in a fall at Le Voreux, then he went on to the pneumonia that had carried off his wife. But through it all he clung to his point: things had never gone well in the past and they never would in the future. For example, they had had a meeting in the forest, five hundred of them, because the king would not reduce working hours; but then he stopped short and began the story of another strike – he'd seen so many of them, he had! And they all finished up under these here trees in the Plan-des-Dames, or else at the Charbonnerie, or further off still, over Saut-du-Loup way. Sometimes it was freezing, sometimes it was blazing. One night it had rained so hard that they had gone home without saying anything. And the king's soldiers arrived and it ended up with shooting.

'We put our hands up like this, and swore never to go back. Oh, I've sworn, I have. . . . oh, yes, I've sworn!'

The crowd was gaping in uncomfortable amazement when Étienne, who had been watching the scene, leaped on to the fallen tree and stood beside the old man. He had recognized

Chaval among his friends in the front row, and the thought that Catherine must be there too had put new fire into him, and a desire to be applauded in front of her.

'Comrades, you have just heard, here is one of our old friends and that's what he has suffered, and what our children will suffer if we don't have it out once and for all with these thieves and murderers.'

His rage was terrifying. Never had he spoken so vehemently. With one arm he supported old Bonnemort, displaying him like a flag of misery and grief, crying for vengeance. In rapid phrases he went back to the first of the Maheus, and told of the whole of this family done to death in the pit, victimized by the Company, hungrier than ever after a hundred years of toil; and then by contrast he pictured the bellies of the directors sweating money, the great crowd of shareholders kept like whores for a century, doing nothing, just enjoying their bodies. Wasn't it terrible to think of? A whole race of people dying down in the pits, sons after their fathers, so that bribes could be given to Ministers and generations of noble lords and bourgeois could give grand parties or sit and grow fat by their own firesides! He had studied miners' occupational diseases and now brought them all out with horrible details: anaemia, scrofula, black bronchitis, choking asthma, paralysing rheumatism. They, poor devils, were just machine-fodder, they were penned like cattle in housing estates, the big Companies were gradually dominating their whole lives, regulating slavery, threatening to enlist all the nation's workers, millions of hands to increase the wealth of a thousand idlers. But the ignorant miner, the mere brute buried in the bowels of the earth, was a thing of the past. In the depths of the mine an army was springing up, a harvest of citizens germinating like seeds that would break through the earth one sunny day. And then they would know whether, after forty years' service, they could dare to offer a hundred and fifty francs as a pension to an old man of sixty, spitting coal and with legs swollen with the water of the coal-face. Yes, labour would call capital to account, capital, that impersonal god, unknown to the worker, crouching somewhere in his mysterious tabernacle whence he sucked the blood of the poor starving

279

devils he lived on! They would go and hunt him out, and make him show his face in the glare of fires, they would drown him in blood, this disgusting hog, this monstrous idol gorged with human flesh!

He stopped, but his arms remained stretched out into space, pointing at the enemy over there, somewhere, wherever he might be in the world. This time the clamour raised by the crowd was so loud that the bourgeois of Montsou heard it and looked anxiously towards Vandame, thinking it was some terrible landslide. Night birds flew up out of the woods and soared into the moonlit sky.

He wanted an immediate decision.

'Comrades, what have you decided? Do you vote for going on with the strike?'

'Yes, yes,' roared the voices.

'Then what steps are you going to take? If any blacklegs go down the pit tomorrow we are bound to be beaten.'

The voices rose again like a hurricane:

'Death to all blacklegs!'

'Very well, then, you have decided to hold them to their duty and sworn word. This is what we could do: go to the pits, our presence will stop the blacklegs, and we could show the Company that we are all in agreement and will die rather than surrender.'

'Right-oh! to the pits, to the pits!'

All the time he had been speaking Étienne had been looking for Catherine among the pale, roaring faces down there. No, she could not be there. But Chaval he could still see, making a point of sneering and shrugging his shoulders, consumed with jealousy and ready to sell himself for a little of Étienne's popularity.

'And if there are any informers amongst our numbers, mates,' Étienne went on, 'let them look out, for we know who they are. Yes, I can see some Vandame men who haven't left their pit.'

'Is that for my benefit?' asked Chaval with a fine show of bravado.

'Yours or anybody else's. But, as it's you who have spoken, you might as well understand that those who have got some-

280

thing to eat are quite a different thing from those who go hungry. You are working at Jean-Bart. . . .'

A mocking voice broke in:

'Oh, he works, does he? No, he's got a woman who works for him.'

Chaval went scarlet and swore.

'Christ! aren't we allowed to work, then?'

'No!' shouted Étienne, 'not when your mates are going through hell for the good of all. We are not going to let people crawl over to the bosses' side just to do themselves a good turn. If the strike had been general we should have been the masters long before this. Ought a single Vandame man to have gone down when Montsou was out? The trump card would be if the whole area stopped work – at Monsieur Deneulin's same as here. Do you see? they're all blacklegs on the coal-faces at Jean-Bart. You are all traitors!'

The crowd round Chaval was getting dangerous; fists were being brandished and cries of death were heard. He had turned pale. But in his furious determination to get the better of Étienne, he suddenly had an idea.

'Just you listen to me now! You come to Jean-Bart to-morrow and see for yourselves whether I am working! We are all on your side, and that's what I was sent here to say. The furnaces have got to be put out, and the enginemen must come out too. And if the pumps give out, all the better! The water will burst up the pits and the whole bloody lot.'

He was wildly applauded in his turn, and from then on even Étienne was edged into the background, as speaker after speaker mounted the fallen trunk, waved his arms about in the din and threw out the wildest proposals. It was now a par-oxysm of blind faith, the impatience of a religious sect, weary of waiting for a miracle and determined to provoke one itself. These people, light-headed with hunger, saw red, had visions of fire and blood in a glorious apotheosis out of which uni-versal happiness was rising before their eyes. The peaceful moonlight bathed this surging swell, and the clamour for blood was hemmed in on all sides by the deep silence of the forest. The frozen moss crackled under foot, whilst the beeches, standing tall and strong, spreading the delicate tracery of

281

their branches black against the sky, were blind and deaf to the poor wretches moving at their feet.

There was some pushing in the crowd, and Maheude found herself next to her husband, and both of them, crazed by the long-drawn-out exasperation of the past months, were backing up Levaque who was going one better than everybody else and demanding the heads of the engineers. Pierron had vanished. Bonnemort and Mouque, both talking at once, were saying vague and terrible things that nobody could hear. Zacharie, just for fun, was agitating for the demolition of the churches, whilst Mouquet was banging the ground with his *crosse*, just to add to the row. The women were quite off their heads: la Levaque, hands on hips, was going for Philomène, whom she accused of laughing; Mouquette talked of putting the police out of action by kicking them up the so-and-so; Ma Brûlé, who had been cuffing Lydie for being without her basket or any salad either, was aiming punches into the air, for all the bosses she would have liked to get hold of. For a moment Jeanlin had been overcome with panic, Bébert having heard from a fellow that Madame Rasseneur had seen them take Poland; but he soon decided to go back and let the rabbit loose at the door of the Avantage, and set about yelling louder than ever, opening and brandishing his new knife and proudly making the blade gleam.

'Comrades! comrades!' Étienne was repeating, at the end of his tether, hoarse with trying to get a moment's silence in order to come to some definite decision.

At last he got their attention.

'Comrades! tomorrow morning at Jean-Bart; is that settled?'

'Yes, yes, to Jean-Bart! Death to the traitors!'

The three thousand voices rose to heaven in a tempest, and died away in the pure light of the moon.

Part Five

•••

[1]

IT was four o'clock, the moon had set and the night was very
dark. At Deneulin's everybody was still asleep, and the old
brick house stood silent and dark, with doors and windows
closed, at the end of the large, untidy garden separating it
from the Jean-Bart pit. The front of the house looked on to the
deserted road to Vandame, a big village hidden behind the
forest, about three kilometres away.

Deneulin, exhausted after having spent part of the previous
day at pit-bottom, was snoring with his face to the wall when
he dreamed that somebody was calling him. When he at
length came out of his dream he really did hear a voice, and
ran and opened the window. It was one of his deputies, standing in the garden.

'What is it?' he asked.

'It's mutiny, sir. Half the men refuse to work and won't let
the others go down.'

He did not quite grasp what was being said, for his head
was still heavy and buzzing with sleep, and the extreme cold
had caught him like an icy shower.

'Then, good God, make them go down!' he managed to
stammer out.

'It has been going on for an hour already,' went on the deputy, 'so we thought we had better come for you. You are the
only one who might be able to make them see reason.'

'All right, I'll come.'

He hurriedly dressed, quite clear-headed now, and very per-
turbed. The house could easily have been burgled, for neither
the cook nor the manservant had stirred. By now frightened
voices were whispering across the landing, and when he came

out the door of his daughters' room opened and they both emerged, having slipped on white dressing-gowns.

'What's the matter, Daddy?'

Lucie, the elder, was already twenty-two, tall, dark, and dignified, whilst the younger, Jeanne, just nineteen, was small, golden-haired, charming and graceful.

'Nothing serious,' he answered reassuringly. 'It seems that some awkward customers are kicking up a row down there, and I'm going to see about it.'

But they protested that he must not go without having something hot, or else he would come back ill, with his stomach all upset as usual. He argued, swore that he was in too much of a hurry.

'Now, listen,' said Jeanne, clinging to his neck, 'drink just a little glass of rum and eat a couple of biscuits. If you don't, I shall stay like this and you'll have to carry me with you.'

He had to give in, grumbling that the biscuits would stick in his throat. They went downstairs with him, each holding a candlestick. In the dining-room they eagerly waited on him, one pouring out the rum and the other running off to the pantry for a packet of biscuits. As they had lost their mother when they were very young, they had been brought up alone and in a haphazard way by an indulgent father. The elder was obsessed by her dream of singing on the stage and the younger mad on painting, in which she displayed daringly individual taste. But when serious business troubles had forced the household to retrench, these apparently harum-scarum girls had suddenly blossomed into sensible and shrewd housewives, with an eye for even a few centimes out in the accounts. And now, for all their bohemian manners, they held the purse-strings, watched every sou, haggled with the tradesmen, constantly refurbished their clothes, and managed to put a decent face on the growing poverty of their home.

'Eat them up, Daddy,' said Lucie.

But, noticing how he relapsed into silence and gloomy thoughts, her fears returned.

'It must be serious, then, for you to pull such a face? Look here, we'll stay at home with you; they can do without us at this lunch-party.'

284

She was referring to an excursion arranged for that morning. Madame Hennebeau was to go in her carriage and pick up Cécile at the Grégoires' and then come to collect them, and they were all going to Marchiennes to lunch at the Forges as guests of the manager's wife. It would be a change to go over the workshops and see blast-furnaces and coke-ovens.

'Yes, of course, we'll stay here,' echoed Jeanne.

But he would not hear of it.

'The idea! I tell you once again, it's nothing much. Be so good as to go back to bed and be ready for nine o'clock, as you had arranged.'

He kissed them and hurried off, and his footsteps could be heard dying away on the frozen earth of the garden.

Jeanne carefully corked up the rum bottle and Lucie locked the biscuits away. The room was bare and clean as all rooms are where the fare is frugal. Then they both took advantage of being down so early to have a look round in case anything had been left lying about since the day before. There was a napkin out, the servant would get a scolding. Finally they went upstairs again.

As he took a short cut along the narrow paths of the kitchen-garden, Deneulin was thinking of his fortune in jeopardy, the Montsou *denier*, the million he had realized and dreamed of multiplying tenfold, and which was now so seriously threatened. He had had an uninterrupted series of misfortunes: enormous unforeseen repairs, ruinously costly working conditions, and finally this disastrous industrial crisis just at the moment when some profit was beginning to come in. If the strike broke out in his pit he would be finished. He pushed open a little gate, and in the pitch darkness the colliery buildings could be guessed at, rather than seen, by the even deeper blackness starred with a few lamps.

Jean-Bart was not as important as Le Voreux, but its modernized plant made it a nice pit, as the engineers put it. Not only had the shaft been widened by a metre and a half and taken down to a depth of seven hundred and eight metres, but it had been newly equipped with a new winding-engine, new cages, in fact completely new plant fitted up in accordance with the most recent scientific developments. And this deliberate elegance extended even to the buildings, for the screening-shed had a carved frieze, there was a clock-tower, and the top landing and winding-house were rounded like renaissance chapels, the whole being surmounted by a chimney adorned with a mosaic spiral in red and black bricks. The pump was installed in the other shaft of the concession, the former Gaston-Marie pit, now used exclusively for drainage. To the right and left of the main winding-shaft Jean-Bart had only two subsidiary shafts, one for the steam ventilator and the other for ladders.

That morning Chaval had been the first to arrive, at three o'clock, and had set about corrupting his mates, convincing them that they ought to imitate the Montsou men and demand a rise of five centimes per tub. Soon the four hundred colliers had overflowed from the locker-room into the top landing, with much shouting and gesticulating. Those who wanted to work were standing barefoot, lamp in hand and pick and shovel under their arms, whilst the others, still wearing their clogs and with their coats on because of the cold, were barring the way to the shaft. The deputies had shouted themselves hoarse in their attempts to restore order, begging the men to be reasonable and not prevent those who wanted to work from going down.

Seeing Catherine in her trousers and vest, with her hair tucked into her blue cap, Chaval flew into a rage. When he got up he had roughly ordered her to stay in bed, but she had followed him all the same because this stoppage of work filled her with dismay. As he never gave her any money and she had to keep both of them, what would become of her if she earned nothing? She was haunted by fear of the brothel at Marchiennes, which was where pit-girls ended up when they found themselves without food and lodging.

'What the bloody hell are you doing here?' he asked.

She nervously pointed out that not having a private income she wanted to work.

'Then you set yourself up against me, you bitch? Go home at once or I'll send you there with kicks up the behind!'

She backed away in fear, but did not go, determined to see how things would turn out.

Deneulin came down the staircase from the screens. In spite of the dim light of the lanterns he took the whole scene in at a glance: the mob of shadowy figures, every one of whom he knew, colliers, onsetters, trammers, haulage girls, and even the pit-boys. In the vast shed, still new and clean, the interrupted work was waiting, the engine, with steam up, was gently blowing off, the cages were suspended from motionless cables, tubs were standing unattended on the iron floor. Scarcely eighty lamps had been taken, and the rest were still burning in the lamp-room. But no doubt a word from him would suffice and everything would start up again.

'Well, well! What's the matter, boys?' he asked in a loud voice. 'What's upsetting you? Tell me all about it, and we'll thrash it out!'

He usually treated them in a fatherly way, though expecting good, hard work. He was brusque and authoritative and always tried first to get his way by bursts of mateyness loud as bugle-calls; and he often won the men's affection, for they respected him above all as a man of courage, always down at the coal-face with them, the first on the scene of danger as soon as any accident alarmed the pit. On two occasions, after firedamp explosions, when even the bravest flinched, he had been let down by a rope tied under the armpits.

'Now then,' he went on, 'you are not going to make me regret having trusted you, are you? You know I turned down an offer of police protection. . . . You can talk quietly, I am listening.'

But nobody spoke, and they all shuffled away in embarrassment. In the end it was Chaval who acted as spokesman:

'It's like this, Monsieur Deneulin. We can't go on working because we want five centimes more per tub.'

He looked amazed.

'What! five centimes? Why this demand? It isn't as though I complained about your timbering. I don't want to impose a new rate, like the Montsou Company.'

'That's as may be, but our mates at Montsou are right all the same. They won't have the new rates and are insisting on a rise of five centimes because it isn't possible to do the job

287

properly under the present contracts. We want five centimes more, don't we, mates?'

Voices backed him up and the hubbub began again, with threatening gestures. Gradually they were closing in and forming a compact ring.

Deneulin's eyes flickered with anger and he clenched his fists, for he was a man who liked strong government, and he was afraid of yielding to the temptation to seize one of them by the scruff of the neck. Better to argue reasonably.

'You want five centimes, and I grant you the job is worth it. Only I can't give it to you. If I did I should be finished, that's all. You must understand that I have to get a livelihood first, if you are to have one. And now I have reached the end, the slightest increase in costs would send me up the spout. Two years ago, you may remember, at the time of the last strike I gave in. I still could, then. But all the same that rise meant ruin to me, and these two years have been a constant struggle. Today I would rather throw up the whole thing straight away than not know where to lay my hands on your next month's wages.'

As he listened to this employer so frankly explaining his position Chaval wore an ugly sneer on his face. The others looked down on the ground, obstinately incredulous, refusing to get it into their heads that any boss did not make millions out of his workmen.

But Deneulin stuck to his point. He told them about his fight against Montsou, which was always on the look-out to smash him if he were foolish enough to over-reach himself. It was fierce competition which forced him to cut his expenses, especially as the great depth of Jean-Bart increased extraction costs, and these unfavourable conditions were not really counterbalanced by the great thickness of his coal seams. He would never have raised wages after the last strike if he had not been obliged to keep level with Montsou for fear of losing his men. He held out the threat of the future – what a fine outcome it would be for them if they forced him to sell, and they came under the terrible yoke of the Company! He did not sit on a distant throne in some unknown temple; he was not one of those shareholders who paid managers to fleece the men and whom the men never saw; he was an employer, he had other things to lose as well as his money – his intelligence, his health, and his life. Stoppage of work would mean death to him, simply that, for he carried no stock and the orders had to be delivered. Neither could the capital tied up in his plant simply lie dormant. How was he to honour his commitments? Who would pay the interest on money entrusted to him by his friends? It would mean bankruptcy.

'So there you are chaps,' he concluded. 'I have tried to show you. You can't expect a man to do himself in, can you? And whether I give you five centimes or let you go on strike, it's like cutting my own throat either way!'

He was silent, and a murmour ran round the crowd. Some of them seemed to hesitate and some moved off towards the shaft.

'At any rate,' said a deputy, 'let everybody have a free hand. How many of you want to work?'

Catherine was one of the first to step forward. But Chaval angrily pulled her back, shouting:

'We're all agreed. Only bloody swine leave their mates in the lurch!'

From then on conciliation seemed out of the question. The shouting began again and men were hustled away from the shaft and nearly crushed against the walls. For a minute the owner tried desperately to fight on alone and force the mob to bend to his will, but he realized that it was stupid and useless. and had to retire. He sat for a few minutes breathless on a chair in the checkweighman's office, so overcome by a feeling of impotence that he could not think of anything to do. Eventually he recovered and told a foreman to go and find Chaval. Then, when the latter had agreed to have a parley, he sent everybody else away.

'Leave us alone.'

Deneulin's idea was to see what there was in this fellow. From the first words he spoke he realized that he was conceited and full of resentful jealousy. He therefore got at him by flattery, expressing surprise that a workman of his calibre should jeopardize his future in this way. From the way he spoke it sounded as though for some time he had singled him out for rapid promotion, and he wound up by making him a direct offer of a deputyship later on. Chaval listened in silence, but his fists, which at first had been clenched, gradually opened. A deep calculation was going on in his head: if he insisted on going on with the strike, he would never be anything more than second-in-command to Étienne, but there was a new ambition opening out before him, to become one of the bosses. His face flushed with pride and he felt exultant. And in any case, the army of strikers he had been expecting all the morning would not come now; something must have stopped them, the police most likely. It was high time to give in. But he went on shaking his head in refusal, posing as the Incorruptible, banging his hand on his heart with a great show of indignation. In the end, without mentioning the arrangement he had made with the Montsou men, he undertook to calm his mates and to persuade them to go down to work.

Deneulin remained unseen and even the deputies kept themselves in the background. For a whole hour Chaval could be heard holding forth and arguing, standing on a tub in the top landing. Some of the men booed him and a hundred and twenty of them went off in disgust, determined to abide by the decision he himself had made them take. It was now after seven and day was dawning, a clear, bright, frosty day. And suddenly the sounds of the pit started up again, and work went on where it had left off. First the crank of the engine began to plunge up and down, winding and unwinding the cables on the drums. Then, amid the clanging of signals, the descent began, cages filled, dived out of sight and rose again. The pit was swallowing its ration of pit-boys, haulage girls, and colliers, whilst labourers pushed tubs about on the iron floor with a rumbling of thunder.

'What the hell are you doing there?' Chaval shouted to Catherine as she stood waiting her turn. 'Will you go down and not stand there messing about!'

When Madame Hennebeau arrived in her carriage with Cécile at nine, she found Lucie and Jeanne quite ready and looking very elegant, although their clothes had been refurbished a score of times. But Deneulin was surprised to see Négrel accompanying the carriage on horseback. What, were men in the party too? Madame Hennebeau, sounding very motherly, explained that they had frightened her with tales about the roads being infested with dangerous characters, and that she preferred a bodyguard. Négrel laughingly reassured them: there was nothing to worry about, the usual threats from the more vocal elements, of course, but not one of them would dare throw a stone through a window. In the first flush of success, Deneulin told them about the insurrection that had been suppressed at Jean-Bart. He was quite confident now, he said. And as the young ladies stepped into the carirage on the Vandame road, everybody was delighted at the lovely weather, little dreaming that in the open countryside a long rustling sound was growing. It was the people on the march, whose trampling feet they could have heard had they put their ears to the ground.

'Very well, that's settled,' repeated Madame Hennebeau. 'You will come and fetch your young ladies this evening and have dinner with us. Madame Grégoire has promised to come and pick up Cécile.'

'I shall be there,' answered Deneulin.

The carriage set off in the direction of Vandame, Jeanne and Lucie leaning forward to smile a good-bye at their father standing at the roadside, whilst the gallant Négrel trotted along behind the flying wheels.

They went through the forest and took the road from Vandame to Marchiennes. As they were nearing Le Tartaret, Jeanne asked Madame Hennebeau if she knew the Green Hill, and she, although she had been in the neighbourhood for five years now, admitted that she had never been that way. So they made a detour. Le Tartaret was a piece of wild moorland on the edge of the forest, sterile volcanic rock beneath which a coal mine had been burning for generations. It went back to legendary times, and the local miners told a story about it. The fire from heaven had fallen on this Sodom in the bowels of the earth where long ago pit girls committed untold abominations, and it had fallen so swiftly that they had not had time to come up, so that to this very day they were still burning down in this hell. The dark red calcined rocks had taken on an efflo-rescent coating of alum, like leprosy. On the edges of fissures sulphur grew like yellow flowers. Doughty souls who were brave enough to peep down these holes at night swore that they could see flames and the spirits of the damned frizzling in the red-hot furnace below. Wandering lights moved over the surface of the ground and hot vapours, stinking of lecherous sin and the disgusting smell of the devil's kitchen, rose unceasingly. And it was here that, like a miracle of eternal spring in the midst of the accursed moor of Le Tartaret, the Green Hill stood forth with its grass for ever green, the leaves of its beech-trees for ever new, and its fields where as many as three harvests ripened. It was a natural hothouse, warmed by the burning strata below. Snow never settled there. Beside the bare trees of the forest the great clump of verdure flourished on this December day, and the frost had not even nipped its edges.

Soon the carriage sped across the plain. Négrel laughed at the legend, and explained how fire usually broke out at the bottom of a pit through fermentation of the coal-dust, and if it could not be dealt with it burned on for ever. He instanced a Belgian mine which they had flooded by diverting a river into it. But he suddenly stopped, for groups of miners had been passing the carriage for the last few minutes. They went by in silence, casting sidelong glances at this luxurious turn-out which forced them to one side. They went past in increasing numbers, and on the little bridge over the Scarpe the horses had to slacken to a walking-pace. What was going on, to bring all these people out on the roads? The young ladies were getting nervous, and Négrel was beginning to suspect that some trouble was brewing in the seething countryside. It was a relief when they reached Marchiennes. Beneath the sun which appeared to dim their fires, the batteries of coke-ovens and lofty blast-furnaces belched forth clouds of smoke which rained down soot eternally.

[2]

Aт Jean-Bart Catherine had been pushing her tub to the relay-point and back for an hour, and she was so dripping with
sweat that she paused for a minute to wipe her face.

From where he was in the depths of the seam, picking away
at the coal with the rest of the team, Chaval was surprised not
to hear the usual rumbling of wheels. The lamps were burning
badly and dust made it difficult to see.

'What's up?' he shouted.

When she called back that she was sure she was going to
melt and that her heart was missing a beat, he angrily bellowed back:

'Don't be so silly, take your shirt off, same as us.'

They were seven hundred and eight metres below ground,
at the north end, in the first gallery of the Désirée seam, three
kilometres from pit-bottom. When this part of the mine was
mentioned, colliers went pale and spoke in hushed voices as
though talking of hell itself, and most often they dismissed the
subject with a shake of the head, preferring not to discuss these
fiery depths. As the galleries dived down northwards,they
went in the direction of Le Tartaret and penetrated into the
underground fire which had calcined the rocks up above. At
the point the team had reached, the temperature at the coal-
face averaged a hundred and thirteen degrees.* It was in the
accursed city, amid the flames which passers-by on the plain
above could see down the fissures, spitting sulphur and noxious
gases.

Catherine had already taken off her jacket, and now she
hesitated, then shed her trousers, and with bare arms, legs, and
her shirt tied round her hips with a piece of string like a
blouse, she began pushing again.

'Anyhow it will be better like this,' she said aloud.

The stifling heat filled her with uneasiness. During the five
days they had been working there, she had been thinking of
the tales she had heard as a child about the girls of long ago

* 45° Centigrade.

293

who were still burning under Le Tartaret, being punished for things you dare not repeat. Of course she was too old now to believe such silly stories, but all the same what would she have done if she had suddenly seen a girl come out of the wall, red-hot like a stove and with eyes like live coals? The very thought brought her out in a fresh sweat.

At the relay-point, eighty metres from the coal-face, another girl took the tub on for another eighty metres to the foot of the incline where the receiver dispatched it with others that had come down from the higher galleries.

'Oh my, you're making yourself comfortable,' said the woman at the relay, a skinny widow of thirty, when she saw Catherine in her shirt. 'I can't, because the kids on the incline start bothering me with their dirty tricks.'

'Oh, I can't help the men!' answered Catherine, 'I feel too rotten.'

Off she went, pushing her empty tub. The worst of it was that in the bottom gallery something else made the heat unbearable, besides being near Le Tartaret. The gallery ran near some disused workings, an abandoned gallery of Gaston-Marie, also very deep, where a fire-damp explosion ten years before had set fire to the seam, which was still burning on the other side of the *corroi*, the clay wall that had been set up there and had to be repaired continually, so as to check the spread of the trouble. The fire ought to have gone out for want of air, but there must have been some unnoticed draughts to keep it alive, and it had gone on for ten years, heating the clay wall like bricks in a kiln till it burned you as you went past. And haulage ran alongside this wall for more than a hundred metres, in a temperature of a hundred and forty degrees.*

After two journeys Catherine was overcome with heat again. Fortunately the tunnel was wide and easy in this Dési-rée seam, which was one of the thickest in the district. The stratum was one metre ninety high and the colliers could work standing up. But they would have preferred a backbreaking job with a little cool air.

'Here you, have you gone to sleep?' roared Chaval again, as soon as he could no longer hear Catherine. 'How the hell

* 60° Centigrade.

294

did I come to get such a bitch. Will you kindly fill your tub and get on with it!'

She was at the foot of the seam, leaning on her shovel, having come over faint, and there she stood looking at them stupidly, and did not obey. She could not see them very clearly in the red glimmer of the lamps, they were as naked as animals, but so black and encrusted with sweat and coal that their nakedness did not worry her. Toiling in the darkness ape-like backs were straining and stretching; it was like an infernal vision of reddened limbs toiling to dropping point amid dull thuds and groans. But evidently they had a clearer view of her, for picks stopped tapping and they chaffed her for having taken off her trousers.

'Now mind how you go, you'll catch cold!'

'She's got a good pair of legs! I say, Chaval, there's room for two!'

'Oh, we want to see the rest. Lift it up – up, up!'

Quite unmoved by the laughter, Chaval fell upon her again. 'Come on, for Christ's sake! Oh, when it comes to dirty jokes she's quite all right. She'd stay there listening to them until tomorrow.'

With great difficulty Catherine made herself fill the tub, and she pushed it off. The gallery being too wide for her to get a purchase against the timbers on each side, her bare feet caught in the rails where they tried to get a hold and she moved along very slowly, with her arms held out stiff in front and her body bent double. When she reached the stretch along the *corroi*, the torture by fire began again, and sweat poured from her in great drops like heavy rain. Before she had gone a third of the relay she was streaming and blinded, and covered with black mud like the men. Her tight-fitting shirt seemed to be soaked in ink, and it clung to her skin and crept up to her haunches with the movement of her thighs; it tied her up so painfully that she had to stop work again.

What was the matter with her today? She had never felt like this before, as though her bones were made of cotton-wool. It must be the foul air. The ventilation did not work properly in this remote gallery. You breathed all sorts of gases that bubbled out of the coal like springs, sometimes in such quantities that the lamps would not burn – to say nothing of the fire-damp which everybody had given up bothering about, for the seam blew such a lot of that into the men's nostrils from one end of the fortnight to the other. She knew all about this foul air – dead air, miners called it – heavy asphyxiating gases at the bottom, light, explosive gases at the top which can blow up all the teams in a mine, hundreds of men, in one thunderclap. She had swallowed so much of it since early childhood that she was surprised to be taking it so badly now, with noises in her ears and a burning throat.

In desperation she felt she must take off her shirt. The material, every fold of which cut and burned her, was becoming a torture. She resisted the temptation and tried to push on, but was obliged to straighten herself and stand up. Then, telling herself that she would put it on again at the relay, she took everything off, string, shirt and all. with such feverish haste that she would have torn her off skin as well if she could. So now she toiled on in pitiful nakedness, brought down to the level of some female beast hunting for food in the mire, and with sooty haunches and filth up to her belly she went along on all fours like a cabhorse.

But to her dismay she found no relief in nakedness. What more could she take off? The buzzing in her ears grew louder and her temples felt as though they were being crushed in a vice. She fell on her knees. Her lamp, standing on the coal in the tub, seemed to go out. One idea rose to the surface of her swimming consciousness: she must turn up the wick. Twice she tried to examine it, and each time as she lifted it down to put it on the ground in front of her, she saw it wane as though it, too, were out of breath. Suddenly it went out and everything whirled away into darkness, a millstone was turning round in her head and her heart grew faint and stopped beating, overcome in its turn by the immense fatigue that had cramped her limbs. She had fallen on her back and was dying in the heavy asphyxiating air at ground level.

'Good God, I think she's slacking again!' growled Chaval.

He listened from the top of the coal-face, but heard no sound of wheels.

'Hi! Catherine, you lazy slug!'

His voice trailed off into the black gallery, and no answer came.

'Have I got to come and make you move?'

Nothing stirred, there was the same deathly silence. He went down in a towering rage, and ran so fast holding his lamp that he nearly tripped over her body lying across the road. He gaped at her. What was the matter? Not a try-on was it, to get a little nap? But when he lowered his lamp to look at her face, the flame nearly went out. He raised it, lowered it again, and finally understood. She must have swallowed some foul air. All his violence was forgotten and gave way to the miner's devotion to a mate in peril. He shouted for somebody to bring her shirt, and seized the unconscious girl in his arms and held her up as high as possible. When some of their clothes had been thrown round her shoulders, he set off as fast as he could, steadying his burden with one hand and holding the two lamps in the other. The deep galleries flew past him as he rushed along, turning to right and left in his quest for the cold air of the plain coming down the ventilator. He was pulled up at last by the sound of water gushing from the rock. He was at a junction with a main haulage gallery that formerly served Gaston-Marie. Here the ventilation was blowing like a hurricane and it was so cold that, when he had set his still unconscious mistress down with her back against the timbers, he was seized with a violent fit of shivering.

'Catherine, come on, for God's sake don't act the fool. . . . Sit up and let me dip this in the water.'

It frightened him to see her so limp. He managed, however, to dip her shirt in the spring and bathe her face. She was like a corpse already buried, with her slim young body still only half formed. Then a shudder ran through her childish bosom and along the belly and thighs of this pathetic little thing, deflowered before her time. She opened her eyes and murmured:

'I'm cold.'

'Ah, that's better! that's the style!' cried Chaval, immensely relieved.

He put her clothes on again; the shirt slipped on easily enough, but he cursed at the trouble he had to get on her trousers, for she could not do much to help herself. She was still bewildered, unable to make out where she was or why she was naked. When she remembered, she was overcome with shame. However had she dared to take everything off! She asked him questions: had anybody seen her like that, without even a handerchief round her middle for decency? He tried to make her laugh by inventing stories, saying how he had carried her along between a guard of honour of all their mates. And fancy her taking him at his word and sticking her behind up in the air! But later he gave her his word that the others could not even have known whether hers was round or square, so fast had he run.

'Hell, I'm dying of cold,' he said, dressing in his turn.

She had never known him so nice. Generally for each kind word he spoke she immediately got a couple of curses. How lovely it would have been to live in agreement! In her tired and weak state she was filled with sentimentality, and smiled at him, whispering:

'Kiss me.'

He did, and lay down beside her to wait until she was fit to walk.

'You know,' she went on, 'you shouldn't have bawled at me down there, because I couldn't go on any more – I just couldn't! It's not so bad for you at the face, but if you knew how baking it is along the roads!'

'Yes, I know it would be nicer under the trees,' he said, 'this pitch makes you feel bad, I daresay, poor kid.'

She was so touched to hear him agreeing with her that she put on a show of bravery.

'Oh, it's just a bad stretch. And then the air is foul today. But you'll soon see whether I really am a slug. When you've got to work, you work, don't you? I'd rather die than give in.'

There was a pause. He had one arm round her waist and was holding her close to his body to keep her from catching cold. Although she now felt strong enough to go back to the job, she was making the most of this delicious moment.

'Only,' she went on very softly, 'I do wish you could be a bit nicer to me. . . . Yes, you're so happy when you love each other a bit.'

She began crying softly.

298

'But I do love you,' he protested, 'otherwise I wouldn't have taken you to live with me.'

She only shook her head. So many men only took women for the sake of having them, and never bothered their heads about their happiness. Her hot tears ran faster and faster as she thought with wistful despair of the wonderful life she might have had if she had come across a different fellow whose arm always took her round the waist like this. Some different fellow? And the vague figure of this other man floated before her in her distress. But no, that was all over now, and all she wanted was to go on with this one, if only he would not be so rough with her.

'Very well,' said she, 'then try to be like this now and again.'

She broke down into sobs and he kissed her again.

'You silly little thing! All right, I swear I'll be nice. Anyway, I'm no worse than anybody else!'

She looked at him and began to smile again through her tears. Perhaps he was right, for you didn't see many happy women about. And although she did not quite believe in his protestations, she gave herself up to the joy of seeing him so kind. Oh God, if only it could have lasted! They were now in each other's arms again, and as they were locked in an embrace the sound of footsteps made them jump up. Three of their mates who had seen them go past had come to see what was the matter.

They all set off together. It was nearly ten, and they had their lunch in a cool corner before going back to sweat at the coal-face. They were finishing their sandwiches and were about to have a drink of coffee from their flasks, when they were alarmed by a noise of shouting in the distance. What, another accident? They got up and ran. Colliers, haulage girls, and pit-boys kept passing them, but nobody knew anything and everybody was shouting – it must be something serious. The panic was spreading all through the pit, frightened shadows ran out of passages, lamps bobbed and danced about in the darkness. Where was it? Why couldn't somebody say?

Suddenly a deputy ran by shouting:

'They're cutting the cables! They're cutting the cables!'

Then real panic broke out, with people galloping madly along the dark galleries. They all lost their heads. Why were they cutting the cables? Who was cutting them, with men still underground? It seemed unspeakable.

The voice of another deputy boomed and died away.

'The Montsou lot are cutting the cables! Everybody out!'

When he realized what it was, Chaval stopped Catherine. The thought that he would meet the Montsou men if he went up paralysed his limbs. So they had come, and he thought they had been arrested by the police! For a moment he thought of going back and getting out through Gaston-Marie, but that shaft was now out of order. He stormed and swore to cover his hesitation and hide his fear, declaring that it was silly to run like that. They were not going to be left at the bottom of the pit, surely?

The deputy's voice called again, nearer and louder:

'Everybody out! Use the ladders! Use the ladders!'

Chaval was carried along by the others. He bullied Catherine and accused her of not running fast enough. Did she want them to stay alone down here and die of hunger? Those Montsou ruffians were quite capable of destroying the ladders without waiting for everybody to get out. This horrible suggestion sent them all clean out of their minds, and it was now a wild stampede along the galleries, a lot of madmen racing to see who could get there first and go up before the others. Men yelled that the ladders had been destroyed and that nobody could get out. And when the terrified groups began to pour into pit-bottom, they hurled themselves towards the shaft like a rushing torrent, crushing one another in the narrow entrance to the escape shaft. But an old ponyman, who had just prudently taken his ponies back into the stable, looked on with contemptuous indifference. He was quite used to spending nights down below and was certain that they would always get him out somehow.

'For God's sake, go on up in front of me!' said Chaval. 'At any rate, then, I shall catch you if you fall!'

After running three kilometres she was breathless and bewildered, soaked in sweat again, and without realizing what she was doing, was letting herself be carried hither and thither by the crowd. He tugged her arm almost to breaking point, and she screamed with pain and burst into tears: he had forgotten his promise already, she would never be happy.

'Go on!' he bawled.

But she was too afraid of him. If she went up in front of him, he would rough-handle her all the time. And so she resisted, and the surge of panic-stricken workmates pushed them to one side. Water seeping from the shaft was falling in huge drops, and the floor of the bottom landing, which was over the sump filled with ten metres of slimy water, was shaking and giving way beneath the weight of stampeding feet. It was here, at Jean-Bart, that, two years earlier, there had been a terrible accident when a cable had snapped and flung the cage to the bottom of the sump, drowning two men. Everybody had this in mind, feeling that they would all end their days there if they kept crowding on to this piece of floor.

'You'd better die, then, you bloody fool,' shouted Chaval, 'and then I'll be rid of you!'

Up he went, and she followed.

From the bottom up to the daylight there were a hundred and two ladders, each standing on a narrow platform stretching across the well, in the middle of which was a square opening just big enough to allow a man's shoulders through. It was like a flat chimney seven hundred metres high, between the wall of the shaft proper and the lining of the cage shaft, a damp, black, endless well in which the ladders were superimposed almost vertically on regularly spaced platforms. It took a strong man twenty-five minutes to climb up this gigantic column, which was never used now except in emergencies.

At first Catherine climbed gaily enough. Her bare feet, hardened by the sharp-edged coal floors of the galleries, were not troubled by the square rungs covered with iron rods to preserve them, and her hands, roughened by tramming, grasped the uprights easily, even though they were too big for her grip. She was even glad to have something to think about and take her mind off her troubles in this unexpected climb, this human serpent moving upwards, three men to each ladder, and so long that its head would reach daylight while its tail was still dragging across the sump. They were not yet as far advanced as that, though, for the leaders could scarcely be a third of the way up. They had all relapsed into silence, and only the dull thud of feet could be heard, and lamps like moving stars stretched up from the bottom in an ever lengthening line.

Hearing a boy behind her counting the ladders, she thought she would count them too. They had already climbed fifteen and were coming to a level. But just at that moment she collided with Chaval's legs. He swore at her and told her to be more careful. The whole column was slowing down now and stopping. What was the matter? What was going on? Everybody found his voice again and began asking frightened questions. Anxiety had been steadily growing ever since they left the bottom, and the nearer they were to daylight the more strongly the fear of the unknown gripped them. Somebody called out that they would have to go down again because the ladders were broken. That was what was in everybody's mind, the dread of coming up against the void. Another explanation was passed down from mouth to mouth: a collier had had an accident and slipped on a rung. Nobody knew for certain and the shouting prevented anybody from hearing. Were they going to stay there all night? Finally, without anything more being found out, the climb began again, slow and painful as before, with the same bobbing of lamps and thudding of feet. They would find the broken ladders higher up, no doubt!

By the thirty-second ladder, as they were passing a third level, Catherine felt her legs and arms go stiff. At first it had been a slight sensation of pins and needles, but now her feet and hands could not feel the iron and wood. A slight pain in the muscles became much more acute and was now like a hot smarting. In the swooning feeling that was coming over her she recalled old Bonnemort's tales about the time before there was a proper ladder-shaft and girls of ten used to bring up the coal on their shoulders by completely exposed ladders, so that if one of them slipped, or even dropped a piece of coal out of her basket, three or four children were knocked down head first. The cramp in her limbs was becoming unbearable, she would never last out.

But fresh stoppages gave her some breathing space, although the panic which came down from above each time added to her distress. The breathing of people above and below was becoming more laboured, and the endless climb was communicating a general feeling of giddiness from which she suffered with all the others. She felt stifled and almost intoxicated by the darkness, maddened by the sides of a well which seemed to be crushing her in. Moreover the wet was making her shiver, for the great drops of water fell on her sweating body. They were nearing the level of the underground springs, and so much water was pouring down that their lamps were in danger of being put out.

Twice Chaval spoke to Catherine without getting any answer. What was she up to down there? Had her tongue dropped out? She might at any rate say whether she was all right. The climb had been going on for half an hour, but so wearily that he was only at the fifty-ninth ladder. Forty-three more. Catherine managed to gasp out that she was holding on somehow. He would have called her a slug again if she had owned up to being tired. The iron on the rungs must be affecting her feet, for it felt as though they were being sawn to the bone. After each movement of her arms she expected her hands would lose their grip on the uprights, for they were so stiff and skinned that she could not close her fingers, and her shoulders were so strained and her thighs so wrenched from their sockets by the continual effort that she felt she was falling backwards. What upset her most was the very slight rake of the ladders, the almost upright position which obliged her to hoist herself up by the wrists, with her stomach pressing against the wood. By now the noise of feet was drowned by heavy breathing, and a great gasping sound, intensified by the walls of this chimney, rose up from below and went on up towards the daylight. There was a groan, and word was passed along the line. A pit-boy had cut his head open on the edge of a platform.

Still Catherine climbed on. They passed through the water level and the downpour stopped, but the air was heavy with mist and smelt like a cellar, a musty smell of old iron and damp wood. She forced herself to go on counting, mechanically, under her breath: eighty-one, eighty-two, eighty-three, still nineteen more. It was only these repeated figures, with their rhythmical swing, that kept her going, for she ceased to be conscious of her movements. Above her, as she looked up, the lamps were going round in a spiral. Her blood was draining away, she felt she was dying and the slightest breath would blow her down. To make things worse, they were pushing up behind her now, the whole column was stampeding, giving in to a growing rage and exhaustion, a frantic determination to see the sun. Some of the leading ones had already reached the top and were out, which meant that no ladders had been damaged, but the thought that somebody might still do so in order to prevent the last ones from coming out when others were already breathing the fresh air above ground, put the finishing touch to their frenzy. And so when a fresh stoppage occurred everybody swore and went on climbing, pushing and shoving over each other's bodies in a last bid to get there all the same.

Then Catherine fell. She had screamed Chaval's name in a desperate appeal. He did not hear, he was fighting mad and kicking one of his mates' ribs with his heels so as to get in front of him. She was rolled over and trampled on. In her unconsciousness she dreamed that she was one of the little girls of long ago, and that a piece of coal dropped from a basket above her had knocked her down to the bottom of the shaft like a sparrow hit by a stone. There were only five more ladders to climb and it had taken nearly an hour. She never knew how she reached daylight, carried on people's shoulders, prevented from falling by the solid mass of humanity jammed in the well. Suddenly she found herself in blinding sunlight, surrounded by a booing crowd.

[3]

SINCE before dawn the villages had been seething with unrest, an excitement which was now spreading far and wide along the roads and throughout the countryside. But the departure had not come off as arranged, for the news went round that the whole plain was being patrolled by dragoons and gendarmes. It was said that they had come from Douai during the night. Rasseneur was accused of having betrayed his comrades by warning Monsieur Hennebeau, and one haulage girl had even sworn she had seen the manservant taking the note to the office. With clenched fists the men watched for the soldiers through their shutters in the wan light of dawn.

At about half past seven, as the sun was rising, another rumour came round to reassure the impatient: it was a false alarm, it appeared, just one of those military exercises which, since the beginning of the strike, the general had occasionally ordered at the request of the Prefect of Lille. The strikers detested this official, whom they accused of having tricked them with a promise of friendly arbitration, which boiled down to marching troops through Montsou once a week to intimidate them. And so, when the dragoons and gendarmes meekly went back along the Marchiennes road after contenting themselves with deafening the villagers with the trotting of their horses on the hard ground, the miners laughed at this ninny of a prefect, whose soldiers took to their heels just when things were about to warm up. Until nine o'clock they stood peacefully about in front of their houses and watched the harmless backs of the last gendarmes disappearing down the road. The good people of Montsou were still in their big beds, sleeping with their heads in their downy pillows. Madame Hennebeau had been seen leaving the manager's house in her carriage, leaving Monsieur Hennebeau working, presumably, for the closed and silent house looked dead. Not a single pit was being guarded by troops: an example of the inevitable lack of foresight at the moment of danger, the usual stupidity in times of emergency, in fact all the mistakes a government can make when a little knowledge of facts is required. At nine the miners finally set out along the Vandame road for the meeting place settled in the forest the night before.

Of course Étienne realized at once that he would not have anything like the three thousand comrades at Jean-Bart that he had counted on. Many of them assumed that the demonstration had been postponed, and the worst feature was that two or three groups had already set out and would compromise the cause if he did not get them under his control. Nearly a hundred of them who had set off before dawn must have taken refuge under the beeches in the forest to wait for the others. Souvarine, whom he went up to consult, merely shrugged his shoulders. Ten determined men did much better than a mob, he said, and turned back to the book he was reading; he refused to have anything to do with it. The thing looked like turning into emotionalism, he added, whereas all that was needed was to burn down Montsou, which was quite simple. As Étienne was going off along the passage he saw Rasseneur sitting by his iron stove, looking very pale, whilst his wife, towering above him in her everlasting black dress, was giving him a piece of her mind in trenchant but genteel terms.

Maheu's opinion was that they must keep their word. An appointment like this was sacred. But the night had cooled everybody down somewhat, and he himself was afraid there would be trouble; therefore, he said, their duty was to be on the spot so as to keep an eye on the others. Maheude agreed. Étienne repeated, with somewhat naïve optimism, that they must act in a revolutionary way but not endanger anybody's life. Before leaving he refused his share of a loaf which had been given him the day before with a bottle of gin, but he drank three nips of the gin straight off just to keep out the cold, and took a full flask away with him. Alzire would look after the children. Grandpa Bonnemort, whose legs were worn out after yesterday's running about, had stayed in bed.

They thought it wiser not to leave in a body. Jeanlin had disappeared long ago. Maheu and his wife went in one direction, cutting across towards Montsou, whilst Étienne made for the forest where he proposed to rejoin the main body of his mates. On the way he caught up with a party of women, amongst whom he recognized Ma Brûlé and la Levaque. As they marched they were eating chestnuts brought by Mouquette, swallowing them skins and all so as to have a little more in their stomachs. But he found nobody in the forest – they were at Jean-Bart already. He ran off at full speed and reached the pit just as Levaque and a hundred others were forcing their way into the yard. Miners were coming in from all sides, the Maheus along the main road, the women across the fields, all higgledy-piggledy, without leaders and without weapons, all flowing there naturally like flood water running down the slopes. Étienne spied Jeanlin perched up on a foot-bridge, in a front seat for the show. He quickened his pace and got in amongst the first. There were scarcely three hundred of them all told.

The onrush was checked by the appearance of Deneulin at the head of the stairway leading to the top landing.

'What do you want?' he shouted.

Having watched the carriage drive away, bearing his daughters who were still smiling and waving at him, he had returned to the pit, full of vague misgivings. And yet every-thing seemed in good shape: the men had gone down and coal was coming up. He was feeling more cheerful and chatting to his overman when somebody pointed out the approaching strikers. He had at once taken up a position at a window of the screening-shed, and at the sight of this flood of men surging into the yard had immediately realized he was powerless. How could he defend buildings that were open on all sides? He could not muster more than a score of his men round him. The game was up.

'What do you want?' he repeated, white with repressed anger, making an effort to accept his doom courageously.

After a certain amount of pushing and muttering in the crowd, Étienne stepped forward and said:

'We don't mean you any harm, sir. But work must stop everywhere alike.'

Deneulin frankly treated him as a fool.

'Do you think you'll do me good, then, by stopping work in my pit? You might just as well fire a gun pointblank into my back. . . . Yes, my men are down below and they are not com-ing up unless you murder me first!'

This plain speaking raised a clamour. Maheu had to re-strain Levaque, who was rushing angrily forward, while Étienne went on parleying and trying to convince Deneulin that their revolutionary action was legitimate. But the latter replied by claiming everyone's right to work. In any case he refused to argue about such nonsense; he meant to be master in his own place. All he reproached himself with was not hav-ing four gendarmes there to sweep all this riff-raff away.

'Yes, it's my fault, and I deserve what has come to me.

With people of your type nothing is any use but force. It's like the government, which thinks it can buy you over with concessions. You will throw it over when it has supplied you with the weapons, that's all!'

Étienne was trembling with rage, but still managed to hold himself in. He spoke more softly:

'I do beg of you, sir, to order your men up. I cannot answer for what my mates might do. It is in your power to avoid a disaster.'

'No, clear off! Who are you, anyway? You don't belong to my concern, you have nothing to discuss with me. You're no better than a lot of bandits roaming round the country robbing houses.'

His voice was drowned by vociferations, and the women, in particular, hurled insults. But he continued to stand up to them, and even found some relief for his pent-up feelings in these harsh and dictatorial words. Since in any case he was facing ruin, he scorned useless and cowardly platitudes. But the numbers were continually growing, already over five hundred men were advancing towards the door and he was on the point of being lynched, when his overman roughly pulled him back.

'For pity's sake, sir! It'll be murder. Where's the sense in getting men killed for nothing?'

Deneulin still struggled and protested, shouting a last word at the mob:

'You're a lot of bandits! You wait and see when we are the masters again!'

He was hurried away just as the first of them rushed the staircase, the banisters of which were twisted by the impact. It was the screaming women who were egging the men on. The door, which had no lock and was simply fastened by a latch, gave at once. But the stairway was too narrow and was jammed by the mob, which would have taken endless time to get in that way if those in the rear of the assailants had not decided to go through the other openings. Then they burst in everywhere, through the locker-room, the screening-shed, and boiler-house, and in less than five minutes the whole pit was theirs. They careered all over the three floors, uttering wild shouts and madly waving their arms in the elation of their victory over this boss who stood up to them.

Maheu was horrified, and ran to the head of the crowd, saying to Étienne:

'They mustn't kill him!'

Étienne was now running too, but when he realized that Deneulin had barricaded himself in the deputies' room, he answered:

'Well, what of it? It wouldn't be our fault, would it, with a crazy fellow like that?'

But he was very anxious, for he was still too cold-headed himself to give in to this mass hysteria. Also his pride as a leader was hurt as he saw the mob slipping out of his control and doing wild things far beyond the cold execution of the People's Will that he had planned. He tried in vain to restore order, saying that they must not put their enemies in the right by committing acts of senseless destruction.

'The boilers, the boilers!' screamed Ma Brûlé, 'put out the furnaces!'

Levaque had picked up a file and was brandishing it like a sword, dominating the tumult with a terrible cry:

'Cut the cables, cut the cables!'

Soon they were all chanting it, and only Étienne and Maheu went on protesting, shouting frantically in the midst of the uproar but unable to command silence. At last Étienne managed to get a word in:

'But there are men down there, mates!'

The din grew even louder and voices answered from all sides:

'Good job too! Shouldn't ever have gone down! . . . Serves the traitors bloody well right! Yes, yes, let them stop down there! . . . Anyhow they've got the ladders!'

When they thought of the ladders they became still more determined, and Étienne realized that he would have to give in. Fearing an even greater disaster he rushed to the winding-house, meaning at any rate to bring up the cages, so that if the cables were sawn through above the shaft they would not fall and smash them to smithereens by their enormous weight. The engineman had disappeared with the few surface workers, and Étienne seized the starting lever and pushed it over while Levaque and the two others were climbing up the iron pylon supporting the pulleys. Scarcely had the cages been secured on their keeps before the harsh sound of the file on steel could be heard. Everybody was silent and this sound seemed to fill the whole pit. They all looked up and listened with deep emotion. Maheu, in the front row, felt a savage joy come over him as though the teeth of the file were delivering them from evil by destroying the cable of one of these holes of misery so that nobody would ever go down again.

But Ma Brûlé had disappeared into the stairway leading to the locker-room, shouting:

'Let's draw the fires! To the boilers, to the boilers!'

She was followed by other women. Maheude ran off to prevent their smashing everything, just as her husband had tried to reason with his mates. She was the most level-headed of the lot: surely they could demand their rights without wreaking destruction on people's property. By the time she reached the boiler-house the women were already driving off the two stokers, and Ma Brûlé, armed with a huge shovel, was squatting in front of one of the furnaces and emptying it for all she was worth, scattering the live coals all over the brick floor, where they went on burning in clouds of black smoke. There were ten furnaces for the five boilers. Soon the women warmed up to the task; la Levaque was wielding her shovel with both hands, Mouquette tucking her clothes up to her thighs for fear of catching fire, and they were all lit up blood-red by the glare, sweating and dishevelled in this witches' sabbath. The heaps of embers mounted higher and higher, and the heat was beginning to crack the ceiling of the huge shed.

'That'll do!' shouted Maheude, 'the store-room's on fire.'

'Good job too!' Ma Brûlé screamed back. 'It'll be a good day's work. By God, I always said I'd make them pay for taking my man.'

At that moment the shrill voice of Jeanlin sang out:

'Look out! I'm going to put the fire out. I'm letting everything out.'

He had been among the first in, and had galloped about in the crowd, thrilled by all the confusion and out for mischief.

And now it had occurred to him to open the steam-cocks and let out the steam. The jets went off like gunshots and the five boilers blew off like hurricanes, with such a thunderous hissing that your ears seemed to be bleeding. Everything was hidden in the steam, the hot coals went pale, and the women became nothing but shadows making half-visible gestures. Only the boy could be seen clearly, up in the gallery behind the clouds of white vapour, looking delighted, grinning from ear tò ear with satisfaction at having unleashed this tornado.

It lasted nearly a quarter of an hour. A few pails of water on the heaps of coal had put them right out and there was no further danger of fire. But the fury of the mob was not appeased, on the contrary it was lashed up. Men came down with hammers, and even the women armed themselves with crowbars; there was talk of smashing boilers, breaking machines, demolishing the whole mine.

When Étienne was told of this he rushed to the spot with Maheu. Even he was getting carried away, drunk with the frenzy of revenge. But he fought it down and urged them to be calm, now that the cut cables, extinguished fires, and empty boilers made all work impossible. But they continued to ignore him, and he was on the point of being overruled again when sounds of booing were heard outside, from a little low door where the escape shaft came up.

'Down with the blacklegs! Look at the ugly cowards! Down with them!'

The men from the bottom were beginning to come out. The first ones were standing there blinking in the strong light. Then off they ran, trying to get to the road and make themselves scarce.

'Down with the blacklegs and cowards!'

The whole crowd of strikers ran up, and in less than three minutes there was not a soul left in the buildings, for all five hundred Montsou men formed a double line so as to force the Vandame blacklegs to run the gauntlet. And as each new miner emerged from the door of the escape shaft, with his clothes in rags and covered with the black mud of toil, he was met with renewed booings and ferocious pleasantries: Oh, look at that one! only three inches of leg and you got to his arse! And this one, look, his nose had been eaten away by the tarts at the Volcan! What about this other one whose eyes were pissing enough wax to make candles for ten cathedrals! And that tall one, all skin and no bum, and as long as Lent! A huge haulage girl appeared, with her bosom hanging down to her belly and her belly looking as though it had slipped round to her backside, and she raised screams of laughter. They wanted to feel, and the jokes began to turn nasty, and to go from nastiness to cruelty. Soon blows would be raining down. And the procession of poor devils went on, shivering and silent in the face of insults, glancing from side to side so as to dodge punches, and happy when at last they could scuttle away from the pit.

'However many of them are there, then?' asked Étienne.

He was amazed to see them still coming up and angry that it was not merely a matter of a handful of men driven to it by hunger and browbeaten by deputies. So he had been lied to in the forest? Almost everybody at Jean-Bart had gone down. But he suddenly uttered a shout and rushed forward, for there was Chaval standing in the doorway.

'Blast you! So this is your idea of keeping an appointment!'

There was a volley of curses and the crowd surged forward to throw itself on the traitor. Why, he had taken the oath with them the very day before, and now here he was down below with the others! Of all the bleeding humbugs!

'Take him away! Chuck him down the shaft! Down the shaft with him!'

Livid with fear, Chaval was trying to stammer out an explanation, but Étienne cut him short, for he was now beside himself with rage and as frenzied as all the rest.

'You wanted to be in this with us, and in it you will be. Come on, you bastard, get a move on!'

But a fresh clamour drowned his words. Catherine had just appeared, and there she was, dazzled by the sunlight and terrified at falling into the hands of these savages. Her legs were giving way after the one-hundred ladders, her hands were bleeding and she was gasping for breath, when Maheude caught sight of her and flew at her with raised fist.

'You as well, you bitch! When your own mother is dying

312

of starvation, you go and betray her for that pimp of yours!'

Maheu seized her arm and warded off the blow. But he gave his daughter a shaking, and like his wife he cursed her furiously for her behaviour, and they both went completely crazy, shouting louder than all their mates combined.

The sight of Catherine had put the finishing touch to Étienne's exasperation. He repeated:

'Come on! Let's get to the other pits! And you're coming with us, you filthy swine!'

Chaval scarcely had time to pick up his clogs in the locker-room and pull his jersey over his frozen shoulders. They dragged him off and forced him to run along with them. Poor Catherine also put on her clogs and buttoned up the old jacket with which she had been covering herself since coming into the cold, and she ran along behind her lover, determined not to leave him, for they were going to murder him, she felt sure.

Jean-Bart emptied in two minutes. Jeanlin, who had found a watchman's horn, was blowing it and making bellowing noises as though he were calling the cattle home. The women, Ma Brûlé, la Levaque, Mouquette, lifted up their skirts so as to run better, whilst Levaque twirled an axe about like a drum-major's staff. They were continually being joined by other workmates and now, nearly a thousand strong, they poured forth again into the road in a disorderly rabble, like a river in spate. The way out was too narrow, so they broke down fences.

'To the pits! Down with the traitors! Stop all work!'

A deep silence suddenly fell on Jean-Bart. Not a soul was left, not a breath was to be heard. Deneulin emerged from the deputies' room and, refusing all offers to accompany him, inspected the pit alone. He looked pale, but quite composed. First he stopped by the shaft and looked up at the cut cables: the bits of steel were dangling uselessly, the file had left a fresh wound like an open sore shining in the black grease. Then he went up to the winding-house and contemplated the motionless crank, like the joint of some gigantic limb stricken with paralysis, and he touched the metal which had already cooled, and its coldness made him shudder as though he had touched a corpse. Next he went down to look at the boilers, walking slowly past the dead furnaces, gaping open and flooded, and when he kicked the boilers they rang hollow. Well, this was the end, he was well and truly ruined. Even if he could repair the cables and relight the furnaces, where could he find any men? Another fortnight of the strike and he would be bankrupt. And in the knowledge of this certain disaster he no longer felt any hatred for the Montsou hooligans, but rather was conscious of universal complicity, sins shared by all for generations past. Brutes they might be, but they were brutes who could not read and were dying of starvation.

[4]

Under a pale wintry sun the mob straggled off across the bare frosty plain, spilling over the edges of the road, trampling down the fields of beet.

From the Fourche-aux-Bœufs Étienne had taken over control. Without calling a halt, he shouted orders and organized the march. Jeanlin ran on in front, blowing outlandish music on his horn. Next came the women in the front ranks, some of them armed with sticks, Maheude wild-eyed, as though she were gazing into the distance for the coming of the promised city of justice, Ma Brûlé, la Levaque, Mouquette, striding along in their rags like soldiers marching off to the war. If they ran into any trouble they would see whether the troops would dare to strike women. After them the straggling herd of men formed a spreading tail, bristling with crowbars, over which stood out the single axe of Levaque, with its edge gleaming in the sunlight. Étienne, in the middle, kept an eye on Chaval whom he forced to march in front of him, whilst Maheu from further back cast disapproving glances at Catherine, who was the only woman amongst all these men, determined to run along near her lover so that they could not hurt him. They were bareheaded, with tousled hair, and no sound could be heard but the clatter of clogs, like the trampling of cattle turned loose and driven on by Jeanlin's wild trumpetings.

314

Suddenly a new cry rang out!

'We want bread! We want bread!'

It was midday, and the hunger of a six-week's strike, intensified by this march across country, was growing acute in their empty bellies. The few crusts of the morning, Mouquette's chestnuts, were now things of the distant past, their stomachs were crying out for food and their suffering put the finishing touch to their fury against the traitors.

'To the pits! Stop all work! We want bread!'

Étienne who had refused to eat his share before leaving the village, was now tortured by an unbearable rending sensation in the chest. He did not complain, but every so often he automatically raised his flask and swallowed a nip of gin, for he felt so shaky that it seemed vital to have it so as to be able to carry on. His cheeks were burning and a flame shone in his eyes. But he did not lose his head and still wanted to avoid pointless destruction.

As they came to the Joiselle road a collier from Vandame, who had joined the band to get his own back on his employer, turned his mates to the right, shouting:

'To Gaston-Marie! Stop the pump! Let the water finish off Jean-Bart!'

The mob was already letting itself be headed in that direction although Étienne begged them not to stop the drainage. What was the point of destroying the workings? Angry though he was, such an idea outraged his conscience as a working man. Maheu also thought it unfair to wreak vengeance upon a machine. But the collier was still yelling for revenge, and so Étienne had to shout louder still:

'What about Mirou? There are blacklegs at work there! To Mirou! To Mirou!'

By a wave of the arm he had managed to drive the crowd back on to the left-hand road, and Jeanlin took the lead again, blowing his horn louder than ever. The crowd swirled round and for the moment Gaston-Marie was saved.

The four kilometres from there to Mirou were covered in half an hour, almost at the double across the featureless plain, which at this point was cut by the canal in a long ribbon of ice. The flat uniformity, stretching out of sight and merging into the sky as if it were the sea, was only broken by the bare trees along the canal banks, transformed by the frost into gigantic candelabra. Montsou and Marchiennes were both hidden by a slight undulation of the ground, so that there was nothing but stark immensity.

As they reached the pit they saw a deputy standing on a footbridge at the screens, waiting for them. Everybody knew Daddy Quandieu, the senior deputy of Montsou, an old boy white of skin and hair, close on seventy and a marvel of health for a miner.

'What do you think you are doing here, you interfering lot of blighters?' he shouted.

The crowd stopped dead. This was not one of the bosses, he was one of themselves, and their respect for an old workman held them back.

'There are chaps working down below,' said Étienne. 'Make them come out.'

'Yes there are,' answered Daddy Quandieu, 'at any rate there are six dozen. The rest were afraid of you buggers. . . . But I'm telling you, not one of them is coming out or you'll have me to deal with!'

Exclamations broke out, men pushed forward and women began to advance. The deputy quickly came down from the footbridge and took up his stand in front of the door.

Then Maheu tried to intervene.

'It's our right, old chap. How can we make the strike general if we don't force all the blokes to come out with us?'

The old man was silent for a moment. Evidently his ignorance about solidarity matched the collier's. He finally answered:

'It's your right, I dare say. But all I know about is orders. I'm on my own here. The men are down there until three o'clock and there they stay until three!'

His last words were drowned by booings. Fists were brandished and already the women were screaming at him and their hot breath blew in his face. With his snow-white hair and goatee beard he stood firm, his head high, and courage so uplifted his voice that above all the din he could distinctly be heard saying:

316

'By God, you shall not pass! As true as the sun is shining.
I'd rather die than let anybody touch those cables. . . . And stop
shoving, or I'll jump down the bloody shaft in front of you!'

The crowd recoiled, deeply impressed. He went on:

'Is there any swine here who can't understand that? I'm only
a working man like yourselves. I've been told to look after
this and I'm looking after it!'

Daddy Quandieu's intellect stopped at that point, in stiff
military discipline, his head was narrow and his eyes had been
dimmed by half a century of black gloom underground. The
crowd of mates stood looking at him, and they were touched,
for what he said called forth echoes of their own soldierly
obedience, brotherhood and resignation in the face of danger.
Thinking they were still unconvinced he said once again:

'I'll jump down the bloody pit first!'

The crowd moved as one man, turned and made off again
along the road that ran on and on between the fields. Once
again the chorus began:

'To Madeleine! To Crèvecœur! Stop all work! We want
bread! We want bread!'

A scrimmage had occurred in the middle of the marching
host. It was Chaval, they said, who had tried to take advantage
of the confusion and escape. Étienne had seized him by the
arm, threatening to do him in if he was thinking of any funny
business. Chaval struggled, furiously protesting:

'What's all this about? Isn't this a free country? I've been
frozen for the last hour and I want a wash. Let me go!'

It was true that the coal stuck to his skin by sweat was beginning to hurt him, and there was very little warmth in his
jersey.

'Just you keep on marching or we'll give you a wash!'
answered Étienne. 'You shouldn't have gone one better than
everybody else and asked for blood.'

They were all running along together and eventually he
turned round and saw Catherine still holding on. It hurt him
to feel her so near and so unhappy, shivering under her man's
coat and with her trousers covered in mud. She must be dead
beat, he thought, but still she ran on.

'You'd better go home,' he said.

She did not seem to hear, but as her eyes met Étienne's they showed a slight flicker of reproach. She did not stop, though. Why did he expect her to abandon her man? Chaval wasn't very nice, she knew that, and he even beat her sometimes, but still he was her man, the one who had had her first, and it made her wild that they should all go for him – more than a thousand to one! She would have defended him if she could, not for love but out of pride.

'Clear off!' said Maheu this time.

This order, coming from her father, made her slacken for a moment. She was trembling and the tears came to her eyes. But in spite of her fear she went back to the same position, still trotting along. After that they all left her alone.

The crowd crossed the Joiselle road, went a little way along the Cron road and then turned up towards Cougny. In this direction the flat horizon was broken by factory chimneys and the road was lined with wooden sheds, brick workshops with large dusty windows. They passed by the low houses of two mining villages, numbers One Hundred and Eighty and Seventy-Six, and from each, at the sound of the horn and shouts of the crowd, whole families ran out, men, women, and children, and joined on behind their comrades. By the time they reached Madeleine, they were full fifteen hundred strong. The road sloped gently downhill and the roaring torrent of strikers had to flow round the pit-bank before spreading out over the yards.

It had scarcely gone two o'clock, but the deputies had been warned and had speeded up the raising of the cages, so that as the mob arrived the men had just finished coming out, and only a score or so were left, who came out of the cage at that moment. They were pursued with stones, two of them were beaten up and one left his coat-sleeve behind. This man-hunt saved the plant and neither the cables nor the boilers were touched. The flood was already heading for the next pit.

This was Crèvecœur, and was only five hundred metres away. And once again the crowd arrived just as the men were coming up. One haulage girl was seized and flogged by the women, who split open her drawers and exposed her buttocks, to the great amusement of the men. The pit-boys were cuffed, and by the time colliers escaped they were black and blue with bruises and had bloody noses. In the growing ferocity of this age-old craving for revenge which was lashing them all into madness, the yelling went on ever more raucous, as they called for death to all traitors, screamed their hatred of ill-paid toil and roared the desperate need of empty bellies for bread. They began cutting cables, but now the file did not bite quickly enough, for everybody was mad to get on, ever on-wards. One boiler cock was broken and water thrown in pail-fuls into the furnaces cracked the iron grates.

Outside they were now talking of a march against Saint-Thomas, the most law-abiding of all the pits, which was so far unaffected by the strike. Nearly seven hundred men must have gone down to work, and that was infuriating – they would wait for them with cudgels in battle formation and see who would remain on the field! But word ran round that the gen-darmes were at Saint-Thomas, the very troops they had laughed at in the morning. How did they know? Nobody could say, but all the same panic seized them and they decided on Feutry-Cantel instead. They veered round again dizzily and found themselves once more on the road, clattering their clogs and rushing ahead. To Feutry-Cantel! To Feutry-Cantel! There must still be a good four hundred blacklegs there – what a game! This pit was three kilometres away and hidden in a depression near the Scarpe. They had already begun to climb the slope of Plâtrières, beyond the Beaugnies road, when a voice, nobody ever found out whose, spread the idea that per-haps the dragoons were there, at Feutry-Cantel. From end to end of the column the word was passed along that the dragoons were there. The march wavered and panic began to spread over this silent, workless land which they had been scouring for ages past. Why hadn't they run into the soldiers? Their very impunity puzzled them and brought to mind the reprisals they felt must be on the way.

Nobody knew where it started, but yet another word of command turned them towards yet another pit:

'To La Victoire! To La Victoire!'

Weren't there any dragoons or gendarmes at La Vic-toire, then? Nobody could say, but they all seemed reassured.

Turning right round, they went back towards Beaumont, cutting across the fields to rejoin the Joiselle road. The railway line ran across their path, but they smashed down the palings and passed over. They were now nearing Montsou and the gently undulating country flattened out, opening up the sea of beet-fields right away to the dark houses of Marchiennes.

This time it was a good five-kilometre stretch, but they were carried along by such elation that they did not notice their dreadful fatigue or their aching, bruised feet. The tail grew steadily longer as more and more comrades were picked up in each village they passed through. By the time they had crossed the canal by the Magache bridge and appeared at La Victoire there were two thousand of them. But it was past three, the men had come up, not one was left underground. They vented their disappointment in vague threats, but all they could do was throw brickbats at the rippers who were coming on to begin their shift. These were easily routed and the deserted pit was theirs. And in their fury at not having any traitors to hit they began attacking objects. An abscess of rancour was bursting, a septic boil of long, slow growth. Years and years of hunger were now torturing them with a lust for massacre and destruction.

Behind a shed Étienne saw some labourers filling a coal-cart.

'Bugger off, will you?' he shouted. 'Not one bit is going out of here!'

A hundred strikers ran up at his command and the men only just had time to get away. The horses were taken out of the shafts, some of the men pricked them in the rump and they made off, whilst others overturned the cart and broke the shafts.

Levaque threw himself at the trestles with his axe, so as to bring down the footbridges. They were too strong, however, so he bethought himself of tearing up the railway track from one end of the yard to the other, and soon the whole mob set about this task. Maheu ripped up the iron chairs, using his crowbar as a lever. Meanwhile Ma Brûlé, at the head of the women, was invading the lamp-room, where they wielded

320

their sticks and covered the floor with bits of smashed lamps. By now Maheude was quite frenzied, and lashing out as hard as la Levaque. They were all soaked in oil, and Mouquette wiped her hands on her skirt, giggling because she was so dirty. By way of a bit of fun Jeanlin had emptied a lamp down her neck.

But these acts of revenge did not feed them, and their stomachs cried out more and more insistently for food. The great lamentation arose once again:

'We want bread! We want bread!'

It happened that an ex-deputy ran a canteen at La Victoire. He had presumably taken fright, for his shack was abandoned. When the women came back from the lamp-room and the men had finished tearing up the lines, they all attacked the canteen, the shutters of which gave way at once. There was no bread there, nothing but two pieces of raw meat and a sack of potatoes. But they discovered some fifty bottles of gin, which vanished like drops of water in the sand.

Étienne was able to refill his empty flask. Gradually an ugly drunkenness, the drunkenness of the hungry, was making his eyes bloodshot and baring his teeth like a wolf's fangs between his pallid lips. And then he suddenly realized that Chaval had slipped off in the confusion. He swore, men were dispatched, and the fugitive was seized hiding behind the wood-pile, with Catherine.

'You dirty swine, so you're afraid of being compromised, are you?' roared Étienne. 'You were the one in the forest to demand a strike of enginemen so as to stop the pumps, and now you want to do the dirty on us! All right! By Christ! we're going back to Gaston-Marie and I'll make you smash up the pump yourself. Yes, that you will, by God!'

He really was drunk now, and launching his troops against the very pump he had saved from destruction a few hours earlier.

'To Gaston-Marie! To Gaston-Marie!'

They all applauded and leaped forward, whilst Chaval, still asking to be allowed to wash, was seized by the shoulders and roughly hustled along.

'You clear off!' said Maheu to Catherine, who had started her running again.

But this time she did not even flinch, but gave her father a defiant look and went on running.

Once again the mob ploughed across the bare plain, doubling back over its own tracks on the long straight roads, over ever-widening fields. It was four o'clock, and the setting sun cast the long, wildly gesticulating shadows of the rabble across the frozen ground.

They avoided Montsou by joining the Joiselle road higher up, and in order to save the detour by La Fourche-aux-Bœufs they passed beneath the walls of La Piolaine. The Grégoires had just gone out, intending to call on their lawyer before going to dinner at the Hennebeaus', where they were to pick up Cécile. The property seemed wrapped in slumber, with its deserted avenue of limes, its kitchen garden and orchard all stripped bare by winter. Nothing was stirring inside the house, the closed windows of which were misty with condensation from the warmth within. The deep silence gave an impression of good natured well-being, a patriarchal sensation made up of the good beds, good food, and carefully regulated happiness in the midst of which the proprietors spent their lives.

The crowd did not stop, but glanced angrily through the railings and along the protecting walls, bristling with broken bottles. The cry went up again:

'We want bread! We want bread!'

The only answer was the fierce barking of a pair of Great Danes with tawny coats, who stood there open-jawed. But behind the closed shutters stood the two maids, Mélanie the cook and Honorine the housemaid, whom the noise had brought there sweating with fear and deathly pale as they watched these savages go by. They fell on their knees and t ought their last hour had come when they heard a stone, just one stone, break a window-pane in another room. It was one of Jeanlin's little games: he had made a sling with a bit of rope and was leaving a little passing greeting for the Grégoires. But he had at once gone back to his horn-blowing, and as the mob receded into the distance the cry grew fainter:

'We want bread! We want bread!'

By the time they reached Gaston-Marie their numbers had

swollen still more: over two thousand five hundred madmen smashing everything, sweeping all before them with the force of a rushing torrent in spate. Some gendarmes had been that way an hour earlier, but had set off for Saint-Thomas, misdirected by some peasants, and in their haste they had not even taken the precaution of leaving a small detachment to guard the pit. In less than a quarter of an hour the fires were drawn, the boilers emptied and the buildings ransacked and laid waste. But it was the pump that they were really after. It was not enough for them that it should stop working when the steam ran out, they hurled themselves against it as though it were a living being whose life they wanted.

'You shall strike the first blow,' said Étienne, putting a hammer into Chaval's hand. 'Come on, you took your oath with the rest of us!'

Chaval recoiled trembling, and in the scrimmage dropped the hammer, but the rest of them, without waiting for him, was already slaughtering the pump with crowbars, bricks, anything they could lay hands on. Some of them even broke their sticks on it. Nuts flew off and pieces of steel were wrenched away like limbs being torn apart. A shovel aimed with full force smashed the iron cylinder and the water ran out with a final gurgle, like the hiccup of a dying man.

That was that, and once again the mob found itself outside and pressing on behind Étienne, who was still holding on to Chaval.

'Death to the traitor! Throw him down the shaft!'

The wretched man, livid and stammering out disjointed words, was still clinging to his obsession with stupid obstinacy: he wanted to wash.

'Half a jiffy, if that's what bothering you,' said la Levaque. 'Look, here's your wash-tub!'

There was a pool made by water leaking from the pump. It was white with a thick coat of ice. They broke the ice, pushed him in and forced him to rinse his head in the freezing water.

'Go on, dive in,' said Ma Brûlé. 'By God, if you don't you'll be chucked in. And now you can have a drink – yes, yes! – like the animals, with your snout in the trough!'

They made him drink on all fours, while they all roared with savage mirth. One woman pulled his ears and another rammed into his face a handful of fresh horse-dung she had found in the road. His old jersey was torn to shreds. He lurched about wildly, lunging from side to side in a desperate struggle to escape.

Maheu had pushed him about and Maheude was among those who warmed up to the job, for they both had old scores to settle with him. Even Mouquette, usually so kindly disposed to all her young men, vented her rage on this one, calling him a good-for-nothing and talking of pulling his trousers down to see if he was still a man.

Étienne stopped her.

'That'll do! There's no need for everybody to take a hand. Now, if you're ready, the two of us are going to settle this between us.'

His fists were clenched and a murderous gleam shone in his eyes; his drunkenness was turning into a lust for blood.

'Are you ready? There's only room for one of us here. . . . Give him a knife. I've got mine.'

Catherine, on the point of collapse, gazed at him in horror. She remembered what he had told her about the desire to kill a man that came over him when he had been drinking, how he went raving mad after his third glass, because his sottish forebears had planted the poison in his system. She suddenly leaped forward and boxed his ears with both hands, shouting into his face in a frenzy of indignation:

'Coward! Coward! Coward! Aren't all these abominations enough for you? So you want to murder him now that he can't even stand up!'

She rounded on her father and mother and all the others:

'Cowards! You're all cowards! Why don't you kill me with him? I'll fly at your faces if you touch him again. Oh, what a lot of cowards.'

She took up her stand in front of her man and defended him, forgetting the life of misery and how he had beaten her, inspired by the thought that she belonged to him because he had taken her, and that it brought shame on her too when he was humiliated.

Étienne had gone white when the girl hit him, and at first had been on the point of striking her down. Then he ran his hand over his face like a man coming round from a drunken stupor, and in the midst of a deathly silence said to Chaval:

'She's right, that'll do. . . . Get out!'

Chaval made off at once, followed by Catherine. The crowd stood thunderstruck and watched them go out of sight round a bend in the road. But Maheude murmured:

'You are wrong. You ought to have kept hold of him. He'll get up to some mischief for certain.'

The mob set off on the march again. It was nearly five, and on the horizon the sun, like a red-hot coal, was setting the whole plain on fire. A pedlar in the road told them that the dragoons were coming down from Crèvecœur. So they turned yet again, and the order ran along:

'To Montsou! To the Manager's! We want bread! We want bread!'

[5]

MONSIEUR HENNEBEAU had stood at his office window to watch the carriage take his wife off to lunch at Marchiennes. For a moment or two his eyes followed Négrel trotting along by the carriage door and then he quietly went back and sat down at his desk. The house seemed empty indeed when neither his wife nor his nephew enlivened it with the sounds of their existence. On that particular day the coachman was driving Madame, Rose, the new maid, had her day off until five, and the only other people left in the house were Hippolyte the manservant, slopping about the rooms in his slippers, and cook, who had been up since dawn having a battle royal with her saucepans, completely taken up with the dinner-party the master and mistress were giving that evening. Monsieur Hennebeau promised himself a good day's work in the quiet, deserted house.

At about nine o'clock, although he had orders to send everybody away, Hippolyte ventured to admit Dansaert, who had come with news. It was only then that the manager heard about the previous evening's meeting in the forest, and the details were so circumstantial that as he listened he thought of the well-known affair with Pierronne, so well-known indeed that he received two or three anonymous letters every week denouncing the overman's goings-on. It was clear that the husband had talked, for this report smacked of the pillow. He even took advantage of the opening and gave Dansaert to understand that he knew all about it, and mildly recommended a little prudence, for fear of a scandal. Taken off his guard by this criticism in the middle of his report, Dansaert floundered about his denials and apologies, though the sudden reddening of his big nose was sufficient confession of guilt. But he did not follow the matter up, for he was glad to get off so lightly, as usually the manager displayed the inflexible severity of a clean-living man when an employee indulged in a bit of fun with a pretty girl in one of the pits. The conversation went on about the strike – this meeting in the forest was only a lot of blusterers showing off, there was no serious danger. In any case the villages would certainly lie low for some days after the impression of fear and respect which the military sortie must have produced that morning.

Nevertheless, when he was on his own again Monsieur Hennebeau was on the point of sending a telegram to the Prefect, and was only held back by his fear of showing himself unjustifiably nervous. He was already painfully aware of having been so completely lacking in insight that he had said everywhere, and even written to the Directors, that the strike would last a fortnight at the most. And, to his great surprise, it had now dragged on for nearly two months, and he was desperate, losing prestige every day, feeling more and more compromised and obliged to think of some sensational achievement in order to regain favour in high places. He had asked the Directors for instructions in the event of trouble, but their reply still had not come and he expected it by the afternoon post. And so he told himself that that would be time enough to send off telegrams asking for military occupation of the pits if these gentlemen thought it advisable. In his view such a step would certainly lead to war, bloodshed, and death, and in spite of his normally forthright nature such a heavy responsibility weighed on him.

He worked on quietly until eleven, and nothing could be heard in the house but the noise of Hippolyte's floor-polisher far away in one of the first-floor rooms. Then he received two dispatches in quick succession, the first informing him about the invasion of Jean-Bart by the Montsou mob and the second reporting the severed cables, extinguished furnaces, and other damage. He did not understand. What were the strikers doing at Deneulin's instead of attacking one of the Company's pits? Incidentally they could sack Vandame if they liked, for it brought nearer to fruition the plan of conquest he had been turning over in his mind. At midday he lunched alone in the big dining-room, served in silence by Hippolyte, whose slippers he did not even hear. The loneliness deepened still more the gloom of his premonitions, and he was feeling sick at heart when one of the deputies who had come hot-foot was shown in and told him of the march on Mirou. Almost immediately afterwards, as he was finishing his coffee, a telegram informed him that Madeleine and Crèvecœur were also threatened. That drew him into a terrible dilemma. He was waiting for the two o'clock post, but ought he to summon the troops at once? Or was it wiser to possess himself in patience so as not to act before knowing the orders from Headquarters? He returned to his office, meaning to read through a note to the Prefect which he had asked Négrel to draft the day before. But he could not put his hand on it and thought that perhaps his nephew had left it in his room, where he often did his writing at night. Before coming to a decision he ran upstairs to look for the missing note in the young man's room.

He was taken aback to find that the bedroom had not been done, either through forgetfulness or laziness on Hippolyte's part. It was stuffy from having been shut up all night, especially as the door of the stove had been left open, and his nostrils were assailed by a strong scent which he thought must come from the wash-basin which had not been emptied. The room was very untidy, with clothes lying about, wet towels thrown over the backs of chairs, and one of the sheets of the unmade bed was hanging down on the carpet. He took all this in absent-mindedly, for he had made straight for a table covered with papers, still looking for the lost note. He went through the papers twice most carefully; it was not there. Where the devil had that crackbrained Paul hidden it?

As he returned to the middle of the room, looking on each piece of furniture, he saw something shining in the middle of the bed, like a spark. He went over mechanically and picked it up. It was a little gilt scent-bottle lying in a fold of the sheet. He recognized it at once. It was Madame Hennebeau's, a little phial of ether which she always had with her. But why in Paul's bed, he wondered. Suddenly he went deathly pale. His wife had spent the night there.

'Excuse me, sir,' came Hippolyte's voice through the door, 'I saw you go up, sir. . . .'

He came in, and the state of the room filled him with consternation.

'Oh Lord, yes, of course, the room hasn't been done! Rose went out and left all the housework on my hands.'

Monsieur Hennebeau had the phial hidden in his hand, clutching it so tightly that he nearly broke it.

'What do you want?'

'Sir, it's another man, from Crèvecœur, with a letter.'

'All right, leave me alone. Tell him to wait.'

His wife had slept there! He bolted the door, opened his hand and looked at the phial, which had stamped its shape red on his flesh. Suddenly he saw and understood. This filthy thing had been going on under his roof for months. His earlier suspicions came back to his mind, the sound of clothes brushing against the doors, of bare feet receding at night in the silent house. Yes, of course, it was the sound of his wife going up there!

He dropped into a chair and for many minutes stared at the bed as though stunned. A noise disturbed him, somebody knocking at the door and trying to open it. He recognized the servant's voice.

'Sir. . . . Oh, you have locked the door, sir!'

'What is it now?'

'It seems it's urgent, sir. The men are smashing everything up. There are two more men downstairs and a lot of telegrams.'

'Clear off! I'll be down in a minute.'

The thought that Hippolyte would have found the phial himself if he had done the room in the morning made his blood run cold. In any case the servant must know all about it, a score of times he must have found the bed still hot with adultery, Madame's hairs on the pillow, disgusting stains on the sheets, and no doubt he kept on interrupting him now out of sheer malice. He had probably listened at the door and enjoyed the debauches of his employers.

Still Monsieur Hennebeau did not move, but went on staring at the bed, seeing the long tale unfold, the tale of suffering, his marriage to this woman, their immediate maladjustment of body and spirit, the lovers she had had unknown to him and the one he had tolerated for ten years as one puts up with a sick woman's abnormal tastes. Then their arrival at Montsou and his fatuous hope of curing her, months of languishing in sleepy exile and the approach of middle age which he had hoped would at last give her back to him. Then the arrival of their nephew Paul, Paul to whom she had played the part of a mother, with whom she had discussed her dead passions, dead and buried in ashes. And fool of a husband that he was, he had foreseen nothing, he had worshipped this woman who belonged to him, whom all sorts of men had had and whom he alone could not possess! He worshipped her with a shameful passion, he would have fallen on his knees before her if only she had consented to give him the other men's leavings. Other men's leavings! She was giving them to this boy.

A distant bell made him start. He recognized the signal that was given on his orders when the postman came. He stood up and in his grief shouted aloud, letting out a pent-up stream of foul language.

'Oh, to hell with them! To bloody hell with the lot of them and their telegrams and letters!'

In his fury he felt he must have some midden to kick all this filth into. The woman was a bitch – he cast round for obscene words to throw in her face. The last straw was this marriage between Cécile and Paul that she was arranging with such smiling calmness. Was there no passion, not even any jealousy left in this inveterate sensuality of hers? By now the thing had

329

become simply a depraved amusement, she wanted men as a habit, a recreation, like dessert after a meal. He blamed everything on to her, almost exculpating the boy, whom she had dug her teeth into with this belated appetite, as one might bite the first green fruit picked up in the road. Whom would she devour next, how low would she sink when there were no more obliging nephews astute enough to come into their household and accept bed, board, and wife?

There was a timid scratching at the door and Hippolyte ventured to whisper through the keyhole:

'Sir, the post. . . . And Monsieur Dansaert has come back. He says it's murder!'

'I'm coming, damn you!'

What should he do to them? Turn them out of his house as soon as they came back from Marchiennes, like stinking beasts that he would not keep under his roof? He would take a stick to them and tell them to take their disgusting copulation somewhere else. The sultry warmth of this room was heavy with their mingled sighs and breath, the pungent scent that had caught his nostrils was the scent of musk from her skin – another of his wife's perverted tastes, this voluptuous desire for strong perfumes. Everywhere he found the heat and smell of fornication, of adultery as a living reality – in the jars lying about, the basins still full, the crumpled linen, the furniture, everything in this vice-infested room. He threw himself on the bed and pummelled it in impotent fury, belabouring the places where he saw the imprint of their bodies, maddened at the coverlets thrown back and the crumpled sheets which yielded soft and passive beneath his blows as though they also were exhausted after a whole night of orgies.

Suddenly he thought he heard Hippolyte coming up yet again, and a feeling of shame pulled him up. He paused one moment more, gasping and mopping his brow, trying to calm his thumping heart. He stood in front of the mirror and his face looked so changed that he hardly recognized himself. He watched it slowly return to an appearance of normality and then by a supreme effort of will went downstairs.

Five messengers were standing there, apart from Dansaert. Each one brought worse news than the other of the march of the strikers from pit to pit, and his overman told him at some length what had happened at Mirou and how it had been saved by the splendid conduct of old Quandieu. He nodded in approval, but was not taking it in, for his mind was still in that room upstairs. He eventually sent them away saying that he would take steps, and when he was alone again at his desk he buried his head in his hands and seemed to sink into slumber. But his post was waiting and he made himself pick out the expected reply from Headquarters. At first the lines danced before his eyes, but he finally gathered that these gentlemen hoped it would come to an open fight: of course they did not actually order him to make things worse, but between the lines they gave him to understand that a certain amount of disturbance would hasten the end of the strike by justifying strong repressive measures. That put an end to his hesitation, and he immediately dispatched wires in all directions: to the Prefect of Lille, to the military headquarters at Douai and the police at Marchiennes. This was a way of escape, for all he had to do was shut himself in, and, in fact, he even let it be understood that he had an attack of gout. And so he lay low in his office all the afternoon, seeing nobody, but reading the endless stream of telegrams and letters. In this way he followed the movements of the mob from Madeleine to Crèvecœur, from Crèvecœur to La Victoire, from La Victoire to Gaston-Marie. News also reached him of the behaviour of the gendarmes and dragoons, who were so flurried that they continually lost their way and turned their backs on the very pits being attacked. What did it matter? Let them murder and destroy! He allowed his head to sink back into his hands and covered his eyes with his fingers, and lost himself in the deep silence of the empty house, only broken now and again by the sound of cook's saucepans as she busied herself with the evening's dinner.

Dusk was already enveloping the room, it was five o'clock and Monsieur Hennebeau was still dazed and listless, with his elbows on his papers, when he was startled by a loud noise. For a moment he thought it was those two wretched creatures coming back, but the tumult increased and as he was going to the window a terrible cry rang out:

'We want bread! We want bread!'

The strikers were invading Montsou just as the gendarmes, deciding that an attack on Le Voreux was imminent, were galloping off in the opposite direction to occupy that pit.

It was just before this, two kilometres from the first houses of the town and a little below the crossing of the main road and the road to Vandame, that Madame Hennebeau and the young ladies had watched the crowd go by. They had had a pleasant day at Marchiennes, with a delightful lunch at the house of the manager of the Forges, followed by an interesting tour of the workshops and a visit to a nearby glassworks to fill up the afternoon. On the return journey, as this lovely winter day was drawing to its radiant close, Cécile had taken it into her head to have a cup of milk at a little farm by the roadside. They had all got out of the carriage. Négrel had gallantly leaped off his horse, and the farmer's wife, flustered by the presence of all these grand folk, was running to and fro and talking of laying a cloth before she served them. But Lucie and Jeanne wanted to see the cow milked and so they had gone down to the cowshed with their cups, making it a rustic excursion and much amused when their feet sank into the deep litter.

Madame Hennebeau, looking quite the indulgent mother, was elegantly sipping her milk when she was disturbed by a strange roaring noise outside.

'What's that?'

The cowshed was built right on the road and had a large door for carts, for it was also a hay-barn. The young ladies craned their necks and were very surprised to see a mob of people pouring out of the Vandame road like a black stream and yelling at the tops of their voices.

'The devil!' said Négrel, who had come out too, 'do these bawlers really mean business at last?'

'I expect it's those miners again,' said the farmer's wife. 'That's twice they've been past. It seems things aren't going too well and that they are the masters now round here.'

She pronounced each word carefully, watching the effect on their faces, and when she noticed how frightened and apprehensive they all looked she hastened to conclude:

'Oh, the ruffians! the ruffians!'

Realizing it was too late to get back into the carriage and

reach Montsou, Négrel ordered the coachman to move the carriage quickly into the farmyard, where the whole equipage was concealed behind a shed. A lad had been holding his horse's bridle and he now took the horse himself and tethered it inside the shed. When he returned it was to find his aunt and the girls panic-stricken and on the point of following the farmer's wife who was offering them shelter in the house. But he thought they would be even safer where they were, for nobody would dream of looking for them here in the hay. But the barn door did not shut very well and there were such wide gaps between its rotten planks that the road could be seen quite clearly.

'Courage!' he said. 'We'll sell our lives dearly.'

This witticism only increased their alarm. The noise was coming nearer; so far nothing could be seen, but a wind seemed to sweep the empty road, like a sudden squall preceding a great storm.

'No, no, I don't want to look,' said Cécile, cowering down in the hay.

Madame Hennebeau looked very pale. She was irritated at these people coming and spoiling one of her pleasures, and was standing well back, casting sidelong glances of disapproval, but Lucie and Jeanne, although trembling, had their eyes glued to a crack, for they were anxious not to miss any of the show.

The thunder drew nearer, shaking the very earth, and then Jeanlin was the first to appear, running along and blowing his horn.

'Get out your smelling-salts, the sweat of the people is going by,' murmured Négrel who, for all his republican convictions, liked to laugh at the common people when he was with ladies.

But his witty remark was lost in the din of the shouting and gesticulating mob. The women had come into sight, nearly a thousand of them, dishevelled after their tramp, in rags through which could be seen their naked flesh worn out with bearing children doomed to starve. Some of them had babies in their arms and raised them aloft and waved them like flags of grief and vengeance. Others, younger, with chests thrown out like warriors, were brandishing sticks, whilst the old crones made a horrible sight as they yelled so hard that the strings in their skinny necks looked ready to snap. The men brought up the rear: two thousand raving madmen, pit-boys, colliers, repairers in a solid phalanx moving in a single block, so closely packed together that neither their faded trousers nor their ragged jerseys could be picked out from the uniform earth-coloured mass. All that could be seen was their blazing eyes and the black holes of their mouths singing the *Marseillaise*, the verses of which merged into a confused roar, accompanied by the clatter of clogs on the hard ground. Above their heads an axe rose straight up amidst the bristling crowbars, a single axe, the banner of the mob, and it stood out against the clear sky like the blade of the guillotine.

'What dreadful faces!' was all Madame Hennebeau could find to say.

Négrel muttered:

'Devil take me If I can recognize a single one! Where have all these ruffians come from?'

And indeed rage, hunger, and two months of suffering, and then this wild stampede through the pits, had lengthened the placid features of the Montsou miners into something resembling the jaws of wild beasts. The last red rays of the setting sun bathed the plain in blood, and the road seemed like a river of blood as men and women, bespattered like butchers in a slaughterhouse, galloped on and on.

'Oh, how wonderful!' whispered Lucie and Jeanne, whose artistic taste was deeply stirred by the lovely horror of it all.

Nevertheless they were afraid and fell back towards Madame Hennebeau, who was leaning for support against a trough. She was appalled as she realized that one glimpse through the cracks in this rickety door would suffice, and they would all be slaughtered. Even Négrel, usually so brave, felt himself grow pale with a fear stronger than his will-power, the fear of the unknown. Cécile continued to lie motionless in the hay. As for the others, try as they might to avert their gaze they could not do so, but went on looking.

And what they saw was a red vision of the coming revolution that would inevitably carry them all off one bloody night at the end of this epoch. Yes, one night the people would break loose and hurtle like this along the roads, dripping with bourgeois blood, waving severed heads and scattering gold from rifled safes. The women would yell and the men's teeth would be bared like the jaws of wolves ready to bite. Yes, it would be just like this, with the same rags, the same thunderous trampling of heavy clogs, the same dreadful rabble with filthy bodies and stinking breath, sweeping away the old world like the onrush of a barbaric horde. Fires would blaze and not a single stone would be left standing in the cities, and after the great orgy, the grand feast, when in a single night the poor would empty the cellars of the rich and rip open their women, nothing would be left but wild life in the forests. Nothing at all: not a sou of anybody's wealth, not one title-deed of any established fortune, pending the day when a new world would be born, perhaps. Yes, this was what was passing them by along the road like a force of nature, they could feel its deadly blast blowing in their faces.

Over and above the *Marseillaise* a great cry went up: 'We want bread! We want bread!'

Lucie and Jeanne clung to Madame Hennebeau, herself almost swooning, while Négrel took his stand in front of them as if to protect them with his body. Could this be the very night of doom for the old social order? What they saw next put the finishing touch to their stupefaction. The main body had gone by and only the laggards were trailing on behind, when Mouquette appeared. She was dawdling in the rear, on the look-out for bourgeois at their garden gates or windows, and when she saw any, not being able to spit in their faces she showed them what was for her the supreme mark of contempt. She must have seen one now, for she suddenly lifted her skirt, proffered her buttocks and displayed her great fat behind, its nakedness lit up by the last gleams of sunlight. There was nothing obscene in this gesture, nothing laughable, it was terrible.

They all disappeared as the stream rolled on towards Montsou, following the bends of the road between the squat, gaily painted houses. The carriage was brought out from the farmyard, but the coachman said he could not take it upon himself to drive Madame and the young ladies back without delays if the strikers kept to the roadway. And the worst of it was that there was no other way.

'But we must get back, the dinner will be waiting,' said Madame Hennebeau, beside herself with vexation and fear. 'Those beastly workmen would choose a day when I have company! You see what comes of being kind to creatures like that!'

Lucie and Jeanne set to work to get Cécile out of the hay, but she resisted, thinking that the savages were still going by and repeating that she did not want to see. But eventually they were all back in their seats. Négrel jumped on his horse and then it occurred to him that they might get home by the back lanes of Réquillart.

'Go carefully,' he told the coachman, 'it's a very bad road. If there are crowds preventing you from getting back to the road at the other end you can stop behind the old pit and we can get in on foot by the garden gate. You can put the carriage and horses anywhere – some shed belonging to a pub!'

They set off. By now the mob was streaming into Montsou. Having seen the gendarmes and dragoons go through twice already the townsfolk were all agog and panic-stricken. Abominable rumours were going round, with talk of hand-written posters bearing threats that the bourgeois would have their bellies ripped open. Nobody had seen these, but that did not prevent their being quoted verbatim. The terror was at its height at the notary's, for he had received an anonymous letter through the post, warning him that a barrel of gunpowder had been buried under his cellar and would blow him up if he did not declare himself on the people's side.

The Grégoires happened to be there when the letter arrived and it delayed them, for they all discussed it and had reached the conclusion that it was a practical joke just as the appearance of the mob threw the house into paroxysms of fright. But they merely smiled, lifting a corner of the curtain and looking out, refusing to admit that there could possibly be any danger, and quite positive that everything would end up amicably. As it was just after five they had plenty of time to wait for the road to clear before crossing over to dine at the Hennebeaus', where Cécile would certainly have returned by now and would be expecting them. But nobody else in Montsou seemed to share their confidence: people were running up and down in terror and doors and windows were being banged to. Over the road they saw Maigrat barricading his shop with lots of iron bars. He was very pale and so shaky that his poor little wife had to tighten up the nuts.

The crowd was drawn up in front of the manager's house and the cry rang out:

'We want bread! We want bread!'

Monsieur Hennebeau was standing at the window when Hippolyte came in to close the shutters for fear of the glass being broken by stones. He also shut up all the ground floor and went up to the first floor, whence the squeaking of hasps could be heard, and shutters slamming one by one. It was not possible to block up the kitchen window in the same way, which was unfortunate because it was a basement window through which, alas, could be seen the red fires under the saucepans and the spit.

But Monsieur Hennebeau wanted to look, and so he went up to the second floor and wandered automatically into Paul's room. It was on the left and the best placed, for it commanded a view along the road as far as the Company's yards. He stood behind the blind, looking down on the crowd. But then he noticed the room again: the wash-stand had been wiped down and set in order and the bed stood coldly there, properly made now with clean sheets. And all the afternoon's rage and his fierce battle in the great lonely silence culminated in an immense weariness. Like this room, his whole personality was now cool, swept clean of the morning's filth and restored to its usual propriety. What was the use of a scandal? Was anything really different? His wife merely had one more lover, and her having chosen him in the family scarcely made the fact any worse – perhaps it was even an advantage because it would save appearances. In retrospect his outburst of jealous rage seemed pitiful. How ridiculous to have gone for the bed with his fists! Since he had put up with another man before he might as well put up with this one now. It would only mean that he despised her a little more. A horribly bitter taste came into his mouth: the futility of everything, the eternal pain of existence, the self-disgust to think that he worshipped this woman and still desired her, even while letting her sink into depravity.

Beneath the window the shouting burst out with renewed violence:

'We want bread! We want bread!'

'Imbeciles!' hissed Monsieur Hennebeau through his teeth.

He heard them insulting him because of his big salary, calling him a pot-bellied good-for-nothing, a dirty swine who stuffed himself sick with good things while the workers were dying of hunger. The women had seen the kitchen, and there was an outburst of invective directed at the pheasant roasting there and the greasy-smelling sauces which tortured their empty stomachs. Oh these bleeding bourgeois! They should be stuffed with champagne and truffles till their innards burst!

'We want bread! We want bread!'

'Imbeciles!' repeated Monsieur Hennebeau. 'Do you think I'm happy?'

His anger boiled up against these people who would not understand. How gladly would he have made them a present of his fat salary if he could have had their tough hide and could have copulated like them, easy come, easy go! Why couldn't he sit them at his table and stuff them with his pheasant, while he went off fornicating behind the hedges, laying girls without bothering about who had done so before. He would have given up everything – education, comfort, luxurious life and his powerful position as manager – if just for one day he could have been the humblest of these poor devils under him and be free with his own body and be oafish enough to beat his wife and take his pleasure with the wives of his neighbours. He found himself wishing he were dying of starvation too, and that his empty belly were twisted with pains that made his brain reel, for perhaps that might deaden this relentless grief! Oh to live like a brute, possessing nothing but freedom to roam in the cornfields with the ugliest and most revolting haulage girl and possess her!

'We want bread! We want bread!'

Over and above the din he shouted in a burst of fury:

'Bread! Do you think that it is all there is to it, you fools?'

He had food in plenty, but that did not prevent his groaning in anguish. His devastated home and the long drawn-out pain of his life – these things seemed to rise and catch him in the throat like the gasp of a dying man. As though everything in the garden were lovely just because you had bread to eat! What idiot imagined that happiness in this world depended on a share-out of wealth? These starry-eyed revolutionaries could demolish society and build a brave new world if they liked, but they would not by so doing add one single joy to man's lot, nor relieve him of a single pain merely by sharing out the cake. In fact they would only spread out the unhappiness of the world, and some day they would make the very dogs howl with despair by removing them from the simple satisfaction of their instincts and raising them to the unsatisfied yearnings of passion. No, the only good was to be found in non-existence or, if one had to exist, in being a tree, a stone, or lower still, a grain of sand, for that cannot bleed under the heel of every passer-by.

In his extremity of torment, tears filled Monsieur Henne-beau's eyes and ran burning down his cheeks. The road was almost lost to sight in the deepening gloom when stones be-gan pitting the front of the house. Feeling no resentment now against these famished creatures, but only maddened by the smarting wound in his heart, he went on gasping through his tears:

'Fools! Fools!'

But the cry of the stomach prevailed, and a howl rose like a tempest, sweeping all before it:

'We want bread! We want bread!'

[6]

CATHERINE's blows had sobered Étienne, but he was still at the head of his comrades. Yet even while he was hoarsely urg-ing them on against Montsou, he could hear another voice within him, the voice of reason, asking in amazement what was the meaning of all this? He had not meant any of this to

339

happen. How had it come about that having set out for Jean-Bart with the object of keeping a cool head and preventing disaster, he now found himself ending a day of violence upon violence by besieging the manager's house?

And yet he it was who had cried halt. But at first his sole idea had been to protect the Company's yards where they were talking of going to smash everything up. And now that stones were beginning to graze the walls of the house, he cast about in vain for some legitimate prey against which to unleash the mob and so prevent still more serious disasters. As he was standing in the middle of the road, feeling alone and powerless, he heard a voice calling him. It was a man in the doorway of Tison's bar, the proprietress of which had hastily put up her shutters, leaving only the door open.

'Yes, it's me . . . now listen a moment.'

It was Rasseneur. Some thirty men and women, almost all from Village 240, had stayed at home in the morning and had now come out for news. At the approach of the strikers they had rushed into the bar. Zacharie was at a table with his wife Philomène, and further in, with their backs turned to the road and their faces hidden, were Pierron and Pierronne. Nobody was drinking, they had simply sought refuge.

Recognizing Rasseneur, Étienne was turning away, but the latter added:

'You don't want to see me, do you? . . . Well, I warned you and now the trouble is beginning. You can ask for bread now, but you'll get bullets.'

Étienne turned back and answered:

'What annoys me is to see cowards looking on with folded arms while we risk our lives.'

'So your idea is pillage over there?' asked Rasseneur.

'My idea is to stick by my friends to the end, and die with them if need be.'

Sick at heart, Étienne went back into the crowd, prepared to die. Three children in the road were throwing stones, and he gave them a good kick, saying very loud, for the benefit of his mates, that smashing windows would do no good to anyone.

Bébert and Lydie had rejoined Jeanlin, who was teaching

340

them how to work the sling. Each one aimed a stone, and the game was to see who would do the most damage. Lydie bungled her throw and cut open a woman's head in the crowd, which made the two boys helpless with merriment. Bonnemort and Mouque were sitting behind them on a bench, watching. Bonnemort's swollen legs were now so bad that he had only dragged himself as far as this with the greatest difficulty, and God knows what curiosity had brought him there, for his face had the ashen hue it wore on the days when nobody could get a word out of him.

Anyhow they had all long since given up obeying Étienne. Despite his order, stones went on flying, and he was dismayed at the sight of these brutes whom he had unleashed, for if they were slow to anger they were terrible when roused, and their ferocity was implacable. All the old Flemish blood was there, thick and placid, taking months to warm up, but then working itself up to unspeakable cruelties and refusing to listen to any arguments until the beast in them was sated with atrocities. In the south, where he came from, mobs flared up more quickly but they did far less damage. He had to fight Levaque to get the axe away from him, and he had lost control of the Maheus, who were throwing stones with both hands. It was above all the women who frightened him: la Levaque, Mouquette, and the rest, who were possessed with murderous fury and fighting tooth and nail, yelping like a pack of bitches and egged on by Ma Brûlé, whose skinny form towered above them.

But there was a sudden lull. A moment of surprise had produced some of the calm that all Étienne's supplications failed to impose. It was simply that the Grégoires had decided to take leave of the notary and cross the road to the manager's house; and they looked so peaceful, as though they thought all this was just a joke on the part of their worthy miners, whose resignation had fed them for a century, that the crowd in its amazement had stopped throwing stones for fear of hitting this old gentleman and old lady who had dropped from the sky. They were allowed to enter the garden, walk up the steps and ring at the barricaded door which nobody was anxious to open. But just then Rose was returning from her afternoon off, joking with the enraged miners, every one of whom she knew, for she was a Montsou girl. And she it was who banged on the door with her fist and forced Hippolyte to open it a few inches. Only just in time, too, for the hail of stones began again as the Grégoires were disappearing inside. The crowd had recovered from its astonishment and was now chanting louder than ever:

'Death to the bourgeois! Up with Socialism!'

In the hall Rose was still laughing, very tickled by the adventure, and she repeated to the terrified manservant:

'They won't hurt you! I know them.'

Monsieur Grégoire methodically hung up his coat and helped Madame Grégoire out of her thick winter wrap. Then he said:

'Oh, I'm sure there is no real malice in them. When they have had a good shout they'll go home with a better appetite for supper!'

Monsieur Hennebeau was coming down from the second floor. Having witnessed the scene he was now hastening to welcome his guests with his customary formal politeness, with only a slight pallor betraying his recent storm of tears. The man in him had been overcome and only the administrator was left, perfectly behaved and determined to do his duty.

'You know,' he said, 'the ladies are not back yet.'

For the first time the Grégoires felt some anxiety. Cécile not back! How could she get in if the miners went on with this nonsense?

'I thought of having a space cleared in front of the house, but unfortunately I am on my own here, and in any case I don't know where to send my man for four men and a corporal to come and clear this rabble away.'

Rose, who was still there, ventured to say yet again:

'Oh, sir, they're all right really!'

The manager shook his head as the tumult outside increased in volume and stones could be heard thudding against the walls.

'I don't bear them any ill-will, in fact I can excuse them, for anybody who can believe that we are out to do them harm must be as foolish as they are. But all the same I am respon-

342

sible for keeping the peace. To think that there are gendarmes parading the roads, or so I'm told, and yet ever since this morning I have been trying in vain to find one!'

He broke off and stepped back to allow Madame Grégoire to pass, saying:

'But please don't stay here, Madame. Come into the drawing-room.'

They were kept in the hall, however, by cook who came up from the basement in a towering rage, declaring that she could no longer answer for the dinner, as she was still waiting for the vol-au-vent cases she had ordered for four o'clock from the pastrycook's at Marchiennes. Obviously he had got lost on the way – scared of the bandits, she supposed. His baskets might even have been pillaged. She had visions of the vol-au-vents held up behind some bushes, besieged by these three thousand ne'er-do-wells who were clamouring for bread, and destined to blow out their bellies. Howsoever be it, the master had been warned: she would rather chuck the whole dinner into the fire than have it spoilt because of the revolution.

'Do be patient,' said Monsieur Hennebeau. 'All is not lost. The pastrycook may still come.'

He was turning back to Madame Grégoire and opening the drawing-room door for her when to his great surprise he saw a man sitting on the hall seat. In the deepening twilight he had not noticed him before.

'What, you, Maigrat? What brings you here?'

Maigrat had risen, and his heavy features were livid and quite changed by fear. Gone was his four-square, calm solidity as he diffidently explained that he had slipped over to the manager's house to ask for help and protection if the brigands attacked his shop.

'You can see that I am in danger too and have nobody here,' answered Monsieur Hennebeau. 'You would have done better to stay at home and guard your stock.'

'Oh, I have put up iron bars and left my wife there!'

The manager was annoyed and made no effort to hide his contempt. A nice guard indeed, that puny creature, worn to a skeleton by beatings!

'Anyhow, there's nothing I can do about it. Try and fend

343

for yourself. And I advise you to get back at once, for they are still shouting for bread. Listen to them.'

The tumult was starting up again with renewed violence, and Maigrat thought he heard his own name. It was too late to go back now – he would be lynched. But on the other hand he was appalled by the prospect of ruin. He glued his face to the glass panel in the front door, sweating and trembling, expecting disaster at any moment. Meanwhile the Grégoires decided to go into the drawing-room.

Monsieur Hennebeau calmly played the attentive host. But in vain did he beg his guests to be seated. This room, closed and boarded up, with two lamps burning while it was still broad daylight outside, was filled with fresh terror at every shout from the street. Muffled by the curtains, the roaring anger of the mob was all the more frightening for being vague. But they made conversation which, however, always came back to this extraordinary revolt. He was amazed at his own lack of foresight, but his information was so at fault that he singled out Rasseneur for abuse, claiming that he recognized the man's hateful influence. Of course the gendarmes were bound to come, for it was impossible that he could be so completely let down. The Grégoires had no thought except for their daughter: poor little dear, and she took fright so easily! Perhaps, in view of the danger, the carriage had gone back to Marchiennes. The wait lasted another quarter of an hour, with the tension increasing because of the noise in the street and the impact of stones on the shutters resounding like drums. The situation was becoming intolerable, and Monsieur Hennebeau was talking of going out single-handed to drive away these bawling creatures and meet the carriage, when Hippolyte appeared, shouting:

'Sir! Sir! Here is Madame! They are killing Madame!'

The carriage had not been able to get out of the Réquillart lane because of threatening groups, and Négrel had carried out his plan of walking the hundred metres from there to the house and knocking at the little garden gate near the outbuildings, for he was confident that the gardener would hear them, or at any rate that there would be somebody to open it for them. At first the plan had worked perfectly, and Madame

Hennebeau and the young ladies were actually knocking when some of the women who had got wind of the manoeuvre rushed round into the lane. From then onwards everything went wrong. Nobody opened the gate and Négrel tried in vain to burst it open with his shoulder. The crowd of women was rapidly swelling, and fearing he might be overwhelmed, he took the desperate measure of pushing his aunt and the girls in front of him and trying to force a way through the assailants to the front steps. But this move led to a scrimmage, for the howling mob would not let go of them, and veered to and fro, not yet understanding why these fashionably dressed ladies were in the middle of the fray. At that moment the confusion was so great that one of those inexplicable misunderstandings occurred. Lucie and Jeanne had reached the steps and slipped through the door which the maid was holding ajar, Madame Hennebeau had managed to follow them in, and Négrel had brought up the rear and bolted the door behind him, under the impression that he had seen Cécile go in first. She was not there. She had disappeared on the way, so panic-stricken that she had turned her back on the house and rushed of her own accord right into the danger.

At once a shout arose:

'Up with the people! Death to the bourgeois! Death!'

Her face was hidden by a veil, and some of them took her at a distance for Madame Hennebeau. Others thought she was a friend of the manager's wife, the young wife of a neighbouring industrialist whom his workmen loathed. In any case it did not matter, for what infuriated them was her silk dress, fur coat and the white feather in her hat. She smelled of scent, she had a watch, she had the tender skin of an idle creature who never touched coal.

'Just you wait!' screamed Ma Brûlé. 'We'll stick that lace up your arse!'

'Those bitches pinch all that stuff from us,' added la Levaque. 'They stick fur on their skins while we die of cold. Strip her bloody well naked, just to show her what life is!'

Mouquette rushed forward.

'Yes, yes, let's whip her!'

345

The women vied with each other in abominations, choking with rage, displaying their own rags and each trying to get a piece of this rich man's daughter. Her bum was no better than anyone else's you bet! More than one of them was rotten underneath her fine feathers. This injustice had lasted long enough, and now they would be made to dress the same as the working people, these harlots who had the sauce to spend fifty sous to have a skirt cleaned!

Surrounded by these furies Cécile was shaking with terror and on the point of collapse. Over and over again she stammered out the same words:

'Ladies – please, ladies! Please don't hurt me!'

But her voice turned into a strangled scream: cold hands had closed round her throat. The crowd had pushed her up close to old Bonnemort who had seized her. Hunger had made him light-headed, he was stupefied by long years of misery, and now he had suddenly emerged from half a century of resignation, spurred on by some mysterious impulse to get his own back. The man who had saved a dozen of his mates from death and risked his life in fire-damp and falls of rock, was now giving way to things he could never have explained, an urge to act like this, the fascination of this girl's white throat. As it was one of his silent days he kept his teeth clenched, looking like some sick and aged animal chewing over his memories.

'No, no!' yelled the women. 'Turn her up, arse in the air!'

As soon as they had seen what was happening, Négrel and Monsieur Hennebeau had courageously opened the door again to rush to Cécile's rescue. But the crowd was now storming the garden fence, and it was not easy to get out. A pitched battle began, watched by the terrified Grégoires, who had come out on to the steps.

'Leave her alone, old boy, it's the young lady from La Piolaine,' said Maheude to Grandpa Bonnemort, recognizing Cécile whose veil had been torn off by one of the women.

Étienne, horrified by these reprisals on a mere child, cast round for some way of heading off the mob. He had an inspiration and, brandishing the axe he had taken from Levaque, cried out:

346

'To Maigrat's, by God! There's bread there! Down with Maigrat's bloody shack!'

He aimed the first blow at random against the shop door. Some of the men followed suit, Levaque, Maheu, and a few more. But the women were not to be put off, and Cécile had fallen from the hands of Bonnemort into those of Ma Brûlé. Lydie and Bébert, led by Jeanlin, were crawling on all fours under her skirt to see the lady's bottom. Already she was being mauled and her clothes torn, when a man on horseback rode up, forcing his animal on and using the whip on anybody who did not stand back at once.

'You lot of swine! So you're hitting our daughters now!'

It was Deneulin, arriving in time for dinner. He jumped down, put one arm round Cécile's waist, and with the other steered his horse with such strength and skill that he used it as a living wedge and split the crowd which fell back before the shying beast. The battle was still raging at the railings, but he won through, breaking limbs right and left. This unforeseen help relieved Négrel and Monsieur Hennebeau, who were in great danger amid the curses and blows. And while the young man at last took the swooning Cécile indoors, Deneulin, covering the manager with his burly frame, reached the top of the steps, but was hit by a stone which nearly dislocated his shoulder.

'That's right!' he shouted. 'Break my bones now you have broken my machines!'

He slammed the door. A volley of stones cut into the wood.

'What a lot of madmen!' he cried. 'Another two seconds and they would have split my head open like a pumpkin. There's nothing you can say to them, is there? They are past understanding and all you can do is mow them down!'

In the drawing-room the Grégoires tearfully watched Cécile come round. She was quite unhurt, without even a scratch, but had merely lost her veil. Their dismay was greater than ever, though, when they realized that their own cook, Mélanie, was standing in front of them, describing how the mob had wrecked La Piolaine. Mad with terror, she had rushed to warn her master and mistress and had slipped in unnoticed through the open door during the confusion. As her

347

interminable story unfolded itself, the single stone thrown by Jeanlin which had broken one window-pane became a full-scale bombardment which had rent the walls asunder. All Monsieur Grégoire's ideas were by now topsy-turvy: they slew his daughter and razed his home to the ground, so it must be true, then, that these miners were capable of resenting his living peacefully on their work!

The maid, who had brought a towel and some Eau de Cologne, remarked yet again:

'It's funny, though, because they're all right really.'

Madame Hennebeau, looking deathly pale as she sat in her chair, could not shake off the shock, but she did manage to smile when Négrel was congratulated. Cécile's parents were particularly grateful to the young man, and the marriage was as good as settled. Monsieur Hennebeau silently glanced from his wife to this lover of hers whom that very morning he had sworn to kill, and then to this girl who would probably soon take him out of the way. He has not in any hurry, but the only thing he feared now was that his wife would sink still lower – some servant, perhaps.

'And what about you, my dears,' Deneulin asked his daughters, 'no bones broken?'

Lucie and Jeanne had had a great fright, but they were glad to have seen it all, and were now merrily laughing.

'Gosh!' their father went on. 'What a day we've had! If you want a dowry you would do well to earn it yourselves, and, what's more, you can count on having to keep me as well.'

He spoke flippantly, but his voice was unsteady, and when his daughters threw themselves into his arms, his eyes filled with tears.

Monsieur Hennebeau had overheard this confession of ruin, and a sudden thought lit up his face. Of course Vandame would now belong to Montsou. Here was the long hoped-for compensation, the stroke of luck that would put him back into favour with the Directors. At every crisis in his life he took refuge in the strict execution of orders, and found his small share of happiness in the military discipline in which he lived.

By now the tension was relaxing and a weary peace was descending upon the room, with the soft light of the two lamps and the warm and deadening effect of the hangings. What could be happening outside? The shoutings had almost died away and no more stones were hitting the walls. Only heavy thuds could be heard, like the distant sound of an axe in the forest. They felt a curiosity to know and went back into the hall to peep through the glass panel in the front door. Even the ladies went upstairs to look through the shutters on the first floor.

'Do you see that scoundrel Rasseneur standing at the door of the pub over there?' Monsieur Hennebeau said to Deneulin. 'I guessed as much, he must be behind it.'

But it was not Rasseneur. It was Étienne, smashing in Maigrat's shop with an axe. He kept on calling to his mates: didn't the provisions in the shop belong to the miners? Hadn't they the right to claim back their own from this robber who had been exploiting them for so long and who starved them whenever the Company told him to? Gradually they all left the manager's house and ran to sack the neighbouring shop. The cry 'We want bread!' began again. They would find plenty of it behind this door. A frenzy of hunger seized them all, as though they had suddenly found out that they could last out no longer without dying there and then in the road. They pressed in such crowds against the door that Étienne was afraid of hurting somebody with each swing of the axe.

Meanwhile Maigrat had left the hall and had first sought refuge in the kitchen. But from there he could not hear anything, and visualized abominable attacks on his shop. So he had come up again and hidden behind the pump in the yard, whence he could clearly hear his door cracking and voices urging each other on to the pillage and pronouncing his own name. It was not a nightmare, then, for although he could not see he could now hear, and he followed each stage of the attack with outraged ears. Each blow of the axe struck at his heart. One hinge must have gone: five more minutes now and the whole shop must be in their hands. He had mental pictures of appalling realism – the brigands rushing in, drawers forced, sacks ripped open, everything eaten and drunk and his home plundered into the bargain – nothing left, not even a stick to go begging with in the villages. No! he would not let them

349

finish him off, he would sooner leave his dead body there. Since he had been standing there he had seen through a side window of the house the puny figure of his wife, pale and distorted through the glass; she was no doubt passively watching the attack like the poor, beaten, dumb animal she was. Below the window there was a shed in such a position that from the garden of the manager's house it could be reached by climbing up the palings on the party wall, and from there it was simple to crawl along the tiles as far as the window. He became obsessed by the idea of getting back home by this route, for he was cursing himself for ever having left. He might still be in time to barricade the shop with furniture – he even thought of other heroic means of defence such as boiling oil or burning paraffin poured down from above. A desperate struggle ensued between love of his stock and fear for his life, and his breath came thick in the battle against cowardice. Suddenly a still louder blow of the axe made up his mind for him. Avarice won: he and his wife would cover the sacks with their dead bodies rather than give up a single loaf.

Almost at once there was a burst of catcalls:

'Look, look! There's the tomcat up there! After him!'

They had caught sight of Maigrat on the shed roof. In spite of his corpulence he had leaped up the palings with feverish agility, heedless of what wood he smashed, and now he was flat on the tiles, working his way towards the window. But the pitch of the roof was steep, his stomach was in the way and his nails were breaking off. Nevertheless he would have dragged himself to the top had not his fear of stones started a fit of trembling, for the crowd, which he could no longer see, was still shouting:

'After him! After the cat! Let's do him in!'

All of a sudden both hands lost their grip, he rolled down like a ball, bounced over the gutter and fell across the party wall so awkwardly that he rebounded from there to the road, where his skull was split open on the point of a stone post, and his brains gushed out. He was killed instantly. The pale, dim form of his wife was still looking down through the window-pane.

For a moment everyone was horror-struck. Étienne stopped

short and the axe fell from his hands. Maheu, Levaque, and the others forgot all about the shop, and all eyes were fixed on the wall, down which a thin red streak was slowly trickling. The shouting had died and a hush spread through the deepening shadows.

Then the yelling began again. It was the women who rushed forward, seized with a thirst for blood.

'Then there is a God after all! You swine, you're done for now!'

They surrounded the warm body and insulted it with jeers, called his smashed head an ugly mug, screaming into his face all the long pent-up hatred of their starved lives.

'I owed you sixty francs. Well, you're paid now, you thief!' said Maheude, now as frenzied as anybody else. 'You won't refuse me any more credit. Just wait a minute, I must fatten you up a bit more!'

With her ten fingers she scratched up the earth, took two handfuls and rammed them into his mouth.

'Here you are, eat it! Go on, eat away like you used to eat us!'

Insults rained thick and fast while the dead man lay on his back, gazing with staring eyes at the wide sky from which night was falling. This earth in his mouth was the bread he had denied them, and it was the only bread he would eat henceforth. A lot of good it had done him to starve poor folk!

But the women had other scores to settle. They sniffed round him like she-wolves, trying to think of some outrage some obscenity to relieve their feelings.

The shrill voice of Ma Brûlé was heard:

'Doctor him like a tomcat!'

'Yes, yes, like a cat! The dirty old sod has done it once too often!'

Mouquette was already undoing his trousers and pulling them down, helped by la Levaque who lifted the legs. And Ma Brûlé, with her withered old hands, parted his naked thighs and grasped his dead virility. She took hold of the lot and pulled so hard that she strained her skinny back and her long arms cracked with the effort. The soft skin resisted and she had to try again, but she managed in the end to pull away the lump of hairy, bleeding flesh which she waved aloft with a snarl of triumph.

'I've got it! I've got it!'

The horrible trophy was greeted with shrill imprecations.

'You bugger, you won't fill up our girls any more!'

'Yes, no more paying you with our bodies! Never again shall we have to go through that, offering our backsides for a loaf of bread!'

'Oh, by the way, I owe you ten francs. Would you like something on account? I'm willing if you still can!'

These witticisms made them shake with terrible mirth. They pointed out to each other the bloody piece of flesh as though it were some nasty animal that had hurt them all and which they had at last squashed to death and now had lying there inert in their power. They spat on it, thrusting forward their jaws, repeating in a furious outburst of contempt:

'He can't do it now! He can't do it now! It isn't even a man they've got left to shove in the ground. Go and rot, you're no good for anything now!'

Then Ma Brûlé stuck the whole thing on the end of her stick, raised it on high and carried it like a standard down the street, followed by a rout of shrieking women. Drops of blood spattered down, and this miserable bit of flesh hung down like an odd piece of meat on a butcher's stall. Up at the window Madame Maigrat was still motionless, but the last rays of the setting sun caught her pale face, and through the distorting glass it seemed to be grinning. Beaten, continually deceived, with her back bent over a ledger from morn till night, perhaps she really was laughing as the band of women hurtled by, with the evil beast crushed at last and stuck on a pole.

This frightful mutilation had been performed in an atmosphere of icy horror. Neither Étienne, Maheu, nor anybody else had had time to intervene, but stood motionless before this stampede of furies. Faces appeared at the door of Tison's: Rasseneur livid with disgust, Zacharie and Philomène horrified at having seen it. The two old men, Bonnemort and Mouque, sagely shook their heads. The only one to giggle was Jeanlin, who nudged Bébert and forced Lydie to look up. But already the women had turned back and were passing the manager's windows. Behind the shutters the ladies were craning their necks. They had not been able to see the scene which had been hidden from them by the wall, and now they could not see anything clearly because it was getting dark.

'Whatever have they got on the end of that stick!' asked Cécile, who had now plucked up courage to look out.

Lucie and Jeanne declared that it must be a rabbit-skin.

'No, no,' murmured Madame Hennebeau, 'they must have looted the butcher's. It looks like a bit of pork.'

Then she shuddered and stopped. Madame Grégoire had nudged her with her knee. They both stood stock still, open mouthed. The girls, deathly pale, asked no more questions, but their eyes watched the red vision disappear into the darkness.

Étienne brandished his axe again. But the feeling of horror could not be dispelled, and now the corpse was in the way, protecting the shop. Many of them had turned away, as though now that their appetites were sated they had lost interest. Maheu was standing in glum silence when a voice whispering in his ear told him to make off at once. He turned and saw Catherine, still in her man's coat, with coal on her face and gasping with anxiety. He pushed her aside refused to listen and threatened to hit her. She hesitated, made a despairing gesture and then ran up to Étienne.

'Run, run! The police!'

He also made as if to drive her off with curses, feeling the blood rush back to his cheeks at the places where she had hit them. But she would not be put off, forced him to drop the axe, and exerting all her strength dragged him along irresistibly by both arms.

'I tell you it's the police! Listen. Chaval went for them and is bringing them, if you want to know. I was disgusted at him, and so I've come. . . . Clear off, I don't want you to be caught.'

Catherine led him away just as a heavy galloping could be heard some way off along the road. At once a shout went up: 'The police the police!' It was a rout, such a wild stampede that in two minutes the road was cleared, absolutely empty, as though it had been swept by a hurricane. Only Maigrat's corpse remained, a dark patch on the white roadway. There was nobody left in front of Tison's except Rasseneur, whose face had lit up with relief and approval of the easy victory of the sabres, whilst in the darkened and deserted town of Montsou, behind their silent, shuttered walls, the bourgeois, with sweating bodies and chattering teeth, still dared not look out. The plain had disappeared in the dense night, and far away in the tragic sky only the glare of the furnaces and coke-ovens remained. The heavy gallop of the gendarmes came nearer and they entered the street in an indistinguishable dark mass. Behind them and entrusted to their protection, came the pastry-cook's van from Marchiennes at long last: a light two-wheeled cart out of which jumped an errand-boy who calmly proceeded to unload the vol-au-vent cases.

Part Six

[1]

THE first fortnight of February came and went and a black frost went on and on. It was a hard winter, pitiless for the poor. Once again the authorities had made a tour of inspection: the Prefect of Lille, an attorney and a general. As the gendarmes had proved inadequate, troops were now occupying Montsou, a whole regiment of them, and the men were billeted from Beaugnies to Marchiennes. The pits had armed guards, with soldiers standing by every engine. The manager's house, the Company's yards and even the houses of some of the bourgeois were bristling with bayonets. The slow marching of patrols was constantly heard along the streets. A sentry was always posted on top of the Voreux slag-heap, a look-out high above the plain in the icy wind, and every two hours the sentries' cries rang out as though they were in a hostile occupied country.

'Who goes there? Advance and give the password!'

Work had not been resumed anywhere. On the contrary, the strike had spread, for Crèvecœur, Mirou, and Madeleine had stopped production like Le Voreux; Feutry-Cantel and La Victoire saw fewer men turn up each morning, and even Saint-Thomas, hitherto unaffected, was now shorthanded. This display of force was being countered by a mute resistance, for the worker's pride had been outraged. In the midst of the beet-fields the villages appeared to be deserted. Not a single workman stirred abroad, and if by chance you met one he would be alone and looking about him furtively, lowering his head at the sight of red trousers. But underlying this universal dreary quietness and behind this passive obstinacy in the face of the guns, there was the deceptive gentleness and patient, enforced obedience of wild beasts kept in a cage, never taking their eyes off the trainer, but waiting to bury their teeth in his neck the moment he turns his back. The Company, faced with ruin, talked of taking on men from the Borinage, on the Belgian frontier, but it had not the courage to do so. The result was a stalemate between the miners shut up in their homes and the dead pits guarded by troops.

This calm had set in immediately after the day of terror, and it concealed such panic that the least possible was said about damage and atrocities. The inquest established that Maigrat had died as the result of his fall, and the fearful mutilation of his body was not insisted upon, though it had already become legendary. The Company did not admit the damage it had suffered any more than the Grégoires cared about exposing their daughter to the scandal of a lawsuit at which she should have been a witness. Nevertheless there had been a few arrests – mere onlookers, of course, as always happens, silly, scared people who knew nothing about anything. Pierron had been taken in handcuffs to Marchiennes, by mistake, and the chaps had never stopped laughing. Rasseneur, too, had nearly been taken off between two gendarmes. The only step taken by the administration was to compile lists of people to be sacked, and cards had been handed back wholesale. Maheu had had his, and Levaque, together with thirty-four of their mates in Village 240 alone. The full weight of official wrath fell upon Étienne, who had disappeared since the evening of the riot without leaving a trace. Chaval had maliciously denounced him though refusing to name the others, for Catherine had implored him not to, in order to save her parents. As the days went on everybody was full of foreboding, for the matter was still inconclusive and they wanted to know what the end would be.

In Montsou now the worthy bourgeois woke up in a panic every night, with imaginary tocsins clanging in their ears and a smell of powder in their nostrils. But they went clean out of their minds when they heard a sermon by the new curé, abbé Ranvier, the lean priest with blazing eyes who had succeeded abbé Joire. How far removed from the smiling diplomacy of that plump and unctuous man whose one aim in life had been to live at peace with everybody. Had not abbé Ranvier had the effrontery to defend these unspeakable brigands who were a disgrace to the neighbourhood? He found excuses for the crimes of the strikers and violently attacked the bourgeoisie, on whom he thrust all the responsibility. According to him it was the bourgeoisie which, by robbing the Church of her ancient liberties and misusing them, had turned this world into an accursed hell of injustice and suffering, it was the bourgeoisie which prolonged misunderstandings and which was leading the world to a terrible cataclysm through its atheism and refusal to go back to the beliefs and brotherly traditions of the early Christians. And he had even dared to threaten the rich, he had warned them that if they went on hardening their hearts, heeding not the voice of God, God would surely side with the poor, He would take away the fortunes of these self-indulgent unbelievers and distribute them to the humble of this world for His greater glory. Pious females shuddered, the notary declared that this was socialism of the most rabid kind, and they all visualized this parish priest at the head of a mob, brandishing a crucifix and smashing the bourgeois society of 1789.

When Monsieur Hennebeau was told about it he merely shrugged his shoulders and said:

'If he makes himself too much of a nuisance the bishop will get rid of him for us.'

While panic was thus sweeping over the plain Étienne was living underground, in Jeanlin's burrow down in Réquillart. Nobody imagined he could be hiding so near, for the cool audacity of this retreat in the mine itself, in an abandoned gallery, had thrown his pursuers off the scent. Up on the surface the blackthorns and hawthorns growing among the fallen timbers of the headgear blocked up the entrance, and nobody ventured there – you had to have the knack of hanging from the roots of the rowan tree and fearlessly dropping on to the rungs of the ladder that were still sound. And there were other obstacles to protect him, such as the suffocating heat of the shaft, a perilous descent of a hundred and twenty metres, then the difficult belly-slide for a quarter of a league between narrow walls before you discovered the robber's cave with its plundered treasures. There he lived in abundance: he had found some gin, the remains of the dried cod and other provisions of all kinds. The big bed of hay was excellent, and there were no draughts in this equable temperature, like a warm bath. The only thing in danger of giving out was light, for although Jeanlin had undertaken to supply him and was delighted to bring all his instinctive prudence and finesse to bear on the task of tricking the gendarmes, the boy who had managed to produce even hair-oil could not lay his hands on a packet of candles.

By the fifth day Étienne could only light a candle when he was eating. Somehow the food would not go down in the dark. His great trial was the endless, uniform, total darkness. It was all very well to be able to sleep in safety and to have plenty of food and warmth, but never had darkness weighed down on him so heavily. It seemed to crush his very thoughts. So now he was reduced to living on stolen goods! For all his communist theories, the old scruples of his upbringing would raise their heads, and he made do with dry bread and measured out his portions. But what else could be done? He had to live, for his task was not yet accomplished. Something else made him ashamed; he felt remorse for his fit of drunken savagery, for having drunk that gin on an empty stomach in the cold weather. That was what had made him fling himself on Chaval with a knife. It stirred up within him a whole world of unknown fears: his hereditary malady, that long heredity of drunkenness which made him incapable of taking a single drop of alcohol without being gripped by this homicidal mania. Would he end up as a murderer? When he had found refuge in this deep subterranean silence he was so overcome by excess of violence that for two whole days he had slept the sleep of a brute, gorged and stupefied; and yet his nausea persisted, and he was still dead-beat, with a horrible taste in his mouth and a sick headache as though he were recovering from a terrible orgy. A whole week passed and still the Maheus, who had been let into the secret, could not send down a candle; and so he had to give up seeing, even to eat.

Now he spent hours lying on the hay turning over vague ideas which he did not recognize as his own, a sensation, for instance, of superiority which set him apart from his mates, as though his intellectual progress had raised his whole being to greater spiritual heights. He had never reflected so deeply, and he wondered why he had felt such disgust after the mad rush through the pits; but he dared not answer his own question, for he was revolted by memories of mean covetousnesses, coarse instincts and the stench of all this poverty which was in the very air you breathed. Horrible though the torment of darkness might be, he would end up, he felt, by dreading the moment when he would have to go back to the village. How sickening! To think of these poor wretches all living in a heap and washing together in the same tub! There was not one of them with whom you could talk politics seriously, it was a bestial existence in that everlasting choking stink of onions! He longed to widen their horizon, raise them up to the comfortable standards and decent manners of the bourgeois by making them the masters. But what a long job! He no longer felt the courage to wait for victory in this prison of hunger. Gradually his vanity at being their leader and the constant necessity of doing their thinking for them was setting him apart and creating within him the soul of one of the bourgeois he hated so much.

One evening Jeanlin brought down a bit of candle he had stolen out of a carter's lantern, and this was a great relief. When the darkness drove him almost out of his mind and seemed to weigh down on his head, he would light his candle for a minute or two, and then, when he had dispelled the nightmare, blow it out again, for he had to husband light as much as food. The very silence made noises in his head and the only sounds he could hear were the scuttling of rats, the cracking of old timbers or the tiny noise of a spider spinning its web. Staring wide-eyed into the stuffy emptiness he constantly came back to his obsession: what were his mates doing up there? It would have been the worst possible cowardice on his part to let them down, and he was only hiding in this way, he told himself, so as to remain free to advise and act. These long meditations had shown him where his real ambitions lay: pending something better he would like to be a Pluchart and give up manual labour in order to work full time in politics.

But it must be alone and in a decent room, and he justified this to himself by reflecting that mental work needs one's full attention in complete peace and quiet.

At the beginning of the second week the boy told him that the police thought he had crossed into Belgium, and so Étienne ventured to come up out of his hole at nightfall. He wanted to reconnoitre and see whether they ought to continue the resistance. He himself was now doubtful about the outcome; even before the strike he had been sceptical but had yielded to the facts of the situation, but now, after the intoxication of rebellion, he was coming round to his earlier doubts and beginning to despair of ever making the Company give in. But he did not yet admit it even to himself, and he was still tortured with anguish at the thought of the sufferings defeat would entail and the heavy responsibility for these sufferings which would fall on him. Would not the end of the strike mean the end of the part he had played, the collapse of all his ambition and the resumption of his brutish life in the pits and revolting existence in the village? And in all honesty, without unworthy calculations and self-deceptions, he struggled to recapture his faith and prove to himself that resistance was still feasible and that capital would destroy itself in the face of the heroic suicide of labour.

Throughout the district ruin echoed ruin. At night he wandered about the black countryside like a wolf sallying forth from its forest lair. He could almost hear the financial crashes from one end of the plain to the other. Along the roads he passed nothing but closed factories, quite dead, with their buildings rotting away beneath the ashen sky. The sugar refineries, in particular, had suffered: the Hoton and Fauvelle refineries, having begun by cutting down their staff, had now crashed one after the other. At the Dutilleul flour mills the last grindstone had stopped on the second Saturday of the month, and the Bleuze ropeworks, which made pit-cables, had been finished off by the stoppage. Round Marchiennes the position was deteriorating daily: all the furnaces had been extinguished at the Gagebois glassworks, the Sonneville building shops were continually putting men off, only one of the three blast-furnaces at the Forges was alight and not a single battery of

coke-ovens was flaring on the horizon. The strike of the Montsou miners, itself the outcome of the industrial crisis which had
been worsening for two years, had in its turn speeded up that
crisis and was now precipitating disaster. To the prime causes
of the trouble, the falling off of orders from America and the
resulting accumulation of capital immobilized in excessive production, was now added unforeseen lack of coal for the few
boilers still working. The mines no longer supplied the
machines with their food, and that meant death. Scared by the
general unrest, the Company had reduced output and starved
its miners, with the inevitable result that by the end of December it had found itself without a scrap of coal in its yards.
Everything hung together and the wind of disaster blew far
and wide: one failure involved another, industries destroyed
each other in their crashes in such a crescendo of catastrophes
that the effects could be felt throughout the neighbouring
cities of Lille, Douai, and Valenciennes, where banks failed and
families found themselves penniless.

Often, in the freezing night, Étienne would pause at a bend
of the road and listen, as it were, to the ruins falling, and draw
deep breaths of night air, filled with the joy of sheer destruction and the hope that the morrow would dawn on the extermination of the old world, the day when the levelling scythe
of equality would pass across the ground and leave no wealth
standing. But in this general destruction the fate of the Company's pits interested him more particularly, and he would set
off again in the blinding darkness and visit them one by one,
rejoicing when he heard of some new damage. As the neglect
of the galleries went on, new falls were continually occurring
and they were more and more serious in character. The subsidence of the land above the north gallery of Mirou was now
so extensive that a hundred metres of the Joiselle road had
fallen in as though there had been an earthquake; and the
Company was so disturbed by the talk these accidents were
creating that it was paying compensation to owners of sunken
fields without any haggling. Crèvecœur and Madeleine,
where the rock was very loose, were rapidly becoming blocked
up. It was said that two deputies had been buried alive in La
Victoire, the waters had flooded Feutry-Cantel, while a whole

kilometre of galleries at Saint-Thomas would have to be bricked up because the timbers were collapsing all the way along for want of repair. Huge sums of money were being lost hourly, making gaping holes in the shareholders' dividends; in fact this rapid deterioration of the pits was bound to end by swallowing up the famous Montsou *deniers* which had multiplied a hundredfold in a century.

In the face of these repeated disasters Étienne's hopes revived and he began to believe that a third month of resistance would finish off once and for all this monster, this beast drowsy with over-eating, crouching yonder like an idol in the secret recesses of its tabernacle. He knew that the troubles at Montsou had unloosed a storm of excitement in the Paris press, a furious polemic between the time-serving papers and those of the opposition. In particular, hair-raising stories had been exploited against the International which the Imperial régime had first encouraged but now feared. The Administration had not been able to go on turning a deaf ear, and two of the directors had deigned to come down and conduct an enquiry, but they had done so unwillingly and without appearing to be in the least concerned about the result – indeed their 'impartiality' was such that in three days they had gone home again, declaring that everything was going perfectly. But from other sources Étienne had learned that during their stay these gentlemen had worked incessantly and with feverish activity, burying themselves in matters about which nobody who had had any contact with them would divulge a word. And so he accused them of play-acting, persuading himself that they had fled in panic. Now he was certain of victory, since these terrible gentlemen were clearly throwing up the sponge.

But the very next night plunged Étienne into despair again, and he felt that the Company's back was too strong to be broken so easily. It might well be losing millions, but later on it would make them up again at the workers' expense by cutting down their livelihood. That night he pushed on as far as Jean-Bart, and guessed the truth when an overseer told him that there was talk of handing over Vandame to Montsou. It was said that the plight of the Deneulins was pitiful – the sordid life of the rich come down in the world – the father ill with frustration and money worries, the daughters struggling on amidst mounting bills and trying to save at least their clothes from the wreck. Even the distress in the famine-stricken villages was preferable to life in this well-to-do home where they shut themselves up so as not to be seen drinking water. Work had not been resumed at Jean-Bart and the pump at Gaston-Marie had had to be replaced; but even then, despite the hasty emergency measures, flooding had begun, and was a source of great expense. Deneulin had at last plucked up courage to ask the Grégoires for a loan of a hundred thousand francs, and their refusal, although expected, had been the last straw. They refused, so they said, out of affection for him, so as to spare him an impossible struggle, and advised him to sell. He still said no, violently. It was infuriating that the cost of the strike should fall on him, and at first he wished he could have a rush of blood to the head, and die of an apoplectic seizure. What then, was to be done? He had considered offers. They haggled, and underrated this splendid prize – a pit entirely modernized in which nothing but lack of ready cash was holding up output. He would be lucky if he got enough out of it to keep his creditors at bay. For two whole days he had wrestled with the directors encamped at Montsou, furious at the calm way they were taking advantage of his difficulties and shouting 'Never!' in his stentorian voice. And there the matter rested – they had returned to Paris to wait patiently for his last gasp. Étienne saw in all this the Company's compensation for its own disasters, and it filled him with fresh discouragement at the invincible power of big capital, which was so strong in battle that, even in defeat, it could still grow fat on the bodies of the less important casualties lying round it.

Fortunately Jeanlin brought some good news the next day. At Le Voreux the lining of the shaft was in danger of giving way and water was coming in through every joint. A squad of carpenters had had to be rushed there for emergency repairs.

So far Étienne had avoided Le Voreux, not liking the look of the sentry whose black silhouette always stood out on top of the slag-heap, overlooking the plain. He could not be dodged; there he stood dominating everything, up aloft like the regimental flag. At about three o'clock in the morning, however, when the sky was very dark, he made his way to the pit, where some of his friends met him and explained the bad state of the shaft lining – they even thought that the whole of it should be replaced at once, and that would put a stop to all output for three months. He prowled round for a long time, listening to the carpenters' mallets banging away in the shaft. It rejoiced his heart that here was a wound needing to be dressed.

At daybreak on his way back he saw the sentry still on the slag-heap, and this time surely the sentry could not help seeing him. As he walked along he thought of these soldiers, recruited from the people and armed against the people. How easily the revolution could have triumphed if only the army had suddenly come over to their side! It was only necessary for the workman or the peasant in the barracks to remember his own origins! The very thought of a possible defection of the troops was the supreme peril, the ultimate terror that set the bourgeois' teeth chattering. In two hours they would be swept away, exterminated, together with all the luxuries and abominations of their iniquitous lives. It was already being said that whole regiments were infected with socialism. Was it true? Were they about to bring justice to the world with the very cartridges issued them by the bourgeoisie? Seizing on a fresh hope, the young man dreamed that the regiment whose outposts were guarding the pits decided to throw in its lot with the strikers, shot the directors to a man, and handed the mine over at last to the miners.

As these thoughts were buzzing round in his head he realized that he was climbing up the tip. Why not talk to the soldier? He would find out what sort of ideas he had. Looking quite unconcerned, he drew nearer, pretending to be gleaning old bits of wood amongst the rubbish. The sentry did not move.

'Hello, chum! Bloody awful weather! I think we are going to get some snow.'

The soldier was a fair-haired little chap with a gentle, pale, freckled face. He looked like a recruit, judging by the awkward way he was wearing his greatcoat.

'Yes, perhaps we shall. . . . I suppose,' he murmured.

His blue eyes stared for a long time at the livid sky. The sooty dawn seemed to weigh down like lead over the distant plain.

'Aren't they daft to stick you up here freezing your bones!' went on Étienne. 'Anybody would think we were expecting the Cossacks to come! What's more, the wind always blows up here.'

The little soldier shivered but did not complain. There was, as it happened, a dry-stone shelter in which old Bonnemort used to find protection on blowy nights, but orders were that the top of the tip must never be abandoned, and the soldier did not move an inch, though his hands were so numbed with cold that he could not feel his rifle. He was one of a detachment of sixty men guarding Le Voreux, and as this cruel duty came round frequently, he had nearly stayed there for good with frostbitten feet. But that was his job and passive obedience had finished the stultifying process. He answered questions with disconnected, stammering words like a sleepy child.

Étienne tried for a quarter of an hour to get him talking about politics, but in vain. He said yes or no without seeming to understand: yes, some of his comrades said that the captain was a republican; as for himself he really had no idea, he didn't care. If he was ordered to shoot he would shoot, so as not to be punished. As Étienne listened he was seized by the people's instinctive hatred of the army, these brothers of theirs whose hearts had been changed by a pair of red trousers stuck on their behinds.

'What's your name?'

'Jules.'

'Where from?'

'Plogof, over there.'

He pointed at random. It was in Brittany, that was all he knew. His pale little face lit up and he began to laugh, quite cheered.

'I've got mother and my sister. They're waiting for me, I'm sure. But it won't be tomorrow. When I left they came with me as far as Pont l'Abbé. We had borrowed the Lepalmecs' horse, and he nearly broke his legs at the bottom of the hill at Audierne. Cousin Charlie met us with some sausages, but the women were crying so much that we couldn't enjoy them. Oh dear! oh dear! What a long way away home is!'

His eyes grew moist although he was still laughing. The lonely moor of Plogof and the wild and stormy Pointe du Raz appeared before his gaze in a golden, sun-bathed vision, in the season of purple heather.

'I say,' he asked, 'if I get no bad marks do you think they'll give me a month's leave in two years' time?'

Then Étienne told him about his own Provence, which he had left when he was still a small child. By now it was quite light and snowflakes were beginning to float in the leaden sky. At length he became anxious, for he was aware of Jeanlin prowling about in the brambles, amazed to see him up there. The boy was beckoning him. What was the use of this dream of fraternizing with the soldiery? It would take years and years, and this vain attempt upset him as though he had counted on its succeeding. But all of a sudden he realized what Jeanlin's beckoning meant: the sentry was about to be relieved. And so he raced off and went to earth in Réquillart, once more heartbroken at the certainty of defeat, whilst the boy, running along with him, accused that dirty old trooper of having called out the guard to fire on them.

Up the slag-heap Jules had not moved; his eyes gazed on at the falling snow. The sergeant came up with the relieving party and the regulation calls were exchanged.

'Who goes there? Advance and give the password!'

The heavy steps receded, marching as though in an occupied country. Although by now it was broad daylight, nothing stirred in the villages. The miners were chafing in silence under the conqueror's heel.

[2]

Snow had been falling for two days, but it had stopped that morning and a sharp frost had turned the plain into one great sheet of ice. The black country with its inky roads, it walls and trees powdered with coal-dust, now seemed to go on uniformly white for ever. Village 240 was as good as buried under the snow. Not one wisp of smoke was coming from any chimney, the fireless houses were as cold as the stones of the road and the thick layer of snow on the roofs never melted. The village looked like a quarry of white stones on the white plain, a dead village, wrapped in its shroud. The only tracks in the slush were the footprints of the military patrols passing up and down the streets.

In the Maheu home the last shovelful of gleanings from the pit-bank had been burnt the day before, and it was now out of the question to think of picking up any more there in this terrible weather, when even the sparrows could not find a blade of grass. Through having persisted in digging in the snow with her poor little hands Alzire was now critically ill. Her mother had had to wrap her in an old bit of bedspread and settle down to wait for Dr Vanderhaghen, to whose house she had already made two fruitless visits, but his housekeeper had promised that the doctor would be round before nightfall. So now she stood watching at the window, whilst the sick child, who had wanted to be downstairs, sat shivering on a chair, deluding herself that it was better there by the empty fireplace. Opposite her old Bonnemort, whose legs were bad again, seemed to be asleep. Neither Lénore nor Henri had come back from tramping the streets with Jeanlin, begging for coppers. Only Maheu was walking heavily up and down the bare room, running into the wall at each end with the bewildered look of an animal that cannot see its cage. The oil had run out too, but the reflection of the snow outside was so bright that it dimly lit the room although night had fallen.

There was a sound of clogs and la Levaque burst into the room in a towering rage, shouting to Maheude:

367

'So it's you who said I forced my lodger to pay me twenty sous when he slept with me!'

Maheude shrugged her shoulders.

'Don't be so silly, I never said anything of the kind. . . . And who told you I said so, anyway?'

'Never you mind who. I've been told that you said so. And what's more you said you could hear our dirty goings-on through the wall, and that my house was hanging with filth because I was always on my back. . . . Now say you didn't say so, go on!'

Every day there were scenes like this owing to the ceaseless gossiping of the women. Between pairs of houses in particular, rows and reconciliations were daily occurrences. But never before had they flown at each other with such spiteful bitterness. Since the strike had been on, hunger had accentuated old rancours and they all felt like hitting the other. Such arguments between two gossiping women frequently led on to murderous fights between their menfolk.

And sure enough, Levaque came in now, dragging Bouteloup by main force.

'Here's our mate. Now let him say whether he has paid my wife twenty sous to sleep with her!'

The lodger protested, hiding his nervous meekness behind his fierce beard:

'Oh no! Never anything like that, never!'

Thereupon Levaque became nasty and brandished his fist under Maheu's nose.

'Look here. I'm not having any of this! If you've got a wife who says things like tha yo : hould hit her. It means you believe what she says, I suppose?'

'But in God's name,' exclaimed Maheu, furious at being shaken out of his lethargy, 'what the hell are all these tales about? Haven't we got enough trouble as it is? Bugger off, or I'll knock you down! . . . And besides, who told you my wife said that?'

'Who said so? Pierronne.'

Maheude went off into a shrill laugh and turned on la Levaque:

'Oh, it was Pierronne, was it? Very well. Now I can tell you

368

what she told me. Yes, she said you slept with both your men together, one underneath and one on top!'

That started a general shouting match. They all lost their tempers, the Levaques countering the Maheus' remarks by saying that Pierronne had had a lot to say about them too, that they had sold Catherine, and that they were all eaten up, kids and all, with a filthy disease Étienne had picked up at the Volcan.

'Oh, she said that, did she? So that's what she said!' bawled Maheu. 'Right! Then I'm going straight over there, and if she says she said it I'll sock her one on the jaw!'

He rushed out, followed by the Levaques as witnesses, but Bouteloup, who hated scenes, slipped furtively home. Maheude, equally incensed by the argument, was on the point of going over too, but a cry from Alzire held her back. She pulled the bits of coverlet over the child's shivering body and returned to her vigil by the window, staring out with unseeing eyes. When would that doctor come?

Maheu and the Levaques met Lydie outside the Pierrons' door, walking up and down in the snow. The house was shut up, but a chink of light was showing through a shutter. At first the child was very embarrassed by their questions: no, Daddy wasn't there, he had gone to the wash-house to meet Ma Brûlé and carry back the bundle of washing. Then she became very flustered and would not say what Mummy was doing, but in the end she blabbed it all out, with a sly, vindictive grin. Her mother had put her outside because Monsieur Dansaert was there and she was in the way when they wanted to have a talk. Dansaert had been going round the village with two gendarmes ever since morning, trying to recruit workmen, brow-beating the weaker ones and announcing to all and sundry that if there was not a general return to Le Voreux by Monday the Company had decided to take on men from Belgium. At dusk he had sent off the gendarmes on finding Pierronne alone, and had stayed with her to drink a glass of gin in front of the roaring fire.

'Sh! be quiet, let's watch them!' whispered Levaque with a smutty leer. 'We'll go into that other business later. You be off, missy!'

Lydie moved a few paces away while he put his eye to the crack in the shutter. He stifled little exclamations and a quiver ran down his back. La Levaque had the next look, but she made a show of wanting to be sick and said it was disgusting. Maheu pushed her out of the way so as to have his look and said you got a good money's worth. And they began again one after the other, each having a squint as at a peep-show. The room was shining with polish and the big fire made it look cheerful, there were cakes on the table, with a bottle and glasses – a real party, in fact. What they saw going on would in any other circumstances have given the two men food for jokes for six months, but now it exasperated them. The fact that she let herself be plugged up to the neck with her skirts in the air was funny. But wasn't it bloody disgusting to treat yourself to that in front of such a big fire, and to get up your strength for it with biscuits when your mates hadn't got a scrap of bread or one single bit of coal?

'Here comes Daddy,' said Lydie, and scampered off.

Pierron was calmly returning from the wash-house with the bundle of washing on his shoulder. Maheu accosted him at once:

'Look here, I've been told that your wife said I had sold Catherine and that we're all pox-ridden in our house. And how much does the gentleman pay you for wear and tear of your wife? He's at it now.'

Taken completely by surprise, Pierron did not understand, but just then his wife, scared by the sound of voices, lost her head and opened the door a little to see what was going on. They caught a glimpse of her, looking very red with her dress open at the neck and her skirt still caught up in her belt, whilst in the background Dansaert was frantically pulling on his trousers. The overman moved off at full speed, terrified lest a tale like this should reach the manager's ears. An appalling din broke out, with laughter, booing, and insults.

'You always say everybody else is dirty,' shouted la Levaque to Pierronne. 'No wonder you are so clean if you get the bosses to scour you out!'

'Ah, she's a nice one to talk!' added Levaque. 'There's a bitch for you! She said my wife slept with me and the lodger, one on top and the other underneath! Yes, that's what I'm told you said!'

But by now Pierronne had recovered her composure and was facing up to the insults with lofty scorn, safe in the knowledge that she was prettier and richer than anybody else.

'I said what I said, and now clear off, see? What business is it of yours what I do? You're all jealous and wild with us just because we put money away in the bank! Get along with you, you can say what you like, but my husband knows quite well why Monsieur Dansaert was in our house.'

And indeed by now Pierron was indignantly defending his wife. The quarrel shifted its ground, and they accused him of being the Company's watchdog and spying on them for money, shutting himself indoors to stuff himself with the good things the Company gave him as a reward for his treachery. He retaliated by making out that Maheu had slipped a threatening letter under his door – a piece of paper bearing cross-bones with a dagger above. Inevitably it ended up in a free fight between the men, just as the women's rows had been doing ever since hunger had turned even the gentlest of them into viragos. Maheu and Levaque had rushed at Pierron with their fists, and they all had to be separated.

By the time Ma Brûlé appeared her son-in-law's nose was bleeding copiously. When she learned what was afoot she merely said:

'That swine is a disgrace to me.'

Peace returned to the empty street and no shadow darkened the bare whiteness of the snow. The village had relapsed into the deathly stillness of starvation in the intense cold.

'Doctor been?' asked Maheu, shutting the door behind him.

'Not yet,' answered his wife, still standing at the window.

'Kids back?'

'No, not back yet.'

He resumed his heavy tramp up and down the room, looking like a dazed ox. Old Bonnemort, sitting stiff in his chair, had not even raised his head. Alzire said nothing either, but tried not to shiver, so as to spare them pain. In spite of her courage in suffering, however, there were times when she shook so violently that the vibration of her poor little sick body could be heard against the coverlet, while her big open eyes gazed up at the ceiling, where the pale reflection of the snowy gardens lit the room with a sort of moonlight.

The house was in its last agony, empty and destitute. The mattress covers had followed the woollen stuffing to the dealer's, then the sheets had gone, and all the linen, in fact everything that could be sold. One evening one of Grandpa's handkerchiefs had fetched two sous. Tears had been shed over each object in the poor home that had had to go, and mother was still bewailing having taken away, hidden under her skirt, the pink cardboard box her sweetheart had once given her, for it had felt like taking a baby to leave on someone's doorstep. Now the home was stripped bare, and they had nothing left to sell but their skins, and those were so worn out that nobody would have given a farthing for them. They no longer even bothered to look for anything, knowing that there was nothing. It was the end, it was no use hoping for a candle, a piece of coal, or a potato, and they were simply waiting to die. Their only feelings of anger were on the children's behalf, for they were outraged by the pointless cruelty of Providence which had struck their little girl down with an illness when she had got to die anyway.

'Here he is at last!' said Maheude.

A dark form had passed the window and the door opened. But it was not Dr Vanderhaghen. They recognized the new parish priest, abbé Ranvier, who did not seem in the least surprised to find this house dead, without light, fire, or bread. He had just come from three neighbouring houses, in a tour of the families, gathering in men of good will, like Dansaert and his gendarmes. He plunged at once into business in his feverish, fanatical voice.

'Why didn't you come to Mass last Sunday, my children? You are making a great mistake. Only the Church can save you. . . . Now just promise me you will come along next Sunday.'

Maheu took one look at him and went on with his weary pacing without uttering a word. His wife answered:

'Mass, Monsieur le curé, what for? Isn't your God laughing at us? Look, what has my little girl done to Him that she

372

should be shaking with fever? We weren't suffering enough already, I suppose, so He had to go and make her ill when I can't even give her a cup of something warm.'

Then the priest stood there and held forth at great length. He was exploiting the strike, with its dreadful misery and the bitter resentment engendered by hunger, and bringing to his task all the ardour of a missionary preaching to savages for the greater glory of his faith. The Church, he declared, was on the side of the poor, one day she would cause justice to triumph by calling down the wrath of God on the iniquities of the wealthy. And that day would soon dawn, for the rich had put themselves in the place of God and were ruling without him, having wickedly usurped His power. But if the workers wanted a fair share of the things of this world they must at once put themselves into the hands of the priests, even as after the death of Jesus the poor and lowly gathered round the apostles. Look what power the Pope would have, what an army the clergy could command when the countless hosts of workers accepted their dictates! Within a week the world would be cleansed of evildoers, the unworthy employers would be hounded out and the true kingdom of God would come, where each man would be rewarded according to his worth and the law of labour would be the foundation of universal happiness.

As she listened, Maheude thought she could hear Étienne when he used to prophesy the end of their woes as they all sat round on those autumn evenings. The only difference was that she never had trusted the cloth.

'What you are saying is all very well, sir,' she said, 'but that's only because you happen to have fallen out with the bourgeois. All our other priests used to dine with the manager and threaten us with hell fire as soon as we asked for bread.'

He began again, speaking of the deplorable misunderstanding between the Church and the people. And in veiled terms he attacked the town priests, the bishops and prelates, sated with luxury and drunk with power, hand in glove with the liberal middle classes in their stupid blindness, not seeing that these very middle classes were depriving them of world empire. Deliverance would come from the country priests, who would rise up as one man to establish the kingdom of Christ, helped by the poor. And he already seemed to see himself at their head, drawing his bony form up to its full height, a partisan leader, a revolutionary of the Gospel, and his eyes shone with such fire that they lit up the dark room. His ardent preaching carried him aloft in mystic words which these poor folk had long since been unable to follow.

'There's no need for so much talk,' growled Maheu. 'You would have done better to bring us a loaf of bread!'

'Come to Mass next Sunday,' cried the priest. 'God will provide!'

He took himself off to catechize the Levaques in their turn, so up in the clouds in his dream of the final triumph of the Church, and having such contempt for mere facts, that he was capable of going about in the villages empty-handed and giving nothing in the midst of this host of starving people, for the poor devil looked on suffering as a spur to salvation.

Maheu was still walking up and down, and the flagstones shook with the regular beat of his steps. There was a noise like a rusty pulley and old Bonnemort spat into the empty grate. Alzire, drowsy with fever, had begun to mutter in her delirium, laughing away and thinking she was playing in the warm sunshine.

'Good God!' exclaimed Maheude, feeling the child's cheeks, 'she's burning hot now. I've given up waiting for that swine, I bet those beasts have told him not to come!'

She was referring to the doctor and the Company. Yet she uttered an exclamation of joy when the door opened again. But her arms dropped limply and she stood bolt upright with a sullen face.

'Good evening,' whispered Étienne, after carefully shutting the door.

He often looked in like this after dark. From the second day the Maheus had known about his hiding-place, but they had kept the knowledge to themselves, and nobody else in the village quite knew what had become of the young man, and this surrounded him with an aura of mystery. They still believed in him, and strange rumours about him were spread around: he would return at the head of an army with coffers full of gold. It was the old religious faith in miracles, in dreams coming true, in a sudden entry into the city of justice he had promised. Some said they had seen him in a carriage with three gentlemen on the Marchiennes road, others affirmed that he would be in England for two more days yet. But in the end they were becoming sceptical and the more frivolous accused him of hiding in a cellar and being kept warm by Mouquette, for his affair with her was common knowledge and had done him no good. There was a gradual falling off in his popularity due to the steady pressure of the pessimistic elements whose numbers were bound to go on increasing.

'Bloody awful weather!' he went on. 'What about yourselves? Nothing new, I suppose, and things not getting any better! I'm told that master Négrel has gone off to Belgium looking for men in the Borinage. God! we're done for if that's true.'

This dark, icy room had given him the creeps, and his eyes had to accustom themselves before he could see these poor devils, whose whereabouts he could only guess from deeper patches of shadow. Once again he felt that sensation of repugnance and embarrassment that assails the workman who has risen above his class, been refined by study and begun to harbour ambitions. What misery! And what a smell! All these bodies huddled together in a heap – the awful pity of it brought a lump to his throat. The sight of this agony upset him so much that he was at a loss for words with which to advise them to give in.

Maheu rushed up to him shouting:

'Borains! The buggers wouldn't dare! If they want us to destroy the pits they had better put Belgians down there.'

Étienne diffidently pointed out that they could not move, and that the soldiers guarding the pits would cover the Belgians' descent. But Maheu clenched his fists, angered above all at having a bayonet in his back, as he put it. So the miners were no longer masters in their own place? They were treated as galley-slaves and forced to work at the end of a gun? He loved his pit, and it hurt him not to have been down for two months, and the thought of this insult, this threat to send foreigners down, made him see red. Also he was heartbroken at having had his card returned.

'I don't know why I'm angry,' he said, 'since I don't belong to the show any more. When they turn me out of here I might as well peg out on the road.'

'Don't be silly!' said Étienne. 'They'll take your card back tomorrow if you want them to. They don't sack good men.'

But he broke off in astonishment, hearing Alzire chuckling softly in her delirium. So far all he had been able to make out had been the stiff form of old Bonnemort, and this sick child's laughter terrified him. This was too awful if the children were beginning to die. He took the plunge and said in a hesitant voice:

'Look here, things can't go on like this. We're finished and we shall have to give in.'

Until then Maheude had been still and quiet, but now she suddenly burst out, shouting in his face in violent language as man to man:

'What do you say? Christ! *You* talk like that!'

He tried to explain, but she would not let him speak.

'Don't you say that again, or God strike me dead if I don't sock you one on the jaw, woman or no woman. . . . So we have starved for two months, and I have sold my home and my children are ill, all to no purpose! And the same old injustice would start all over again! Oh! the very thought of it is enough to give you a fit! No, no, now I would burn everything and kill everybody rather than give in.'

With a grand and threatening gesture she pointed at Maheu in the dark.

'Listen to me! If my man goes back to the pit I'll wait for him myself in the street and spit in his face and call him a scab!'

Étienne could not see her, but he felt something like the hot breath of a baying hound, and he recoiled in horror from this frenzy that was his own handiwork. She was so different that she did not seem the same woman; she had been so sensible and used to blame him for being violent, saying that one ought never to wish for anyone's death, and now she was refusing to listen to reason and talking of killing people. Instead of himself it was she who was talking politics, wanting to sweep the bourgeois away at one blow, demanding the republic and the guillotine to rid the earth of these wealthy robbers grown fat on the toil of the starving masses.

'Yes, I would strangle them with my own fingers. . . . We've had about enough of it! It's our turn now, you used to say so yourself. When I think that father, grandfather, and grandfather's father and all the past generations have gone through what we are suffering now, and that our sons and our sons' sons will go through it all over again, it drives me mad and makes me want to take a knife. . . . We didn't go far enough the other day, we ought to have torn that bloody Montsou to the ground, every brick of it. Do you know, there's only one thing I regret, and that is that we didn't let the old man strangle that Piolaine girl. They let hunger strangle my children!'

Her words fell like axe strokes in the darkness. The closed horizon had refused to open for her, and the unrealizable ideal was turning to poison in this brain crazed by grief.

'But you have misunderstood me,' Étienne at last managed to say, now on the defensive. 'We ought to come to an understanding with the Company: I know that the pits are getting seriously damaged, and that might make them agree to some arrangement.'

'No! Nothing!' she screamed.

At that moment Lénore and Henri came home empty-handed. Yes, a gentleman had given them two sous, but the sister had kept on kicking her little brother and the coins had dropped into the snow, and as Jeanlin had joined in the search they had not been found again.

'Well, where is Jeanlin?'

'He ran away, Mummy. He said he had some business.'

Étienne listened with aching heart. She used to threaten to kill them if they begged in the street. Now it was she who sent them out, and she talked of their all going, all the ten thousand Montsou miners, with sticks and wallets like aged beggars, roaming the panic-stricken countryside.

And now the anguish in that dark room was still further intensified because the brats had come home hungry and wanted something to eat – why wasn't there anything to eat? They grumbled and threw themselves about, ending up by stamping on the feet of their dying sister, who uttered a groan. Their mother furiously lashed out at them in the dark, not seeing or caring what she hit. That made them howl and beg for bread louder than ever, and she suddenly burst into tears, collapsed on to the floor and hugged them all together, dying sister and all. In a nervous reaction she wept and wept until finally, limp and exhausted, all she could do was moan the same phrase over and over again, calling on death: 'Oh God, why don't you take us? Oh God, for pity's sake make an end of it!' Grandpa was still rooted in his place like an ancient tree, gnarled by wind and rain, whilst father tramped on between the fireplace and the cupboard, never looking round.

The door opened again, and this time it really was Dr Vanderhaghen.

'Devil take it!' he said, 'your eyesight won't be ruined by candle-light. . . . Make haste, I'm in a hurry.'

As usual he grumbled all the time, for he was cruelly over-worked. Fortunately he had some matches, and the child's father had to light six, one after the other, and hold them for the doctor to examine the patient. She had been uncovered and was shivering in the flickering light, looking as puny as a bird dying in the snow, so thin that all you could see was her hump. But she smiled all the same, with the vague smile of the dying, her great eyes were staring and her poor little hands clutching her hollow chest. And as the grief-stricken mother was asking whether it was right that this child, the only one who ever helped in the house, and so intelligent and so gentle, should be taken before her, the doctor impatiently rapped out:

'Look, she's gone! Your wretched brat has died of starvation. And she's not the only one. I've just seen another down the street. You all call me in and there's nothing I can do. Meat is the medicine you want.'

Maheu dropped the match which was burning his fingers, and darkness fell again on the little warm corpse. Already the doctor had hurried off. All Étienne could hear in the blackness of the room was Maheude crying out again and again for death in her endless mournful lament:

378

'Oh God, it's my turn, take me! Oh, God take my man, take us all, for pity's sake, and make an end of it!'

BY eight o'clock on that Sunday evening Souvarine was left to himself in the bar at the Avantage, sitting in his usual seat with his head against the wall. There was not a single miner left now who could put his hand on the two sous for a beer, and the pubs had never had so few customers. Madame Rasseneur sat motionless at her counter in irritable silence whilst Rasseneur, standing in front of the iron stove, appeared to be intently examining the reddish smoke of the coal.

The stuffy silence of the overheated room was suddenly broken by three little taps on the window, and Souvarine looked round. He leaped to his feet, recognizing the signal that Étienne had used several times to call him, when from outside he had seen him sitting at an empty table smoking a cigarette. But before he could reach the door Rasseneur had opened it, saying to the man he recognized in the beam of light from the window:

'Are you afraid I shall give you away? You would be more comfortable talking in here than outside in the street.'

Étienne came in. Madame Rasseneur politely offered him a beer, but he waved it away. The publican went on:

'I guessed long ago where you were hiding. If I were a sneak as your friends say, I should have put the police on to you a week ago.'

'No need to tell me that,' the young man answered, 'I know you've never eaten that sort of bread. People can have different ideas and still respect each other.'

Silence fell again. Souvarine had gone back to his chair and was sitting back to the wall, gazing dreamily at his cigarette smoke, but his nervous fingers were fidgeting anxiously along his thighs, feeling for the warm fur of Poland, who was out that evening. He was unconsciously looking for something missing, without quite knowing what.

Étienne was sitting opposite him. Eventually he broke the silence:

'Work begins again tomorrow at Le Voreux. The Belgians have arrived with young Négrel.'

'Yes,' murmured Rasseneur, who was still standing. 'They were unloaded at dusk. So long as it doesn't lead to any more of this killing!'

Then, raising his voice:

'Now look here, I don't want to start arguing again, but we shall run into trouble if you go on being obstinate. You know, what's happened to you is exactly like what's happened to this International of yours. I met Pluchart the day before yesterday in Lille, where I had to go on business. It seems that this stunt of his is coming to grief.'

He went into details. It appeared that the Association, having begun by enrolling the workers all the world over by a vigorous propaganda campaign, at which the bourgeoisie was still shivering in its shoes, was now being undermined and steadily destroyed by internal dissensions through vanity and ambition. Since the anarchist elements had dominated it and overridden the evolutionists of the early days the whole thing was going to pieces, and the original object of reforming the wage-system was being obscured by sectarian wranglings. The intellectuals were disorganized because they refused to knuckle under to discipline. Already it was easy to foresee that this mass rising, which for a brief moment had threatened to sweep away the corrupt old world, was simply going to peter out.

'It has made Pluchart quite ill,' he concluded, 'though in any case he has ceased to count at all. But he still talks a lot and wants to go to Paris and do some more talking there. . . . And no less than three times he said to me that our strike was a wash-out.'

With downcast eyes Étienne let him have his say. He had had a talk with some of the chaps the day before and had sensed the first signs of bitterness and suspicion, the beginnings of the unpopularity that precedes defeat. He sat there sullenly, trying not to admit his own despair in front of the very man who had prophesied that his turn would come to be howled down by the mob as soon as it wanted a scape-goat.

'Yes, the strike is a wash-out, no doubt. I know that as well as Pluchart,' he said. 'But we foresaw that. We had to decide on a strike against our will, and never expected to finish the Company off. . . . Only you get carried away and begin to hope and then when it all goes wrong you forget that you ought to have foreseen, and squeal and argue as though it was a disaster from heaven.'

'But,' asked Rasseneur, 'if you think the game is up why don't you make your mates see reason?'

The young man looked him straight in the eyes.

'Now listen, let's cut this out! You have your ideas and I have mine. I have come into your house to show you that I respect you all the same. But I still think that if we go under, our starved bodies will do more for the people's cause than all your prudent politics. . . . If only one of those bleeding soldiers could land a bullet in my heart, what a fine end it would be!'

His eyes were moist as he betrayed the secret wish of the defeated for a refuge where all torment would be finished for ever.

'Well said,' applauded Madame Rasseneur, putting all her uncompromising radicalism into a scornful glance at her husband.

Souvarine, whose eyes were lost in dreams and whose fingers were still nervously drumming, did not seem to have heard. His fair girlish face, with its thin nose and little pointed teeth, had taken on a savage expression, reflecting his mystic dreams about the International and bloody visions. Answering a remark of Rasseneur's that he had caught in the middle of the conversation, he began thinking aloud:

'They are all cowards. There was only one man capable of turning their show into a terrible instrument of destruction. But it is the will that is needed, nobody has the will, and that is why the revolution is going to misfire once again.'

He proceeded in disgusted tones to bewail the imbecility of mankind, whilst the two others felt like intruders upon the secrets a sleepwalker was confiding to the shades of night. Nothing was going right in Russia; the news he had received

381

was heartbreaking. His former comrades were all turning to politics; the famous nihilists who had made Europe tremble – sons of village priests, or of middle-class parents, or shop-keepers – now dared not venture beyond national liberation and seemed to think the world would be set free when they had killed their own particular tyrant. And as soon as he spoke to them of mowing down the old society like a ripe harvest, or even pronounced the childish word republic, he felt misunderstood, looked upon as a dangerous man who had stepped out of his class, and whom they ranked with the failures, the broken-down princes of revolutionary cosmopolitanism. But he still had lingering qualms of patriotism in his heart, and it was with painful bitterness that he repeated his favourite word:

'Balderdash! They'll never get anywhere with their poppy-cock!'

Then in an even softer voice he ruefully spoke of his old dream of fraternity. He had given up his own rank and fortune and thrown in his lot with the workers for one reason only: the hope of seeing a new society founded on communal work. For a long time all his spare coins had been given to the village children, he had always shown brotherly affection to all the miners, smiling when they hesitated to accept him and winning their trust by his air of quietness and efficiency. But it was none the less true that they did not mix properly, he remained a foreigner to them, with his contempt for all human ties and his determination to stay pure and uncorrupted by pride or pleasure. And since he had read an item in the morning papers he was reduced to exasperation.

His voice changed and his eyes lit up as he turned and addressed Étienne:

'Can you understand this? A couple of hat-makers at Marseilles have drawn the lucky number in a lottery – a prize of a hundred thousand francs – and straight away they have invested it in annuities, saying they were never going to work any more! Yes, all you French workers have that one idea: you want to dig up a treasure and live on it for evermore in selfish and lazy isolation. You make a great song against the rich, but when fortune gives you some money you haven't the guts to give it back to the poor. You will never deserve to be happy so long as you have personal possessions, and your hatred of the bourgeois simply comes from your mad desire to be bourgeois yourselves in their place!'

Rasseneur laughed outright, for the thought that the two workers of Marseilles ought to have refused to accept the first prize struck him as ridiculous. But Souvarine turned pale, and his features twisted into a horrible expression, the expression of one of those fanatical religious passions that can exterminate whole nations.

'You will all be mown down and thrown on the rubbish-heap,' he shouted. 'The one who will destroy your race of cowards and sensualists is at hand. Look at these hands of mine – if they could do so they would take hold of the world like this and shake it into little pieces so as to bury the lot of you under the wreckage!'

'Hear, hear!' said Madame Rasseneur, with her usual air of polite conviction.

Another silence. Then Étienne came back to the subject of the Belgian workmen. He asked Souvarine what arrangements had been made at Le Voreux. But by now the mechanic had relapsed into his daydreams and scarcely answered any questions; all he knew was that cartridges were to be issued to the soldiers on guard. At this point the nervous drumming of his fingers became so marked that he finally realized what was missing – the soft, soothing fur of the tame rabbit.

'Where's Poland?' he asked.

The publican laughed once again and glanced at his wife. After an awkward pause he took the plunge.

'Poland? she's been hotted up.'

The plump rabbit had no doubt been injured by her adventure with Jeanlin, for ever since then she had only brought forth stillborn offspring, and so as not to have to feed a useless mouth they had decided that very day to serve her up with potatoes.

'Yes, you had one of her legs this evening. . . . You licked your fingers after it, didn't you?'

For a moment Souvarine did not understand. Then he went very pale, retched convulsively, and for all his stoical strength of character his eyes filled with big tears.

But his emotion passed unnoticed because the door had been flung open and in had come Chaval, pushing Catherine in front of him. He had been drinking and showing off in all the pubs in Montsou, and now it had occurred to him to come to the Avantage and show his former friends that he was not afraid of anybody. As he came in he said to Catherine:

'By Christ, I tell you you're going to have a drink in here, and the first man who starts looking me up and down gets one on the jaw!'

Seeing Étienne there, Catherine started and turned pale. When Chaval saw him he said with a nasty leer:

'Two beers please, Madame Rasseneur. We're celebrating the start of work!'

She served him without a word, for she never refused beer to anyone. Nobody spoke and the publican and the two men did not move.

'I know people who said I was a scab,' Chaval went on arrogantly, 'and I'm waiting for these people to say so to my face so that we can have a bit of an explanation.'

Still there was no answer, the men turning away and looking at the walls.

'There are some as do their job and others as don't,' he went on, raising his voice. 'I've got nothing to hide. I've left Deneulin's dirty hole and tomorrow I start at Le Voreux with twelve Belgians they've put me in charge of because they think well of me. And if that upsets anybody he can say so, and we'll talk it over!'

As his provocative remarks were greeted with the same contemptuous silence he took it out of Catherine.

'Are you going to drink or not, for Christ's sake? Here's the toast: to hell with all the dirty swine who won't work!'

She put her glass to his, but her hand trembled so much that the two glasses made a continuous tinkling. He had taken a handful of silver out of his pocket and was spreading it out with tipsy ostentation, saying that he had earned it with the sweat of his brow and that he challenged the slackers to show ten sous. Finding the attitude of the others exasperating he resorted to direct insults.

'So the moles come out at night? The police must be asleep then, as the thieves seem to be abroad!'

Étienne rose to his feet in quiet determination.

'Now listen. I've had enough of you. Yes, you are a sneak and your money stinks of some new treachery. I don't want to dirty my hands on your skin, you Judas! But still, I'll take you on. It's high time one of us finished the other one off!'

Chaval clenched his fists.

'Come on, then! What a lot of talking it needs to warm you up, you cowardly bugger! I'm ready to take you on alone, and you are going to pay for some of the bloody insults I've had to put up with!'

Catherine tried to rush between them, raising her arms in supplication, but they did not even have to bother to push her back, for she realized that this fight had to be, and slowly stepped back of her own accord. She stood with her back against the wall, silent and so paralysed with anguish that she no longer trembled, but simply stared with her great eyes at these two men who were going to kill each other for her sake.

Madame Rasseneur removed the glasses from the counter in a businesslike way to save their being broken, and then sat on her seat again without showing unseemly curiosity. But two old comrades could not be allowed to kill each other like this, and Rasseneur insisted on trying to stop them until Souvarine took him by the shoulder and led him back to the table, saying:

'This is none of your business. . . . There isn't room for both of them, and it's up to the stronger to survive.'

Without waiting to be attacked, Chaval was already punching the air wildly. He was taller, a great gangling figure of a man, and he aimed at Étienne's face with furious slashing movements, using both arms as though he were wielding a pair of sabres. And he talked all the time, playing to the gallery, with a running fire of insults which also kept his own courage up.

'You bloody pimp! I'll get your nose and stick it up you know where! Let me have a go at your pretty face that all the tarts like looking at! I'll turn it into pigs' mash and then we'll see if the bloody women run after you!'

Étienne said never a word but, holding his slim body taut and setting his teeth, took up a correct position, guarding his face and chest with both fists and watching for his chances, when he let them fly like springs with terrible straight punches.

At first they did each other little harm. The waving windmill strokes of the one and the cool watchfulness of the other prolonged the fight. A chair was knocked over and the sand on the stone floor crunched beneath their heavy boots. But in the end they were both winded, and their breath came in snoring gasps, while their faces seemed to be inflamed with an inner fire, the flames of which showed in the whites of their eyes.

'Got him!' yelled Chaval. 'Trumps on your carcase!'

And indeed his fist, working slantwise like a flail, had grazed along his opponent's shoulder. Étienne checked a howl of pain, and the only sound was the soft thud on his bruised muscles. He countered with a straight punch to the heart which would have been a knock-out had the other not protected himself by his ceaseless jumping about. But the blow landed on his left side and there was still so much power in it that he staggered, gasping for breath. Feeling his arms weakening he went mad with rage and charged like a wild beast, aiming at Étienne's groin with a kick from his heel.

'That's for your innards!' he gasped. 'I'll pull them out into the daylight!'

Étienne dodged the kick, and this fouling of the rules of decent fighting so enraged him that he broke his silence.

'Shut up, you brute! And no kicking, or by God I'll pick up a chair and smash you!'

From then on the fight took a more desperate turn. Rasseneur was disgusted and would have interfered again, but was dissuaded by a warning look from his wife: had not two customers the right to settle their affairs in the house? So he contented himself with standing in front of the fire for fear of their falling into it. Souvarine had calmly rolled himself a cigarette, but he forgot to light it. Catherine was still motionless by the wall, but her hands had risen unconsciously to her bosom, where they automatically twisted and untwisted and clutched

386

at the stuff of her dress. Her whole being was concentrated in an effort not to scream out and so kill one of them by showing her preference. By now she was so distraught that she had no idea which one she did prefer.

Chaval soon tired: he was bathed in sweat and hitting out at random. Furious though he was, Étienne never relaxed his guard but parried almost every punch, though some of them grazed him. One of his ears was split and a nail scratch had cut his neck which smarted so much that he began swearing too, and let fly another of his terrible straight punches. Once more Chaval avoided a chest blow by jumping, but in doing so he ducked and Étienne's fist flattened his nose and closed one of his eyes. Blood at once spurted from his nostrils and the eye swelled up and went blue. Blinded by the red stream and dizzy from head-punches, the wretched man was wildly beating the air when another blow, a real body-blow this time, finished him off. There was a crash and he fell on his back with a thud like the sound of a sack of plaster being unloaded.

Étienne waited.

'If you want some more, get up and we'll start again.'

Chaval made no reply, but after lying dazed for a few seconds, began moving on the ground and stretching his limbs. He wearily dragged himself up on to his knees, where he stayed a moment huddled up, but his hand was doing something deep down in his pocket. The he got to his feet and made another mad rush, with the muscles of his throat standing out as he yelled like a savage.

But Catherine had seen, and in spite of herself a great cry rose from her heart, like the admission of a preference unknown and astounding even to herself:

'Look out! He's got his knife!'

Étienne just had time to parry the first stab with his arm. His woollen jersey was cut by the heavy blade, one of those blades fixed into a boxwood handle by a brass ferrule. He seized Chaval's wrist and a deadly struggle ensued; he knew he was lost if he let go, and the other kept trying to jerk himself free in order to strike. Slowly the knife came lower and lower as their strained limbs grew more tired, and once Étienne felt the cold touch of steel on his skin. By a supreme effort he squeezed Chaval's wrist so tightly that the knife fell out of his open hand. Both flung themselves at it, but Étienne picked it up and brandished it in his turn. He had Chaval down under his knee and made ready to slit his throat.

'You bloody traitor! It's coming to you now!'

A horrible, deafening voice was rising within him, coming up from his very entrails and banging like a hammer in his head. It was a sudden insane desire to murder a man, a lust for blood. He had never had it so badly before, and yet he was not drunk this time. He fought against his hereditary taint with the frantic paroxysms of a man mad with lust struggling on the verge of rape. He managed to get himself under control, threw the knife behind him, and muttered hoarsely:

'Get up and get out!'

This time Rasseneur had leaped forward, taking care, however, not to get between them for fear of catching a nasty blow. He did not want murder in his house, and he protested so loudly that his wife, still enthroned behind the counter, pointed out that he always shouted too soon. Souvarine, who had almost had the dagger in his lap, made up his mind to light his cigarette. It was all over, then? Catherine was still staring bewildered at the two men, who were both alive.

'Get out!' Étienne said again. 'Get out, or I'll finish you off!'

Chaval got up, wiped his bleeding nose with the back of his hand, and with his face smeared with blood and his eye blackened, slouched off in the bitterness of defeat. Catherine automatically made as if to follow him. He turned back and his hatred poured itself out in a stream of obscenities.

'Oh no you don't! As he's the one you want, go and sleep with him, you bloody bitch! And don't you bloody well put your foot inside my place again if you value your life!'

He slammed the door. The only sound that broke the silence in the warm room was the roaring of the fire. The overturned chair was still on the floor, and splashes of blood were soaking into the sand.

[4]

ÉTIENNE and Catherine left Rasseneur's and walked on in silence. It was beginning to thaw – a slow, cold thaw, dirtying the snow without really melting it. The sky was leaden and a full moon could be dimly seen behind high banks of cloud, like black rags blown along very fast by a gale. But down on the ground there was not a breath of wind, and only the dripping of the gutters could be heard, or the soft thuds of lumps of snow falling from the roofs.

Étienne felt awkward with this woman who had been handed over to him, and in his embarrassment could find nothing to say. It seemed absurd to take her with him to his hiding-place in Réquillart. He had offered to take her home to her parents, but she had recoiled from the suggestion in terror: no, no, anything rather than go back to be a burden to them after the dirty trick she had played by leaving them in the lurch! So neither of them said another word, but tramped on along the roads which were now rivers of mud, not knowing where they were going. First they went down towards Le Voreux, then turned right between the pit bank and the canal.

'But you must sleep somewhere,' Étienne said eventually. 'If I had a room I would gladly take you. . . .'

But he could not complete his thought, checked by a strange fit of shyness. He remembered their past, their passionate desires and the delicacy and timidity that had prevented their coming together. Could it be that he still desired her, since he felt so disturbed, with a new longing gradually warming his heart? The recollection that she had slapped his face at Gaston-Marie now made him excited rather than resentful. To his surprise it now seemed quite natural to take her to Réquillart, and quite easy to do so.

'Come, make up your mind, where do you want me to take you? Do you hate me so much then, that you won't come with me?'

She was slowly following him, her clogs slipping in the ruts, and without looking up she murmured:

389

'I've enough trouble as it is, don't make more for me! Where would it land us, what you are asking for, now that I have a man and you have a woman yourself?'

She was referring to Mouquette, thinking he had taken up with her, for everybody had been saying so for a fortnight. When he swore it was not true she shook her head, remembering the night when she had seen them kissing each other.

He stood still and said in a low voice: 'Isn't all this nonsense a great pity? You and I would have got on so well together!'

She faltered slightly, but answered:

'No, there's nothing to be sorry about. You haven't lost much. If only you knew what a miserable little scrap I am – no fatter than two sous' worth of butter, and such a botched-up job that I shall never be a proper woman, I'm sure!'

She went on without embarrassment, accusing herself as though her long-delayed puberty were a crime. Although she had had a man it seemed to lessen her worth and relegate her to a place among the kids. At any rate there is some excuse when you can have a child.

'Poor little thing!' Étienne muttered to himself, overcome with pity.

They were at the foot of the pit bank and hidden in its huge shadow. An inky cloud was passing across the moon and they could not even see each other's faces, but their breath mingled and their lips sought each other's, longing for the kiss each of them had desired for months to the point of obsession. But the moon suddenly came out again and there, standing above them on the summit of the white cliffs of light, was the upright figure of the sentry. And without having even kissed each other at long last, they drew back out of modesty, that old modesty of theirs, compounded of anger, a vague feeling of repugnance and a great deal of friendship. They trudged on again, ankle-deep in slush.

'Then that's that, you don't want to?' asked Étienne.

'No,' she said, 'not after Chaval. And then there'd be somebody else after you, I suppose? No, it all disgusts me, and as it doesn't give me any pleasure what is the point of it?'

They fell silent again and walked another hundred paces or so.

'But anyway, do you know where you are going? I can't leave you out of doors on a night like this.'

She replied quite simply:

'I'm going back. Chaval is my man, and I can't sleep anywhere else.'

'But he'll half kill you!'

There was a fresh silence. She had merely shrugged her shoulders in resignation. Of course he would beat her, and when he was tired he would stop, but wasn't that better than roaming the streets like a whore? And besides, she was getting used to beatings, and consoled herself by reflecting that eight girls out of ten were no better off than she was. If he married her some day it would be nice of him, though.

They had instinctively turned towards Montsou, and the nearer they came to it the longer their silences were. It was as though they were not walking together any more. It hurt him terribly to send her back to Chaval, but he could not think of any argument to convince her. He was heartbroken, but he had little better to offer her himself: the existence of a penniless fugitive and maybe a night with no morrow if a soldier's bullet found his head. Perhaps after all it was wiser to bear one's present sufferings without taking on new ones. And so here he was taking her back to her lover and hanging his head in misery. He did not protest when she stopped on the main road at the corner of the yards, some twenty metres from Piquette's, and said:

'Don't come any further. If he saw you there would be more trouble!'

It was striking eleven. The bar was shut, but light showed through the slits in the shutters.

'Good-bye,' she whispered.

She had given him her hand and he would not let it go; she had to wrench it away with slow determination. She did not look back, but let herself in by unlatching the little side door. He did not go away, but stood where he was, looking at the house, anxiously wondering what was happening. He listened intently, dreading to hear the screams of a woman being beaten. But the house was dark and still, and all he saw was a light appearing at a first-floor window. The window opened and recognizing the slender shadow leaning out he stepped forward.

Catherine whispered very softly:

'He isn't back yet. I'm going to bed. Do go away, please!'

He went. It was now thawing more quickly and the water was running off the roofs in a steady stream. Damp was running like sweat from walls, fences, and all the nondescript buildings of this industrial area only half visible in the night. His first thought was to make for Réquillart; sick with fatigue and distress his one desire was to disappear underground and be lost. But then he thought of Le Voreux again, of the Belgian workmen who were to go down, and of his friends in the village who were furious with the soldiers and determined not to have foreigners in their pit. Once again he waded through the pools of slush along the canal towpath.

When he was back by the pit bank the moon came out very bright. He looked up at the clouds scudding by before the high wind far up in the sky, but now they were whiter, thinner and broken, mistily transparent in front of the moon, like troubled waters, and they followed each other so rapidly that the moon was only veiled for a moment at a time and always coming out again in its full brightness.

Étienne's eyes were dazzled by this pure light and as he lowered them something caught his attention on top of the bank. The sentry, stiff with cold, was now walking up and down – twenty-five paces towards Marchiennes and then back towards Montsou. His bayonet gleamed white above his dark outline which stood out against the pale sky. But what interested Étienne was a shadow moving behind the hut where Bonnemort sheltered on stormy nights, a creeping, watchful animal that he at once recognized as Jeanlin by his long thin weasel's back. The sentry could not see him and it was clear that this devilish child was meditating some prank, for he detested the soldiers and was always asking when they would be rid of these murderers who were sent with guns to kill people.

For a moment Étienne had half a mind to call out and stop him from doing anything silly. As the moon went behind a cloud he had seen the boy gather himself up ready to spring, but then the moon came out again and he was still crouching

392

there. At each turn the sentry came as far as the hut and then turned his back and marched away. Suddenly, as another cloud threw everything into darkness, Jeanlin leaped on to the soldier's shoulders with one bound, like a wild cat, clung on with his nails and plunged his open knife into his throat. The soldier's stiff collar was in the way and Jeanlin had to ram the handle with both hands and press with all the weight of his body. He had often bled chickens he had found behind farm buildings. It was all so rapid that there was only one muffled cry in the darkness, and the rifle clattered to the ground. The moon was already shining again, very bright.

As he watched, Étienne was rooted to the spot with horror, and the shout stuck in his throat. Above him the slag-heap was empty, and no shadow now stood out against the scurrying clouds. He ran up as fast as he could and found Jeanlin crouching on all fours by the corpse, which was on its back with arms outspread. In the brilliant moonlight the man's red trousers and grey greatcoat contrasted harshly with the white snow. There was not a drop of blood, for the knife was still buried up to the hilt in the man's neck.

In a burst of ungovernable fury he knocked the boy down beside the corpse.

'Why did you do that?'

Jeanlin pulled himself up and crawled along on his hands, his thin spine arched like a cat's. His big ears, green eyes, and prominent jaws were quivering and ablaze with the excitement of his evil deed.

'In God's name, what did you do that for?'

'I don't know, I just had to.'

He stuck obstinately to this reply. He had wanted to for three days. It had tormented him, and his head had ached, just there behind the ears, with constantly thinking about it. Was there any need to be so particular about these bloody soldiers who came and bullied miners in their own homes? Of all the violent speeches in the forest and the cries of destruction and death yelled in the pits, he had retained five or six words, which he repeated like a street-arab playing at revolutions. And that was all he knew; nobody had put him on to doing this, he had thought of it by himself, just as he might suddenly take it into his head to steal onions in a field.

Horrified at this mysterious growth of crime in a child's mind, Étienne kicked him out of the way as though he were some irresponsible animal. He was terrified lest the muffled cry of the sentry might have been heard in the guardroom at Le Voreux, and each time the moon came out he glanced towards the pit. But nothing had stirred, and he bent down, felt the cooling hand and listened for a beat of the still heart under the greatcoat. All that could be seen of the knife was the bone handle on which, by way of a sentimental motto, the single word Love was engraved in black.

His eyes went from the knife to the face and at once he recognized the young soldier: it was Jules the recruit with whom he had talked one morning. He was filled with deep pity at the sight of this gentle, fair face, thickly mottled with freckles. The blue eyes were wide open and staring at the sky with the same fixed stare with which he had seen him look over the horizon towards the land of his birth. Where was this Plogof which he saw in a sun-bathed vision? Over yonder, over yonder. Somewhere far off the sea would be roaring on this stormy night. This wind blowing high in the sky had perhaps swept across his native heath. Two women were standing there: his mother and his sister, holding on their blowing coifs, and they were looking, too, as though across the intervening leagues they could see what their boy was doing at this moment. They would wait for ever now. What a dreadful thing that poor devils should kill each other for the benefit of the rich!

But the corpse must be disposed of. At first Étienne thought of throwing it into the canal, but it would certainly be found there, and he gave up the idea. As the minutes rushed by he became intensely anxious, for some decision must be made. He had a sudden inspiration. If he could carry the body to Réquillart he could bury it there for ever.

'Come here,' he said to Jeanlin.

The boy was suspicious.

'No, you'll hit me. Besides, I've something else to do. Cheerio!'

As a matter of fact he had arranged to meet Bébert and Lydie in a hidey-hole they had made under the timber stack at Le Voreux. They had worked out a grand adventure – a night away from home so as to be on the spot if the Belgians were stoned when they went down in the morning.

'Now listen,' repeated Étienne. 'Come here, or I'll call the soldiers and they'll chop off your head.'

The boy made up his mind and came. Étienne rolled his handkerchief into a pad and tied it tightly round the soldier's neck without pulling out the knife which was preventing the wound from bleeding. The snow was melting and there was no sign on the ground of either bloodstains or footprints of a struggle.

'You take the legs!'

Jeanlin took hold of the legs and Étienne lifted the shoulders after tying the rifle to the soldier's back, and they went slowly down the pit bank, taking care not to dislodge any stones. Fortunately the moon was hidden again, but it came out brightly as they were going along the towpath, and it was only by a miracle that the guards did not see them. They hurried on in silence, but the swaying of the corpse made progress difficult, and they had to put it down every hundred metres. At the corner of the Réquillart lane a sound petrified them with fright, and they only just had time to hide behind a wall to avoid a patrol. Further on a man took them by surprise, but he was drunk and went on his way swearing. By the time they at last reached the disused pit they were bathed in sweat and so unnerved that their teeth were chattering.

Étienne had foreseen that it would be no easy matter to lower the soldier down the escape shaft. In fact it was appalling. To begin with, Jeanlin had to stay at the top and slide the body down while Étienne, suspended from the bushes, went down with it in order to get it safely past the first two ladders where some of the rungs were missing. Then the same performance had to be repeated at each ladder: he went down first and received it in his arms. For two hundred and ten metres, down thirty ladders, the body was continually falling on him. The rifle grazed his back, and he had not let the boy go ahead and find the candle-end, which he was hoarding like a miser. In any case what would have been the point, for a light would have been a nuisance in this narrow shaft. All the same, when they reached the bottom, breathless, he did send the boy for a candle, while he sat down in the dark beside the corpse and waited with pounding heart.

When Jeanlin came back with the candle, Étienne asked his advice, for the child had explored these old workings and been right into crannies where men could not pass. They set off again, dragging the body for nearly a kilometre through a maze of collapsing galleries. Eventually the roof became so low that they found themselves on their knees under some crumbling rock supported by rotting timbers. It was a sort of long box, like a coffin, and here they laid the young soldier, with his rifle by his side. Then they managed to break the props by kicking them away, at the risk of staying there themselves. The rocks broke up at once and they only had time to crawl out on their knees and elbows. When Étienne turned round to have a last look the roof was still falling in and slowly crushing the body under its enormous weight. And then nothing was left but the solid mass of the earth itself.

When they were back in Jeanlin's robbers' cave the child threw himself on the hay and stretched himself out exhausted, murmuring:

'Dammit, the kids will have to wait. I'm going to have forty winks.'

Étienne had blown out the candle, for there was only a little end left. He also was knocked up with fatigue, but not at all sleepy, and sinister, nightmarish thoughts were hammering away in his head. Soon they resolved themselves into a single thought which tormented and wearied him with an unanswerable question: why hadn't he killed Chaval when he had him at his mercy under the knife, whereas this child had just slain a soldier without even knowing his name? It upset all his revolutionary beliefs about the right to kill, the courage to kill. Was he a coward, then? The child had begun to snore in the hay; it was like the snoring of a drunken man, as though he were sleeping off the intoxication of murder. He was irritated and disgusted at having the boy there and having to listen to him. Suddenly he shuddered. Fear had breathed into his face.

A slight rustling sound, a sigh seemed to have come from the depths of the earth, and the vision of the young soldier lying there with his rifle beneath the rocks sent a shiver down his back and made his hair stand on end. It was absurd, he knew, but the whole pit was full of voices and he had to light the candle again, and only recovered his self-possession when he could see the empty galleries in its pale light.

He meditated for a quarter of an hour, fighting out the same battle with himself, with his eyes fixed on the burning wick. Then there was a sizzling sound and the wick fell into the molten grease, and everything was dark again. The shuddering returned and he felt like hitting Jeanlin to stop his loud snoring. He found it so unbearable to be near the boy that he ran off, filled with an imperious desire for fresh air, hurrying through the galleries and up the shaft as though a pursuing shadow were panting at his heels.

When at last he found himself above ground in the ruins of Réquillart Étienne could breathe freely. As he had not the courage to kill it was up to him to die, and the thought of death, which had already vaguely passed through his head now returned and took possession of his mind as a last hope. A plucky death, death for the revolution, would end all, and by settling his account, whether good or bad, would prevent his thinking any more. If his mates attacked the Belgians he would be in the front line, where he might be lucky enough to be knocked out. So he boldly walked back, intending to lurk around Le Voreux. It struck two, and loud voices were issuing from the deputies' room, where the detachment of troops guarding the pit was billeted. They had been thrown into a panic by the disappearance of the sentry: somebody had been sent to wake up the captain, and after a careful examination of the scene they had decided that the soldier had deserted. Listening in the darkness Étienne remembered the republican captain the young soldier had told him about. Supposing he could be persuaded to go over to the people's side? The troops would raise the butts of their rifles in the air and that would be the signal for the massacre of the bourgeois. Carried away by this new vision he thought no more of death, but stood there in the mud for hours, with the drizzle of the thaw wetting his shoulders, feverishly hoping that a victory might still be possible.

He waited for the Belgians until five. Then he realized that the Company had artfully arranged for them to sleep on the premises. The descent was already under way, and the one or two strikers from Village 240 who were posted as pickets did not know whether to warn their comrades or not. He told them about the Company's trick and off they ran, leaving him watching out on the towpath behind the slag-heap. By now it was six, and the leaden sky was lightening into a red dawn when abbé Ranvier emerged from a path, holding up his cassock and showing his spindly legs. Every Monday he went to say early Mass in the chapel of a convent on the other side of the pit.

'Good morning, my friend,' he said in loud tones, after looking the young man up and down with his fiery eyes.

But Étienne did not answer. In the distance he had noticed a woman passing between the trestles of Le Voreux, and he rushed off anxiously, for he thought it looked like Catherine.

She had been tramping the slushy roads since midnight. Finding her in bed when he came in, Chaval had got her up with a box on the ears and bawled at her to get out through the door at once unless she wanted to be thrown out of the window. Half dressed and in tears, with her legs bruised by kicks, she had had to run downstairs and had been thrown out with a final punch. Bewildered by this brutal separation, she had sat down on a stone, watching the house and waiting for him to call her back, for surely he must be looking at her and would tell her to come back when he saw her shivering like this and cast off without anybody to take her in.

But after two hours she had made up her mind, for she was freezing to death sitting still like a dog turned out into the street. She walked out of Montsou, then returned, but did not dare to call out from the street or knock at the door. In the end she went off along the straight main road, meaning to go back to the village and her parents. But when she got there she suddenly felt so ashamed that she ran along the gardens, afraid of being recognized by somebody, although in fact everybody was asleep behind closed shutters. From then on she simply wandered about, startled by the slightest sound and fearful of being picked up and taken as a vagrant to the brothel at Marchiennes, the threat of which had haunted her like a nightmare for months. Twice she stumbled into Le Voreux, took fright at the loud voices of the guards and ran off breathlessly, looking behind to see whether she was being followed. The Réquillart lane was always full of drunks, but nevertheless she went back there in the vague hope of meeting the man she had refused a few hours earlier.

Chaval was to go down to work that morning, and with this in mind Catherine made for the pit once again, although she realized it was useless to speak to him: it was all over between them. All work had stopped at Jean-Bart and he had sworn to throttle her if she went back to a job at Le Voreux, because he was afraid she might make things awkward for him. Then what was she to do? Go somewhere else, die of starvation, or fall a victim to the brutality of every passing man? She dragged herself on, tripping over the ruts, with aching legs and mud up to her waist. The thaw had now turned the roads into rivers of slush and she paddled through it, on and on, not even daring to find a stone to sit on.

Daylight came. She had recognized Chaval's back as he was cautiously rounding the pit-bank, and then she saw Lydie and Bébert peeping out of their hiding-place under the timber-stack. They had been on the watch all night, not daring to go home because Jeanlin had ordered them to wait for him, and while the latter was at Réquillart sleeping off his blood-lust the two children had been lying in each other's arms to keep warm. The wind whistled through the chestnut and oak poles, and there they curled up as if it were some abandoned wood-cutter's hut. Lydie dared not voice aloud all the sufferings she had endured like a little beaten wife, any more than Bébert found enough courage to complain of the cuffs from the captain which made his cheeks swell up; but in the end he had gone too far, making them risk life and limb in crazy forays and then denying them any share in the spoils. So now they had rebelled, and had ended by kissing each other although he had ordered them not to, risking the blow from the unknown that he had promised would surely come, and they went on gently kissing each other in all innocence, putting into their caresses all their long, frustrated passion, all their poor, martyred, affectionate natures In this way they had kept each other warm all through the night, so happy in their hidden lair that they could not remember ever having been so happy before, even on Sainte-Barbe when everybody ate fritters and drank wine.

A sudden bugle-call made Catherine start. She looked up and saw the guards taking up their guns. Étienne was rushing up, Bébert and Lydie had leaped out of their hiding-place. In the growing daylight a band of men and women could be seen coming down from the village, furiously waving their arms.

[5]

ALL the entrances to Le Voreux had been sealed, and the only door left open was guarded by sixty soldiers standing with ordered arms. This was the way into the pit-top, by a narrow flight of steps on to which the doors of the locker-room and deputies' room opened. The captain had lined them up two-deep against the brick wall so that they could not be attacked from the rear.

At first the band of miners from the village kept its distance. There were not more than thirty-five of them and they were arguing violently among themselves.

Maheude had been the first to arrive, all dishevelled, with a kerchief tied hastily round her head and Estelle asleep in her arms. She was furiously repeating:

'Don't let anybody go in or come out! Catch them all inside!'

Maheu was backing his wife up when old Mouque came along from Réquillart. They tried to prevent his going through, but he insisted, saying that his horses went on eating oats just the same and didn't care two hoots about a revolution. Besides, a horse had died, and he had to see about bringing it up. Étienne managed to free the old ponyman, whom the soldiers allowed into the pit. A quarter of an hour later, as

400

the band of strikers was growing larger and more threatening, a wide door opened on the ground floor and some men appeared, hauling out the dead animal, a pitiful carcase still tied up in the rope net, and they left it in the middle of the puddles of melted snow. The sensation was so great that nobody thought of preventing their going in again and barricading the door behind them. For they had all recognized the horse, his head stiff and bent back against his side, and whispers ran round.

'It's Trompette, isn't it? Yes, it's Trompette.'

It was. He had never been able to accustom himself to life underground and had remained dismal and unwilling to work, tortured by longing for the daylight he had lost. In vain had Bataille, the father of the pit, given him friendly rubs with his side and nibbled his neck so as to give him a little of his own resignation after ten years underground. Caresses only made him more doleful and his skin quivered when his friend who had grown old in the darkness whispered secrets in his ear. And whenever they met and snorted together they both seemed to be lamenting – the old one because he could not now remember, and the young one because he could not forget. They lived side by side in the stable, lowering their heads into the same manger and blowing into each other's nostrils, comparing their unending dreams of daylight, their visions of green pastures, white roads, and golden sunlight for ever and ever, Then, as Trompette, bathed in sweat, lay dying on his straw, Bataille had begun to sniff at him with heartbroken little sniffs, like sobs. He felt his friend grow cold, the pit was taking his last joy away, this friend who had come from up there, all fresh with lovely smells that brought back his own young days in the open air. And when he saw that the other was lying still he broke his tether, whinnying with fear.

Mouque had been warning the overman for a week. But who bothered about a sick horse at such a time? In any case these gentlemen disliked moving the horses about. But now they had got to make up their minds to move him. The day before Mouque and two men had spent an hour roping Trompette up. Bataille was harnessed to haul him to the shaft. Slowly the old horse dragged his dead friend along through such a narrow gallery that he had to proceed by little jerks, at the risk of grazing the skin off the corpse, and he shook his head in distress as he heard the long brushing sound of this mass of flesh bound for the knacker's yard. When they un-harnessed him at pit bottom he watched with melancholy gaze the preparations for the ascent, as the body was pushed on to cross-beams over the sump and the net was tied to the bottom of a cage. Then at last the onsetters rang the meat-call, and he raised his head to see his friend go, gently at first and then with a rush up into darkness – lost for ever up the black hole. There he stood craning his neck, his shaky old memory recall-ing, maybe, some of the things of the earth. It was all over now, and his friend would never see anything again, and he would be done up himself into a dreadful bundle when the day came for him to go up there. His legs began to shake and the open air from that far country seemed to catch his throat, and he plodded back to the stable unsteadily as though he were drunk.

Up in the yard the miners stood round sadly looking at Trompette's body. One woman said softly:

'At any rate a man only goes down there if he wants to!'

A new crowd was coming down from the village, led by Le-vaque, followed by his wife and Bouteloup. Levaque was shouting:

'Death to the Belgians! No foreigners here! Down with them!'

They all surged forward, and Étienne had to check them. He went up to the captain, a tall, thin young man not more than twenty-eight, looking desperate but determined, and reasoned with him, trying to win him over, watching the effect of his words. Why risk useless slaughter? Was not justice on the miners' side? They were all brothers, and ought to work together. When Étienne mentioned the word republic the captain made a nervous gesture, but he kept his military stiffness and rapped out:

'Stand back! Don't force me to do my duty!'

Étienne tried three times, but his friends behind him were getting restive. The word ran round that Monsieur Henne-beau was at the pit and somebody suggested letting him down by the neck to see if he would hew his own coal. But the rumour was false; only Négrel and Dansaert were there, and they both appeared for a moment at a window of the pit top, the over-man keeping in the background, for he had been very sub-dued since his adventure with Pierronne. The engineer, how-ever, boldly looked down at the crowd with his sharp little eyes, smiling with the contemptuous mockery with which he regarded all men and all things. But he was booed and they both disappeared. The only face that could now be seen was that of the fair-haired Souvarine. He was on duty, not having left his machine for a single day throughout the strike. But he had become more and more taciturn and absorbed in some fixed idea, which seemed to gleam like steel in his pale eyes.

'Stand back!' shouted the captain again. 'No, I can't listen to anything. My orders are to guard this pit and I'm going to guard it. And don't start hustling my men, or I'll find some way of making you get back!'

But in spite of his firm tone he was becoming increasingly uneasy as he saw the ever rising tide of miners. He was due to be relieved at noon, but fearing that he would not be able to hold out until then he had just sent a pit-boy off to Montsou for reinforcements.

He was answered by a storm of yells.

'Down with the foreigners! Death to the Belgians! We want to be masters in our own pit!'

Étienne turned back, sick at heart. So it had come to this, and there was nothing left to do but fight and die. He gave up trying to hold his mates back and the crowd rushed the little detachment of troops. There were nearly four hundred of them now, and more were pouring out of the neighbouring villages and running down to swell the numbers. They were all shouting the same war-cry, and Maheu and Levaque were furiously addressing the soldiers:

'Go away! We've no quarrel with you. Go away!'

'This is nothing to do with you,' added Maheude. 'You let us mind our own business!'

Behind her la Levaque screamed in her more violent way: 'Have we got to kill you so as to get past? Just you bugger off!'

403

And even the shrill little voice of Lydie could be heard coming from the thickest part of the fray, where she and Bébert had managed to worm themselves:

'Look at those silly old sausages of soldiers!'

Catherine was standing a little in the rear and listening in bewilderment to all this new violence into which ill-luck had thrown her. Hadn't she had enough trouble already? What had she done to be constantly dogged by misfortune? Even up till yesterday she had not really understood what all the anger of the strikers was about, thinking that when you have your own fair share of beatings it is silly to go looking for more. But now her heart was full of hatred, and remembering what Étienne used to say during those evening talks at home she tried to understand what he was now saying to the soldiers. For he was treating them as friends, reminding them that they were men of the people too, and that they should side with the people against the exploiters of the people's sufferings.

Just then the crowd swayed violently and an old woman emerged. It was Ma Brûlé in all her skinny hideousness, neck and arms outstretched and running so fast that wisps of grey hair blew into her eyes.

'By Christ, I'm in this!' she panted. 'That rat Pierron tried to keep me locked in the cellar!'

Without more ado she fell upon the soldiers, belching abuse from her black mouth:

'You lot of blackguards! You dirty lot of sods! Look at them! They lick their masters' boots and can only be brave against poor people!'

The others joined in the volleys of insults. A few still shouted: 'Up with the soldiers! Throw the officer down the shaft.' But soon the only shout was: 'Down with the red trousers!' However, these men who had heard appeals for fraternity and friendly attempts to enlist them on the people's side with still, impassive faces, not batting an eyelid, kept their same passive stiffness under the storm of abuse. Behind them the captain had drawn his sword and as the crowd closed in more and more, threatening to crush them against the wall, he gave the order to present bayonets. They obeyed, and a double hedge of steel blades pointed at the chests of the strikers.

'The bloody bastards!' screamed Ma Brûlé, but she fell back.

But they all returned to the charge immediately, heedless of death in their frenzy. Women rushed forward, Maheude and la Levaque shouted:

'That's right! Kill us, Kill us! We want our rights.'

Levaque, at the risk of cutting himself, took three bayonets in his hands and tried to pull them towards him and wrench them off the rifles. In his rage he stood there twisting them with ten times his normal strength, but Bouteloup, regretting having followed his mate, stood quietly on one side, watching.

'Come and have a look at this! Come on, look at this if you are good chaps!' said Maheu.

And he unbuttoned his coat and opened his shirt, displaying his bare chest, hairy and tattooed with coal. In a terrible outburst of insolent bravado he pressed himself against the points of the bayonets and forced the soldiers back. One point pricked him in the nipple and so maddened him that he forced it further in so as to hear his ribs crack.

'Cowards! you daren't do it! There are ten thousand more behind us. Yes, you can kill us, but there'll be ten thousand more to kill as well!'

The soldiers' position was becoming critical, for they had had strict orders not to use their arms except in a desperate emergency. But how could they prevent these madmen from running themselves through? Moreover there was no room left, as they now had their backs to the wall and could not retire any further. The little handful of men held firm against the rising tide of miners, however, coolly carrying out their captain's brief commands. He stood there nervous and tight-lipped, with only one fear: that all this abuse would make his men lose their tempers. Already a young sergeant, a lanky fellow whose four hairs of moustache were bristling, was blinking his eyes in an ominous manner, and near him a veteran, tanned in a score of campaigns, had turned pale on seeing his bayonet twisted like a straw. Yet another, probably a recruit, still smelling of the farmyard, flushed crimson every time he was called a shit and a blackguard. But the abuse went on and on, with waving fists and abominable words: shovelfuls of accusations and threats hit them in the face. It needed all the force of their orders to keep them standing there in the lofty, gloomy silence of military discipline.

Just as a collision seemed inevitable, Richomme the deputy could be seen coming out behind the soldiers. His kindly white head was bowed down with emotion. He addressed them in a loud voice:

'Oh, for God's sake! This is getting silly! This damn nonsense can't go on!'

He threw himself between the bayonets and the miners.

'Listen mates. You know I'm an old workman and that I've always been on your side! Very well, then, I promise you that if they don't deal fair with you I'll tell the bosses some home truths myself. But you're going too far, and it won't do you any good to bawl a lot of filthy words at these good chaps and try to get your own bellies ripped open.'

They listened and hesitated. But as ill-luck would have it Négrel's strong profile appeared again just then at an upper window. No doubt he was afraid they would accuse him of having sent out a deputy instead of risking his own skin, and he tried to speak. But his voice was drowned in such a frightful outcry that he could only shrug his shoulders and leave the window again. From then onwards it was useless for Richomme to try to reason with them on his own account and repeat that the matter should be settled between friends; he was suspect and shouted down. But he stuck to his guns and stayed with them.

'What the hell! I don't care if I'm smashed up with you, but so long as you are so stupid I shall stick to you!'

Étienne, whom he had asked to help him make them see reason, made a gesture of impotence. It was too late now; there were more than five hundred of them, and not only the fanatics who had charged down the hill to turn out the Belgians, but onlookers and people who thought the battle was a good lark. Some way back Zacharie and Philomène were standing in the middle of a group watching as if it were a show, and so unconcerned that they had brought the two children,

406

Achille and Désirée. A new wave of strikers arrived from Réquillart, including Mouquet and Mouquette; he at once went and clapped his friend Zacharie's shoulders with a grin, but she was very worked up and ran off to join the front row of the malcontents.

The captain was continually glancing towards the Montsou road. The reinforcements he had requested had not yet come, and his sixty men could not hold out much longer. It occurred to him to stage a demonstration that would strike the imagination of the mob, and he ordered his men to load their rifles in full view. The soldiers obeyed, but it only increased the tension and gave rise to further mockeries and provocations.

'Look, they're off to target-practice!' sneered the women, Ma Brûlé, la Levaque and the rest.

Maheude, holding Estelle to her breast (she had woken up and was crying) came so near that the sergeant asked her what she thought she was doing, with a poor little kid and all.

'Mind you own bloody business!' was her answer. 'Shoot her if you dare!'

The men shook their heads in scorn. Nobody believed they could be fired at.

'They've only got blank cartridges,' said Levaque.

'Do you take us for Cossacks or what?' shouted Maheu. 'You don't fire at Frenchmen, dammit!'

Others said that when you had served in the Crimea you weren't afraid of lead, and they all went on throwing themselves at the rifles. If these had gone off at that moment the mob would have been mown down.

Mouquette, now in the front row, was almost speechless with indignation at the idea that soldiers could mean to cut open women's bodies. She had exhausted all her obscene vocabulary on them, and could not think of anything when suddenly she bethought herself of the supreme insult to fire at the troops, and showed them her backside. She lifted her skirts with both hands and displayed her great round buttocks, making them as huge as she could.

'Look that's for you, and it's too clean by half, you lot of swine!'

She bobbed and somersaulted and turned about so that everybody had a good view, and at each thrust of her bum she repeated:

'That's for the officer! That's for the sergeant! That's for the privates!'

A storm of laughter went up, and Bébert and Lydie were convulsed. Even Étienne, despite his gloomy forebodings, applauded this insulting exhibition. Everybody, scoffers and fanatics alike, now joined in booing the soldiers as though they were splashed all over with excrement, and only Catherine stood apart, on some old timber, saying nothing, but feeling such bitter hatred rising within her that her breast seemed about to burst.

There was a scuffle. The captain had decided to take a few prisoners in order to give his men something to do to relieve their feelings. With one bound Mouquette darted off between some of the men's legs and was gone. Three miners, including Levaque, were seized from the thick of the fray and taken off under guard to the deputies' room. Négrel and Dansaert called from above to the captain to come in and barricade himself with them, but he refused, feeling that these buildings, the doors of which had no locks to them, were bound to be taken by assault and that he would have the humiliation of being disarmed. Already his little company was chafing with impatience, and they could not run away from a rabble in clogs. Once again the sixty were back to the wall and facing the mob with loaded rifles.

At first the strikers were impressed by this display of force and fell back in silence. But then a shout went up demanding the immediate release of the prisoners. Somebody said that they were being killed in there. And at once, without any sort of concerted action, everybody had the same impulse, the same thirst for revenge, and they all made a dash for the stacks of bricks nearby. The marly soil provided the clay, and these bricks were baked on the premises. Children carried them one by one, women filled their skirts with them, and soon everybody had his own ammunition dump at his feet and the stoning began.

Ma Brûlé was the first to join battle. She broke the bricks

408

across her bony knee and hurled the two pieces with her right and left hands together. La Levaque nearly dislocated her shoulders, for being so fat and soft she had to go very near in order to aim straight, heedless of the pleadings of Bouteloup, who tried to pull her back in the hope of taking her home now that her husband was out of the way. The women all warmed up to the job, and Mouquette, finding it annoying to be all bleeding through trying to break bricks over her soft, fat thighs, had given it up and was throwing them whole. Even the children entered the fray. Bébert showing Lydie how to bowl them underarm. The thudding bricks made a noise like gigantic hailstones. Suddenly Catherine appeared in the midst of the furies, waving her arms in the air and hurling her bricks with all the strength of her young arms. Though she could never have explained why, she was bursting with an impulse to slaughter everybody. Wouldn't this accursed life of misery soon be over? She had had enough of it, what with being beaten and cast off by her man, paddling about the muddy roads like a stray cur and not even being able to ask her own father for a bite or a sup because he was starving as well. Things had never taken a turn for the better, but had gone on getting worse ever since she had known anything. So she broke her bricks and flung the pieces anywhere with the one idea of smashing everything up. She saw red and did not care whose jaw she broke.

Étienne, still standing in front of the soldiers, nearly had his head split open. His ear began to swell up, and he turned round and realized with a shock that the brick had come from Catherine's frenzied hands. At the risk of his life he stayed there and watched her. Similarly many others were so enthralled by the battle that they simply stood with their arms dangling by their sides. Mouquet was adjudicating the throws as though it were a cork-throwing contest: oh, well aimed! or oh, hard luck! He was entering into the fun of the thing, nudging Zacharie, who was having words with Philomène because he had clouted Achille and Désirée and refused to take them up on his shoulders to give them a better view. In the background the road was lined with crowds of onlookers. At the top of the hill, where the village began, old Bonnemort had just come into view, hobbling along on his stick, and his motionless form was now outlined against the rust-coloured sky.

As soon as the brick-throwing had begun, Richomme had taken up his stand again between the soldiers and the mob, entreating one side and exhorting the other, heedless of danger and so heartbroken that great tears were running down his cheeks. But the noise drowned his words, and only his big grey moustache could be seen moving up and down.

The hail of bricks became thicker, for the men had now followed the women's example.

At that moment Maheude noticed Maheu standing in the rear, sullen and empty-handed.

'Here, what's up with you?' she shouted. 'Are you scared? Are you going to stand there and let your mates be taken to prison? If I hadn't got the child I'd show you!'

Estelle was clutching her neck and bawling her head off, preventing her mother from joining Ma Brûlé and the others. And as her husband still did not seem to understand she kicked some bricks towards his legs.

'Are you going to pick them up, for God's sake? Have I got to spit in your face in front of everybody so as to put a bit of pluck into you?'

He went very red and broke some bricks and threw the pieces. She lashed him on with her tongue, dazed him with words, stood behind him howling for death and almost crushed the life out of the child at her breast, until he had moved forward right in front of the rifles.

The little squad was nearly lost to sight under the hail of stones. Fortunately they landed too high and merely pitted the wall above. What was to be done? For a moment the captain considered retreating into the buildings, but the very thought of showing his back to the mob made his pale face flush – and in any case it was no longer practicable, for if they made the slightest movement they would be lynched. A brick had just broken the peak of his cap and blood was trickling down his forehead. Several of his men were wounded, and he realized that they were at the end of their tether and had reached the stage of instinctive self-defence when they would no longer obey their superiors. The sergeant had let out an oath when his shoulder had nearly been put out and his skin bruised by a heavy thud that sounded like a dolly banging the washing. The recruit had been grazed in two places, his thumb was smashed and his right knee was smarting: how much longer were they going to put up with this? One brick had bounced up and hit the veteran in the groin, and he had turned green and was raising his rifle with his thin arms. Three times the captain was on the point of ordering them to fire. He was torn with perplexity, and for some seconds an apparently endless struggle within him shook all his ideas, his sense of duty and his beliefs as a man and a soldier. The bricks rained thicker still, and just as he was opening his mouth to shout 'Fire!' the rifles went off of their own accord; first three shots, then five, then the whole volley of a platoon and then, long afterwards, a single shot in the midst of silence.

There was a moment of stupefaction. They had really fired, and the crowd stood motionless, unable to believe it. Then piercing shrieks arose, while the bugle sounded the cease fire. And then a wild panic like the stampede of cattle before machine-guns, a frantic rush through the mud.

With the first three shots Bébert and Lydie collapsed on each other, the girl shot in the face and the boy with a hole under the left shoulder. She was killed instantly and lay still. But he went on moving for a while, and in his dying convulsions seized her in his arms as though wanting to take her again as he had taken her in the dark retreat where they had spent their last night on earth. At that moment Jeanlin, still puffy with sleep came skipping along from Réquillart through the smoke, just in time to see Bébert embrace his little wife and die.

The other five shots which followed had brought down Ma Brûlé and the deputy Richomme. He had been shot in the back while still imploring his mates, and had sunk to his knees. He fell on one side and lay gasping on the ground, with his eyes still full of tears. As for the old woman, her breast had been torn open and she had fallen stiff, crashing like a bundle of dry wood, vomiting a final oath with her life-blood.

Then the volley swept the whole area, moving down the groups of onlookers as they were enjoying the battle and

411

laughing a hundred paces away. A bullet went into Mouquet's mouth and bowled him over with his face smashed in. He fell at the feet of Zacharie and Philomène, whose children were spattered with red spots. At the same moment Mouquette had two bullets in the stomach. She had seen the soldiers raise their rifles, and, good soul that she was, she had instinctively flung herself in front of Catherine, warning her to look out. With a loud scream she fell on her back, knocked clean over by the blow. Étienne rushed up meaning to lift her and carry her away, but she waved him off as though to say she was done for anyway. Then she hiccuped, still smiling at them both to show she was happy to see them together now that she was going.

All was over, or so it seemed, and the bullets were all spent, some of them as far away as the walls of the village, when the last single shot went off.

It went through Maheu's heart. He spun round and fell with his face in a puddle of black water.

Maheude stooped down, bewildered.

'Here, come on, old chap, get up! It's nothing, is it?'

She was still encumbered with Estelle, and had to tuck her under one arm so as to turn her husband's head.

'Say something, do! Where does it hurt?'

His eyes were staring expressionless and a bloody foam was coming from his mouth. She understood. He was dead. And she sat down in the mud, with her baby still under her arm like a bundle, looking at her old chap, dazed.

The pit had been cleared. The captain had nervously taken off his cap which had been cut by a stone, and then put it on again, but even in the face of the great tragedy of his life he kept his stiff military bearing, while his men silently reloaded their rifles. The horrified faces of Négrel and Dansaert could be seen at the window. Behind them was standing Souvarine, his brow deeply furrowed as though the answer to his terrible problem had etched itself there. On the horizon at the edge of the plateau Bonnemort was still standing, leaning on his stick with one hand and shading his eyes with the other so as to see more clearly the slaughter of his own flesh and blood down below. The wounded were groaning and the dead freezing into twisted postures, muddy with the liquid mire of the thaw and sinking in places into the inky patches of coal now reappearing here and there out of the wastes of dirty snow. In the midst of these human corpses, looking so small and pinched and poor, lay the corpse of Trompette, a huge and pitiful heap of dead flesh.

Étienne had not found death. He was still waiting for it by the side of Catherine who had collapsed with fatigue and grief, when a sonorous voice made him start. It was abbé Ranvier coming back from his Mass. There he stood with arms raised like an inspired prophet of old, calling down the wrath of God upon the murderers, foretelling the age of justice and the coming extermination of the bourgeoisie by fire from heaven, since now it had committed the foulest crime of all and caused the workers and the penniless of this world to be slain.

Part Seven

─────────────────────

[1]

THE shots at Montsou had resounded far and wide, even in
Paris. For four days the opposition papers had been in an
uproar of indignation, covering their front pages with harrowing stories: twenty-five wounded, fourteen dead, including
two children and three women, and there were prisoners
besides. Levaque had become a sort of hero to whom they
attributed an answer to the examining magistrate worthy of
some sublime figure of antiquity. These few bullets had hit
the Empire in the vitals, but it affected an omnipotent serenity,
all unconscious of the gravity of its own wound. There had
simply been a regrettable incident, it was alleged, an obscure
scuffle far away in the black country, a long way from the
Paris streets where public opinion was formed. It would all
be forgotten quite soon; the Company had been unofficially
instructed to hush up the whole affair and put an end to this
strike which by dragging on in such a tiresome manner was
turning into a social problem.

Hence it came about that on the following Wednesday
morning three of the directors were seen arriving in Montsou.
The little town, which was so unnerved that it had not dared
to rejoice openly at the massacre, now breathed again and
tasted the joy of being definitely saved. Moreover the weather
had turned fine, with bright sunshine, one of those first sunny
days of February which touch the lilac shoots with warmth and
tinge them with green. All the shutters of the office block had
been thrown back and the great building seemed to have come
to life again. Most reassuring rumours came therefrom to the
effect that these gentlemen were very touched by the disaster

and had come to extend loving paternal arms to the poor misled sinners in the villages. Now that the blow had fallen, albeit a heavier blow than they had wished for, they devoted themselves to their mission as saviours and decreed excellent if belated measures. They began by discharging the Belgians, and made a great noise about this extreme concession to their workpeople. Then they called off the military occupation of the pits which in any case were no longer in any danger from the crushed miners. Thanks to them, also, the enquiry about the sentry who had disappeared from Le Voreux was hushed up. The whole area had been searched and neither the rifle nor the corpse had been found, and so it was agreed to write the soldier off as a deserter, although everybody suspected a crime. In every way they strove to attenuate what had happened, for they were full of fear for the morrow, and felt it impolitic to admit how irresistible was the savage strength of a mob running amok among the tottering foundations of the old order. Not that all this work of conciliation prevented their pushing ahead with purely administrative matters, for Deneulin had been seen going to and from the office, where he had discussions with Monsieur Hennebeau. Negotiations were in progress for the purchase of Vandame, and it was confidently expected that he would accept the gentlemen's offers.

But the great sensation in the neighbourhood was the big yellow notices which the directors had had posted on all the walls. They bore these few lines, in very bold type:

WORKERS OF MONTSOU!

WE DO NOT WANT THE ERRORS OF WHICH YOU HAVE RECENTLY SEEN THE DEPLORABLE CONSEQUENCES TO DEPRIVE GOOD AND LOYAL WORKERS OF THEIR LIVELIHOOD. WE THEREFORE PROPOSE TO REOPEN ALL PITS ON MONDAY NEXT, AND, WHEN WORK HAS BEEN RESUMED, TO EXAMINE WITH DUE CARE AND CONSIDERATION ALL CASES WHERE THERE IS ROOM FOR IMPROVEMENT. WE SHALL DO EVERYTHING THAT IS RIGHT AND THAT IT IS IN OUR POWER TO DO.

In one morning the ten thousand miners filed past this notice. None of them said a word, many shook their heads, and others slouched off without having moved a muscle of their stolid faces.

Until then Village 240 has persisted in its fierce resistance. The blood that had reddened the mud of the pit barred the road for the survivors. Scarcely ten had returned underground, Pierron and a few toadies of his type, whom the others watched set off and return with sullen faces but with neither a gesture nor a threat. The notice stuck on the church wall was treated with deep mistrust. There was not a word on it about returned cards – was the Company going to take them back? They still stood out stubbornly through fear of victimization and the feeling that they must hang together and protest against any dismissals of their more compromised brethren. It all seemed fishy, it needed looking into, and they would return to work when these gentlemen condescended to say exactly what they meant. The squat houses were wrapped in silence – even hunger meant nothing now, and they might as well die since violent death had passed over their homes.

But one house was more dark and silent than all the others. The Maheus were overwhelmed with grief. Since she had followed her man to the cemetery Maheude had never opened her mouth. After the shooting she had let Étienne bring Catherine back home, half dead and covered with mud, and as she was undressing her in front of the young man before putting her to bed she thought for a moment that her daughter had been shot in the stomach too, for her chemise was stained with large patches of blood. But soon she realized that it was the pent-up flood of her puberty released at last by the shock of that dreadful day. Yet another stroke of ill-luck, this! A nice thing, indeed, to be able to have children for the gendarmes to slaughter later on! Not that she said a word to Catherine, any more than to Étienne. The latter was now sleeping with Jeanlin again at the risk of being arrested, for the thought of going back to the darkness of Réquillart filled him with such dread that he preferred prison: the very thought of it made him shudder – the horror of darkness after all these deaths and his unacknowledged fear of that young soldier sleeping beneath the rocks. Moreover, in the bitterness of defeat he dreamed of prison as a haven of refuge. But nobody came for him, and as the weary hours dragged on he tried in vain to tire out his body. Sometimes, however, Maheude would look at them both in a resentful way as though she were about to ask them what they were doing in her house.

Once again they all slept in a heap. Grandpa Bonnemort now had the bed the two children used to sleep in, and they shared with Catherine now that poor Alzire was no longer there to stick her hump into her big sister's ribs. It was at night that the lonely mother felt the emptiness of her home in the cold spaces of the bed which was now too big for her. It was of little avail to take Estelle in with her to fill the gap; she did not take the place of her man, and she quietly cried to herself for hours. Life went on again as before: still no bread, and not even the good fortune to die once and for all, for odd bits picked up here and there did these poor wretches the disservice of keeping them alive. Nothing had changed in their existence, nothing except that her man was not there.

On the afternoon of the fifth day Étienne, depressed beyond endurance by the sight of this silent woman, went out of the house and wandered slowly down the cobbled street of the village. This irksome inactivity drove him to take endless walks with his arms hanging idle and his head down and always the same torturing thoughts. He had been walking round like this for half an hour when he had the still more uncomfortable sensation that his mates were coming out on their doorsteps to look at him. What little popularity remained to him had been blown away by the shooting, and now he never went out but he was followed by looks of hatred. If he raised his eyes he saw men standing in threatening attitudes and women pulling back their little curtains and, subjected to this so far inarticulate accusation and the pent-up anger of these staring eyes widened still more by hunger and weeping, he became self-conscious and could not walk properly. The mute reproaches behind him grew steadily more embittered and he was so afraid that the whole village would come out and scream its misery at him that he went indoors, all of a tremble.

But there he was greeted by a scene which upset him even more. Old Bonnemort had been glued to his chair in front of

418

the cold fireplace ever since the day of the massacre, when two neighbours had found him lying on the ground with his stick broken in pieces, laid low like an old tree blasted by lightning. While Lénore and Henri, in an attempt to deceive their hunger, were making a terrible din scraping an old saucepan in which cabbages had been boiled the day before, Maheude, having put Estelle down on the table, was standing erect and brandishing her fist at Catherine.

'Just you say that again, by God! Just you repeat what you said!'

Catherine had announced her intention of going back to Le Voreux. Each day she was finding it more unbearable not to be earning her keep, to be tolerated in her mother's house like some useless animal in the way. Had she not feared trouble from Chaval she would have gone back on Tuesday. She nervously began again:

'What do you want me to do? I can't live without doing anything. And at least we should have some bread to eat.'

Maheude cut her short.

'Now listen. I'll strangle the first one of you lot who goes back to work. Oh no! that would be the last straw, to kill the father and then go on exploiting the children! No, I'd rather see every one of you taken off between four planks like the one that's gone already!'

Her long silence broke into a furious torrent of words. A nice help that would be! Catherine would bring in thirty sous at the most, and you could add to that twenty sous if the bosses were willing to find some job for that little varmint Jeanlin. Fifty sous and seven mouths to feed! The kids were good for nothing but swallowing soup. As for Grandpa, he must have busted something in his brain when he fell down, for he was quite potty now, unless it was the sight of the soldiers shooting his friends down that had given him a fit.

'They've finished you off, haven't they, old chap? It's all very well to have your strong arms still, but you're done for!'

Bonnemort looked at her dully without understanding. He sat like that staring in front of him for hours on end, and the only sign of intelligence he had left was that he did spit into a tray of ashes they had put down beside him for the sake of cleanliness.

'And they haven't fixed up his pension either!' she went on. 'I'm sure they won't give it him because of our ideas. No, I tell you it's too much to put up with from these cursed people!'

'But still,' Catherine ventured, 'they have promised on the notice. . . .'

'Will you shut up, you and your bloody notice! That's only a bit of birdlime to catch us and do us in! They can afford to be ever so kind now that they have shot us down.'

'But, Mother, where shall we go? They won't let us stay in the village, that's certain.'

Maheude waved her arm in a vague and terrible gesture. Where could they go? She didn't know, and tried not to think about it, for it drove her mad. They'd go somewhere . . . somewhere. And as the scraping of the saucepan became unbearable, she fell upon Lénore and Henri and boxed their ears. Meanwhile Estelle had crawled along the table on all fours and fallen off, which redoubled the commotion. Her mother whacked her and made her stop; it would have been a good job if the fall had killed her! She began talking about Alzire and wishing all the others could have had her luck! Then suddenly she thrust her face against the wall and burst into hysterical sobs.

Étienne had been standing by, not daring to interfere. He did not count now in this house; even the children turned suspiciously away from him. But this poor creature's tears pierced him to the heart, and he said:

'Oh, now, now, courage! We'll get over it somehow.'

She did not seem to hear him, for she was pouring out her grief in a low, continuous moaning.

'Oh, for pity's sake, can you believe it? We still managed to keep going before all these horrors. We only had dry bread, but at any rate we were together! Oh, God, what has happened? What have we done to deserve such trouble, with some of us dead and buried and the rest of us only wishing we were dead, too! It's true that we were harnessed to the job like horses, and it wasn't fair that our share was always the

420

kicks and cuffs, and we swelled the fortunes of the rich, with no hope of ever having the good things ourselves. There's no pleasure left in being alive when there's no hope left. Yes, I know it couldn't go on like that; we had to breathe a bit. . . . But if only we had known! Is it possible that you can make yourself so miserable simply by wanting to see justice done!'

Her immeasurable grief seemed to rise up from her breast in convulsive sobs and choke her voice.

'And then there are always clever people about to promise you that everything will be all right if only you put yourself out a bit. . . . And you get carried away; you suffer so much from the things that exist that you ask for what can't ever exist. Now look at me. I was well away dreaming like a fool and seeing visions of a nice friendly life on good terms with everybody, and off I went, up into the clouds. And when you fall back into the mud it hurts a lot. No! none of it was true, none of those things we thought we could see existed at all. All that was really there was still more misery – oh yes! as much of that as you like – and bullets into the bargain!'

Every tear in this outpouring of grief filled Étienne with remorse. No words of his could calm Maheude, for her terrible fall from such a high ideal had left her utterly broken. She came back into the middle of the room and, looking straight at him, let fly a final cry of rage:

'And what about you? Are you thinking of going back to the pit too, after you've landed us all in this bloody mess? Oh, I'm not blaming you. Only if I were in your shoes I'd have died of shame long before this for having done so much harm to my friends.'

He felt like answering back, but he shrugged his shoulders in despair: what was the use of going into explanations which she would never understand in her grief? And so, finding it too painful to stay where he was, he went out and resumed his desperate walk.

But outside the whole village seemed to be waiting for him, the men on their doorsteps and the women at their windows. As soon as he appeared a hostile snarl ran round and the crowd thickened. A whispering campaign that had been steadily intensifying for four days now burst out in a universal malediction. Fists were brandished, mothers pointed him out to their children with vindictive gestures, old men looked at him and spat. It was the inevitable reaction after defeat, the necessary reverse side of popularity, a feeling of execration that had come to breaking point after all these sufferings endured to no purpose. He was paying the price of hunger and death.

Zacharie, who was coming along with Philomène, deliberately bumped against Étienne as he was leaving the house and sneered evilly:

'Look, he's getting fatter! Other people's dead bodies seem to be doing him good!'

La Levaque was already outside her door with Bouteloup. Referring to her boy Bébert, killed by a bullet, she called out:

'Yes, there are some cowards in the world who get children murdered! If he wants to give me back my child he'd better go and look for him under the ground!'

She was not bothering her head about her husband in prison, for her home was still carrying on as Bouteloup was there. But now she suddenly remembered him and screamed:

'Get out! Rogues like you walk about scot free while good men are locked up!'

In trying to dodge her, Étienne ran into Pierronne, who had rushed up across the gardens. She had welcomed her mother's death as a blessed relief, for the old woman's violent behaviour threatened to get them all hanged. Neither was she particularly grief-stricken for Pierron's girl, that little minx of a Lydie, good riddance to her! But she sided with her neighbours so as to get back into their favour.

'What about my mother? And the poor little girlie? We saw you hiding behind them when they stopped the bullets meant for you!'

What could he do? Throttle Pierronne and the others, and then take on the whole village? For a moment Étienne was tempted to try, for the blood was singing through his head and he could now see how brutish his mates were, and it made him mad to see that they were so stupid and thick-headed that they blamed him for the logic of events. How ridiculous! But he was disgusted also at his own powerlessness to dominate them once again, and so he quickened his pace and turned a deaf ear to their insults. Soon it became a headlong flight, every household booed him as he went by, they dogged his steps, and the curses of the whole community rose to a thunder of unleashed hatred. He was now the exploiter, the murderer, the sole cause of all their woe. He rushed away from the village, pale and terrified, with the yelling crowd at his heels. A few of them gave up the chase at the main road, but some were still persisting when, at the bottom of the hill, just in front of the Avantage, he ran into another group coming out of Le Voreux.

Old Mouque and Chaval were among them. Since the death of his daughter Mouquette and his son, Mouquet, the old man had gone on with his job as ponyman and had never uttered a word of regret or complaint. But suddenly on seeing Étienne he was seized with fury, the tears streamed from his eyes, and a spate of oaths burst forth from his mouth, black and bleeding through chewing.

'You filthy tike! You swine! You bleeding bastard! Wait a minute, you've got my poor kids to pay for. You're going the same way too.'

He picked up a brick, broke it in two, and threw the pieces.

'Yes, yes, let's wipe him off the slate!' grinned Chaval, overjoyed at this chance of getting his own back and working himself up into a rage. 'Everyone gets his turn, and now it's yours to be up against the wall, you dirty sod!'

He also made a rush at Étienne with stones. A savage clamour went up and each of them picked up a brick and broke it, trying to disembowel him as they had hoped to do to the soldiers. He was too dazed to try to run away, but faced up to them, trying to calm them down with words. His old speeches, once so warmly applauded, now came back to his lips. He repeated phrases with which he had had them spellbound when he held them in the palm of his hand like a flock of sheep. But the old magic had gone, and the only answer was brickbats. Already his left arm was injured, and he was backing away in deadly peril when he found himself driven against the wall of the Avantage.

Rasseneur had just come out on his doorstep.

'Come in,' was all he said.

Étienne hesitated, hating to go there, of all places, for shelter.

'Come in. I'll talk to them.'

He accepted the situation and went in and hid at the back of the bar, while the publican blocked the doorway with his broad shoulders.

'Look here, chums, be sensible. You know I have never let you down. I have always been for peaceful methods, and if you had listened to me you wouldn't be where you are now, and that's a fact.'

He stood there, rocking his shoulders and belly, and for a long time poured out his facile eloquence, gentle and soothing like warm water. All this old mastery came back, he regained all his former popularity in a natural, effortless way, as though his mates had never booed him and called him a coward only a month ago. Voices exclaimed in agreement: very good! yes we're with you there! that's the style! There was a thunderous burst of applause.

Inside the bar Étienne felt sick and his heart was full of bitterness. He remembered Rasseneur's prophecy in the forest, when he had warned him about the ingratitude of the mob. What stupid brutality! how abominable to forget all he had done for them! They were like a blind force constantly feeding on itself. But underlying his indignation at these stupid brutes who were wrecking their own cause was chagrin at his own collapse and the tragic end of his own ambition. So it was all over already! He recalled how under the beech-trees he had heard three thousand hearts beating in time with his own. On that night he had grasped popularity with both hands, these people had belonged to him and he knew he was their master. At that time he had been drunk with grandiose visions: Montsou at his feet, Paris beyond, returned to Parliament perhaps, blasting the bourgeoisie with his oratory, the first speech made in Parliament by a working man. All over now! This was the awakening, to find himself miserable and ostracized – his own people had driven him off with brickbats.

Rasseneur's voice rose to fresh heights:

'Violence has never succeeded. You can't make a new world in a day. People who have promised you to change everything at once are either leg-pullers or rogues!'

'Hear, hear!'

Who are guilty then? This question which Étienne asked himself put the finishing touch to his misery. Was it really his fault, all this suffering which made his heart bleed, the misery of some and the death of others, all these women and children wasting away with starvation? One night, before all these disasters, he had seen this dire vision, but at that stage he was already uplifted by a strength outside himself, and had been carried away like his comrades. And it was not true that he had ever imposed his will on them – on the contrary they had led him and made him do things he would never have done himself without the momentum of the crowd behind him. Each outburst of violence had appalled him by the logic of events which he had neither wanted nor foreseen. How could he ever have foretold, for example, that a day would come when his own faithful disciples would stone him? These crazy people were lying when they accused him of having promised them a life of eating and idleness. Behind this self-justification and these arguments with which he was trying to stifle his remorse a suspicion was nagging away at him, the vague feeling that he had not proved himself equal to his task, those misgivings of the half-educated which had always pursued him. But his courage was at an end, for he now no longer even spoke the same language as his mates, and was afraid of them, afraid of the huge, blind, irresistible weight of the people, sweeping on like a force of nature, wiping everything out irrespective of rules and theories. Gradually, as his own tastes had become more refined and all his instincts had been slowly raising him towards a higher social class, these people had nauseated him more and more.

Rasseneur was ending his speech amid shouts of enthusiasm: 'Up with Rasseneur! He's the only one for us! Bravo!'

The publican shut the door and the crowd dispersed. The two men looked at each other and shrugged their shoulders without a word. Then they had a drink together.

On the same day there was a grand dinner at La Piolaine to

celebrate the engagement of Négrel and Cécile. Ever since the previous day the Grégoires had been having the dining-room polished and the drawing-room dusted. In the kitchen Mélanie was in her glory, watching the roasts and stirring the sauces, and the smell filled the house right up to the lofts. Francis the coachman was to help Honorine wait at table, the gardener's wife was to wash up and the gardener open the gate. Never before had such a gala turned the big, comfortable, patriarchal house so completely upside down.

Everything went off splendidly. Madame Hennebeau was charming to Cécile and beamed at Négrel when the notary gallantly proposed the health and happiness of the bride and bridegroom to be. Monsieur was also at his most affable. All the company was struck by his happy and carefree manner, and it was whispered that he was now quite in the directors' good books again and would soon be made an Officer of the Legion of Honour for the energetic way he had dealt with the strike. They carefully avoided any reference to the recent troubles, but the general gaiety smacked of triumph, and the dinner was taking on the character of an official celebration of victory. They were out of danger at last and could begin to eat and sleep in peace again! A very discreet allusion was made to the dead whose blood had scarcely soaked into the mud of Le Voreux: it was a necessary lesson, they said, and all looked very touched. The Grégoires added that it was the duty of all to go and heal the wounds in the villages. They had recovered their placid charitableness and made excuses for the worthy miners, whom they could already see back under-ground giving a good example of age-old resignation. Various notabilities of Montsou, feeling secure once more, agreed that the wage problem should be cautiously looked into. By the time they were having the roast, victory was assured when Monsieur Hennebeau read out a letter from the bishop announcing the removal of abbé Ranvier. All the bour-geois of the province were indignantly discussing this priest who treated the soldiers as murderers. As dessert was being served the notary resolutely took up his stand as a freethinker.

Deneulin was there with his two daughters, forcing himself to hide his grief at his own ruin in the midst of all this gaiety.

That very morning he had signed the sale of his Vandame concession to the Montsou Company. With his back to the wall and a knife at his throat he had agreed to all the directors' demands, handing over the prize they had coveted so long for a sum hardly sufficient to pay off his creditors. He had even agreed at the last moment, as a piece of singularly good fortune, to their wish to keep him on as a divisional engineer, resigning himself to accepting a salaried post at the pit in which he had sunk his fortune. This sounded the knell of small private enterprise, of proprietors soon doomed to disappear, devoured piecemeal by the insatiable maw of capital, lost in the rising tide of great combines. He was the only one to pay for the strike, and he felt that in toasting the decoration of Monsieur Hennebeau they were drinking to his own disaster. His only slight consolation was the fine, devil-may-care attitude of Lucie and Jeanne, who were looking charming in their altered clothes, laughing amid the ruins, scorning money like the pretty hoydens they were.

As they passed into the drawing-room for coffee Monsieur Grégoire took his cousin to one side and congratulated him on his courageous decision.

'What can you expect? Your great mistake was to jeopardize the million of your Montsou *denier* in Vandame. You have let yourself in for all this terrible trouble and the money has all melted away in a life of unspeakable toiling and moiling, whereas mine, which has sat tight all along in a drawer, still keeps me quietly doing nothing, as it will my grandchildren's children.'

[2]

At nightfall on Sunday Étienne slipped out of the village. A cloudless sky, jewelled with stars, shed a bluish twilight over the land. He went down to the canal and made his way slowly along the towpath towards Marchiennes. This was his favourite walk, a grass path two leagues long running in a straight line along this geometrical waterway stretching out like an endless bar of molten silver.

Usually he never met anybody, but this time he was vexed to see a man coming towards him, In the pale starlight the two lonely walkers did not recognize each other until they were face to face.

'Oh, it's you!' said Étienne.

Souvarine nodded silently. They stood still for a moment and then set off side by side for Marchiennes. Each seemed to be pursuing his own line of thought as though the other were not there. Étienne was the first to break the silence.

'Did you read in the paper about the success Pluchart has had in Paris? After the meeting at Belleville the crowds waited for him on the pavement and gave him an ovation. Oh, he seems to have made his mark now, and will get wherever he wants to, catarrh and all!'

The mechanic shrugged his shoulders. He despised people with the gift of the gab, who take up politics as others go in for the law, to make big money out of phraseology.

Étienne was now reading Darwin – that is to say he had read extracts in a popular five-sou synopsis – and this half-digested reading had inspired him with revolutionary ideas about the struggle for existence, the survival of the fittest, the strong people devouring the effete bourgeoisie. But Souvarine violently condemned all that and talked at some length about the stupidity of the type of socialist who accepted Darwin, the apostle of scientific inequality, whose famous natural selection was only fit for the aristocratic intelligentsia. His friend stuck to his guns, however, and wanted to argue the thing out, and so he expressed his doubts in a hypothesis: suppose the last crumb of the old order had been swept away; well, wasn't there a danger that the new world as it grew up would be slowly corrupted by the very same injustices, with some people sick and others flourishing, some, the artful and intelligent ones, turning everything to their own advantage, and others, stupid and lazy, relapsing into slavery? In the face of this vision of misery without end Souvarine fiercely cried out that if justice was not feasible for mankind, mankind would have to disappear. For every corrupt society a massacre, until the last human being had been exterminated. Then they fell silent again.

Souvarine walked on for a long time on the soft turf, head down and so absorbed in his own thoughts that he was following the very edge of the water, with the calm assurance of a sleep-walker on a roof. Then he started without any visible reason, as though he had run into a ghost. He looked up, and his face was very pale. He said softly to his companion:

'Did I ever tell you how she died?'

'Who?'

'My wife, in Russia.'

Étienne made a vague gesture, astonished that this normally insensitive fellow, so stoically detached from others and even from himself, should now be speaking in a trembling voice and feel a sudden desire to confide in him. All he knew was that the 'wife' had been a mistress and that she had been hanged in Moscow.

Souvarine began his tale, while his dreamy eyes followed the white canal as it stretched on and on between the bluish colonnades of tall trees: 'Our plans had gone wrong; we had spent fourteen days in a hole in the ground, undermining the railway line, and then instead of the Imperial train it was an ordinary passenger train that blew up. . . . Then they arrested Annushka. She used to bring us food every day, disguised as a peasant. She it was, too, who had lit the fuse, because a man might have attracted attention. For six days I followed the trial, hidden in the crowd.'

His voice faltered and he had a choking fit of coughing.

'Twice I almost shouted out and leaped over people's heads to join her. But what use would that have been? One man less is one soldier less, and I could tell that each time her big steady eyes met mine they were saying no.'

He coughed again.

'On her last day I was there, in the public square. The pouring rain had made the clumsy devils bungle the job, and they had taken twenty minutes to hang four others: the rope broke and they could not finish off the fourth. Annushka stood there waiting for her turn. She could not see me, although she continually scanned the crowd. And so I stood on a stone

429

and she saw me, and our eyes never left each other again. Even after death her eyes were still upon me. I waved my hat and walked away.'

There was another pause. The canal stretched on like a white road, out of sight, and they walked along with light, noiseless tread as though each were alone again. On the horizon the pale water seemed to pierce the sky with a narrow gash of light.

'That was our punishment,' Souvarine went on, but his voice was now hard. 'We were guilty of loving each other. Yes, her death was a good thing, for her blood will inspire heroes and I have no weakness left in my heart. Nothing at all: no family, no wife, no friends, nothing to make my hand falter on the day when I have to take other people's lives or give my own!'

Étienne shuddered and stood still, and the night felt very cold. He did not argue, but just said:

'We've gone a long way, shall we turn back?'

They slowly retraced their steps towards Le Voreux, and after a little while Étienne said:

'Have you read the new notices?'

The Company had put up some more big yellow posters that morning. They were more conciliatory and less vague, promising to take back cards of miners who returned to work the next day. Everything would be overlooked, and a free pardon was extended even to the ringleaders.

'Yes, I've seen them,' answered Souvarine.

'Well, what do you think?'

'I think this is the end. They'll all troop back like a flock of sheep. You are cowards, all the lot of you.'

Étienne hastened to excuse his comrades. One man alone can be brave, but a starving crowd is helpless. They had now reached Le Voreux, and standing in front of the black buildings he swore that he would never go back himself, but he forgave those who were going to do so. Then, as there had been a rumour that the shaftsmen had not had time to repair the shaft lining, he asked about it. Was it true that the pressure of earth against the timber jacket of the shaft had made it bulge so much that one of the cages fouled the sides

430

for a distance of over five metres? Souvarine, who had gone pensive again, explained in a few words. He had been at work the day before, and it was true that the cage caught against the sides – in fact the engineman had had to increase speed in order to get past this place. But when it had been pointed out to the bosses they had all snapped back the same remark: they wanted coal, consolidation could come later.

'You know it's going to give way,' said Étienne. 'It'll be a nice do!'

Gazing at the shadowy pit Souvarine quietly concluded:

'If it does, your mates will know about it. You've advised them to go down again.'

The clock at Montsou was striking nine, and when Étienne said he was going home to bed his friend added, without even holding out his hand:

'Well, good-bye. I'm going.'

'Going? What do you mean?'

'What I said, I've asked for my card back. I'm off somewhere else.'

Étienne stared at him in amazement and grief. There was his friend, saying this after they had been walking together for two hours, and so calmly too, whereas the mere mention of a sudden separation filled him with sadness. They had become friends and worked hard together, and the thought of parting for good is always sad.

'You're off? Where are you going, then?'

'Oh, somewhere, I don't know.'

'But I shall see you again?'

'No, I don't expect so.'

They stood looking at each other for a moment, and could find nothing else to say.

'Well, good-bye.'

'Good-bye.'

While Étienne went up to the village Souvarine turned round and went back to the towpath and walked on and on alone, with head down and so much a part of the inky darkness that he was but a moving shadow of the night. Now and again he stopped to listen to the clock striking in the distance. When it struck midnight he left the towpath and made for the pit.

431

At this hour of the night it was empty, and he only met one sleepy-eyed deputy. The furnaces were not to be lit until two, in readiness for the resumption of work. He began by pretending to go and look for a coat he had left in the back of a cupboard. Rolled up inside the coat were tools: a brace and bit, a very sharp small saw, a hammer and chisel. Then he went off, but instead of going out through the locker-room he went through the narrow corridor leading to the escape shaft. Holding the rolled coat under one arm he softly went down without a light, judging the depth by counting the ladders. He knew that the cage was catching at three hundred and seventy-four metres, against the fifth section of the lower lining. When he had counted fifty-four ladders he put out his hand and felt the bulge in the timbers. This was the place.

Then, with the quiet skill of a good workman who has carefully thought out the job, he set to work. He began by sawing a panel out of the partition separating the escape shaft from the main winding shaft. By the short-lived flame of one or two matches he was able to ascertain the state of the lining and the extent of the recent repairs.

Between Calais and Valenciennes the sinking of pit shafts met with appalling difficulties because they had to pass through enormous subterranean lakes that lay at the level of the deepest valleys. The only way to hold back these gushing springs was to construct linings of pieces of timber joined to each other like the staves of a cask. These linings isolated the shafts in tunnels through the middle of the lakes, the dark and mysterious waves of which lapped against the outside of the walls. When Le Voreux was sunk two distinct linings had had to be made; the one for the upper part of the shaft where it went through the shifting sands and white clays found near chalky soils, and these were riddled with fissures and soaked with water like a sponge; and the other lower down, immediately above the coal measures, through yellow sand as fine as flour, flowing like liquid. Behind this lower lining was the Torrent, the underground sea that was the terror of the pits in the Nord department – a sea with its own storms and wrecks, unexplored, unfathomable, the black rollers of which heaved more than three hundred metres below ground. Normally the linings were secure against the enormous pressure, and the only real danger came from the settling of earth in the vicinity when it was disturbed by the continual movement of disused galleries caving in. When the rocks sank in this way fissures were sometimes produced which slowly lengthened until they met the timbers, and they eventually warped these and forced them inwards into the shaft. Therein lay the great danger, the threat of collapse and flooding which could fill the pit with an avalanche of soil and deluge of spring-water.

Straddled across the opening he had made, Souvarine found a very considerable bulge in this fifth section of the lining. The planks of wood were bellying out from their framework, and some were even right out of their shouldering. A great many leaks, *pichoux* as the miners called them, were squirting out of the joints, through the tarred cotton waste with which they were packed. And the shaftsmen, being pressed for time, had simply put angle-irons across the corners, and so casually that they had not even put in all the screws. Clearly there was a considerable shifting going on behind the sands of the Torrent.

Then with his brace he undid the screws in the angle-irons so that one last push would tear them all out. The job demanded an incredible nerve, and a score of times he all but overbalanced and fell the hundred and eighty metres to the bottom. He had had to get a hold on the oaken guides in which the cages slid up and down and, hanging over the void, to move along the cross-pieces which connected them at intervals. He slipped along, sat down, and even turned upside down, simply buttressing himself with an elbow or a knee, and with a cool contempt for death. A mere breath would have upset him, and three times he just caught himself in time without so much as a shudder. First he explored with his hands and then did his work, only lighting a match when he had lost his bearings among these greasy timbers. Having loosened the screws he attacked the planking itself, and the danger became even greater. He had found the key piece which held all the others and concentrated on that, boring, sawing, and thinning to lessen its resistance, and all the time water spurted through the holes and slits in fine jets of icy rain which blinded him and soaked him through. Two matches were put out and then the whole box got wet, and there was nothing but impenetrable night.

Then he worked like one possessed. The breath of the invisible elated him, and the black horror of this rain-swept cavern filled him with a frenzy of destruction. He attacked the lining at random, hitting wherever he could, using his brace and bit or his saw as though his one idea were to rip everything open there and then on top of him. He put into the task the sort of ferocity with which he might have driven a knife into the flesh of some living being whom he loathed. He would kill this foul beast in the end, this pit with the ever-open jaws that had swallowed down so much human flesh. The bite of his tools could be heard as he stretched himself out, crawled along went down, came up, holding on by a miracle, in continual movement like some night bird flying in and out between the beams of a belfry.

But he forced himself to take things calmly. Surely he could keep a cool head? He quietly waited to recover his breath, and then moved back into the escape shaft, filling up the gap by replacing the panel he had sawn out. That would do. He did not want to raise the alarm by doing too much damage at that moment, for they might have tried to repair it at once. Sufficient that the beast was wounded in the vitals, and whether it would still be alive by the next evening remained to be seen. What was more, he had put his signature to the job, so that a horrified world should know that the pit had not died a natural death. He still took his time, methodically rolling up his tools in the coat and slowly climbing the ladders. Having emerged from the shaft unseen, it did not even occur to him to change his clothes. It was three o'clock, and he stood in the road, waiting.

At the same time Étienne, who could not sleep, was disturbed by a little noise in the darkness of the bedroom. He could hear the light breathing of the children, the snores of Bonnemort and Maheude, whilst at his side Jeanlin was whistling like a flute. Thinking he must have been dreaming, he was nestling down once more when the noise began again.

It was the crackling of a palliasse; somebody was trying to get out of bed noiselessly. He supposed Catherine must be feeling unwell.

'Is it you? Are you all right?' he whispered.

There was no answer, no sound except the snoring of the others. Nothing stirred for five minutes, and then there was another crackling. This time he was sure he was not mistaken, and he crossed the room, holding his hands out in front of him to feel for the opposite bed. Great was his surprise when he touched Catherine, sitting up, and holding her breath in tense watchfulness.

'Well, why don't you answer? What are you up to?'

At last she spoke.

'Getting up.'

'What, now?'

'Yes, I'm going back to work at the pit.'

Étienne felt strangely moved, and had to sit down on the bed beside her while she explained. It was too upsetting to live like this, doing nothing and feeling reproachful eyes always on her. She would rather risk being rough-handled down there by Chaval. And if her mother wouldn't take the money she brought in, well, she was big enough to fend for herself and get her own food.

'You go back to bed, I want to dress. And don't say anything, will you? Please!'

But he did not leave her, for he had put his arm round her waist in a caress of pity and concern. As they sat together on the edge of the bed still warm with the night's sleep, they were huddled so close that they could feel each other's hot flesh through their shifts. At first she had tried to free herself, but then had begun to whimper softly, and in her turn she threw her arms round his neck and drew him near her in a desperate embrace. And there they stayed, with no other desire, and behind them was the past, with their unhappy unsatisfied love. Was it all over between them? Would they dare to love each other some day, now that they were free? If only they could have experienced a little happiness together they would have forgotten their reticence, this awkward reticence that kept them apart because of all sorts

435

of odd ideas which they could not quite make out themselves.

'Go back to bed,' she whispered. 'I don't want to light up, it would wake mother. It's time I got on, let me go.'

He paid no attention but went on holding her close, and his heart was overflowing with unspeakable sadness. He felt a longing for peace and happiness at all costs: he saw himself married, with a nice little home, and no other ambition but to live and die there together. He would be content with dry bread, and if there were only enough for one it should be hers. What was the good of anything else? Was life worth it?

But she freed her bare arms.

'Let me go please!'

Then in an impulsive movement of love he whispered:

'Wait for me. I'm coming with you.'

He himself was amazed at having said this. He had sworn never to go down again. Then why this sudden decision which had tumbled out of his mouth without a moment's thought or discussion? Immediately he felt such a sense of calm and complete release from his doubts that he clung to it like a man whom a mere chance had saved and who had at last found a way out of his dilemma. He refused to listen when she took fright, realizing that he was sacrificing himself for her, and dreading the insults with which he would be greeted at the pit. He laughed it all off; the notices promised no victimization, and that was enough.

'I want to work, that's how it is. . . . Let's get dressed and be quiet about it.'

They dressed in the dark, taking a thousand precautions. She had secretly put her working clothes ready the day before, and he found his coat and trousers in the cupboard. They did not wash for fear of moving the basin. Everybody was still asleep, but they had to cross the narrow passage where her mother's bed was. As ill-luck would have it, on their way out they knocked a chair. Maheude awoke and asked sleepily:

'Eh, what's that?'

Catherine stood stock still, trembling and squeezing Étienne's hand very hard.

436

'It's me, it's all right. I feel stuffy and I'm going out to get some fresh air.'

'Oh, all right.'

She fell asleep again. Catherine dared not move for a long time, but eventually went downstairs to the living-room, where she cut in two a slice of bread she had saved from a loaf given by a lady in Montsou. Then she softly closed the door behind them and went off.

Souvarine was still standing at the corner by the Avantage. For half an hour he had been watching the miners returning to work, tramping by in the darkness like a herd of cattle. He was counting them as a butcher might count animals going into the slaughter-house, and was surprised how many there were, for even in his pessimism he had not foreseen that there would be so many cowards. The line stretched on and on, and still he stood watching, stiff and cold, with clenched teeth and shining eyes.

Then a shudder ran through him. Among these men going past, whose faces he could not make out, there was one he recognized by his walk. He stepped forward and stopped him.

'Where are you going?'

Étienne was so startled that instead of answering the question he said:

'What! haven't you gone yet?'

Then he owned up. Yes, he was going back to work. Of course he knew he had sworn not to, but it was no life at all to wait with folded arms for things that might turn up in a hundred years' time – besides, he had personal reasons.

As he listened Souvarine was deeply troubled. He seized Étienne by the shoulder and spun him round towards the village.

'Go back home, do you hear? I mean it, do you understand?'

But Catherine came up at that moment, and he recognized her too. By now Étienne was protesting that he was not going to let anyone else set himself up as a judge of what he did. The mechanic's eyes travelled from the girl to his friend, and he stepped back with a sudden gesture of surrender. When a man's heart was tied up with a woman he was finished and might as well die. Perhaps he caught one more fleeting vision of his

437

mistress hanged in Moscow, the severing of the last bond of
his flesh which had set him free to dispose of his own life and
those of others. He merely said:

'All right.'

Étienne, feeling very awkward, stood about trying to find
some friendly word so as not to leave his friend like this.

'So you are still going away?'

'Yes.'

'Oh, well, shake hands, chum. Good journey! No ill
feeling!'

The other held out an icy hand. No friend, no woman . . .

'Good-bye for good this time, then.'

'Yes, good-bye.'

Standing motionless in the darkness he watched Étienne
and Catherine go into Le Voreux.

[3]

THE descent began at four. Dansaert himself was in the
time-keeper's office in the lamp-room, writing down the name
of each miner as he appeared and seeing that he was given a
lamp. He accepted everybody without comment, keeping the
promise made on the notices. However, when he saw Étienne
and Catherine at the window he went very red and was on
the point of angrily refusing to take them on, but he contented
himself with a sneer of triumph: oh, oh! so the great strong
man was down, then? There was some good in the Company
after all, since the terrible prize-fighter of Montsou was back
begging for bread! Étienne held his tongue, took his lamp and
went up to the top landing with Catherine.

But that was where Catherine feared there would be trouble
from the others. As soon as she went in she saw Chaval in the
middle of a group of twenty or so, waiting for a free cage. He
was bearing down on her in a fury, but saw Étienne and
paused. Then he put on a sneer and shrugged his shoulders in
an offensive manner. Oh well, right-oh! He didn't give a bugger,
evidently the other chap had entered into occupation while

the place was still warm. Good riddance, he said! It was the gentleman's own business, if he liked left-overs. But behind the display of contempt he was trembling with jealous anger and his eyes were blazing. Nobody else moved; they all stood in awkward silence, looking at their feet. They merely cast a few sidelong glances at the newcomers and then turned back in stolid dejection and stared at the shaft, lamp in hand and shivering in their thin coats while draughts blew continuously through the huge shed.

At last the cage settled on its keeps and they were told to get in. Catherine and Étienne piled into a tub where Pierron and two colliers were already sitting. Beside them in the next tub Chaval was observing to Mouque at the top of his voice that the administration was making a mistake in not seizing this chance to rid the pits of mischief-making blighters, but the old ponyman, who had already resigned himself to this dog's life and forgotten his anger at the death of his children, simply made a conciliatory gesture.

The cage dropped down into the darkness. Nobody said a word. Suddenly, when they were two-thirds of the way down there was a terrible grating sound and a creaking of iron. The men were thrown in a heap.

'Christ!' growled Étienne, 'do they want us all to be flattened out? We shall all stay down there for good thanks to their bloody lining! What's more, they make out it has been repaired!'

However, the cage had passed the obstacle. But now it was going down through such a deluge of water that the miners listened anxiously to the downpour. Surely there must be a lot of new leaks in the caulking of the joints?

Pierron, who had been working for some days already, was asked what he thought, but not wanting to show any fear that might be interpreted as criticism of the directors, he answered:

'Oh, there's no danger! It's always like that. They just haven't had time to stop up the leaks.'

The torrent was roaring down on their heads, and when they reached pit-bottom it was like a veritable waterspout. Not one deputy had thought to go up the ladders to find out what was amiss – oh well, the pump would cope with it and the shaftmen would look at the joints the next night; in any case they had quite enough trouble getting work reorganized in the galleries. The engineer had decided that before letting the colliers return to the coal-faces everybody should put in five days' work on certain urgent maintenance jobs. Falls were imminent in all directions and roads had deteriorated so much that propping had to be repaired over distances of several hundred metres. And so at pit-bottom they were making up teams of ten men, each with a deputy in charge, and setting them to work at the most dangerous places. When everybody was down, three hundred and twenty-two men were counted or about half the number working when the mine was in full production.

Chaval happened to make up the number in Étienne and Catherine's team, and this was no coincidence, for he had lurked behind some of the others and had then forced the deputy's hand. This team went off to the extremity of the North Gallery, a distance of nearly three kilometres, to clear away a fall of earth blocking a road in the Dix-huit Pouces seam. They attacked the fallen rock with pick and shovel. Étienne, Chaval, and five others cleared while Catherine and two lads trammed the stuff to the incline. Few words were exchanged, for the deputy was supervising them all the time, but in spite of that Catherine's two lovers almost came to blows. Chaval kept on muttering that he had done with the trollop, but at the same time would not leave her alone and slyly pushed her about, which made Étienne threaten to give him what for unless he kept his hands off her. They glared at each other and had to be separated.

At about eight Dansaert came round to see how the job was going on. He was clearly in a terrible temper and took it out of the deputy: nothing was right, props should be replaced as you went along, work like this was no good at all! He flounced off, saying he would come back with the engineer. He had been waiting for Négrel since first thing, and could not understand why he was so late.

Another hour went by. The deputy had called off the clearing so as to put everybody on to propping the roof. Even

440

Catherine and the two lads stopped tramming and prepared and handed up pieces of wood. In this blind gallery the team was like an outpost at the extreme limit of the mine, and quite out of touch with the other workings. Three or four times strange noises like people running in the distance had made them turn and listen: what was the matter? It was as though the roads were emptying and their mates were knocking off already, and as fast as they could. But the sounds died away into deep silence and they turned back to drive home props in a whirl of hammering. Then they resumed the clearing and the tubs began moving again.

But Catherine came back from her first journey looking very frightened, saying that there was nobody left at the incline.

'I called out, but there was no answer. They've all cleared off.'

They were so horrified that all ten of them threw down their tools and ran, panic-stricken at the thought of being abandoned alone in the pit, so far from the shaft. They had taken only their lamps, and ran along in a line, men, boys, and the girl. Even the deputy lost his head and called out loudly, for the silence in this endless wilderness of galleries un-nerved him more and more. What was going on? Why wasn't there a living soul anywhere? Had some accident carried all the others off? The very vagueness of the danger increased their terror, for they felt an unknown threat hanging over them.

When at last they were nearing pit-bottom a rushing stream barred the way. In a moment water was up to their knees, and they could not run, but had to wade painfully along, knowing full well that one minute's delay might mean death.

'God Almighty, the lining's given way!' cried Étienne. 'Didn't I say we should stay down here?'

Ever since they came down Pierron had been anxiously watching the steadily increasing deluge down the shaft. While loading tubs into cages with two other onsetters he kept glancing up, and his face was splashed with water and his ears deafened by the thundering of the waterfall above him.

But he got really frightened when he saw that the ten-metre sump below him was filling up: the water was already splashing on to the ground and creeping over the sheet-iron flooring, which proved that the pump could no longer keep up with the leakages. He could hear it panting and gasping with fatigue. He warned Dansaert, who swore angrily and said they must wait for the engineer. Twice he returned to the attack, but all he could get out of Dansaert was shrugs of exasperation: very well, if the water was rising it was rising, and what could he do about it?

Mouque appeared, leading Bataille to do his turn. But he had to hold him with both hands, for the sleepy old animal had suddenly reared and stretched his head towards the shaft, whinnying a death-cry.

'What's up, old philosopher? What are you worrying about? Oh, because it's raining, I suppose! Come on, it's none of your business.'

But the horse stood there shuddering all over his body, and he had to be dragged to work by main force.

Almost at the same moment as Mouque and Bataille were disappearing into a gallery there was a crash high up in the air followed by a long noise of falling. A section of lining had come loose and was bouncing down against the sides of the shaft for a hundred and eighty metres. Pierron and the other onsetters just had time to dodge out of the way and the oak planking merely smashed an empty tub. Simultaneously a great chunk of water fell down like the bore from a burst dam. Dansaert wanted to go up and see, but even while he was saying so a second piece of timber came down. Appalled by the imminent catastrophe he came to a decision and ordered the pit to be evacuated, sending deputies to warn the men in the workings.

Then there began a fearful stampede. Streams of men rushed in from all the roads and fought their way into the cages, crushing each other to death in order to get taken up at once. Some of them had thought of going up the escape-shaft, but they came down again shouting that it was already blocked. After each cage left the rest stood there in terror: that one had got past, but who could say whether the next one

442

would, for the shaft was filling up with debris. The collapse must still be going on up above, for through the continuous and ever-growing noise of falling water could be heard a series of muffled detonations and the splitting and cracking of timber. Soon one of the cages was out of action; it was smashed in and wedged between the guides, which were probably broken too. The other one was catching so badly that the cable would certainly snap soon. And the hundred men still to be taken up were fuming with impatience, spattered with blood and half drowned, clinging on for their lives. Two were killed outright by falling planks. A third hung on to the underside of the cage, lost his grip and fell fifty metres to his death in the sump.

Nevertheless Dansaert was still trying to keep some sort of order. He seized a pick and threatened that the first to disobey would have his head split open. He tried to make them form a queue and ordered that the onsetters must be the last to leave, after seeing the others off. But they would not listen – in fact he had just prevented Pierron, pale and shaken, from slipping off among the first. Dansaert had to knock him aside each time the cage left. But his own teeth were chattering: one more minute and he would be buried alive, for everything was caving in and coming down like a river in spate, with a murderous hail of timbers. A few more men were still to come when he went mad with fear himself and leaped into a tub, letting Pierron tumble in behind him. The cage went up.

At that very moment Étienne and Chaval's team reached pit-bottom. They saw the cage disappearing and hurled themselves forward, but had to fall back before the final collapse of the lining. The shaft was blocked and the cage would never come down again. Catherine began whimpering. Chaval swore till he choked. There were still a score of them; were those bloody bosses going to leave them to die? Old Mouque had slowly brought Bataille back and stood holding his reins, and there they stayed, the old man and the animal, both appalled by the speed with which the flood was rising. Already it was up to the men's thighs. Étienne, silent and with set jaws, lifted Catherine in his arms. With upturned faces the twenty stood there vacantly gazing up the shaft, now a mere hole that had caved in and was spitting forth a river. No help could come from there, but they went on screaming in terror.

As he emerged into the daylight Dansaert saw Négrel running up. By a stroke of fate, that particular morning, as he and Madame Hennebeau were getting out of bed, she had delayed him in order to look through some catalogues of presents for his bride. It was now ten o'clock.

'Well, what's the matter?' he shouted, still running.

'The pit is finished,' answered the overman.

He stammered out the story of the disaster, but the engineers looked quite incredulous: oh, come! how could a shaft lining just collapse of its own accord like that? They must be exaggerating, it must be looked into.

'Nobody left at the bottom, I trust?'

Dansaert faltered. Er . . . nobody . . . that is to say, he hoped not. And yet perhaps some of the men might have got delayed.

'Then why the hell did you come up? You can't leave your men in the lurch!'

He at once ordered a count of the lamps. Three hundred and twenty-two had been issued that morning, and only two hundred and fifty-five could be accounted for; but several men admitted that in the panic they had dropped theirs and left them down below. They tried to have a roll-call, but it was impossible to reach an exact figure, for some of the miners had rushed off home already and others did not hear their names. Nobody could agree who was missing – there might be twenty, but then again there might be forty. Only one fact was clear to the engineer: there were men left down there, and, indeed, if you hung over the mouth of the shaft you could hear their screams through the rushing of water and the crashing of timber.

Négrel's first thoughts were to send for Monsieur Hennebeau and to try to shut the pit. But it was already too late, for the miners who had rushed off at once to Village 240, as though still pursued by crashing timber, had spread the alarm among the families, and crowds of women, old men, and children were running down the hill, crying and shouting. They had to be pushed back, and a cordon of inspectors was

444

told off to hold them and prevent them from hampering operations. Many of the rescued miners stood there in a daze, forgetting to change, transfixed by fear in front of this dreadful cavern in which they had nearly stayed for ever. They were surrounded by frantic women imploring them for names. Was so-and-so there? and so-and-so? and somebody else? They could not remember, they muttered meaningless phrases, shivered convulsively and made insane gestures – gestures which tried to push away the abominable, haunting vision. The crowd rapidly swelled, and a great lamentation went up from the roads near by. And all the while, up on the pit bank, sitting in Bonnemort's shelter, was a man – Souvarine. He had not gone away. He was watching.

'Names! tell us the names!' wailed the crowd of women. Négrel appeared for a moment and said:

'As soon as we know the names we shall let you know. But we mustn't give up hope yet. Everybody will be saved. I am going down myself.'

The crowd began waiting in silent agony. For with quiet confidence the engineer was preparing to go down. He had had the cage disconnected and ordered a skip to be attached to the end of the cable instead, and expecting that the water would put out his lamp he had a second lamp hung underneath the skip which would keep it dry.

The deputies who helped him with these preparations had white and terrified faces.

'Dansaert, you're coming down with me,' said Négrel curtly. But seeing how frightened they all were, especially the overman, who in his terror was staggering as though he were drunk, he pushed him contemptuously aside.

'No, you would get in the way. I'd rather be on my own.'

He had already stepped into the narrow bucket swinging on the cable, and holding his lamp in one hand and the signal rope with the other, he shouted to the engineman:

'Easy does it!'

The engine began to turn the drums and Négrel vanished into the abyss, from which the screams of the trapped men could still be heard.

He found nothing wrong with the upper part of the shaft

where the lining was intact. Dangling in space, he shone his
lamp on the sides as he spun round and round, and there
were so few leaks between joints that the lamp was not
affected. But when he reached three hundred metres, where
the lower section of lining began, his lamp was extinguished as
he had foreseen, and the skip filled with water. From there onwards his only source of light was the lamp hanging underneath, which preceded him in the darkness. Brave though he
was, he began to shudder as he realized the full horror of the
disaster. Only a few pieces of wood remained in position; the
others had gone down, frames and all, and where they had
been there yawned enormous cavities, from which the fine,
flour-like yellow sand was pouring in large quantities, whilst
the waters of the Torrent, the underground sea with its
mysterious storms and wrecks, were gushing forth like a weir.
He went lower still, amidst ever-widening chasms, tossed and
whirled about by waterspouts, and so ill lit by the red star of
the lamp beneath him that the great moving shadows took on
the shapes of streets and crossroads in some far away, devastated city. Any further human action here was out of the
question, and there was only one thing left to hope for: to try
to save the men in peril. As he went down their shrieks grew
louder. But suddenly he had to stop, for the shaft was blocked
by an impassable obstacle; a mass of timber, the broken beams
of cage-guides, split partitions of the escape-shafts, all
tangled up with supports torn from the pump. As, with aching
heart, he was examining the wreckage, the shouting below
him suddenly stopped. The poor devils must have taken fright
at the rapid rise of the flood and fled along the galleries, unless
the water had already stopped their mouths.

Négrel had to admit defeat and tugged the signal rope to
be drawn up. But then he ordered another stop. He was still
baffled by the suddenness of the accident, the cause of which
passed his understanding, and anxious to find out the reason
he began to examine the few pieces of the shaft lining still in
place. From a distance he had been amazed by the rents and
nicks in the wood, and as by now the wet had almost put out
his lamp, he felt with his fingers and recognized unmistakable
saw-cuts, holes bored by a bit, in fact a fiendishly complete job

of destruction. It was obvious that the disaster had been deliberately planned. As he was gazing in amazement the remaining pieces crashed down with their framework in a final collapse which almost carried him away. All his courage had vanished – the thought of the man who had done this made his hair stand on end and froze his blood with the superstitious dread of evil, as if the man were still lurking there monstrous in the shadows, expiating his unspeakable crime. He shouted aloud and tugged madly at the signal rope; and it was high time, for a hundred metres higher up he noticed that the upper lining was also beginning to move: the joints were widening and their caulking was coming adrift, letting in jets of water. Now it could only be a matter of hours before the shaft would lose the whole of its lining and cave in.

At the surface Monsieur Hennebeau was anxiously waiting for him.

'Well, what about it?' he asked.

But the engineer could not answer. His voice had gone and he was almost swooning.

'Impossible!' said Monsieur Hennebeau. 'Such a thing is unheard of! Did you have a good look?'

Négrel nodded, but gave him a warning glance. He would not go into it in the presence of one or two deputies within earshot, and led his uncle ten metres away, decided that was not far enough, and went further still. Then in a whisper he told him about the outrage, how the planks had been sawn and bored, in fact that the pit had had its throat cut and was bleeding to death. The manager paled and also lowered his voice with the instinctive need to speak quietly about monstrous orgies and dastardly crimes. There was no point in appearing to tremble in front of the ten thousand employees of Montsou – later on they would see. The two men went on whispering, appalled that any man could have had the nerve to go down there and hang over the abyss, risking his life twenty times over to do his dreadful work. They could not even conceive of such insanely intrepid destruction, and refused to believe in the very face of proof, as one is sceptical about famous escape stores in which prisoners apparently fly out of windows thirty metres above the ground.

447

When Monsieur Hennebeau rejoined the deputies his face was drawn by a nervous twitch. With a gesture of despair he ordered the pit to be evacuated at once. Everybody began to leave in funereal gloom, silently abandoning the pit, casting backward glances at the great empty brick buildings still standing but doomed beyond any possibility of salvation.

The manager and the engineer were the last to leave the pit head, and the crowd greeted them with its monotonous clamour:

'Names! Names! Tell us the names!'

By now Maheude had joined the waiting women. She recollected the noise in the night: her girl and the lodger must have gone together, and they were down there for certain. Although at first she had declared that it was a good job and that they deserved to stay there, the heartless wretches, she had rushed off just the same and was now in the front row, shuddering with dread. In any case she dared not doubt any longer, for the talk going on around her told her all too plainly. Yes, yes, Catherine was among them, and Étienne too, one of their mates had seen them. But there was less general agreement about the others. No, no, not him – but so-and-so – perhaps Chaval? But then a pit-boy swore he had come up with Chaval. La Levaque and Pierronne had nobody in peril, but wailed as loudly as the others. Zacharie had been one of the first up and in spite of his cynical pose had burst into tears as he kissed his wife and mother, and now stayed by his mother's side, sharing her sorrow, and showing un-expected depths of tenderness for his sister, refusing to believe she was down below until it was officially confirmed.

'Names! Names! For God's sake tell us the names!'

Négrel could stand it no longer and shouted in a carrying voice to the cordon of inspectors:

'Oh, do shut them up! It's enough to kill you! We don't know any names yet.'

This had been going on for two hours already. In the first shock nobody had thought of the other shaft, the old Réquillart one. Monsieur Hennebeau was in the act of announcing that they would try to carry out rescue work from Réquillart when a new rumour ran round: five men had escaped from the flooding by climbing up the rotten ladders in the old disused escape shaft, and old Mouque's name was mentioned, which was a surprise, as nobody thought he was below. But the story of the escaped five only renewed the weeping, for that meant that fifteen others had been unable to follow them, having lost their way through falls of rock, and they could not now be rescued because the water in Réquillart was already ten metres deep. All the names were now known, and the air was filled with the groans of a slaughtered people.

'Oh, stop them, for God's sake,' Négrel repeated furiously. 'And make them stand back! Yes, yes, a hundred metres back! It's dangerous, push them back.'

The poor devils had to be driven back. They imagined fresh horrors – that they were being driven off so that other deaths could be concealed – and the deputies had to explain that the buildings themselves would be swallowed up by the shaft. They were so aghast at the thought of such a thing that they fell silent and let themselves be forced back step by step, but the cordon had to be doubled in order to hold them, for in spite of themselves they continually crept forward as though fascinated. A thousand people were now pushing and jostling in the roadway, and still they were coming in from the villages, and even from Montsou. And high up on the pit-bank the fair man with the girlish features smoked cigarette after cigarette in his impatience, and his pale eyes never left the pit for a moment.

Then the wait began. It was noon, nobody had had any food, but nobody went home. Russet-coloured clouds drifted slowly across the grey, smoky sky. From behind Rasseneur's hedge came the loud and incessant barking of a big dog, upset by the living scent of this crowd. The crowd itself had gradually spread from one field to another, and now surrounded the pit at a distance of a hundred metres, and in the centre of this empty space stood Le Voreux, in lonely isolation without a living soul or sound, its gaping windows and doors showing its deserted interior. A stray ginger cat, sensing the ominous solitude, leaped from a stairway and disappeared. The furnaces could not have gone out yet, for thin wisps of smoke were still issuing from the tall brick chimney and could be seen floating against the sombre clouds, whilst the weather-cock squeaking in the wind with a little high-pitched scream was the only plaintive voice from these vast buildings condemned to die.

Two o'clock and no change. Monsieur Hennebeau, Négrel, and other engineers who had hurried to the scene, formed a frock-coated and black-hatted group in front of the crowd. They could not tear themselves away any the more, though their legs ached with fatigue and they felt sick and ill at their own powerlessness in the presence of such a cataclysm. There they stood, occasionally exchanging a whispered word, like watchers at a deathbed. The upper lining must now be finally collapsing, for they could hear sudden crashes reverberating in the deep chasm, followed by long silences. The wound was steadily opening as the landslide, having begun at the bottom, was rising to the surface. Négrel was seized with unbearable nervous impatience; he felt he must see, and he walked forward alone into the awful empty space, but the others seized him by the shoulders – what was the good? he couldn't do anything. However, one miner, an old hand, dodged through the cordon and ran to the locker-room. But he calmly reappeared, having been to recover his clogs.

Three o'clock, and still no change. Nobody in the crowd had moved a step, in spite of pouring rain. Rasseneur's dog had begun barking again. Not until twenty past three did the first earth tremor occur. Le Voreux shook slightly, but it was strongly built and stood firm. But a second shock followed at once and a long shout came from the astonished crowd. The tarred screening-shed lurched twice and collapsed with a deafening crash, and in falling its huge weight rubbed the broken beams together so hard that fountains of sparks flew up. From then onwards there were continuous tremors, and shock followed shock as underground subsidences rumbled like a volcano in eruption. The dog in the distance had stopped barking and was now howling mournfully as though heralding the earthquakes whose approach he could feel, and the women and children could not hold back cries of distress as each tremor shook them. In less than ten minutes the slate roof of the tower fell in, and gaping holes appeared in the walls of

450

the top landing and winding-house. Then the noises ceased for the time being, and the buildings stopped falling. There was another deathly silence.

For an hour Le Voreux remained in this state, as though it had been breached by a horde of barbarians. The ever-widening circle of onlookers was reduced to watchful silence. Smashed tips and broken and twisted hoppers could be seen under the heaps of splintered beams that had once been the screening-shed. But the greatest pile of debris was on the top landing, where bricks had rained down and whole walls had crumbled into rubble. The iron scaffolding of the headgear had sagged and half disappeared into the shaft: one cage was hanging in mid-air and a bit of cable was dangling loose, and everywhere there was a churned-up mass of tubs, sheet-iron, and ladders. By a strange chance the lamp-room to the left was still intact, with its twinkling rows of little lights. And the engine could be seen through the walls of its house, still squarely set on its foundation of masonry. its copper-work still gleaming and its massive steel limbs looking like inde-structible muscles: the great crank had stopped in mid-air, resembling nothing so much as the powerful knee of a re-cumbent giant, confident in his strength.

When this respite had lasted an hour Monsieur Hennebeau began to feel hope returning. The shifting of the earth must have stopped, and they might be fortunate enough to save the engine and the rest of the buildings. But he still forbade any-one to approach, wanting to wait patiently for another half hour. The suspense was becoming intolerable, for renewed hope sharpened anxiety, and all hearts beat faster. A dark cloud coming up from the horizon had brought on an early twilight, a sinister nightfall over this wreck left by the earth's tempests. Everybody had been there for seven hours without moving, without eating.

And then, as the engineers were cautiously moving for-ward, they were suddenly thrown back by a supreme convul-sion. There was a volley of underground detonations, a monstrous cannonade in the bowels of the earth. On the surface the last buildings toppled over and crumpled up. First a sort of whirlwind blew away the ruins of the screening-shed and top landing. Then the boiler-house burst asunder and disappeared. Next the square tower containing the gasping pump fell on its face like a man shot down. And then a terrifying thing: they saw the engine, torn from its bed, wrestling against death with dislocated limbs. It moved, stretching its crank, its gigantic knee, as though it meant to rise, but it fell back dead, smashed to smithereens, and was swallowed up. The only thing that remained standing was the thirty-metre chimney, and that was swaying like a ship's mast in a hurricane. They expected it to break up and collapse into dust, but suddenly it plunged down in one piece, swallowed whole by the earth, like a giant candle that had melted away. Nothing was left showing, not even the point of the lightning conductor. This was the end, The evil beast, crouching in its hollow, sated with human flesh, had drawn its last long heavy breath. Le Voreux had sunk into the abyss, every bit of it.

The crowd fled, screaming. Women ran along holding their hands in front of their eyes. A wind of terror blew men along like a heap of dry leaves. They tried not to shout, but shouted all the same, with bursting lungs and waving arms as they beheld the immense hole that had opened up. A crater like an extinct volcano fifteen metres deep stretched from the road to the canal, at least forty metres across. The whole yard had followed the buildings, great trestles, bridges with their rails, a whole train of tubs and three railway trucks, as well as the store of pit-props, a forest of cut poles, all swallowed up like straws. In the bed of the crater only a tangled mass of wood, bricks, and plaster could be seen, frightful wreckage, pounded, twisted, and blackened by the fury of the catastrophe. The hole was still spreading, throwing out fissures from its edges far away into the surrounding fields. One of these ran as far as Rasseneur's bar and cracked his wall. Would the village itself be engulfed? Where could shelter be found on this fearful evening, under the leaden sky that looked as though it meant to join in as well and crush the world?

But Négrel uttered a cry of grief, and Monsieur Hennebeau, who had fallen back a little, burst into tears, for the calamity was not yet complete. The canal bank gave way and the water poured like a boiling stream into one of the fissures,

vanishing like a cataract falling into a deep chasm. The pit
drank up the stream, and that meant that the galleries would
be flooded for years. Soon the crater filled up and the place
that had been Le Voreux was a muddy lake, like those lakes
beneath which lie evil cities destroyed by God. In the terrified silence nothing could be heard but the waterfall roaring
down into the bowels of the earth.

At that moment Souvarine rose to his feet on the shaken
slag-heap. He had recognized Maheude and Zacharie sobbing
together in the presence of this total collapse which must be
pressing with its stupendous weight on the heads of those
poor wretches dying down below. He threw away his last
cigarette and walked off into the darkness without so much as
a glance behind. His shadowy form dwindled and merged into
the night. He was bound for the unknown, over yonder,
calmly going to deal violent destruction wherever dynamite
could be found to blow up cities and men. Doubtless, on that
day when the last expiring bourgeois hear the very stones of
the streets exploding under their feet, he will be there.

[4]

On the very night after the collapse of Le Voreux Monsieur
Hennebeau had left for Paris, determined to give the directors
the full story himself before the papers could publish even the
bare news. When he returned on the following day he was
quite calm, and wearing his normal administrative air. It was
clear that he had disclaimed all personal responsibility, and
did not even seem to have lost favour – on the contrary the
decree naming him an Officer of the Legion of Honour was
signed twenty-four hours later.

But though the manager's position was safe, the Company
was reeling under the terrible blow. It was not the loss of a
few millions that mattered, but the wound in the vitals, the
haunting, relentless fear of the morrow in view of the slaughter
of one of its pits. Once again the panic was such that it was

felt that the affair must be hushed up. Was there any need to stir up all this abominable mud? If the criminal were discovered why make a martyr of him, for his horrible heroism would turn other men's heads and might beget a whole progeny of incendiaries and murderers. In any case they did not suspect the real culprit, but eventually decided that it must have been the work of a large number of accomplices, finding it impossible to believe that one man alone could have had the daring and the strength to carry out such a design. This was at the bottom of the Company's obsession that an ever-growing threat hung over their pits. Accordingly the manager had been instructed to organize a vast network of espionage and to dismiss quietly, one by one, any dangerous characters suspected of complicity in the crime. It was thought to be politically wise and prudent to limit action to a purge of this kind.

There was only one immediate dismissal, Dansaert the overman. In any case he had been impossible since the scandal with Pierronne, and the reason now given was his attitude in the face of danger, tantamount to the cowardice of a captain abandoning his crew. It was, moreover, a tactful concession to the miners, who abominated him.

However, rumours had spread among the general public, and the directors had to send a letter to one paper correcting a version of the story which had mentioned a barrel of gunpowder fired by the strikers. Already, after a cursory inspection, the government engineer had reached the conclusion that the lining had given way of its own accord owing to shifting pressure of earth, and the Company had preferred to keep quiet and accept a reprimand for inadequate inspection. By the third day the Paris press had added the disaster to its stock of catchpenny sensations, and people talked of nothing else but miners dying at the bottom of the pit and greedily scanned the dispatches in each morning's issue. In Montsou itself the worthy bourgeois turned pale and silent at the mere name of Le Voreux, and a legend was forming which made the stoutest hearts quail as they whispered it into each other's ears. The whole neighbourhood was full of pity for the victims, and parties made excursions to the wretched pit, whole families treating themselves to the awe-inspiring spectacle of the ruins which weighed so heavily on the heads of the poor creatures buried beneath.

Deneulin had been appointed divisional engineer and had begun his duties just in time to have to deal with the worst of the disaster. The first thing was to turn the canal back into its proper course, for every hour this torrent of water was aggravating the trouble. Very extensive work had to be done and he at once set a hundred men to construct an embankment. Twice the swirling waters washed away the first dams, and now pumps were being installed and there began a desperate fight to recover the lost land inch by inch.

But the rescue of the buried miners was even more enthralling. Négrel was responsible for making a supreme effort, and he had a host of helping hands, for all the miners rushed to offer themselves in a burst of fraternal devotion. The strike was forgotten and pay did not matter; they did not mind working for nothing, all they asked was to risk their lives since there were comrades in danger of death. They all came with their tools, eagerly asking where they were to use them. Many of them were still suffering themselves from the shock of the accident, with nervous twitches, cold sweats, and incessant nightmares driving them mad, but they got up just the same, and showed themselves the most furiously determined to fight against the earth as though they had an account to square. Unfortunately the trouble began over how to set about doing something really useful: what could be done? how could they get down? whereabouts ought the attack on the rock to be directed?

In Négrel's opinion not one of the victims could still be alive, all fifteen must certainly have perished from drowning or asphyxia, but in mining disasters the rule is that men walled in underground must always be presumed to be alive, and he acted on this supposition. The first problem he set himself was to work out which way they could have gone to take refuge. The deputies and old hands whom he consulted were unanimous on this point: in an emergency their mates would certainly have climbed from gallery to gallery until they reached the highest coal-faces, therefore they would probably be trapped at the end of one of the uppermost roads. Moreover that tallied with the information from old Mouque, whose involved story even suggested the theory that in their panic the escaping miners had broken up into little groups which would have scattered fugitives over all the levels. But when it came to discussing ways and means the deputies differed among themselves. As the nearest roads to the surface were a hundred and fifty metres down, the sinking of a shaft was out of the question. That left Réquillart as the only means of access, the one line of approach. The worst of it was that the disused mine, being also flooded, was no longer in direct communication with Le Voreux, for the only clear roads above water were short galleries running from the first level. Since it would take years to drain the pit the best course was to inspect these galleries and find out whether they ran near to the flooded roads at the end of which the marooned men were thought to be. But before logically reaching this conclusion there had been a great deal of discussion in order to rule out a host of impracticable suggestions.

Négrel at once disturbed the dust of the archives, and when he had discovered the old plans of the two pits he studied them and decided from which points the investigations should be carried out. The rescue work had gradually fired him with enthusiasm and like everybody else he became possessed by a frenzy of self-sacrifice despite his usual ironical indifference to men and things. They ran up against preliminary difficulties at Réquillart, where the approaches to the shaft had to be cleared: the mountain ash had to be cut down, the blackthorn and hawthorn cleared away, and the ladders had to be repaired. Then exploration began. The engineer took ten workmen down and made them tap with their iron tools on certain parts of the seam which he pointed out, then in absolute silence they all put an ear to the coal to listen for distant answering taps. They went all over every gallery they could reach, but to no purpose; no answer came. Their quandary was worse: whereabouts should they start cutting the seam? whom should they make for, since nobody seemed to be there? But they went on doggedly with the search, in ever-increasing exhaustion and anxiety.

From the first day Maheude had gone to Réquillart every morning. She sat down on a log near the shaft and never moved until nightfall, except to jump up whenever a man emerged from the pit and ask him the same question with her eyes: Nothing? No, nothing. And she sat down again without a word, to continue the wait with hard, stoical face. As they were invading his territory Jeanlin had also been prowling round with the scared look of a beast of prey whose depredations are about to come to light in his lair. The young soldier was on his mind, too, and the fear that his slumber under the rocks might be disturbed – but that part of the mine was under water and in any case they were digging further to the left, in the west gallery. At first Philomène had come as well with Zacharie who was in the rescue squad, but she had soon tired of catching cold for no rhyme or reason, so now she stayed in the village, where she dragged herself sloppily through the days without bothering her head about it, coughing from morn till night. But Zacharie could not stop even to live, and would have devoured the earth itself to find his sister. He shouted out in the night: he saw and heard her, emaciated with hunger and with her lungs worn out with shouting for help. Twice he had tried to dig against orders, saying she must be there, he could feel it. The engineer finally stopped his going down, but he would not leave the forbidden shaft, neither could he sit still and wait with his mother, but had to run round and round looking for something to do.

They had been at it for three days. Négrel, in despair had resolved to abandon the search that evening. At midday when he was returning after lunch to make one last effort with the men, he was astonished to meet Zacharie coming up out of the shaft, looking very red, gesticulating and shouting:

'She's there! She answered me! Come on, come on!'

He had dodged the watchman and slipped down the ladders, and he swore that somebody had tapped an answer down in the first gallery of the Guillaume seam.

'But we have already been twice all over the part you're talking about,' said Négrel incredulously. 'Still, we'll have another try.'

Maheude had risen to her feet and she had to be prevented

457

from going down herself. She stood waiting on the very brink of the shaft, staring down into the darkness.

When they reached the spot Négrel himself tapped three times at long intervals, then put his ear to the coal, enjoining absolute silence. Not a sound came, and he shook his head obviously the poor fellow had been dreaming. Zacharie tapped frenziedly himself: he heard it again and his eyes blazed and he quivered with excitement. Then the others tried again in turn, and they were all overjoyed to hear a distant answer quite clearly. The engineer was amazed, he listened again, and eventually his ears did catch a faint sound faint as a breath, a scarcely audible rhythmical drumming to the well-known tune of the miner's recall which they beat out on the coal as a danger signal. Coal transmits sound with crystal clearness over great distances; a deputy estimated that the mass between them and their comrades must be at least fifty metres thick. But now it seemed as though they could reach out and touch them, and their joy knew no bounds. Négrel had to give orders to dig in that direction at once.

When Zacharie saw his mother again at the mouth of the shaft they fell into each other's arms.

'You mustn't get too excited,' Pierronne was cruel enough to say. She had come that way for a stroll just to have a look round. 'If Catherine weren't there it would be such a disappointment.'

It was quite true, Catherine might be somewhere else.

'Shut your bloody mouth, can't you?' roared Zacharie. 'Of course she's there, I know she is!'

Maheude had sat down again silent and expressionless. She resigned herself to another wait.

As soon as the story was known in Montsou a fresh crowd of people came out. There was nothing to see, but they stayed there all the same, and sightseers had to be kept back. Below ground work went on night and day. For fear of meeting some obstacle the engineer had had three descending tunnels cut through the seam, converging on the point where the imprisoned miners were believed to be. Only one collier at a time could hew away at the head of each narrow tunnel, and he was relieved every two hours. The coal was loaded into baskets which were passed back by hand along a line of men which lengthened as the excavation went on. At first the work made rapid progress: six metres in one day.

Zacharie had got permission to be one of the chosen few to work on the face. It was the position of honour which they all coveted. When they tried to relieve him after the regulation two hours he violently resisted. He cheated the others out of their turns and refused to hand over his pick. His tunnel was soon ahead of the others, and he battered against the coal with such furious energy that from right back at the entrance to the tunnel they could hear his heavy, snoring breath, like the bellows of a forge. When he staggered out, drunk with fatigue and covered with black mud, he fell at once to the ground and had to be covered with a blanket. Then he would rush back to the job, still unsteady on his feet, and the struggle would be resumed, with heavy muffled blows, muttered oaths, like the fury of a soldier hacking his way through slaughter to victory. Unfortunately the coal was becoming harder: twice he broke his pick on it in his rage at not being able to make so much headway. The heat was an additional torture, for it grew with every metre he advanced, and down in this narrow hole, where the air did not penetrate, it was unbearable. It is true that there was a hand ventilator in working order, but it could not really circulate the air, and three times men were brought out unconscious.

Négrel lived underground with the men. His meals were sent down and occasionally he snatched two hours' sleep on a bale of straw, rolled up in a coat. The men's determination was maintained by the supplications of the poor wretches on the other side of the barrier, whose tapped-out appeals to hurry were becoming more and more distinct. By now they were very clear, with a musical quality something like a harmonica. This note was their guide, and they advanced towards the crystalline sound as an army in battle advances towards the cannon. Each time a collier was relieved Négrel went in, tapped and listened, and each time, so far, the reply had been prompt and imperative. There was now no doubt in his mind that they were advancing in the right direction, but with what deadly slowness! They would never get there in time. At the outset they had, it is true, covered thirteen metres in two days, but on the third day the rate had fallen to five, and on the fourth to three. The coal was becoming so much denser and harder that now they only penetrated two metres per day, if that. By the ninth day, after superhuman efforts, the total advance was thirty-two metres, and they calculated that there were at least twenty more ahead. It was the twelfth day for the prisoners – twelve times twenty-four hours in icy darkness without bread or fire! This dreadful thought made their eyes fill with tears, but put more muscle into their arms for the job. It seemed impossible that Christian folk could live any longer: the distant taps had been weakening since the day before, and every moment they dreaded to hear them no more.

Maheude still came regularly and sat at her place by the mouth of the shaft, bringing Estelle in her arms, for the child could not be left from morning till night. Hour after hour she followed the work, sharing in the hopes and disappointments. The waiting groups, and even people at Montsou, were now in a state of feverish tension and talked of nothing else. Every heart in the neighbourhood was beating with those others under the ground.

At lunch time on the ninth day Zacharie did not answer when he was called to be relieved. He was tearing away at the job with oaths, like one possessed. Négrel came along for a moment but could not make him obey, and the only other people left were a deputy and three miners. At that moment, perhaps, Zacharie, in his fury at being slowed down in his task by the dim and flickering light, committed the folly of opening his lamp, in defiance of strict orders, for it was known that fire-damp had been escaping, and large pockets of gas had collected in these narrow, ill-ventilated passages. Suddenly there was a thunderous roar and a spout of fire issued from the hole like a flash from the muzzle of a gun loaded with grapeshot. Everything burst into flame; the very air caught fire like a train of gunpowder from end to end of the galleries. The torrent of flame, sweeping aside the deputy and three miners, leaped up the shaft and high into the air like a volcanic eruption, spewing out rocks and bits of timber. The sightseers scattered, and Maheude jumped to her feet, clutching the terrified Estelle to her breast.

When Négrel and the others came back from lunch they fell into paroxysms of fury, stamping on the ground like some unnatural woman slaying her step-children with no other reason than the insensate whim of her hatred. To think that they went to the help of their comrades, putting aside all thought of self, simply in order to lose yet more of their number! When at last, after three long hours of struggle and danger, they made their way back into the galleries, they set about the gruesome recovery of the victims. Neither the deputy nor the three men were dead, but they were covered with terrible burns which gave off a stench like charred meat; they had swallowed fire and the burns went right down into their throats, and they moaned incessantly, begging to be finished off. One of the three miners was the man who during the troubles had aimed the final blow with his pick that had smashed the pump at Gaston-Marie, and both the others still had scarred hands and grazed and cut fingers from having pelted the soldiers with bricks. As they were carried by, all the onlookers, pale and trembling, took off their caps.

Maheude stood waiting. Zacharie's body at last appeared. The clothes had been burned away and the body was black, charred and unrecognizable. The head had been blown off. The horrible remains were laid on a stretcher and Maheude followed them listlessly, with dry, burning eyes. Still holding the sleeping Estelle in her arms she moved away, a tragic figure, with her hair blowing in the wind. When they reached the village Philomène was stupefied for a moment and then at once found relief in floods of tears. But the mother went straight back to Réquillart; she had brought home her son, and now she was going back to wait for her daughter.

Three more days went by. The rescue work had been resumed in unspeakably difficult conditions. Fortunately the explosion had not wrecked the approaches, but the galleries were full of such hot, heavy, and foul air that fresh ventilators had to be installed. Now the colliers had to be relieved every twenty minutes, but they were creeping forward, and scarcely two metres were left between them and their comrades. But they were working with death in their hearts, and if they still hit out hard it was only in a spirit of revenge, for the sounds had stopped, there were no more little rhythmical calls. It was the twelfth day of the rescue work and the fifteenth since the disaster, and ever since morning there had been a silence of death.

The new accident had revived the keenest interest in Montsou, and people were organizing excursions with such enthusiasm that the Grégoires decided to follow the fashion. An outing was arranged, and it was agreed that they would go to Le Voreux in their carriage and meet Madame Hennebeau, who would take Lucie and Jeanne in hers. Deneulin would conduct them round his salvage work, and then they would return by way of Réquillart, where Négrel would let them know exactly how far the tunnelling had reached and whether he still entertained any hope. And they would finish up by all dining together in the evening.

At about three, when the Grégoires and their daughter alighted in front of the ruined pit, they found that Madame Hennebeau had arrived first. She was dressed in sea green and holding a parasol to protect her complexion from the pale February sun. The sky was clear and the weather springlike. Monsieur Hennebeau was there with Deneulin, and as the Grégoires arrived she was listening absent-mindedly as Deneulin was explaining the efforts they had made to dam the canal. Jeanne, who always had her sketchbook with her, had begun to draw, for the horror of the subject was most exciting, whilst Lucie, sitting beside her on the remains of a truck, was prattling away with pleasure and calling it all 'thrilling'. The dam was only half finished and still leaking in many places, and foaming streams rushed along and fell headlong into the enormous hole into which the buildings had subsided. And yet the crater was gradually emptying as the waters soaked away into the earth, and the appalling wreckage at the bottom was coming into sight. Beneath the pale blue sky on this lovely day it looked like a cesspool, or the ruins of a stricken city that had sunk into the mud.

'And we've come all this way to see that!' exclaimed Monsieur Grégoire, feeling decidedly let down.

Cécile, in the pink of health and enjoying the pure fresh air, joked away merrily, but Madame Hennebeau, pouting with distaste, observed:

'The fact of the matter is that it isn't at all pretty!'

The two engineers began to laugh. They tried to entertain the visitors by taking them all round, explaining how the pumps worked and how the pile-driver hammered in the baulks of timber. But the ladies were beginning to get restive. They shuddered on learning that the pumps would have to work for years – perhaps six or seven – before the shaft could be reconstructed and all the water drained from the pit. No, they preferred to think about something else; these upheavals only gave you bad dreams.

'Let's go,' said Madame Hennebeau, making for her carriage.

Jeanne and Lucie protested. What, so soon? And before the drawing was finished? They wanted to stay there, saying that their father would bring them on to dinner in the evening. So Monsieur Hennebeau was the only one to join his wife in the carriage, for he wanted to ask Négrel something too.

'Very well, you go on ahead,' said Monsieur Grégoire. 'We'll follow you, we have a little five-minute call to pay up there in the village. . . . Go on, go on, we'll be at Réquillart by the time you are.'

He climbed up after Madame Grégoire and Cécile, and as the other carriage sped off along the canal theirs slowly climbed the hill.

It was one of their little charities, which they had thought of to complete the outing. Zacharie's death had filled them with pity for the tragic Maheu family whom all the neighbourhood was discussing. They had no sympathy for the father, for he was a villain, a killer of soldiers who had had to be destroyed like a wolf. But the mother touched their hearts; this poor woman had just lost her son after losing her husband, and perhaps by now her daughter was a corpse down below. And besides, there was some talk of a sick grandfather and a boy crippled in a fall, as well as a little girl who had died of hunger during the strike. And so, although to some extent this family had brought its troubles upon itself through its detestable ideas, they had resolved to show how broad-minded their charity was and how they were willing to forgive and forget by bringing some little help with their own hands. Two neatly packed parcels were stowed under one of the seats.

An old woman pointed out the Maheus' house to the coachman – No. 16 in the second block. But when the Grégoires had been set down with their parcels they knocked in vain. They banged on the door with their fists, but still no answer came – nothing but a hollow, mournful echo from a home that seemed to have been emptied by death, frozen, dark and deserted long since.

'There's nobody there,' said Cécile, very disappointed. 'Isn't that tiresome! What are we going to do with all this?'

But suddenly the next door flew open and la Levaque appeared.

'Oh, Monsieur and Madame, I beg your pardon! excuse me, Mademoiselle! If you are looking for my neighbour, she isn't in, she's at Réquillart.'

She told them all about it in a torrent of words, saying that we must all help each other, that she was minding Lénore and Henri so as to let their mother go and wait down there. Her eye had been caught by the parcels, and that led her to speak of her poor widowed daughter, to expatiate on her own poverty with a covetous gleam in her eyes. Then, in a different way, she murmured:

'I've got the key. If the lady and gentleman would really like to go in the grandfather is there.'

The Grégoires looked at her incredulously. What, the grandfather was at home all the time! But nobody answered! Was he asleep, then? But when la Levaque had opened the door the sight that met their eyes pulled them up short.

There was Bonnemort alone, sitting on a chair in front of the empty grate, staring wide-eyed in front of him. The room seemed larger than it really was, now that it was no longer cheered up by the cuckoo clock and the varnished furniture. The only things left on the garish green walls were the portraits of the Emperor and Empress, wearing an official smile of benevolence on their rosy lips. The old man did not move, neither did his eyelids blink in the sudden light of the opening

464

door; he was an imbecile and had not apparently even noticed all the people coming in. At his feet was his tray of ashes, like those put for cats to do their messes in.

'You mustn't mind if he's not very polite,' said la Levaque obligingly. 'Something's gone cracked in his head, it seems. He's never said no more than that for a fortnight now.'

At that moment Bonnemort was shaken by a mighty hawking that seemed to come up from the pit of his stomach, and he spat into his tray – a thick black spittle. The ashes were soaked with it, like coal-mud, all the coal from the pit was being heaved up out of his throat. Then he fell back into his stillness. He never moved now, except once in a while to spit.

Although they were deeply shocked and almost retching with disgust, the Grégoires tried to find a few friendly and encouraging words:

'Well, my good man,' said Papa, 'so you have a cold?'

The old man never moved his head, and his eyes stared at the wall. A heavy silence fell.

'They ought to make you a little tea,' said Mamma.

He remained stiff and dumb.

'Oh, I say, Papa,' said Cécile, 'they did tell us he was infirm but we forgot about it.'

She stopped, feeling very awkward. Having set down on the table some stew and two bottles of wine, she undid the second parcel, out of which she took a pair of huge boots. This was the present intended for the grandfather, and she held one in each hand, puzzled and dismayed as she looked at the swollen feet of the poor old man who would never walk again.

'They've come a little late in the day, haven't they, my man?' went on Monsieur Grégoire, trying to cheer things up a little. 'Never mind, they'll always come in.'

Bonnemort did not hear, did not answer. His face was terrifying to behold, as cold and hard as stone.

So Cécile stealthily put the boots down by the wall. But in spite of her care the hobnails made a clinking noise on the floor, and the huge boots were an eyesore in the room.

'Bless you, he won't ever say thank-you!' exclaimed la

Levaque who had cast deeply envious glances at the boots. 'You might as well give a pair of spectacles to a duck – begging your pardon!'

She talked on, trying to lure the Grégoires into her own house, hoping to touch their hearts. She finally thought of a pretext; she praised Lénore and Henri, who were such nice, sweet children, and so clever, too, answering any questions you asked, just like little angels! They would tell the lady and gentleman anything they wanted to know.

'Are you coming in for a moment, girlie?' asked her father, glad of a chance to get out.

'Yes, I'll come on in a minute,' she replied.

Cécile remained alone with Bonnemort. She stayed behind, spellbound and all of a tremble, because she thought she had seen the old man somewhere before – where could she have come across this square, livid face, all tattooed with coal? And suddenly it came back to her; she saw a sea of yelling people all round her and felt cold hands closing round her neck. Yes, this was the man, she was certain of it as she looked at the hands resting on his knees – the hands of a worker who crouches at his job and whose whole strength is in his wrists, still powerful in old age. Slowly Bonnemort seemed to come back to life; he noticed her and in his gaping way appeared to be examining her, too. His cheeks flushed fiery red and a nervous twitch pulled open his mouth from which dribbled a thin trickle of black saliva. They gazed at each other in fascination, she, buxom, plump, and pink from the long days of well-fed idleness of her race, he blown out with dropsy, hideous and pathetic like some broken-down animal, ravaged by a century of toil and hunger passed down from father to son.

Ten minutes later the Grégoires, wondering what had happened to Cécile, went back into the Maheu home. They uttered a piercing shriek. Their daughter was lying on the floor, blue in the face, strangled. Round her throat were the red marks of a giant's grip. Bonnemort, tottering on his useless legs, had fallen beside her and could not move. His hands were still clutching and he stared at them with bulging, unseeing eyes. In his fall he had broken his tray and spilled the ashes, and the black mud of his spittle had splashed over the room. The pair of boots were still standing by the wall, safe and sound.

It was never possible to establish exactly what had happened. Why had Cécile gone near him? How could Bonnemort have seized her throat, glued as he was to his chair? Obviously once he had got hold of her he had hung on relentlessly, his grip had stifled her cries and he had rolled over with her until the last gasp, for no sound or cry had been heard next door through the thin party wall. It could only be supposed that he had suddenly gone out of his mind and yielded to some inexplicable impulse to murder at the sight of the girl's white throat. People were horrified at such savagery from this broken old man who had lived the respectable life of a beast of burden, quite different from these modern ideas. What kind of rancour, unknown even to himself, could have slowly festered in his vitals and risen to his head? In their horror they could only conclude that he had had no idea what he was doing, that it was the crime of an imbecile.

The Grégoires, on their knees, were sobbing and speechless with grief. The daughter they adored, the daughter for whom they had longed for so many years and then loaded with all their riches, whom they went on tiptoe to watch sleeping, who never seemed well enough fed, never plump enough! Their very life had collapsed; what was there left to live for without her?

La Levaque screamed wildly:

'Oh, the old devil! What *has* he done? Fancy such a thing happening . . . did you ever? and Maheude won't be back until this evening. . . . Shall I go and find her?'

The father and mother were too overwhelmed to answer.

'Perhaps I'd better, eh? All right, I'll go.'

But before going she eyed the boots. The whole village was agog and already a crowd was pushing in. They might get stolen. And anyhow there wasn't a man left in this house who could wear them. She quietly took them. They looked just the right size for Bouteloup.

At Réquillart the Hennebeaus waited a long time for the Grégoires. Négrel had come up from the pit and was giving them a detailed account: it was hoped to get through to the prisoners that very night, but he was sure that they would only bring out their dead bodies, for the deathly silence had not been broken. Maheude was sitting on her baulk behind the engineer's back, white with fear at what he was saying, when la Levaque arrived and told her about her old man's nice trick. All she did was raise her hands in a great gesture of impatience and annoyance. But she followed her home.

Madame Hennebeau nearly fainted. How abominable! Poor, dear Cécile! She had been so merry that day, so full of life only an hour before! Monsieur Hennebeau had to take his wife into Mouque's shack for a moment. He loosened her corset with fumbling hands, for the scent from her bosom excited his senses. In floods of tears she clung to Négrel, who was horrified at this death which put an end to his marriage. And as her husband watched the two of them sharing their grief, a great load fell from his mind. This tragedy settled things nicely: better keep his nephew, for fear it might be the coachman.

[5]

At pit-bottom the water was now waist-deep and the marooned victims were shrieking with terror. The noise of tumbling water was deafening, and the last pieces of lining to fall sounded like the crack of doom. But what turned their terror into horror was the whinneying of the ponies shut up in the stable: the blood-curdling, unforgettable death-cry of animals being slaughtered.

Mouque had let Bataille loose. The aged horse stood trembling and staring with dilated eyes at the ever rising waters. The bottom landing was rapidly filling, and the flood showed greenish in the red light of the three lamps still burning near the vaulted roof. All of a sudden, as the icy water penetrated his coat, Bataille galloped off madly and disappeared down one of the galleries, and the men followed him in a wild dash for safety.

'Nothing doing this way,' shouted Mouque. 'Try Réquillart.'

They were all swept along by the one idea that they might still get through the adjoining disused mine if they could get there before the way was cut off. The twenty of them pushed and shoved each other in single file, with lamps held high to keep them away from the water. Fortunately the gallery sloped slightly upwards and for two hundred metres they struggled on without the water gaining on them. In their frightened hearts old slumbering beliefs came back to consciousness, and they called upon mother earth since it was she who was taking her revenge by bleeding from her veins because a man had cut her arteries. One old man was muttering forgotten prayers and turning out his thumbs to appease the evil spirits of the mine.

A dispute arose at the very first junction. The ponyman wanted to take the left fork, but others swore it would be shorter to the right. A minute was lost.

'Oh, stay there, then, and die, for all I care!' said Chaval brutally. 'I'm going this way.'

He took the right fork, followed by two of the others. The rest ran ahead after old Mouque who, after all, had grown up in the Réquillart pit. But even he was not sure of his bearings, and did not know which way to turn. They were all losing their heads, and even the old stagers could no longer recognize the roads, which seemed to have twisted themselves up into a tangled skein before their very eyes. At each junction they were pulled up by indecision, and yet they had to make up their minds.

Étienne was bringing up the rear, slowed down by Catherine, who was paralysed by weariness and fear. He would have taken the right-hand fork with Chaval, for he thought it was the right way, but he had let him go, even if it meant staying down there for good. And in any case the party went on breaking up, for some others had struck off on their own, leaving only seven following old Mouque.

'Put your arms round my neck and I'll carry you,' Étienne said to the girl, who looked on the point of fainting.

'No, leave me here,' she murmured, 'I can't go on. I'd rather die straight away.'

They had dropped fifty metres behind the others and he was

on the point of picking her up to carry her, willy-nilly, when the road was suddenly blocked: an enormous slab or rock fell in and cut them off from the others. The flood water was already percolating into the rocks and causing falls on all sides. They had to retrace their steps and in so doing they lost their sense of direction. That put an end to any idea of climbing out via Réquillart, and their only hope was to reach the upper levels where they might be rescued if the floods abated.

At last Étienne recognized the Guillaume seam.

'Good!' he said. 'Now I know where we are. Good God! we were on the right road all the time, but it's all one now! Look here, if we go straight ahead we can climb up the chimney.'

Progress was very slow because the water was now up to their chests. So long as they had a light they would not despair, and so they put out one of the lamps in order to save oil, intending to empty it into the other. As they reached the chimney, a noise behind them made them turn. Had the others also been cut off and forced back this way? There was a distant sound of stentorian breathing, like an approaching storm lashing the water into foam. For a moment they were mystified, then they uttered a scream of terror as a gigantic whitish mass loomed up out of the darkness, fighting its way towards them through the narrow timbers between which it was nearly jammed.

It was Bataille. On leaving pit-bottom he had galloped along the black galleries, panic-stricken, but still sure of his way in this underground city where he had lived for eleven years, for his eyes could see quite clearly through the eternal night in which he had spent his life. On and on he galloped, lowering his head, lifting his feet, speeding through these narrow warrens where his great body could only just pass. Roads followed roads and junctions forked this way and that, but he never hesitated. Where was he bound? Over yonder, maybe, towards that dream of his youth, that mill on the Scarpe where he was born, that distant memory of the sun burning up there like a big lamp. He wanted to live, his animal memories came back to him; a longing to breathe once again the air of the plain carried him on, straight on, in the hope of that hole which led out into the light of day under the warm sky. His lifelong resignation was swept away in a fierce revolt against this pit that had first blinded him and now was trying to kill him. The water was pursuing him: now it was lashing his thighs, now licking his rump. But as he plunged onward the galleries narrowed and the roofs came lower, the walls jutted out. Nevertheless he galloped on, grazing his flanks and leaving his bleeding flesh on the jagged timbers. The mine was pressing it on him from every side: it was going to get him and crush the life out of him.

As he came nearer, Catherine and Étienne saw him wedge himself finally between the rocks. In stumbling he had broken both his forelegs. With one last effort he dragged himself a few metres along, but his haunches would not pass through, and there he was, snared and garrotted by the earth. He craned forward his bleeding head, still looking for some crack with his great frightened eyes. The water was rapidly rising over him, and he began to whinney, with the same long-drawn-out, agonized cry with which the other horses had perished in the stable. It was a fearful death; this poor old animal, mutilated, held prisoner, was struggling his last struggle in the bowels of the earth, so far from the light of day. His cry of distress never stopped, and even when the flood reached his mane it still went on, only more raucous, as his mouth stretched upwards, wide open. Then there was a final snoring sound, and a muffled gurgling like a barrel being filled. Then silence.

'Oh, God! take me away!' sobbed Catherine. 'Oh, God, I'm frightened, I don't want to die. Take me away!'

She had looked on death. Neither the collapsing shaft nor the flooded pit had filled her with such horror as this death-cry of Bataille. It went on echoing in her ears and sent a shudder through her whole being.

'Take me away! Take me away!'

Étienne seized her and carried her off. It was high time, for they were in water up to their shoulders as they began to climb up the chimney. He had to help her up, for she had no strength left to hold on to the timbers. Three times he thought he was going to drop her into the deep, swirling waters below.

They were able to stop for a few minutes' breathing space when they reached the first level, where it was still dry. But the water caught them up, and they had to hoist themselves still higher. And so the climb went on for hours as the flood drove them from level to level, always forcing them upwards. At the sixth there was a respite which filled them with excitement and hope, for the water seemed to remain stationary. But then it rose more quickly than before, and they had to climb to the seventh, and then the eighth. There was only one more left, and when they reached that they anxiously watched every centimetre that the water rose. Unless it stopped, was this to be their death, crushed against the roof with water filling up their lungs – like the old horse?

At every moment some new fall re-echoed. The whole mine was convulsed, for its entrails were too weak to hold all this liquid on which the creature was gorged, and they were bursting. Pockets of air, compressed into blind galleries, went off in terrible detonations, splitting the rocks and overthrowing great blocks of earth. This terrifying din of internal cataclysms was like those prehistoric upheavals when deluges turned the earth inside out, burying the mountains under the plains.

Catherine, dazed and shaken by the continuous earthquake, wrung her hands and repeated her never-ending refrain:

'I don't want to die! I don't want to die!'

Étienne tried to reassure her by swearing that the water had stopped moving. Their flight had lasted a good six hours, and somebody was bound to come down to their rescue. He said six hours, but he had no real idea, for they had lost their sense of time. In reality a whole day had already passed while they were climbing through the Guillaume seam.

Wet through and shivering, they settled down to wait. She did not hesitate to take off her clothes and wring out the water, and then put on her jacket and trousers again to dry on her. She was barefoot, and he made her put on his clogs. They had plenty of time ahead of them now, and so they turned the wick of the lamp down until there was only the feeblest glimmer left. It was not until now that gnawing pains in their stomachs reminded them that they were dying of hunger.

Until then they had not had time to notice. They had not had their lunch when the accident occurred, and now they found their sandwiches soaked with water and turned into a mere sop. She had to be angry with him to make him accept a share. As soon as she had eaten she fell asleep, exhausted, on the cold earth. But he was tortured by wakefulness and sat with his head in his hands watching over her.

How many hours went by like this? They could not have said. All he knew was that there in front of him the creeping black water had reappeared at the mouth of the chimney, as though the malignant beast were arching his back so as to reach them. At first it was only a thin trickle, like a sinuous lengthening serpent, but it broadened into the back of a sinister, crawling animal, then it caught them up and soon the sleeping girl's feet were in the water. He could not decide whether to wake her up, for it seemed cruel to drag her from rest, from this happy oblivion which was perhaps lulling her in dreams of open air and life in the sunshine. Besides, where was there to go? As he pondered he remembered that the incline serving this part of the seam communicated with the one serving the next level. There was a way out. But he let her sleep on as long as possible, keeping an eye on the advancing water, waiting for it to hound them on. Then he gently lifted her, and she shuddered:

'Oh, so it's true then! My God, it's starting all over again.'

As it all came back to her and she saw death drawing near she began crying out in a loud voice.

'No, keep calm,' he said softly, 'I'm sure there is a way through.'

In order to reach the incline they had to walk bent double and were soaked once again right up to the shoulders. Another climb began, but this was a more dangerous one, as the tunnel was a hundred metres long and timbered throughout. They began by trying to pull the cable so as to make one of the trucks fast at the bottom, for if the others were to come down while they were climbing they would be smashed to smithereens. But something had fouled the mechanism, and it would not move. So they had to risk it, not daring to hold on to the cable, which got in their way, breaking their nails on the smooth, slippery timbers. He followed her and when she slipped back with bleeding hands steadied her with his head. Suddenly they ran into a splintered beam which barred the way up. There had been a fall of earth and they could not climb any higher. Mercifully there was a doorway just there, and they came out on to a road.

They were thunderstruck to see a lamp burning in front of them and to hear a man's voice shouting angrily:

'Some more clever Dicks who are as silly as I am!'

It was Chaval, cut off by the same fall that had blocked the incline and killed the two others who had set off with him. He had been injured in the elbow, but had had the courage to crawl back and take their lamps and search them for their sandwiches. As he was making his escape a final collapse had blocked the gallery behind him.

His first thought was to swear to himself that he would never share his provisions with these survivors from below. Sooner strike them dead! Then he recognized them and dropping his blustering manner he began to laugh, an unpleasant gloating laugh.

'Oh, it's you, Catherine! So you have come a cropper and want your man back again. Well, well! We're in for a fine old time together!'

He pretended not to see Étienne, whose first reaction had been an instinctive move to protect the girl clinging to him. But the situation had to be faced, and Étienne merely asked his mate, as though they had parted the best of friends an hour before:

'Have you explored the other end! Can't we get out by the coal-faces?'

'The faces? Lord, no, they've fallen in too, and we're between two walls, in a proper trap. But you can go back by the incline if you're a good diver.'

It was true; the water was still rising and they could hear it lapping. Their retreat was already cut off. He was right, they were caught in a trap, a length of gallery cut off at each end by heavy falls of rock. No way out: the three of them were immured together.

'So you've decided to stay?' jeered Chaval. 'Well, it's the

best thing you can do, and if you don't interfere with me I won't even talk to you. There's still room for two men here. We shall soon see which dies first, unless somebody comes to the rescue, which looks unlikely to me!'

Étienne went on:

'If we tapped somebody might hear.'

'I'm sick and tired of tapping. You have a go yourself with this stone!'

Étienne picked up the piece of sandstone that the other man had already half worn away, went to the end and beat out the miners' recall, the long roll used by men in peril to show where they are. Then he put his ear to the rock and listened. He went on obstinately a score of times. No answer came.

Meanwhile Chaval was ostentatiously settling himself in. First he put his three lamps down in a row against the wall; only one burning, the others were for later. Then he set out on a piece of timber his two remaining sandwiches. That was the sideboard. With due care he could last two days on that. He turned round and said:

'You know, Catherine, half of this is for you if you get too hungry.'

She said nothing. This was the last refinement of misery, to be back again between these two men.

The dreadful existence began. Neither Étienne nor Chaval opened his mouth, although they were sitting on the ground almost side by side. Once Chaval made a remark and Étienne put out his lamp, which was a useless luxury; then they relapsed into silence. Feeling uncomfortable at the way her former lover was looking at her, Catherine took up a position near Étienne, lying at his side. As the hours dragged on the only sounds were the lapping of the steadily rising water, and from time to time distant shocks and reverberations as the mine finally caved in. When the lamp gave out and they had to open another to light it, the thought of fire-damp made them hesitate for a moment, but they preferred to be blown up at once than to last on in darkness. However, there was no gas and no explosion. They lay down again and the hours of waiting went on.

A noise startled Étienne and Catherine and made them look

up. Chaval had decided to have some food: he had cut a sandwich in two and was chewing very slowly to resist the temptation to swallow it all at once. They watched him, tortured by hunger.

'You're sure you won't have any?' he asked Catherine in a provocative way. 'You are making a mistake.'

She lowered her eyes for fear of giving in, for the pain in her stomach was so agonizing that she had tears in her eyes. But she understood what he wanted. Once already that morning he had breathed down her neck. One of his old fits of lust had come over him through seeing her near the other man. She knew that flicker in his eyes as he invited her, it was the old flame of his jealous rage when he used to fall on her with blows and accuse her of committing abominations with her mother's lodger. But she did not want to, fearing that if she returned to him the two men would fly at each other's throats in this narrow cave where they were all facing death together. Oh God, couldn't they end up as friends?

Étienne would rather have starved to death than beg a mouthful of bread from Chaval. The silence grew more and more ominous, and eternity seemed to stretch out before them as the slow, monotonous minutes went by one by one, hopelessly. They had lived shut up together for a whole day. The second lamp burned low and they lit the third.

Chaval began his second sandwich.

'Come on, silly!' he growled.

Catherine shuddered. Étienne turned away so as to leave her free. But still she did not move, and he whispered to her: 'Go on, my dear!'

Then the tears she had been holding back gushed forth and she cried for a long time, too weak to get to her feet or even to know whether she was hungry or not, for by now the pain was torturing her whole body. Étienne got to his feet and paced up and down, vainly tapping out the miners' call, lashed to madness by the thought that what little life he had left was to be spent tied to this detestable rival. Not even room to get away from each other to die! He could not walk ten steps without having to turn round and collide with this man. And the poor girl – they were still fighting over her even in the

476

depths of the earth! She would go to the survivor, and if he went first this man would rob him of her yet again. It went on and on, hour followed hour, and the promiscuity of their lives became more and more disgusting, what with their foul breath and the stench of the bodily needs they had had to satisfy in front of each other. Twice he made a rush at the wall of rock as though he expected to split it open with his fists.

Another day drew to its close, and Chaval was sitting by Catherine, with whom he was sharing his last half sandwich. She was painfully chewing each mouthful, and he made her pay for each one with a kiss, in his jealous determination not to die before he had possessed her in front of the other man. In her exhausted state she was beginning to yield, but when he attempted to take her she cried out in pain:

'Oh, leave off, you're hurting me!'

Trembling with emotion, Étienne had thrust his face against the pit-props so as not to see. But now he jumped round in a rage:

'Take your bloody hands off her!'

'What's it got to do with you?' said Chaval. 'She's my woman, and I can do what I like with her, can't I?'

He seized her again and held her tight in his arms, out of bravado, crushing his red moustache to her mouth. Then he said:

'Leave us alone, see! Kindly buzz off!'

Étienne, pale to the lips, shouted:

'If you don't leave her alone I'll throttle you!'

The other stood up at once, realizing from the tone of Étienne's voice that he was determined to make an end of things. Death seemed too slow for them, and one of them had to make way for the other at once. The old feud had come to a head again here in the earth where they would soon be sleeping side by side; and space was so cramped that they could not even raise their fists at each other without grazing them.

'Look out,' snarled Chaval. 'This time I'm going to get you!'

Then Étienne went mad. A red mist swam before his eyes

477

and blood surged up to his head. The blood-lust was upon him, as imperious as a physical need, as a lump of phlegm in the throat that makes you cough. It rose up in him and his will-power was swept away before the onrush of his hereditary taint. He laid hold of a flake of shale in the wall, tugged it from side to side until it came away. Huge and heavy though it was he raised it in both hands, and with superhuman strength brought it down on Chaval's skull.

He did not even have time to jump back, but went down with his face smashed in and skull split open. His brains spattered the gallery roof and a red flood streamed like a steady flowing spring, making a pool which reflected the smoky flame of the lamp. Darker shadows seemed to invade the narrow enclosed space, and the black corpse on the ground looked like a heap of slack.

Étienne stood over him, staring with dilated eyes. So he had done it, he had killed a man! All his past struggles swam through his consciousness; the unavailing fight against the latent poison in his system, the slowly accumulated alcohol in his blood. And yet he was far from drunk now, unless it were with hunger. The drunkenness of his parents long ago had sufficed. Though his hair stood on end at the horror of this murder, though all his upbringing cried out in protest, his heart was beating faster with sheer joy, the animal joy of an appetite satisfied at last. And then there was pride, the pride of the stronger. He had a fleeting vision of that young soldier's throat slit by a knife – killed by a child. Now he had killed, too.

Catherine, standing motionless, uttered a wild shriek.

'Oh God! He's dead!'

'Are you sorry?' asked Étienne brutally.

She gasped and made incoherent sounds, then swayed and fell into his arms.

'Oh, kill me too! Let's die together!'

She wound her arms round his shoulders in a fierce embrace, which he returned, and they wished they could die. But death was in no hurry, and they loosened their embrace. She hid her eyes while he dragged the body along and threw it down the incline, so as to clear the narrow space where they had to go on living. Life would not have been possible with that corpse in the way. They were horrified when they heard it plop into the water, splashing up a cloud of spray. So the water had already filled that great hole? Yes, they could see it now, it had overflowed into the gallery.

A new battle set in. They had lit the last lamp, and as the oil was burning away they could see the water mounting steadily, relentlessly. First it touched their ankles and soon it had reached their knees. The road ran uphill and they retreated to the upper end which gave them a few hours' respite. But the water caught them up, and now it was waist-high, Standing with their backs to the rocky wall they watched it rise and rise, and still rise, knowing that when it reached their mouths it would be all over. They had hung up the lamp and it cast its yellow light on the tiny wavelets of the advancing flood, but as the flame waned all they could see was a rapidly shrinking semicircle on which the darkness was encroaching with the rising water. Then suddenly the blackness enveloped them as the lamp went out with a final splutter. Now it was total, absolute night, the darkness of the earth where they would sleep without ever setting eyes on daylight again.

'Bloody hell!' swore Étienne.

Catherine crept close to him, as though she had felt the shadows snatching at her. In a quiet voice she repeated the miners' proverb:

'Death blows out the lamp.'

And yet their instinct fought on, and the very will to live gave them strength. He began jabbing at the shaly wall with the hook of the lamp, and she helped him with her nails. They made a sort of high shelf, and when they had hauled themselves up on to it they managed to sit there with their legs dangling and their backs bent, for the roof forced them to lower their heads. Now it was only their heels that were frozen by the water, but before long they felt its icy touch on their ankles, up their calves, on their knees, as it continued its inexorable advance. They had not been able to level out the seat properly, and when it was wet it became so slippery that they had to hold tight for fear of slipping off. This must surely be the end, for how long could they go on waiting with no space except this niche on which they dared not move, and exhausted and hungry, with no food or light left? The darkness tormented them by denying them even the sight of approaching death. There was no sound: the mine was now saturated with water and was lying still. The only thing they were conscious of was the tide silently rising from the depths of the galleries.

Hours followed black hours, though they could not keep an exact account, as their sensation of time grew more and more confused. Instead of making the minutes drag, the torments they were enduring made them fly swiftly by. They thought they had been buried for only two days and a night, whereas in fact the third day was already drawing to its close. They had given up all hope of being rescued, for nobody knew they were there and nobody could possibly come down. Hunger would finish them even if the flood relented. They thought of tapping out the signal one last time, but the stone was under water, and in any case who could hear?

Catherine was sitting in hopeless resignation, with her aching head propped against the wall, when she suddenly jumped and said:

'Listen!'

At first Étienne thought she meant the lapping of the rising water. He lied, trying to reassure her.

'No, it's me, moving my legs.'

'No, no, I don't mean that. Over that side, listen!'

She put her ear to the coal. He understood and did the same. They held their breath for seconds together. Then they heard three taps, widely spaced, very soft and very far away. But still they could not believe it – there were noises in their ears, or it might be the coal cracking. And they did not know what to answer with.

Étienne had an idea.

'You've got my clogs. Take them off and tap with the heels.'

She did, beating out the miners' signal. They listened again, and again they heard the distant three taps. They did so a score of times, and each time the answer came. They burst into tears and embraced, at the risk of overbalancing. At last

480

their comrades were there, they were coming. All the torments of the long vigil, the frustration of endless tapping with never a reply, were forgotten in an upsurge of love and joy, as though their rescuers had only to pick away the rock with one finger and let them out.

'Wasn't it a bit of luck that I rested my head against the wall!' she laughed.

'Oh, you certainly have an ear! I didn't hear anything.'

From then on they took it in turns to listen and answer the slightest signal. Soon they heard the noise of picks: they were beginning to cut a way through, opening up a gallery. Not a sound escaped them. But their joy was short-lived. It was all very well to laugh and try to deceive each other, but despair gradually overtook them. At first they went in for elaborate explanations: they were coming via Réquillart, the gallery they were hewing ran downhill into the seam, perhaps they were opening up more than one, for they could hear three men at it. But they talked less and finally relapsed into silence as they began to work out the enormous thickness of earth between them and their comrades, each one mentally calculating the days and days it would take a man to pierce through such a mass. They would never get through in time, and both of them would be dead twenty times over. Not daring to exchange a word in their increasing agony of mind, they gloomily answered the signals by tapping with the heels of the clogs, but it was without hope, and simply out of an automatic instinct to show the others that they were still alive.

Another day passed, and another. They had now been underground for six days. The water had stopped at their knees, neither rising nor falling, and their legs seemed to be melting away in this ice-bath. They could lift them out for about an hour, but by then the unnatural posture brought on such unbearable cramp that they had to let them drop down again. Every ten minutes they had to lift their buttocks with a jerk for fear of sliding off the slippery ledge. Jagged edges of coal stuck into their backs and they had acute and ceaseless pain in the back of the neck through having to keep their heads constantly bent forward under the low roof. The

481

atmosphere became more and more stifling because the water had compressed the air into the sort of cloche in which they were imprisoned. If they spoke the muffled tones seemed to come from a great distance. Noises in their heads sounded like the jangling of bells gone mad, or a herd of animals galloping on and on in pelting hail.

At first Catherine suffered unspeakable tortures of hunger, and clawed desperately at her breast while her breath came in long agonizing moans, and her stomach felt as if it were being dragged out of her with pincers. Étienne, suffering the same pains, was desperately feeling in the darkness when his fingers touched a piece of rotting timber which broke up as he scratched it. He gave Catherine a handful which she swallowed voraciously. For two days they lived on worm-eaten wood, finishing the whole piece, and when there was no more they almost tore themselves to pieces trying to eat other bits that were still solid wood and too hard. As their torments grew worse and worse they were furious to find that they could not chew the cloth of their garments. His leather belt gave them some slight relief. He bit it into small pieces and she chewed them up and forced herself to swallow them. At any rate it occupied their jaws and gave them an illusion of eating. When the belt was finished they returned to the cloth, sucking it for hours on end.

In time, however, the violent paroxysms passed away, and hunger became just a dull, deep-seated pain, the sensation of a slow and steady draining away of their strength. They might have succumbed earlier had they not had as much water as they wanted. They only had to lean forward and drink from their hands, and this they did over and over again, for they were parched with a thirst that all this water could not quench.

On the seventh day Catherine was leaning forward to drink when her hand touched an object floating in front of her.

'Look here, what's this?' she said.

Étienne felt in the darkness.

'I don't understand. It feels like the cover of a ventilator door.'

She drank the water, but as she was taking up some more

the object touched her hand again, and she uttered a terrible shriek.

'It's him! Oh God!'

'Who?'

'Him. You know. I felt his moustache.'

It was Chaval's body, which the rising water had borne up the incline and washed up to them. Étienne put out his hand and felt the moustache and smashed nose, and shook with horror and disgust. Seized with a terrible nausea Catherine spewed out the water still in her mouth. She felt she had been drinking blood, that all this deep water in front of her was that man's blood.

'Wait a minute,' said Étienne. 'I'll push it away.'

He gave the corpse a kick and it floated off. But soon it was hitting their legs again.

'Go away, for Christ's sake!'

But after a third time Étienne had to let it stay, for some current kept bringing it back. Chaval would not go; he was determined to stay with them, right up against them. This gruesome companion added his foul stench to the vitiated air. All through that day they did not drink, but fought down their thirst, preferring death, but the next day their sufferings won, and they moved the body aside for each mouthful. What had been the use of killing him if he was still to come between them with his obstinate jealousy? He would always be there to prevent their coming together, even in death, even to the end.

Yet another day, and another. With each wavelet Étienne could feel the gentle touch of the man he had killed – just a touch to remind him he was there. And each touch made him shudder. Étienne constantly visualized him, swollen and green with his red moustache in his smashed face. Then his memory began to play him tricks; perhaps he had not killed him after all, he was swimming and about to bite. Catherine had now given way to long fits of weeping, followed by a state of semi-consciousness. In the end she became invincibly drowsy. He would wake her up, but she would only say a few disconnected words and fall asleep again without even opening her eyes, and so to prevent her falling into the water he kept one arm round her waist. Now he alone answered the signals which were coming nearer behind him, but his own strength was failing and he had not the heart to go on tapping. They knew they were here, so why go on tiring oneself? He no longer cared whether they came or not. The long wait had so stupefied him that for hours together he did not even know what he was waiting for.

There came one slight relief. The water receded a little and Chaval's body went away. The rescue party had been at work for nine days and they themselves were able for the first time to walk a few steps along the gallery, when a fearful explosion threw them to the ground. They felt their way to each other and stood clinging together in terror, not understanding what had happened and thinking that the catastrophe was beginning all over again. But there was not another sound; the noise of the rescuers' picks had ceased.

In the corner where they were sitting side by side Catherine suddenly broke into a little titter.

'It must be lovely outside. Come on, let's go out.'

At first Étienne tried to fight against this delirium, but even his stronger head began to catch the contagion, and he lost his sense of reality. All their senses were beginning to play tricks on them, especially Catherine's, who was now wandering in her mind and finding relief in incessant chatter and fidgeting. The noises in her head were now babbling brooks or warbling birds, she could smell a strong scent of newly trodden grass and clearly see big yellow things waving in the air, so big that she thought she was out by the canal in the cornfields on a bright sunny day.

'Isn't it hot here? Take me, and let's stay together always and always!'

He held her tight and she nestled up against him for a long time, chattering like a happy child:

'How silly we have been to wait all this long time! I would have loved you from the very beginning, only you did not realize it! You sulked. . . . And then do you remember how we couldn't sleep at night, but lay with our noses in the air listening to each other's breathing, and all the time dying for each other?'

Her gaiety was infectious, and he too began joking about memories of their unspoken love.

'You hit me once. Oh yes you did! On both cheeks.'

'That was because I loved you. But, you see, I wouldn't let myself think about you. I told myself it was all over between us. But all the time I really knew that we should come together some day. All we wanted was a chance, just some lucky chance, didn't we?'

A cold shudder ran through him, and he wanted to shake her out of this dream of hers. But he went on:

'It's never all over. All you need is a little happiness, and it begins all over again.'

'Then will you keep me? It's the real thing this time, isn't it?'

She was so weak that she fell limp in his arms, and her voice died away. He was frightened, and he held her close to his heart.

'Are you ill?'

She started up in surprise.

'No, of course not. Why?'

But the question had wakened her out of her dream. She looked round in the darkness, clasped and unclasped her hands and burst into a fresh fit of sobbing.

'Oh God! How dark it is!'

Gone were the cornfields, the scent of the grass, the song of the larks, and the golden sunshine. She was back in the flooded pit, in the stinking darkness, the lugubrious drip-drip in this cavern in which they had been dying for so many days. Her hallucination made it all the more horrible, and she went back to the superstitions of her childhood and saw the Black Man, the old miner who came back from the grave to wring the necks of bad girls in the mine.

'Listen. Did you hear?'

'No, nothing. I can't hear anything.'

'Yes, I tell you! It's the Man . . . you know . . . look, there he is. The earth has let all the blood out of her veins, out of revenge for having an artery cut. And there he is, look! blacker than night. Oh, I'm afraid, I'm afraid!'

She stopped, but was shaking violently. Then she whispered:

485

'No. It's still the other one.'

'What other one?'

'The one who's still with us. The one who's dead.'

She was haunted by the vision of Chaval, and rambled on about him, about their cat and dog life together, the one day when he had been nice to her, in Jean-Bart, and the other days of alternate caresses and blows, when he half-killed her with his embraces after nearly beating her to death.

'He's coming, I tell you he is, and he is going to stop our being together yet again. It's still the same old jealousy. Oh, send him away, and keep me – all of me!'

She clung impetuously to him, found his mouth and pressed it passionately with hers. The darkness rolled away, she saw the sun, and laughed the serene laugh of a young girl in love. Feeling her half naked body through her rags, so close to his, his virility returned, and he took her. This at last was their wedding night, in this tomb, on this bed of mud. They could not die before having their happiness, they must live and pass on life one last time. They loved each other in despair, in death itself.

There was no sequel. For hour after hour Étienne sat in the same corner and Catherine lay quite still on his knees. For a long time he thought she was asleep, but when he felt her she was very cold, she was dead. Even so he did not move for fear of waking her. He dwelt with deep emotion on the thought that he had been the first to possess her womanhood, and that she could now bear a child of his. And other thoughts came, but so vaguely that they merely touched his brow like the very breath of sleep – how lovely to set off with her, the happy things they would do later on. For he was weakening and only had strength left to make a little stroking movement with his hand to feel whether she was still there, stiff and cold, like a sleeping child. Everything sank away, even the darkness itself. He was nowhere, beyond space and time. And yet something was still tapping near his head, and the taps were getting louder; but at first he had felt too lazy to reply, too tired, and now he hardly knew, but somehow dreamed that she was walking in front of him and that he could hear the light tap of her clogs. Two days passed in this way and she had not stirred, but he stroked her automatically, glad to know she was so quiet.

He felt a shock. Voices were murmuring and stones were rolling down at his feet. Then he saw a lamp and burst into tears. He blinked at the light and kept his eyes fixed in ecstasy on the little red flame that scarcely dispelled the gloom. Now his friends were carrying him along, he allowed them to pour a few spoonfuls of broth between his clenched teeth. He was already in the Réquillart gallery before he recognized one of them: Négrel, the engineer, standing in front of him. And the two men, who had despised each other, the defiant workman and the sarcastic, sceptical chief, embraced and wept together, pouring out the deep springs of their common humanity. Into their bitter grief entered all the misery of countless generations, all the immeasurable sorrow of human life.

At the surface Maheude fell down beside her dead Catherine and uttered cry after cry, long, endless moans. Several other bodies had already been brought up and laid in a line on the ground: Chaval who, it was assumed, had been crushed by a fall of rock, a lad and two colliers smashed in the same way, with the brains gone from their skulls and their bellies swollen with water. Women in the crowd went out of their minds and tore their clothes and scratched their own faces. When they brought Étienne up at last, after having accustomed him to lamplight and given him some food, he was a skeleton with hair as white as snow. People in the crowd turned away, shuddering at the sight of this old man. Even Maheude stopped her wailing and looked at him stupidly, with great staring eyes.

$$\lceil 6 \rceil$$

I⊤ was four o'clock in the morning. The warmth of approaching day was beginning to succeed the cool April night and the stars were waning in the clear sky as dawn touched the east with red. Only the faintest stir animated the black, slumbering countryside, the vague sounds heralding reawakening life.

Étienne was striding along the Vandame road. He had been six weeks in a hospital bed at Montsou. Though he was still very pale and thin, he felt strong enough to go, and he was going. The Company, still trembling for the safety of its pits and carrying out successive dismissals, had notified him that he could not be kept on. This had been accompanied by the award of a grant of one hundred francs, with paternal advice that he should give up work in the mines which was now too strenuous for him. But he had refused their hundred francs, having already had a letter from Pluchart calling him to Paris and enclosing his fare. His old dream had come true. After leaving hospital the day before, he had slept at the Bon Joyeux, at widow Désir's, and he had got up very early, with only one thing left to do: say good-bye to his friends before catching the eight o'clock train at Marchiennes.

Étienne stood still for a moment in the middle of the street in the rosy light of dawn. It was good to breathe the pure air of early spring, and it was going to be a lovely day. As it grew gradually lighter the life of the earth began to rise with the sun. Then he walked on again, loudly striking the ground with his dogwood stick, and watching the distant plain emerge from the mists of the night. He had seen nobody: Maheude had come to see him once at the hospital, but had no doubt been prevented from coming again. What he did not know was that the whole of Village 240 was now working in Jean-Bart and that she had gone back to work there herself.

Gradually the deserted roads filled with people, and silent, pale-faced miners continually passed Étienne. He had heard that the Company was taking advantage of its victory. When they returned to work, beaten by hunger after two and a half months of strike, the miners had had to accept the separate rate for timbering, that disguised wage-cut which was now more hateful than ever, being stained with the blood of their friends. They were being robbed of an hour's work and made to break their oath never to yield, and this enforced perjury stuck in their throats with the bitterness of gall. Work was beginning again everywhere: at Mirou, Madeleine, Crèvecœur and La Victoire. Everywhere, in the morning mist, along the shadowy roads, the trampling herd could be seen, lines of men plodding along with their noses to the ground like cattle being driven to the slaughterhouse. They were shivering in their thin cotton clothes, their arms folded for warmth, shambling and hunched up so that the *briquet*, held between shirt and coat, looked like a deformity. But behind this mass return to work, these silent dark shapes with never a smile or glance to the side, you could sense jaws set in anger and hearts bursting with hatred. They had only knuckled under because compelled to by starvation.

The nearer he came to the pit the more of them he saw. Most of them walked alone, and those who were in groups followed each other in single file, tired out already, and sick of themselves and everybody else. He noticed one old man with eyes blazing like burning coals under his livid brow. Another, quite young, was panting as he walked, and it was like the breath of a pent-up storm. Many had their clogs in their hands and he could hardly hear the soft pad of their stockinged feet. The stream flowed on endlessly, like the forced march of a routed army, tramping head down, sullenly absorbed in its fierce determination to fight again and be revenged.

As Étienne reached Jean-Bart the pit was emerging from the shadows and the lanterns on the trestles were still burning in the growing daylight. Above the dark buildings rose the white plume of an exhaust, delicately tinted with carmine. He took the stairway of the screening-shed and made his way into the pit head.

The descent was about to begin, and men were coming up from the locker-room. He paused for a moment in the midst of the din and bustle. Rumbling tubs shook the sheet-iron flooring, drums were turning, unwinding cables to the accompaniment of shouting megaphones, the ringing of bells and the clatter of the signal hammer. Here once again was the monster gulping down his ration of human flesh, cages emerged and plunged down again into the abyss loaded with men, bolted down tirelessly by the insatiable giant. Since the accident he had a nervous dread of pits, and as the cages went down his stomach turned over. He had to look away, he could not stand it.

489

In the great dark shed, only dimly lit by the guttering lamps, he could not make out a single face he knew. The miners waiting there barefoot, lamp in hand, looked at him with wide enquiring eyes, and then looked down or turned away in embarrassment. They evidently knew him, but, far from bearing malice, they seemed to be afraid of him, reddening with shame as though he were reproaching them for cowardice. Saddened by this attitude, he forgot that these were the brutes who had stoned him, and found himself dreaming once again of turning them into heroes, leading the people, that force of nature feeding upon itself.

A cage filled with men and disappeared, and as others moved up he at last recognized one of his stalwarts of the strike, a good fellow who had sworn to die before surrendering.

'You too!' he said, deeply shocked.

The man looked confused and mumbled vaguely, then said apologetically:

'What else can I do? I'm a married man.'

He knew all the next group to move up.

'You too! You too! You too!'

They all muttered shamefacedly:

'I've got my mother . . . my children . . . we must eat!'

As the cage did not come up at once they stood about gloomily waiting, so depressed by their defeat that they avoided each other's eyes and looked steadfastly at the shaft.

'What about Maheude?' asked Étienne.

Nobody answered. One made a sign that she was coming. Others raised their arms in a pitying gesture as if to say: oh, poor woman! what she was going through! But the silence was unbroken, and when he held out his hand in farewell they all shook it vigorously and put into this silent grip all their bitterness at having had to give in and fervent hopes of revenge. The cage came up, they got in and were swallowed in the abyss.

Pierron came on the scene, wearing the open lamp of a deputy in his leather cap. A week since he had been promoted to master haulier, and the workers moved to one side, for promotion had turned his head. He was taken aback at seeing Étienne, but came up to him and was very relieved when he learned that he was leaving. They had a chat. His wife now managed the Progrès bar thanks to the gentlemen who were all so kind to her. But he broke off to read a lecture to old Mouque, accusing him of not having brought up his horse-dung at the regulation time. The old man humbly listened with bowed head. But he was outraged by this reprimand, and before going down he also shook Étienne's hand with the same long, warm grip, full of suppressed anger and eloquent with promise of future rebellion. Étienne was so touched to feel the old man's hand trembling in his, showing that he bore him no ill-will for the death of his children, that he watched him go without a word.

'Isn't Maheude coming this morning?' he asked Pierron.

At first Pierron pretended not to understand, for there were times when it seemed to bring him bad luck even to talk about her. He began to move off, on the pretext that some order had to be given, but relented and said:

'What? Maheude? Yes, here she comes.'

Yes, here she was, coming from the locker-room with her lamp, wearing trousers and coat and with her head covered by a cap. The Company, touched by the poor woman's sad plight, had made a special exception in her favour and allowed her to work underground at the age of forty. But as it seemed difficult to put her back on to tramming she had been given the job of working a little hand ventilator that had been installed in the North Gallery, in those infernal regions under Le Tartaret, where the air never circulated. And there, for ten back-breaking hours, she turned her wheel in a tunnel of fire, roasting in a temperature of over a hundred degrees.* She earned thirty sous.

Seeing her standing there, a pitiful sight in her men's clothes, with her stomach and bosom distended with water from the pit, Étienne was so deeply moved that he could hardly find words to tell her that he was off and had come to say good-bye.

She looked at him without taking in what he was saying, but said at length:

'You are surprised to see me here, eh? It's true I said I

* 40° Centigrade.

would strangle the first of mine to go back again, and here I am going down, so I should strangle myself, I suppose? Ah well, I would have done so before this if I hadn't got the old man and the children at home!'

She talked on in her quiet, weary voice, not trying to make excuses for herself but just saying how things were. They had almost starved to death and she had had to make up her mind to it, otherwise they would have been turned out of the village.

'How's the old man?'

'Still very quiet and clean. But his head is quite cracked. He wasn't found guilty of that business, you know. They wanted to put him in the madhouse, but I wouldn't have it. They'd have finished him off with a dose of something in his soup. But it has done us a lot of harm, because they'll never give him a pension now – one of the gentlemen told me it would be immoral to give him one.'

'Is Jeanlin working?'

'Yes, the gentlemen have found him a job above ground. He gets twenty sous. Oh, I don't complain. They have been very kind to me, as they have pointed out. The boy's twenty and my thirty make fifty – enough to live on if there weren't six of us. Estelle is weaned now and has to be fed, and the worst of it is that there are another four or five years to wait before Lénore and Henri are old enough to go down the mine.'

Étienne could not withhold an expression of grief.

'Them too!'

Maheude's pale cheeks coloured and her eyes blazed. But her shoulders sagged, as though weighed down by destiny.

'What can we do? They'll have to go after the others. All the rest have left their dead bodies in the job and now it'll be their turn.'

She had to stop as some labourers rumbled their tubs past them. Daylight was filtering through the grimy windows and the lamps shed an uncertain glimmer in the grey light. The engine started up every three minutes, the cables unwound and the cages went on swallowing men.

'Come on, you lazy devils, hurry up!' shouted Pierron. 'Get into the cages, or we shall never be done today.'

He looked at Maheude, but she did not move. She had

already let three cages go, but now she seemed to wake up from a dream, remembering Étienne's first words.

'So you're off?'

'Yes, this morning!'

'You're right. Better go somewhere else if you can. And I'm glad I've seen you, because anyhow you'll know that I don't bear you any ill-will. There was a time when I could have killed you, just after all that slaughter. But you have second thoughts, don't you? And then you realize that in the long run it isn't anybody's fault. No, no, it isn't your fault, it's everybody's fault.'

Now she could talk quite calmly about her dead: her husband, Zacharie, and Catherine, but her eyes did fill with tears when she mentioned the name of Alzire. She was once again the sensible, phlegmatic woman she used to be, taking a reasonable view of things. It wouldn't do the bourgeois any good, she reflected, to have killed so many poor people, and some day they would be punished for it, because everything has to be paid for. There wouldn't even be any need for them to do anything about it, for the whole show would blow up of its own accord, and the soldiers would shoot the employers just as they had shot the workers. In the resignation and disciplined subservience that she had inherited from a century of forebears a change had come about: she was sure now that injustice could not last much longer, and that if God was no more, some other Force would assuredly spring up and avenge the downtrodden.

She was speaking softly and furtively looking about her. Then as Pierron came within earshot she went on in a loud voice:

'Ah well, so you're going! You will have to pick up your things at home. There are still two shirts, three handkerchiefs, and an old pair of trousers.'

Étienne waved away this offer of the few things of his that had not gone to the dealers.

'No, don't bother about them, they'll come in for the children. I can get fixed up in Paris.'

Two more cages had gone down, and Pierron made up his mind to address her directly:

493

'Look here, you, we're waiting. Have you nearly finished your little chat?'

She turned her back on him. What right had this traitor to be so zealous? The descent was none of his business anyway, and the men on his level hated him enough as it was. . . . So there she stayed, lamp in hand, freezing in the draught, although the weather outside was so warm.

Neither of them could think of anything else to say. They stood looking at each other, and their hearts were so full that they wished there was something else to put into words.

She finally said something just for the sake of talking:

'La Levaque is in the family way. Levaque is in prison, and so meanwhile Bouteloup is taking his place.'

'Bouteloup, oh yes, of course!'

'Oh, and did I tell you? Philomène has gone off.'

'Gone off! Where?'

'Gone off with a miner from the Pas-de-Calais. I was afraid she might leave the two children with me, but she has taken them with her. What do you think of that – a woman spitting blood and looking as though she were going to kick the bucket at any moment!'

She mused for a moment and then went on in her drawling voice:

'The things they said about me! You remember, they said I slept with you. Of course, after my man died it could very easily have happened if I'd been younger, couldn't it? Still I'm very glad now that it didn't, because I'm sure we should have regretted it.'

'Yes, we should have regretted it,' was all Étienne could say.

And that was the last thing they said. There was a cage waiting and she was angrily told to get in or else be fined. She then decided to shake hands and go. Looking at her, so faded and old, with her bloodless face and untidy wisps of greying hair showing under her blue cap, and her body, the shapeless body of a female worn out with bearing young, all flabby under her cotton coat and trousers, he felt sad beyond words. But in this last handshake of hers he felt the same long, affectionate grip, with its silent promise to be there on the

494

day when the struggle was resumed. He read the message of calm faith in her eyes: good-bye until the big day.

'Of all the bloody lazy creatures!' shouted Pierron.

She was hustled into a tub pell-mell with four others, the signal-rope was pulled for the meat-call, the cage fell away into the darkness and nothing was left but the flying cable.

Then Étienne left the pit. On his way down, in the screening-shed, he saw an individual sitting on a thick bed of coal with his legs stretched out stiff in front of him. It was Jeanlin, working as a cleaner of large coal. He held a large block of coal between his legs and hammered away bits of shale, and he was so enveloped in a cloud of fine, black dust that Étienne would never have recognized him had he not raised his monkey face and shown his protruding ears and green eyes. He laughed out of bravado, broke his block with a final blow and vanished in a rising cloud of blackness.

Back in the open air, Étienne walked along the road absorbed in a welter of confused thoughts. But he also took deep breaths of the pure air and rejoiced in the space and sky. The sun was mounting triumphant over the horizon and the whole countryside was awakening to a new and happy day. From east to west across the measureless plain everything was bathed in a golden haze, and on all sides life was springing up warm and vigorous. Its youthful ectasy was made up of the rustling sounds of earth, the song of birds and the murmur of streams and woods. It was good to be alive; the old world meant to live through another spring.

Full of this hope, he slackened his pace and let his eyes wander from right to left, taking in the gaiety of the new season. He thought about himself, and knew that he was now strong, matured by his hard experience down in the pit. His apprenticeship was over, and he was going forth fully armed as a fighting missionary of the revolution, having declared war on society, for he had seen it and condemned it. In his joy at meeting Pluchart once more, and becoming, like Pluchart, a leader whose word commanded attention, he began thinking of speeches and putting phrases together. He considered how he could broaden his programme, for the bourgeois refinement that had raised him above his own class now filled him with a greater refinement of hatred for these bourgeois. The poverty-stricken smell of the workers might displease him now, but he would surround them with glory, he would show the world that they alone were great and pure, the only nobility and strength in which humanity could be tempered anew. Already he could see himself on the rostrum, sharing the people's triumph – unless he were the people's victim.

The song of a lark high in the heavens made him look up. The last vapours of the night were melting as rosy wisps of cloud into the limpid blue, and they vaguely reminded him of the faces of Souvarine and Rasseneur. No, it was clear that everything must go wrong as soon as any one man sought power for himself. Hence the fiasco of this much-trumpeted International which, instead of creating a new world, had merely witnessed the piecemeal break-up of its mighty army through internal strife. Was Darwin right, then, was this world nothing but a struggle in which the strong devoured the weak so that the species might advance in strength and beauty? The question disturbed him although as a self-styled scientist he could only settle it one way. But his misgivings were dispelled by one idea, a most attractive ambition: to go on with his old cherished examination of basic theory on the first occasion when he spoke in public. For if one class had to be devoured, surely the people, vigorous and young, must devour the effete and luxury-loving bourgeoisie? A new society needed new blood. In this expectation of a new invasion of barbarians regenerating the decayed nations of the old world, he rediscovered his absolute faith in a coming revolution, and this time it would be the real one, whose fires would cast their red glare over the end of this epoch even as the rising sun was now drenching the sky in blood.

On he walked, lost in these dreams, hitting stones with his dogwood stick. On looking round, however, he saw the familiar landmarks. At the Fourche-aux-Bœufs, just over there, he remembered taking over command of the crowd on the morning they had stormed the pits. And today the brutish, deadly, ill-paid toil was beginning all over again. On the other side he thought he could hear the distant sound of

496

picks, very soft, but regular and insistent, seven hundred metres under the ground: it was his mates whom he had just seen go down, his black comrades tapping away in silent rage. They might be beaten, they had lost their money, and some of them their lives, but Paris would never forget the gunshots at Le Voreux, for they had inflicted a mortal wound from which the Empire itself would lose its life blood. Even if this industrial crisis blew over and the factories reopened one by one, a state of open war had been declared and henceforth peace was out of the question. The miners had numbered their forces and measured their strength, and their cry for justice had stirred the workers throughout France. That was why their present defeat brought no comfort to anybody, and least of all to the bourgeois of Montsou, whose victory was poisoned by the uneasy fears that strikes always bring in their wake, and who were looking over their shoulders all the time to see whether their inevitable doom was not lurking behind this ominous silence. They realized that the revolution would always be raising its head anew – perhaps tomorrow there would be a general strike, an understanding between all workers, whose fighting funds would enable them to hold out for months and eat as well. This time their old, tottering society had received a jolt and they had heard the ground crack beneath their feet, but they felt other jolts on the way, and yet others, and so it would go on until the old edifice was shaken to pieces and collapsed and disappeared into the earth, like Le Voreux.

Étienne turned to the left along the Joiselle road, where he remembered having prevented the mob from storming Gaston-Marie. In the bright sunshine he could see the distant headgears of many pits. Mirou to the right, Madeleine and Crèvecœur side by side. From all quarters came the hum of work; and the tapping of picks that he had thought he could hear deep down in the earth could now be heard from end to end of the plain. Under these fields and roads and villages now smiling in the sunshine, one blow, then another, then blow after blow were being struck as the work went on in the black prisons so deep down beneath the rocks that you had to know what was going on down there before your ear was attuned to its heavy sigh of pain. And now he began to wonder whether violence really helped things on at all. Cut cables, torn-up rails, broken lamps – how futile! Rushing about, three thousand strong, in an orgy of destruction – what a waste of energy! It was dawning on him that some day legal methods would be much more terrible, for now that his blind hatreds had had their fling his intelligence was coming of age. Yes, Maheude was right when she said in her sensible way that that would be the big day, when they could legally band together, know what they were doing and work through their unions. Then, one morning, confident in their solidarity, millions of workers against a few thousand idlers, they would take over power and be the masters. Ah, then indeed truth and justice would awake! Then that crouching, sated god, that monstrous idol hidden away in his secret tabernacle, gorged with the flesh of poor creatures who never even saw him, would instantly perish.

Leaving the Vandame road Étienne came out on the high-road. To the right he saw Montsou running down its hill into the valley out of sight. Before him were the ruins of Le Voreux, an accursed hole which three pumps were draining night and day. And on the horizon the other pits, La Victoire, Saint-Thomas, Feutry-Cantel, whilst northward the lofty blast-furnaces and coke-ovens smoked in the limpid air. If he meant to catch the eight o'clock train he must put his best foot forward, for there was a six-kilometre walk ahead of him.

Deep down underfoot the picks were still obstinately hammering away. All his comrades were there, he could hear them following his every step. Beneath this field of beet was it not Maheude, bent double at her task, whose hoarse gasps for breath were coming up to him, mingled with the whirring of the ventilator? To left and to right far away into the distance he thought he could recognize other friends under the corn, the hedges and young trees. The April sun was now well up in the sky, shedding its glorious warming rays on the teeming earth. Life was springing from her fertile womb, buds were bursting into leaf and the fields were quickening with fresh green grass. Everywhere seeds were swelling and lengthening, cracking open the plain in their upward thrust for warmth and light. The sap was rising in abundance with whispering voices, the germs of life were opening with a kiss. On and on, ever more insistently, his comrades were tapping, tapping, as though they too were rising through the ground. On this youthful morning, in the fiery rays of the sun, the whole country was alive with this sound. Men were springing up, a black avenging host was slowly germinating in the furrows, thrusting upwards for the harvests of future ages. And very soon their germination would crack the earth asunder.

Everyman's Library, founded in 1906 and relaunched in 1991, aims to offer the most complete library in the English language of the world's classics. Each volume is printed in a classic typeface on acid-free, cream-wove paper with a sewn full cloth binding.